CW01080773

For the real Katina.

Sam

Magnetite

Magnetite

◆ ◆ ◆

A Voyage across Seven Continents over Three Centuries

A Novel

San Cassimally

Okapi Press
Edinburgh
2017

© 2017 San Cassimally
All rights reserved.

ISBN: 197836671X
ISBN 13: 9781978366718

Contents

Book 1

Prologue

(Kilmahog, Scotland, The mmPresent)

IF TWO SOLUTIONS of differing concentration are separated by a permeable membrane, the solute diffuses through the membrane from the solution having the greater concentration into the solution having the lesser solute concentration whilst water diffuses into the solution having the greater solute concentration.

Osmosis is the diffusion of water across a membrane into a solution having a greater solute concentration. The two processes only stop when the concentration on either side of the membrane is equalised.

Katrina Crialese slowed down as she read the sign: Kilmahog 4. Nearly there. She had been cycling for two hours. The guide book suggested a stop at The Hamish, if only to see its famous resident - also called Hamish, a hirsute Highland bull in the paddock there, its star attraction. The book said nothing about the quality of the food though. Grandma Gina ("Don't call me Angelina cara, there's nothing angelic about me") used to say, "the taste of the food is the least important thing to the Eeeng…lish, as long as eet looks nice". I hope I do not speak like a music-hall Italian; she knew that she had unconsciously picked an American accent in the two years she was in Washington, which she had promised to get rid of whilst over in Scotland.

The morning mist had lifted and she had an unimpeded view of the various shades of green of the forests on either side of the winding shiny blue-tinted, asphalt road. From the distance the outlines of munros and corbetts began to emerge like a photograph in the final stages of processing. Time was when she enjoyed printing her own photographs, now with digital it seems a bit pointless, although when asked to supply a pic for a magazine or an exhibition, she insisted on doing everything herself on her trusty Voigtlander. She still had a dark room. You had to go on-line to lay hands on black-and-white films though.

If I don't put something inside me soon I am going to pass out. Fact was that there was no fear of that; she liked to think of herself as a healthy strong girl - no, a healthy strong woman. She had been volley ball captain of her university team, was no mean exponent of the martial arts. A personal fitness trainer had described her once as a perfectly tuned human machine. She didn't think that he was only saying this so he could charge her more. Or might he have been trying to come on to her? She could have been an Arctic explorer (she had not entirely given up hope of achieving that adolescent ambition), or an Everest climber. Dream on Modesty Blaise… She knew the Dolomites in Italy where she grew up, inside out, and had in fact first seen the famous hairy Highland bull there.

She sometimes fantasised about roaming the mountains and forests of Africa, or India, looking for birds which had not been seen in the last few years, presumed extinct. Perhaps she could initiate some scheme to promote their survival. She would dearly love to see a blue swallow, or a Bulo Burti bubou - there cannot be too many of them left.

For three years she had worked with Professor Marcello Giardino at Italy's National Institute of Physics Matter on STARFLAG, Starlings in Flight, a European project involving physicists, biologists like herself and economists. For years scientists as well as those irksome twitchers, had been puzzled by bird formation, by how they arrived at keeping such precision in their flying patterns, how millions of them could fly across each other without colliding. Just compare that with the chaos produced on any motorway in the world, with less than 0.1% the number of cars, fitted with all the newest electronic devices. Obviously there was some sort of communication between them. STARFLAG had set itself the task of finding out the mechanism of their flight.

When she joined the international team engaged in this activity three years ago, a lot of work had already been done, and Chiara Cavagna at the Centre For Statistical Mechanics and Complexity in Rome already had impressive data. When Katrina arrived to join the team in Rome fresh from her research fellowship at the Smithsonian Bird Center in Washington, they were planning to carry out a detailed study of the skies of the Stazione Centrale di Termini in Rome. For two years she and her colleagues kept track of the millions of starlings that haunt the area, taking photographs, making 3-D models, studying them and analysing all aspects from all possible angles. Finally the team had arrived at the conclusion that each starling kept track of seven others, which made more sense than the original hypothesis that each bird was in contact with all the members of the flock, explaining why not a single bird is ever left isolated in case of predatory attack.

The results had been published in the Proceedings of the National Academy of Sciences, and she had moved on. Last spring Jolyon (Professor McMasters) had come to Rome to participate in a seminar on Bird Migration, and they had got on famously. He had mentioned that Aberdeen had funding for two fellowships, maybe three, and had more or less offered one of them to her. As she was not one for dilly dallying, she made up her mind on the spot to accept. She was delighted to be able to spend some time in the land of her birth, for she was born in Britain, although the family had left for Italy before she was five, when papa was made redundant.

She had arrived in London a few weeks early as she needed a holiday, not having taken one in almost two years. She had always found the Scottish Highlands fascinating in photographs, imagining virile red-bearded men in tartans and comely lassies dancing the Highland Fling on a carpet of heather, and now she was going to see for herself. Too bad the heather was not going to be in full bloom until much later.

Although she hardly ever wore make-up and had little dress sense, men seemed to find her attractive, and clearly this had advantages. She had full lips, possibly inherited from her African slave ancestor. Her rich gold tan was no doubt due to Gina's island lover, but she could only have inherited her blue eyes from her Nazi ancestor who shot the dying in Babi Yar...

She pedalled on with renewed vigour now that she knew that she was going to stop soon. Kilmahog - Kill my hunger! There were three coaches in the car park and chattering tourists were merrily feeding the famous bull which was famous for being famous, bits of apple, pear, carrot or whatever, which the mollycoddled bovine took as his due, with a negligence bordering on impudence. Some of the younger folks in the precinct eyed her fancy bike with envy, something she was very proud of, having splashed out almost half the advance Aberdeen had sent her on it. She chained the prized mount to the cycle rack and made for the toilets. Whilst washing her hands, she noticed in the mirror that she still had her helmet on, and laughed. Gina proudly called her "our little absent-minded professor". She went back and dropped it in her pannier, entered the café and ordered a pot of tea. Never drink their coffee, the grandmother had advised, unless you badly want stomach ache, usually adding, "and it tastes like a sick bull's piss". Hamish's?

She asked the Polish chap behind the counter for a croissant and took a small plastic pot of apricot jam. She picked a handful of sachets of sugar as she liked her tea extra sweet, and groaned as she read "tastes like real cream" on the tub of the substitute. Croissant and jam. And the croissant looked surprisingly fresh too.

What a treat! She loved everything sweet. She did not have to worry about her weight, for she was something of a fitness freak, and even if she had not had a personal trainer since Washington, she was constantly on the move and did not have one gram of excess fat in her body. Gina used to encourage her to eat sweets, explaining that her own sour nature was because as a child she had been deprived of the good things of life, like sweets and lemonade. Katrina smiled, for if there was a thing which the old dear did not have, it was one sour gene in her body. Yes, she did have a colourful speech, and was rather fond of mild expletives when she wanted to show off, but nobody she knew had a more optimistic nature or was less ill-tempered. Now, with her stroke, she was using swear words all the time, and her granddaughter suspected that she knew that she would get away with this, as everybody would put her swearing on the back of her condition. Gina sometimes spoke disparagingly about family, neighbour or friend, but in reality she bore malice towards none. It was as if once she had said something nasty this had absolved the target of her diatribe of whatever crime they were supposed to have committed. I hope the old thing does not die on me while I am over here.

As she was munching away thinking of random things, poor mum, with her pains and aches, her sleepless nights, dad and his ulcers, Donald

Robertson walked in, looking around him like a little boy lost, killing Chinamen. Killing Chinamen was what her family called blinking. Zio Mario, dad's cousin, a master of trivia, had once informed the table that in China, every time someone blinked a Chinaman died, thus giving the family their overused code.

Donald was thin, tall and gangly and had a strange walk. He never seemed to take two strides of the same length, as if he had to make a conscious decision about each step. It seemed to take him all the skill God gave him to avoid walking into chairs and tables, but unlike Katrina, he had remembered to take his helmet off, carrying it gingerly, like it was a basket of eggs of near extinct birds. She watched him surreptitiously, saw a red maple leaf on his pale blue blouson, and assumed that he was Canadian. Do I have anything on me to identify me as an Italian? She found him an interesting if bizarre specimen, and suspected (wrongly, as she would discover shortly) that even if she was staring at him, he would be unlikely to notice. She recalled seeing a cyclist sitting on a rock some ten kilometres from Kilmahog, obviously entranced by the carpet of bluebells which punctuated the scenery, and deduced that he was none other than Mr Charisma here.

The behaviourist in her watched him as he ordered his coffee, bacon and eggs. She noticed how he jerked his head involuntarily, unable to stand still, as if he had ants in his shoes and something in his collar irritating his neck. The Pole served him his coffee, told him to go sit down, saying that someone would bring him his egg. Hope he doesn't come and sit at my table. The Canadian hesitated before picking up his coffee, twitching his lips for a split second, in what must have been the ghost of a smile, put his helmet on his head, and holding his coffee with both hands, walked towards a table next to the counter with cutlery, sugar, creamer etc, and served himself, after which he walked in her direction. She noticed him slowing down, looking at her furtively, blinking uncontrollably, almost tripping, as if the sight of her had caused him some mild shock. However, this did not seem to deter him from considering joining her at her table. She gave him no encouragement, and hesitatingly he made for the table by a window diagonally opposite her, pretending that that was what he had been meaning to do all along, like Karl Lorenz's dog going blind not recognising its master approaching, beginning to bark aggressively, and then on realising the truth, pretending he had been barking at some small non-existent creature in the grass all the time.

The Canadian took the spoon in his right hand in an attempt to stir his drink, but remembering that he had not put the sugar in yet, he panicked, blushed and started blinking. He picked the sachet of sugar with his left hand, realised that he needed both hands to tear it open, put the spoon down, tore the sachet, emptied half of it in his coffee, and then with a contented smile picked the spoon anew and used it to stir his coffee. He then looked right and left, and inevitably their eyes met. Surprisingly he did not immediately look away as she had expected, but when he did, after a decent interval he looked at her again, and again their eyes met, launching another thousand blinks. He stared at her clumsily, as if he was trying to remember where he might have seen her. She was used to being stared at, specially by effete Italians with macho pretensions, and paid no more attention to the fellow cyclist, who however, was clearly no Italian macho, pretend or otherwise. Which did not mean that he was unattractive. He was tall and lanky, had a pleasant enough face with frank and innocent eyes and a good crop of unkempt brownish hair. One could even call his features rugged, but the tenseness and his unrelaxed body language were all too obvious and worked against him. She had not ruled out finding a man some day, and if pressed would have admitted (to herself) that he had two pluses in his favour. He had a good physique, and manifestly also had vulnerability, which, she supposed appealed to her maternal instincts. That, however, was the sort of thing she preferred to keep to herself.

As there was nothing more she wanted to know about the subject, she switched him off and concentrated on her tea instead. The milk substitute wasn't all that bad. Although she had given up smoking three years ago, in a situation like this one, on holiday, after a physical effort and a pleasant breakfast, she felt an urge to light up, but she was not gasping for it, and in any case, she prided herself on her will-power and had never once succumbed in those three years. Still, the yearning was all too recognisable. One does not ever become a non-smoker, just an abstainer. When she rose, Donald looked up, like a timid animal quietly engaged in eating, at the approach of human footsteps. Their eyes crossed again, and she was sure that in his she read this mute plea, Please don't go yet, I want to talk to you. She was perplexed and flattered, smiled vaguely but walked away. She was even more bewildered when she found another Revolutionary Country Traveller, next to her own bike. She immediately guessed that it was the blinking Canadian's, for why else would he have a cyclist's helmet? He must have guessed that the first bike belonged to her, with the gear she had on, and this was no doubt why he had made that weak attempt at coming over to talk to her. Now she felt a bit mean at having discouraged him. She was not usually unsociable, but today, the cycling had tired her and she preferred her own company.

There was a bright sun in the sky above, and it was nice and warm, and the rise to Strathyre was quite gentle. Take it easy now, ragazza.

◆ ◆ ◆

Donald Robertson took another sip of the coffee. 3.5 out of ten, he judged, but that was only because he was pissed off because the girl had left; 4.3 really. He had invented this game when he discovered sex at eleven, but the rules had been modified over the years. It had begun with ranking and now it was points out of ten. Sex never lost its prominence at the top of the table; it was 10 out of 10. Sneezing was usually second (7.5), but there were times when scratching took over. This was itself categorised and sub-categorised. An itch between the shoulder blades below the neck which was only reached by dint of almost acrobatic contortions was clearly more valued than a common or garden itch between the toes. Water was probably the most difficult one to judge. There was spring water and tap water. First thing in the morning, with meals, after a strenuous run. They were different allotropes. Food was a mere five, but you did not need a PhD to know that apples were worth more than bananas. Nova Scotia Golden Delicious was way higher up than the McIntosh. What a nerd am I? I should be thinking of better things. He smiled.

The Revolutionary Country Traveller belonged to her, but she had made it clear that she did not want company. He easily imagined arriving at her table, opening his mouth and finding it impossible to articulate those simple words, may I join you. Niagara in winter!

He had a gnawing conviction that he had seen her before, maybe a couple of years ago. Could it have been through the glass partition between incoming and departing passengers at some airport? Yes, that was it. He suddenly located the memory file and downloaded it. He had indeed seen her and had stared at her, stopping briefly, which had caused a minor collision with the lady behind. He was sure of that. Probably at JFK. He travelled rather a lot and had trained himself to Delete and send to Trash any file he was not likely to need in the immediate future, in the knowledge that one can always double-click on the Trash icon to recover most things. He would have dearly loved to get to know her. He was no ladies' man, he knew that, but seeing her again he was instantly drawn to her, and wished that he had Cousin Alex's gift of the gab. Clearly she was no bimbo. Her appeal stemmed from a face and bearing that seemed to breathe intelligence and self-assurance.

He imagined that, like him, she was someone who worked in some scientific domain and had little doubt that she was one hundred percent dedicated to whatever she worked on. Well-built but not masculine. Perfect proportions. Mediterranean tan. All combined to make her an impressive figure. Just thinking of her gave him a sexual frisson, but then, involuntary celibate that he was, everything did.

Women and sex were always on his mind, and he sometimes despaired of getting either. If only there was some celibate agnostic order for him to join! He had once confided in his sure-footed cousin that he knew that because of his physical impediments he had to lower his heights and not aspire to the perfect womanhood of his dreams, conceding that he would have to settle for second best. Wrong! Alex had laughed. It's the ugly stupid ones who are the most difficult. You would stand a better chance making a bid for your ideal woman. Who was he to contradict Alex?

Although he was fit and strong, as a result of a difficult birth, he had some minor disabilities. His coordination had much improved after years of therapy, but as a toddler he could not take two steps without falling over. When he did manage to walk properly, he was always bumping into furniture and walls. Dad said he was clumsy but mum showed him her claws and fangs and he backed off. The paediatrician had whistled in admiration when he had read the psychologist's report and seen his IQ results and had said that his less than perfect coordination was due to a minor trauma at birth caused by internal cranial bleeding, and this was compounded by his naturally tense nature, which, the doctor suggested, was often the price to pay for high intelligence. The specialist had also said that his stammering and his blinking were two allotropes of the same phenomenon, and were by-products of his intense nature compounded by his minor physical problems. To mum's relief he had added that this condition usually improved with time. True enough, it had, up to a point. He had great will-power, and everybody marvelled at how, against all odds, he managed not only to learn to ride a bicycle when he could scarcely walk, but to do so with such aplomb. If only people knew what effort of concentration he had to put in the process. Sometimes when he switched off but for a split second, his grip on the handlebar would loosen, and the consequences were dire but not disastrous enough to dampen his determination. He looked upon his bruises, scratches and scars as badges of honour. On top of everything, he did not know how to relax properly. Fortunately while most people get tired of work, Don found it relaxing. He did not know how to talk to girls, knew that he did not create a good first impression. Alex told him once that first impressions were difficult to erase. If a girl forms the view that you are an OK guy, she would not easily believe the negative things all her instincts will warn her about you. And conversely.

Those hussies who have not leapt upon you, Ida said, do not know what they're missing. Serve them right! If only you were not my brother, grrr... Ida did outrageous to perfection.

He had more or less made up his mind that some day he would have no option but to go to a Dating Agency, all his clumsy attempts at finding a woman on his own having failed. Dr Robertson, famous ornithologist, a virgin at 28!

Now there was this awesome cyclist - a soulmate if ever there was one... was it just a coincidence that they had the same bike? Ach, why waste energy thinking about her? She never even looked at him, did not even know he existed, or cared. In any case she's gone now. Yet he had seen her before, years ago, so who knows? No, Robertson, it's the Agency for you, buddy!

He was not much given to melancholy. His passion for science and learning, birds in particular, left him with no time to sit and mope, there was so much to do, so many places to visit, India, Madagascar, the Philippines, all those near extinct birds to photograph, perhaps help conserve. So many birds, so little time! He ate his food mechanically, and once he had finished, he came out and saw a crowd photographing the well-groomed Hamish. Why snap some tame bull in a paddock when all along the route, in a natural environment there were any number of more impressive and ragged specimens? He really only understood birds...

His Revolutionary Traveller seemed a bit forlorn on its own... oh, I'll name him Hamish, he decided, on a sudden impulse. The scientist in him loved giving names to everything. He wondered whether the girl had a name for her mount. Come on Hamish, sorry to interrupt your rest, we have to be on our way, pal. He rather liked that much used Scottish word. Dad who had never been within a few thousand miles of the land of his ancestors (he wondered why) used it all the time, forcing himself to say aye, I dinnae ken or cannae dae this, pal.

He found himself cycling more lustily, and suspected that it was either because he was invigorated after a good meal, or possibly, subconsciously he was trying to catch up with the woman who had a good ten minute start, hoping that they was heading the same way.

The sun and the gentle breeze made it ideal for cycling, and he pedalled briskly, enjoying the view. The Trossachs most certainly deserved their reputation for beauty. The vegetation glows in luminescent green contrasting magnificently with red ochre patches of the Highland cattle gently grazing randomly, whilst the waters of the lochs gleam with silvery splendour and bluebells and gorse punctuate the harmony of the rolling slopes. The so-called "crooked" Loch Lubnaig, one of the many jewels in the crown of the Trossachs nests beautifully in it surroundings. He had done his homework before leaving Halifax. He revelled in trivia, no wonder they called him The Anorak! Well, Ida did. He didn't mind. He looked upon the appellation as a badge of honour.

He thought that it was a bit irrational trying to catch up with the woman. Was she going north or south? Would he even be able to catch up with her? Worst of all, he knew that he wouldn't know how to approach her even if he did.

When he had cycled a couple of kilometres along the Loch Lubnaig, he stopped and sat on the beach to take in its splendour. He leant Hamish against a solitary birch, sat on a rock, and took a long sip of water from a bottle. He did not believe in buying bottled water, he usually filled his aluminium litre flask ("We write aluminum like the Yanks, but litre like the Brits") with tap water and was none the worse for it. The gentle ripples on the nearly smooth surface reminded him of the old Mi'kmaq maid Mary, a born story-teller, who told him that the ripples were made by angels invisible to all but a privileged few, dancing on the water to the tune of their feet on the surface and the lapping. As a child, Don had little difficulty seeing them. He half closed his eyes and looked at the surface, and this time a single shape appeared, and it was not an elf, but the beautiful cyclist, like Christ, walking on water.

In the distance he could see Ben Shian (572 metres). There was no habitation in sight, and traffic on the A84 was sparse. He closed his eyes and listened to the music of silence - that was what he called the silence of deserted spots after hearing John Cage's famous piece, 4'33. The loch was unusually tranquil, but a discerning ear could detect the timid lapping of the waves on the beach. He thought of this as the lake breathing. He then became aware of the intermittent whispers of the breeze among the trees, and for a while the two sounds melded as in a concerto for two instruments, and leaning his head against the bark of the birch he listened to that. In vain he waited for a bird or two to manifest themselves. This part of the Highlands was not too hospitable to them, mainly because of reforestation. The native trees growing randomly had been replaced over the years by larches, cypresses and spruce, and in order to maximise profits, they had been tightly packed, causing the original insects to migrate or die, making it difficult to sustain a healthy bird population. The signs were there for all to see. He had read that you could still see the occasional black and red grouse, choughs, crossbills, dippers, great spotted woodpecker, even kingfishers and ptarmigans, as well as the inevitable magpies and crows. At this very moment a couple of bad tempered crows above croaked, bringing in a discordant note to the melody which was gently building up. It was still early, with a good few hours of sunlight left. He was in no hurry, and this terrain seemed as good as any to pitch one's tent on. Get real, forget that exotic princess. Wonder if she is English…

He had all the time in the world, and if the fancy took him, he might go up the Shian although he did not have proper boots. Or consider doing Cycle Track 7. How heavenly it would be to be doing that in the company of that soulmate of his (who did not know she was!) Imagine the statistical probability of two persons meeting in the Scottish Highlands both having a Revolutionary. Only marginally more that of seeing a penguin flying over the Atlantic. Multiply that by the probability of the same two persons having met each other in some airport, one coming in and the other leaving. That probability was fast going to zero. The same as the probability of one of your father's sperm hitting the jackpot, but that order of magnitude didn't stop you being here.

Yes, he would camp on the bank of Lubnaig for the night. He pitched his Gelert Eiger ("Easy to Pitch, a bargain at $76.99") under a diseased spruce showing all the signs of being on its last lap, uncharacteristically growing on its own. He unloaded his rucksack and equipment and stored them in there, and lay down outside the tent under the shade of a chestnut tree.

Inevitably he again began to think of that woman in the café with the same bike as him. Donald Robertson, Obsession is your middle name. Thank you Ida, I love you too, dear sister. This cyclist is the woman I have been looking for all the time - which explains why I have never hit it off with anybody else before. Yep, that makes sense. I would give anything if I could just talk to her. O.K. Ida, stammer to her. There was something uncanny, bordering on the mystical in coming across her. The fact that she had gone plus the fact that he had no idea where she was heading, did not seem too relevant. He had this conviction based on nothing but his intuition, that he was going to see her again. As a scientist he valued intuition, although he knew that it was a tool and not the master of research. In this case, however, he was willing to put his blind trust in it. What was it Ida had said about intuition? She could read him inside out, his sister could. Although he tended to be secretive, she had the capacity to worm anything out of him. Even when they were kids, although he was a year older, she had a wisdom beyond her age. She always assumed an insouciance which belied her devotion to the causes she believed in. She always treated him like a younger sibling who needed her protection. She never shone at school like he did, but she always claimed that she had intuition which was worth more than its weight in gold. He must devise the means of measuring the weight of intuition some day. Ida was the person he loved most in this world. He admired her zest for life, her optimism and her common sense, her good causes. How he wished he could see more of her, but she had gone and married MacKenzie, her lobster fisherman, who unlike him had no speech impediment, not that it would have mattered in his case, as usually he only grunted. He was a rum figure, his ancestor had arrived in Pictou on the Hector in 1773 and he had Pictou blood in his veins. What Ida saw in him, Don would never understand, but she clearly saw a lot, for after the first time she met him she informed him that he was the man she was going to marry.

Mum was sweet and lovely, but once she had taught Don to stand on his own two legs - literally - she lost interest in parenting, and that was fine, as he rather liked not being fussed over. She now spent her time gardening, knitting, patchwork quilting, reading. She was a dab hand at the cryptic Crossword in the Star, and she played Bridge. Whatever time was left after these activities, she devoted to the many good causes that she espoused rather aggressively. Nobody he knew had such a perfect control of time. Dad was always busy making money, learning Scottish history and inventing excuses for not visiting the land of his forbears. Don suspected that he preferred the ideal view that he had nurtured, and did not want it tarnished by reality. Or maybe he was simply scared of air travel. Or again, he did not want to miss an occasion for making a killing. The Robertsons seemed to produce scientists and money-makers in alternate generations. Dad was devoted to his family, but did not know how to manifest his love.

Don often wondered whether his sister knew how much he valued her. All this sentimental rubbish made him melancholy, and he took out his copy of Tagore's Gitanjali from his rucksack, and read a couple of poems aloud without stammering. Grandad was often quoted as saying that with an Indian great great great grandmother, the family should honour the Hindu poet and Nobel Prize winner as much as Shakespeare.

He had not known too much about him and decided to look into this, for historical if not sentimental reasons, and had picked the weather-beaten tome in an Oxfam shop when he stopped in Peterborough on the way north.

He must have dozed off, and when he woke up, the words of the poem

and when old words die out on the tongue
new melodies break forth from the heart;
where the old tracks are lost,
new country is revealed with its wonders…

reverberated in his head. The sun was still high up in the sky but he knew that it was late afternoon. He played on his harmonica for a bit, trying to produce melancholy Highland strains that he had heard. The mouth organ seemed very appropriate. The sounds he produced must have been quite doleful, as he ended up with, if not quite tears rolling down his cheeks, at least a lump in his throat. Later he decided that he would go to the Munro Inn, which he had spotted earlier. It seemed like a reasonable place for a drink and would give him the opportunity of a discreet look at the natives. Time was when he refused to set foot in a pub or restaurant, hating the idea of drinking in a glass or eating off a plate that had been used by others, but as he grew up, it was either conform or starve. In India two years ago, he had been impressed that there, when you bought a cup of tea (they called it chai), it came in a rudimentary earthenware bowl which you threw away afterwards.

He had many phobias. He hated books with dog ears or frayed spines, which is why whenever anybody asked to borrow one of his books, he usually said to keep it as he had finished with it. He would then go buy a new copy. He never used to buy second hand books. It was sheer willpower which enabled him to shed many of his shibboleths, and he was sure that if he tried hard enough he would be able to deal with the remaining ones. So it was going to the Munro Inn.

He knew that he would find it difficult, maybe even impossible to start a conversation with anybody, and the dour Scots were not reputed to be over fond of engaging in verbal jousts with strangers, so he would have to sit in a corner, eat a sandwich, drink a pint or two and discreetly watch and listen.

He was pleased to find that the inn had catered for cyclists, and he parked Hamish in the rack. It was after nine and there was a goodly crowd inside. The locals scarcely acknowledged his presence. He mumbled his order of a pint of Tennent's and a grilled salmon supper with chips and water-cress salad. With all the lakes around, he was sure that he would get excellent fare. The barman told him to go sit down and he would send his supper over when it was ready.

Some people stared at him but one or two others gave him a hardly perceptible nod. He took his pint and sat himself under the obligatory stag head on the wall. The furniture was of massive dark varnished oak, and smelled of wax polish. Apart from one or two small groups sitting in corners, couples mainly, there was one enclave of noise at the far end of the room. A fair number of the locals had gathered around an immaculately kilted old man who was merrily holding forth, glowing in the certainty that his every word was a nugget falling into the lap of his audience. He was tall and thin, had a sunburnt tan, laughing eyes, and everything about him exuded an energetic intensity surprising for someone of his age.

Don made an effort to catch his drift, but the mixture of an alien accent, the distance and the loud laughter of the crowd made that a vain exercise. His salmon was delivered by a comely Scottish lassie in a fetching tartan, with the regulatory red hair, and he dug into it with relish. Six and a half out of ten overall. He did not immediately become aware of a man standing by his side, waiting to start a conversation.

'Canadian, aren't you, pal?' He was surprised and looked at the man rather blankly, blinking furiously.

'Aye,' he said. As a stammerer, he had worked on a number of strategies to disguise his impediment, and at an early stage in his entry in Scotland, he had realised that "aye", a word widely used in his family, was much better than "y-y-y-yes!" A godsend! And without blinking, he added, 'how d-d-did you know?'

'I am Bell,' the man said. He was in his mid thirties, wearing sandals, shorts and a thick flannel shirt. He briefly wondered whether the reason why he knew that Don was Canadian was because he was called Bell. He had worked out Bell really meant Bill.

'D-on,' he managed to say, hardly stammering. He sometimes practised saying "don, don, don, don…" when he had nothing to do, in the hope that an automatic and mechanical delivery would obviate the stutter, but the strategy did not always work. However if he did begin to stammer, the strategy was to say d-on! You said d, stopped and then added on. He knew that this sounded incongruous, but people understood him more easily. He was grateful that in the adult world, nobody make jokes about you because of your impediment.

'Right,' said Bill, 'right! How did I know you're Canadian? You see, I am a driver stroke guide for Heart of Scotland Tours, and I meet all the nationalities on earth, and I have learnt to tell.' They then exchanged some pleasantries about the beer and the salmon, Bill venturing a remark about the Munro always serving Norway's best! Don found it surprising that he was not wishing the man would go away. The Scotsman asked what he did, and he explained that he was going to be joining a team at Aberdeen, working on a bird migration project, but that at the moment, as he had six free weeks, he was just touring the Highlands of his ancestors.

'Ach yes, most Canadians have Highland ancestors,' said Bill.

'I don't know about most Canadians, but I certainly do,' Don formulated in his head, but was pleasantly surprised when a helpful nod had beaten his half open mouth, forcing the words back in. He was forever indebted to St Nod, patron saint of stammerers.

It had been much less of a strain talking to the tourist guide than he would have thought. To his surprise, Bill leant towards his plate, took a chip and put it in his mouth, making a hum of appreciation as he munched it. There was a time when that would have stopped the flow of Don's digestive juices, but now, he found it friendly and reassuring. He smiled, and by a gesture consisting of a twitch of the head and a widening of his eyes, indicated that Bill would be welcome to serve himself. His companion shook his head and after a while decided to go rejoin the crowd, hesitating as he began moving away.

'If you want an educational - and fun - experience, Don, you could do worse than to come listen to Auld Fergus. He is well into his nineties, and I know of no one who can keep an audience entertained… even enthralled,' adding that the man was an expert on any topic under the sun…, 'well come and hear for yourself.' Don nodded in a non-committal manner and Bill walked away in the direction of Auld Fergus and his disciples. While he was finishing his meal, he noticed the tour guide looking in his direction, making encouraging signs for him to come over. So, a short while later, he stood up and noticed that almost everybody in the crowd was turning round to look at him. Oh God, I can't face this, I have to go now, was his first reaction. But he understood that they were willing him on, inviting him over, and blinking at the rate of six per second (he had timed himself once, so he knew), he walked towards Bill, and the people opened up to let him through. His new friend who was much shorter than him, put a protective arm around his shoulder, which must have been a comical sight, and Auld Fergus himself bent slightly forward in his direction, nodded at him and offered him a hand to shake, without stopping his flow.

He noticed that the old man had a black object no bigger than a golf ball in his hand. When Fergus saw the Canadian looking at it, he took two steps forward and forcibly put it in his hand. Don looked at it and saw that it was a stone, and instinctively he twiddled his fingers around it to get its feel. Then he looked at it again, and saw that it had the imprints of a fossilised fern embedded just below the surface.

'Guess how old this is?' Auld Fergus asked. Don knew that the answer would be in millions of years, although fossils was an area of darkness for him.

'Two hundred years,' he said with a straight face, injecting a note of awe in his voice. And Ida thinks I am a humourless academic. Everybody laughed. Was it because they appreciated the joke, he wondered. It was funny how when he was putting on an act, the stammer went overboard. When asked to read Shakespeare at school, he would get into character and read flawlessly. Although not much given to levity, aye, I am humourless, he found that when he spoke with a mock Italian or Russian accent, he could stand and deliver like a politician.

'That's forty million years old,' said Auld Fergus authoritatively, 'not a day less, but perhaps a good few years more.' Don had guessed that would be the order of magnitude, but he opened his eyes wide in mock awe at this statement.

'And what does it tell us, my friend?' This time, Don really had no idea and shook his head. The old man took the stone back and displayed it to his audience.

'See this fossilised fern here, it is not a Scottish fern, not even European… It is an African equatorial fern, and remember,' he said brandishing his fore-finger, 'this stone was picked in Ayrshire, so what does it tell us?'

'That Scotland has drifted over the years.' That was Bill.

'Exactly!' Auld Fergus said. 'You see, my young transatlantic friend, it's not just your birds that migrate, continents migrate too.' Don was delighted with this observation. Fame at last! Bill must have told them about him.

'Time was, when the British Isles were way down south, below the equa-tor, enjoying the warm climate, then it decided that it did not like the heat and embarked upon a million year trek. Do you know where it arrived?' This was addressed to the whole audience, and Don was quite pleased that he rec-ognised that this was a signpost for a joke, as did the locals.

'No, Fergus, tell us,' they chorused.

'Up north, where North America is.' The audience nodded its apprecia-tion, but perhaps they had heard the story before.

'Do you know what happened then?'

'No, tell us what happened next Fergus.'

'It did not like it much there with all the MacDonalds and Coca Cola signs, and decided that its real habitat was over here. So it took another few million years to get back here.' He seemed as unrehearsed in what he was going to say as those extempore stand-ups.

'Where it found more MacDonalds and Coca Cola signs of course.' Suddenly Don found a fresh pint thrust in his hands, and even before he had touched it another man had brought him yet another pint. He had little option but to indulge. He offered to buy a round for everybody but was sol-emnly warned that as a guest, his duty was to be treated by them and that under no circumstances would he be allowed to disburse. Growing up in what the family loved to call a Scottish household, he was glad that he had never believed the stories of Scottish avarice. ("Get behind your lover, faith-less woman so I can shoot you both with one bullet") He was a little bit wary of getting drunk, so he held the glass in one hand and took very small sips.

It was Fergus, ever willing to augment the sum of his knowledge who suggested Don explain bird migration to him. He knew why birds migrated, he said, everybody wants to go somewhere where food is plentiful. Stands to reason.

What he wanted to understand was the logistics and mechanism of the flights. Where did they stop for a refill when the tank was empty? How did they guide themselves? Why did they not get lost? Bump into each other? Don had often had to read papers to his peers, and it had always been agony before the day arrived. He would spend long sleepless nights learning his text off by heart, not because he would have any problem with the facts, he had a prodigious, near photographic memory, but he had to work jolly hard to get the delivery right. Knowing the exact words facilitated delivery. Now, with goodness knows how many pints inside him, he had no problem at all. He knew that he had a sympathetic audience and already he was enjoying it. He took a deep breath and swallowed half the beer in his near full pint pot in one go, but before he could start, Fergus had a last question.

'Tell me Donald… Don…, am I right that even Aristotle believed that when birds disappeared in winter, it was because they went into hibernation?' It was clear to everybody that the old man did not need an answer to this. Don was reminded of that old Hollywood director who used to say to his board, "Gentlemen, for your information, can I ask a question?"

'That's r-r-ight sir, no one could imagine that b-b-birds actually flew thousands of kilometres to find feeding grounds.' Auld Fergus glowed with pride and looked around him. Man does not live by bread alone, he also needs approval. Mercifully the stammering was under control.

'Right! The f-f-fuel question first. B-b-birds p-repare themselves for the b-big trek. In an experiment we c-c-carried out at the USGS, on the Alaskan bar-tailed godwit, we found that at the start of their big migration, 56.85 percent of their body weight was fat.'

'USGS? wha's that when it's a' haem?'

'United States Geology Survey.' He paused before continuing. 'Next… eh… how do they guide themselves? F-f-f-or a long time we only had in-complete answers to this question. We we we… now believe that we more or less know the f-f-full story.' He took a deep breath, and was pleased that everybody was hanging on to his every single word. He was hardly stammering. If only he could talk with the same self-confidence to that woman.

'There are broadly three distinct means,' he pursued. 'First, what one would expect, I mean sight. They recognise rivers, m-m-mountain ranges, c-c-coastlines, forests, stars and the sun. We... we are assuming that the first time round they just followed the more experienced members of the f-f-flock...' He paused and had another sip before he continued.

'Smell, counts for a lot too. Birds are very sensitive to smells and are guided by them.'

'They better not have a blocked nose before they set off, then,' someone cackled rather drunkenly, and thankfully, this fell flat.

'But the most crucial navigational aid is m-m-magnetite.'

'Magnetite?'

'Aye, magnetite, I have heard about magnetite,' boasted Auld Fergus, nodding gravely.

'Aye, magnetite. M-migratory birds have tiny grains of a mineral c-called magnetite in their heads. That is an established fact.'

'So they are guided by the earth's magnetism?' asked Auld Fergus, because he was both an inveterate seeker after knowledge and at the same time a show-off. Still, for a man used to the limelight, to whom everybody turned when they wanted an explanation, he was surprisingly generous in his attitude towards the visitor. Maybe because he knew that he would be around long after the young man had cycled away into the Highland mist. Don was grateful to Fergus for not resenting him and gave him a nod of appreciation. Nothing would stop him in his tracks now that he was in full flow.

'Nobody can p-prove this with certainty, b-b-but...' The audience kindly signified that they knew what he meant and he saw that there was no need to finish the sentence, enabling him to put his thoughts in order before continuing.

'Eh... also, they use two electroma-ma-magnetic tools actually... eh... in their search for their destination. One is innate while the other is a learning process. You see, the bird flying for the first time, following the flock, f-f-flies in a direction dictated by the earth's m-m-magnetic field, but has no idea of the length of the journey. It makes use of something called the r-r-radical pair mechanism, which is easy to understand.' The look on his audience showed that it was probably not so.

'It is a m-m-mechanism whereby chemical reactions in special photo p-pigments sensitive to long wavelengths are affected by the f-f-field. The inexperienced bird learns to map by the magnetite in its trigeminal system which tells it how strong the f-field is.' He noticed that the people who so far had seemed enthralled by what he had to say at the start were now beginning to switch off, and he began to stutter. He realised that he had probably lost them. Bill came to his rescue, winking at him in a conspiratorial manner. Ida had told him that only when he had learnt when not to include technical details would he be able to talk to girls properly, adding that it was vital for him to learn that skill.

'Thanks Don, that was most interesting, I think we get the picture...' He felt a little bit sore. What he was about to go into was simplicity itself, if only people would listen. Gamely he shrugged. He had enjoyed the evening and he was not going to spoil it by unwarranted resentment. He had no sooner made the resolution to stop drinking when someone pushed a pint in his hands, saying, 'I really learnt a lot today, pal.' This cheered him up a bit, and he forgot the resolution. It was Auld Fergus who would not let go.

'Tell us about the Arctic Tern, Donald,' he entreated. 'I want to know more.'

'Aye, the Arctic Tern,' said Bill, 'he's the champion, isn't he?' Don took a deep breath. Having been part of a team studying bar-tailed godwits, he was not going to let this notion go unchallenged. Indeed the Arctic Tern, the *Sterna paradisaea* is a champion migrator, he explained. Each year it travelled nineteen thousand kilometres, from its Arctic breeding grounds to the Antarctic. Unique among living creatures, it saw two summers a year... certainly no creature on the planet sees more sunlight. He was beginning to enjoy himself again.

'What about those filthy rich Russian oligarchs who follow the sun in their yachts?' That was the obscene cackler.

'Och, shut up wee man and let the erudite scientist talk,' said Auld Fergus good-naturedly.

The average tern travels a distance of 800,000 kilometres in its lifetime, Don continued merrily.

'What's that in miles?'

'A bloody lot,' said Auld Fergus dismissively. 'That's like going to the moon and back.' Don marvelled at the speed (and accuracy) of the remark.

Now, explained Don, although the Tern does nineteen thousand kilometres a year, and has some claim to the title of champion, there is one thing that works against it. It does land on the ocean to feed itself during its odyssey. Don paused dramatically.

'I think you're about to tell us that the bar-tailed godwit has a greater claim to being the champion migrator,' said Auld Fergus opening his eyes wide.

'The *Limosa lapponnica*?' quizzed Don with fake incredulity. 'I have worked with godwits, believe me they are lovely creatures. When you hold one in your hands, he seems so v-v-vulnerable, but still you immediately get the f-f-f-feeling that you are holding someone who is a c-credit to the feathered species. Proper flying machines, they are.'

He went on talking about what was fast becoming his favourite bird, and to his surprise nobody yawned. He took a deep breath and another large sip.

'Just before leaving for the United Kingdom, I was part of a team researching the bar-tailed godwit. Most of our previous studies had ended inconclusively, mainly on account of b-battery failure, but this time, our dear E7 did us p-proud.'

'E7?' asked Auld Fergus, with the enthusiasm of a teenage nerd in a Science lesson. One could almost hear the unsaid, "Please sir". Someone said it sounded like a food additive.

'Aye,' said Don, who by now had completely forgotten that he stuttered. 'We usually call our specimens by some prosaic name. This young female beauty was christened E7. She was fitted with a transmitter in the Firth of Thames in New Zealand. This time we were able to follow her complete journey, and it was a first. We were so excited, we were able to verify many established conjectures.' All eyes were now on him, and all ears wide open.

'And we followed her every movement from the 7th of February to the day she returned to the Firth on the 6th of September.'

'That's seven months!'

'Aye, seven months… covering 29,181 kilometres.'

'Incredible!'

'She flew non-stop from New Zealand to Yalu Jiang in China, a distance of 10,219 kilometres. From there she flew non-stop to Alaska, a p-paltry 6,459 kilometres. She then went to Manokinak, her breeding ground, where she stayed for two months, fattening up for the return journey. Her last lap was from Avinof to Piako in New Zealand, which she accomplished in eight days and twelve hours non-stop, beating her previous record, clocking 11,570 kilometres!' It surprised him when the whole pub burst into spontaneous applause, as if the heroic bird had just entered the bar.

'I don't think I had even heard of the godwit,' admitted Auld Fergus, and everybody stared at him. Some gasped in disbelief, as if in the middle of his sermon, the priest had suddenly admitted that he was not sure whether he believed in the Holy Trinity.

Next morning, when he woke up in his tent, he had no clear recollection of how the night had ended. He knew that he had rambled on for what seemed like hours. He only hoped that he had not said anything outrageous. He felt frustrated until he began gradually recalling images of Bill helping him into his van. He was a bit less comfortable when he remembered incoherent sentences about the princess in Kilmahog.

Hangover or not, he certainly had never felt so relaxed in his life. Tomorrow he will be on his way to Ullapool for no other reason than the name of the place had the same resonance as Allapur, where he knew the Indian ancestor had come from, although he did not know the details. He also remembered telling Bill about his great great… can't remember how many greats… grandfather who was the king of the Gypsies!

CHAPTER 1

❖❖❖

The Ancestors

ALLAPUR, THE MOST charming little gaon in the Gaya district of Bihar! Everybody agreed that the Allapur was the loveliest tributary of the Ganga, clear sweet pure water from the Himalayas, home to the best fish, prawn and crayfish in the country. Even the magnificent mahseer, the biggest fresh-water fish known to man, could sometimes be caught in its crystalline stillness as the swelling of the monsoon began to recede. The regular floods of Mother Ganga and the monsoon rains which were as dependable as sunrise, vied with each other, to soak and bathe this luxuriant paradise with their sacred waters, turning it into the most fertile land on earth, enabling it to breed the healthiest gai and goats, chickens and ducks, and produce the reddest tomatoes and the plumpest beans. Except when they politely told each other, after you Ma, no after you, Monsoonji, and then everything dried and shrivelled up.

Parsad's ambition had been to become a teacher, but there were no schools when he was a boy. His Pitaji who knew book, had taught him what little he knew and had given the youngster his great love of learning which, unfortunately remained limited, but this did not stop him claiming that he valued learning above earning. Parsad never let slip any opportunity for picking up a new knowledge. The two books that Pitaji had given him, now protected from rains and insects by a pillowcase, volume 7 of The Upanishads and volume 3 of The Laws of Many, were in a sorry state, as he had read and re-read them a thousand times. He would ask questions of those who were able to provide answers, and considered it a pity if on any given day he had not learnt at least one new fact, or if a new thought had not crossed his mind. He was, however, quite content to carry on doing what his father and grandfathers had done before him, and settled down to the life of a peasant farmer. It was a noble calling and he worked on his fields with a fervour which, at the end of a hard day, found him in the same state of exaltation which religious devotees experienced after an intense puja session in the Mandir.

◆ ◆ ◆

He had always thought that the land where he was born was paradise on earth, but lately the sky, like an angry woman who wanted to punish her husband for something she suspected that he had done, but would not spell out what it was, had decided to withhold its bounty. Every time you looked at the land, the small chinks zigzagging across the once smooth surface of the earth turning it into smaller and paler fragments, seemed darker and deeper than the day before as the drought and the scorching sun squeezed the life out of them. However, he always put his trust in Bhagwan who knows what He does. Not that he associated Bhagwan with the Mandir or the Pandit. He always felt uneasy in the company of the latter. Not that he did not believe in prayers and offerings, but he knew that he only prayed as a duty. It was the exaltation that made all the difference. He only truly felt elevated at the sight of little shoots pluckily forcing their way up having miraculously breached the crust of the earth, at the sound of the first bleat of a new-born goat, or the insouciant moo of his cow as she saw him approaching, at the warmth of a freshly laid egg. In those things he clearly saw Bhagwan's bounty, and this Bhagwan, he worshipped with all the fibres in his body.

However, three successive years of parsimonious monsoon and drought had turned his land, once famous for its fertility, into a gnarled resentful patch which would respond to neither coaxing nor cajoling. You break your back carrying water from the river to the plants, but when you came back with a fresh bucket, the blazing sun had drunk it all. The seedlings had shrivelled up and died. Of the good-sized herd that he once possessed, the bulk had perished through lack of water and fodder. Still, he had been luckier than most people who had lost everything. Hundreds of villagers had slowly succumbed to the effects of starvation, especially the elderly, their existing ailments made worse by persistent hunger as the crops failed. However, Bhagwan in his wisdom, had saved his family and had even provided him with the means of saving the two remaining cows and one bullock if little else.

In the old days, he would whisper nice words to the growing tomatoes, lovingly caress their roundness and they would blush visibly and yield their delectable ripeness to him. Whilst in the old days, he would be all smiles, every pore of his body exuding gratitude for nature's munificence when he stood in front of his fields, happy that this earth that he loved as much as he loved God, his wife and the yet-to-be-born sons, now he had only a mute curse, whenever he approached his bigha of land, "arrey sukkha chooth day-in!" - dried-cunt witch, taking care not to say these words aloud.

Although it had been his dearest wish to have a son, now that Parvatti had finally done it right, he was dreading his arrival. The timing was un-fortunate. How would they feed him, clothe him, keep him warm when the temperature went down in the night, and when the cold winter rains came trickling in through the leaky roof? People he knew had moved to Jharkhand, where he had heard things were much better. There, one had not only the possibility of cultivating one's own land, but as an insurance against unpredictable weather conditions, people said that there was the possibility of finding work on tea plantations, or becoming a carpenter, a trade he was familiar with, having taught himself by watching Vinod Chacha.

With the help of his friend and cousin Sukhdeo, he had built a boat which the two of them went fishing in, the fish caught, either providing for the two families or bartered or sold to the villagers. Now even the fish was gone as the water level had receded. First the clear water had turned into mud and finally the mud had caked up into dry rock hard bricks.

The two of them had been friends for ever. They had grown up together, had got married in the same year, shared everything, and had no secrets from each other. Parvatti was wrong when she said that Sukhdeo's fields had a lower yield than theirs because he and Lalita were work-shy. She did not take into account that they had help from Parsad's widowed sister Umma who lived with them. The way he looked at things, if he harvested more, it was his duty to share some of his crops with his friend. He would do the same for me, he told the sceptical Parvatti. He knew that Sukhdeo would die for him as easily as he would for him, if, Bhagwan forbids, the life of either was under threat. He knew that it was in a woman's nature to doubt everything. Parvatti would smile sarcastically whenever he told her how devoted to him Sukhdeo was. Whenever there was any problem, like most men, he would discuss it with his friend rather than with his wife. She was a woman and wouldn't have any idea. He trusted her in household matters. It was not a woman's fault, but Bhagwan did not make women as clever as men.

The two friends met regularly under the peepul tree enjoying a bidhi, a reefer, on which each pulled with comical intensity, blowing the smoke out of their noses, nodding gravely at some half-formed idea before passing it on to the other, and sharing the last half of a bottle of toddy. The dry season had wreaked havoc on palm trees as well, and toddy was just as scarce as everything else. After two sleepless nights thinking about it, he had made up his mind to ask his friend what he thought of moving to Jharkhand.

'Tell me, Sukhdeo, who are we?'

'Why you ask? Have you forgotten?' Sukhdeo was not known for his wit, but sometimes he could surprise his friend. The latter laughed and gave him his hand to clap.

'No, I mean our race, our people, who are we? Where do we come from?'

'Oh, I see. Do you mean Bihar… we are Bihari?'

'Bihari! Good. Tell me, what does Bihari mean? In Sanskrit?'

'Arrey, why you ask? Am I the one who knows book?'

'In Sanskrit, Bihari means traveller. So, you see, we are natural born travellers.' Sukhdeo still had no idea what he was driving at, but from Parsad's grave tone, he suspected that he had something important to say.

'So?'

'With the conditions the fields are in, there is not much point staying in this dump. Sukkha chooth dayin! I think we should sell up and go.'

'Go? Go where?

'Have you observed the weeds growing on our land? What do they do when they encounter rocks?' He did not give his friend time to respond. 'When there are rocks in its path, the weed will produce longer stems and tendrils allowing it to circumvent the rock in its quest for soil, is all I am saying.' Sukhdeo did not always understand his friend's drift, but he was full of admiration for his way with words. Parsad then mentioned Jharkhand, and the good things he had heard about the place.

'Oh, Lalita would never agree, all her relatives are here.'

'Relatives, yes, of course,' Parsad said as if he had never given any thought to them

'Why you ask?' Sukhdeo suddenly said in alarm. 'Are you thinking of going there?' He stared at his friend for a while and then almost wailed. 'No, you cannot go without me…'

'Arrey yaar, I will never go anywhere without you, you know that.'

'Lalita won't budge, so best not to talk about it again.'

Sukhdeo is my friend, and I cannot do anything without him, he thought as he lay in bed listlessly, on his third consecutive sleepless night. Parvatti found it difficult to sleep when her man kept sighing and tossing about.

'Arrey, you are not sleeping, you keep sighing and scratching, why don't you go to sleep?' It should be obvious to anybody that one does not choose insomnia for the fun of it, but now that she had this little boy growing inside her, he was even more tender and loving to her. He just smiled to himself in the dark. She was such a fine person and he loved her so much, even if she was not all that bright.

'Piari,' he said, 'we are producing nothing here.'

'Yes, father of our unborn child,' she immediately agreed. 'Have you thought of how we are going to feed this extra mouth?' At the same time she caught his hand and placed it on her round belly. It was smooth and warm, and he could feel it pulsating as she breathed in and out.

'I have thought we could move to a better place, but the relatives? How can we leave them?'

'Arrey, relatives, belatives!' she said dismissively. 'Will they feed the baby when he will have no food?'

'That's what I told Sukhdeo,' he lied. He sensed her anger and knew immediately that she resented the fact that he had first talked to his friend, but it was an age-old thing.

'Maybe we should go to Calcutta,' she said. 'I have heard that the Angrezi have big plans and that people there are doing very well.'

'Don't talk to me about the Angrezi,' he said bitterly. 'After the battle of Buxar, where my Pitaji lost an arm, they claimed diwani rights, took people's taxes and promised to govern fairly, but what did they do?' He paused for breath, and with uncharacteristic indignation fired his last salvo. 'They cannot even guarantee rain, pteh!'

'You say there is no work here? You are a good carpenter…'

'There is nothing. I have asked everybody. When no one earns anything, people don't wants chairs and tables. They sit on the ground and beat their chests. There is only one thing left to do.' He took a deep breath but said nothing. Parvatti turned her head towards him in expectation, but he seemed lost in thought.

'Haa..n?' she questioned. All he could think of was to say, 'Tomorrow we go to the Mandir and pray. Buy some bananas and coconut.'

'Arrey, you men are so clever,' Parvatti said. 'We have no money, and the only remedy you can think of is to spend what little we have buying bananas and coconuts for Gods.'

He did not approve of her flippancy, but said nothing; she had not finished. 'If Bhagwan wants to help, does he really want us to waste what little savings we have on him? Arrey, he can get all the bananas and coconuts he wants up there in Svarga,' she said. And he probably has no time for bananas and coconuts anyway, he must be gorging himself on good expensive cakes from London England that come in tins with pictures on them.' This time she was going too far.

'Be careful what you say, piari. Sometimes you are so lacking in respect,' he tut tutted. 'No, we go to Mandir tomorrow.' She said nothing for a while. If he wants to go to the Mandir, it is a waste of time, but I am too sleepy to argue.

'Jharkand,' she said suddenly. 'My cousin Bhobesh, he went there, and auntie says he is doing all right. A mosquito began to buzz in the far corner of the room. They kept quiet in expectation for its next move. The little buzzer buzzed for a bit and finally landed on her forehead. She slapped it and of course missed.

'You should have spat on your hand first,' he said. She had no idea what he was talking about, and turned to him to ensure that he had not lost his marbles.

'My Pitaji... Oh Piari, what a saint that man! He used to say that if you have wet hands, it's much easier to swot mosquitoes. You should have spat on your hand.' Mysteriously the mosquito flew away, at least for a while.

'But Sukhdeo doesn't want to go to Jharkhand.' Parsad said tearfully. Parvatti was unable to hide her anger this time. She pushed his hand away from her belly, sat up in one quick movement, was on the point of giving him a mouthful, but decided to express herself more moderately.

'You mean, father of my unborn child, you mean you have discussed this with him first? Is he your wife or am I?' He could not see why that was a problem, but he was not insensitive enough to voice his true reasons: women do not understand these things. It is well-known that they have smaller brains. The Pandit said so. Still, sometimes she surprised him and he had begun to wonder whether Parvatti might not be an exception to this age-old rule.

'I have known him so much longer,' he said weakly. 'Anyway he says Lalita will not move from here.'

Parvatti shook her head and said that she did not understand his stance. If Sukhdeo wanted to stay in this dump, he was welcome to it, but to her, there was no choice. She would never let her baby starve because Lalita's relatives lived in Allapur. Anyway doesn't she hate them all? As far as Parvatti was concerned, they should leave for Jharkhand, and the sooner the better, because in a matter of days she would be in no position to travel. He said nothing, but he was not happy.

Women did not understand about the friendship between men, and seemed jealous of it. This bond was something as sacred as the love between a man and a woman, but on a different level. A man needed a woman for her beauty, her body, to cuddle and to make love to, to look after the family's needs, to bear and rear children. There was no greater pleasure than to link your two bodies together and be one for a while, and sleep with your arms around each other, at least when it was not too hot. With a man, it was everything else, you can talk to a man, make jokes, tell stories, share a smoke and a drink, discuss serious matters. You can expect a man friend to lay down his life for you, and he can expect the same from you. You are of course ready to lay down your life for your woman, but may Bhagwan preserve good men from the shame of a woman giving her life for you.

Think of the boy, she said. Surely we want to give him a good start in life. Parvatti had a point there. She had insight, she was indeed sometimes as clever as a man. He must find a way to convince Sukhdeo.

Fortunately next day, it was Sukhdeo who surprisingly said that Lalita was of the opinion that there was no future in Allapur or Gaya, or even Patna, and that they should go to Calcutta. The battle was won. The details could be worked out later. Umma, with whom nobody discussed anything, had no choice but to accompany her brother and Parvatti to wherever they decided. Nobody asked her opinion, she was not expected to have any. Not only was she a woman, but she was also a widow, and as such, she had no rights. Brothers looked after their widowed sisters, as a sacred duty. However, in this case, Umma knew that it was with grace and generosity that her younger brother did this, because he was a good and loving man. She remembered how they used to tie a rakhi, a ribbon, round each other's wrists every year before she got married, swearing eternal protection to each other. He knew that if fate had wished it, roles might have been reversed. He could have been the victim of a serious accident and Umma would have looked after him with the same devotion. Of course she worked in the fields, did more than half the housework, washing and mending the family's clothes, cooking and cleaning.

Parsad listened to his friend, and then explained that Jharkhand was nearer, and made it possible to come back and visit friends and relatives, not too often, maybe once or twice a year. Sukhdeo said that Lalita would like that, said that he would ask, and was surprised when she agreed. The friends stared at each other for a few seconds, unable to speak, as if under a spell, then suddenly they nodded to each other. Yes we will take the plunge. Go to Jharkhand in the first instance, and if that did not work out, then they could always go further.

Sukhdeo had next to nothing, and depended on his friend who still had his two cows and a bullock and a cart. He also had some money and besides, Parvatti had jewellery. It was a tradition when the going was good, for a husband to buy jewellery for wife and daughters, which they would wear at their leisure, but there was always an understanding that in an emergency, they could be used to bolster family finances, by pawning or selling. Lalita, for her part had none to speak of. They took no more than a week to prepare for the departure.

Parsad had enquired from people who claimed they knew about the road, and had even made a sort of map. At first he had no idea about the daunting distances involved, but by the time he realised the enormity of the project ahead, the momentum had become unstoppable. The two men had hoped that they might have made some good money by selling their land, but the only big zamindar who had expressed an interest, knowing they were desperate, offered very little and they had no choice.

They said their tearful good-byes to everybody and loaded their possessions on the cart, and the five of them left Allapur with an equal mixture of optimism and foreboding. It was very much a shot in the dark, but the wretched condition of Allapur made them see the unknown place they were aiming for, which nobody knew much about, as a land of plenty wrapped in all the colours of the rainbow and where the aroma of jasmine and gulab filled the air.

As there was only enough room for two people in the cart, in view of the possessions of the two families, they sat inside and walked in alternation. The resolute Parvatti tried to make a case against the preferential treatment everybody, Lalita included, insisted upon for her, and was voted down. Suddenly, without warning, it began to rain. It was not just a drizzle, but a downpour, and the travellers looked at each other wryly, none having second thoughts, and they did not look back.

After two days, they reached Bodh Gaya, and as none of them had seen this marvel, they spent a whole morning looking at it from all angles, together with hundreds of pilgrims. They sat under the Bodhi tree and meditated, praying for guidance and prosperity. Parvatti collected a few seeds, intending to plant them when they found a place to settle in.

'Yes, good idea,' said Sukhdeo. 'Our new house will be blessed.'

'All I am interested in, is a nice big tree like this one, to provide shade for us,' said Parvatti. Sometimes Parsad despaired of his wife, loving and lovely though she was. First she was not all that bright, and now she is being disrespectful to the Supreme Being. Lalita ordered Sukhdeo to pick Bodhi seeds too, as she did not want to lose out, either on blessing, wealth or on shade.

After Bodh Gaya, they made for Sagarpur, and that was a never-ending, bone-shattering journey. The heat was relentless and the wind dusty and dry. The pregnant Parvatti, who should have been taking things easy felt the strain, but she did not complain half as much as Lalita. As long as I do not have a miscarriage, she thought. Please Bhagwan, she cried aloud one night, be merciful, do not let my unborn baby pay for my impious thoughts. Bhagwan is not vengeful, piari, Parsad said, taking her hands in his, He knows you do not mean those impolite things you say. She did not tell him, but she did. She often used to think that if just some of the thousands of gods paid the slightest attention to the millions of poor people who prayed to them so frequently and with such fervour, it would impossible to understand why there was still so much poverty and wretchedness on this earth. Live to be a hundred, she will never understand what her Pitaji had done to deserve Bhagwan's ire and all the afflictions visited upon him in his lifetime.

Lakhaipur, Fatehpur, Danua followed, and the travellers were bearing up quite well. Except that Lalita never stopped moaning: When it was hot, it was too hot, she was being fried alive! When at night it freshened up, it was too cold she could feel her bones turning to ice; when the atmosphere was heavy and still, she sweated and complained, and when there was the slightest breeze, the wind was blowing dirt in her eyes! Parsad was so proud that the pregnant Parvatti never complained. They ate what they could find to buy, they fished and sometimes, they stole from vegetable patches at night, promising themselves that when they were in the money, they would pay back what they had stolen with interest to the Pandit for his Mandir, swore that they would never shoo away beggars, even if their blindness or crippled condition were fake. On some rare occasions they found work on fields and Parsad mended broken wheels or fixed tables and chairs for some villagers who gave them food in return. The cows gave them milk and they spent memorable nights, often sleeping in the open air, under the protection of stars, sometimes around a wood fire over which they roasted a wood pigeon or a small hare when they caught one. Parsad did not have to be begged to tell them stories of Birbal and the Mahabharatha that his father had told him. He had a special fondness for Birbal, and regaled them with the tales of Akbar's confidant, clown and adviser, leaving everybody in good spirits, enabling them to sleep better and thus wake up refreshed in the morning. Everybody, Lalita included, fussed over Parvatti and there was never one cross word exchanged between them until now.

It took them over a month before they reached Hazaribagh which proved true to its name of place of a thousand gardens. Parsad's first reaction on seeing the hilly slopes with its breathtaking patches of colour, was to cry out to Parvatti, Look Piari, the moon collided with a rainbow in the night and the bits have fallen over the vales. Marigolds and poppies, wild hibiscus and a multitude of flowers unseen in Allapur, and the undulating hills which reminded him of lovers intertwined, were one rhythm locked in another. Do we need to go further? Parsad asked in a tone which left no one in any doubt as to where his own inclinations lay.

They had all fallen in love with the place, although Lalita, perhaps wisely for once, said, flowers are nice to look at and smell, but can one eat them? They found a nice sheltered corner in the forest and decided to stay there whilst they investigated the place. They were aware of the dangers lurking in the surroundings. They knew about tigers and pythons, wolves, jackals and wild boars, and hoped that a fire kept going all night long would be enough to deter those beasts. They found some alti kachu, cocoyam, growing on the banks of a small stream. They caught a one-year old nilgai, killed it, skinned it and roasted it together with the yam over a wood fire, spreading an aroma which blended with the forest's own distinct smell of dried and decaying leaves which they would later be able to recall effortlessly, and had an unforgettable feast. They arranged to sleep round the ghari, needing only thin sheets to cover themselves with, and for the first time since they had left Allapur, they felt relaxed and slept soundly, unperturbed by the buzzing of mosquitoes. They were all surprised at how quickly their muscles got used to their daily walking marathons.

The people had seemed nice enough, and had assured the newcomers that water was plentiful. They explained that the place not only benefited from a generous monsoon, but was blessed with waters of the Ganga Jamna and the Damodar as well as a multitude of their tributaries. The soil was dark and rich, and they made up their mind to start looking for land. They found a family who had a small plot to sell and started negotiations with them. It was smaller than what they had hoped for, but it would have to do for a start. With Bhagwan's blessings they would use the profits to extend and buy more land. Parsad and Sukhdeo were convinced that they within a day of agreeing terms with the prospective seller.

On their second night their optimism had become uncontrollable, and they spent a whole night round a fire, in great spirits, watching the golden yellow flames dance merrily to the tune of the cracking music of the embers, making plans and telling stories. There was an abundance of trees, fruit trees, pines and banyans as well as other common denizens of the forest. At one point, as their fire was going out, the men went to find more wood, and in the semi-darkness they thought that it would be easiest to cut a few branches from an old jackfruit tree. They had not slept as soundly as this since before the onset of the drought.

In the morning however, they were woken up by a big racket, and to their consternation, they saw a small crowd of men, women and children brandishing sticks and making angry noises, surging towards them, nothing about their shouting and the expression on their faces indicating that they were well-disposed to the newcomers. Lalita said that the people might be thinking that they were chamars, untouchables, who were soiling their environment and were bent on driving them away. Tell them we are not chamars, she urged the men, tell them that we come from the best families in Bihar. Parsad felt stupid, but with Sukhdeo's help, they tried to convey that information to the mob, but they realised that their bhojpuri was hardly understood. They had no nagpuri, which seemed to be the language of the mob. A young stalwart with a pleasant enough face, contrasting with the hostile scowls and pursed lips of the crowd, finally managed to explain in bhojpuri that they were to follow them, leaving them no choice. They meekly did what they were told, spurred on by the angry and menacing crowd. Some of the younger men began prodding them in the ribs with sticks, but they were ordered to stop by an elder.

They were led to where the two Bihari men had cut some wood from the jackfruit tree. It was then that Parsad noticed that all the trees in the area had a pink string tied round them. Everybody began talking and expostulating at the same time, and the young bhojpuri speaker explained that they had broken a sacred law of Jharkhand. They had damaged a protected tree. How could they not have seen the rakhi strings tied round them, they were asked. Parsad explained that it was not their intention to break their laws, that they were peaceful people, Bihari folks who did not know the local customs, and in any case, they had not seen the pink strings in the dark. Tell them to pack up their things and leave, shouted a small group, tell them they are not wanted here. Biharis are worse than Chamars, shouted a small group in nagpuri. The young interpreter then explained about Rakhi. Rakhi? Meaning no offence, wasn't the rakhi for brothers and sisters? Parsad asked. The young man smiled and shook his head, and translating the cacophonous flow of words from the crowd, explained that in Jharkhand, people considered trees as their own flesh and blood, effectively their brothers and sisters. If everybody chops down trees wantonly, in no time at all there would be none left, someone said and the young man translated. So the folks tie a rakhi round chosen trees and expect everybody to respect them. Even picking a single leaf from a protected tree was an inexcusable offence against sacred Rakhi lore.

They apologised profusely, pleading ignorance and promised that never again would they show disrespect to the local people and their customs. The young stalwart translated and the group dispersed, although no one except one or two men smiled and nodded to the pregnant Parvatti as they left. No great harm done, sighed Parsad, we've salvaged our honour, but he was wrong. It seemed that the whole of Jharkhand had heard about their misdemeanours. People who had previously received them graciously now turned their backs on them. The farmer withdrew his offer to sell them land, and they knew that no one else would.

They had said from the start that if Hazaribagh proved unsuitable, they would make for Lohardaga, but they all asked themselves one question: Why would Lohardaga be any better than Harazibagh? Only Lalita voiced her reservations. She started screaming that she wanted to go back to Allapur, that she was always against that stupid idea, and for the first time ever, Parsad heard his friend tell his wife to shut up.

'Do you want to go back to that place where we have nothing, and starve? Go by yourself if you must!' He regretted his outburst and tried to bring a conciliatory note in proceedings by saying that he had heard that the Subarnarekha river had made Lohardaga prosperous, that there was rich soil all along the banks of its many tributaries. You just take a look at the dark soil, he said.

The optimism at the start of their trek was now in tatters, revealing the extent of the nakedness of their prospects, but they had no choice. In Lohardaga, which they reached after an exhausting trek, they were advised that they might be able to buy some land at a good price in a small village called Hundru, and ended up there.

They thought that it was a promising place, and believed that they could be happy here. A zamindar on the Subarnarska river had some land he wanted to sell, and they went and had a look at it. Even the naturally fault-finding women were bowled over. The zamindar was marrying his first born, which was why he needed the money. Parvatti, forgetting that one does not address a male stranger, suddenly asked if Zamindarji was not planning to give the newly weds some almaris and tables. The man was so stunned that he forgot to frown, and there and then an agreement was reached, whereby the land changed hands for a mixture of money and furniture.

Hundru seemed like a really good place to start a little their new life. The friends ended up with about two bigha of prime land each. They began by building a small hut for each family and dug an irrigation canal which would bring water from a tributary of the Subarnarska to their fields. They were very optimistic about making a real go of this new situation. As luck would have it, another rich landowner was also marrying his daughter, and Parsad was again asked to make an almari, a bed and two chairs for the couple. This was an unexpected bonus which helped him buy a couple of goats and some hens for himself, and the same for Sukhdeo. ("He would have done the same for me, piari".) They sowed vegetables, beans and pulses, built pens for goats and in anticipation of better times, a stable for yet to be purchased cattle. The hens roosted on trees.

The crops were excellent, the cows gave good milk, the hens laid eggs a-plenty and they made good profit. However, gradually they discovered that the people of this new place were no better than those of Hazaribagh. They were now openly hearing people saying things like "Ek Bihari Sau Bimari" (one Bihari hundred diseases). The news of their success was making folks in the area jealous, and they found that the goodwill which they thought they had earned by their hard work, was but an illusion. Still things were looking up for the pioneers, and to crown it all, Parvatti was delivered of a fine little boy. They all saw this as a happy omen, good things on the horizon. The boy was called Rajendra Parsad, and known as Raju. The birth was difficult, and Parvatti, already exhausted by the long trek became very weak after the delivery.

It was the baby, more than anything which made the place tolerable to them, but the land also continued to produce good yields. My boy has brought good fortune to us all, Parsad told everybody. However, less than a month after Raju's birth, Parvatti caught a chill in the rain one morning. Parsad was distraught, and prayed day and night for her recovery. The neighbours surprisingly rallied and recommended a Sadhu, who they said had a gift for healing second to none, but even he had to admit defeat. You wasted valuable time, he chided the distraught husband. You were crass and stupid! You should have sent for me straight away, now by your fault, the devil's work has gone too far, there is nothing even I can do now. Pray to Bhagwan to forgive you your stupidity. He spat on the ground, muttering, Stupid Bihari, what else can you expect from them!

That night, Parvatti was in a sweat, feeling hot and cold at the same time. Parsad was disconsolate and knew not what to do. He sat by her side, took her hand in his, every now and then wiping her brow with a cold compress. He could see that she badly wanted to say something. He tried to discourage her, but she smiled wanly and insisted on talking. 'Tell me, how... what you did when your Pitaji told you that he was getting you married to his friend's daughter... to me?' She smiled wanly and he did not fail to detect an impish glint in her near lifeless eyes. He felt uneasy, turned his head away, and with a guilty smile he admitted that he had run away because he had not wanted to marry someone he had never seen. She shook her head, the glint in he eye slightly more pronounced. You thought I had buck teeth, she managed to say with a large smile. 'Yes, some liar had said... but the moment I cast my eyes on you, piari, I knew I wanted to share my life you,' he said, making an effort to keep his voice from breaking. 'I know,' whispered Parvatti letting go of his hand, but the smile was still there. 'Even if you had buck teeth, I would have wanted no one else,' he muttered, but she never heard him. Parsad never cried in public, not even in front of Sukhdeo, but the death of his beloved wife shook him to the very foundation. Although he had qualms about widows feeling obliged to commit suttee by throwing themselves on their husband's funeral pyre, he felt that he would not have needed much en-couragement to do the same, as Parvatti's human remains rose up in smoke on their way to Svarga. Bhagwan would surely accept her in that blessed place. He was not vindictive. He surely knew that she liked to laugh and say things she did not mean, but she was a good woman, the best.

It did not take him more than one week of marriage before he became convinced that he could not have had a better life companion. He had wrong-ly thought that like all women, she was not terribly bright, but as he sat under the guava tree on his own at sunset on the day of the immolation, he could remember any number of occasions when she had dazzled him by her com-mon sense. Her fortitude during that exhausting trek was an example to everybody, and no doubt it was the fatigue which had sapped her strength and finished her off. What had possessed him to contemplate this reckless adventure? Nobody could understand the magnitude of his sadness, the gnawing regret, the guilt, the depth of his loss. He had lost not only a wife that he loved to distraction, but his best friend. He wondered if she knew the strength of his devotion to her. Did she understand that when he had seemed to be putting her down, he had only been joking? He knew that he had not known how to express his unbounded love for her properly; he was a clumsy man. She was such a forthright woman, had such generosity. Never once had she made poor Umma feel unwanted. How many wives would have been so willing to share the little they had with a third person? Only now he realised fully what a sound head she had on her shoulders. He had been such a brute. If it was possible to put the clock back, he would do things so very differently, he would cherish her as she deserved, and make sure that she knew what his real feelings were. He knew now what an admirable woman she was. How could Bhagwan be so heartless?

From that day, although he would continue to recite prayers, no one would ever hear him praise the Lord. As his copious tears streamed down his cheeks, he could feel the sorrow deep inside his belly as a real physical pain. Were it not for the little boy, he would have prayed for death so his aatma, his soul, could go and join hers.

Umma was a devoted mother substitute to Raju. They tried to rebuild their lives, but Parsad became disenchanted with Hundru. To his surprise, his greatest ally in this was Lalita. She had never stopped hankering after Calcutta, and now he found himself listening sympathetically to her constant evocations of that paradise on earth. In the past he had always dismissed whatever she said as the rantings of a mad woman. Besides he regularly heard people talking about the capital of British India, and how easy it was to make a good living there, how everybody was so much better off than the poor peasants of Hundru or Lohardaga, and so on. Calcutta was very much in everybody's mind. Raju was two years old by now, and had turned into a healthy and spirited little boy, cherished by everybody, with the possible exception of Lalita, who would have dearly loved to have a son of her own, and as a result resented the toddler. Parvatti, who mistrusted her husband's friend, would have been surprised at how fond of the boy Sukhdeo was.

One fine day, the two men did it again. They took the decision to move to Calcutta. Lalita now declared that she was against the move, but the men were adamant. You are lacking in ambition, Sukhdeo said to his wife. You women can only see where the next meal is coming from. Men have to think of the future, and the future was Calcutta, where the British East India Company were working miracles for the benefit of the people of this land. Parsad was still dubious about those Angrezis, but said nothing.

Umma yet again had no say in the matter, but she had found a new role in her life, that of mother substitute to the toddler. Nothing else mattered. Parsad readily agreed with everybody who said that no mother could have done better for his little boy. Her devotion to both of them was total. This time the farewells were less tearful, and the trek was much more strenuous, but their determination was just as strong.

CHAPTER 2

◆◆◆

Inhambane

THE CHOPI PEOPLE had always had a unique relationship with elephants whom they called their forest cousins. The elders told of how their first ancestor suddenly appeared in the forests of Inhambane amidst a herd of elephants and started the Chopi tribe. Midala even had his own elephant, Bobo Big Ears, and he took great pride in the fact that his little boy Abo could handle the big beast with the same ease as the tribe's champion rowers their canoes. They were the husbands of all the teams from Mambone to Inharrime. Even as a toddler, the boy had never been afraid of the big beast, laughing his head off when one day, Bobo suddenly wrapped his trunk around him, raised him high up in the air and gently rocked him from left to right, to the consternation of his mother. It was as if the boy and the big-eared beast could read each other's minds. Abo assured Midala that Bobo not only understood Chopi, but also spoke it. Doting father that he was, he had only smiled condescendingly, and this had upset the son who hated being disbelieved. 'I know you don't believe me, but it's true,' he had said indignantly.

'Well, Abo, my beloved, the day I hear you two talk I will believe you, I promise,' the warrior had said, making an effort not to laugh. The little boy was not easily pacified.

'But my father, how can you hear him talk to me? He only talks to me in my sleep.'

If Bobo was almost family, the rogue elephants which ran amok over everything, demolishing huts and fences, devouring crops, were an altogether different matter. Sometimes they even trampled unwary people to death.

Elephant patrols had been in existence ever since man came into contact with their big cousins. Their hunger drove them to seek sustenance wherever they could and they trampled over crops rendering them useless. Thus all able-bodied men and some of the more daring women began guarding the plantations at night, armed with spears and torches. At the approach of the crop raiders, they would holler at the top of their voices, and brandish the flames in order to frighten the attackers, but it took more than noise to stop the fearless pachyderms, fuelled by their great hunger. Spears and arrows had little effect, and it was agreed that there was little anyone could do against this calamity. It was like stopping huts leaking during the harmattan. Or smoke rising. Sadly, many valiant people were trampled to death for not much.

Midala was not only the commander of the Cojo's warriors, but he also had the reputation of being the brainiest man around, invariably finding solutions to the tribe's problems. He was the one who had thought of using chillies to which the big beasts were averse. He asked everybody to plant the pungent plant around their crops of maize, okra, cassava or tomatoes, and this had indeed kept the famished beasts at bay, if only for a short time. Elephants, however, are resourceful and clever, for weren't they related to the Chopis after all? It was not long, as Midala had anticipated, before they had learnt to uproot the chillies, discard them and then trample and devour the defenceless crops.

For weeks Midala had used all his mental resources to find another solution, and after spending many sleepless hours in deep thought, he had come up with a modified system which he was now ready to put to the test. The crops had flourished and the big-eared beasts had been seen inching towards the plantations. Midala was going to act.

He had instructed people to weave thick ropes from sisal plants which grew in abundance on the slopes of the hills surrounding the village and had despatched the near redundant Elephant Patrol, augmented by an ever-willing army of kids who usually hampered more than helped into the forest. Their mission was to collect as much dung as they could find. When the destructive cousins were getting ready for a raid, they drew nearer and nearer to the settlements providing dung aplenty, and this, ironically was now going to be used against them. We fight them with sticks, we fight them with stones and now we're gonna fight them with their own shit, the people said merrily.

In the morning all able-bodied men and women had been asked to assemble in the fields around the strangler fig. Kids did not have to be dragooned in, they just turned up, to help prepare for the final and decisive combat. Midala had been on his feet since the roosters had begun to crow, preparing the ground and giving out instructions. The women prepared the mixture of dung, game fat and crushed chillies mixed with ash and straw, and then the men wrapped this mix all along the ropes, held by older children, like one does the skewer with meat before roasting.

The application of the paste was a delicate operation, for often, no sooner had a fair length of the rope been primed than a previously done length would see its wrapping plop to the ground. Midala thought that he really should work on finding a way of getting the paste to stick. Perhaps he should experiment with different amounts of ash.

With the new system now ready for inauguration, there was no need for an elephant patrol the size of an army. Goja, the palm-wine tapper who claimed he never slept a wink at night had volunteered to stand guard with Midala. Abo begged to go with him, swearing that he would not go to sleep on his legs as Rolena, his mother, claimed he would. Midala remembered how excited he had been when his own father had taken him night hunting for the first time, and pleaded with his wife to let the boy have his wish for once. He understood that the history of the village was in the making that night and wanted his son to be part of it. That was how the traditions and histories of the tribe were transmitted from generation to generation.

The ropes were placed around the field, suspended at regular intervals by posts fixed to the ground or to trees. Together, father and son, and the self-proclaimed insomniac waited, although the latter leaning against a tree was soon snoring blissfully. It was not long before they heard a distant rumble. Clearly the elephants were on the march and their stampede was gathering speed. With the help of Abo, Midala lit the ropes one by one, with torches. A pungent smell immediately filled the air, but by sheer will-power the boy kept his cough in. Unfortunately the wind was blowing in the wrong direction, and the raiders were protected from the irritating stench rising and floating away in the opposite direction, and kept approaching. Would all the work the tribe had put in produce any result? The rumble grew louder. Father and son held their breaths, and to their dismay the shapes of the beasts began appearing in the moonlight, growing bigger and more threatening by the second. Suddenly, what must have been the leader of the herd stopped and gave out an angry growl. Thankfully the wind had changed direction at the right time. The whole herd began groaning and ground to a standstill, and to Abo's delight, they turned round and with howls of despair, they ambled away, defeated. Midala felt the grip of his boy's hand on his grow tighter, and never would he be prouder of his son. Never again would the raiders pose such a threat to the tribe. Now that they had a system, he would modify and improve things all the time. Goja suddenly woke up and jumping in the air shouting merrily, we did it, we did it!

No sooner had the tribe neutralised the danger from their rampaging cousins, than the tom-toms began rumbling one morning. The message originated from Massingwé and was being successively relayed by tribes living near Morrumbene, Pembe, and then Maxixe until they reached Mambocké. Most people had understood the broad thrust of what was happening. Ships had been sighted by the folks of Massingwé, heading towards their lands, and it was not good news.

This was a complete surprise to the tribe. The Cojo who was supposed to be the protector and chief of the tribe was known to be in league with the slave-traders, and he quite shamelessly sold his own people to them. For baubles, fire-water, and hats. He had a predilection for gaudy headwear. This time, it was clear that he had not been informed of the impending visit from his so-called friends, Sheikh Yahaya Ibn Qalb and Captain Flyte-Camilton. As a rule he was warned of their visit in good time, to enable him to assemble the number of slaves required by his associates. When the captives brought home from the wars were not enough, he fulfilled his quota by putting the tribe under all sorts of pressure that Midala, the military commander did not approve of. He started by taking treacherous measures, getting his corrupt courts to send minor miscreants to the escape-proof clay pit from which they could more easily be sold to his two partners. The sinister Zanzibari and his equally hateful English partner in crime could manipulate the Cojo, who always loudly proclaimed that he was appointed by the Great Spirit to protect and guide his people. As if the admirable masata the tribe had elaborated over centuries, from cashew nuts and tangerines were not good enough, the Cojo had become addicted to English fire water. The moment the visitors dangled a bottle of gin in front of him, he became weak in the knees, like a hunter coming home after a week in the forest, stalking some game, approaching the bed of his favourite wife at full moon. They could mould him in any shape they wished, like the best potters in the tribe, their clay.

Midala was torn between his military duty and his conscience, his oath to obey his Chief blindly at all times conflicting with his view of what was right and wrong. Responsible for his fighters, he had to keep to himself his qualms about the senseless ventures the Cojo embarked upon. The Spirits who had appointed the Chief must surely have their reasons, although these eluded Midala. Fortunately he had Rolena, and she was a wise woman. To her he would reveal all his reservations, but he had not approved of her suggestion that he ought to work towards the elimination of the Cojo with like-minded elders. He could never contemplate or condone treason. He was himself the son of a warrior who had taught him everything he knew about obedience, to the Spirits, to the Chief, to his people. His life was at their disposal. He had once believed with all the fibres in his body that the Cojo's person was sacrosanct, but the seed of doubt sown in his mind by his wife over the years had sprouted, and was thriving with the waters and fertilisers from his own conscience. Which is why he was so full of torment, why his jaws were never relaxed, why he never had a full night's sleep, why he no longer laughed as heartily as his erstwhile cheerful nature dictated.

It was clear to any thinking man of the tribe that the Cojo was in thrall to the slave traders. He seemed unaware that the foreigners were cheating him, with their glass beads and hats, their colourful textiles and their gin. Midala, as military chief had often asked for guns and ammunition, to be used in the many wars the Cojo initiated, but the sinister pair kept promising them for the next time, and failed to deliver, no doubt determined to keep the tribe weak. Over the years they had brought a handful of guns with very little ammunition, and these were defective and seemed to be a greater danger to the user than to an enemy.

He no longer relished fighting the Cojo's wars when he did not understand their necessity. Military man though he was, after the many senseless killings that he had been party to, he had turned into a man of peace, believing in negotiation and thinking it much more satisfying to ensure that his fellow tribesmen had plenty to eat, to win wrestling and regatta competitions with the neighbouring tribes than to be constantly fighting and killing them. Unfortunately his allegiance had to be to the paramount chief and his duty to fight his enemies, arrest criminals, and carry out whatever task the Cojo wanted done. As he was no yes-man, he was never in the inner circle of the Cojo and his advice on policy was rarely sought. The chief only listened to his own coterie of toadies.

The Cojo usually gave him his orders, which he would carry out without questioning, for that had always been the tradition of fighting men. That was what his father had taught him. The Cojo wanted a war with the Hopparis. He was a soldier, he owed the Hopparis nothing. He prepared his army in the best way he knew, planned his strategy, and attacked the enemy. Until now, the Spirits be praised, they had always seen to it that his men came out victorious. Our boys need wives, go kidnap some women from the Jaba tribe, the Cojo would order. Midala would set out with his commandos and come back within a week with reluctant brides for his fellow villagers as well as captives who could provide labour, and again be sold as slaves. Until now, he rarely questioned the rights or wrongs of the matter. His belief was that if the Spirits did not approve, they would be roundly defeated. Would the Spirits favour the wicked against the good? Besides what would happen if everybody questioned the orders of the leader? He imagined how difficult it was to keep a tribe going smoothly. Discipline was of the essence, for without it, anarchy and chaos would end up clogging the system, like weeds strangling the crops, if they were not exterminated the moment they emerged from the soil.

The council of elders who was appointed to judge those accused of theft, of causing grievous bodily harms, of murder or rape, were noticeably readier to pronounce the guilty verdict on little or no evidence whenever Ibn Qalb or Flyte-Camilton were due for a visit. One more slave meant one more bottle of English gin.

The men on the ships had an insatiable demand for slaves, and he knew that the arrangement with the Cojo notwithstanding, if the latter could not deliver, they would not think twice about forcing their way in and taking what they needed. They had guns against which spears and arrows could do little. Rolena had seemed shocked by what she heard. The man must be stopped, she said. I think you should throw a big rock in front of his canoe. Was this really high treason or common sense? A mortal sin in the eyes of the Spirits or a selfless act in the defence of the tribe?

'Father,' Abo asked him in the morning, 'what are those monsters from the sea that everybody is talking about?'

'Monsters?'

'Everybody talks of slavos, coming to capture and kill us. I saw them, they were giant monsters dribbling slime form all over their slimy green bodies.'

'You saw them? Where?'

'In my sleep my father, but I was not frightened.'

'No, they are human, and it's slavers, not slavos, but don't worry. Daddy and his army will stop them, trust me.' He knew that it was an empty promise. He did not usually indulge in that, but what does one tell an apprehensive child? He wondered whether his duty towards his children outweighed his duty towards the Spirits.

CHAPTER 3

— ◆◆◆ —

Year of the Sheep

Hugh Breac Mackenzie greeted the news with mixed feelings, but he had always wanted to become a father. His own father had provided him with a role model, in the sense that he knew that if he did the opposite of what Da did, he would be bound to be a great father. Mam said not to be too harsh on the old sot, that he was not born a drunk and that all men turned to the devil drink when they found that God sided with the lairds. He was an intelligent man who had read books, she reminded him, and spoke English like them folks doon sooth. She was as upright a woman as ever breathed the cold Highland air, but whilst she knew what motivated the greedy lairds, she could not understand the mind of God. How could a just and loving God allow so much misery on His earth? She went to church like everybody else only because she hated to have fingers pointed at her. She had heard stories of women being burnt as witches for much less, but her heart was never in it. She liked Father Anthony Ross as a man but only because he was the son of Molly Ross, a good childhood friend. She had known Anthony as a bairn, and had always liked his cheerful disposition and his ready laughter. He let her air her feelings about "your God" when there were no strangers around. The priest knew that Mrs Mackenzie meant every word she said, but cleverly made as if it was all banter and laughed it off, grateful that the woman was intelligent enough not to put him on the spot when in company. He tut tutted with feigned severity and winked at her as they parted. Having made her point, she was willing to leave it at that.

'No, Martha, I am truly delighted,' Hugh assured his wife when she told him that she suspected that she might be with child. It's probably the wrong time, the expectant mother said, as if to excuse herself. For the likes of them, Hugh mused, could there ever be a right time? 'No, lassie,' he said, 'I've always wanted a bairn in the house, rest assured, we will find the means to feed him.' She had laughed and said how did he know it was going to be a he. He had protested, a wee girl would be just as good. Hugh was as hardworking and upright a man as walked the rugged rocky glens of Strathrusdale. He had been brought up by his no-nonsense mother Mhairi after his father Kenneth had walked out and disappeared into the Highland mist. In spite of her ambivalence, she had encouraged Hugh to go to Father Ross and learn the 3 R's, with a handful of other ragamuffins of the glen, and the boy seemed to delight in it. She had some reservations about the bible the man of cloth allowed the boy to take home sometimes, but knew that it was his only chance of improving his reading skill. Anyway, she never failed to air her views about Father Ross's so-called all-loving and omnipotent God to the boy, just to provide a balanced view.

It was a great source of joy to Hugh that his formidable mother and his meek Martha, who was all sweetness and light, got on so well. Not that Mam kept her criticisms of what she saw as the failings of the younger woman to herself. She was wanting in organisational skills, used too much soap when she did the laundry, spilled too much oatmeal when she made bread, but Martha shrugged these pinpricks off because she knew the old lady meant well, and hardly gave them any thought. Mam would often think that she should keep her thoughts to herself, but although she resolved to do this, she always forgot herself when she saw what she thought was a weakness in the daughter-in-law. When Hugh teased his wife about the drubbing she endured at the hands of the old dear, she would only smile and say, 'If you think that was a drubbing, Hugh Breac Mackenzie, you should listen to what my Mam says to oor Rabbie's wife. The granny-to-be was overjoyed at the news of the new addition, but in keeping with her no-nonsense nature, her first reaction was, 'What? Another mouth to feed!' Still she shook her head and smiled, saying, Father Ross's God will provide. Then she pursed her lips and frowned for a bit, saying, 'It's all right for the wean to call me Granny when she begins to speak, but you are not to call me anything but Mam, I am not your granny, you hear? Och, and another thing, I hate baby talk… yup yup glig glig choop choop…' Hugh winked at Martha.

He whistled a tuneless and indeterminate air as he went out to collect Big Eyes and Sniffer, from their pasture. They were his lifeline, these two black cows, generous with their milk which provided for the family, when traded for oat and turnips with other cotters. Besides there was an arrangement whereby some of the women brought her their share of milk and Mam made butter which she took to the market in Boath every Friday.

Ever since the Cameron brothers of Lochaber had rented a massive stretch of land from Sir Hector Munro, the crofters knew that dark clouds were gathering. The brothers began by moving their sheep to Culcairn, and ordering the tenants to move out. Then seemingly relenting they changed their minds but demanded a big increase in rent instead. Soon after, came the coup de grace: they were limiting the available pasture to the tenants on pain of having their cattle poinded if they strayed outside the permitted area. Life had taken a turn for the worse. So far Hugh had escaped the fate of poor John Aird, whose cattle had ventured on Cameron land, and who had to pay fines of seventeen shillings, a sum which exceeded what the poor man made in two weeks. He was a good friend, John, and whenever Hugh took his cows whoring, as John said, he would laugh and say it was for him to pay Hugh, and not the other way round. Why Hugh, he would say, the whores of Edinburgh would charge less, my Jupiter had his wicked ways with your Big Eyes, and now you are paying me! Not that the God-fearing and virtuous John would know anything about the whores of Edinburgh. In any case he had never even set foot in that wicked city. He loved using bad words as a way of compensating for his sedate and unblemished life.

Hugh had never been entirely sure of where to stand in the controversy between Mam and Father Ross. Sometimes he found it expedient to believe in a benevolent God watching over His people. Certainly that afternoon, the heart of the father-to-be ringing with joyful little bells that he believed he could hear as he went to meet his two lovely cows, he believed in Him with all the fibres in his body. Yes, God would see to it that the wee boy would come out healthy, that dear sweet Martha would not suffer too much, that by the time the boy had become a strapping young man, the world would be a better place. It was bound to be. Father Ross often said that there were enlightened voices making themselves heard these days, which were bound to put right the iniquities on this earth. He only went to Sunday Mass in Boath once in a while, and only to placate Martha anyway. Mam said that if God was so kind and just, why would he need to be begged favours? Wouldn't he provide for his creatures without asking?

'God knows,' she said laughing at herself for taking His name, 'when you were a helpless wee bairn, you did not have to beg me to give you what was in my power to give you. I would steal to feed you, eggs and potatoes, turnips. I even used to milk the farmer's cow behind his back for you. Why would God only help you if you begged him?' Somehow, Hugh could not quite picture the dignified Mhairi Mackenzie furtively hiding behind a bush, bowl in hand, waiting for the farmer's wife to be out of away so she could sneak into the stable to do some illegal milking.

John Aird was always only too willing to give them a seat on his cart, and Mary Aird was always happy to see her good friend Martha. It made him so happy to see the two girls laugh and exchange gossip, although these poor dears led such a humdrum existence that he could not imagine what they had to talk about. He felt so guilty about her having so little joy in her life. Next Sunday he would definitely go, and he would pray to the good Lord to see to it that his yet-to-be-born boy grow up healthy, and implore him that if he was ever minded to visit some ailment or misfortune on the boy, to direct his wrath against him instead. Why could he only contemplate having a boy? He must be careful not to air his preference in Martha's hearing. It was selfish, but he could not control his thoughts. It was not altogether selfishness, he was sure of that, for if anything should happen to him, a boy would be more able to look after his mother than a girl. No doubt Martha would be dreaming of a little girl, and he must do nothing to make her feel bad if it was a girl, he must watch his words. To be sure, I would love my little girl just as wholeheartedly. Would I though? he wondered. From a distance he could see Loch Morie, and the shiny sheet of gold floating on its surface told him that the sun was going to set shortly, and he knew that he would soon reach the place where he had left the cows to roam in the morning. Sniffer! She made him smile, always lifting her head and sniffing disdainfully.

He kept walking at a brisk rate, trampling over the heather, absently hitting small pebbles with his walking stick, making them fly. On an impulse he decided to do the hitting with the knobby end, tightened his grip, chose a nice round granite pebble at his feet, and raising the stick above his head, he let go with all his might. The contact was perfect, he thought, and to his amazement the stone rose up in the air as if it had wings and flew away in a curve, landing at a good distance from him. Nice little game this, I'll teach the boy, he thought. Now where were Big Eyes and Sniffer? Where the hell were they? He began to fret a bit. Had they fallen into a crack somewhere? Into a bog? Suddenly it hit him like a cold blast in the face on a winter morning as one tentatively puts one's head outside the bothie. The hard-hearted Cameron brothers! At first no one believed that they would have the nerve to turn their words into actions, but had they not poinded John Aird's cattle? Where would he find the five shillings he would have to pay to get them released? Maybe as this was a first offence, Captain Cameron would let him off with a warning. With John they had been merciless though. Perhaps John had rubbed them the wrong way. He has a certain brusqueness that people in his position had better take great care to hide when dealing with the lairds and their henchmen. Hugh would keep his head down, explain that the cows had strayed inside the lairds' enclosure by mistake, that he would make sure this would not happen again. Still, God knows they had grazed all the grass on the allowable pastures, it was hunger that drove them outside their borders. What would they feed on? The brothers were not going to make it easy for him, since it was clear as the Highland air on a sunny morning that they really wanted was to be rid of everybody. Where would he go? How was he to feed his family? What would the wee one eat?

The optimism of the morning was instantly washed away by a relentless tide of gloom. He could see no way out of his predicament. As he directed his steps towards the Camerons' farm, despair had taken over completely, and the lump in his throat made it difficult for him to speak properly. He was greeted at the big iron door of the estate by Big Jim Davidson.

'What are you doing here, Hughie? Do you want to be poinded too?' And he burst out laughing.

'What can you be meaning, Jimmy?' Hugh said angrily. 'Why talk about poinding? I left my cows in pastures agreed upon by contract.'

'Ah, you must be thinking of the verbal contract between me and you. Don't you know, Hughie boy, a verbal contract isn't worth the paper it's written on, wee pal.' Big Jim guffawed aloud at the witticism, but recognising the pain he had caused, he relented.

'It's like this, Hughie, I was the one who settled this matter with you, but when I told the Captain he was reet furious. Why did you go and give those peasants so much leeway? he said. The land between the stream and crest is out of bounds for those ruffians under any circumstances, he said.'

'But Jimmy, where would my cows go to drink? They-'

'I only carry out his orders, that's what the captain said, Hughie.'

'But that's wickedness... a sin... shouldn't be allowed...' Hugh was now so confused that he could only mutter disjointed phrases.

'Listen to me Hughie, why don't you do what you should have done already? Leave the area, there is no future here for you, the brothers want yous all out and you know it. They've got the law on their side, they have all the power and you can't do nought. Why do you think they decided to stop you men from watering your beasts? They want you oot.' Although he had softened his tone, Hugh was mighty angry with him.

'You've sold your soul to the devil Jimmy Davidson!'

'Don't be saying things like that, Hughie, I have a wife and bairns. I sold the only thing I had left, to feed them, man. Masel!'

It was at that moment that Captain Allan Cameron appeared. He ignored Hugh completely and addressed himself to his man.

'What's happening Jim? Why are you not tending the new-born lambs?'

'Why Captain sir, this man Mackenzie is complaining about his cows being poinded, Captain sir.'

'Did you not tell him that his cows trespassed on enclosed pastures.'

'That's what I was explaining, Captain, sir.'

'Captain Cameron, sir, we agreed... with Jimmy here... that the cows need access to water. It is against God's laws to stop his creatures from drinking...'

'Tell the man that I am not stopping his cows drinking, but they must not trespass on my land.'

'But Captain, sir, it's well nigh impossible for the beasts to get to the water sir, for them crags and sheer drops, unless they-'

'Tell the man that he should have thought of that when he refused my generous offer.' Never once had the laird cast a glance at Hugh, and he found that attitude gross and insulting. Cameron then curtly turned away, playfully decapitating some marigolds with his whip, adding as an afterthought, 'Tell him we do not mean to keep his cows, he can have them if he pays the usual fine, that's seven shillings per cow.'

'But I don't even have seven pence Captain...' wailed Hugh, but it is doubtful whether the man heard, and certain that, had he done so, he would have been delighted, in the knowledge that his ploy was working, for his ill-concealed aim was indeed to drive away all the crofters so he could bring in the more lucrative Cheviot sheep.

As Hugh descended the hillock, prey to the darkest thoughts, he was almost at touching distance to the men before he realised that John Aird and Alistair Mor Wallace were engaged in excited conversation underneath the big oak where they were sheltering from the rain, which in his agitated state Hugh had been unaware of. He noticed that the two men had glum faces too, and even before he heard a single word of what they were saying, he had gathered that they were in the same boat as him. Their cattle had also been poinded and for the same reason. In Aird's case for the third time.

'Are there no means of stopping them lairds riding roughshod over our needs?' Wallace was saying.

'It's them and their kind that make the laws,' said John Aird, 'so who's to stop them?'

'Who's to stop them, you ask?' Hugh said in a booming voice which surprised himself. Then in a hoarse voice the words, 'If we don't, nobody else will!' were heard. Hugh did not immediately recognise them as his own. Alistair Wallace looked at Hugh intently and nodded gravely.

'Hughie, are you saying we should take the law unto our own hands?' Hugh had not meant that, it was just an expression of despair, but that was how the seed for what was to happen in the following months saw the light of the day. After the connotation Wallace had put on the words of the father-to-be, the decision for action had become inexorable. It was like a rock balancing on the top of a snow covered cliff at the moment of thaw, nothing could prevent its plunge into the abyss below. With uncharacteristic bravado, he pursed his lips, lifted his nose slightly and assumed a harsh expression.

'Aye, that's what I was saying, Cousin Wallace, what else do you think I was meaning? We must indeed take the law unto our own hands.'

CHAPTER 4

❖ ❖ ❖

Granddaughter of the King of the Gypsies

ANNIE GREEN _ ONLY, having changed colour through no fault of her own, she was Annie Browne now _ was mighty scared when she saw the blood spidering down her legs. It was her first time. She was on the point of screaming but was immediately assailed by the thought of what would become of the little 'uns if she bled to death? She dropped her pail, stared at the red lines, stunned, and finally sat down under the chestnut tree in a daze. She dried her tears almost immediately, remonstrating with herself. Blood flowing from down there and tears coming from her eyes at the same time simply won't do, Annie, she told herself, I cannot cope with both. Clearly I can do nothing about the blood, but I sure can stop the tears, I have done that often enough in the past. Maybe I ain't gonna bleed to death, she hoped. Please God, she added as an afterthought, I'll be ever so good if you spare my life. I'll stop thieving, stop pulling my tongue at haughty old ladies. Who is going to look after young Michael Michael and sweet little Queenie (her first words had been Makel Makel)? They'll starve to death if their Annie snuffs it. Sure enough the tears dried up, and she was relieved when the flow down below slowed down too. She did not want to draw attention to herself and furtively wiped the blood off with the hem of her skirt. It was so soiled already that no one would notice the difference.

Suddenly she remembered what Old Isaac had said. We'll do it proper once you've had your bloods, I ain't no brute me. So that's what he meant. Not that he didn't do it "proper" shortly after the first time. It did not feel proper. Ah the pain!

She had looked after the two little 'uns for almost as long as she could remember. They had set off from Quedgeley with Mama Yolanda one morning, Queenie hanging precariously on her frail haunch with the bigger Michael Michael on Mam's back. They had walked all day, slept in the woods, and next day they had reached Stroud. There was a fair and Yolanda had settled her and the little 'uns under an oak tree with a piece of stale bread whilst she went to get them something more to eat, but she never came back. Annie had been desperate, and when one or two bystanders seeing her crying had asked, she had explained that her Mam had been lost. Some offered sympathy of course, but no more. The others just laughed. She cannot remember clearly what happened next, how they survived the cold nights and the hunger. Fortunately Yolanda had taught her about berries and fungi, but the body needs much more.

At first she had wasted her compassion, feeling sorry for Mam. Had she been picked up by the new Charleys for vagrancy? Had she had a fall and bled to death in some ditch? Later it dawned upon her that she had done a runner on them. She damn well planned to abandon them to their fate, for why else would she have said, 'Remember, you are Annie Green, you are nine years old, your little brother is Michael Green and the girl is Queenie Green. And remember your grandfather was the King of the Gypsies.'

When some time later the truth dawned upon her, her sorrow turned to bitterness, but not for long. The poor cow was at the end of her tether and felt that she had no choice. She sometimes longed for a cuddle from her, but she rarely pined for her. Instead she comforted herself by cuddling the little 'uns. She knew that they adored their Annie. The two of them were her whole life too.

Fortunately Stroud had a weekly Fair. Later, thinking about it, she would realise that Mam had chosen the town for that very reason, believing that the children would at least manage to have a half full belly there. All sorts of tradesmen from the villages of Gloucestershire arrived early on a Friday and set up their stalls on the Market Square. They came in oxcarts and horse-carts, some came on foot pushing their laden barrows. Yet more came in boats up the canal. They came with poultry, goats and sheep, piglets, bread and cakes, peas and tomatoes, potatoes and cabbages, cheeses and honey, apples and pears, woollen and cotton clothing. They brought kettles, pots and pans, jingling merrily as the cart went over a bump on the road. They had ropes, nails, paints, trinkets. There were fortune-tellers and sellers of miracle cures, there were jugglers and magicians, acrobats, singers and story tellers, and of course there were cutpurses and muggers too. Everything that the good citizens and villagers might have needed was available if you had the money. Yolanda had guessed right. Those with no money could beg for work, or just beg, sometimes steal, and it was not impossible to get by.

Annie made a few pennies every week by doing odd jobs at the Fair, fetching and carrying, plucking chicken or gutting fish for the market vendors, fanning their charcoal fires, driving away flies round meats. Some paid in kind, scraps of left overs, bread, fish, a chicken leg, an old rag which somehow she fashioned into something for the mites to wear. So, there were always a few scraps for them and herself. They had found refuge in a disused barn until one morning they was discovered and chased away. She had begged for food, stolen a loaf and an apple when the opportunity arose. They were always hungry and cold, and Michael Michael's nose always dripping with yellow stuff, but the three of them had survived.

The bleeding had completely stopped now, but she did not feel able to get up and move on. Suddenly she noticed that she was just outside the mansion of Sir George, whoever he might be, where she had been caught stealing apples only a few weeks ago. She shuddered at the memory.

She had been mesmerised by the dark pink of the fruits on the apple trees, and had thought that she might easily slip through the hedges and go serve herself. There were bound to be a good windfall on the ground and surely nobody was going to miss them, she had thought. Certainly she and the little 'uns would love to have them. She had dropped her pail, squeezed through the hedge, and in a trice she was inside the orchard. She saw plenty of shiny pink fruits nesting in the moist green grass, begging to be picked. She looked round, saw nobody and began to serve herself: six of the best she had thought, two for each of us. She picked them and put them in the fold of her skirt, and was walking towards the breach where she had forced an entry, when she heard voices and saw what was obviously a gardener and a portly gentleman sporting the finest garments that she had ever seen. They had seen her, and the gardener was rushing towards her angrily, followed by the portly gentleman. In the scramble, the apples fell off and she was not sure what to do. Never one to give up, she thought that she might just be able to grab two of them, one in each hand before reaching the hedge, but she tripped over a stump and came crashing, face down on the ground. Before she had picked herself up, her ear was firmly gripped between two vicious fingers belonging to the gardener. By now the portly gentleman had reached their level, out of breath and was jumping up and down as if he had ants in his silk trousers. He nodded to the owner of the vicious fingers whereupon he generously offered his master the prized ear. He was still out of breath but harrumphing and nodding happily as he took possession of the offering. He twisted it two or three times in quick succession, raising and turning her head to provide eye contact with the girl who was out to ruin him. With his free hand, he took a kerchief from his pocket and wiped his sweaty brow.

'Filth!' he spat out, and Annie stared at him, not immediately catching the word.

'Absolutely, Sir George,' said the gardener, 'filth indeed. Those gyppos hate the sight of water as much as they like thieving.' I don't, mused Annie, there's nothing I love more than the sight of a cool stream when I am thirsty. And I am not any gyppo! My grandfather was the King of the Gypsies.

'It's prison for you now, my dear,' Sir George said merrily, opening his eyes and shaking his head from left to right comically. O Lordie! Who will look after the little 'uns if I go to prison, Annie had thought. No, she was determined not to go to prison. On an impulse, she bit Sir George's hand. Anyone hearing his squealing would have thought that he had just lost a whole arm. He let go of the ear, and jumped up in the air, as if he had just stepped on live coals, which was surprising in view of his bulk. Annie made a dash for the hedge with the gardener closely behind. At first she could not see the breach that she had made, and had to run randomly, like a hare in order to mislead the pursuant. Sir George having regained his composure joined in, and for a while, the crows in the sky, if there had been any, would have been mightily amused by the sight of the girl running like a hare, the gardener chasing her in the most curious fashion, unable to change direction seamlessly, having to brake off suddenly before aiming for a new path, and Sir George bobbing up and down and then forward, unable to decide whether to follow the gardener or the girl, ending up by spinning round like some German mechanical toy. Demented, the crows would have cawed to each other. Suddenly Annie saw the gap, but instead of going straight through it to liberty, having espied two seductive apples on the ground, she went back a few steps towards the gardener in close pursuit, exposing herself to being caught again, pounced on them and only narrowly evaded capture, richer by two apples. The scratch on her face as she scraped herself out was well worth it, she thought. The men inside gave up the chase, and she was able to grab her pail and kept running until the mansion was out of sight. That was weeks ago.

She decided that it was not a safe place to have your first bloods. She placed her prized apples in the pail. I'll wash them after, she told herself, and started running for dear life, not that there was any chance of her being caught now. She did not have a single penny to her name, and she had no doubt that the little 'uns would be starving. And the pail isn't even half full, she thought glumly.

She decided to go on looking for more dog turds. What was happening to them dogs these days, she wondered, are they all blocked? Time was when all you did was bend down and you could pick and choose plump droppings the size of a sausage. The tannery owners were pretty picky and would sometimes refuse to pay you for your day's work if they did not like the result of your toil. Still she managed to fill her pail and was pleased when Mr Balchin said here's two shiny pennies for you girl. I would have liked three rusty ones better, she thought. With just one more penny she could have got some cheese to go with the bread. With bread only, half an hour after you have eaten, the beast starts gnawing at your insides again. Today was going to be a feast with the apples. She went to the town centre, put on her look of suffering and approaching the burghers going about their business, she made hammering motions at her half open mouth with her tiny tapered fist, in a show of hunger. In an hour all she got was two farthings and a score of insults. Her heart ringing with joy, she put the bread and cheese in the unwashed pail beside the fruits, and ran towards the canal where she had lodged Queenie and Michael Michael.

Old Isaac the lock-keeper still allowed them to stay in a disused hut next to his own shack, where he kept tools. The little 'uns had to be reminded all the time that they had to stay inside when she when she went out earning their keeps. It was a complicated arrangement.

It had started when Old Isaac had taken pity on them one wintry night and invited them to shelter in his lock-keeper's shack. He was an old childless widower, living alone, and had seemed kindly and well-disposed towards the waifs. That first night, he had made them sausages and mashed potatoes and for the first time in a long time Annie remembered going to bed on a full belly. He did not have beds but provided blankets and old sails for them to keep warm. Annie had not even thought of the possible dangers of accepting the hospitality of a stranger, but Old Isaac had assured her that he was not an old brute waiting for the chance to take advantage of the weak and defence-less, but a god-fearing Christian. However, once she was safely tucked in, he approached her with a candle and asked if he could sit down next to her, just for a talk, mind you. He rambled on and on. She knew that she had to show some gratitude for the man's kindness, but she could not help yawning. He kept repeating that he was not a brute but a god-fearing Christian, and this was what alerted the girl to the possibility of something sinister. He asked her if she had enjoyed the sausage that he had offered them, and she nodded enthusiastically. It was then that he offered to show her his own sausage. Annie had no idea what he meant, and was completely uninterested. Sausages are meant to be eaten not looked at, she had thought but shrugged, where-upon he dropped his trousers and held his erect penis up with two fingers. Instinctively she knew that this was wrong, but thought that he would now leave her alone to go to sleep. He asked if she wanted to touch it, and she shook her head. It's nice, he said, soft and warm. She had no great inclination to do what he said but thought that if she did, he would then go away. She was trembling a bit, but forcing a smile, she took his member in his hand. It's so nice when you do that, he said. She frowned, wondering what was nice about that, and Old Isaac closed his eyes and groaned with pleasure. Stroke it gen-tly, he urged, but not waiting for her to take the initiative, he took her hand gently and wrapped her frail fingers around the member and began sliding it up and down. The girl had not the slightest inkling about what this was all about, but knew that it was wrong. She also knew that she had no choice. I am not a brute, he said again, but this will not hurt you, take it in your lovely little mouth. Annie did not want to, and feeling instinctive revulsion at what was being proposed, felt a lump in her throat. She was now fighting a losing battle against her tears which were ready to cascade down. He stroked her head gently and told her she was such a sweet good little girl, that he would make sure they would never go hungry, that he would look after them like a real father. Annie was too stunned to say anything. I am a God-fearing man, Old Isaac said, I will never let anybody harm a single hair on your head. She had felt that she had no choice, and fighting her tears, she opened her mouth, and he pushed the sausage in. He spurted in her mouth, and he gave her a bowl of water to rinse it. Now we will pray to the good Lord to forgive us for our sins, he had said, and had made her kneel down with him. She was trembling all over and it took her a lot of effort to stop her tears.

'Lord,' he had said closing his eyes which did not stop his own tears streaming down his cheeks, 'you who know the inside of our hearts must know that I did not offer these unfortunate children my hospitality with any thought of committing a sin. Lord, remember that anybody else would have done worse, but I am not a brute. Forgive her for tempting me and me for succumbing. Give me the strength not to want more from this sweet innocent child.' Suddenly he stood up like a man in a trance, and began to shake his raised fists and scream. 'Lord, why did you give me sinful desires? I do not want them, I did not ask for them, take them away from me. Why Lord? Answer me!'

She did not know why, but felt that she was soiled and dirty, and wished that Old Isaac would not want to do all this again. But of course he did. Next night he asked her to let him see her little pussy, promising that he was not going to do anything but the looking, as he was not a brute. She felt cornered and lifted her skirt and he stared in rapture. The night after, he asked if he could just stroke it, nothing more, he was no brute. The following night he asked if she would sit on his erect member and stroke it with her pussy, swearing that he wanted nothing more, adding mysteriously, not before you have had your first bloods. She was too scared and too exhausted to resist.

It was on the next night that he tried to penetrate her. She pushed him away screaming and tried to run away, but he seized her, placed a hand over her mouth to stop her screaming. Do you want to wake up the little angels? he admonished, and carried her trembling and struggling little body to his bed. He promised that he was not going to hurt her, that it was going to be nice, that he would put it in gently. The little 'uns began to scream, but he held her firmly and she was helpless. It hurt so much when he put it in. She bled profusely and he was ever so gentle as he washed the blood away and cuddled her, tears streaming down his wizened face, repeating nice things, calling her little angel and little devil at the same time, sometimes laughing as someone who had lost his mind, which did not stop the flow of his tears. Fortunately the mites had wept themselves to sleep.

She cried herself to sleep too, and next morning, Old Isaac having gone to have a look at the sluice gates, she grabbed hold of the little 'uns and left, but he soon caught up with them. He was alarmed. Where are you going? He asked, who will look after you, who will protect you? It's a treacherous world, come back home, he entreated, promising that he will never repeat what he did last night. I will promise on the Bible he said, I will take a knife and cut off this evil member of mine. Annie was adamant. Never will she go back, she had no wish for anyone to cut off their member on her account. He begged and entreated her, went down on his knees, cried hot tears. She shook her head and kept walking away. I am so lonely, he cried, I liked having you around. What's to become of me? Annie kept walking. Suddenly, as they were passing near a small shack in which he kept tools and things, he grabbed her hand.

'You don't even have to stay in the house, you can stay here, it will provide you with shelter... I will not let you go hungry... all I want is for you to sweep the floor in the house, perhaps darn my clothes... cook for me... not even everyday... please, say yes.'

Annie shook her head, struggled to free her hand, and went on her way with the little 'uns, leaving a disconsolate Old Isaac behind. They went to the city square, and it rained all day. Michael Michael sneezed and seemed to be having a temperature, and she was greatly alarmed. She begged when she could, and all she got was a penny and two farthings, and advice to clean herself. Queenie began to cry, she was cold and hungry and Michael Michael was shivering. Finally she decided that she would sneak into the Lock-keeper's tool shack for the night. Old Isaac saw them and brought them hot soup and bread.

Annie began earning a few pennies doing odd jobs for the people at the Fair and begging when there was no work. She was not averse to a little thieving when the opportunity arose. She could not guarantee that they had a full belly everyday, but they rarely had a whole day without at least something inside them. The lock keeper did not make any more demands upon her. He sometimes came around and offered them food and rags, and she had no choice, but she hated having to accept his help. Inevitably the men she came in contact with at the Fair would sometimes offer her a penny or two if she would go behind a tree with them, but she always spat on the ground when they made their lewd suggestions. If anybody tried to grab her, she would scratch bite and swear and they would laugh, saying that she was too dirty anyway and leave her alone.

Today, as she was wending her way home - that's what she called the tool shack - the blood on her legs now dried up, she heard a big commotion and saw the circus which had been in town the whole of last week, all packed in their colourful carts, leaving. She had hoped to take the mites to have a look-in, but had never got round to it. She stopped near a small crowd of cheering children and watched the clowns and acrobats doing their farewell antics, waving at them merrily.

She now had some bread and cheese as well as a banana in the pail - she should have thought of washing it. The thought of seeing the little 'uns filled her with joy. Yes, she loved them with all her heart, they were her pride and joy, even if they were always doing things that she forbade them to do. She could never raise her voice to them. All the little reprobates had to do was to look at her with those hurt little eyes of theirs and she would stop chiding them and give them a cuddle instead. Clearly she could not ferry them around for a whole day when she was out working, and had no alternative but to leave them in the shack. Although she made no demands on Old Isaac, she knew that he would pop in now and then and see that they were all right, give them a scrap to eat. She was uneasy about this, and often feared that he might do to Queenie what he had done to her. She swore that if he did, she would stick a knife in him and crush his head with a stone and then drown herself and the mites in the canal.

She was thoroughly exhausted when she opened the door of the shack saying, your Annie's back my little darlings. There was no response. They never do what I tell them, she said wearily, always making me sweat a little more. She went out and shouted their names, and this produced no result. She went on the canal and in the woods, her panic rising as her calls remained unanswered. She became desperate, and in the end had no choice but to go look for Old Isaac and ask for his help.

The sun had set when she finally saw the lock-keeper tottering ahead in a drunken stupor. In the old days he never drank, calling it the devil drink. He took to it after the rape. He seemed not to understand what she was saying, but when he finally did, he started crying, beating himself on the chest and saying that it was all his fault. He made a weak and vain attempt at finding the lost babes.

Next day, when Isaac had a clearer head, he remembered that he had seen two strange men lurking around in the last week, but had thought nothing of it. Now he became convinced that they had kidnapped the little 'uns. Annie became hysterical and wanted to know more, but the lock-keeper could say no more. Strange men, he said incoherently, two of them, might have been three. Why would anybody steal my little babes? Annie asked tearfully. To sell them into slavery, the old man suggested, or worse. No, no, she screamed, how can you say that? You are an 'orrible man! She knew that there was no one to help and was at a complete loss.

A day later, Isaac suggested that the kidnappers might have been circus folk. He remembered that they had colourful scarves. They had a reputation for stealing small children so they could train them to become acrobats or pages. Annie clutched at that straw. It was definitely the circus folk. She was determined to go find them and beg them to let go of her little 'uns. She would tell them that she could not live without them. They will surely understand. They could not be heartless. With new heart, she went to the market and asked questions, and when someone said that the circus usually headed for Gloucester after Stroud, she determined to follow them there.

She heard that Harry the tailor, who had a cart, went to Gloucester regularly as he had clients there, and approached him, explaining about her lost siblings. Harry was surprisingly sympathetic, saying that he was going in two days' time and would gladly take her with him, which filled her heart with gladness. However, just as she was leaving, he stopped her. There is one thing, Annie, he said, I'm entertaining my daughter's prospective in-laws in a week, and seein' as you work in the market, couldn't you get me a plump 'en? Her heart sank. Everybody in the market knew of her thieving reputation, and Potter the poultryman had threatened to slash her face for her if he but saw her go within sight of the coops. How was she going to steal one of those noisy pests without getting caught? She did not know that it was possible to spend a sleepless night, and also have nightmares! She woke up resolved that she would get that plum 'en for Mr Potter or a scar on her face. As she was so small, she was able to mingle in the crowd and creep towards Potter's stall unseen. She hid behind a drum and watched the poultryman's every movement, knowing that he was bound to want to go ease himself behind the giant chestnut sooner or later. The moment he did, she boldly made for the coops, opened the door and grabbed a plump four-pounder, but the stupid bird made such a racket that the whole market's attention was drawn to what was going on. People began shouting, Thief! Chicken thief! Stop the Gyppo! Potter stopped in his tracks, picked up his trousers, and still holding to them, rushed back towards the coop where Mrs Wipps the ribbon merchant was holding Annie's head tightly between her fat thighs. There was no point struggling. She tried to tell them about Michael Michael and Queenie, but no one was listening.

Old Isaac was distraught when he heard, and promised that he would do all he could to help, but there was little he or anyone else could do. The whole market was willing to testify against the pestilential Gyppo brat who was out to destroy the whole fabric of society. But worse was to come.

When three days later, she appeared at the Assizes Court in Gloucester, she found that the Magistrate was none other than the Sir George whose hand she had nearly amputated. He recognised her immediately, and rubbed his hands in glee.

'What's your name?' she was asked.

'Annie Green, sir,' she said in a firm voice, 'and my grandfather was King of the Gypsies.' The whole court laughed.

'You're more brown than green,' Sir George said to renewed laughter.

'Shall I enter her name as Annie Browne then, your honour?' the clerk of court asked.

'Brown or Black, you choose,' Sir George said. She had lost her siblings but had gained a new name, she mused.

When the charge was read, the magistrate, Sir George Culjohn-McRoe adjusted his spectacles and demurred.

'A four pounder hen costing seven shillings and sixpence?' he cried, 'rubbish! I bought one only last week and was charged ten shillings and... fourpence... change it to ten shillings and a penny, clerk,' he bawled out in a Stentorian tone.

'Your honour, you can't!' shouted Old Isaac, and, addressing the unsympathetic court, added, 'He wants to transport 'er to the end of the world...' It was an established practice to pass a sentence of transportation to thieves guilty of stealing goods worth more than ten shillings. A law officer grabbed Isaac and took him away. Four people came forward and testified to Annie's thieving habit, and there was no one to speak for her. Culjohn-McRoe shook his head in mock disbelief.

'Annie Browne,' he said, 'if at the tender age that you are, you have already done all those horrible things we have heard, I am willing to wager... eh... an apple to an orchard... hum... that by doing the rightful thing and sentencing you to seven years' transportation to New South Wales, there to reflect upon your sinful and guilt-ridden life, when you return to this blessed land of ours, you would have sincerely repented of your sins and made yourself ready to lead a new life of honesty. I am in fact saving you from a sentence of hanging which you would have handsomely merited for some serious crime which you would indubitably commit if left to your own device.' Annie had no idea what the man was saying but conceded that he spoke very well. Still she felt that she had to say something as she was being led away.

'My name is Annie Green and I am a granddaughter of the King of the Gypsies.'

CHAPTER 5

— ◆ ◆ ◆ —

Tolpuddle

JAMES HAMMETT HAD planned to do some serious poaching with Jonas that day, and his friend had promised some of his illicit brew. So, when John mentioned the two men sent by the London Union to show them how to organise The Friendly Society of Agricultural Workers, the younger brother demurred. John had a tendency to preach and although he claimed that it was up to the younger man to decide, he made it clear that he was disappointed, reminding him of the injustice and contempt with which they and their fellow labourers were treated by the bosses. He loved making speeches, did dear John and never missed an opportunity, even to an audience of one. He had the facts at the ready: It was a miserable life for all but the land-owning class. Children were bow-legged, small, with poor constitution because of malnutrition. They were prey to disease, because their bodies lacked so many nutrients, and obviously their kind had a very short life expectancy. Everybody dreaded winter as they could not afford to heat up their leaky and draught-ridden hovels. Wasn't James aware of the practice whereby seven neighbouring families arranged for one of them to light a fire once a week, when the other families would bring their kettles to boil so they could have some tea to keep themselves warm, before hurrying to their icy mattress-less beds? Many people, the Lord grant them wisdom to know better, thought that death was preferable to that sort of existence. When John started preaching he was most loth to stop.

The average rent for something which bore only passing resemblance to a shack, was one shilling and tuppence, bread for an average family, 9 shillings, tea 2 pence, potatoes one shilling, sugar three and a half pence, soap three pence, candle three pence, coal and wood nine pence, butter four and a half pence, salt half a penny, and that did not include meat or fish which they rarely had anyway. That made for a sum which was in excess of what either brother took home in one week, in fact about one and a half times. Of course their combined earnings gave them an advantage at the moment, but surely James wished to have his own family someday, and with the new baby on the way, how would they manage? No wonder many supplemented their meagre incomes by poaching or illicit brewing. John abhorred the devil drink, but turned a blind eye to his younger brother's occasional indulgence. With the Lord's help James sincerely hoped that he might give it up entirely too, but not yet.

Young James was not insensible to the realities of life as an agricultural worker. He did not need John to tell him that the labourers were getting a raw deal from the bosses and that something had to be done. He was one hundred percent behind the schemes of George Loveless, but not today! He really meant it when he said that he was going to join the society, but he wanted a few hours of fun now and then. John had his own family to occupy his thoughts, a loving wife, two cheeky little boys and who knows who was playing peek-a-boo behind sister-in-law Madge's round tummy?

Later he would remember the drink and the larking about with Jonas, but not if they had bagged anything that day. Still he remembered the proceedings of the meeting under the giant sycamore tree as if he had been there and stone cold sober too, such was the exaltation and intensity of John's narration. James had nothing but love and admiration for the older brother, he was sure no finer man existed. He was a devoted husband, father and brother and although he abhorred the conditions of employment, never did the idea occur to him that he could give less of himself than one hundred percent. He was generous to a fault, but what the younger brother admired above all else, was that staunch follower of the teachings of George Loveless though he was, his generosity was rooted in his natural goodness and not his piety. He made James laugh when he produced a book the man from London had offered the Society and which George had urged him to borrow: "The Life and most Surprizing Adventures of Robinson Crusoe of York, Mariner." He had said that if they had a spare candle, he would have started reading it that very night so he could tell the little ones a new story. He stared at his young brother earnestly as he explained, clearly quoting the men from London who had come with a gift of books for the Society, in a clear move to encourage reading. A book is like rain water which the good Lord provides. One used it, drank it, and when it evaporated, it became clouds which became rain and fell on earth again and again. James was not quite sure what he meant, and his brother recognised this by his perplexed look, so he elaborated.

'I read the book, and tell the story to the wee 'uns eh, James, then I do not need to read it again to tell it to the one to be born, and they will in turn tell it to their own little 'uns... you see... like the rain!' His eyes glowed as he said this. If dear John had one failing, it was an undeveloped sense of fun.

The Society was running smoothly, but the bosses did not look upon it with favour. George Loveless had told everybody to watch their step, to always act within the law. James readily agreed to accompany his brother to the fateful meeting in the church hall a few weeks later. George who was a quiet and unflappable man, had seemed quite upbeat that time. Things are beginning to move, he told everybody. The Reverend Thomas Warren who did not have too much time for Loveless, himself a lay Methodist preacher, had surprisingly agreed to chair a meeting with agricultural workers and the landowners. It was going to be in the spirit of co-operation and fairness. A new era was in sight and nothing but good can come out of that.

Indeed, James was surprised at the peaceful nature of the assembly when he got there. Everybody smiled and talked politely to each other. The Reverend began by inviting George to have his say, and, in a dispassionate manner, quoting prices and earnings, he made a strong case for a need to review past practices. The reverend nodded sympathetically at everything he heard. The representative of the farmers, Sir Tobias then took the floor. Although Malfysing spoke calmly and in measured tones, James could not help guessing that he was inwardly seething with rage at having to share a platform with his obvious inferiors. He understood what Loveless was saying, he said, but let people not think that they were the only ones who were having trouble making ends meet. It would be a good thing if the workers learnt some discipline. They could not expect that every time they over-spent they could claim a rise, this was unrealistic. James saw that Reverend Warren was nodding at these sentiments too. We are all in this together, the landowners were under severe strain too, he pursued. He was not saying no to their requests, but the people he represented needed to discuss the matter properly before arriving at a conclusion. George stressed that he had not come in a spirit of confrontation, but pointed out with a little laugh, that he could not believe that people who had stables where the horses were fed better than the workers for the sole purpose of chasing hares and foxes could claim to be under any sort of strain. Sir Tobias' face changed colour, he scowled but said nothing. George then expressed concern at rumours to the effect that the landowners were thinking of decreasing their average wage by a whole shilling a week. Malfysing tut tutted and said that it was wrong to listen to rumours, whereupon George, who had been the picture of calm and self-control until now challenged the baronet to deny that this had been discussed only a week ago, not revealing that he knew the place, the time and exact words used on the occasion. For the first time Malfysing lost his cool and retorted that he had come to the meeting in a spirit of conciliation and not confrontation, and would not tolerate being cross-examined.

'All I am asking for my men,' said George helplessly, 'is that we be paid the same as folks in neighbouring districts. We are the lowest paid workers in Dorset.' He paused for breath and James could clearly see that he was measuring his words for a final salvo.

'Gentlemen,' he said finally, 'it is with regret that I say this: the law now gives us the power to withhold our labour-' He was not allowed to continue. Malfysing and the other landowners stood up brandishing clenched fists and making indignant noises. Reverend Warren had to call everybody to order. He enjoined George to use more temperate language. The lay preacher managed to put across a final but crucial point, concerning the disparity between the wages of people of Tolpuddle and their neighbouring districts. There was no earthly reason why parity could not be established, seeing that they all did the same type of work, producing comparable yields.

The reverend was seen conversing with Malfysing, after which he stood up, beamed a no-grudge-borne sort of smile to George and solemnly declared that speaking in the name of the other employers, he saw no impediment to their wages being aligned with those of the folks in surrounding districts in the very near future. Now, the men from London had instructed George never to accept anything from the bosses except if it was on paper and signed, so respectfully he asked that an agreement be drafted there and then, and signed by all the parties. To his dismay, the bosses smiled to everybody and said that there was no need for papers between friends, for he considered every man in the hall as a true son of Dorset, and as such his friend. George was not sure, but the reverend came towards him, grabbed him by the shoulders and James heard him clearly utter those words that the man of the cloth would later deny: "I am witness between you men and your masters, that if you will go quietly to your work, you shall receive for your labour as much as any men in the district. If your masters should attempt to run from their word, I will undertake to see you righted, so help me God!"

What happened next stunned the whole of Tolpuddle's workforce. They had been living in hope of a prompt implementation of the agreement reached in the village church hall, but Malfysing told whoever would listen to him that no agreement had been reached. He swore that he had only given "that rabble" as he called the workers, the assurance that at some point in the future, when things got better for the struggling land-owning class, he would discuss a review of the wage system for the workers. In the meantime, he regretted to say, that as a temporary measure, in view of the rising cost of seeds and feeds, the average wage of the workers would decrease by no more than one shilling a week. No one regretted this measure more than he.

George appealed to Reverend Warren and reminded him of the word of honour given to them by Malfysing at the church hall. What word of honour? the man of the cloth asked. He swore that no undertaking had been given, and confirmed the lie Malfysing had been propagating, namely that all that was agreed was that a review will be considered at a later date, when "things got better".

The anger of the victims could no longer be contained, but worse was to come. In the knowledge of their power and what was obviously a show of their contempt for the workers, the bosses decided to lower the wages by three whole shillings, bringing the average wage down to seven shillings. George agreed that the only thing left was to go on strike. Though still not a member of the Union, James was vociferous in his support for his peers and condemnation of the land-owners. Although others were clearly acting in breach of the law, damaging threshing machines and burning small fields of wheat and a barn or two, resisting his own inclination, he refrained from acting in any way which he thought brother John would disapprove of.

One morning a breathless George Loveless turned up at their dwelling and informed the Hammett brothers that the ring leaders of the Union were on the point of being rounded up. Clearly there was no point in running away when one had a family, he said. In any case, he said, apart from one or two lawless acts, the strikers now had the law on their side. At worse it would mean a week or two behind bars. John who did not have too much trust in the new law went pale on hearing the news. What will happen to Madge, he said, with the new baby coming, how is she going to manage? The three men were staring at each other helplessly when they beheld six law officers bearing muskets coming towards their shack. They let the uniformed men in and waited for the worse.

'I have a warrant for the arrest of six individuals,' the lieutenant said addressing George Loveless.

'I am George Loveless,' George said.

'Yes, I have a G. Loveless on my list… you are under arrest, Loveless.' George meekly tended his two hands together to be handcuffed by one of the men.

'You must be J. Hammett,' the lieutenant said to John, but before he could answer, James took a step towards the men, tending his two hands.

'I am J. Hammett,' he said, winking at John. Madge who was next to John retained him by pulling him by the sleeve, in case he did anything stupid.

'And who might you be, my man?' asked the lieutenant of John.

'I am… his brother,' he replied in a state of confusion which James instantly recognised.

'I've only got one Hammett on my list,' the officer said.

James knew his brother to be a man of honour to whom justice was the most important consideration in the world, and he read the torment inside him as an open book as he debated within himself the pros and cons of the situation. Was it fair to let his younger brother, who did not even belong to the Society, take the rap? On the other hand, who would take care of Madge and the babies if he was not there for them? James was single and had selflessly offered himself. The look on Madge's face did not escape James either.

It was a mixture of gratitude as well as an unneeded apology for the resentment she had often manifested when at the death of the elder Mr Hammett, she had to share the meagre resources of the family with him, thus diminishing the portions of her own little ones. Even at an early age, James had never borne her any grudge, understanding what mothers did and felt. He saw his brother take one step forward and his round-bellied wife retaining him yet again, whereupon he said loudly and with mock negligence that prison did not scare him, seeing that he had already tasted it. This earned him a sharp poke in the ribs from the lieutenant's musket, and although it hurt, he made light of it and smiled wryly.

James felt strangely elated as he followed the soldiers to the dungeon where he was being taken with George. They would be joined by four others the next day. Mr Frampton the magistrate in charge of the case, had never been coy in expressing his conviction that the workers were the enemy within, waiting for their moment to turn this green and pleasant land into the anarchic mess that France had become since the events of 1789. He told everybody within his hearing that he had written to Lord Melbourne, the Home Secretary to communicate his fears to him, and had obtained his blessing to deal with the scoundrels as he thought fit. Besides, his lordship had expressed to him the view that, the poor had only their lack of discipline to blame for their condition.

The judge appointed for the trial was Baron John Williams, and Frampton had impressed upon him the necessity to find the six accused guilty, pour l'exemple!

The hearing was to take place at the Spring Assizes in Dorchester on the 15th of March 1834. Mr Butt, the counsel for the defence began by pointing out that the Combination Act proscribing appurtenance to a trade union had been repealed, and this stumped the Baron Judge, but not for long. Ah, yes, he conceded, but what about the Mutiny Act 1820, which stipulates that people swearing secret oaths are guilty of treason? For which the penalty is death by hanging, he added darkly. The defence pointed out that the aforesaid Act was passed to stop sailors and soldiers swearing an oath to make a concerted move towards gaining better pay, or perhaps mutiny, and was clearly not aimed at agricultural workers or journeymen, but this left judge and jury, comprised solely of landowners, unimpressed. Several witnesses were called by the prosecution and James could hardly believe that people who openly professed their attachment to the teachings of Our Lord Jesus Christ could so unashamedly commit perjury and tell such barefaced lies, no doubt for rewards promised by the farmers. The defence called character witnesses who all testified to the good character of George Loveless and his followers in fulsome terms, but as Dissenters, they were seen by the jury as representatives of the fiend on earth. It was clear to James from the beginning that all this was a charade. Indeed the Foreman of the jury, the Hon. Ponsonby after a quick deliberation with his panel pronounced the guilty verdict.

The six men were stunned as they heard that they were to be transported to Botany Bay for seven years. If at first they had thought of a short jail sentence, it had become clear to them as the trial went on that they could expect anything, including the ultimate penalty. They were put in chains and taken to the hulk York in Portsmouth separately. George Loveless stayed there for a while and was then conveyed to the brig William Metcalfe, and on the 5th of May began a gruesome voyage to Van Diemen's Island.

CHAPTER 6

❖❖❖

Sunderban

RAJU'S MEMORIES OF his pre-Sunderban days, was a mixture of half-remembered facts and stories told by elders which had become more real every time he heard them. Did he really remember the interminable walk across deserts and swamps? Or being found under a rock one sunset crying his eyes out, by uncle Sukhdeo, after being lost for a whole day? Phoopi Umma never tired of telling him stories of his childhood. As he never knew his mother, all his life he would endow her with all the qualities of the best women he knew. Phoopi was the best model of course. Widowhood had turned her hair prematurely grey and Raju thought that she looked very dignified like this, frail and thin though she was. Because of a back problem resulting from long hours of bending down over her nets in her quest for Bagda Chingris, knee deep in muddy waters, she walked with a stoop. A proud woman, she disliked this much more than the pains in her body since these she could keep hidden from the world. An all too visible stoop was a weakness which was there for all to see. She always spoke in deliberate and measured tones, taking trouble to articulate every syllable clearly. Some people said that when one was a pauper dependent on a brother, putting on airs was like farting through one's navel. It hurt Raju that a woman who never uttered one malicious remark about others, could attract such obloquy. When the boy commiserated with her, she would smile wanly, and say that she was like kochu leaves. When you poured water on that cocoyam plant, the drops danced merrily on them like live silver jewels and leapt away. Try as much as you want, you cannot wet a kochu leaf. When one is a poor widow, one learns how not to hear bad words. He would later understand that people said hurtful things because poverty and hunger made them mean-spirited in their speech, but it was rare that anybody would do bad things to you. In reality, when you were in any sort of distress, the whole village would forget past rancours and jealousies and rally round to offer succour, however modest.

Even after Baba Parsad had married Ma, Phoopi, a few years older, remained the head of the household, deciding on what to eat and what to wear. He never knew his Ma Parvatti, but he saw her regularly in his dreams and knew exactly what she was like. Of course she was the prettiest, kindest and wisest of all humans. In appearance she could have been Phoopi's twin sister, but not as dark-skinned, with infinitely gentle eyes, wrapped in a glow of white light wherever she went. Raju imagined that Phoopi and Ma had been the best of friends, that their relationship was one of sweetness and light, laughter and love, the older woman giving advice and encouragement to the younger one, who in turn would massage her neck and tired legs when necessary. It was true that Phoopi and his Ma were always the best of friends.

According to the aunt when the migrants finally arrived in Calcutta, a few years after leaving Allapur, people in this new place had looked upon them as Bhojpuri-speaking beings from another world, therefore uncouth intruders who talked funny, ailé gailé, kaa ba, kon chi ba? and had awful habits. Bengalis have class, they are poets, musicians, their middle name is Probity. Biharis are bandits, vagabonds who were unable to stay in one place.

What little money they had possessed, was now all gone. Work was harder to find than fish up a tree. They had been discouraged to stay where they wanted, and had been forced to leave for the least salubrious part of the city, the outskirts, where, if they found work, it was laborious and badly paid. Parsad and Sukhdeo had ended up miles from the centre in Roshankhali, one of the islands of the Sundarbans. It was situated near Sonarkhali where the mangrove forests can be said to begin, where because of the salt contents of the earth almost nothing grew but weeds and shrubs. Besides all sorts of dangers lurked in every corner, coming in all shapes and sizes: mosquitoes, man-eating tigers, crocodiles which left their shores and roamed the land in search of prey, sharks, cobras, rats as big as cats. On top of everything, in the rainy months the monsoon reigned supreme. The women in the village used to say that the monsoon was like husbands. A woman needed one if she did not want to starve, but then you have to put up with his exigencies. Without water, the land dies, but with the monsoon, it rained all the time, you walked knee-deep in mud. The cyclones joined in to cause more havoc. They were able to lift people or cattle up in the air and hurl them to their deaths against trees or rocks cracking their skulls, or into the boiling sea where they drowned. They wrecked boats and caused more drowning. Any little extra grain that people kept as an insurance against the lean months were often irreparably damaged when the rains came in through the leaky roofs, or unimpeded if the roof had been blown away. When the floods came, they drove away everything in their path, they uprooted trees and carried away people and habitations, leaving bleakness and misery around.

The Allapuris were left with no choice but to endure all this, and after two years, they settled in this new life and were not doing too badly for themselves, although they did not always have two square meals a day. Of course when the weather was good, it was the most glorious place on earth. It was like a husband in the first month of marriage. The place would be ringing with the singing of birds, luxuriating in a green splendour that was unparalleled in the country, with a wealth of vegetation and flowers of every colour under the sun. A stranger could not easily imagine that this paradise could metamorphose into hell if the cyclones had made up their minds to upstage Bhagwan's munificence.

Parsad would tell the boy how he regretted all his life that he had prayed so hard for a boy that he had forgotten to pray for Parvatti's health. Aunt Lalita lost three babies in succession, and Uncle Sukhdeo despaired of ever becoming a father. In the beginning he had looked upon Raju as his own, and had indeed assumed that if one day he ended up rich, the boy would inherit it all at his death. Still husband and wife prayed assiduously to Durga, begging her to give them even a girl, but sometimes the gods turn a deaf ear to one's pleas. Many people said that this was why Lalita had turned sour, while others whispered between themselves that the wise Durga Devi knew what she was doing. She knew that Lalita, with her bad character, would make a terrible mother.

Lalita never looked upon the friendship between the two men with favour. She obviously resented the fact that her husband seemed to prefer the company of his friend to hers.

Phoopi had looked after the boy with love and care. She couldn't do enough for her little prince. Oh he is so handsome, so sweet-tempered, she would say to herself as she gazed at him endlessly as he slept in the little wooden cot that his Baba Parsad had made for him from kankra wood with the help of his good Musselman friend the Hakeem who made his living as a carpenter. He had sawed and planed the wood Parsad had brought from the forest when he went honey picking.

Raju grew up without serious complications, learnt to walk and speak, sing and run and in no time at all he was well able to row and punt the little boat all by himself. As he had no siblings, he decided to adopt a little orphan boy two years younger than himself called Jayant, who, having lost both parents during a monsoon storm, lived with a boatman uncle and his wife. This boy was devoted to Raju, and called him Bhayya, big brother.

Phoopi was never at ease when Raju took the boat out, saying that it was leaky and falling apart. Baba, who seemed to have an answer for anything, taught the boy to swim. She then started worrying about sharks, and this time, all his Baba could do was to laugh, since he realised, after a quick calculation, that he would never be able to kill all the sharks. Baba always talked about teaching the boy some reading and writing but never got round to it. It was left to Phoopi to teach him, but fact was she did not know too much herself, although she had an amazing capacity for counting in her head. Often Sukhdeo, who would develop a talent for making money, but had no head for figures, would call on the family, tell Phoopi how much of such and such he had bought, what he had sold, who owed him what, and ask her to calculate his takings. Apparently she never put a foot wrong.

When Raju was growing up, the family was squatting on some land which seemed to belong to nobody, and made a living by growing and selling their own vegetables, tomatoes, beans, bhindi, brinjal, palak, onions etc, bartering some with other villagers for things they did not grow in salty earth, like aloo and dudhi. They also had some hens which produced eggs for the family. Baba was a very skilful fisherman and the waters were teeming with the tastiest fish in the land, bhetki, parshe, pabdam bacha and many others, and he knew how to lure them into the traps he made from golpata fronds or at the end of his hook. They filleted easily, and when salted and

dried could be sold in the Parganas or even Calcutta, although the wholesalers paid a derisory price. The Bagda Chingri found in the muddy waters near
the shore were much sought after, and these too dried easily and brought a
small income. That was Phoopi's job, and she was happy to do it, feeling that
she made a contribution. Baba was not too happy about this, saying that he
had seen sharks lurking in the area, and people told of how some unfortunate women regularly lost a leg there. On top of everything, the best Bagda
Chingri were those caught during the monsoon when the currents were
dangerous, and a good few women had been carried away by the torrents.
However, unless one took risks, one starved.

The most lucrative pursuit was honey gathering in tiger-infested country. Raju learnt at an early age that constant danger was as much a part of life
as manure was to agriculture. Part of the fun of eating fish was sucking on
the bone avoiding getting one stuck in your throat. Raju was so proud that
his Baba and his Phoopi were completely fearless, and had no doubt that Ma
was made from the same clay. Bihari folks know no fear, Baba often said.
Bengalis said Bihari folk had big mouths.

Raju was always disappointed that when he went fishing with Baba, they
saw not one single crocodile, not one shark. He sometimes dreamt of meeting a massive crocodile at the riverside and that he had beaten it away with
nothing more than his oar, ramming it down the beast's throat. He often
bragged that his arms were so strong that if one day a crocodile had the misfortune of encountering him, he would grab its upper jaw with one hand and
the lower jaw with the other and pulling with all his might, he would tear
the brute's head apart. He could not understand why the adults in the village
were in such awe of the reptile.

When he loudly proclaimed all those imaginary feats, Baba would smile
and nod approvingly, although Phoopi would sometimes bite her lips and
shake her head. She feared that his intrepid nature would land him into trouble one day.

Baba was adamant when the boy announced that he was joining the honey gatherers. No, he said, not before you turn fifteen, it's too dangerous. He
argued that he had often heard Baba swear to the needlessly apprehensive
Phoopi that honey gathering was completely safe if only one watched every

single step one took. Baba continued to say no, and in the end when the boy
would not give up, he promised him a slap on the face that will tingle for
weeks if he did not shut up. That was usually the last thing Baba said when
he was at a lost for words. He had never raised a hand to the boy and knew
that crocodiles would grow wings and fly before he would. Still, that threat
issued at some crucial point usually shut the boy up- for a whole hour. He
must have been just over ten one day, when to Phoopi's horror, Baba said,
'Raju, beta, you have been pestering me for so long now, if you promise
you will do exactly as I tell you, I will bring you along next time.' Although
Sukhdeo owed money to Baba, his influence had grown to the extent that
the honey pickers, all Bihari men in their early thirties, as well as the buyers,
considered him as the boss. Baba had a team of eight working under him.

The boy thought that the risk of being attacked by a man-eating tiger
was the pinnacle of excitement. He was not afraid of Dakshin Rai, he'd pick
up a sharp stick and drive it through his throat, he would! He had killed
many a crocodile in his dreams, and a tiger was not half as fearsome…

He had been unable to sleep when he woke up hours before dawn, fearing that Baba might forget his promise. It was the most unforgettable day
of his life. Every step one took was a thrill. First there was the lengthy boat
journey which would take them to the islands where the bees made the best
honey. Although he was already a dab hand at being in charge of a boat, and
thought no more of rowing or punting than going out for a walk in the bush,
the knowledge that this time, it was only the beginning of an odyssey added
extra chillies to the sauce. It was like a ride on that magic jaggarnath on the
way to the stars in Baba's stories, full of unexpected twists and turns. The
most fun of all was the wearing of the face mask. Baba had made a small one
for him, from half a coconut shell, had carved it, painted two fierce larger-
than-life eyes. To fix it to the head, he had made two holes through which
ran some rope made of coconut fibre which Phoopi had weaved, for home use
and selling. You wore it at the back of the head to fool Dakshin Rai the tiger.
Tigers never attack men from the front. They pounce on their quarry from
the back, aiming fangs and claws for the spot just below your neck where the
spine begins, causing instantaneous death. When they see a human face staring at them, they wait for them to turn round. This strategy allowed their

prospective victims to escape. At an early age, when Raju heard the story of the mask, he wondered why mask or no mask, he never stopped hearing stories of tigers killing honey gatherers, but he kept this thought to himself. Anyway no one from Baba's team had ever had a brush with Dakhsin.

When they reached the island, the first thing they did was to make for the shrine of Bon Bibi to placate the Goddess with a gift of bananas and coconut milk and to beg for her protection and blessing. Everybody knew that with Bob Bibi's protection, Dakshin Rai all but became toothless. Forget Bon Bibi, and you were as good as dead, for the forests had more dangers than just man-eating tigers. Apart from king cobras and crocodiles, there were swamps which swallowed a fully grown man in seconds and countless other hazards.

The boy relished wading knee-deep in muddy clay which gave one a feeling of being twice as heavy as you pulled your feet up- the very opposite of swimming, which made you weightless. It was true that even as a child he had been fearless. He had the certainty that if he willed it, he could walk through a raging fire unscathed, that a massive tree falling on him would do him no damage; he would hold his breath and contract his muscles and the trunk would simply bounce off his body. He noticed that everybody was talking loudly and making a lot of noise, and understood that this was a tactic used to let Dakshin Rai know they were around so he would keep away. He watched every step, and was convinced that if Dakshin Rai had not shown up on that first day, it was because of his extraordinary vigilance.

Gloriously, he was the first one to spot a massive honeycomb hanging from a leafy keora. That boy has got the eyes of a tiger, everybody said loudly (the more noise the better! he was told.) For no reason everybody fell silent now, and wordlessly the team began to set alight the leaves and sticks they had been carrying with them, with a Lucifer match, to create smoke to stun the bees and make them fly away in confusion, buzzing angrily, but attacking no one. Once the preliminaries were out of the way, everybody came to the boy and tapped him on the shoulders, saying "Shabash! Shabash!" "Ya Bhagwan, the boy is a natural, spotting that honeycomb like that!" Now you watch for Dakshin Rai, with your fantastic eyesight, you won't miss him if he approaches. He would have wished to be given the honour of making the first harvest, as he had spotted the honeycomb, but Baba made ready.

How proud he was to see his old man put the curved knife in his mouth, his basket dangling on his left shoulder, walk towards the tree with a smile on his face, wrap his arms and legs around the bark and begin to hoist himself up with the speed of a young boy tearing down a sandy slope. He watched him in admiration. When he was level with the honeycomb, he stopped, held himself on a branch with one hand and firmly entwined his legs round it. With the knife in the other hand, he began to slice chunks off it, dropping them in the basket. That day they bagged a record harvest, and their spirits rose as they realised that they would be making good money. How everybody laughed and jumped about as they sampled their harvest, smearing each other merrily, chanting Bhojpuri songs and prancing about.

They left it for three days to give the honeycomb time to replenish itself before they returned. It was on this second trip that Raju saw his first tiger. He was stunned by its awesome beauty and by its size. It seemed to him that he was the length of a grown man. He was sleek and moved in utmost silence, his paws scarcely touching the ground. The boy was specially drawn to the way shoulder bones of the beast stuck out and went in as he moved. The men made the biggest racket they could, and Dakshin looked at them, yawned, turned round and walked away in disgust, as if bored by the shenanigans of humans.

Apart from honey gathering, Sukhdeo was involved in a large number of other commercial activities and Baba was his right-hand man. Time was when Parsad was the driving force behind the two-men partnership, but at the death of Parvatti, his erstwhile vitality had dried up like a nimbu squeezed out of all its juice and then left in the punishing sun. His mind had lost its sharpness, and he was quite content to play second fiddle to a man he had so clearly towered above in every respect in the old days. Many villagers grew various things on small plots of land on which they were squatting, and Sukhdeo had an arrangement with them whereby he handled their produce for them. At first, according to Phoopi, he was reasonably equitable, but once he discovered that he could, he began to demand a bigger cut. He and Baba were best friends, but he proudly repeated that business was one thing and friendship was another. If Baba was ever in need, he'd sell his soul to help, but under normal circumstances Parsad should not expect preferential treatment. He still conveniently forgot to repay the loans Parsad had made to him when they had left Allapur. When Phoopi mentioned this, Baba expressed his disapproval by drawing some air through the nose, sniff and turn his face round as he expelled it, shaking his head almost imperceptibly, saying nothing.

Sukhdeo sometimes provided small crafts for people who wanted to fish, and Raju did not understand why Baba who was so full of resources, never made a boat himself, or at least get his friend the Hakeem to help him make one for him. As a result, more than half his catch automatically went to Sukhdeo.

Fortunately Phoopi was quite expert at fishing for shrimps and prawns which needed no boat, as these grew near the muddy shores. She also made her own basketwork and used them deftly to land in good catches, which she dried in the sun and bartered with other villagers for other commodities which they produced.

Although Sukhdeo was noticeably much more prosperous than the other villagers, he had not as yet bought any land. He had not yet made enough money to be in the same league as Ishwarlal. The zamindar had arrived in Bengal a few years earlier, and had ended up owning valuable land. The jealous Sukhdeo loudly proclaimed that Ishwarlal was a crook. This conclusion was based on his oft-repeated conviction that no one ever became rich by honest means. One day, he promised, I am going to have more money than that crook.

It was that same year that Sukhdeo began to lay the foundation of his wealth, although Raju would only understand the ramifications much later. He was there, and later he would remember everything. The honey-picking season lasted no more than two months every year, as the moment the flowers began to wilt, the honey turned bitter, and was of no use to man or beast.

One day, as Parsad and Sukhdeo sat under the peepul tree, pulling on their bidis with furrowed brows, and enjoying a cup of toddy, the latter wondered aloud about the possibility of removing the bitterness from the late honey, perhaps by adding something to it, so it could still be sold. Baba suggested, half in jest, that they could give people some good honey to taste first and then sell them the bitter stuff. Sukhdeo laughed, but said that this could prove dangerous, as the buyers might make trouble next time round. Baba gave no more thought to bitter honey.

A few days later, Sukhdeo came to their little hut and said that he had found a foolproof method for making money with bitter honey.

'Yes?' said Baba. 'Kaho, kaho!'

'It's like this: we will go to Calcutta and sell the bitter honey and tell people it is a miracle drug which will cure anything.'

'Anything?' Yes, pains and aches, winds, colds, you name it.' Sukhdeo said. Baba thought the scheme might just work. After all people believed that the more bitter the medicine the more potent it was.

'We could get your friend the Hakeem to come with us and testify to the quality of the product,' said Sukhdeo, but Parsad shook his head.

'That man will never tell a lie, not for all the water in the Zam Zam, as he says.' Sukhdeo was not so sure, but suddenly Parsad's face lit up.

'Your mentioning the Hakeem gave me an idea, listen with both your ears.'

'I am, yaar, I am.'

'The Hakeem told me about something he read many years ago. Tell me, yaar, what does a man want value more than anything else in the world?'

'Money?'

'Money, yes. But money cannot buy everything.'

'No?' Sukhdeo paused for a very short while. 'Course it can, what can it not buy? Tell me, yaar.'

'If you were an old man and were no longer able to… eh… perform, would any amount of money make it stand up again?'

'Methi Paak? Garlic?' Methi Paak was a prized sweet containing fenugreek and nutmeg.

'Doesn't always work.'

'I wouldn't know,' laughed Sukhdeo, 'I don't need it yet. Do you?'

'Any man would give an arm and an eye to be able to do at fifty what he could do at twenty five.'

'Bilkul!' Absolutely.

'And what I am saying is that bitter honey is that miracle product.'

'Is that true? I never knew,' Sukhdeo said foolishly.

'Listen, yaar, people may not believe true and simple things, but when it comes to a promise of… how shall I put it…? Becoming younger…' and Parsad made a fist and pumped it backwards and forwards a few times, in a familiar sexual gesture, 'they will readily believe you.'

'You think?'

'The idea came from the Hakeem, it was he who told me that he had read about a type of honey from the Himalayas which indeed had the ability to raise the dead. We can tell people our bitter honey will help them get it up again… they will believe us.'

But it was Sukhdeo who carefully elaborated the nuts and bolts of the operation, thus justifying to himself that it was his idea, and keeping the ill-gotten gains for himself.

They made for a part of the Hooghly river where hawkers from all over the area came to sell their wares. They used to sell a small earthenware pot of their best honey for two pise, but this time they asked for twice the price. One whole anna? People asked, how come? Sukhdeo winked and asked the hesitant customer if to him bed was just for resting his tired bones now. At the end of the day, their stock was depleted and Sukhdeo went back home with a small fortune. They were not sure how they would be received on their next visit, but prospective buyers were already queuing up, swearing to the potency of this Sunderbans Bitter. Sukhdeo surprised Baba by his quick-ness of mind, explaining that his suppliers were asking for more, and that one pot would now cost two annas. They were surprised when people readily disbursed. Many clients were all smiles and swore that the miracle drug was indeed potent, and with little encouragement recounted to all and sundry how they had kept their wives awake all night every night since they sampled the product. The Hakeem who did not condone such practices, explained that in such matters, often all one needed was faith and self-belief.

At first Sukhdeo had shared half the gains with Parsad, but Lalita frowned upon what she called her husband's stupidity, and soon put an end to that. Arrey, why you give this lay-about so much? Why do you always put his in-terest first? What about me? Do I not work hard? Are you calling me lazy? Is that what you are saying? In the beginning, nothing she said made any difference, but gradually he started mentioning imaginary expenses, and ended up by keeping a bigger share of the loot for himself.

'Friendship is worth more than money, Didi,' was Baba's explanation to his older sister.

However, almost imperceptibly the relationship between the two men became strained. They still met regularly under the peepul tree by the stream to smoke their bidis and indulge in their toddy, more by force of habit than anything else. They were not heard to laugh as much or as heartily as in their carefree Allapur days.

By now, Raju was considered grown-up enough to start doing man's work. Everybody agreed that he had Parsad's dexterity, and he took great pride in holding the curved knife between his teeth like Baba, as he climbed the honey tree to cut off chunks of honeycomb. He knew how to entwine his legs around the trunk before hoisting himself up. He had learnt all the rules and all the tricks. Above all else, he knew what only the best gatherers knew: when to stop. You did not cut the whole honeycomb off in one fell swoop, you needed to leave enough behind for the bees to rebuild on. Often the greedy or inexperienced gatherer took too much and spoiled it for themselves.

Many a time they had spotted Dakshin Rai, and managed to keep out of his way. In five years Raju had not witnessed a single mauling. The young man was never to lose his great love for honey-picking, not even after what happened to Baba.

Parsad was, as ever, terribly proud of his boy, and he would declare this openly to all and sundry. When he started making rash statements, his team mates became uneasy, although opinions were divided. When you say Dakshin Rai can come for me now and do his worst, some argued that it was inviting tragedy, whilst others maintained that on the contrary, when Dakshin heard this, he knew that the speaker had a fearless soul and should be left well alone. Anyway, Baba began saying, with a laugh of course, that as his boy could do this job as well as he, Parsad, Dakshin could come for him now. He should not have said that, for Bon Bibi must have misunderstood and thought Parsad no longer wanted her protection. The villagers would argue endlessly about the cause, but the fact was that Dakshin acted upon this.

One morning, Baba was unusually happy and relaxed, although he had been quite tired lately. His good humour was infectious, for everybody in the team was relaxed and was singing humming, and telling stories. It is said that a relaxed atmosphere was prone to attract danger, as people lowered their guards. Dakshin Rai appeared suddenly from a bush and almost before his presence was registered, ignoring the face mask at the back of Baba's head, he pounced on the unfortunate man from behind and made for the top of his spine, which is what he usually does. Death was almost instantaneous. Baba fell down, his eyes wide open. He just whispered, "Bodh Gaya!" and expired with a smile on his lips. The others fearlessly drove the killer away with massive sticks, but it was too late. Sukhdeo cried like a child and everybody else began beating their chests, crying their eyes out, except Raju. He kept shaking his head. No, he kept saying to everybody, my Baba is tired, he's just gone to sleep but he will wake up soon and none the worse for the attack. Why was everybody crying? For three whole days, even after Parsad was cremated, Raju was convinced that something mysterious had occurred, and that Baba would turn up soon.

Raju avoided people. Whenever anybody said anything to him, he stared at them with vacant eyes and seemed not to hear. The only person whose presence he tolerated was the Hakeem. He would walk to his little hut by the water and sit on the ground quietly, saying nothing, watching the man Baba admired above everybody else sawing or planing wood. The Hakeem was not given to making long speeches, and would leave the boy to his thoughts. Only when he was going back to Aunty Umma after maybe two hours, would the older man take him by the shoulder and hug him. One day he grabbed his hand as he was walking away.

'You know beta, I have not seen you cry for your Baba, why?' The young man did not answer.

'It is not shameful to cry for your dead father, even the bravest warriors shed tears for their dead comrades.'

'I know,' he had said weakly. On the way home, a thought struck him. If I cry now, I will feel less sad tomorrow, but I want to feel sad for the rest of my life. I will keep my tears in, I will never cry for my Pitaji so I can be always sad. This made him remember how loving Baba was. All his life he would remember the stories he had told him. He specially cherished the memory of how he would press him to his heart before he fell asleep. He would force the tastiest piece of bhetki in his mouth, saying, eat, beta, eat, when you eat Baba's hunger is gone. He remembered how he had carried him on his shoulders from Jharkhand to Calcutta, singing his funny ditties. Prey to all those remembrances, he had to sit down under a bush. The clouds which had gathered in his skull suddenly burst and rained tears which burst through the banks of his eyes. He did not know for how long he had cried, but when he woke up, the sun had set. This gave him a lot of comfort, and did not make him feel bad. It felt like a homage to the dead man. Later he would try to relive the events, but it was never the same.

Sukhdeo said to everybody that as long as he lived, his friend's son and sister would want for nothing, but only once did he give Phoopi Umma some money. He loved saying things like this when there were people around, and he would loudly proclaim that whenever she wanted any help, be it midday or midnight, all she had to do was to ask, in the hope of seeing admiration in the eyes of the bystanders. Midday or midnight, yesterday or tomorrow, admiration was what he craved for. After that first time, he never gave or offered her anything, and she never asked. The proud Phoopi had told herself that she would starve before taking any money from a man she had always despised.

Raju was not really able to earn a reasonable living by himself, as Sukhdeo gave him less than the other honey pickers, saying that grown-up men and youths could not be paid the same rate, although the boy did the work of two.

On top of her fishing activities, Umma made a few more annas by offering her services as cook to the richer folks when there was a festival, or by darning other people's clothes, knitting woollen bonnets for babies. Still, most of the villagers were even less fortunate than themselves. In any case, it was rare for anybody to go hungry in the Sunderbans if one was prepared to eat the same fare day in and day out, there was any number of comestible greens as well as nuts and roots growing abundantly around.

Unsurprisingly, the Hakeem who himself barely scratched a living from the little carpentry that came his way, making a boat now and then, supplementing his meagre takings by his healing work, which he did mainly for free, was always there for them. People thanked him by bringing him eggs or beans, milk or curd and similar things, and these he happily shared with the orphan and his aunt. More than that, he became a second father to Raju, giving him guidance, but most of all he taught him about the magic plants of the Sunderbans. In the beginning, he would go to the forest with the teenager to reveal to him the secrets of the flora, and tell him stories associated with them. The old man was a fount of wisdom, and taught him which plants were good and which to avoid.

'Never walk under this tree,' he told, as they were approaching a nona jhaw, 'it brings bad luck. You see, it bears no fruit, and if a woman walks in its shade, she becomes barren.'

'But I am not a woman,' Raju protested in jest.

'Well,' the Hakeem winked, 'do it, and you'll never become a father.' The most unforgettable experience the lad had was with the bhola flower, a type of hibiscus which prospered in the marshy salty soil. It immediately filled you with delight when one suddenly leapt at you in the forest. It is the prettiest flower one is likely to come across, golden yellow petals with a red centre.

'Look at this one here,' ordered the Hakeem, 'stare at it and concentrate.' For five minutes nothing happened, then suddenly, Raju could not believe his eyes when the yellow petals started darkening, first becoming golden yellow then orange. Raju was not one to keep his surprise silent, and began to exclaim his appreciation, but the Hakeem ordered him to be quiet and to keep looking. The deep orange now turned red, and in a matter of minutes, the whole flower detached itself from its stem and fell to the ground. He had never witnessed such a miracle in his life.

Thus it was that Raju became an expert in the field, and in gratitude he would bring his mentor whose knees made walking more difficult everyday, a regular stock of his medicinal leaves, roots, bark and seeds: Lata hargoza seeds which he needed for people to cleanse their blood, Passur for stomach pains, math goran for ulcers, harguja with was the most effective remedy against rheumatism as well as a large variety of other plants like amur, kripa, or dabur.

Sukhdeo did not view this friendship with a good eye, and one afternoon he arrived in Roshankhali on Jayant's boat and made for the little hovel where aunt and nephew lived.

'This Musselman is trying to convert the boy to Islam and make him eat beef,' he told Phoopi, but fortunately the wise old woman told him that the Hakeem often told the boy stories from the Ramayana, although he himself was not a Hindu, so how could he be trying to convert the boy? Sukhdeo was not going to give up too easily.

'The man is a charlatan I tell you,' he exclaimed in desperation.

'I know you went to see him about your flatulence and you're still spoiling the air whenever you go anyplace,' thought Umma.

'How can you be saying that? So many people he has been curing,' she said instead.

'Nonsense, if he was such a great Hakeem, how come he cannot be curing himself of his bad knee?' Phoopi was stumped, but only for a short while. 'Sukhdeo Bhai, no one can be cured of old age.' The malicious man was still not beaten.

'He is only using the boy to bring him all those quack herbs he uses to fleece people,' Sukhdeo said. 'He is wearing rags and telling everybody he is poor, but I have heard that he has rupees and gold sovereigns hidden in the ground.' Umma and Raju both knew that "Somebody" was another word for Lalita, and Raju's aunt pointed out that everybody extols the virtues of the man who never charged anything for his healing work.

'But people are always giving him things,' Lalita's husband said, 'dried bhetki, eggs, chicken even... I am not knowing, so many things...' Umma thought that it was best to keep quiet.

'Your Baba who was more than a brother to me,' he told the boy, 'was a friend of the Hakeem, but he would not wish his son to associate with a Musselman like this, specially as I am a second father to you.'

Raju was very astute. 'Chacha Sukhdeo, remember the Hakeem cured you of those pains in your knee, he's a good man to have as an ally.'

'Cure me, you say? hraak! All he does when anybody has an ailment is to get you to eat cabbage, put cabbage on your aching knee, chew cabbage when you have toothache, drink cabbage water when you have stomach pains... all that cabbage does is to make me fart, your aunty Lalita says...'

'It's not the cabbage, Chacha, everything makes you fart,' the boy was going to say but bit his tongue in time to stop the hurtful words.

'Chacha Sukhdeo,' he said instead, 'I am thrice blessed, for I have three fathers: my poor Pitaji who always watches over me, your good self, my second father, and a Musselman for a third father!' The older man was very angry, but thought that he would bide his time.

Now, when Raju went honey picking, he came back loaded with the good things of the mangrove, the excellent golpata shoots, hental dates, not only gila roots and nuts, but also its bark which is used as soap, khalsi or du-lya bayen twigs which proved to be excellent firewood, edible fruits, passur twigs which he gave to friends who had stomach problems, keora leaves for the goats and cows, and their edible fruits which Phoopi boiled or roasted, or cooked with sojne. The Hakeem had taught him how to collect the tasty ashilata beans which made one strong ('you'll understand when you are older, beta'). But make sure that you did not let the hairs touch your body, as they had an itchy effect on one, he warned.

He knew how much Sukhdeo resented the Hakeem, and understood that he viewed it as an affront to himself, as if he could not be friends with both of them. Gradually the older man's attitude towards him hardened. It was as if he wanted to end his personal relationship with his best friend's son, but Raju knew that the man needed his sweat. The astute businessman swallowed his resentment and began involving him in his multifarious commercial activities, the sort of thing Baba had been doing for years. Clearly Lalita had made sure that he did not pay him a full wage.

It was this which prompted Raju to think of new schemes. He would build a boat with the Hakeem's help, and use it to go fishing on his own account. Sukhdeo reacted angrily to this, told the boy that as his guardian, he should have been consulted before embarking upon something so reckless. Did he not know the dangers? Did he wish his Phoopi Umma to be left destitute if something happened to him? He reproached the young man for treating him with such little respect. He had never once done the p'rnaam to him, never prostrated himself in an attempt to kiss the older man's feet like one is expected to do to an elder to whom one owed respect and allegiance. If Raju had thought that was what was expected of him, he would have done it for form's sake, but the idea had never occurred to him. It was true that he never asked for advice, even the doting Phoopi had to accept that her nephew thought he knew it all.

Gradually, by his commonsensical approach to work, the boy had ended by earning the older man's grudging admiration. He sometimes forgot himself and declared that if Bhagwan had given him a son, Raju would have made a good model, but he quickly changed the subject. Deep down he could never forgive him.

It was Sukhdeo who suggested to the young man one day that it was time to marry, and went as far as to suggest that he would find him a suitable bride. Raju liked the idea and giggling happily, agreed. When the older man mentioned the daughter of a honey-picker called Kamla, Raju remembered her as a very plain sort of girl who he had never found in the least attractive, and said so. Who do you want as a bride then? Sukhdeo had asked angrily, Ishwarlal's daughter Shanti? Raju's eyes opened wide. He had always dreamt of Shanti, but expected that the daughter of the rich zamindar would end up marrying the son of a rich man from Calcutta. No, Uncle Sukhdeo, I am too young to marry at the moment, but the seed of an impossible romance had fallen on fertile soil.

It was Phoopi who now began to have a go as well. She said that Raju could tell her if there was anybody he liked. Cheekily he only mentioned Shanti's name, in the hope that she'd leave him alone. He reasoned that Ishwarlal who had always treated him with disdain would never agree to such a union, but Phoopi said, why not? With little to lighten her gloomy existence, she often found solace in the fact that back in Bihar their ancestors had once been rich landowners and were of a much higher standing than Ishwarlal's. She told her nephew, 'Your grandfather was a poet, we had hundreds of bigha of land. Ishwarlal comes from a family of dhobis, earning their living by washing other people's dirty linen,' adding that nobody forgets things like that. She was convinced that Raju would have been an excellent match for anybody. He was a respectable and handsome young man with excellent prospects. If anything, her nephew was too good for that family.

One morning, she scrubbed herself, washed her hair with soap and put on a white widow's sari, found an old pair of dried up chhampals that she had not worn since she arrived in Roshankhali, cleaned it, mended it, found it bit her now bigger feet, but decided that for her nephew she had to look good. With determined steps, she came out of the house and made for Ishwarlal's. She had once been friends with Radha in Allapur, but this was the first time that she was going to visit her here.

She suddenly remembered her stoop and stopped suddenly. She took a deep breath, straightened her back at great cost to herself, and pursued her route. Radha received her with great warmth and courtesy. Although she expected no less, she was flattered. She went straight to the point. Good husbands for our daughters are very hard to find, she began, and Shanti's mother agreed. Feeling encouraged, she launched into an elegy of her nephew, which, because it was so heartfelt, struck the other woman as very convincing. Yes, Umma didi, conceded Radha, so I have heard. She had? He is going to go far in life, assured Phoopi. Radha said she would mention her visit to their father.

Ishwarlal, a sound businessman used to weighing the pros and cons of all deals, agreed that Raju was poor but had great potential. He remembered that the boy reacted with maturity when he gave him a hard time as a child, he neither cried, nor looked at him insolently.

'Yes, the boy has great potential. When I buy a piece of land,' he told the bemused Radha, 'I do not look at the rocks and stumps and dismiss it as barren. I wouldn't be who I am today if I did. On the contrary, I visualise it after the impediments have been removed and after I have tilled the soil, watered it, ploughed in the best cow shit. Yes, piari, you can call me a man of vision if you insist. The boy will indeed make a good husband for our beloved daughter.' He decided on the spot that the young man should come work for him, for each other's mutual benefit.

Sukhdeo was flabbergasted when he heard about the proposed union. His feelings for his dead friend's son were so confused. Sometimes he loved him like the son he never had, and at others, he felt an inexplicable anger mount in his breast and had to stop himself doing him physical harm. He admired his devotion to work, but at the same time was jealous of this capacity.

However, this prospective marriage gave him no joy. He wanted the boy to do well, but not that well. Lalita saw it as a union between two different and unequal species like between a dog and a lioness. No good can come out of this, mark my word, she said. This thought gave her husband a jolt. No piari, he admonished, don't be like that. Don't be the goat's mouth that turns everything bitter on the vegetable patch by just one bite. Parsad's boy needs our blessings.

There were problems from the very beginning. When Ishwarlal told Raju to come work for him, Phoopi told the boy that it was never a good idea to work for your in-law, pointing out to him that he had excellent prospects and did not need patronage. 'You do not want to be beholden to them.' she advised. 'You work for your father-in-law, and you become clay in the hands of your wife. She will never let you forget that you owe her family everything, they turn you into a burbak.'

The zamindar was in a fix. First Radha had become sold on the idea. Worse, they had told everybody about the impending wedding. A break at this stage would make Shanti unmarriageable, as tongues had already begun wagging. Ishwarlal decided to shrug this incomprehensible stance, telling himself that the boy was bound to come round soon enough.

Then it became apparent to aunt and nephew that plans were being made for them to move in Ishwarlal's house until he had another house built for them. This time it was Raju who did not relish the idea. He wanted to be the boss in his own house. On learning this, Ishwarlal thought that enough was enough. In a fit of anger he shouted at Radha, accused her of going ahead with a hare-brained plan without talking to him, and proclaimed that the wedding was off. But Radha had taken a shine to the young man, and although she did not defend herself against Ishwarlal's unjust remarks, she knew that in the end, she would have her way. All that happened was that the wedding was postponed for three whole months until Raju had finished the repairs on his dilapidated dwelling, under the supervision of the Hakeem and with Jayant's help.

Ishwarlal was not a happy man when the big day came, but he had no choice. Shanti, on her part said nothing, but after what she had heard of Raju and seen of him, she was hopeful that he would make no worse a husband than those of her married friends.

Shortly after the wedding, Phoopi Umma died suddenly. She woke up fit and cheerful, took ill at noon and in keeping with her nature, died without fuss within an hour. It was as if she had decided that Raju was now in good hands and she could let go. It was her dearest wish to see her grandchildren before she died, but Shanti only discovered that she was pregnant a week after she died.

Ya Bhagwan, cried Raju as he watched the flames rise from the ignited body of the dead woman, how could you be so mean to such a saint? Parvatti had never been more than a picture to him, but Phoopi was flesh and blood. All mothers loved their children, he thought, they had no choice, but Umma's love for him had not been forced upon her. It was love in its purest form. She had never once raised her voice to him, never said one unkind word. Her every single action was dictated by her need to protect her boy and make his life happy. He allowed his tears to flow freely this time, but knew that he would carry the memory of the woman who had been both father and mother to him in his heart until he breathed his last.

CHAPTER 7

◆ ◆ ◆

Insurrection in the Highlands

THE SEED FOR the insurrection had scarcely been put into the all too fertile soil of discontent, had not even been watered by illicit brew, than it had sprouted. Hugh Breac Mackenzie made his way to John Aird's ramshackle home, part of which everybody but the law enforcers knew, housed a still for the brewing of illegal but much sought after uisghe beatha. The surprise was that the God-fearing John himself was quite abstemious. If he indulged in the occasional wee dram, no one had ever seen him drunk. He could have made himself a tidy little sum by this cottage industry, seeing he was taking all the risks, but he chose not to. More often than not, he gave away the product of his labours or charged just enough to cover the expenses.

Mackenzie found about a dozen men (most of whom were called Ross) had preceded him and to his surprise, Fergus Davidson, Jimmy's wee brother was holding forth about the iniquities to which they were subjected. The tension between Highlanders and lairds had one root cause. With the great demand for wool, everybody wanted to change over to Cheviot Sheep. They grazed wherever they could, did not have to be looked after, needed no green pastures, produced wool every year and could also provide meat. All the lairds who had changed over were overjoyed at the size of their profits. Obviously all that happened at a price. To the poor crofters. One of the Rosses cackled in an unpleasant manner, 'Fergus, go tell that to your brother Jimmy who is at one with the lairds.' Fergus protested that he was not his brother's keeper. 'Oor Jimmy will answer to the Lord for his action hissel,' he said. Hugh knew that Fergus too had been in the employ of the Camerons, but he had been sacked for looking the other way when the Black Cattle of the small tenants had encroached upon the pastures of the sheep owners. No turncoat he. Hugh wondered whether if matters came to a head, he himself would not take the Camerons' shilling. Would he let the bairn that was coming starve out of his stubbornness? Mam was right. Damn the God that would inflict such mental torments on his creatures!

Although Aird had set aside a generous amount of his brew for his guests and fellow conspirators, he had made it clear that they would agree on any action envisaged, uninfluenced by the brew. Fergus, probably eager to show he was on side, made an impassioned appeal for action. We have nothing to lose, he went on. If we do nothing, the situation will get worse, but remember that if we take action, we might draw the attention of the men in Dingwall, or even London. I don't want to spend my life in a prison, one of the Rosses said, I despise the notion of transportation to Botany Bay. To this, another Ross spat on the ground muttering enigmatically, Faintheart never turned oat into porridge. Another Ross added, 'Or rye into malt'.

Mor Wallace, called the Gentle Giant because of his gentle nature and huge size then sprang forward and to everybody's surprise, growled angrily. 'What I say is that doing nothing is not an option.' Aye, aye, chorused the assembly. Action is what is called for, the giant said in his big bass bellow, and everybody nodded.

Hugh can write a letter to Mr Robert Dundas, the Lord Advocate of Scotland, John Aird suggested. Father Anthony will correct his spelling mistakes, teased a Ross merrily. The Lord Advocate will do what he always does, Hugh said, he burns all petitions from us crofters.

'See,' said Michael Ross, 'he is already backing out of writing the letter.' Hugh knew that the man was only teasing, but there were times when he did not like jokes.

'I will have you know that my spelling and my handwriting are both up to scratch, Michael Ross, it's just that I know and you all know that letters carry no weight.' Michael nodded and raised his hands apologetically.

'There is only one thing,' said Wallace. 'We enlist the help of all men who refuse to kowtow to the lairds, fearless men, who I know Highlanders are, and we go and free our cattle.' The men from the other parishes will join us if we ask them, suggested another Ross. 'Then let us send them word,' said Hugh. Everybody marvelled at his capacity for taking quick but sound decisions. Only at the end of the discussions were the whisky bottles produced. As every Highlander knows, once whisky is poured, like the genie, there is no way it can find its way back into the bottle. The drinking, carousing and merrymaking lasted all night long.

Hugh said not one word about what was afoot to either Mam or Martha, but inevitably they learnt about it, and neither expressed disapproval.

On the next day, a small group of less than twenty men, small tenants, peat cutters, destitute men with no work, gathered on the bank of River Oykel and Fergus who had been in the employ of the brothers from Lochaber and knew that the impounded cattle were kept in a guarded enclosure at the western end of Loch Morie, explained to the men the best way of getting to the bank. The men who had touched not one drop of whisky between them, listened to Hugh attentively. He had emerged as a natural leader without seeking the role.

Someone suggested cutlasses and sticks, but Hugh shook his head forcefully, saying that their best course would be to use no force, just make a show of their resolution and try to talk the Cameron brothers into releasing what was theirs. They all readily agreed. They climbed over the long moor down the shoulder of Carn Beag to the meadow at the head of Loch Morie, and singing lustily to keep their spirits up, they arrived at the gate of the pen where they were met by the Captain, his brother, about ten shepherds and five or six men of undefined status. The Captain and his brother had their muskets, and the former also had a fierce-looking one-foot long dirk. The men had nothing more than sticks and iron bars.

'We have come to talk, Captain, why are you and your men armed?' asked Hugh in a firm voice. For all answer Captain Cameron fired his musket into the air.

'I do not talk to rabble,' he said haughtily. 'Get your men off my land, or you will live to regret it. You churls only understand one language...' he left the sentence in the air, cocked his musket once more, this time pointing it at the crowd. This was too much for the Gentle Giant. Big though he was, he had the agility of a goat. Suddenly he sprang forward and threw himself at the Captain, who taken by surprise, backed two steps and stumbled on his brother, whose musket went off, seemingly of its own accord. Some of the Cameron men seeing this ran away in a panic, but were pursued by the bog-cutters. The consumptive Alexander Cameron seemed to have hurt himself when his brother fell on him, and Jimmy Davidson rushed to his aid. The Captain regained his balance, and was trying to use the musket, not to shoot, but as a weapon to hit Wallace with, whereupon the irate giant growled, grabbed the weapon and smashed it on his knee, bending it in the bargain. Amazed at his own strength, he held it high for all to see, and everybody cheered loudly. The party ran after the shepherds and the other men, their intention of causing grievous harm clear for all to see. It took Hugh all the authority he could muster to call them to attention.

'Do not hurt anyone who does not attack you,' he urged, but that did not stop one or two of the Camerons' men getting kicks in the arse, humiliating and painful, but not really injurious. Wallace grabbed the Captain by the neck, lifted him up in the air, then suddenly pushed him down unceremoniously, with such vigour that the man expected that he was going to be buried in the earth half way up the knees. The man who claimed to have fought in foreign wars for king and country was left whimpering like a drenched puppy, hands raised over his head like a Highland laddie parrying a punch in the face by his drunken da. Alexander finally helped him to his feet and the brothers just walked away towards their mansion, heads bent down, their tails between their legs. The men of the strath were at liberty to do as they wanted, but all they did was to liberate their cattle. Michael Ross, who rarely parted from his pipe, played a triumphant tune as they went down the hill to shelter their prized cattle in the comfort of their own stables.

The action of the tenants had much outraged the lairds and inevitably the authorities decided to act against the perpetrators, to scotch any nascent revolutionary zeal in the egg. In a dawn raid two days later, Wallace and three others were arrested, although inexplicably neither Hugh Mackenzie not John Aird was. A preliminary hearing called a procognition was set up to determine the feasibility of a legal trial. Witnesses contradicted each other. When one man swore that one Robert Macdonald had tried to set fire to the Cameron barn, it was established beyond the shadow of a doubt that the said

MacDonald had been immobilised for the last three weeks on account of a broken leg. Wallace who had undeniably inflicted some serious injury to the Captain's pride if nothing else, said that they had come to parley, and that it was the military man who had a gun and had threatened to use it. I had no choice, he explained, a man has to defend himself. One witness said the men were armed with crooks, to which a Ross said that they were cowherds. What's a cowherd without his crook? A laird without money? He asked to universal merriment. It was decided that there was insufficient basis for a trial.

The Camerons were dismayed and petitioned everybody. They urged McLeod of Geanies to use his influence to get the case reviewed. They wrote to the Lord Advocate, promised favours to some, threatened others, but it came to nothing.

The tenants were kept informed of all this, and flaunted their victory over enslavement, as they called it. They took their cattle over the erstwhile forbidden territory to water in the Morie, and the Camerons were helpless to stop them. The brothers finally begged Lord Adam Gordon to see them, and after much entreaty, the Commander of Forces in Northern Britain agreed, and they travelled hopefully to Fort George in Ardersier.

The Commander was a large rugged man who had seen action all over Europe, and nevertheless had the reputation of being someone of great intellect with a great sense of justice. He was not known for his enthusiasm for what the sheep farmers seemed to be doing to the Highlanders. He saw himself as a tactician who was responsible for matters of national and international importance, and did not like wasting his time on trivial matters like disputes between small tenants and lairds. However, he owed a favour to the elder Cameron, now dead, and so he agreed to hear what the sons had to say. The moment Captain Allan opened his mouth, Lord Gordon took an instant dislike to him.

'I am not here to speak about my own trivial problem,' he said immediately he was seated on the large velvet armchair, 'but for a much greater cause.'

He went on about what he saw as a struggle to the end which pitted order and decency against the forces of anarchy. If the rabble were not stopped, the younger Cameron added, this great country might well go the same way as France.

'So you are not really striking a blow for yourselves, but doing your patriotic duty in helping preserve the monarchy and all that it stands for, eh what?' the Commander said, and the brothers failing to detect the irony nodded enthusiastically.

Feeling encouraged, they explained about Culcairn and the sheep, the Black cattle and the difficulty of coexistence of these two species. The peasants no longer showed their class the respect to which they were entitled. They were becoming arrogant and disobedient. Something had to be done, and done quickly, they urged.

'We're thinking of petitioning His Majesty in Buckingham Palace,' Alexander said suddenly. He regretted saying this the moment he saw how Gordon reacted, no doubt perceiving it as a threat to his authority.

'My dear fellow, do you think that after the events in Paris, His Majesty has time to look at petty parochial matters which could have been dealt with by your good selves with a little compassion and good sense?' he asked. The brothers knew then that their trip to Ardersier had been a waste of time, and on the way back, the brothers refused to talk to each other, each blaming the other for saying the wrong thing. They knew when they were beaten, but they were sure that the time would come when they would be able to avenge the ignominy to which they had been subjected.

The following week Michael Ross' daughter was getting married to John Aird's cousin Wullie, and there was much merriment and carousing at Aird's house where the nuptials were taking place. The men were still basking in what they saw as their triumph over the forces of reaction, but further lubricated by the illicit brew, the dancing and the singing became lustier by the hour. To say nothing of bragging and bluster.

'We have been too timid in the past,' said someone, 'we didn't know our own strength.' Everybody ayed.

'We'll drink to that,' was the automatic response to this, and action followed words. In no time at all, apart from Hugh, who made it a point of never drinking immoderately, no one could think clearly. Even the usually abstemious Aird had, exceptionally, in view of the occasion, partaken of rather too much of his own medicine.

'We are a powerful force,' said someone, 'and if we can't defeat those Cheviot sheep, we're not worthy of the name of Highlanders.' Aye, Aye, we'll drink to that. It was thus that the seed for the second harvest of hatred, justified though it was, was sown. This group of drunken men took the decision, there and then, to get rid of the pestilence that had invaded their land. Each pronouncement immediately became a solemn undertaking, a declaration of intent. We'll gather a force of hundreds. Easy! We'll enlist men from the other parts. Done! We'll march on the sheep farms. Let's go now! Hugh had to put a stop to that one. No, he urged, we must organise ourselves first. He did not entirely disagree with the principle of what was being mooted, and he half hoped that after the effects of the illicit brew wore off, the militancy of the people would give way to a more sober but determined resolve. By God, we will organise, they chorused. They will be powerless to stop us! Of course, we'll be hundreds! No, at least a thousand!

When sobriety seemed not to have dampened the revolutionary spirit of the crofters, Hugh decided that he had better do some organising. He talked to John Aird and to Father Anthony. The man of cloth demurred, and preached the virtues of forbearance and patience. Taking the sort of action that they were planning was against the laws of God. The men are drunk, give them a couple of days to sober up and clarify their cobwebbed brains and they will see the error of their ways and back out. Come talk to me in two days' time, he said, and if they are still bent on doing something, we'll talk again.

After the two extra days that Father Anthony had demanded, Hugh found that the eagerness of his friends, far from being blunted, had gathered momentum, and not one man had had second thoughts. He was not surprised. Once he took the decision to act, no power on earth could have stopped him.

Thus it was that, Mackenzie, Aird, Father Anthony, Michael Ross, Fergus Davidson and some others met secretly in the church hall to thrash out the minutest details of what was obviously going to be an insurrection. Hugh knew that he was expected to come up with a plan, and indeed one was already taking shape in his head. Risks had to be taken, but caution was necessary in order not to exact extreme retribution by the powers that be.

Volunteers were despatched to Alness, Boath, Creich, Kincardine, Lairg, Resolis, Urquhart, to spread the word, and wherever there were aggrieved men, that is, everywhere, they were received rapturously. They claimed that they had always hoped that some day someone would organise just such a movement as seemed to be now afoot, and vowed that they would do everything in their power to right these wrongs, even if it meant transportation to Botany Bay. Or worse.

Thus it was that upwards of four hundred men gathered on the banks of River Oykel on the following Tuesday. Hugh Mackenzie, who knew the lie of the land, and Michael Ross who was well-informed about the sheep walks, had produced a map. The eventual aim was to collect as many sheep as they could, drive them across the Beauly River and there set them free. They would thus be striking a serious blow to those who had planned a proxy war against them, by dispatching these wooly creatures south, where they came from. In one fell swoop they would be solving their problems for good. Hugh, as de facto leader, had expressly forbidden any firearms, but some hotheads had decided to ignore this order. Men were dispatched all over Easter Ross with specific instructions to collect the sheep and drive them south, but the movement soon gathered surprising momentum. Some men were even sent to faraway places like Lairg in Sutherland. Hugh, who had some gifts of the tactician, thought that it would be politic not to include the sheep of Donald McLeod of Geanies in his plans, for the man was the Sheriff Depute of Ross. As such, he had earned the respect of the small tenants for some of the risks that he had taken in the past on their behalf.

At first the action went on as planned. The sheep farmers were caught unawares. The whole of the Highlands seemed to reverberate under the massive stampede of fifty thousand sheep, all going south at a speed. Ten thousand sheep were seen moving south to Boath. Five thousand from Cromarty, two thousand from Novar, thousands more from Culrain, Tulloch, Cadboll. The reversal of the sheep migration from north to south seemed unstoppable. People all over the country were kept informed of the mass exodus, by word of mouth as well as by the newspapers of Edinburgh.

As the sheep were all converging towards the River Beauly, the forces of law and order began collecting themselves for the inevitable onslaught against the determined but ineffective men. They had no intention of resisting any government action by force, for they knew what the punishment for that would be. They were counting on the Lord Advocate understanding the magnitude of their grievances, which might be enough for a review of the deplorable process of replacing people by sheep in the Highlands, which was clearly the intention of those who had the upper hand.

Hugh knew that even if they were armed to the teeth, they would be no match for the might of the forty-second Regiment. The moment the word reached him that three companies were being despatched to stop them in their tracks, he knew that the game was up. At the same time he received news that Martha was in labour. He had a short parley with John Aird who was at hand, and as had been planned in advance, word was sent to all the groups to cut short the action and go in hiding until things cooled down. It had been decided from the start that no sheep would be mishandled, and indeed there was not one case of ill-treatment. The men never killed a single sheep even when they were short of food, and of the fifty thousand odd sheep which were displaced by the angry tenants, all but a handful would be returned safely to their folds in the end.

Hugh made his way to Kilmorie and found Martha in agony. Fortunately Mhairi Mackenzie was well-versed in the techniques of midwifery, and assured her son that there was no need to worry. It was just a matter of waiting, but no sooner had she spoken than men in uniforms appeared on the horizon. Mam urged her son to go into hiding, but he, knowing that when you have a family, it is impossible to stay on the run, decided that he would offer no resistance.

He was waiting for the arrival of the guards when Mam approached him and said she had something to give him.

'It's a letter from your da,' she said. 'It's addressed to you, but you were only a bairn when it arrived...' Hugh looked at Mam, stunned.

'It's full of lies anyway, for a start he wasn't even born at the Battle of Culloden.' Hugh said nothing, and extended his hand to receive the letter, but Mam withheld it for a bit.

'The only thing he said in this letter which was true, was that he loved you. Don't you be judging him too harshly.'

Hugh would have liked to read the letter on the spot, but there was no time. He just committed it into his cloth bag. When the armed men arrived, he smiled at them and gave them his hands to tie.

Mr McLeod had given express orders to the troops to treat the prisoners with dignity. He was taken to a cell in Dingwall, where he found John Aird, Alexander Mor Wallace, Michael Ross and Fergus Davidson. The Sheriff Depute had said not to bother with the foot soldiers of the rebellion, but to concentrate on the men whose names he gave the soldiers, and who were known to be the ringleaders.

Martha gave birth to a premature baby girl the same night, and whether the little bairn was going to survive or not was very much in the balance. Hugh was given the news in his cell, and all night he prayed that the baby would thrive. Even if I do not live to see her, may she prosper and grow up to live in a better and more equitable world, he prayed. He kept the letter from his father in his small bag, and it was a surprise that the guards had allowed him to keep it. The cell was damp and dark, but not dark enough to stop him reading his da's letter.

CHAPTER 8

◆ ◆ ◆

Pictou

Hughie dear boy, the letter began, *I am writing to you from Pictou in Canada, where I have been these last few years. I am writing to tell you that I never meant to abandon you and your Mam, but when God made me, he used two different types of clay, so part of me is weak-willed, whilst the other part is a man of surprising strength and courage. Sometimes the weak clay is stronger than the strong clay… I mean the weak man wins, like when I got drunk and thrown in jail and was too ashamed to confront your Mam. Honest to God, laddie, I worshipped the ground she trod, but anything above that ground, I was dead scared of. You see I had made a promise to her that I would never touch the devil drink for as long as I lived, and couldnae keep it. One advice I will give you, Hughie, never make such a promise, it is the devil itself to keep! I have touched no alcohol today, and mean to write a sensible letter to you, to say sorry to you and to explain how I came to land in this blessed place, for it is indeed blessed. I have to stop to pour myself a drink to toast that land, but no more than one, I swear.*

Ha! Yes. As your Mam must have told you, time was when I was hoping to become a preacher; I was always very good with words, they told me, I was good at book learning and had a memory like a sponge that absorbed everything I saw and read. They said I drank like a sponge too, and I am afraid it's true. Yes, I never became a man of the cloth, as I lacked discipline, they said. I liked my drink, I preferred playing the pipe to reading the good book, and I loved telling bawdy stories. Mam will explain to you what that means. But I never harmed no man. Sorry, I mean to write proper grammatical language, I meant I never harmed anybody! Anyroad, I became a crofter, but as you must know, I was no good at it. When I started playing my pipe, I forgot everything, and let the cows stray. Were it not for your Mam, the oats and turnips would have withered and we would have starved. I knew what was wrong, and prayed to the Good Lord to help me stay on the path of righteousness, but the weak clay was stronger than the strong clay. Och I said that already… As your Mam would say, God's ears are deaf to the supplications of the poor. Your sister Morag died in her infancy, and it was my fault. I was heart-broken – Hugh had almost forgotten Morag!

When you was born, Hughie, I thought that it was the end of my woes, I prayed that I would have the strength to do right by you. I knew I could be strong. As you know at the Battle of Culloden, I came to within inches of slaying the Duke of Cumberland- which would have altered the course of history. Sorry, I need a drink to drown my sorrows here, I saw so many good people lay down their lives for Auld Scotland in this battle. I promise you, no more now. I am not going to describe to you how I chased the wicked Duke with my axe, managed to unhorse him… I will tell you all that in my next letter. Hugh smiled as he recalled what Mam had said.

I want to stick to my story. I got drunk in Boath once, and lost my way. I found myself in jail for rowdy behaviour. I was too ashamed to go back home and face your Mam, so I roamed the land, playing on my pipe, drinking and making merry. That was when I found myself in Loch Broom. It was mid-July when I met some good people who told me that they were meaning to go to Canada where there was land aplenty to be given free to us Highlanders who were willing to seek their fortune beyond the seas. Kenny, I said to myself, this is what you have been waiting for all your life. You were a bad crofter because you had to give half of everything you produced to the laird; if you had your own land, you would surely take greater care of it. Aye, I thought, I would take the plunge, go to Canada, claim that land, build the best farm anybody had ever seen and send for you and Mam.

Honest to God, that was my sworn purpose. The ship was the "Hector." I watched it coming in from Greenock, and my heart was aflutter. It was mighty big, I thought, almost one hundred feet long, three- masted, two hundred ton, Dutch made, and they know how to build ships them Hollanders, but folks said it was old and damaged, and many said that there was no guarantee that it would survive the raging storms on this eight week journey. But nothing was going to stop me, my mind was made up, I was going to *take my chances. But there was one impediment to my aspiration, Hughie, I had not one brass farthing to my name, and Captain Speirs demanded three whole pounds sterling to take me on board. I begged him to let me come on board, swore that I would work for my passage, clean the deck, play music to entertain passengers and crew in times of hardship and danger, do anything, but he had a rock for a heart. The passengers coming in to join the ship took to me, as I would play my tunes on my pipe to entertain them while they waited. First the ship had to be rigged and when that was done, they had to wait for propitious winds. They took to me, the passengers, and would have raised the money for my passage, but with the uncertainty ahead, they were loth to part with the little they had themselves. On the day of the departure after the passengers had pleaded with all their might, the Captain's heart melted. A true Scot heart is generous in spite of a hard exterior, Hughie, remember that.*

The ship had appeared quite big to me as I saw it enter the Loch, but the moment I set foot on board, I could not believe that two hundred souls were going to be accommodated in an area half the size of our stable in Strathruthsdale, but arrangements had been made for people to sleep in bunk beds four storeys high. It was pandemonium, dear laddie, how were the people going to manage? I wondered. How were they going to scramble on their allocated bunks without murdering each other? I decided to act. I did my utmost in calming down frayed nerves, repeating, No need to panic, dear friend, there is room for everybody if we organise ourselves. I succeeded in stopping any fighting that would surely have resulted without my intervention.

Shall I tell you about the voyage? Yes. The first few days went well; at first, everybody including the captain was sea-sick, except me, so from the beginning I played an important part in the running of the ship. I was the one who took the helm and avoided a head-on collision with an iceberg off Greenland when the captain was being sick. Thankfully we had a good wind but no storm. Mind you, we were two hundred souls altogether on that small brig, and it took a while before we got used to the stench, the crying of children, the moaning of the sick, the constant battering and buffeting we had to endure. We were fed more or less properly, nothing fancy, salt beef, oatcakes, turnips; the Captain had assured us that we need not go hungry, as there was adequate food for the two months the trip was going to take; the crew treated us well, and Captain Speirs was civil and sensible. I played my pipe every afternoon, to the obvious delight of passengers and crew, who could not have enough of my tunes, many of which I made up myself. I might have made a fortune as a composer! After I had avoided that rock that I mentioned earlier, the captain's respect for me never stopped growing; he never took an important decision without consulting with me.

The first death from cholera took place a week after we had left Loch Broom, and eight people died in the next few days and were buried at sea; miraculously the epidemic did not spread, as the captain had feared. Naturally we mourned the untimely death of our comrades, but I urged everybody not to let gloom and despondency take over, and I am happy to say that they heeded my advice.

For six weeks or so, although it was not plain sailing we made good progress and the Captain confided to me: 'Mr Mackenzie, eh, can I call you Kenneth?' he said. 'Keep this to yourself, I don't want to give false hope to the folks, but I strongly believe that we would get to our destination a few days early.' But I thought that it would be kinder to tell everybody, as this intelligence would make it easier for them to overlook the many hardships we had thus far encountered. 'You're a man of great wisdom, Mr Mackenzie,' Captain Speirs said to me. I wish I had not prevailed, for all this was about to change.

Now words fail me as I attempt to describe what happened when we were within sight of the coast of Newfoundland. A storm the like of which none of the hardened sea dogs on board swore they had ever witnessed, started brewing. One child was thrown overboard, and the captain had to restrain me from throwing myself in the boiling seas to attempt a rescue. Some four people died of fractured skull as they were flung against the hull by the violence of the storm. Some more were to die in the same manner in the next few days. Although it was midsummer, a roaring cold cutting wind blew pitilessly, and the leaky Hector was in danger of keeling over and sink with complete loss of life. All the sailors were exhausted and had no strength left in their arms to work the pump. Thus the brig kept taking in more water than *they were capable of pumping away, but for my timely intervention. Captain Speirs, I shouted, let me help. The sailors looked at me and made a passage for me. I do not know where I got the strength from laddie, but there was I, working like a demented soul at this Herculean task, and everybody looked at me in amazement. Surely they must have been asking where does such a frail man get all this energy. All the time, the storm was raging with hellish fury, the passengers were screaming and praying, Lord Help Us, Save Our Children, Why Did We Leave Our Dear Highlands? The ship was soon completely out of control and just drifted where the winds blew it.*

It was at this very moment that the good lord chose for Anna McClean who had been big with child when she boarded the brig in Loch Broom, to go into labour. Everybody panicked; Captain Speirs who usually doubled up as ship surgeon was not in any condition to attend to her; he was a bundle of nerves; he already had too much on his plate, what with having to keep the ship afloat. There was no one around who could or would help coax out the little bairn that was dying to come see what a storm looked like. It seemed that I was the only one with any sort of qualification. I had after all had some farming experience and had delivered calves. I will do it, I said. Everybody gasped. Is there any limit to what the man can do, they must have been asking themselves. Someone brought me a basin of sea water to wash my hands with, and I immediately set to work. I made people move away, and Anna looked at me with gratitude. She seized my hand and pressed it, and I smiled at her and talked to her gently to reassure her. Trust him, he is a good man her husband Rabbie said to her needlessly. The good Lord guided my hands and I was able to deliver her of the prettiest little girl you ever saw. Everybody cheered aloud when she began to cry. She probably did not like the look of that storm! Someone gave me a pitcher of ale to which I did immediate justice. Friends, I said, this new arrival is a good omen; she has come to tell us that the new life waiting for us in Canada is going to be a good life, and everybody cheered.

When after three days the storm finally abated, the Captain called me and confided in me. Kenny, he said, keep this to yourself, I do not wish to cause panic, but we are lost. I have no idea where we are, my instruments are broken. It was a clear starry night and we were smoking our pipes and watching the sky. Suddenly I had an idea: Captain Speirs, I said, isn't that the northern star up there? I said pointing to that star. Aye, he grunted. And that constellation there? I asked. The Plough, he said. Need I say more? I said happily. You're a good man, Mackenzie, I am glad I've got you on board. You understand, dear boy, that gave him the idea to work out where we were, and what course to take after the sails had been mended and the masts repaired. The ship had lost two weeks, for that was what it took us to get back to the point where the storm had started playing havoc with us.

Now the real trouble started, for provisions were getting low on account of the lengthening of the voyage, and I advised Speirs that there was only one thing left: rationing. But they're all going to protest, he said. Not if you tell them that it was either that or starvation when the rations were completely exhausted. He recognised the wisdom of my words and acted accordingly. *As I had expected, everybody agreed that there was no other course of action possible, and ate stale bread that was turning green.*

The 189 souls who had survived the trip. It was a sad sight that greeted us, Hughie; the landscape was flat and dreary in the extreme and looked quite unwelcoming. Now, we had been promised food for the next few weeks, until our seeds were able to produce, but the Captain admitted that there was practically no food left, a high proportion of the seeds having rotten away in the storm. He was going to set sail for Philadelphia as soon as possible, he said, in order to get us food and seeds.

When we landed, there was chaos and panic as the Captain was in a great hurry to leave us. The plots we had been promised were swampy and overgrown with thorns and thickets, and we had no equipment to make a propitious start. Discontent was rife and the prevailing anarchy might have deteriorated into riot and murder were it not for my taking charge.

We knew about English immigrants who had arrived some ten years before us and had settled in the region of Truro, but they were a hundred miles from where we had landed. Nearer there were Pictou Indians, and my idea was that we could ask them for help. The others proposed attacking them and taking what we wanted by force. I was against that course of action on two grounds; we had come to their country and had no right to ride roughshod over them, and on the more practical level, we were not properly armed for conflict, having but two guns between us.

Many people were for walking to places like Truro where our English cousins might give us employment, food and shelter. I was the only one in the group who could speak English properly, but I was not willing to beg. Make up your own minds, I told them, you follow your own ideas. Some of our numbers kept arguing that the natives had only axes and at least we had two guns, but I opposed violence with great vehemence. The settlers' anger turned on me.

'What are you going to do then?' someone asked, 'go to them natives on bended knees and beg?'

'Its worth a try,' I said without great conviction. They were very sceptical; many then decided to leave and go look for work and food. Fortunately the cold weather had not yet reared its ugly head. About half of our numbers took to the road. I do not know what happened to them; did the English treat them with sympathy? How many starved before they got anywhere safe? Did bears or other wild beasts make a meal of those poor creatures looking for a meal? I have no idea, Hughie, dear boy.

With a small party of volunteers from those who stayed behind, we made our way gingerly to where the natives were encamped, raising our hands in a gesture of peace as we saw them, but they immediately surrounded us, banging on their drums, brandishing spears and sticks with plumes on them, shouting and talking incoherently and jumping up in the air like demented creatures The party began to curse me for my stupidity, and I daresay many would have gladly stuck a knife in my back. Some began praying to the Good Lord to spare us.

'They are preparing to kill us,' someone said, and everybody agreed. 'Maybe it's their way of welcoming us,' spat one vociferous fellow venomously. 'Aye,' said I, more in hope than with conviction, 'maybe that's what they're doing.' Suddenly amid the throng we saw a party of young women nearing us with meats and fish, and made it obvious to us by signs and incoherent words that we were to partake.

Needless to say, we sat down and devoured their offering. When we were sated, the Chief approached me and explained, by dint of sign language and some hardly recognisable English words, that they had but very little themselves, that the buffaloes had practically disappeared from the area, that the salmon and the muskellenge seemed to have deserted their waters too, and that there was very little lake rice to be found. They introduced us to the dulse, a reddish seaweed which could be picked up on rocks and which grows in the area between low tide and high tide. It is very nourishing but we found it difficult to eat this at first, it has a strange taste, however we soon not only got used to it but became very fond of it.

The Pictou natives told us that they had watched the "Hector" come in, with dismay and foreboding wondering what we were going to do in the land of their forefathers, but they were not hostile and gave us some food to take back to our companions, explaining that they did not have much to give.

We went back to the beach and our friends were surprised at what we had to tell them. The Pictou Indians had given us some good advice on where to find food, dulse and wild turnips, and it was thus that we managed to survive. We were not idle and set to work on our plots, working with our bare hands to clear the land, and when the first shoots appeared, our joy was great. Now, I have an admission to make. It had never been my intention to desert your Mam and yourself, but from the very first I noticed that Wahamaha, Chief Red Stag's youngest daughter could not keep her eyes off me. Why, I will never understand, for I was never a handsome man; maybe she recognised my inner qualities. I will not beat about the bush, Hughie, we ended up getting joined in matrimony. You now have a young brother whom we named Robert Pictou Mackenzie, and a sister, Morag Wahamaha Mackenzie. I am now a very happy man- for the first time in my life. I am not going to say that I do not touch the devil drink anymore, but I now drink only moderately. I have never stopped loving you, Hughie, and it is my dearest hope that one day you will join us here, if your Mam will let you. I now have over one hundred acres of forest and land under cultivation, and will send you some money soon, and will write regularly.

I DON'T SUPPOSE he ever got round doing that, Hugh mused, Mam never said.

CHAPTER 9

◆ ◆ ◆

The Enemy Approaches

MIDALA HAD SLEPT not a wink all night. Shortly after the first crow of the cock, the tom toms had begun to rumble. This time things were happening nearer home, in Owambane, two days' walk away. They told of how they were threatened and felt powerless against the force poised to attack, how those who did not flee into the bush and those who did not die resisting were captured and taken on the ship in fetters, and how their village was looted and burnt to the ground.

This time the Cojo seemed taken aback, but assured his people that he had everything under control. There was no need to worry, he said. An assurance which was was, like a talking drum: the hollower one was, the louder its sound. The warrior had no doubt that the Cojo ought to be doing something. The danger was real and imminent. Only a fool could fail to read the signals. Was the Cojo a fool? Could the Chief be considered a criminal, a traitor to his people, in his dereliction of duty? The Spirits had clearly wanted him to lead them and protect them, and he was selling them down the river. Would the Spirits forgive an honest man who had no axe to grind if he worked towards the elimination of a corrupt and useless Chief? For once he did not chase away the disturbing thoughts breaking the banks of his mental defences and flooding his conscious.

The people were famous for their optimistic disposition, as could be evidenced by their relaxed bearing, their jaunty walk which suggested that they were on the point of breaking into a dance, their ready smiles which brought comfort even to the gloomiest among them. They were a fun-loving people, much given to singing, dancing and music making. The heavenly sounds coming out of their timbila and their horns could produce the same effect as the brews they made from fermenting tangerines and cashew nuts. Now, with this calamity looming large, you never saw a smile on the lips of the folks, they walked with their heads bent down, and were forever looking behind their shoulders as if they feared someone was going to jump on them from behind. Everywhere Midala saw long faces, defeated looks, shaking heads, and hands flung up in the air in a gesture of helplessness. At his approach excited conversations turned into low whispers, and murmurs into nervous coughs, for nobody wanted the commander of their army to know how afraid they all were. From a distance he saw people arguing, and for once, he had the feeling that they were actually listening to each other, for the Chopis had the reputation of talking and laughing a lot, but of rarely listening.

Midala would have liked to send his wife and children into the bush for safety, but anybody leaving the village would have been seen as a traitor and dealt with accordingly. Whilst he was around to defend them, no harm would be done to them was what he promised. Disobedience was tantamount to treason. It was widely known that the Chief had spies everywhere, so when people talked they had to be ever so careful. There was a saying about trees having ears, and sending messages on their leaves carried by treacherous winds to the Cojo. Midala smiled as he remembered young Abo saying that he had spent hours looking at trees in order to discover where their ears might be, and had not found any.

At night, after the children were all asleep, Rolena pointed out to him that his forehead had become narrow with frowning, and he repeated that he was not worried, that the Spirits would look after them. I trust the Spirits, Rolena said, it's the Cojo I do not trust. Then to her surprise he asked her whether she thought it would be a good idea for her and the little ones to run away, to the bush somewhere, until he could come and join them after. Her response was not unexpected. Angrily she asked him if he really believed that she would do this. No, my man I will stand and fight by your side. What about the children? he said simply. He whistled in admiration as she came up with her suggestion: Pack them on Bobo Big Ears, and he will take them to safety across the river. Indeed Abo could almost talk to that lovely beast. They did not take long to decide that the best solution was indeed to send the kids away to safety in Chokwé.

As it was full moon, he and his wife started preparing for their children's flight straight away. They packed food and clothing, animal skins to be used as blankets, and water, and whilst Rolena woke the little ones, he went to get Bobo who usually retired into the hollow in a strangler fig tree for the night. Rolena told Abo that he was going to take the little ones to Chokwé on Bobo Big Ears, and he had to look after them for some time whilst they helped defeat the enemy, after which they would come for them. Midala read his son readily. On the one hand the boy was sad and slightly apprehensive, as he knew that he would miss his parents, but on the other hand, he was going to have a big responsibility, and this he relished. Midala explained that Bobo would take them to Chokwé by the river side and that the tribe there would welcome them when they told that they were Midala's children. Without further ado, the children were on their way.

A few hours later, the tom-toms from the tribes across the river began to rumble again with unusual vigour and persistence, which probably meant that the slavers were getting nearer. It turned out that Mara Mara, the settlement just across the river had been burnt to the ground, to teach a lesson to others that resistance against their might was pointless. We tried to resist, but sticks and spears were no match against cannons, guns and treachery. It will be your turn next, the tom-toms warned, may the Spirits of the Ancestors give you strength so you can fight the enemy with greater success than your unfortunate neighbours. May you die spear in hand, brothers and sisters, for death is sweeter than subjugation!

Midala finally accepted what he had always known, that the Cojo had much to answer for. He, it was who had drunk from the same cup as the devil and had not bothered to turn the cup round first. Or maybe he was the devil! The warrior had served him loyally, because he was taught by his father that the Chief got his authority from the Spirits of the Ancestors. Suddenly he dismissed from his mind the notion that he had held sacred until now: that the Cojo was the descendant of a river god and had taken human shape in order to lead their tribe to greater glory.

He, who used to treat his subjects with singular lack of courtesy, always shouting at everybody and scowling, had a totally different behaviour towards the sinister slave traders. He was all bows and smiles with them and their men, of course sir, sure thing sir, whatever you say sir. He fed them like kings, offered them maidens to comfort their beds, and let them drink half the gin he had bought from them. Ibn Qalb who claimed to be a true believer of the koran would invariably laugh as he dipped a finger in his gourd and shake away one drop of the forbidden drink, saying, "A single drop of alcohol shall not cross your lips, O ye faithful… and there goes that drop." But their allegiance was shallow. All concerned knew that the foreigners were friendly to the Chopis and their Cojo only when it suited them.

Another thing which sorely tested Midala's loyalty was the Cojo's dishonourable order to re-arrest liberated slaves, so they could be handed over to the slavers in order to make up the numbers. Midala and one or two of the braver councillors had pointed out that this was both illegal and immoral. The Cojo had shouted that he was the one who decided what was legal or moral. Who was the nephew of the River God? Midala or he the Cojo? Midala had executed the order, but had never been happy about it. He knew that he was not going to put up with the excesses of his chief much longer. The Spirits would understand that his action was motivated by honour. It seemed obvious to him that the Cojo had no plans to stop the fiendish Arab and his wicked English accomplice.

After the news of the overwhelming of Mara Mara, Midala, Nkilo and Mossane went to see the Cojo in the Palaver Room. He did not like people asking to see him. Usually he was the one asking to do the seeing, but these were the three most powerful men in the tribe, and he knew that he had to hear them. Mossane had offered to shoot the first arrow.

'O Cojo, nephew of the River God, hear us.'

'Speak, Mossane, brother of my first wife.'

'We are sure our leader has plans to stop the attack—'

'What attack? There's not going to be an attack. The ships coming in belong to my friends, people I trade with, why are you afraid like a woman?'

'But they attacked Owambane, Mara Mara,' Nkilo said impatiently.

'The Marzuk of Owambane is a fool, he was asking for it. Ibn Qalb and the white people respect us, they are our friends.'

'We know that the Marzuk also believed the same thing,' said Midala.

'That Ibn Qalb and his white partners respect us and are our friends?' laughed the Cojo, 'he is right!' It was only after he had said this that his audience joined in the laughter with a singular lack of enthusiasm.

'My little joke,' he explained, 'yes, we have developed an understanding with the slave traders, and there is nothing like a little diplomacy to solve problems.'

Then suddenly he frowned and nodded at his three visitors.

'Let us just suppose that you have a point, that there is some danger, what would you propose? Are we in a position to defend ourselves?'

'It's a bit late in the day, O Cojo, Nephew of the River God,' said Midala.

'You see!' said the Cojo, happy to be vindicated.

'We should have prepared for this weeks ago… they have guns and cannons, we have nothing.'

'So, isn't my way the best?'

'Your way,' shouted Mossane, trying to control his temper but failing to do so, 'means certain death and capture for the tribe.'

'Will you fight them with sticks and stones? Tell me.' The Cojo was now quite angry, 'There is no way of stopping them if they have made up their minds to destroy us,' he said, adding after a short pause, 'trust my powers of persuasion.'

There was a short silence, which Midala broke.

'I have a plan,' he said, 'I cannot guarantee that it will work, but I believe that it is the only course of action left.' The Cojo waved his hand at him dismissively, and turned his head away testily.

'Midala is no fool, O Cojo,' said Nkilo and Mossane in unison, 'you must listen to the words of his mouth.' The Cojo said nothing, but looked at the military man wearily. The latter took it as permission to hold forth.

'We do not know how many attackers there will be, we have to plan for a force of one hundred. They are hardly likely to number more than that. With their guns, they do not even need that many. Although fully armed, they are seamen, not soldiers. We'll get one hundred of our best men, proven in battle, and they are in good shape and condition since we fought our last war only a short time ago—'

'Midala's plan is a very good one, O Cojo!' said Mossane enthusiastically.

'Anybody coming to attack us must necessarily pass under the strangler fig tree.' The Cojo seemed interested for the first time, and nodded thoughtfully.

'Our men will be armed with spears, machetes and bows and arrows, and will be waiting on top of the strangler, hidden by the foliage.'

'I see,' said the Cojo merrily, 'that's damn very clever,' he admitted, 'then our men pounce on them from above, disarm them, seize their guns and we kill each and everyone of them.'

The four men laughed happily, as if the victory had already been won.

'So you like my plan?' asked the Cojo suddenly. The three wise men knew their Cojo, but were relieved that he was hijacking their plan, which meant that he was seeing reason for the first time.

'But we need to train, practise the jump, we need to hone in our shooting skills, there's such a lot to do.'

The Cojo suddenly jumped on his feet, and squealed with joy.

'And when we have killed them, everything in their ships will belong to me! Their gin, their guns, their gold. We will live like white men!'

'Yes, we will have their guns, so when their friends send a force to avenge their deaths, we will have the means of defending ourselves.' said Nkilo.

'I will make a big speech to the tribe and tell them that there is no cause for worry, that I have got everything in control.'

'We must start preparing immediately,' said Midala, 'we cannot afford to waste time.'

The Cojo blanched on hearing this. He looked at Midala with his piercing eyes and wagged a finger at him.

'Your father never dared talk to me like this! Are you suggesting that listening to my speech is a waste of time?' he asked.

'No, of course not, O Cojo, nephew of the River God, but they will be here tomorrow, and we—'

'They won't be here for another three days,' said the Cojo decisively.

'But O most exalted Cojo, how do you know?'

'My fortune teller said so. He said that the ships would be becalmed for three days, the Spirits of the Ancestors have been appeased, so don't worry, you'll have all the time in the world to practise.'

'Your fortune-teller? That man is a fraud,' said Midala.

'When he predicted floods, we had a drought,' said Mossane.

'When he said your new wife was going to have a son, you had twin girls,' said Nkilo.

'When I order silence, I get silence!' screamed the Nephew of the River God. 'I have been kind enough to listen to you, I have granted you leave to bad-mouth my friends… against my better judgement, but I order you all to come to listen to my speech! Then you can put my plan in action.'

'But Lord Cojo,' Midala had protested, 'what if—' The Cojo stopped himself flying into another fit of rage.

'I will not hear another word! Just come to the strangler tree before the sun disappears behind the Meira Hills.'

Now, the three would-be saviours of the tribe were condemned to a fate worse than death: listening to the Cojo's speech. It was a secret to nobody that the three things the Cojo loved above everything, were, and in that order, himself, flattery, and speechmaking. It must be said that he had a great booming voice and spoke in pleasant rhythms. He loved to use beautiful, nice-sounding words, the meaning of which most people, including himself often did not know. Obviously, to him, words meant whatever he wanted them to mean.

CHAPTER 10

Sunderban Memories

As a child, Shanti had instinctively sensed Raju's apprehension whenever he came to their house. Her Pitaji treated the boy with contempt, as if he had just caught him in the act doing something forbidden. She even remembered him giving the boy an undeserved clip on the ear on occasions. He always had a sneer on his lips, dauntingly suspicious eyes, which, immediately must have dampened the boy's obvious bold spirits. So what were you doing the other day when I caught you lurking behind that neem tree? Were you thieving again? He never even let the boy answer. He would just purse his lips and nod knowingly in a manner calculated to frighten the child, although she noticed that the boy was not all that troubled. Or, I suppose that rascal Parsad thinks this rotting bhetki is worth two pise. He s-s-said four pise, Seth Ishwarlal, the poor boy would stutter, looking away. It took some guts to do that, she thought. Father would bellow with laughter. One whole anna? Why not a rupiah? These people, he would say, to an invisible presence above his head, just bend down and pick fish you put in the sea, and then the man has the gall to want one whole anna, ya Bhagwan, the badmash will ruin me! And he would give the boy two pise and turn his back and walk away. The boy would stare at the coins, and for a whole minute he would just stay there, unwilling to leave without the one anna that Baba had mentioned. He would grudgingly walk away, stopping every now and then, looking back in the vain hope that the rich man would have changed his mind. He was always an optimist. Pitaji's attitude left the young Shanti perplexed, for she knew that he was a loving father and an honest man. Still it must be true that if one were not careful people took advantage of one's kindness. She had often heard him tell Ma that people often mistook kindness for stupidity.

Shanti who loved skipping would watch from behind a jackfruit tree in silence, her rope dangling in her hands. Raju did not dare raise his head in her direction, no doubt for fear of having his ear pulled by the irate zamindar. She certainly believed the saying that poor kids would have been better off if they were born with an extra ear put there just for pulling. Still the boy was not easily daunted, and would often sneak a furtive look in her direction. He obviously liked what he saw, and she rightly suspected that her tiny little person was what made the weekly visit bearable to the boy. She was not sure if she was pleased or not that Raju seemed to like her, or whether, on the contrary, she should be annoyed with him for daring to have a soft spot for someone who was so much above his own station. Yes, she was a haughty little minx then.

For Raju, the visit to the rich zamindar's gradually transformed itself from what, to begin with, was just a bearable chore, into a desirable interlude, and from there, it progressed to something which had become a gnawing imperative. On his way home, if he had caught a glimpse of the rich girl, (Raju would tell her later when they were married) he would put the recent humiliation at the back of his mind, and skip and whistle merrily, danced round trees, dreaming the impossible dream. If this was a fairy tale, Shanti would have been smitten by the boy too, and the two would find the opportunity of playing together, running round the jackfruit tree, holding hands, maybe singing a duo, admiring their images in the limpid pond. In spite of her reservations, Shanti could not help liking the boy's laughing eyes, but she thought that he was uncouth and could do with a bath. She could never entirely believe her Pitaji who said that the boy's father was an extortionate fish seller, out to ruin him.

However when a few years later Pitaji told her that he was arranging for him to marry Raju, her initial reaction was one of surprise rather than shock. She never understood how the man that she had finally discovered to be a proud and haughty boor, a bully, could contemplate marrying his daughter to someone who possessed nothing, but understood that it was her mother Radha's doing. She had scrutinised all the eligible young men in the village, and although Raju was a near pauper, she had recognised in him the qualities which she felt would make him an ideal husband for her daughter. Besides she knew that he came from a more distinguished family than Ishwarlal's or hers, and ancestry was not something to be sneezed at. Naturally Ma thought that money was very important too, but she used to say that a poor man can become rich one day, and vice versa. However, a visit from Raju's aunt Umma was what was needed to start the marital ball rolling. From what Radha had heard, Raju had the potential to make his way into the world, all he needed was the opportunity. Everybody she had talked to said that he was a polite, intelligent and dependable young man.

She had cleverly poured that notion into Ishwarlal's ears, and, like many an astute wife, she had succeeded in making him believe that it was his idea. She got a lot of satisfaction when she later heard her man explain to surprised friends and relatives his reason for picking the penniless Parsad's boy for his Shanti. I would not be where I am today if I was not the most astute man in Roshankhali, she heard him boasting. I have enquired about all the young men in the area, and found out that young Raju Varma is the hardest working of the lot. He is an ambitious young fellow, comes from one of the top families in the whole of Bihar, his grandfather was a poet you know, and I therefore have every reason to expect him to do well in time. In the end class will tell… always, bilkul. I see him as an investment who will bring in big dividends. She did not mind him passing her ideas off as his own. A wife knows and accepts her husband's weaknesses. She is never surprised by anything he does or says. She sees him naked, hears him farting, smells his breath first thing in the morning. She knew that many a woman, like herself, gets untold satisfaction when she watches the bullying husband snore and dribble helplessly just before he wakes up.

Shanti knew that the boy had always been enamoured of her, but she had never been a dreamer, had never had a crush on anybody like some of her friends, had never questioned herself about the suitability of such and such young swain. She had reservations about marrying a man who could barely scratch a living, but she agreed to the union cheerfully — not that she had much say in the matter, but she knew that Ma thought he was a good prospect and she trusted her judgement as she never trusted Pitaji's. She caught herself once thinking that if Raju is the opposite of Pitaji, he can't be that bad.

Of course she had seen Raju around at all the stages of his life and liked his cheerful disposition. She did not dislike his appearance or his wiry frame, or the fact that he wore drab dhotis and darned shirts. Her mother Radha often said that poverty was often a temporary condition not a vice. She had regretted that he was a bit on the small side, but he was all muscles and energy. Could that mean that deep down she had already been half in love with him as a youth? Who knows? Moreover she had heard from servants and friends that her intended was well-liked and highly thought of by everybody. He was polite without being obsequious, funny without being disrespectful. They said he was fearless and was not afraid of tigers and crocodiles, and knew about medicinal plants. Certainly even the shrewd Ishwarlal had finally thought him good enough to be his son-in-law. She had been told that even older people sought his advice on diverse matters. The few negative things that she had heard about him seemed insignificant. Some said that he was always making jokes, that even at funerals he sometimes made people laugh by whispering stories about how the poor dead man used to scratch his bum or how pathetic he was at hiding it when he farted, or how he had a squeaky effeminate voice. One or two voices were heard suggesting that his reputation for fearlessness was entirely based on his own boastful accounts of imaginary encounters with Dakshin Rai.

When she did fantasise about an eventual beau, she could not help invoking the image of someone who was basically Raju, had the same features, but was rather taller, fairer, and dressed in fine clothes. No, she had not disapproved of him. She was not overly apprehensive about the impending wedding, but then neither did she count the days. Girls, like beggars could not be choosers.

But things had not worked out like Ishwarlal had planned. First, Raju's Phoopi Umma had warned against their moving to a house the prospective father-in-law was planning to build for them. He will end up by putting your soul in his pocket if you let him, were her words, and Raju readily agreed with her. He decided to spend all his savings and some money the hakeem, who had no children of his own, had forced him to accept, and all his spare time, on improving the house Baba had built, to make it fit to receive a princess bride from a rich family.

Ishwarlal could not believe his ears when he heard that an offer he had made out of the kindness of his heart had been spurned by those paupers who did not even possess the skin on their arses! There was no love lost between him and Parsad's sister. That wretched woman is always watering my fields with sea water, he cried. The fact that Raju refused to play the son-in-law game, the astute Radha said, proves that he has got character, didn't her husband agree? The next day she heard him say to a visitor that he thought that his future son-in-law was a boy of character. Can you imagine a young man who refuses to move in his his father-in-law's house?

Raju turned down Ishwarlal's offer to work for him too, hating the idea of being the ox pulling his father-in-law's cart. This was one stick in his spoke too many. Radha was unable to pacify him this time, he flew into a violent rage and said that it was her fault, suddenly remembering that it was her idea that their daughter should marry that boy who went around in rags. He swore that he would not lift a finger to help them even if they were starving. Raju was heartened when he discovered that Shanti had not disapproved of his independence.

Raju would always harbour a lingering suspicion that deep down she was disappointed in him because he was not able to provide for her in the manner to which she had no doubt been accustomed, growing up in the household of the richest man in the Sundarbans, although he never gave up the hope that some day he would be able to match his opulence.

However, soon after the marriage, it was discovered that the land everybody thought was Ishwarlal's had been illegally occupied. There were many irregularities in the papers. The British East India Company was not going to accept any more nonsense from the natives. They had to respect their land laws, buy their land formally, pay the diwani taxes, or else move out. Shanti's brother Mohan was becoming more and more erratic and unreasonable, claiming that he heard voices ordering him to go beat the cows with a stick and break their legs, or to set fire to the barn. The Pandit said that he was possessed by some evil spirit, and that getting rid of it would be a lengthy and costly affair. Preoccupied by more earthly problems, the distraught father did not know where to run, earning him constant rebuke from Radha, that he did not care for anything but money. He began by relinquishing some of the best pastures that the Company demanded. Then he had to sell some of his cattle, and never attended to Mohan's problem.

However, for the newlyweds, this was a period of bliss as they got to discover each other. Shortly after the wedding, two children were born in quick succession. Raju had always called the girl by the nickname of Sundari because to him she was the prettiest little girl on earth, a miniature Shanti. The boy, Pradeep, was born eleven months later. Ishwarlal had now practically gone bankrupt. After threatening to hang himself or go throw himself in the Matla, and watch the ungrateful Radha make a living by begging in the village, he finally compromised and took the family back to Allapur instead. Shanti missed her mother, but took their departure without undue grief. From the beginning of married life, she had been dazzled by the extent of Raju's love for her. He could not keep his eyes from her, extolling her virtues to everybody. She never knew she had so many qualities! It was like worship, it made her feel like a goddess. Radha had smiled and told her to enjoy the moment, for it never lasted more than six months. Still, they had now been married six years, and his adoration never waned. On her part, she was undemonstrative, but deep down, she too worshipped her man, thought that he was the kindest man she knew, was almost devoid of real malice, although he often said outrageous things about some people. Yes, he thought that he knew everything, hated to be in the wrong, but didn't all men? Even the weak-minded Mohan who could not tell his right hand from his left foot, did not hesitate to lecture her and Ma.

Raju did not doubt that she loved him very much too, but he wished that she would be more demonstrative, that she would laugh more when he was being funny, say flattering things about him to the children. He was always saying things like, isn't your mother as beautiful as a peri, doesn't she cook like a Maharajah's bhandari? Being a demonstrative person himself, he imagined that her restraint was due to a less than blind devotion on her part. He suspected that she was disappointed because he could barely provide for her and the two little ones. One of his idle thoughts was that she was just that little bit jealous of the unbounded love the little ones had for him. It was true that she was just that little bit jealous of their joy as they recognised the speck on the horizon, being no other than their dear Baba, as they stood outside the little hut, open-mouthed, watching it grow bigger as it passed the three coconut palms and assume his shape.

The three of them were her whole universe, but she did not feel the need to climb on the roof of the house to shout this information to the world. Still her great love for him did not stop her being less than enthusiastic about his capacity for work. He was not what she would call lazy, sometimes he would come back from the fields or from a trip in a state of near exhaustion. He could be counted upon to deliver the goods, but when he had the occasion to sit and smoke his bidi, on which he pulled with loving intensity, joking with Jayant or some other mates, he often forgot himself. He himself was always taken aback by the duration of his bidi break. I never realised I took so long, he would say, smacking his forehead with the palm of his right hand. Can we afford for him to smoke? Shanti sometimes asked herself, not daring to question her man. If she asked him to mend a chair or cut some wood, his stock response was, not just yet, Rani, in a short while, and again it would be the bidi. He would forget himself for hours sitting under the jackfruit tree like in a trance, sucking on that stinking thing. He was not a drunkard, he did not partake of the toddy, one lota after another, but he loved to sip one slowly every afternoon. She could never understand why men needed to fill their insides with smoke, and crave for a drink which tasted like paraffin. As a teenager, intrigued by father's attachment to the weed, she had found a smouldering bidi once, and as there was nobody around, she had put it in her mouth and inhaled deeply. She thought she was going to choke to death. There was nothing the least bit pleasant about the smoke. She had thought that maybe it would be aromatic and nice-tasting, and found that it was nothing of the sort, it was acrid and she compared the experience to that of having to swallow a spoonful of castor oil every two months. She would never even dream of tasting toddy, its smell was enough to put her off. But she never questioned him. She had grown up in a family of men, an authoritative father and two brothers. All those years, she had wrongly thought of her mother as a dormouse who never questioned her menfolk. Arrey, she would say to herself finally, all men need their bidis, why am I such a drag?

At that time, Sukhdeo had become the legal owner of the fields, having been able to pay the Company what they demanded, and with Ishwarlal out of the frame, he was now the richest man in Roshankhali. He owned several fields rented out to tenant farmers, including Raju. He produced crops according to the boss' directive, kept a small percentage for themselves but gave the bulk of the harvest to him as rental. He kept a close watch over his crofters, did Sukhdeo, since the more they produced, the bigger were his profits. The tenants were expected to be at the zamindar's disposal for so many days a week, leaving their wives to work on their own patch, so they could work on his much bigger plantations. Sometimes, when he knew that the boss was not going to be around, instead of tending the tomatoes and baiguns, Raju would leave her to work on the fields by herself, quietly take a day off, embark the children on the boat and go fishing with them round the islands, although he caught but few fish. Shanti knew that fishing was just a pretext. All he wanted to do was laze about in his boat, sail aimlessly, talk non-stop to the kids, showing them the mangrove plants and gharials. And she would shake her head and have a quiet chuckle. OK, he would concede, today we didn't catch any, but how many birds we saw, tell mama, kids. And the boy would make a long list which usually included the chai, the kokil, but it was the colourful parrots in full flight that they dreamt of catching sight of. Shanti was always apprehensive because of what happened to Baba Parsad. Everybody knew that tigers could swim, and were known to attack boatmen. Surprisingly, Raju seemed to bear no grudge to Dakshin Rai. He maintained that he had eaten his Baba by mistake, and that he had promised to make amends by leaving his descendants well alone. How did he know this? she had asked. He had laughed. Dakshin comes to me in my dreams and talks to me, he had explained, he apologised to me with tears in his eyes. At other times, he maintained that as a child, there was a tiger who had befriended him, and played with him. In any case, if there was some unforeseen danger, a noor, a special light, came out of his eyes, a gift of the saintly Parvatti, and this made the danger disappear. In any case, tigers are not really dangerous, he said, they want to be our friends, but everybody avoids them. Wouldn't you be angry if you wanted to be friends with someone and they avoided you? They've got feelings too, and if you hurt their feelings, how do you expect them to act? Shanti understood that Raju had carefully thought out this seeming piece of nonsense. He knew about the danger of tigers all right, but he had to make a living in this dangerous environment, and his bravado was just an act, to stop her fretting whenever he was away.

What worried her, was that the mangrove was known to be haunted by snakes, and rats, scorpions, spiders, poisonous plants, marshes which will swallow a grown man in seconds. But they will never attack me, he would explain with great conviction, giving one of his oft repeated reasons. Yes, Shanti thought wryly, he does talk too much, and a lot of nonsense too sometimes. Of course she lived in fear of a tragedy happening at the mangrove, for the simple reason that her man was so relaxed. Every time he had to go to Calcutta or the Pargannas with a load of produce for the zamindar, she had sleepless nights imagining an encounter with his so-called friends. It's not the fault of the tiger, it was Bhagwan who gave him strong teeth…

Raju never stopped reminding her that Parvatti had died after giving birth to him, and that after his father's accident, it was Phoopi Umma who had made sure they never went hungry. Given to romanticising, one day he declared that he knew for sure that the old aunt went hungry herself when there was not enough, so he could have a full stomach. She must have, he said with great conviction, when he recognised the scepticism in her eyes. She knew that in the Sundarbans, rain or shine, it was next to impossible to go hungry. There were so many edible leaves, roots, nuts, fruits, and, more interestingly, fish or shrimps. Every now and then he would embroider on the theme of Phoopi's selflessness, but although she did not like to contradict him, she did not believe everything he said, for she could not imagine the dignified woman sneaking into some rich homestead stealing eggs from the chicken coops or milking a cow in a field for her nephew. But she had no doubt that in time Raju would make up more and more glorious exploits of the old woman who would, like Parvatti, end up a Devta, a Goddess. But it was true that she knew how to sew and knit. Unfortunately there was little demand for knitwear, so she made a few pise, or a handful of rice or dal by darning rags for the villagers who were not much better-off than herself. She was quite an expert at coaxing Bagda Chingris from the mud too. Although she had not known her all that much, the intensity of Raju's love for the old woman had been enough to colour her judgement of her. She would have tears in her eyes whenever he began talking about her.

Shanti had known all along that life with Raju was not going to be all falooda and Ghulab Jamun, but she never complained, in the belief that one day her new husband would end up rich and prosperous. Everybody said he would, Ma, family friends, even her hard-nosed Pitaji who never forgave Raju his independent spirit. After she married, there had been good times and bad times. Sometimes there had been good harvests, sometimes the monsoon ruined everything. Who can explain the sea? Sometimes the waters teemed with fish. You throw in your net and pull it up, and it shone like a gigantic pulsating silver jewel, but there were times when the fish simply disappeared. Who can explain people's tastes? Sometimes people wanted to eat fish and there were times when it seemed nobody cared for even the best hilsa.

Although she had led a life of luxury in her palatial wooden house with glass windows, painted doors and corrugated iron roofs, surrounded by servants, malis to look after the garden, dhobis to wash their clothes, and bandharis to cook their food, never having to do any sort of hard work herself, once married she had to go down on her knees to wash and scrub, till the land with a spade, water the shoots, and she did all that without complaining. To her surprise, she found physical work stimulating. As a child it was her ambition to learn to milk a cow, but of course she was never allowed to. They had acquired a cow and a few goats just after they married, and Phoopi had taught her to milk them. The goats had died since, and the cow had been sold when a child was dangerously ill, and there were too many people chasing too little honey. There had been more lean years than years of plenty, but still they never went hungry, mainly because she was good at housekeeping, knowing how to use yesterday's leftovers to enhance today's meagre fare, making acchar, pickling extra vegetables or fish in times of plenty, so no one went hungry when there were shortages.

Raju was a good, kind man, she wanted no one else, but he was worse than that rooster, always wanting to do horizontal exercises, as he put it. Not that she minded, although it had taken her some time to get used to that. She had to admit that she caught herself more and more often, anticipating a little... eh... exercise herself. But of course women had no right to expect things like that, you submitted to your husband's demands, and if you had some pleasure, so much the better. However, that was not how Raju saw things. Me, I do not feel pleasure if my woman behaves as if my ministrations were a prelude to yawning. At first she had tried hard to keep her own feelings under wraps. It had seemed unladylike to do what had to be done in other than perfect silence, but inevitably she forgot herself and dropped her guard, and too late caught herself resonating with his hoos and haas, which had made Raju so ecstatic. Good, that's so much more fun, he had said. He often boasted that no one he knew was better in bed than him. He never explained how he knew, and she did not ask, but she believed him.

Pitaji, was a stout dark man with an oval head tapering upwards, reminiscent of a coconut. He had a darker patch like a scar on his forehead, and people called him the pahelwan on account of his bulk, but it was more flab than sinew. He had a black toothbrush moustache, unsullied by the slightest trace of grey, which he got Radha to trim for him everyday. For a man of his size, his voice was surprisingly high-pitched, but he was tough and hardhearted, and in his pursuit of lucre, he was ruthless, although his daughter had refused to see this first. She had not missed him when the family went back to Bihar. Ma was altogether different. She had a fair complexion of which she was very proud, and often sighed that it was a shame her daughter had inherited her father's skin colour.

Now the sun was not going to be long setting, and the kids' father wasn't home yet. He had gone to Sonarkhali to work on Sukhdeo's fields today. The little ones were getting excited, and already they had asked a few times when their Baba was going to be home. How do I know? she had snapped, do I have eyes at the back of my head? She knew that even with eyes at the back of her head she still wouldn't be any the wiser, but that was what you said when your kids pestered you, and when you yourself were fretting. Arrey, Rani, don't be hard on little children, he would admonish her softly when he heard her snap at the little ones. She never answered back, but her inner voice provided some solace. You're never around to put up with them, constantly talking or pulling on my sari, wanting this or that, so you can talk! But it was true that he never raised his voice to them, answering all their questions, telling them stories, making them laugh their silly little heads off. Yes, he was a good father and a good husband. A good man! The children were really very reasonable, if they were better behaved, she would begin to wonder whether there wasn't anything wrong with them. She wished she would be less impatient with them. Raju told them that if they had been good nine times, it was all right to be a lee..ttle naughty the tenth time. She had to admit that this system worked wonders, for whenever there was any trouble brewing up between the siblings, she would show them five or six fingers, and they would understand that they had to be good another four or five occasions. Raju laughed and said it was also the best way to teach them a little arithmetic.

The sun behind the hut had now turned bright orange, and the food was ready. She had managed some fried onions for the dal today, and put a handful of curry leaves and a couple of drumsticks in it. The children liked sucking these noisily as they ate. As a special treat, she had boiled some ashilata nuts in salt water, the kids loved them. Often it was only boiled dal with a little salt and a little haldi. There were no vegetables, but it was not for want of trying. The earth was parched and no amount of watering could remedy this, and whenever there was a little rain and some green shoots appeared, the goats from next door or the chicken, would just wander in and serve themselves. You shooed them away, but they always found their way back. It was a pointless exercise, like catching smoke in a bag, or stopping a dog wagging its tail when it saw the master. There was no oil left after she had fried the onions, so she was going to grill the chapatis on the tawa with water only. They were going to be hard and brittle, but when dipped in the dal they would become easy to munch and swallow. She would have made some sojne data sag from the drumstick tree, that grew everywhere, but without oil, it tasted like raw grass and it left a lingering bitter taste. Sojne data was what the poor survived on when there was nothing else. You plucked a few branches, removed the small round green leaves by sliding three fingers over the stems and when you had nothing else, you boiled this and at least you did not starve, your hunger dissolving the grass taste. Cooked with oil, onions, garlic, haldi, and chillies, it was a very tasty dish and even rich folks liked it.

Suddenly the little ones became excited, and she knew that they had recognised their Baba approaching. She had a funny feeling in her belly, and admitted to herself that she too was excited at the coming home of her man. She slightly resented this, thinking that a grown woman had got no business getting excited just because her man was approaching, but she could not help it. Her love for Raju easily matched his, although she could never convey this to him. The women of her acquaintance always had some grievance against their men. Ma always grumbled at whatever Pitaji was doing. Didi, her sister-in-law never stopped making sarcastic remarks about poor Bhiku, her female cousins often said disparaging things about their men, they talked too much and did little, they made too little money and spent too much on themselves. Shanti suspected that those whose husbands were good in bed complained less. She had heard sarcastic remarks about 'that pahelwan who talks big and cannot deliver.' She had not immediately understood the tenor of those words, but the meaning was now clear to her. Raju was no pahelwan, but she suspected that few men were as loving and caring in bed.

Her peers had often talked about their fears of what was going to happen on their wedding night, but Shanti had always rather looked forward to hers, albeit with some trepidation, feeling that that mysterious feelings she often experienced all over her body would respond to whatever was going to happen, in a good way. Her breasts had just started to develop when she had found that when she was unable to go to sleep, stroking between her legs made her feel good and helped send her to the land of dreams, although she could not dispel the gnawing feeling that she was doing something wicked. No doubt a man was going to make her feel even better, she had hoped. Raju had been so nice, had kept telling her not to be afraid. If you tell me to stop, I will, he had promised. The first time there was some blood which terrified her. Oh Bhagwan, I am bleeding to death, she had thought. It's nothing, he had said, it's always like this. How did he know? Had he done it to someone else before? She had not dared ask him then, but later he would tell her that the hakeem had explained everything to him before he got married. She had felt the same sensation take possession of her body as when she stroked herself — the practice had become very regular over the years — but this was so much better. It was like the downpour outside during the monsoon compared to the trickle that came in through the leaky roof. The memory of the experience left her in a daze the next day. It was so good to be alive! But she had decided that it was unseemly to show your man the extent of your enjoyment of sex, she was no nautch girl. She therefore tried to mute her enjoyment… until the inevitable day when she dropped her guard.

After a week, Raju began to talk about other things that they could do. She did not understand, but she was too shy to ask what he meant. One night, he suddenly grabbed her, pulled her head towards him, and kissed her. She liked being kissed, and responded with measured enthusiasm, but this time he prised her lips open with his tongue and introduced it inside her mouth, and got her to put hers in his at the same time. She had demurred, but found this almost unbearably exciting, her whole body filled with a sensation of well-being that she had never experienced before, and she readily shed her frock and waited for him to start proceedings. But he did not. Instead he began to stroke her and put his finger inside her. Is he mistaking his finger for the other thing? Arrey what are you doing? She was on the point of asking, but she was experiencing yet more pleasant sensations and turned her head away. Women too have a little danta, he explained, and he made her whole body tingle as he found it and twiddled it. He suddenly slid down and used his tongue down below too. Though shocked, she had liked it, so when he directed her head down towards his loins, she knew what he wanted, and pretending reluctance, she took his swollen danta in her mouth. She had liked the feeling. It was nice and warm, had a lovely consistency, and she had sucked him, at first timidly, but more lustily afterwards. Her tongue began to tingle, then her whole mouth. This new feeling spread across her whole body and she thought she was going to pass out when he finally put his danta inside her. He taught her that there was no shame in liking liking for sex, but although he would often talk about it in his all-knowing manner, she never talked about it except to answer his questions. Shrugging, and with the shadow of a smile on her face, she would say things like, Yes, it's all right, but I prefer a good fish curry with baigun and chillies. I can't promise you fish everyday, but if it's meat you're after, you can have it as often as you wish. Yes, he was a bit of a boast, but in this case he was totally justified.

He was no doubt going to want it tonight, they had not done it in three days (why?). As usual she would demur when he would make his intention clear, it was a game, she felt she had to pretend. She never understood why. Sometimes she wished she could tell him how much she loved their lovemaking, but it must be a woman thing. Fifty generation of female reti-cence cannot disappear overnight. She wondered whether he realised how much this part of their life together meant to her. Arrey what was she think-ing, that he was going to want it tonight? She wanted it just as badly.

She began listening to the children. The girl who was only four was saying that Baba was going to tell them a story tonight, he had 'cromised,' she said. It's not 'cromise,' you silly owl, it's 'gromise,' why don't you learn to talk proper, said the boy who was a year younger, but she noticed that he had already, like all males, assumed a natural superiority in all matters. You shut your mouth, she snapped, and she heard them pushing and pulling, but there were no tears. Yes, Raju liked telling them stories. He was a gifted sto-ryteller, and remembered loads of stories from his childhood. His father read books and had told him lots of stories, as did Phoopi Umma, and it seems that when he went to visit the old man, who was now almost a cripple, the old man would indulge in storytelling over a bowl of chai.

More often than not, he would start on a well-known tale, but would be un-able to resist messing with it, chopping bits and changing. She had to admit that sometimes his new version was so much more refreshing and had even her in stitches. The youngsters would squeal happily, remembering a previous version. Baba, that's all wrong, you're doing it on purpose, you're saying it all wrong. Raju would then assume a serious pose. Yes, you are quite absolutely, perfectly, and entirely right! One hundred and one percent! And he would scratch his head in mock earnest and pretend to revert to the old scenario. This would redouble the wailing. We like the new one better, the children would then scream.

As a child, Shanti loved stories too. Old Nani Laddoo used to arrive in her precarious little boat which she paddled herself as she went visiting her customers with her sweetmeats every week, and often, neighbours and their children would beat a path to their door on the off-chance that the old crone had a story to tell. Radha pretended a complete lack of interest in these proceedings ('Arrey, stories are for kids, na.') but she would sit on her mat, woven from hental fronds, spread under the veranda and informally preside. Some ladies who had won her favour would be invited to join her and Nani on the mat, and the others would sit on the floor, and wait. The old dear knew how to play with her audience.

'Once upon a time', she would start, but she would immediately stop. Could some child fetch me a lota of water please? The children would jostle and push, each wanting to be the one to carry out this welcome task, possibly in the hope that during the narration Nani Laddoo would apostrophise her, and create the illusion that she was the one the story was being told to, that the others were just being offered crumbs. Shanti usually won.

'As I was saying,' the old dear would start again, after having taking a sip, 'once upon a time…' and she would stop again. The children would begin to protest at this unwarranted stoppage.

I am not telling stories to children who are asleep, she would admonish. We are not asleep, the children would chorus. Why am I not hearing you respond then? She loved telling stories, but she exacted one price, and it was just one syllable: 'Unh!' every time she paused for breath. This was what showed her that her every word was being hung to.

'Once upon a time—'

A chorus of 'Unh!'

'There was a king, his queen and their three sons.'

'Unh!'

'They were very happy, of course, but the queen longed for a daughter.'

'Unh!'

'They tried every magic potion, every prayer, but still there was no baby.'

'Unh!' Sometimes the children would play tricks on her.

'An old man disguised as a fruit seller appeared at the castle one morning—'

She would stop suddenly and wait for the 'Unh!', but it was not forthcoming. Shanti never understood how the synchronisation worked, nobody said a word, no signals were exchanged, and yet the 'Unh' tarried on their collective lips at the same precise moment. Nani would cup her hand behind an ear, and repeat.

'An old man disguised as a fruit seller appeared at the castle one morning…' A resounding silence sometimes breached by an imperfectly repressed guffaw.

'Well, I am going home now, you children have all fallen asleep…'

At this point, all the children would burst out laughing, explaining that they were teasing the old dear, they were only pretending. Ma did not approve of this.

'Do you children have no respect for your elders? Teasing Nani like this? How dare you?' But Nani would spring to the defence of the little ones.

'Arrey beti, if my own grandchildren cannot have a little fun teasing me, then who can?' And the narration continued in the same vein until the whole story had run its course, until good had defeated evil, the queen had borne the child she was longing for and the prince married the princess and they lived happily ever after.

On more than one occasion, Shanti remembered a very unusual stoppage. The first time, she was in the middle of the story of Bol Bida Raja, and the princess had just espied her beloved prince metamorphosing into a Cobra.

'He had black crystalline eyes,' she was saying, 'his body was shiny, like a massive jewel, and oh,' she wailed alarmingly, and addressed Ma, 'tell me, beti, what do you do when your very destiny is rotten.'

The children and everybody else stared at the narrator open-mouthed, not understanding what was going on. The first time, Ma frowned but she liked to be thought of as a woman of wisdom who was able to dispense advice. By now, the storyteller was in tears.

'It's the bahu?' Ma asked, knowing that relations between the old woman and her daughter-in-law were always strained.

'Who else?'

'That's because your son is a half-man who cannot control his wife,' Ma said with great finality.

'You've put your finger on it,' the old widow nodded appreciatively, having dried her tears. 'As you say, it's all my fault, I didn't bring them up firmly enough.' Suddenly the tears began to flow again.

'But what could I a helpless widow do? Why did their father suddenly decide to die on me, why didn't Bhagwan take me instead? I am so useless.'

Ma was not usually one to give credit to others too lightly, but this time she was quite lavish.

'Aunty, what are you saying? You were never a helpless woman, when that useless husband of yours was killed by lightning, what did you do? Did you throw your hands up in the air and wail? No, you decided to earn a living for your little ones. You toiled all the hours of the day cooking your laddoos, and putting them in your basket and you rowed miles and miles on the waters in your boat, in sunny or stormy weather selling them to the rich families, how can anybody say a woman like you is useless, come on pull yourself together.'

The other women in the audience made assenting and appreciative noises, and the old cake vendor poured out her grievances. The daughter-in-law told lies about her to her husband and the ungrateful son believed her. She answered back, she was sullen, she was slatternly, never putting things in the right place... Then just as suddenly she stopped, dried her tears and without warning, picked up the thread of her narration, as if there had never been any interruption.

'He tried to look away when he realised that the princess had seen him, but the game was up. He loved his princess and the last thing he wanted was to make her unhappy, but there was nothing to do. His serpent eyes became filled with tears... Why did you say my husband was useless, it wasn't his fault that lightning struck him down?' This was addressed to Ma, who often spoke without thinking.

'No, I didn't mean he was useless, what I meant was why did he have to die. I mean a man dies and leaves a widow and children to look after themselves. You know what I mean? I didn't mean to say useless.' Nani was unconvinced, but decided to let it go.

'... because the princess had discovered his secret...'

Everybody marvelled at the precision of Nani's storytelling. If she told the same story twice, there would never be one word changed.

Raju had a totally different style of narration. The plot was never sacrosanct. To him everything was in the telling of the tale. Do dafa ka zikr hai... Twice upon a time, he would sometimes begin. This made the kids scream with mock indignation. But Baba, it's not twice upon a time, stories always begin with Ek dafa ka zikr hai... once upon a time! No, no, he would explain, sometimes it is twice upon a time, sometimes it is once upon a time, and believe me, sometimes it can even be three times upon a time.

His favourites were the Birbal stories, but Raju was never one to tell them straight. His version of the story of the well, that Shanti had heard from Nani Laddoo as a child, did not feature an ordinary well with water in it, no sir, Raju had to bring in a gold well.

'A gold well, Baba?' the children would ask in wonderment.

'Yes, a gold well. Let me explain, you throw your pail in and when you pulled, you had a pail full of liquid gold, but of course once you took the liquid gold out, you had massive shiny gold lumps.'

'Baba, you're teasing us again, how can—'.

'Shut your face, you don't know better than Baba. Go on, Baba, tell us.'

'Well, it was like this. As I said, there was this diamond well—'

Now both kids would squeal their objection in unison, Baba, you said gold, now you're saying diamond.

'Diamond? Did I say diamond? Ma,' he would ask Shanti, 'did you hear me say diamond?' And she, trying hard to repress her laughter, managed a few words.

'Children, remind me tomorrow to put a drop of coconut oil in your ears, you seem to be becoming deaf. I never heard your father say diamonds, he said gold.'

'You see!'

The children loved it when Ma joined Baba to tease them, happy that dad and mum were on the same side.

'Anyway, the owner of the well, was a very greedy man, a greedy man and a cheat! And he a wicked plan. I will sell the well, he thought, ask for a lot of money for it.

'Many people were keen to buy the well,' Raju went on, 'specially as they all knew that it was a gold well, and he sold it to a good man from Bihar.

'Biharis are the best!' He always got that bit in all his stories.

'The man from Bihar had paid a lot of money, but he knew that he was on to a good thing. So immediately the sale had taken place, he went to the well with his wife and brothers, each carrying a pail. His intention was clear, he was literally going to collect gold by the bucketful, and start leading the life of a Mughal emperor.

'But do you think he was able to do that?' he asked the children. The boy, always the optimist shouted yes, but the more cautious girl glumly shook her head, and said no.

'Ask your Ma.' Shanti pretended to agree with the boy. Raju shook her head sadly and smiled.

'My Sundari is right. They were stopped by the man who had just agreed to the sale.'

'The man had no right,' said the boy indignantly. She loved the boy's indignation, taking it to be a manifestation of his sense of justice. 'He had bought the well, so it belonged to him… the man from… from Mihar!'

'Bihar, stupid,' the girl corrected, pulling a face at her brother.

'He had no right, he had no right, the man from B-Bihar had bought the well.'

'Yes, the cheating seller countered, he had bought the well, but… listen to this… not its contents. The well belongs to you, but the gold is mine, he said.'

'But that's not fair,' the little ones chorused, and Raju demurred sadly.

'So, the seller and the man from Bihar — oh, what a lovely place, Bihar, the Bodh Gaya… arrey, don't get me started on my lovely Bihar, or I'll never finish. Yes, they agreed to go to the court of Emperor Akbar and ask the wise Birbal to arbitrate.'

'Who was the wise Birbal, Baba?'

'He was the emperor's diwan, the wisest man in the court. Even the emperor asked him to take decisions for him. So, to cut a long long story short short, each one tells the story and Birbal listens intently. When they finish, he shakes his head first, then nod. He makes a sign to a hookah wallah standing by…' Raju paused very slightly, his eyes twinkling with anticipation, for he knew the children wanted to ask a question.

'What's a hookah wallah?'

'I knew they'd ask,' he addressed her first, then turned to the children. 'Children,' he said happily, 'whenever you don't understand anything, just ask.' But he did not answer the question.

'First Birbal turns to the seller, and asks him to repeat that he had legally sold the well to the man, in front of witnesses. The cheat nods, saying "But sarkar, no one said anything about the contents. The well belongs to the man from Bihar, but the gold belongs to me."

'Birbal turns to the man from Bihar. "When the man sold you the well, did he also sell you its contents? Was that point raised?" The man from Bihar turns ashen and admits that only the well was mentioned, whereupon the seller's face glow with happiness.

'"The well belongs to the man from Bihar, but the gold belongs to the first man.

'"My Lord Birbal, everybody says how wise you are, and now I can add my voice to this chorus. Today I have witnessed justice as it is dished out at the court of the good emperor Akbar." The man from Bihar looks like he is about to faint and collapse.'

'"So," Birbal tells the seller, "as the gold is yours, I have to ask you to re-move all of it within twenty four hours, leaving not one drop behind, or the man from Bihar will be entitled to charge you rent for allowing you to keep your property in his well. Remember, not one drop!"'

"R-r-r-r-ent?" the seller wails, in a falsetto voice, which the storyteller gave an excellent version of.

'Rent?' the little ones asked, 'what is rent?'

'I knew you'd ask. Rent is something you pay, usually money, when you make use of something belonging to someone else.'

'Like we live in this hut and work on the fields, growing beans baigun and bhindi, but neither the land nor the hut belongs to us,' Shanti started.

'I know,' the girl said, 'everything belongs to that bloodsucker, Uncle Dukhdeo—'

'Arrey, where did you learn language like that, Sundari? You mustn't say things like that,' Raju admonished her mildly.

'Uncle Sukhdeo... his name is not Dukhdeo,' Shanti replied uneasily.

'But Baba calls him that bloodsucker Dukhdeo,' protested the boy.

'Don't say rude things like that about people,' she had entreated her man who smiled apologetically and shrugged. Not that she believed for a moment that he would mend his ways, Bhagwan forbids! He made her laugh so much, and wouldn't want him different. You had to laugh, Sukhdeo becoming

Dukhdeo. It was so obvious to all that the name of the man was completely inappropriate, as Raju said, Sukh being happiness and Dukh pain.

'Anyway,' explained Raju, 'the land is his, and I cultivate it with Ma, and we give him more than half of everything we harvest. That is a sort of rent.'

The boy began to air his indignation, saying that it wasn't right, since Baba and Ma did all the work, but Raju did not want to start a big palaver, and asked them whether they wanted to hear the story or not, to which they screamed their positive response.

'"R-r-r-r-rent?" said the cheating seller in dismay. Yes, rent, Birbal echoed. The man's face suddenly brightened.'

'"Oh yes, I can pay rent. A fair rent of course, just say it."'

'"Of course, a fair rent." Birbal concedes. The seller looks at Birbal, then at the man from Bihar, and then again at Birbal.'

'"Let me think," says Birbal, closing his eyes for a while. When he opens them again, he nods and smiles.'

'"I have given the matter serious consideration—"'

'"Yes, yes," interrupts the cheating seller', "what, may I kindly ask your worship, would the rent be when I am coming to take my liquid gold out?"'

'"For every pail you get out, you will pay the man from Bihar a rent of two pails of liquid gold." The seller frowns, opens his mouth, but not one word comes out.'

'"You m-m-m-mean," he stammers finally', "I have to draw three pails each time, take one for myself and give the man from Bihar two?"'

'Birbal shakes his head. "No," he says, "that's not what I said, if you draw out three pails of gold, you will owe the man from Bihar six pails."'

'"Then I must draw nine pails," wails the cheating seller.'

'"Nine pails? No, if you draw out nine pails, then you must pay the man eighteen."' The children squealed with joy at seeing villainy confounded. But Raju was in full flow.

'"But… but…but that can't be, how can I do that?"'

'"I will close my eyes," says Birbal', "and count to ten, if when I open them you are gone, I will forget the whole case, and forget that you came here, otherwise…"'

The children squealed with delight, the boy almost ended up crying, so happy he was. The girl loved the story no less, but she had a streak of realism in her which belied her age, and when she managed to stop laughing, she said, almost to herself, I don't believe that a well can contain liquid gold.

CHAPTER 11

Inverness and Cromarty

'It's a sorry business this,' Lord Gordon said to Hugh Stewart at breakfast. He had invited the handsome young Captain to join him for a spot of deer hunting at his estate in Ardersier. The younger man made a grimace and shook his head in dismay. He had strong views about people who thrived on the misery of others, and it was not often that he found someone in his circle who shared his views.

'If I had my way,' the Captain said, 'after we have dealt with the rioters, I'd like to look into the action of the landlords too, they are far from blameless.'

'Really?'

'My Lord, you and I know that the Highlander is no less strongly attached to Christian values of live and let live, to his home and surroundings, as we are. Nobody asked him whether he wanted sheep to invade the land of his forefathers by stealth... what was he to do?'

'Yes, dear boy, but we cannot let them burn and destroy property with impunity.'

'But they did nothing of the sort my lord,' said Hugh Stewart more vehemently than he had wanted, 'they did very little damage. Did you know that they never killed not one single sheep for food.'

'Really? That's extraordinary. I wasn't told.'

'But I was there, my Lord, and I can vouchsafe for their forbearance... I wish I could testify to that in court, but nobody called me as a witness.'

'Lord Stonefield is known for his sense of justice, my boy, I am sure he will listen to all the accounts and direct the jury to a fair verdict.' Stewart demurred but said nothing.

The Cameron brothers had, however, prevailed upon the Lord Advocate to revive the original case against Wallace and his fellow rioters who had attacked him and his farm in Culcairn to liberate their Black cattle, and on the twelfth of September 1792, the court in Inverness sat to try two different if not unconnected cases.

The town was full of peasants from all the nooks and crannies of Ross and Sutherland, in a show of support for their fellow victims.

Stonefield did not hide how much he disliked revisiting a case which had been closed, and knew that it was only because the brothers' influence. But he was going to do a thorough job, allow both sides to present their views. In his summing up, he said that the animals in question were cows and horses which had been removed from their own pastures and illegally poinded, since insufficient legal notice had been given to the tenants as to the change that had been applied to existing pastures. The men were not armed and the Cameron brothers had met them with guns. In his view the defence was right to claim that it was self defence. The men were acquitted.

When the well wishers roaming the town heard the news, their cheer was loud enough to reach the skies. The times are a-changing, they said, the common man is no longer to be taken for granted. They drank many a toast to that and made merry, singing lustily, to the consternation of the landowners and the amusement of the townsfolk.

But their merriment was short lived, for soon after, the second trial began. The prosecution counsel, Mr Anderson opened up by firing his relentless salvo. The seven men on trial had riotously and feloniously instigated their fellow men to invade the property of law abiding landowners and farmers who had obtained their property by lawful means. They had made seditious proclamations at churches where worshippers had come to pray and hear sermons preaching peace and strict adherence to the laws of God and government. Instead they had been urged to seize upon and drive the lawful property of men of honour, defenceless flocks of sheep into the open, with a view to dispersing them and causing great loss of income to these honest men. Anderson's oratory was very impressive and the jury, comprising mainly of the landed gentry could not help nodding in agreement to everything they heard. Hugh and John exchanged glum looks, and Michael Ross stared in front of him, amazed at what he was hearing.

The Jury must take into account the fact that these dangerous men came armed to the teeth, after spending £26.00 on gunpowder when they reach their verdict, the counsel said with great flourish of his arm. At this point the defence counsel jumped to his feet.

'My Lord,' said Mr Reid, 'my learned friend is making claims that he cannot substantiate—'

'I am going to call witnesses to testify to that, I am not in the habit of making wild claims.'

John Speirs, a gunsmith from Inverness was called, took his place at the bar and was sworn in and questioned.

'Yes,' he agreed, 'on the day before the insurrection, a man came into my shop and bought gunpowder.'

'You remember that you are under oath when you maintain this?' Yes, he did.

'How much did he spend, Mr Speirs?' asked Mr Reid before the judge could tell him to wait for his turn in order to cross-examine the witness.

'Sixteen pounds… I think.'

'Was it twenty-six, sixteen or even only six pounds? Remember you are under oath.'

'Aye, six pounds… I cannae remember… I meant to write it in my book, but I ran out of ink.'

'Will the jury remember that most interesting fact, to wit, that Mr Speirs meant to write it all down, but, calamity of calamities, he ran out of ink.' Even the people who had come to support the lairds were unable to keep a serious face.

'Mr Speirs, the man who bought twenty-six, or maybe sixteen or maybe only six pounds worth of gunpowder… or even sixpence for that matter, can you see him here among the accused.' Speirs hesitated, he studied the seven men intently but finally dwelled upon John Aird.

'He looked very much like this man here,' he said glumly pointing at Aird.

'Looks very much like this man… John Aird. Did he look as much like this man here as sixpence looks like twenty-six pounds? But you still cannot swear that it was him… remember you are under oath.'

'It was not him, but he looked like him.'

'You are in a court of justice Mr Speirs, and these men's fates, nay, lives are in your hands. Are you willing to condemn a man on the strength that he looks like a man who spent twenty-six pounds or—'

'Will then learned counsel refrain from his tedious and repetitious remarks. Just say spent some money, will you?' That was his Lordship.

'You are willing to condemn a man on the strength that he looks like a man who spent eh… some money… buying gunpowder.'

'The man could have been the cousin of the accused, and might have been buying the gunpowder for the rioters,' Speirs said, in a desperate attempt at juggling his wish to see the men condemned with his need to avoid perjury.

Lord Stonefield was aghast at this notion and ordered the jury to discard the testimony.

Mr Reid was an adept at reading legal runes, and he knew that in spite of fighting the good fight, his men had no chance of being let off, so he set his sights on saving their necks. These were poor men driven to act rashly by the plight they had been subjected to. Thirty seven families had been evicted and those who had not starved to death were slowly getting there. These were God-fearing men, law-abiding and decent folk. None of them did what they did in a spirit of wantonness. Yes, they were misguided, but one does not get the full force of the law visited upon one for the sin of misguidance!

But there was no escaping the overwhelming testimonies of the respected proprietors of a number of settlements ranging from Allagrange to Scotsburn who spoke of the helplessness with which they saw their poor sweet lambs being mercilessly driven away, bringing tears to the eyes of the landed jury.

Demanding the ultimate penalty for the accused, Mr Anderson appealed to the jury to remember their responsibility as custodians of order in the land and not to let sedition of that magnitude go unpunished.

'A lenient sentence,' he said in vibrant tones, 'was a key which people who had no respect for the laws of the land would indubitably use to open the gates of anarchy. If those dangerous men be allowed to go Scot-free, who knows to what dangers our sacred king and country may not be exposed. Do we wish the country to go the way of poor France? The members of the jury have no doubt witnessed with alarm the threatening behaviour of the people who have descended upon this peaceful town. All they want is a leader and the powder keg will light up and blow us all sky high and to smithereens.'

Lord Stonefield was not a happy man. He wished the accused men could be found not guilty, or that he had a humane sentence at his disposal, but his hands were tied by statutes, and it was clear that the law had been broken.

John Aird and Hugh Mackenzie were found guilty on all charges. Although a death sentence was within Lord Stonefield's power to dispense, he could not make himself wear the black cap. Instead, he pronounced a sentence of transportation. Michael Ross and Fergus Davidson were found guilty of some of the charges and condemned to two years imprisonment. The charges against three others were unproven and they were discharged.

The condemned men were taken to the Tollbooth in Inverness, waiting for transportation. Hugh had not even been able to see his little girl, and was so distraught that he felt sure that he was not going to survive the perilous voyage to the other side of the world. He would willingly have traded a week in the bosom of his family, with Martha, Mam and the little girl, for what was left of his life. When he talked to John Aird, he never responded, it was as if he had not heard. He spent all his time praying to a God whose ears were turned away from the poor, Hugh would have said.

By now Hugh had lost whatever little faith he had, seeing with great clarity what Mam had said over the years. It was kinder to believe that there was no God, than to believe in a God who allowed such cruel things to happen in his world.

However, unbeknownst to either men, Lord Gordon had again asked Captain Stewart to visit him in Fort George, with instruction to keep this summons secret. When Hugh arrived, the good Lord ushered him in his study, ordered tea and locked the door. He reminded the younger man of a conversation they had had only a couple of weeks before about the Insurrection.

'These men are being sent to their death in that hell hole that is Van Diemen's Land,' Lord Gordon said glumly, as he poured his visitor a glass of whisky. The Captain concurred.

'And I say we cannot let that happen,' said the Commander of His Majesty's Armed Forces north of the border to the Captain's amazement.

'There is nothing we can do now, my Lord,' cried Stewart in desperation.

'Dear boy, there always is something to be done, and you are going to do it, and do it with your usual thoroughness and discretion,' Lord Gordon said with absolute finality. And he would not elaborate, he smiled meaningfully and shook his head every time Captain Stewart emitted an opinion or asked a question. When they were saying good-bye, Lord Gordon kept Captain Stewart's hand in his for a while, and whispered the cryptic words, 'Carte Blanche, dear boy!'

On his way home after the enigmatic encounter, Stewart decided that the good Lord Commander was telling him, nay ordering him, to save the men, to help them escape and do everything in his power to convey them and their families to safety, and he immediately set to work, elaborating a watertight plan in his head.

Captain Stewart and his trusted lieutenant Robert Howie went to the Tollbooth in Inverness, and told the guards there that the prisoners were to be entrusted unto their care. Obviously nobody dared question officers wearing such fine uniforms and hats. Mackenzie and Aird were convinced that within hours they would be in the damp dank hold of some hulk, bound for the end of the world. The guards nodded and disappeared, coming back shortly after, pushing and shoving the two prisoners, prodding them in the ribs with their muskets. Seeing this Captain Stewart said in a firm and authoritative voice that the men had been condemned for transportation and not to abuse by prison guards. It was not too common for anyone to notice the rough treatment prisoners received at the hands of gaolers, and the men were quite surprised. And their surprise turned to shock when Captain Stewart ordered them to unshackle the men completely, and they carried out the instructions keeping whatever sceptical thoughts they might have entertained to themselves. They condemned men were led to their coach, where Lieutenant Howie told them to be seated. He then gave them some bandages and liniments and told them to dry and clean their wounds. They took these and just kept them in their trembling hands doing nothing. John Aird's fell from his hand and he did not even notice this.

They were too tired and confused to notice that there was no coachman, and that it was the Lieutenant who was seated at the driving seat. Although it was not cold, their teeth were chattering and they were trembling all over. I always thought I was a brave man, Hugh Breac Mackenzie was thinking, but adversity drains all courage from all but the bravest. Aird was benumbed and had no thoughts at all. The coach was bumping along on the uneven roads, and the men who had very little experience of this form of travelling had just started getting used to this when the Captain spoke.

'Mackenzie, Aird, listen to me carefully, and do exactly as you are told. If they catch you, it isn't going to be Botany Bay, but the gallows.'

Aird began to shake and whimper, not understanding what was happening.

'Stop this, man, you are being rescued!' Mackenzie was not sure that he had heard the word "rescued," the captain's Gaelic being rusty, and was perplexed, but Aird heard not one word, and continued shaking.

'John Aird,' said the captain suddenly, seizing the man by both shoulders and shaking him firmly, 'you are now safe, you are not going to Botany Bay!'

Mackenzie was still unsure. No way, he thought, if at any point in his life he had been minded to believe in miracles, Mam had made sure she taught him how to expel the notion. No, the bosses are up to their usual tricks, although what they were, he had no idea. But the captain and his lieutenant had treated them with a greater courtesy than he had ever experienced from their class.

'Some important people believe that you have been hard done by, and it has been decided to stop them sending you to Botany Bay, do you understand?'

Hugh's doubt began to dissipate, though only gradually, like the morning mist lifting over the glen on a cloudy day as the sun began spreading its largesse around. Aird heard but did not immediately register their meaning. Then he made an effort to recall what he heard and understood that they were not going to be sent to Botany Bay.

The good Lord has answered my prayers, John Aird muttered to himself almost inaudibly, and with trembling hands, he suddenly seized Hugh by the shoulder and fairly shouted the same words:

'D'you hear Hughie, the good Lord has answered our prayers, I knew He would, I told you He would!' Hugh nodded and said nothing. The Captain and his lieutenant were smiling broadly at each other, pleased at having done what both thought was a worthy action.

'Are you taking us to our wives, Captain, sir?' asked Hugh, 'are you taking us to our homes?' Then suddenly turning to John Aird, Hugh burst into tears.

'I am going to see her John, my wee bairn, do you hear? My wee baby… thank you O Lord!' He was surprised to hear himself say that.

'No,' said the Captain, 'we are not taking you home, it's too dangerous, that's the first place Sheriff McLeod's men will be searching, but don't be afraid, your loved ones have been taken care of and you will see them sooner than you may think.' The men did not understand what was happening, but they now felt growing confidence in the two soldiers. No, they both decided, there is no trickery, and exhausted, they loosened up and leant their aching shoulders against the backrest of the coach, finding the regular bumping comforting if you took care not to let your head hit the roof of the coach. Aird had stopped shaking. Soon they were skirting the Beauly Firth, although ignoring the geography of the area they did not know this. The coach was heading for Dingwall and stopped just outside that town, reaching the destination before nightfall. The Captain gave the men a tent which they pitched outside the coach, and blankets, cheese and oatcakes and a bottle of whisky, and they were grateful that the October weather was not unbearable.

It had been decided that they would continue the journey at crack of dawn next day. When they were again on their way, the Captain explained to them that as they were wanted men, they could no longer bide in Ross safely and even in another county. If caught, they would be hanged. They would have to have new names and identities, and he had already arranged for Hugh to be given the papers of Angus Smith. As for Aird, he was to be called Fergus Hicks. Ideally they should go live in another country beyond the reach of the harsh laws of this country. It would be easy to get them over to Nova Scotia. That was the safest option, how did they like that? John Aird immediately said that if his family could join him, he would be more than happy to go there. Hugh was lost in thought, and said nothing. The captain took this for acquiescence, and said that he had already made provisional arrangements for a quick departure, as long as they made as if they did not know each other for the duration of the crossing, seeing that their descriptions will have been in circulation. In the meantime, they would be lodged in a safe house on the coast, near Cromarty, until their ship was ready for departure. He paused to let the information sink in, and noticed that Hugh seemed confused. He asked him if he had arrived at the same decision as John Aird. No sir, he said thoughtfully, I am a Highlander and anywhere else I would be lost. Like a Black Cattle in a peat bog.

The Captain showed great understanding for Hugh's position. Yes, he said, he did not think it was right to dictate to free Scotsmen how and where they should live. And I wouldn't mind saying that it was this spirit which moved me to undertake this venture so enthusiastically, albeit on the prompting of someone very high up who I am not at liberty to name. In the meantime you will both have to go to that safe house on the coast that I mentioned. It is derelict to some extent, but it still has roofs and walls, and no one is going to find you there. He did not explain that it was part of a lot that the Duchess of Sutherland had acquired, with the intention of turning it over, in the not so distant future, to dispossessed tenants, as they transformed themselves into fishermen, so as to make way for more sheep. Hugh who had a suspicious nature, and who seized on the house being located on the coast, was suddenly assailed by the thought that they were being tricked into something, but fortunately he was able to dismiss this idea.

The captain had said that he would see his family soon enough. What did he mean by soon? He missed Martha more than he thought he would, what a fine woman! He knew that she understood why he had to go to set his cows free from the Cameron brothers, but he suspected that when they were planning the big insurrection, she was not at one with him, even if she never said one word. And his little girl… he loved her with all his heart whatever Martha might think. Mam! That he loved her, he had not the slightest doubt, but he knew that he was still in awe of her, she was a tough no-nonsense woman, no wonder Da felt the same. She was such a tower of strength, was so full of common sense, was so upright even if she had no time for the God of the rich. Knowing that she was around made him fear less for the safety of Martha and the baby.

'Captain Stewart, sir, my wife, my wee bairn—'

'Mackenzie, trust me they are well, and you will see them, I promise. Soon.'

The carriage rolled on all night and reached a small abandoned hamlet west of Cromarty a little after sunset. The house seemed empty from outside, but when a horse neighed, it suddenly sprang to life and the doors were burst open and Hugh could swear that time stood still as he saw an image that would stay with him for the rest of his life: Martha with the baby wrapped in a grey blanket in her arms, running towards him, her shawl unable to keep up with her speed gently giving up and drifting towards the ground behind her, her lambent hair, glowing in the moonlight rippling like waves, giving her the appearance of a female warrior poised to strike at her foe. He had never seen her more beautiful. Mrs Aird and Mam must have been there, but he never saw them. Tears of joy gushed out from all eyes. So that was how soon the admirable captain meant by soon!

Stewart and Howie exchanged congratulatory looks, and looked at the joyous reunion with great happiness. Mam Mackenzie immediately decided that after such a long journey, what the travellers needed was a nice large bowl of porridge, and the women set about turning this into reality. Hugh had deftly prised the little wean from her mother's arms and experienced a sensation akin to ecstasy as he pressed the fragile little body to his own.

The military men declined an invitation of a rest before their return journey, but did full justice to Mam's porridge. The admirable pair then said their good-bye and Hugh Stewart promised that he would be back when other arrangements were made.

The condemned men could hardly believe their good fortune. Aird was convinced that going to Nova Scotia was the best solution. Hugh, infected by the enthusiasm of his cousin, began to waver in his determination to stay in the land of his birth come what may. Mam said she would willingly go where Hugh wanted them to be. This time he asked Martha, but the woman, never used to being asked her opinion, was taken aback, and agreed with Mam, You are the master of the house, Hugh Mackenzie, it's for you to decide.

A few days later, the captain showed up and said that the Northern Star was setting sail from Cromarty for Montreal in six days' time, and that there was still time for MacKenzie to change his mind. No one, least of all Hugh himself knew what his reaction was going to be, and he was as surprised as the others to hear him say with unnecessary indignation, 'We are Highlanders born on this Scottish land of our fathers, we have drank Highland waters and breathed the cold fresh air of the glens, we have been nourished by oats grown on our rocky fields, no Captain, no one can make me leave this land.' Martha nodded, but only because she knew that he was speaking in such an uncalled for aggressive manner in order to convince himself of the righteousness of his decision. The Captain was puzzled but said that the choice lay with him.

He took John Aird aside, gave him some papers and money, reminded him that there was no chance of his ever coming back, and instructed him on the steps to be taken regarding their big adventure. Aird nodded and smiled happily, clutching the papers like they were his lifeline, which they were. He then gave Hugh some papers and money, and explained about a waterway which was planned.

'We are at the dawn of a new age,' he said with an almost religious fervour, 'soon the country will be unrecognisable, it will be the age of machines and industry. A sort of revolution, if I may say so. The people in London have plans for the union which will ensure that we stay the topmost nation of this world until the end of time. You have not heard of Mr Watt, Mackenzie, but that man is a genius of the sort that comes into this world but once every three or four centuries. Like us he is a Scotsman… Many years ago the government entrusted him with the study of a bold plan to create a waterway, a navigable canal if you like, here in this part of the world, which will, in the first instance, create jobs for you people being cruelly driven from your tenant farms, but as you know, there is a sad shortage of good roads in the country… and by God, Mackenzie, we will need these roads, I can tell you! And London has finally approved the plans for its construction, and put another son of our soil, Mr Thomas Telford in charge of the project.'

Hugh remembered the knocks he had taken on the head as they were travelling to Cromarty, and smiled. The Captain was so carried away by his enthusiasm and continued breathlessly, 'It will carry goods which will be manufactured all over the country, it will be wide enough to enable the free passage of wide cargo boats.' Hugh was beginning to wonder whether the good Captain was not deluded about his capacity. In what way was he going to be part of this scheme, he was no craftsman, he only knew how to raise cows and grow oats. The Captain explained that he had written a letter to Patrick Gordon, the son of an old family retainer who was the foreman at a site near Fort Williams, where he understood there was always a need for strong and willing arms, as there was a lot of digging to be done, in order to analyse the soil and rock formation. It is a government project, so the pay will be fair and regular, I'll warrant you. He demurred slightly at this point, unsure of what he was warranting, but he had won Hugh over. Yes, he would take his family to Fort Williams, accept the new name the good captain had given him, and never again would he have to depend on the dubious bounty of greedy landlords.

CHAPTER 12

❖❖❖

Raju and Shanti

SHANTI KNEW THAT whatever Raju said about the boss, his tedious Sukhdeo Dukhdeo jokes and his taking offs of the man notwithstanding, he did not dislike him half as much as she did. It was a visceral dislike verging on hatred, based on nothing but her instinct, for she almost never had anything to do with the man. She understood that Chacha Sukhdeo had been very much part of Raju's childhood. He had been like a doting uncle to him at one time, bringing him sweetmeats, ruffling his hair up every time he saw him, playfully pinching his cheeks. His friend's little boy was very much the son he never had. Whenever the child had a fever or was a tad pallid, he would fret like an old mother hen, suggest herbs, pujas, urging Parsad to ask his friend the hakeem for help, reprimanding him for not taking the boy's condition seriously. The older man would always have a soft spot for the young man, but after Parsad's death, he had reacted to what he considered was Raju's lack of respect and consideration for the self-appointed father-substitute. He had a lingering loyalty to his dead friend, but as his horizons had changed, he had decided that sentimentality was a millstone round people's neck, and told himself that the boy was nothing more to him any longer, that he was just someone who worked for him. He was a good worker, and it was in his interest to overlook what he took to be his lack of courtesy. Early on he had made it clear to the boy and his haughty aunt that they were not to expect preferential treatment. I am the landlord and the employer, and I have many tenants and many employees, and as a lover of justice I cannot treat one differently from another.

He was a big man with floppy arms, thick calves and a massive stomach which could be seen pulsating and forming waves on the surface of his translucent white cotton kurta whenever he was panting for breath, which was whenever he was not standing still. His fat round face was patchy, like an archipelago of small black islands in a brown sea. He had a strong bodily odour, and was always scratching his hind parts. He had a crop of black prickly hair, made shiny with generous applications of coconut oil which sometimes dripped down his face in the heat, and accounted for the unmistakeable smell of stale oil which Raju never failed to mention when telling stories about him. Everybody in the village talked of his legendary appetite. Aunt Lalita was thin like a drumstick, and one immediately picked an aura of sour, unripe fruit about her. She was always complaining about the climate, it was either too hot or too cold, there was too much rain or it was too dry. People were either hypocrites or ingrates, and those people who claimed to be poor had more money than they needed, they were just extravagant. She had a pinched nose as if her nostrils were perpetually invaded by bad odours, small piercing eyes, and Raju had told Shanti that as a child, he always had the feeling that he was naked in front of her.

Pitaji had told her once that that dung carrier Sukhdeo had been lucky to have found work the moment he arrived in the Sunderbans; but grudgingly he admitted that the man had shrewd business sense. Parsad, he had said, seemed like a good man, but was totally lacking in drive. When they arrived in this place, Pitaji was willing to help him, but the newcomer was too proud to ask. Aunt Umma later explained to her that because of the status of their family, Parsad could not go with a begging bowl to her father, tradition demanded that Pitaji be the one to make the offer. The old woman had been quite serious. Your father should have approached my brother to pay his respects, and welcome him to Roshankhali and suggest that as he was in need of people to work for him, would Parsad consider helping him? But people have lost their good manners now, she had sighed. Shanti had laughed, she will never understand this rigmarole.

Sukhdeo had sworn publicly that he would never let his friend's son and sister go hungry. He would look after them like his own, he told everybody. In the beginning he did help once or twice, but gradually, as Aunt Umma began to experience more and more difficulty, the man who was accumulating land and cattle almost by the hour, became more and more tight-fisted and distant, until finally he cut off all but business contact with the near destitute woman and nephew.

The tenancy of a holding was on a strictly commercial basis. He charged his usual exorbitant rent in kind, demanded an excessive number of hours' work on his fields, which was why the normally conscientious Raju did as little work as he thought he could get away with. Still this was how the family had survived. When they married he had offered them the tenancy of a rather bigger and more profitable concern. The arrangement was clearly beneficial to the shrewd landowner, in the knowledge that the new wife would provide an extra pair of hands towards his enrichment.

Dukhdeo was always ruing something. He should have asked for a better price for this or that commodity, should have made his tenants take better care of the land, the yield should have been so much higher. He was insanely jealous of his less prosperous competitors, and was always complaining about how they had undercut him, how he never had any money. She was very impressed by Raju's summing up of the man: the rich always believe that they have less money than they were worth, and that the poor more than they deserved. Sadly, she had discovered that this had been true of her own Pitaji as well. When his onions or beans were growing nicely, Dukhdeo had trouble sleeping, so worried was he of thieves. It either rained too much, draining his rich soil away, or too little, causing his vegetables to wither. He had problems digesting food, and Raju said that the perfect remedy would be for him to eat less. The Muslim hakeem had indeed told him the very same thing, but the man was convinced that the jealous villagers, were secretly indulging in witchcraft and satanic pujas in order to harm him. His own guru, Pandit Biswas confirmed that belief, craftily advising the sacrifice of a plump black rooster in order to combat the imaginary malefic practices. Shanti, however, like everybody else, knew that it was Aunt Lalita who put all those malevolent notions into his head. Radha used to say that Sukhdeo on his own was not a bad fellow, and that it was his wife had turned him into a nasty old man.

She had been quietly rejoicing about tomorrow, when Raju would be staying at home, for it had rained a lot lately and there was no need to water the plants. She smiled to herself as she remembered how one rainy day he had suddenly said, Rani, bring me my umbrella. An umbrella? she has asked, but we don't have an umbrella, what do you want an umbrella for, you're not going out? Oh yes, I am, he had said seriously, just because it's raining it doesn't mean the plants need not be watered. Remind me to buy an umbrella when I go to Calcutta next time. How the babies had screamed with laughter. There was always weeding to be done, but when it was muddy you needed to wait for a day or two for the field to dry up. In the meantime, there were always chores that would keep him at home, mending fishnets or sharpening tools and greasing them, making new wooden handles for axes and spades and the like.

Raju had no idea how much she loved having him around, but even after six years of marriage, she was still shy and in any case had always found it difficult to open up to anybody. She only really felt that she was communicating perfectly with him when they made love in the dark, when the feeling of his warm pulsating body around hers gave her a sort of out-of-body experience. She was never good with words.

The tenants had their own work on their rented fields and were responsible for how they exploited it, but the zamindar kept a close watch over their comings and goings. He did not hesitate to evict tenants when he thought that they were not doing everything to maximise his profits. There were loose rules about what proportion of the yields Raju had to hand over to the proprietor, but the latter felt free to bend those rules on a whim. When there was little demand for a certain produce, he would take a benevolent air and declare that because he was not a heartless zamindar like some people thought, he had decided to let the tenant keep a larger proportion of his harvest, but when it was known that there was a shortage of something or other, he demanded more. His principle seemed to be to keep his workers just short of starving, making them forever beholden to him, thus strengthening his dominion over them. Her own father used to do the same thing. The immediate result of this regime was that it discouraged honesty. Everybody felt that as they were being hard done by, they were entitled to retaliate. Everybody naturally learnt how to conceal the real yield in order to lessen their contribution. When the opportunity arose, they would even grab the odd pot of milk or put away a sackful of wheat.

As part of his job, Raju was often required to accompany Sukhdeo to Calcutta or the Pargannas, a four or five-day ride by oxcart from Sonarkhali, to sell his ghee and groundnut oil, hental mats, tamarind, beans, moringa and ashilata seeds, onions, ginger, pumpkins and dudhi, haldi and those crops that did not go bad too quickly. Bayguns and bhindis, tomatoes, palak, karela and similar produce which quickly lost their freshness in the hot climate, were mainly cultivated for the locals. Some islands had such salty earth that practically nothing grew there, and they had to buy everything they ate. But Raju had learnt the ropes and often when Sukhdeo did not feel like a trip, he asked him to go by himself. Raju readily admitted to her that he was no more honest than the others, but he was more crafty, and had forged for himself a reputation of trustworthiness that he did not deserve. The others, he explained to her, stole unintelligently — not he. He remembered the story that Aunty Umma had told him many a time: when she was a child in Bihar, there was a village idiot whom everybody laughed at because when given a nice ripe mango and an unripe one and asked to choose, he would always pick the green one. So people who wanted a laugh would come to him with two such mangoes and laugh their heads off as he invariably spurned the nice red one. One day Umma told him off for being so stupid. Don't you know the ripe one is better to eat? she asked him. Yes Didi, said the idiot boy, of course he knew, they all called him idiot but he was no fool. Why don't you pick the nice red one then? If I pick the good one, the idiot boy answered, they would stop coming to me to make me choose.

'Then I am keeping the green mango in straw for two days, when it is ripening. Don't tell anyone, didi.'

You see, Rani, I am like that idiot boy, if I steal a great deal, Dukhdeo would find out and stop trusting me, so when I can steal five sackfuls of wheat, I only steal two, when the man from Calcutta gives me forty eight rupees for a cartload of onions, I don't take eight rupees and give him forty, I take one rupee and eight annas and give the man forty-six rupees and eight annas. I trust Raju, he says, and we eat at least one good meal a day, the children and us. A fool, her husband was not.

Unexpectedly, as they were watching the river that morning, they saw a speck on the water in the distance, and she guessed that it was Jayant's boat, and indeed the baleful figure of the pain-giver soon emerged. She knew instinctively that she had better forget her hope of Raju spending quality time with her and the babies. He undoubtedly had some chore or errand for her man. She cursed under her breath and told Raju of the impending arrival of the spoilsport. The children were looking gloomily at the approaching boat, and knew what it meant. Jayant had moored the craft and was scooping out seepage. The fat man was making for their hut, half running, and pausing for breath regularly. He was now just level with he crooked coconut palm tree which Raju called the kind-hearted tree, because its slant made climbing up it easier.

He had a bad back, Sukhdeo explained, and did not feel up to going with Harish, as he had planned, and did not trust that halfwit to go on his own, so Raju would have to go by himself. He would be taking a cartload of produce to the market town, deliver to clients, take some of the money, buy things which the zamindar had made a list of, rice and spice, tea and atta flour, nails and rope, Lucifer matches, paraffin and paint, tools and corrugated iron sheets, thread and needles. These he traded with his tenants for their crops, at an exorbitant rate of course. He normally allowed his reps ten to twelve days for the round trip. Although he paid extra for this service, Shanti knew that Raju hated being away from her but they took comfort in the financial benefits.

'Namaskar, beti,' he greeted Shanti breathlessly the moment he caught sight of her.

She said nothing, but mechanically joined the fingers of her hands together and raised the two joined members to her forehead, bowing slightly, in the customary show of respect that one owed one's elders. She became aware of a strong smell of sweat in the air. Sukhdeo panted heavily in an attempt at regaining his breath and said nothing because he needed a whole minute before he could speak. Raju appeared and beamed at the zamindar. He is such a hypocrite, Shanti thought. Anyone would be convinced that Sukhdeo was the man her husband admired most in this world.

'What an honour, Uncle, what an honour! Shanti make some tea for our esteemed guest.' Fortunately before Shanti could react, Sukhdeo managed to say that all he wanted was a lota of water. With the acidity in his stomach tea would make him burp. Anyway, she had limited rations of luxurious commodities and did not like the idea of lavishing them on the undeserving, when her own babies had to go without. Raju invited the zamindar to sit down on a rickety chair he had made himself with some jele goran from the forest, which usually resided under the mango tree by the side of the stone spice crusher, except in the rainy season. He he squatted opposite the big man.

'To what do we owe this honour, Chacha?' he asked, draining his voice of the slightest trace of sarcasm. But now he knew. He too had been looking forward to spending quality time with her and his little princes, but he understood that this bloodsucker had other plans.

'Calcutta,' he said, suddenly starting to sneeze.

'You must have caught a cold, Uncle,' the younger man said with mock sympathy, 'when it is hot, you sweat and in the breeze of the Sunderbans your body cools and you catch colds.' Sukhdeo frowned, unsure as to whether a boy giving him information was disrespectful. But Shanti knew that the rich man still grudgingly had a soft spot for her wag of a husband. To the older man, Raju was not a shirker, although like everybody else, he could obviously put in more effort in his work, but he also believed that he was above board in money matters, convinced that he had inherited Parsad's inherent honesty. He had often thought that his dead friend would never have done anything dishonest had it not been for his nefarious influence. No, the young man was thoughtless, his father died too young and never had the opportunity of sharing with him his enormous wisdom, but disrespectful he was not.

'Yes, there was a good breeze. Your children they are well?'

'Bhagwan and your prayers be thanked!'

'Raju,' Sukhdeo said in unnecessarily conspiratorial tones, looking right and left for indiscreet ears, 'I was going to Calcutta with Harish, but I have this pain in my back, feel the lump...' he bent forward a bit, and Raju went through the motion of seeking out the focus of the pain and tut tutted dutifully, as an expression of his deep sympathy, after which the older man briefed him.

'And when does Chacha want me to go?' he asked, adding what he knew was unrealistic optimism, in the knowledge of how quickly produce deteriorates, 'tomorrow?'

'Raju, my boy,' Sukhdeo said, moving his head right and left several times, 'you know my principle,' and here his eyes twinkled as they always did when uttering this stale witticism, 'never do today what you could have done the day before yesterday.' A stupid adage, thought Shanti who had heard it many times before but Raju nodded as enthusiastically as if this was his first time, raising his hand up and shaking his head from left to right, closing his eyes instinctively, in a wait-a-second gesture, as if to beg the man to stop overwhelming him with such wisdom and witticism so early in the morning, laughing merrily.

'Ha! Ha! Yes, never do today... eh... ha! ha!' his voice trailing off in a sort of sound tunnel from which only the words "day before yesterday" emerged.

Yes, Sukhdeo thought to himself, Raju is a good intelligent boy, a bit lazy, but intelligent and honest. And respectful deep down!

'It's mainly onions this time, there are fifty sacks. Maybe Shri Bannerjee will give us sixty rupees, but ask for seventy two.' Shanti recognised the look on her husband's face, which seemed to be saying, He'll be lucky if he gets forty, but then he frowned thoughtfully and nodded seriously, to indicate that the instruction had sunk in. I'll leave you now, but I expect you to be at the house before the sun gets to there, and he pointed at a position in the sky a little to the left of the midday.

'I cannot wait for you, as I have business in Sonarkhali and must rush,' he said, adding, 'you've got your own boat, so I won't send Jayant to come back to pick you up.'

When the fat man left, Raju pursed his lips and looked at Shanti glumly.

'That man thinks he owns us,' she said, her throat aching with repressed anger.

'Yes, that he does, my Rani, that he does, and he is probably right, but never mind, we'll reap some benefit from this, you'll see.'

She knew that she had to cook something, for the early part of his trip at any rate. He would exchange some of the stuff he was carrying for something to eat, and if that proved difficult, he could always spend some of his money in those roadside stalls that have recently sprouted, selling food to wayfarers. She also had vegetable and fish pickles, made in advance with his trips in mind. These kept for much longer, as they were preserved in salt, mustard oil and juice of lime and spices and chillies. She had to make sure that he had some clean clothes to change into once he reached Calcutta. She also knew that she would have to plan her tasks properly if the tight deadline that Sukhdeo had set, was to be met. She knew that if he started early enough, he would not have to be on the road at night, with dacoits and cut-throats, tigers and cheetahs on the prowl. He normally stopped in a hamlet outside a mandir before dark, and he said that it was safe as there were devotees there at all hours of the night. They knew very well that a dreaded encounter with a dacoit meant not only all Sukhdeo's money gone, a life-threatening beating, and the certain loss of the tenancy. This was because the zamindar had made an example of one-eyed Basdeo, who was attacked by dacoits, robbed and left for dead. Sukhdeo had immediately dismissed him, justifying this by declaring to one and all that there was never any dacoit, that Basdeo and his cousin had planned everything, faked the beating and stolen the ghee destined for Calcutta. The disconsolate one-eyed man had lost his mind and went to hang himself on the tamarind tree on the other side of the river, now known to everybody as the hanging tree. People had seen and heard his ghost wailing there many a time, protesting his innocence.

It was not that her man was thoughtless, and unwilling to help, although he was a bit, but when she had a rush job to do, she preferred him out of the way.

'As you will be gone for so many days, go play with the babies, but first can you get me some sojne from the drumstick tree near the stream as it gives a nice tang to the palak, doesn't it?'

He playfully grabbed the little ones under the waist, one in each hand, and hopped outside merrily. Raju loved the sojne, but she suspected that it was because it had the reputation of making men more virile — not that he thought that he needed anything of the sort himself — and he was right. It was a week after they were married that he turned up one day with a cutting of the moringa not taller than himself, and with tender and loving care, he had chosen a nice spot for it, not too near the mango tree with its reputation for taking more than its fair share of the nutrients in the soil, and had planted it. She had not been too pleased about this, not because she had anything against drumsticks or their leaves, but everybody knew that ghosts liked no tree better to make a home in, with the possible exception of the tamarind. But she had said nothing, for she knew that he would pooh pooh the notion, because Mr Know-all maintained that ghosts only dared show themselves to the weak-minded.

In the beginning, every morning he would take care of it. If the winds had so much as caused it to lean to one side by a hair's breath, he would tut tut, and push it to its former position, add more earth to the base and stamp on it to tighten it. She used to laugh at his ardour, but at the same time she had thought that if he was the sort of man who worried so much about a paltry sojne data, there was every reason to believe that he would make a wonderful father. Once she did refer to the tree as a paltry thing, and he was very sore about this. I don't know why you despise the Sojne data, so much, he said solemnly, when you have so much in common with the plant.

'?'

'You are both Ranis, my piari, the sojne, a Rani among plants and you a Rani among women.'

Encouraged by her wide-eyed wonderment, he had elaborated. Its trunk and branches may be scraggy, but you tell me what other tree, apart from the coconut palm, has so many uses. First its little green leaves makes the most excellent sag, its drumstick cooked in dal tastes so heavenly… she had not spelled out that he should bring some drumsticks as well, and knowing him, the thought would simply not occur to him… the seeds of the drumstick when roasted and slightly salted is such a treat, to say nothing of what extra powers it gives to a man, not that the pleasure I give you every night depends on it, I'll have you know! We can eat the leaves, the drumstick, its seeds and the flowers. I'll teach you how to fry the flowers like Umma Phoopi used to do, it's so delicious that it doesn't need any haldi or chillies. From the seeds you get cooking oil, that's what ben oil is, did you know that? Once he got started, Raju could go on and on, like a cart without an ox when it begins to slip downhill. And not that you need anything to make you beautiful, piari, he went on, but some women in the big town use ben oil to make their skin beautiful and soft. And the hakeem was telling me that when you deliver the child — for she was pregnant with the girl at that time — nothing can ensure that you produce good quality milk, as the products of that tree you despise. She knew that he knew that she did not despise the sojne data, it was his way of teasing her for being lukewarm towards something that he felt so passionate about.

She would make rice, sag and dal and fry some dried fish. There was also some bhetki vindaloo acchar that she had pickled and stored in a large clay jar with a tight lid. If he came on time with the leaves and brought one or two drumsticks, she would put them in the dal, otherwise she had some dried powdered leaves of the plant which gave extra tang to the soup. She knew how much he appreciated her cooking and hated to disappoint him.

Instinctively she knew the order in which things had to be done, in order to complete the task in the least possible time, which today, was of the essence, but she had a sound head on her shoulders, and was in the habit of thinking things out. Raju often aired his admiration of her prowess, how, for instance, she used leftovers from yesterday to enhance today's sauce, how in rare times of plenty, she could prepare a three or four course meal in under an hour.

She set herself to work straight away. First she lit the wood fire in a furnace under the peepul tree, consisting of two specially chosen boulders of roughly the same size, placed at some distance from the peepul to avoid singeing it, but not too far, in order to benefit from its shade, as she dedicated herself to her chores. She was quite an expert at doing this, and prided herself that even in the strongest of winds, she never used more than one Lucifer. She had only four sticks left in the box, which Raju was given as a present from his Gujarati friend Mahendranath. If she ran out of these magical sticks, she would have to use the flint and lock, which was always more difficult. She fanned it with a pankhah made of dried palm fronds, woven together for that purpose — a legacy of Phoopi, and by occasionally blowing on the recalcitrant flames with a bamboo pookhni.

She viewed a starting fire, much as a toddler who kept stumbling and falling over, it needed dried sticks and fanning and blowing before it got going, just like the toddler who stumbled, needed to be picked up, kissed on the knee to soothe the pain he got as he fell down, told how clever he was, before he finally learnt to walk. She knew exactly how to nurture her fire, when to add more sticks just as surely as she knew how to feed her two kids. It was also important not to smother the flames by putting too much wood on, in the same manner that one did not gorge one's kids with too much food. When the fire was going nicely with healthy red flames shooting out of every piece of wood, it was like a heathy child growing safely into adolescence — best to leave them to fend for themselves. She quickly put water on the boil for the dal as that was the thing which needed the most time. She then put the dried salt-fish in a bowl, stole some warm water for soaking the fish, otherwise on frying they became as hard as wood, and was too salty. She now washed the rice from which she had already removed bits of stones and earth, and let it soak. She was not going to just sit and watch the fire, so she went to wash a shirt and a dhoti for her man. She did this at lightning speed, beating them furiously on a rock next to the basin, to expel the dirt which had become encrusted in them and put them out to dry on the rope stretching between a mango tree and the depleted drumstick tree. There was a good breeze and in the hot sun and they would dry up in no time. She then rushed to pick some palak or spinach growing behind the hut. In a matter of minutes, she had prepared her mixture of garlic, ginger, coriander, turmeric and chillies by crushing them over the special stone slab with line grooves chiselled out, resting on a tamarind stump hit by lightning and meticulously planed by Raju, with the funny cylindrical stone crusher which had gone as smooth as a baby's bottom with use. This paste she would then put in everything she was cooking.

Whilst the dal was gurgling happily on the healthy fire, it was time for the latter to produce its own child. She placed some twigs in the second furnace by the side of the first one, deftly extracted a couple of burning embers from the fire by first spitting on the tips of her fingers, placed them over the twigs, fanned it and blew upon it until these were ignited, and she fed the baby fire with more of the same. She replaced the embers stolen from the first fire with some fresh sticks, smiling as she remembered how Raju fussed over her when she was carrying the babies, stealing good things in order to force-feed her. Then she chopped the onions, washed and cut the greens. The dal was once more chirruping happily on the revived fire, occasionally spitting tiny droplets around. Whilst waiting for the new fire to pick up, she checked that they the eddoes or cocoyam left over from yesterday were still good, peeled them and put them in a catora with some coriander and chilli chutney. By now the new fire was thriving and she put the rice on. She added more wood to the fires and alternated fanning with blowing. The second fire was now able to give birth to its own fire child, which the midwife Shanti delivered into the third stone furnace also by the side of the first one, which was hardly ever used but today was an emergency. A second birth is always easier than the first one, as the mother fire and the grandmother fire were both there to help nourish it. By now the dal is cooked, and all it needed was to have the fried onion mix which she would do later. As she had a free fire, she heated her massive pressing iron, a present from her mother, on it, and ironed his shirt and dhoti as they were not completely dry. She now fried the onions with some jeera in the frying pan which was without a handle, and at the same time Raju came back with the kids laughing their heads off at some joke. He had the sojne all right, but he had not remembered the drumsticks. She was on the point of carrying out the precarious task of adding the fried onions to the dal, and Raju seeing her struggling with that lethal invalid pan with the help of a safi, which was what she called the kitchen rag, rushed towards her, took the rag from her hand, and deftly poured the savoury mix into the dal.

'I promise you that this time I will definitely… perhaps… get you a new frying pan,' he said. He had been promising this to her ever since they married.

The rice was next, and that was a simple task. As a teenager at home, she had watched the naukars cook rice in the traditional manner, which was to get it to boil lustily, drain the water away and then dry the half-cooked rice on a very low fire, a process known as the dam. Phoopi had taught Shanti her method, which was to soak the rice first, bring it to the boil in only a small amount of water and then allow it to cook on a very low fire until all the water was absorbed. The hakeem had told Raju that this was a much better method of cooking rice, as one did not throw any of the rice's natural goodness. By now, the dal was cooked, so that the first fire was available for the sag. While the rice was cooking, all four of them sat round in a circle and each one taking a branch of sojne in their hands, depleted it of its small leaves, collecting them in a large dried calabash. Thus it was, that juggling the three fires like a magician, she completed her cooking tasks in record time.

She then transferred pickles into smaller catoras for the trip. As a rule a pickle can last two weeks without spoiling, and was ideal for the sort of trip that Raju made regularly. There was vegetable acchar, nimbu acchar and bhetki vindaloo acchar.

She now had tears in her eyes, as she knew that the moment was drawing near when her man had to leave. May Bhagwan preserve him from the dangers of the road! She tried not to let him see her tears, but it was difficult to hide things like that from him as he had sharp eyes and was good at reading the signs. She did a p'rnaam, bending down in an attempt at kissing his feet — he always stopped her with fake disapproval — as he was about to cross the threshold into the open. He liked the p'rnaam but only because it showed how much she respected him. Not all wives did the p'rnaam to their husbands. He never stopped repeating that she was everything to him, his sun, his other self, his munn or soul mate, that he had the certainty that in the history of the world, no man had ever loved a woman as much as he loved her. Not even the Shah Jehan could have loved his Mumtaz half as much as it is claimed. If he had that emperor's resources, he would build an even more splendid monument than the Taj Mahal for his Rani. She was not a demonstrative woman, she did not have the words, but she could not imagine a woman loving a man more either. If only he knew!

Whistling with fake bonhomie, he turned away and began walking towards the little pier where he moored the boat, on the way to Sukhdeo's house in Sonarkhali, not turning round even once to have another glimpse of his wife and children, he did not believe in unending farewells. She stifled a tear taking care not to let the children see it, and felt a lump in her throat. There were so many dangers on the road. She was a worrier, but the dangers were real, you heard of so many mishaps and accidents, often fatal.

She was apprehensive when Raju took Pradeep and Sundari to what he called that piece of paradise which fell to earth — the estuary and the mangroves. It was indeed the prettiest place she had set eyes upon. You had two rivers meeting in a passionate and vociferous embrace, like long lost lovers reuniting after a long absence, generating the sort of passion which was theirs when he came back from Calcutta. That's what Raju said anyway. She wiped off the remnants of her tears and smiled as she imagined the homecoming of her man and everything that was to follow. I have become so shameless, she chided herself.

Seated in his little craft which Baba Parsad had made all those years ago, although so many bits had been replaced since that he wondered if there remained a single plank from the original, he felt strangely elated. A Sunderbani had a lot in common with a gharial, he felt as much at home on water as on land. The vegetation on the small islands around was lush and luxuriant, there were blue lotus, moss and ferns, hibiscus, oleander and lantana intertwined like legs of lovers — yes he was a sex fiend, he had nothing else on the mind. There were banyan trees, peepuls, fruit trees, bramble, thorn bush, palmyra, bamboo.

The forest he was going to cross in the oxcart was host to all sorts of creatures, monkeys and mongooses, toads and snakes, cheetahs and tigers. Gharials lurked in the waters, sometimes they ventured on land. On the trees you had all the birds imaginable. He had surprised his wife of a week when he had told her that the kak or common crow was his favourite bird. She had been surprised when he claimed that he found its thick velvety black feathers prettier than those of the rainbow coloured humming birds.

As a child, he was staying with a family friend when Baba and Phoopi had gone to a funeral in Sonarkhali. Moti, the little boy who was the same age as himself, had hit a kak dead with a stone, and had left it under a coconut tree at some distance from their hut. Shortly after this, a flock of kaks had descended upon the place, surrounded their dead companion, hopping madly, wailing and cawing their accusations threateningly, and would not go away. They gradually moved nearer and nearer to the hut where he and Moti were, to all intents and purposes, besieging it, cawing with increased vehemence, until the two little boys were terrified out of their wits, unable to figure out why they were making such a racket, and convinced that if they ventured outside, the irate birds would tear their eyes out. Moti's father had attempted to shoo away those impudent and fearless creatures without any success. If only humans cared for each other half as much, Moti's father had said with a sigh. He understood their concern, sorrow and anger, and it was from that moment that his admiration for them had sprouted. They were still there in the morning and it was late on the next afternoon that the last one flew away.

It takes a good man to find a kak beautiful, Shanti had told herself when he had related the episode to her. That was when she knew that she loved him.

His love for the kokil, the cuckoo, was more understandable. It had a beautiful melodious voice — the male actually, the female made a raucous and unpleasant sound. He loved them all, the ghugha, chais, shaliks, nilkhonthos. He knew about birds. How proud he was when he overheard Shanti telling the little ones the story of how, when their father was a kid, he used to trap nilkhontos for the rich villagers in order to make a few pise, because, for Durga Puja, it was considered propitious to release one as a messenger to Heaven. He would never, not for a whole anna, have trapped and caught any bird, if he thought people were going to keep it in a cage, for even if you see them hopping about in their beautiful cages, a trapped bird's soul is already dead. This he believed with all the fibres in his body, birds are made for trees and the sky, not cages.

The mangrove was also host to the spectacular and most colourful parrots, green feathers with red beaks. They flock together for protection against snakes, monkeys, rodents, and above all Man…

Whatever he told Shanti, he was well aware that this corner of Paradise was also full of danger. Everybody said that nowhere in the land were the tigers more cruel. It was said that because the water they drank was salty, it made them mean and bad-tempered. There were so many stories of poor fishermen trying to eke out a living on the waters, being pounced upon, mauled and killed by Dakshin Rai, but he still believed that what happened to Baba notwithstanding, tigers are not wanton killers — not that he planned to take any risk. To pacify Shanti he told her those fantastic stories. No tiger can ever harm me or anybody who is with me, he had told her. Surprised, she had asked why. In a previous life, I was a tiger. She tut tutted, beginning to understand his jokes and fantasies, they were harmless and they amused her, but he tried to look serious. How do you know you were a tiger once? She had asked. He had pretended to be taken aback by the question, as if someone was questioning how he knew that the sun would rise on the next morning. I just know, you tell me why would I not have been a tiger? She was not used to his arguing style. But mean, he was not and hated putting her down. I'll tell you how I know, he explained, sometimes I dream of my past lives, I often dream of a tiger, always the same. That doesn't mean that you were a tiger, just because you dreamt of one, she had countered. No, Rani, in my dream I know the tiger is me, I can feel it.

Later, when talking about cobras and snakes, he would say that he was not afraid of snakes because in a previous life he used to be a cobra. Shanti laughed and shook her head. So you don't believe me? No, she had said, I don't, you said you used to be a tiger, now you say you used to be a cobra. Arrey, Rani, you don't just have one previous life, in one I was a tiger, in another I was a cobra, why is that so surprising? I think in another previous life, you must have been an ulloo, an owl, she said with a laugh. He was taken aback, just a bit offended at being called owl, but pleased that she was beginning to show signs of learning how to defend herself. Yes, a pushover, his Rani was not.

He knew that all those things he told her did little to stop her fretting and worrying about him, imagining all sorts of disasters, for when he came back from his trip, it always shocked him to find her looking so haggard and careworn.

It was shortly after midday, and the sun was at its hottest when he had finally finished loading the onions on the cart, and started on the trip. Dukhdeo and Lalita had given him such a long list of dos and donts that his head was fairly spinning. Ask for a high price and when the client demurs you can bring it down, but a little at a time. How clever of them! I was planning to offer a low price and haggle upwards. But he beamed at the pair as if they had just revealed to him the secret of turning earth into gold. When you buy goods for us, shop around, make sure they don't overcharge you, always tell them they are asking too much, pretend you're walking away, they will call you back, people are so dishonest. Take your time, my first law of business… he was not listening. Your first law of business is to give little and ask for much, you leech! At the same time Lalita was saying the opposite, come back quickly, there is plenty of work to be done here, but take care of the Roshni. How can I take care of the ghai? I will make sure I feed her and give her plenty of water, but I can't sing a lullaby to her and massage her tired legs like my Shanti does to me. He nodded his assent to everything being said, beaming heartily but feeling like a half-wit. She is an old and tired animal, they are saying, then why aren't they giving him a younger one?

After all those sermons, he was finally seated in his ghari, and even the heat of the midday sun was a relief. In any case the mangrove was shaded and the trees will provide some welcome breeze, he thought. He had not started speaking to himself yet, there might be some villagers around, and they would everybody that he talked to himself like a pagla. Usually when he went on a long trip like this one, after a while, he felt free to voice his thoughts, gesticulate with his hands, shrug, smile or even laugh aloud, have imaginary conversations with Shanti. My Rani, I know you are too good for me… You should have married a rich man who would cover you in jewels — at least buy you a proper frying pan, and feed you sweetmeats dripping with honey and ghee… Such class, such poise… That woman is a real peri!

'But it's been my aim,' he heard himself say aloud, in answer to a question which flashed across his brain in no time at all, 'to buy her some nice silver bangles some day…' He laughed, admitting to himself that he would never in a million years find the money for that, 'You need your head examined my friend, you are a bit pagla.' Must definitely buy her that frying pan with a nice handle, I'll never forgive myself if she burns herself one day.

He paid little attention to the intense heat and the sun above, in the knowledge that in only a short while, he would be once more in the mangrove area, with its fresh vegetation and its shade. Also the sight of the birds and monkeys always filled him with joy. He loved all animals, but monkeys above all else. Here in this mangrove you only had langurs, but they happened to be his favourite among all apes. Isn't it funny how I classify things, the kak my favourite bird, langur the monkey I like best, the jack my favourite fruit, fried onions the smell I like best after my Shanti's slightly sweaty smoky smell.

The moment he was in the mangrove, he began to sing a song he made up as he went along. It was a song about how good it was to live, to love and be loved, how beautiful everything was, and as there was no one about. He felt free to sing loudly and lustily, to himself, to the cow, even jumping in and out of the cart every now and then, dancing and prancing around the trusty old cow, stroking her face, leaving her to negotiate the narrow rocky path with its protruding roots, on her own. He skipped and hopped merrily, hugging trees, winking at the langurs, making flying signs with his outstretched arms as he saw some crows. They will say I am childish if they saw me prancing about.

He breathed more freely, he always liked the smell of decaying vegetation that was a feature of mangroves. It was much fresher now, and there was a very welcome breeze, and for a good stretch now, he would be sheltered from the punishing sun. In any case the sun would be setting once he left the tip of the mangrove that was his chosen route. He sometimes came here with Rani and the kids. Yes, he was a very fortunate man to have such a family. Of course life was a struggle, you had to work until you could hardly remain on your legs — Phoopi had a grand expression, you work until you cannot tell which is your right hand, which your left. Was he not twice blessed to have had such a wonderful woman taking care of him? Had he been a prince nobody would have done more for him. Of course he was poor, had no possessions. He needed nothing himself, he had his wooden karpa in his feet, his dhoti, his turban and his kurta, and wished for nothing more, but he regretted not being able to buy pretty things for Rani and Pradeep and the lovely little princess. She was going to be as pretty as her mother some day. Will she find someone to love her like I do her mother? But the important thing was that they were never went hungry. There was always rice, dal, and atta in the house, and Shanti grew some vegetables. There was karela, although he didn't like it too much because of its bitter taste, but cooked with ripe tomatoes, plenty of green chillies and an egg, it was tasty enough. Bhindi grew well even when there was little water, beans often wilted before producing anything, there was dudhi, pumpkin, baygun, palak, and of course sojne — what would the poor do without that prince of shrubs? How stupid of him to have forgotten the drumstick today.

The hens did not lay as much as he would have wished — the small ones needed meat and eggs in order to grow big and strong, but where was the money to buy goat meat? Always eggs, and they make you fart. The fish seemed to be boycotting the river these days — when he was a child they used to jump to the hook before it hit the water! But the hakeem said dal was good for growing children. Shanti said it made him produce bad smells. It's funny, but it did not seem to have the same effect on her. He could not re-member her ever farting, although he supposed she did. When he was lucky he caught one or two fish, but in the mangrove he always found crabs, some-times shrimps. The little money that he made enabled him to buy coconut oil from Basdeo's widow — that woman was so admirable, since her man's death, she does everything herself, including climbing coconut palms and pressing for oil, the family seemed better off than when the poor man was alive. When you have tomatoes, dhanya and jeera, you could always produce a tasty dish. The thought of food began to make his mouth water, although he had eaten a big meal just before starting out. He rummaged though his jute bag and found a catora in which she had some boiled cocoyam for him, she had even peeled them, she was a pearl. The sauce was absolutely out of this world, crushed into the finest paste. What would people do without their crushing stone? He smelled the chutney, and detected, coriander, to-matoes, garlic, coconut and tamarind. That woman could have cooked for the Emperor Akbar himself.

Thinking about her, combined with the rocking of the cart, as he knew from experience that it would, produced its effect in his dhoti. Bhagwan knew he tried to live a righteous life and strove to keep impure thoughts at bay, but he could not help it. When all was said and done, he was a weak man, and there was nothing he could do, he did not invite these lusty images into his head, they just came in uninvited, like a burglar who finds a door open. At almost any time of the day, he felt a presence in his dhoti, like an uninvited but welcome guest, and he had to recite a special mantra his friend Ranjit, who dreamt of becoming a holy man, had taught him in order to get back on track, but sadly it didn't always work. Sadly? he wondered.

Sometimes, he was ashamed to admit, the craving was such that the mo-ment he arrived home after a day in the fields, if the kids were out of sight, playing somewhere, he would grab Shanti by the arms, she laughing and struggling, making a pretence at protesting, he would throw her on the floor and they would be at it. He knew that she liked it as much as he did;, and for all he knew, whilst cooking or washing, she too might well have been visited by these impure thoughts, but she was very shy and would never talk openly about things like that. The hakeem had explained to him once that women had the same needs and desires as men. He had been surprised, but after a few years with Shanti, and having studied her reactions, he convinced himself that the Musselman was right. Come to think of it, why were the thoughts impure? He felt a little discomfort in his chest as he realised that it would be another eight to ten days before he would see his beloved wife, hold her two mangoes in his hands, lie with her, put his hands between her legs, caress her roundness and enjoy her body. He would try to make it eight, but Roshni was no longer as young as she used to be. We'll see, he said aloud.

Dukhdeo had said he should get fifty rupees for the onions, he always expected to get more for less and pay less for more, which was how he made his money. I am a fortunate man of course, Bhagwan, but a little more money is all I ask for, I don't ask for hundreds of rupees, just one or two extra now and then. I must not forget that frying pan before my Shanti burns herself. No, I have no qualms about pocketing a small percentage of Dukhdeo's takings, the man is a glutton, why does he need all that money? Surely Bhagwan cannot consider what I do sinful, it would be a sin if I did it for myself, but perhaps a greater one if I didn't, for then I would be making my children suffer and go hungry. The poor mites were almost always hungry, dal and atta are not enough for growing children. The hut was too small, a real chicken coop, but it was all he wished for, although he knew Shanti who was used to living in a bigger house with a veranda and windows would have preferred a bigger one — not that she had ever said anything.

But I am a rich man, he thought. My loved ones are my treasures, we have so many good things, we are healthy, we are never ill, we sleep well, we play, we laugh a lot and have no enemies. Suppose some God came to me and said, Raju, you can trade places with Dukhdeo, have everything he possesses (but not his wife,) but for that you must lose an arm. Arrey Bhagwan, I'd say, to become Dukhdeo even with both my arms, is a calamity. No, no, Bhagwan would say, you get me wrong, you can have the man's riches but you do not have to become the man, you can be yourself and keep your family, but you must lose an arm. Never! Who can judge the value of an arm? No earthly possession can make up for a good healthy arm. That's a man's real wealth, the things he already has. Take the eyes. Can the Nizam of Hyderabad, if one day he became blind, with all the diamonds in Golconda, order the learned men and sages at his court to make him a pair of eyes so he can see the beautiful things he owns, his palace, his jewellery, his fine silks and his fine women? If I was the Nizam, I'd give my whole fortune for a pair of eyes if I went blind! And I would need another fortune to make me hear the song of the koel, the rustle of wind through the leaves, the sound of thunder, the laughter of my children at play, or my Shanti greeting me in her peculiar manner as I come in with a So you're finally home, eh, come sit here, I'll make you tea. Or the sound of her groaning quietly with pleasure as we do it. How many diamonds are worth the ability to taste the good things my Shanti can cook? Would all the diamonds of the Nizam be able to buy me my taste buds if I were to lose them? The human body is so full of wonder. Look at the things a man can do with his fingers, can even those clever Angrezi invent a machine that can do all that? My nose, even if I curse it when I catch a cold… what riches would I trade my ungainly flattened nose for? The nose that permits me to smell my children, my Shanti's cooking, raat ki rani after sunset. The list of the things man has inherited at birth is endless. How can any normal human being can say he is poor?

CHAPTER 13

❖❖❖

Strathnaver

THE FAMILY, LIVING as Smiths, had done well in Fort Williams. Martha and Mam had never lived so comfortably, for Angus — as Hugh was now called — earned reasonable money on a regular basis, doing a variety of jobs on the Caledonian Canal site. Thomas Telford had designed it and was now building it, but the hard slog, under far from pleasant weather conditions, was the work of people like Hugh. The work was tiring, but he and his fellow Highlanders were not afraid of hard work.

Many, like him, had been dispossessed crofters, but they knew him by his new name, and no one suspected that the mild-mannered Angus might have been the legendary figure that he had become. It was quite funny listening to people telling him how he had (a) jumped into the raging sea from the ship taking him to Botany Bay, and was living as a white Rajah in India (Hugh never learnt how to swim!), or (b) had organised a mutiny on the ship, taken it over, and was now leading a prosperous life on some South Sea Island or (c) had gone to France after a daring escape from a port where his ship had stopped, and was being trained to come back to England to organise a French style revolution which would put the masses in power, and tragically (d) had been tricked by the Duchess of Sutherland, lured to some dark corner by her hired assassins, and there garrotted, his body thrown in the sea.

John was born in Fort Williams, and however tired Hugh was after a gruelling day digging, hearing his little boy's ringing laughter completely reinvigorated him. Martha was delighted that after the initial disappointment of not having a son, he had taken Kitty to his heart, and she could not imagine him loving a boy more.

Still Hugh had always felt like a cuckoo in the nest working on the Canal. He was a farmer, he understood cattle and oats, and he missed the land.

Martha and Mam, accomplished mistresses of husbandry, were able to put aside a not inconsiderable sum of money in five years, and when they decided to move back north, Hugh was satisfied that after the years the authorities had forgotten about him. Thus it was that the family arrived in Strathnaver, again, to live the life of crofters on land belonging to the Duchess of Sutherland.

Soon after settling in his new croft, he was able to purchase six Black cattle, and his oats and potatoes were doing well. Angus Smith quickly earned himself the reputation of an honest hard-working no-nonsense if dour Highlander. The children, John and Catriona were growing up nicely. They had shoes and socks, and were warm at night, they were well fed, went to school and were healthy and lively. Sometimes too lively. Mam was frail and weak, but her mind was as sharp as ever, her hair had gone completely white, but her piercing blue eyes had lost none of their shine, and still commanded respect. Hugh remembered how as a child, she didn't have to open her mouth to convey her disapproval of something he had done. A flick of an eyelid, the shadow of a frown followed by a piercing look was all it took. Although he had always loved her with a longing that often brought a lump to his throat, although he had always known that she would gladly put herself in the trajectory of any lethal blow to stop harm coming to him, he had always been in awe of her, he had lived in the fear of her disapproval. Not that she raised her voice to him or ever spoke sharply to anybody. It had to be those eyes. Now, years later, he realised that he had wrongly read the disapproval he thought he saw there. It was a natural flaw which gave out the wrong signals. As an adult he would encounter people with laughing eyes who had no joy in them, people who looked as if they were on the point of bursting into tears, but who had joyful souls. What was clear was that John and Catriona were not in the least overawed by those piercing eyes. There must be people who are not meant to be mothers, but grandmothers.

John was a sweet enough wean, but he was a moaner. To the chagrin of Martha, ten minutes after a copious meal that he had often claimed he could not finish, he would be complaining of hunger. There was never any shortage of food, but Martha had a Highlander's loathing of waste. There had been lean times, but she made sure the two children had an almost full stomach, even at the expense of sometimes going hungry herself, pretending that she had partaken of a big plate of leftover oat porridge whilst weaving.

Although no one went hungry, the fare was pretty monotonous, border-ing on the unappetising, almost always oat, turnip, a little potato now and then, sometimes a cabbage, and very rarely meat or fish. They only had meat if some poacher brought them a joint which the family paid for with some turnips or oats. Salmon was becoming as rare as warm days in December. Time was when Hugh would spend an hour or two at some loch and come back with a trout or some perches, sometimes a salmon, but as tension be-tween the Duchess and the crofters grew, she hired more wardens to put an end to what she called indiscipline and lawlessness. Still it was as difficult to stop the Highlander bent on doing some honest poaching as it was to stop smoke coming out of a fire. The Highland poacher was a resourceful and tenacious operator, and without him, the likes of the Smith family would forget what meat or fish tasted like.

As Mam grew older, her appetite grew smaller. She often said that old folks needed just a few mouthfuls of food as they were not going to grow any bigger, and that the lighter one was, the better it was for the heart anyway. Have you ever seen a fat old woman, she would ask? Fat people die young.

In a selfless attempt at making sure the kids were not deprived, Hugh would always deviate a part of his share to Kitty's and John's plates. Kitty would usually stop him, but John never protested, even if he knew that he would struggle with what was on his plate.

Hugh and Martha, as well as Mam, had often hoped that John would outgrow what they called his sour nature. He seemed selfish and had a re-sentful nature, was mean to his older sister. Martha called it thoughtlessness. He never missed an opportunity for pointing out that Kitty had had a bigger share of oatcake or whatever. Once when they were both quite small, when told that there was a piece of oatcake for him and one for Kitty, he said, can I have Kitty's? When rebuked over anything, he usually sulked and said that when Kitty did the same thing, they let her get away with it. Hugh tried a reasoned dressing down whilst Martha tried tenderness and reasoning, nei-ther worked.

One night Mam surprised everybody by telling the young pair that if they stopped fighting, she would tell them a story. Hugh did not remember her telling him and Morag, now dead, stories, when they were bairns. After she told her first story, Hugh asked her how come she knew stories now, and she seemed completely stumped, scratched her head thoughtfully, and admitted that she did not know how. She just decided on the spur of the moment to make one up, and then the story took over and narrated itself, so to say.

It was a cold rainy night, and after the evening meal, they were all seated in the big room, as they called it, a small fire burning, providing a little warmth and a glimmer of light. Martha was weaving in one corner, and Hugh smoking his pipe was deep in thought about some scheme for improving yield, and Mam surprised everybody.

The storytelling soon became a family tradition. Although Mam aimed her stories at the children, Hugh and Martha sitting at the far corner of the room supposedly doing their own things, like weaving or smoking a pipe, paid attention to every word. All the stories featured two cousins who were recognisably modelled on John and Kitty. In the first story, Ekko the John character was a selfish and thoughtless meanie and Trina (Kitty) was all sweetness and light, but in the next story it was the other way round. Next day, it was Trina who was the wicked one, and Ekko was a noble and heroic figure. Mam who obviously knew Kitty inside out, was not blind to her faults, and made Trina a proper little minx, resentful and self-regarding. There was little doubt that the protagonists recognised themselves in Mam's tales.

Hugh had often wished that he knew how to help the boy. He sometimes reacted angrily when the lad whined and whinged, but he managed to stop short of hitting him, although he had been often tempted. He had slapped him once when he was four, it had not been a hard slap but the four red marks left on the poor boy's face had shocked him, and he had vowed that never again would he hit his boy. Da used to beat him regularly, hitting him with a yew stick on his bottom, and paid no attention to Mam's objections, until one day she said to him, Kenny, if your words cannot enter into the boy's head, it is unlikely that wisdom would enter his head through his arse! Da had been surprised, had looked at Mam angrily, then shook his head, smiled as the meaning of the words sank in, and nodded. He never hit him again. John was born with these negative characteristics and no amount of talking to helped. Did it mean that later in life he would be left behind, a victim of his own shortcomings?

Hugh recognised that Mam's stories were obviously conceived with great care. When Ekko was good, Mam was showing him what a worthy person he can be, how "being good" made one happier, and when Trina was reprehensible, it was like a warning — watch it young missie, or you might be turning into her.

It did not take him long to realise that her aim was to teach the boy a few qualities she thought he was sadly devoid of. Martha agreed with him, adding that she thought John had inherited many of the traits of her brother Jamie who nevertheless grew up into a kind and thoughtful man, but he had died of gangrene when his broken leg had not mended properly and had festered. Hugh thought highly of his wife, knew that she was a thoughtful woman with a lot of common sense.

Thus it was that every night before the kids went to sleep, Mam would make up a story with the two cousins living in that land which was even further north than the North Pole. Some of the stories Mam told were simplistic, but on some days she was truly uninspired, and even the kids responded by an early yawn. She claimed that the story had not been as good as she had intended because the kids were obviously tired, as demonstrated by their yawn. She needed to know that her tale was being treated with the respect it deserved, otherwise it just withered away. Wonder what came first, Hugh remarked to Martha, the yawn or the faltering of the tale.

The two siblings grew up, fighting as usual, but anyone could see that they fought out of habit. Imperceptibly they had grown closer, and when the animosity with which they fought was boiled away, the residual was usually good-natured childish banter. The moment one was in trouble, with parent or peer, the one would jump to the other's defence. Martha said, rather optimistically that John had shed many of the negative sides of his character, and she, for one, would not have wished for a more decent young man as a son.

No power on earth would shake Hugh's conviction that if the boy had turned into an upright young man, it was entirely down to Mam's subtle indoctrination, and Martha said she agreed with him.

At fifteen, John had grown into a handsome and well proportioned man, responsible and hard-working like his father, as good with cows and oats as he was with carpentry or repairing and making ploughs and rudimentary machines. He was not a brilliant student as Kitty, but he was well able to read and write. Hugh had always told him that he should aim for something better than the life of a crofter. At one point, having talked to his mates, he had started thinking of the 93rd as an obvious home for his brawn, but he hated the Duchess for what he called her avariciousness and her treatment of her tenants and would never dream of being part of her regiment. For one thing, Grand Mam had never made it a secret to anybody that she thought that if there were no soldiers, there would be no wars and people would not be killing each other leaving a trail of misery and desolation. She often said that even the enemy soldier had a mother who would be heartbroken when she heard that her son had died fighting for his king. Why don't the kings fight each other, if they loved fighting, she asked. Hugh and Martha were not keen on losing their only son on some foreign battlefield either.

When one day he came home and started talking about the Earl of Selkirk and his plans to ship Highlanders to the Carolinas and Canada, the family, with the exception of Mam became greatly alarmed. Hugh spoke to him about the Caledonian Canal which was still not completed. He had often thought that if he had stuck with that a bit longer, he might have gotten used to it. Everybody was greatly relieved and pleased when the lad finally made up his mind and went to Fort Williams.

CHAPTER 14

◆◆◆

Calcutta

THE ROAD FROM Sonarkhali across the Pargannas to Calcutta could be fraught with all sorts of danger, none of the oft-repeated assurances to the contrary that Raju gave Shanti in an attempt at stopping her fretting could hide that. He knew that she did not believe the stories that he told her about being immune to Dakshin Rai's claws. A joke never did anyone any harm, but still he had the instinctive certainty that Bhagwan would never let him go the same way as Baba. He had never heard of two members of the same family become victims of the man-eater, although he knew of a banyan tree in the Parganas which had been struck twice by lightning, whatever people said. Still every time he was on his way to Calcutta, he dreaded coming face to face with dacoits. It seemed a miracle that so far he had managed to avoid them. The closest shave was about a year ago. It was a pitch black with no moon, and he had just gone past Habra when a strong gust blew out his lamp. He was about to swear when he heard a noise and at the same time saw a light. Dakus, he had said to himself, and I don't even have a light to guide me to safety. Then he realised that Devi Phoopi must have been watching over him, for if his light was shining, the dakus would have surely spotted him. He took evasive action and held his breath, praying that the cow would not suddenly decide to moo. Bhagwan be blessed, the ghai stayed silent as a fish. Naturally! It was the proof, if proof was needed that he was under Phoopi's protection. Then he began to hear the dakus speak. In Bihari Bhojpuri of course. He had heard that the highwaymen were often the folks from the land of his ancestors.

'I told you I saw nothing, madr chhott, you must have imagined it all.'

'Shut your arsehole, shit-eater, I saw an oxcart in the dim light of an oil lamp, I tell you.'

'Must have been a ghost,' a third voice chipped in.

'You really should lay off the ganja madr chott motherfucker.'

'Bengt chhott, madr chhott!' someone spat out for no obvious reason, and another man sneezed.

Raju's heart was beating in his calves as he realised that he was no match for three or four colossal Biharis. The voices grew louder as the men drew nearer, and he said to himself, Provided I don't suddenly feel the need to sneeze too. And as usual, having formulated that hope, he was immediately seized by an irresistible urge to do just that. Phoopi Devi, he begged silently, please control my sneeze. She was probably not able to, but saw to it that a gust of wind suddenly began blowing, and he was able to sneeze in its wake. The men were now almost close enough to touch, and they kept arguing and swearing. Suddenly they had slowed down, as if sensing that their quarry was at hand, and kept moving in a circle.

'Do you think he is some merchant laden with goods?'

'What an idiotic question? You are speaking through your mother's chhott.'

'Why don't you bengt chhott sisterfuckers stop arguing and use your energy trying to locate the madr chhott instead?'

At that point the cow began to feel restless as if its legs were full of ants.

'What was that… did you hear that?'

'Some rat or snake,' one of the three answered casually.

'I hate rats! I don't mind snakes, but madr chhott rats… ya Bhagwan, how I hate them. Let's not stay here.'

'I can feel the presence of the madr chhott right here,' an authoritative voice pronounced.

'Stay if you want to be eaten alive by rats, I am leaving.' And the men, defeated by the dark finally put some distance between themselves and Raju. He breathed a sigh of relief, and the cow made a tentative moo at the same time. The three men stopped in their tracks. 'What was that? Did you hear it?' Two voices answered, 'Rats!'

That was a year ago. Phoopi Devi was clearly watching over him. He felt confident that she would never let him down. He was halfway between Hasnabad and Bashirhat when the aroma of Shanti's cooking in the morning wafted into his nostrils, as smells sometimes do, from nowhere. It was funny about the memory of scents and odours. Years after having smelled something — not necessarily nice — and not thinking about it either, a smell can suddenly invade your nostrils. The seductive aroma of Nani Laddoo's fine sweetmeats can magically spring forth twenty years after the event, just as if she had just landed from her small boat with a thali of her sweetmeats finely balanced on her head. As unfortunately could also the stench of dead carcasses on an island when they went honey gathering. But Shanti's culinary masterpieces were a daily occurrence, and the smell did not take him by surprise, specially as he had been working an appetite. He had told himself that he would stop for a bite, but not yet, but once the aroma was there, there was nothing he could do. It was like the thought of Shanti's body opening the floodgates of impure thoughts which invariably resulted in the little dog behind his dhoti starting to wag its tail.

He stopped the ghari in a small clearing under a massive tamarind tree by a stream, got off and stroked the cow on the head. He fetched some water in a rusty pail for her, and she drank, but with no great relish. She cannot be well, poor thing, he reflected. Although there was lush vegetation for her to indulge in, she made no effort to bend down and serve herself. Come, on, Mr Cow, Ghaiji, he said, it's for your own good, you need some strength, we have a few more days of this before we're done. He pulled out a few strands of grass and remembering how he used to coax the little ones to eat, he made some funny sounds with his mouth and managed to attract the attention of the tired animal, and she finally condescended to open her mouth to take in a small tuft which she started chewing with a singular lack of enthusiasm. You'll eat when you are hungry, he shrugged, and left her alone. He lit a small wood fire and warmed his dal, he hated cold dal, it did not matter about rice or tarcari. When the dal began boiling, he tipped some rice in it, smacking his lips as he discovered the fried saltfish that Shanti had obviously not failed to pack in; she had fried the fish exactly right, adding the right amount of salt, haldi and crushed chillies. He had filled his lota with cool water from the stream, and leaning against the tamarind tree, took a deep breath, was about to convey the first handful of food into his mouth when he saw three figures emerge. Ghosts in broad daylight! But he knew they were no ghosts, for spirits from the netherworld had their feet turned the other way round, did not touch the ground, but floated just above it. Dakus, he deduced. He knew that they had seen him. Each one had a thick club in one hand, and Raju had no doubt that they also had knives hidden on their bodies. They were walking towards him unhurriedly, in the certainty that there was now no chance of his escaping. He stood up and in his most friendly voice, he shouted in Bhojpuri, 'I was just about to start eating my meal on my own... Aren't I lucky to be able to share it with three Biharis brothers?' The men seemed taken aback by this overture and slowed down momentarily. They were now hovering over him but the menace was more subdued.

'Do wash your hands and we can begin, you must be starving, I know I am,' he said with fake bonhomie, having decided that volubility would be the best weapon against those sinister pahelwans. By now, the men seemed to have inhaled the fumes coming out of the offering, and he went on, 'there is more than enough for all of us. And your bhabi also packed in some bhetki vindaloo acchar... you have to taste it to believe how good it is... your sister-in-law Shanti thinks of everything... Raju, she says, I am putting in some bhetki acchar in case you have the good fortune of meeting some wayfarers on the road... she is like that... thinks of everything... do sit down. It does not matter about washing your hands, I am sure they are clean...' The men said nothing, but looked at each other dubiously.

'How come you speak Bhojpuri?' one of the men asked, 'are you Bihari?'

'You sisterfucker, didn't you hear what the motherfucker said?' They were clearly the same men from last year. Raju laughed immeasurably at this.

'I hate those fucking Bengalis,' one man said, spitting on the ground. Raju smiled, and made a disparaging grimace, which he knew was expected of him, on hearing the word Bengali.

'My father was from Gaya,' he said, and suddenly he decided to lie about the rest, 'I was born there... Allapur... Bihari to the core, that's me...' Unsure as to how that had gone down, he immediately added, 'But here I am nattering on whilst my brothers are starving, I entreat you.' And without a smile or thank you, they plonked themselves down, served themselves and began to eat, noisily and quickly, obviously with great enjoyment. Raju was happy to see them enjoying Shanti's cooking, even if he knew that he might have difficulty feeding himself later.

'You gentlemen are... eh... travellers?' Raju said tentatively.

'Listen sisterfucker, you know very well who we are, so cut the crap, we are dakus, and we plan to kill you.' Raju was surprised by his own reaction. He shook his head and burst out laughing, as if the men had told him the funniest story he had ever heard.

'But you can't do that, brothers, you must not, not after having agreed to accept my nimak.'

'Nimak?'

'In civilised places like our beloved Bihar, when you accept food from someone, you have eaten his nimak… eh… the salt in the food, if you see what I mean.'

'So?'

'Men of Bihar are not Nimak haram like those ungrateful sisterfucking Bengalis here my friends. If you had wanted to kill me and rob me, you should have done it first thing, then if you eat my salt… because once I am dead, I own nothing, the nimak isn't mine. But as you have eaten my food, your soul will be damned for eternity if you do me any harm.' One man shook his head, refusing to believe this nonsense, but the one who was obviously the leader was lost in thought. The first man was twiddling his club in his itchy hand, clearly in readiness for an assault.

'Am I not right, Sarkar?' Raju asked the chief, 'once you have eaten a man's nimak, you can't _'

'You Choottias should have thought first,' the chief said to his two companions, 'but ben chhott sisterfuckers, you can only think of your stomach… The man is right.'

Raju then offered them some bidis and they relaxed, sat down like old friends, passing the smoke round after inhaling it with great intensity. And when one of the men asked him a couple of questions, he started telling them the story of his life on the Sunderbans, the tigers, the honey and the men listened enthralled. The battle is won, Raju said to himself, truly when an aunt becomes a Devi and looks after you, what harm can befall you? But the chief thought he had a final arrow in his quiver.

'My friend,' he said suddenly, 'if we steal from you and beat you up, I understand that it would be all wrong, as you say, we Biharis are not nimak haram.' Raju nodded uneasily.

'But supposing… just supposing, you understand… supposing you were to give us your merchandise—'

'But why would I do that? We are friends, we have shared a meal together—'

'Yes, yes, I know that, but we are bad people, we might forget the rules of hospitality and attack you all the same—'

'I know that you won't,' said Raju, making a superhuman effort at laughing at the notion, 'we are Bihari brothers—'

'Exactly,' said the chief, 'we are Bihari brothers, and you won't let us starve, will you? You see we make an honest living as Dakus, we do not go about beating women and children, we hurt nobody but our victims — it's the only thing we can do — and if we do not have anything to show for a night's work, then we starve, my Bundhu! So I suggest you give us some of your wares of your own volition.' Raju laughed, again with fake merriment, and did a lightning quick mental calculation at the same time.

'But you didn't think I was going to let you go away empty-handed? I was already thinking that I could explain to my Sarkar, that I had an accident on the road and lost a big bag of onions…' The Chief stared at him with his piercing eyes.

'And… and a b-bag of dried fish…' he stammered. The Chief did not indicate ecstasy, on hearing this.

'And a large demijohn of coconut oil.' The Chief stared at Raju and suddenly burst out laughing.

'And all given under no duress?' asked the Chief.

'No duress at all, I am the one making the offer. No convention broken.'

'Throw in an extra bag of aloo, eh?' Raju nodded.

The Dakus took possession of the agreed articles, and left singing bawdy songs. He waved them goodbye heartily, but the moment they were out of sight, he collapsed on the ground and cried. Dukhdeo is going to have the skin off my arse now, he is never going to believe me, he'll say I am dishonest, he'll say that I have sold those things and pocketed the money, he'll never trust me ever again. Without his trust how am I going to steal from him? We'll won't survive, my wife and kids.

Wearily and with a heavy heart he set forth for Barasat. Where was Devi? he wondered, but his loyalty to the dead aunt was such that he immediately answered himself: Were she not around, I would never have got the idea about how to trick those... madr chott... He aimed at stopping outside the Mandir there, where on any given night there were pilgrims and worshippers, thus making it less obvious as a target for dacoits.

Nothing much of interest happened on the rest of the journey. He made an effort not to let the recent encounter with dakus depress him overmuch. He knew that there was always a way out. Over the years he had played his cards well and had earned the trust of Sukhdeo. Provided that ogress Lalita did not put bees in his ears.

When he reached Howrah, he saw the various people he had dealings with. It was always a lengthy process negotiating with the wholesalers, but he rather enjoyed the banter and the bravado.

'So what happened to your onions this time?' asked Mr Bannerjee, taking a few bulbs in his hands and rolling them over playfully, 'did you put feathers in them? They are so flimsy.'

'Shri Bannerjee, what are you saying, sir? We do not put feathers, but small stones to make them heavier so we can charge more, how come you cannot feel them?' The man laughed, and extended his open palm for Raju to clap. He liked the boy, he was a cheerful young rascal. They argued for a bit, and Bannerjee sent for some chai which they drank noisily. They agreed on a price for the 12 bags, and Raju carefully put away the sixty six rupees the older man gave him. Maybe I'll tell Sukhdeo that the onions fetched sixty five rupees for the 13 bags, five rupees per bag, and then I can still pocket the extra rupee. Would the boss swallow that? The man had his ears close to the ground and was usually well-informed. There's plenty of time to think of some foolproof scheme. Maybe in the light of what happened I'll have to forego my little bonuses this time.

When he arrived at the Gujarati man's stall, the round-faced jovial looking man spat a massive blob of betel mush on the ground, saying sorry as some droplets landed on Raju's dhoti.

'Namasté, Chacha Mahendra, Saroo Chhey,?' Raju said using the few Gujarati words he knew.

'Saroo Chhey, Maroo Chhey, poyka.' the old man laughed happily, he loved being greeted in his own language. He also liked Raju, having known him ever since he was a teenager.

'We were told there is a great shortage of coconut oil in town,' said Raju who had heard nothing of the sort, 'so I thought I would take my stock to Chacha Mahendranath first.' The old man did not believe him for one second, but nodded happily, and gave him his open palm to clap. So I was right. I'm gonna get a good price for the oil and would be able to absorb the loss of the one missing amphora. They sat down opposite each other, and the Gujarati man sent his boy to get some chhai from a vendor who had recently started the business of selling tea in a ramshackle stall at a stone's throw from the Mahendranath's shop. The two men sat down on canvas chairs which had become fashionable in Calcutta. The host got rid of his sandals and put one bare foot on the other knee and began stroking it and scratching between his toes. From the shop they could see the traffic on the river Hoogli. There was a large number of crafts of varying shapes and sizes sailing up and down, with brown men in dhotis moving and gesticulating all the time.

'I hear a big Angrezi ship is coming in later today,' Mahendra tells him in excited tones. Raju loves looking at these big sailing ships going to unimaginable places, and welcomes information about them. The chhai comes and they start sipping it noisily.

'This ship coming in,' says the Gujarati man, 'is picking up people to take them to faraway countries.' And he explains that the Angrezi had many colonies, like Mareeshush, Feejee, and Damrara, and wanted men to go work in those countries. The people who want to go, he explained, do not have to pay anything, they travel for free, but they have to work on the land there for a number of years, with food, clothing and housing guaranteed. Then when they have become rich, they can come back and do what they want, with money in their pockets, he says, moving his head left and right, opening his eyes wide. Thousands of people are leaving every month, he adds, and he had been told that a small trader like himself could easily trade with the migrants, selling them the things that they needed, and make a handsome living. He was certainly thinking of packing it in here to go seek his fortunes in the colonies.

'Where would you like to go?' Raju asks.

'Mareeshush or Feejee,' says Mahendra without thinking. He meant Mauritius or Fiji.

Suddenly there is a big commotion, and people begin to shout excitedly. It turns out that the English ship had just been sighted, and was now entering the mouth of the Hoogli, and coming up river to the port. The two men lean forward and see the majestic Startled Fawn sail in.

'Do you think they will take somebody like myself...' Raju ask. Let me see, says Mahendra laughing: two sound arms, two good legs, good eyes... arrey, Raju my boy, they will receive you with open arms. And he, impulsive as ever, having never once until now contemplated leaving his little village, decides there and then that he would be on that boat before the year was out, although he says nothing. Finish with this wretched life, always depending on the whims of the ungrateful Dukhdeo, dakus and cyclones. What was there in Bengal for him? It was not even the land of his fathers. He loved the Sundarbans, but when you cannot even provide for your wife and children...

For the first time since he left Roshankhali, he felt the pain of Shanti's absence. It will be at least five more days before I will see her again, he said to himself. And mischievously he touched his hardening organ. How am going to live with this for four more days? he asked himself aloud. He made up his mind to do what had to be done in record time. Buy the long list of stuff which the astute businessman needed for resale to the villagers at an exorbitant profit. People think I am extortionate, Sukhdeo often explained, but what they don't bear in mind is that a lot of the stuff I get in for you people often remain unsold in my godown — a complete untruth!

Having got all the stuff he needed, he decided to follow Sukhdeo's instructions, never do tomorrow what you could have done the day before yesterday.

He set off at first light next morning, hoping to reach Kalyanpur before sunset. The cow was not in great shape, but she did not have a limp or anything. She's just a lazy old thing and needed to be coaxed and cajoled all the time. Still they proceeded at a fair rate, and managed to get as far as Malikpur before night made it impossible for them to continue.

He slept in the ghari, wrapping himself in some old gunny bags as the night turned out quite chilly. In two days I will be in the Pargannas, he said to himself. Bhagwan give me the patience to endure being away from my lovely wife with this big protuberance between my legs that won't go away. Will it even allow me to sleep? I'll have to tell Sukhdeo about the Bihari gangsters, there is no other way. I'll tell him that I could have run away to save my life, but instead I tried to use my wits to safeguard his interest. And the price to pay was minimal. He will have to believe me, he knows I am honest… well he believes I am anyway.

He woke up at first light and decided to hit the road promptly so as to make sure he got home before sunset tomorrow. He had a long journey ahead; the roads were rough and uneven; you had to negotiate roots and rocks, potholes and subsidence. And then there was the dreary Pargannas to contend with before the cosy familiarity of the Sunderbans. He knew that the unfortunate encounter on the way out did not preclude another similar disaster on the way back. He could not see how he could get away with it a second time. He kept half the money hidden in a small frayed bag dangling negligently under the ghari, the top of which was filled with grain as a special treat for the ghai. The other half he kept under his seat where he knew any prospective attacker would look straight away. His thinking was that highwaymen would know that a man coming from Calcutta would have been going there with goods for sale, and would have money on his way home. They would obviously never leave him until they had found his takings. If he hid all the money, the bandits would keep looking until they found it, never in a million years would they have shrugged and accepted that there was nothing to rob. In frustration, they might even kill him. So if he let them find half the loot, there was a chance that they might be persuaded that that was the lot and leave him with the remaining half, and his life to boot.

But again, Devi Umma must have been watching over him, for the feared robbers were put off scent by her vigilance, but there was nothing he could do to coax the ghai out of her torpor. She would simply proceed at her own pace and when Raju got down to talk to her, urging her to rush a bit, explaining how hard it was to keep body and soul together when one had to contend with a massive erection, she simply stared at him with her cow's eyes and made no effort to change her speed. Nothing doing, Raju conceded, but they still managed to reach Sonarkhali before sunset on the tenth day. Sukhdeo and Lalita looked at them in surprise.

'We were not expecting you until tomorrow night,' Aunt Lalita said suspiciously.

'I hope you did not push the poor cow beyond her limit,' said Sukhdeo, 'we warned you that she was tired and old.'

'You also said not to waste time,' thought Raju, but thought it impolitic to say so.

Raju suddenly noticed how frail and thin the cow looked. She was foaming at the mouth and no sooner had he detached her from the cart than she plonked herself on the ground. When he rushed to get her some water, she turned away. As a rule she was up to two buckets of water on these occasions.

'No, I forgot, I gave her a big bucket of water just half an hour before we got home,' he lied, 'no wonder she is not thirsty.' Sukhdeo pursed his lips and shook his head wearily.

Aunt Lalita began fidgeting, and had to make a great effort not to lash out verbally at the young man.

'I had a stroke of luck on the way,' Raju said negligently, looking away, and casually he mentioned his misadventure with the dakus. Sukhdeo exploded. What did he mean a stroke of luck? There he, Sukhdeo was going bankrupt and he called this luck. Raju expounded, and ended up with the final transaction whereby he had felt obliged to hand over some of the produce to the Bihari badmen.

'And you call this a stroke of luck?'

'Of course,' replied the crafty Raju, 'I managed to salvage the bulk of the merchandise.'

'Lies!' shouted Lalita, 'don't believe a word of this, it's all lies! He has been in league with those badmash for years now, I have been telling you all along, but you are never believing me, the word of a fellow who doesn't even posses the skin of his arse are meaning more to you than mine!'

'Arrey choop!' said Sukhdeo, be quiet, 'who says I am believing him?' The two spouses quarrelled, and Raju was relieved to have the pressure momentarily lifted from him, but unfortunately it was not for long.

'You have to deduct the money from his earnings,' Lalita said with great finality.

'And what will my children and my wife live on? Those goondas could have killed me and all you think about is your money.' He felt that this could not be left unsaid.

Raju felt that as long as the wife was around, there was no way of talking Sukhdeo out of his insistence that he be made to pay for the shortfall. He made a non-committal grunt and turned his back on them and left.

As it was a moonlit night, he felt able to continue the journey home by boat, and reached Roshankhali in the middle of the night. After all his travails and upsets, the moment Shanti opened the door, he collapsed in her arms and cried like a baby, telling her his woeful tale incoherently. She hardly understood what had happened, but felt that this was a major blow, for never had she seen him cry so disconsolately. She bathed his feet and washed him with a wet cloth, gave him a clean shirt, and comforted him like a child. She made chai with the milk that she had been saving for his arrival for some days, keeping it from going bad and at the same time making it thick and tasty by dint of boiling it two or three times a day. The milk having thickened, acquired a slight burnt taste, and made the tea extra delicious, specially with one crushed cardamon in it, just as her man liked his tea. She was expecting a big broad grin on his face as she came back with it, but the poor exhausted man was snoring like a storm beginning to brew. She sat by his side, watching him tossing right and left uneasily. Suddenly he woke up in a panic, not knowing where he was, shouting 'the ghai has run away, the ghai has run away!' Then he shook his head and smiled. I was having a nightmare, he said apologetically. Drink the chai, she urged, having dismissed the alternative of going back to warm it up as she feared that he might fall asleep once more. In any case it was still reasonably warm and he drank it with great relish, sipping it in noisily.

'Oh my rani,' he said, 'no one makes chai like you… all my woes are dissolved in its perfection.' Suddenly he remembered why he had been in such a hurry to get home, and felt a physical response to this. He smiled, and Shanti, reading her man like an open book smiled back, pinching her lips and shaking her head sightly as a mark of pretend disapproval. She huddled up close to him and gently caressed his back, getting hold of a small chunk of flesh between the two shoulder blades between her thumb and her index finger, and pinching it lovingly. He introduced his hand under her blouse and the touch of her bare skin made him shudder with excitement.

'Every single day I thought of this moment, when you and I would be one, and we would celebrate our reunion like this.'

'You are a bad man,' she giggled.

The children were sleeping soundly. He stood up, walked towards them and bending down, he rubbed his cheeks against theirs. Then he came back, and Shanti, who was lying on the mattress raised her arms to wrap him up. Dukhdeo can go to hell, he said to himself as he slipped into those welcoming arms.

It was an accepted practice that after a Calcutta trip, one was entitled to a day's rest at home, so Raju was in no hurry to get out of bed that morning, but thinking it was the middle of the night, he was tossing sleepily when he heard Shanti talking to an excitable Sukhdeo. He jumped out of bed in a confused state. It had always been like this, when he got out of bed, for the first minute or so, he had no idea who or where he was. He would tense up his muscles, and if anybody was out to harm his family, they ran the risk of having all the bones in their body turned into haldi powder! Chacha Sukhdeo, he said, grinning, what can you want in the middle of the night?

'Arrey, stupid boy, now look what you have done,' wailed the older man, 'the cow is dead.'

'Poor ghai!' said Raju, feeling sorry for the poor beast, for he had known Roshni for years, and the two of them seemed to have a mystical understanding of each other. Whenever he had to take her to Calcutta, he would walk towards her, and she would let forth a low moo and lift her head up, waiting for him to take an ear in each hand and fondle it, and stroke her wet nozzle. On the way when the fancy took him, he would get off the ghari, and she would just toddle along, and he would prance about, singing to her, dancing around her, giving her a pat now and then. 'She was old,' he sighed.

'It's your fault!' accused Sukhdeo. Raju knew exactly what the boss meant, knew that he had pushed the old thing too far in his attempt to be home a day early to indulge in his carnal passion. But he put on such an act that even Sukhdeo, reinforced by Lalita's certainties though he was, was invaded by doubt. 'My fault, Uncle? How can you say that? Nobody treated Roshni better, gave her water even before myself, fed her grass and grains... How can it be my fault?'

'I... eh... we warned you, told you to take it easy, not to push her, and now she is dead, and it's your fault.'

'Well, if uncle says it's my fault, I have to come bury her...'

'Arrey, chhootya, bury yourself,' Sukhdeo bellowed so loudly that Deep and the girl began crying. 'Make them shut up,' ordered Sukhdeo relentlessly. Raju's Pa's so-called best friend, had never before called him a chhootya, and that hurt. Neither was he in the habit of swearing in front of Shanti.

'So, what else is there to do?' he asked, feeling a painful lump in his throat. Surely Dukhdeo was not going to ask him to pay damages.

'Uncle,' he said, 'I'll come cut the cow, and we can sell the meat to the Musselmans, telling them it's halal—'

'Madr Chhott, the whole village knows she is dead, why are you talking such rot?'

'You say it's my fault, right... I'll come dig a hole and bury her.'

'I always say, when a man makes a blunder, he must pay for it.' Surely he did not mean literally. Money?

'And I cannot believe that story about your being attacked by goondas, those bastards would have taken everything—'

'No, uncle, I was not attacked, I explained that. I tricked them, I saved the bulk of your goods—'

'Choop! First you steal from me, next you want a medal. But listen to me, I am known throughout the region as a fair man — a tough man, yes, but fair, right?' He did not give Raju the opportunity to agree or disagree with him. The latter thought it expedient to produce a non-committal cough.

'Your aunt Lalita... hum... also a tough woman, but known for her piety... and fairness... thinks I should ask you to pay the full price of the cow, and for those stuff that... how shall I call it? Disappeared. I am not saying stolen... As Bhagwan is my witness, I didn't see you steal them...'

Shanti who had retired in a corner, trembling with foreboding, would not, as a rule, interfere, in the knowledge that Sukhdeo would take it amiss, but she was unable to resist. Coming forward with polite determination, she had her say.

'Chacha Sukhdeo, you know that my Raju has worked very hard for you all those years. I know nothing about the ghai, but you must know that he is incapable of stealing from you and pretend that it was something else.' Sukhdeo looked at her in surprise, then cast a rapid glance at Raju, in the hope that he would order his wife to keep out of men's matters.

'Chacha, as my Shanti says, have I ever stolen from you before?'

'Your Aunt Lalita says… I mean we have no proof,' he paused, adding slyly, 'that you haven't.'

'Chacha, we have no proof that you…' Shanti began, but she was going to say, 'killed that cow yourself,' but realised in time that this would have made matters worse, and much to Raju's relief, stopped herself in time.

'Arrey proof groof! What I want to know is when you are going to pay me damage. I reckon the ghai is worth…' and he mentioned an extravagant price, which made Raju's eyes pop out of his head.

'Where will I find the money? I don't have a single paise, and that is the truth.'

'So what did you do with the money you sold those goods you stole from me?' Raju was dumbfounded.

'And two bag of onions, one bag of…' and he mentioned what according to him these missing commodities would have fetched. Raju just shook his head and smiled wearily.

'Chacha, where am I going to find this money to pay you? I will have to work one whole year to pay you. How am I going to feed my kids, my wife,' adding as an after thought, 'myself?'

'No, you heard wrong, I didn't say I was going to wait for one whole year, we want the damage paid now now.'

'Now, now?' asked husband and wife in unison, looking at each other.

'Yes, you heard right, now now!'

'Where do I find the money?' asked Raju.

'Some people say you may not have money, but you have… possessions…' said Sukhdeo looking away self-conscientiously. Raju pretended he did not understand, but he knew that he was referring to Shanti's jewellery. Shanti had also read Sukhdeo's thoughts very early on. Most of the jewellery she had been given at her wedding had been sold over the years as the children were growing up, but apart from a pair of jhumkas in solid gold, there were one or two gold plated bangles and rings which were worth next to nothing. But he was damned if he was going to force Shanti to part with her most prized possession.

'But chacha, we have nothing, you know how much money I earn, I have two children and a wife—'

'I-I don't know,' Sukhdeo said with some pretend hesitation, 'what about... I don't know... possessions?'

'Possessions! What possessions?' He was damned if he was going to let Sukhdeo get away without having to spell out what he was after.

'I-I... how am I knowing? I-I mean... things you can sell, perhaps, valuable things...' It was Shanti who decided to put the old man out of his misery.

'Sukhdeo Chacha means my jewellery, Pradeep's father.' And she turned away and went rummaging among some bundles under the bed.

'But there's nothing left, it's all gone, you remember when my little girl was between life and death, we—' said Raju.

'Only your Chachi Lalita said...' Sukhdeo interrupted, as Shanti came back holding a pair of glittering gold earrings in her hands. They were small miniature crowns the size of a cat's eyes from which small chains of a fineness rarely seen and the length of a child's thumb cascaded at the rim, a masterpiece of craftsmanship, made by the one-legged Hamidullah, the Bihari goldsmith whose forefathers made jewellery for Bihari Maharajahs. The man was such a perfectionist, that when a piece he had been working with had not matched his expectation, he went into deep depression and committed suicide by swallowing a small crystal of the potassium cyanide that he used in his work. And Hamidullah himself had said that he was never prouder of anything that he had ever made. Sukhdeo's eyes popped out. Even Lalita did not own such a splendid item! On the one hand he did not relish depriving his best friend's son and wife of this unique piece, but this had to be put against the constant vituperations of Lalita if he did not take a firm stand.

'Theek!' he said, extending his hand in order to receive this offering, 'with regret I will have to accept.' He stopped short, and dropped his hand, adding, 'If only you knew how I hate doing this to you, but... eh... business is business, and sentiments is sentiments!' Business is business indeed, said Raju to himself, which is why, Madr Chhott, you eat so much and end up with ulcers and us poor eat mud!

With a slight hesitation, but shrugging slightly, the older man raised a hand and left it just under Shanti's, as someone holding a bowl anticipating the pouring of water into it. Shanti looked at Raju who felt tears welling up in his eyes. Shanti was completely dry-eyed. She looked at the old zamindar and dropped one earring in his hand. The old man frowned tentatively, and left his hand in the same position, ready to accept the second item. Shanti withdrew her hand, but said nothing. It was Raju who came to her rescue.

'I think, boss, you will find that the one earring more than covers the rather exorbitant price you are asking for the ghai... and I never stole those goods, I swear on Devi Umma's soul.'

Sukhdeo protested suggesting they went to Pandit Biswas for arbitration. First, that sanctimonious hypocrite knew nothing about gold, Raju thought, but worse of all, knowing that being on the side of the rich was more profitable to him, he would not dare find against the zamindar. Finally they decided to go see an expert jeweller, Baldeo, who happened to be Sukhdeo's cousin but who, strangely for a jeweller, had a reputation of honesty second to none in the community. Shanti reluctantly gave Raju the second piece, and there and then the two men made for the boat where Jayant was waiting for the boss. They made their way to Sonarkhali, Jayant following the two men who seemed oblivious of his presence. Raju trusted that, cousin or not, Baldeo was going to be scrupulously fair. The young jeweller's eyes popped out when he came face to face with such magnificence. He had never seen anything so well-crafted, he said. He took the pieces in his trembling hands shaking his head in disbelief. He was lost in thought for a whole minute, then he shook his head apologetically to his older cousin and said that owing to the rising price of a tola of gold, one earring on its more than covered the cost Sukhdeo had mentioned. The zamindar looked disappointed but had no choice but to accept the verdict. Raju to whom Baldeo had returned the earring then handed it over to Sukhdeo.

'If you find the money within a month, I will gladly return this piece,' he said. Hypocrite, pretending generosity, thought Raju.

Sukhdeo then, in a gesture of magnanimity ordered Jayant to take Raju back to Roshankhali.

'No, thank you, uncle, I will swim…' sad Raju with a bitter laugh, and Sukhdeo looked at the boy he had much loved, with respect and admiration, that he could make a joke — albeit a bitter one — under the circumstances. He stepped on the boat, and Jayant who had been following the proceedings in silence, had tears in his faithful-dog eyes. Raju found himself inexplicably annoyed at this, but said nothing.

For a while, neither man said a word. Jayant rowed his little craft thoughtfully whilst Raju sat with his head in his hands, prey to black thoughts the like of which he had never entertained before. Suddenly he raised his head and caught Jayant's gaze. Why am I angry with Jayant? He was always my true friend. He smiled at him apologetically. After Sukhdeo had got off, Jayant grabbed his friend's arm and squeezed it in a gesture of solidarity.

'Jayant, I will tell you a secret, keep it to yourself. I am not going to stay in this fucking place anymore,' and he told him about Mahendra, and the places beyond the sea where a man could live in dignity and make a fortune. Yes, he would go to, what was the name of that place the Gujarati man had mentioned? Mareeshush, Marsheesh? Jayant's eyes opened wide. He wanted to know more, and Raju told him what little he had learnt, whereupon the boatman, also an impulsive man, asked if he could join him. He had lost his parents in the floods and had no one to depend upon him, and Raju was his best friend and mentor. Raju was considerably cheered by his friend's sudden decision. We'll go together, he said joyfully.

Shanti was surprised when she saw Raju looking so pleased with himself, and supposed that it was because a big burden had been taken from his shoulders. Negligently he handed over to her the salvaged earring, and told her what Baldeo had said. Being a pessimist by nature, she had assumed that Sukhdeo would have ended up with both. That was the moment he chose to reveal to her his intention of leaving the Sunderbans. Shocked by the suddenness of it all, she lost her calm and asked him if she had lost his reasons. She was flabbergasted, said nothing and took to her bed with a wifely headache.

Raju had not expected her to react like this. Why did she not understand that there was no future in this weather-beaten, disease-ridden, dangerous mangrove forest with its man-eating tigers and cobras, its mosquitoes and its nauseating odours, where you walked knee-deep in shit and mud. Why could she not see that sometimes one had to take risks. This place Mahendra had talked about seemed like a paradise. Suddenly he realised that Shanti was not necessarily against the idea of leaving here, but hated not being asked for her opinion about leaving, first. He had to make amends, he tiptoed towards the bed and lay besides her and put an arm around her, but she pushed it away.

'Rani, I was thinking about you, about the children, we have no future in this place.' And he gently he pulled her towards him, and this time she did not resist. He tickled her under her armpits and she smiled reluctantly. This place, Mar...sheesh, he explained, was exactly what they needed, it is nice and warm, there are no beasts, no floods, and there is always work, no one goes hungry, the Angrezi makes sure everybody has a full belly, and you work a few years and when your pockets are bulging with Rupayyahs, you come back and start your own business.

'Arrey Pradeep's father, you are such a dreamer, how can such a place exist? How are we to get there? Who is to pay the boatman? How long does it take to get there?' Raju laughed and told her all he had heard, that the Angrezi paid the boatman and it took no more than a day or two... it could not take more, could it? I never asked about the distance.

By now, she was in his arms, and whilst talking he had been holding her tighter and tighter, and neither was surprised when in no time at all they found themselves intertwined and aroused like they had rarely been before. As he penetrated her he was filled with an elation which he felt no king living in his palace, covered in diamonds and eating badam halwa, full of almonds and ghee all day long had ever felt before. Shanti too was overwhelmed by a well-being she could not think was possible on the day when she had lost her most cherished material possession. Her man certainly knew how to do things. Yes, she thought, my man is right, we have no future here, if he takes me to the edge of the world and beyond no harm will come to me or my children. His heart is so pure and innocent, how can any God not protect him? And may God burn the ears of that horrid woman like hot coals when she wears my mother's gift to me.

CHAPTER 15

◆◆◆

Dunrobin

ON THAT COLD spring afternoon, with scattered snow still covering the tops of ridges, Sir John Sinclair sat in his coach dressed in his finest, feeling that he had at last made it. Chief Guest to dinner at Dunrobin! He had met the Duke briefly when he was Marquess of Stafford, had curtsied to him and received a nod of approval which had gladdened his heart so much that he had been unable to sleep that night, repeatedly recounting to Lady Sarah every detail which he could remember. This was surprising indeed, in view of his own pedigree and superior intellect, but he had yearned for the day when he would meet the legendary Elizabeth Gordon, who had become Duchess of Sutherland at the age of one, and later Duchess of Stafford — surely her blood must be as blue as my specially tailored blue velvet cape, he had thought. Lady Sarah had been aggrieved when it was made clear that the invitation did not include her, that this was not strictly speaking a social occasion. The noble couple had made it plain to him that they wanted to hear his views on the Improvement. He had explained that as surely as Loch Brora thawed in spring, the time would come when she would be presented to the Duchess and eat at her table, for after all they were themselves nobility, albeit of the minor variety, he having only been born in Thurso Castle and a descendant of the obscure Duke of Lauderdale. Obviously they did not invite comparison with the Staffords and Sutherlands, but John was aware of his sound intellectual worth and calibre. He was recognised as one of the finest brains of his age, having been a brilliant scholar at Oxford. His tutors, had included Adam Smith, whose thoughts on the free market he had espoused with singular enthusiasm. He deeply held the view that the more money the rich make the more they can help ease the burden of the poor, who, self-evidently had no talent for making money themselves. The eminent Father of Economics had further predicted an extraordinary future for him. Which is no doubt why the good Duchess Duchess had invited him.

He ordered the coachman to speed up. It's much better that we arrive half an hour early, Rabbie, he had explained, when we can wait outside the castle and take in its splendour, than be even half a minute late. He took out his gold watch from his waistcoat pocket and was satisfied that they would indeed get to Dunrobin in good time.

The Improvement! That was what was going to bring untold wealth to our part of the world, he had thought. Nowhere in the world were the rights of proprietors so well defined and protected, and he exulted in this. Which was what motivated his clarion call, "Colonise at Home!" He rehearsed his views in his head, picked words and sentences which he felt were going to impress the noble pair. He was a deeply religious man and would never do anything to harm a fellow Christian, but can those slothful Highlanders, given to illicit distillery, poaching and swearing — and no doubt worse — be called Christians? If God in his wisdom made eggs, it was because he wished us to enjoy the savour of the omelette, but the first step is to break the eggs. So, yes, some folks are going to suffer initially, but the end result is going to make it worth all the pain and sacrifice. Yes, he would expound his views and the country would thank him for the benefits of the Improvement, which would mean more money for enterprising people, and result in the eradication of famine and unemployment. Money for investment in the many projects he had looked at was there for the taking. Wasn't the Marquess the richest man in the union? The one problem was getting the message across to the dullards inhabiting the glens. The Duchess had impeccable Scottish credentials, which would make the pill easier to swallow. People who knew her spoke of her charm and magnetism, her extraordinary intelligence, but the best thing about it all was that the English Marquess was besotted with his Scottish spouse.

As expected, they arrived early and waited about half an hour before entering the precincts of the Castle. He looked out of the carriage, admired the structure and the recent renovation which was tastefully carried out. Half an hour was not enough to take it all in, but no doubt the opportunity will arise soon for other visits, perhaps with dear Sarah. Since the Marquess had moved north to Sutherland, he had invested heavily in the modernisation of the seat of his beloved wife's ancestral home. The castle had been built by the first Earl of Sutherland in the mid thirteenth century as nothing more than a fort, where he and his descendants had lived more or less peacefully until the Jacobite uprising which had damaged it considerably. The impoverished residents had not been able to afford repairs and modernisation, but it was the avowed aim of the new lord and master to turn his abode into the most lavish castle in the Highlands, to transform it from the fort that it was into a castle of fantasy that would match Versailles itself in splendour. However, as the noble pair wanted minimal disruption to their daily life, progress was slow. It was very much a long term project, and the Marquess said to all his friends and well wishers, 'I guarantee that every time you come visit, I will have to show you at least one major innovation.'

Sinclair was politely ushered into the petit salon — small for Dunrobin — and served a glass of port by a flunkey and left alone to savour it. He was somewhat taken aback by this minor slight. Shortly afterwards, two other men joined him. They were introduced to him as William Young, a pleasant looking man of about his own age, and a younger man, Patrick Sellar, who had the strange eyes of a religious zealot. They too were served a glass of port and told that their Highnesses were going to join them shortly. They sipped their port quietly, hardly glancing at each other. A few minutes later the sound of raucous laughter was heard outside and when the door was opened, a garrulous and slightly dishevelled Duke walked in, a shock of platinum hair protruding out of his badly fixed wig. Sir John who was a stickler in matters of decorum and etiquette was somewhat surprised that his highness had taken such little care with his appearance. His face was red and shiny, and it was obvious that though not drunk, he had overindulged at lunch. He was looking very jovial and harrumphed his way in, extending both hands towards his guests, almost colliding with a large Chinese vase but stopping in time, wagging a finger playfully at the inanimate object, and reprimanding it for standing in his way. Sir John smiled, the two men laughed loudly and Stafford nodded approvingly.

'The Chinese may have slitty eyes,' he said gruffly, 'but that does not stop them producing masterpieces like that vase here, eh what? Or is it an urn?' The three men nodded their agreement wholeheartedly. He greeted each guest by extending a limp hand for them to shake, but understandably for a man who had to keep so many balls in the air, he called him Sir James instead of Sir John. He believed that it was impolitic to point out this insignificant slip, but even after they had known each other quite well, the good Duke would always have difficulty remembering whether he was Sir Peter, Sir James or Sir John. He even allowed the suspicion that his lordship did this on purpose, as a sort of private joke, to contaminate, albeit ever so slightly, the good opinion that he had formed of the man from across the border.

He took a seat opposite his guests, snapped his fingers and a footman walked towards him gravely, bowed his head slightly and nodded as he acknowledged an order and left. He came back with a decanter on a silver tray and poured some port in a Murano crystal glass, and was about to offer it to his highness when the latter shook his head and with a sign indicated that he wanted more of the stuff in. The footman complied and Stafford happily grabbed the glass and immediately took a large sip from it, rather noisily, Sinclair thought. The two other men, Young and Sellar seemed unable to take their eyes off their host, and their admiration for him seemed boundless. They were no doubt taking it all in, already anticipating the admiration in the eyes of a putative audience to whom everything would be narrated in the near future. Sinclair was not one to pass judgment on his betters, but would have been happier if gravitas was more evident in the proceedings than frivolity, but he had no doubt that the good Earl knew what he was doing. Sinclair did not owe his success in life by questioning the action of his betters.

Duchess Elizabeth did not put in an appearance in the salon, but when a footman came in to invite them into the dining room, she was there at the door, smiling broadly at her guests, extending a hand to be kissed, and bidding them welcome to Dunrobin in the sweetest and most gracious of tones, and in an accent which was as English as it is heard at Buckingham Palace. Sinclair was stunned by her poise and elegance — class will always tell. He noticed her unique beauty, the shapely bosom, the wasplike waist, the peerless hazel eyes, the high cheekbones, the pointed chin, the lips that went on forever at either ends, the long legs and the statuesque physique. I will make a note of what she is wearing later, so I can tell Sarah, he said to himself.

Feverish with expectation, the learned man was unable to enjoy the fare, excellent though it was. The salmon, the Duke explained, came from Loch Brora. No, he wagged a finger to forestall any wrong conclusion that his guests might have arrived at, I did not fish it myself, but waylaid a poacher with a basket of my fish! I had him stopped and I whipped him myself — not as much as you would have thought —

The good Duke stopped at this point, and William Young, as if on cue expressed surprise that the noble lord would carry out the punishment himself and not hand the villain over to his gamekeeper, whereupon the good Duke laughed so much that he spluttered into his plate, to the amusement of his consort who shook her head merrily. For a whole minute the guests were left enjoying the manifestation of their host's high amusement, and no words were exchanged. The Duke almost had tears in his eyes, and raising a knife as a mute prayer to the table to bear with him, as what he was going to say would be absolutely stunning, he finally managed to blurt out, 'Cripes! Get the gamekeeper to whip himself like some demented saint?'

'It was the gamekeeper himself who was the poacher,' explained the Duchess needlessly. When the Duke had calmed down, he shook his head and began another wave of hysterical laughter.

'You won't believe this, but the venison roast had a similar provenance, but sad to say, it was Auld Tam this time, and my better half here has a soft spot for that particular villain, for the simple reason that she had known the fellow since she was a… wee bairrrn, as she put it… why that should white-wash the man's trespasses, I shall never know, but then I am a lover of women and do not claim to understand them, eh what! So we let him go… even after the rascal refused to promise that he would not recommence! 'No, sirrr,' he said, 'I cannae see why I shall refrain from serving masel of the good things the good Lord put on this good earth for ma sake, just because a man puts a fence roond the forests and declare that they belong to hissel!' By now he had calmed down and solemnly added, 'You've got to admire the spirit of the Highlander, eh what!'

They adjourned to the salon, where to Sir John's mild surprise, it seemed that it was the Duchess and not the Duke who was going to preside. Her spouse was surprisingly quiet, and kept nodding off.

Sir John was asked to expound his views on the Improvement, and did so in clear concise words which came easily to him as he had given the matter much thought over the years.

'As my mentor Adam Smith used to say,' he began, but the Marquess interrupted him with a great burst of hilarity.

'Did I hear you say Smith, my dear fellow? How can a man called Smith have anything sensible to say about anything, what piffle!' The Duchess gave him a withering look which forced its way through a superficial smile, and he coughed, closed his eyes and began snoring instantly.

The Highlands which he knew intimately, Sinclair said, was singularly underexploited. It was wrong to believe that because the soil was not among the most fertile, that it could barely support crops like oat and turnips, that it had to be left to go to blazes. It was able to provide for a restricted number of Black cattle, he explained, but Highlanders are too set in their ways, too mentally lazy to think ahead and plan. The future was Cheviot sheep! He had worked out the arithmetic. The statistics, he called it —

'Statistics?' queried the Duchess, 'what's that, Sir John?'.

'Aye, a new word I coined myself,' he said proudly, 'to describe how numbers can be used to give us an idea, using the notion of probability, of what outcome to expect in studies in various fields. Some clever mathematicians have made interesting discoveries in that area and we can gain a lot by making use of their findings. And I can demonstrate that a change from Black cattle to Cheviot sheep, what with the demand for wool in Lancashire, profits… eh… productivity, would be increased fourfold at a stroke.'

'No one can accuse me of being hardhearted,' said the Duchess with some vehemence, 'when they were starving, I was there with my handouts. How did they pay me back? By refusing to join my Sutherland Fencibles. Either they were cowards refusing to fight for King and country, or they were ungrateful dogs who preferred other regiments to the one my dear father, their biggest benefactor had created.'

'Aye, an idle and useless lot, ma'am.' agreed Patrick Sellar, who had said next to nothing all evening.

'Like everybody else, the Highlander is deeply attached to his land and his ways,' said William Young in a slightly dissenting tone, 'but he needs to be persuaded. We need time.' Sinclair began suspecting that the man was only trying to exhibit a compassion that he did not really possess.

'Time!' roared Sir John losing his cool for the first time, 'we do not have that commodity. We are richest nation in Europe and if we intend to stay that way, we cannot let lesser nations like France, Spain and Holland catch up with us, and they will unless we deal with the millstones round our necks by shedding them off, as soon as possible.'

'We need to be sensitive,' implored William Young, 'we need to respect the people's traditions.' Sinclair was now convinced that Young was only mouthing these sentiments in order to convince himself and the audience that he was a thinking man and not a heartless exploiter. Sir John was not going to moderate his views.

'God made eggs,' he began on his familiar theme, and found it hard to hide his annoyance when Patrick Sellar interrupted him.

'In my experience of Highlanders, they only respect force. If they know you are going to be easy on them and tackle them in a spirit of conciliation, you become putty in their hands.'

'My first consideration in everything I undertake,' began the Duchess thoughtfully, 'is the well being of my Sutherlanders. They know they can depend on me, and as you're all aware, when their crops fail and penury casts its chill upon them, it's I and no one else who make sure they get a full belly... I wouldn't let a single man on my land starve, even if they have disappointed me many a time. I am not vindictive, not even against those who have opted to join other regiments.' Yes, indeed an admirable woman, Sir John thought.

'What I was going to say,' she pursued, 'is that if people have to be relocated, then so be it. But I will make sure that any hardship inflicted upon them will be minimal. But sorry Sir John, go ahead.'

Sir John took a deep breath and explained about alternative sources of revenues for the undisciplined tenants. New fishing colonies that could be established on the west coast, kelp production, boat building, lime and chalk production. The vacated area would then be entirely dedicated to sheep, and everybody would be richer and, dared he say, live happily ever after.

'And if anybody does not wish to accept relocation and new openings, then they can emigrate to Canada or the Carolinas,' said Sellar.

'Or transported down under!' guffawed the irrepressible Stafford, suddenly waking up.

'Mark my word, ma'am' said Young gravely, 'Highlanders will not just pack up their things and go away because it suits us that they do.' Perhaps he might be sincere after all, mused Sir John, sincere but misguided, but the Highlanders will have to do as they are told.

'Piffle and balderdash my dear Young, if you allow me to say so — I've said it anyway, ha! ha! Piffle, balderdash and poppycock! The Highlander, from what I have seen of him, is workshy, mentally dead and lacks backbone. He will jolly well do as we tell him. Have you seen their children? If it was rather more than their mouths which were black from eating earth, they couldn't be distinguished from the piccaninnies of our colonies.' I would not have put it like that myself, thought the scientist, but I can't disagree with the sentiments.

'I think, your Lordship underestimates the enemy,' said Young. Ha! I was right after all, he calls them the enemy.

'What do you think, Sir John?' asked the Duchess. Sinclair, ever the rational man, said that he had insufficient data to make a valid pronouncement, but he was sure that there would be problems, but equally sure that problems of that nature were not insurmountable.

After some deliberation, Sinclair said he had to inform his highnesses that there would be not inconsiderable costs to the exercise, whereupon the Duchess solemnly said that for the welfare of his Sutherland Highlanders, she would not hesitate to disburse however much was needed, which triggered another blast of hilarity from the Duke.

'Dear heart,' he said good-naturedly, 'the first reason why you would not hesitate to disburse, is that it's my money,' but to the relief of everybody, he quickly added, 'but what is mine is yours of course.' He took a deep breath and continued, 'And the second and probably more important reason is that you know that any amount spent is an investment which will indubitably double in a year.' Everybody laughed heartily, nodding their agreement with the assessment. I wish he'd go back to sleep, thought Sir John.

Sellar explained that he was speaking in the name of William Young as well, he hoped. If the Duchess meant to implement her plans, then they, her representatives, must be given free rein to act as they thought fit.

'What can you mean, Mr Sellar?' asked Elizabeth Gordon.

'There is only one thing to do once the tenant has been legally evicted, and I take no pleasure in saying this your Highness, their habitation needs to be burnt down, or they would come back and no one will be able to stop them reoccupying their former abode.' For the first time the Duke assumed a serious pose, bit his lips and frowned. Then he shook his head glumly.

'I can see that this course, heartless as it might seem on the surface, cannot be avoided. But I must strongly emphasise that I want no more than minimal violence, and under no circumstances will I tolerate loss of life.'

'Dear heart,' the Duchess said, 'haven't Mr Young and Mr Sellar already impressed us by their compassion, their common sense, and their attachment to our Christian values? They are not men who are going to cause unnecessary harm to those churls.'

'Your ladyship can trust us on that score,' Young assured her, 'I am a man of peace myself, as the tenants well know from the long association I have had with many of them. We will handle this matter with utmost judiciousness and delicacy,' adding, after a pause, 'firmness and... eh... delicacy.'

'There is one important thing I must make clear to you,' said the Duchess earnestly, 'when the churls are resettled in fishing villages, they are not to be given leases.'

Everybody looked at her in surprise. She smiled with self-satisfaction and explained that this would make it easier to evict them legally if they are troublesome. Surprise immediately turned to admiration. What intelligence, what manly determination! They shook their heads and smiled. The Duke positively glowed with pride at his wife, and beamed at her lovingly. The footmen then served dessert.

'Gentlemen, you will love this special creation by François, our new directeur de cuisine. It is something our illustrious Gallic neighbours called Crêpe, and he has himself invented this new sauce which he makes with a heavenly liqueur created by monks, called Green Chartreuse.' Everybody partook of this excellent offering and pronounced it... heavenly.

The session ended on an upbeat note, and Sir John went home happy in the thought that he had laid the foundation stone to greater things to come, a new departure for a deprived area. With the admirable work Thomas Telford was doing, building a canal through the Great Glen which would facilitate transport of goods, the people who had advanced the views that Lanarkshire would become another Lancashire before the middle of the century, were soon going to be proved right. He was quite sanguine about that.

Young and Sellar were asked to come back to Dunrobin within a week, when the Duchess would consult with them about the nuts and bolts of operations. But not tomorrow, she said, explaining that she had promised her godson who had come over to spend part of his vacation at Dunrobin, with two Etonian friends that she was going to devote the whole day to them.

Unbeknownst to all those clever people, Albert the footman had picked a fair bit of what had gone on, and what he had missed out was soon filled in by patchy intelligence from attendants, cooks, other footmen and lackeys. Albert was one of the few friends of Angus Smith. Hugh had been extremely discreet and careful, for he had known from the very outset that a slip on his part could mean recapture, resulting in hanging. He constantly repeated this to his wife and Mam, and made them swear on the good book that under no circumstance would they reveal the truth about what had happened to them, even to the many good friends that they had made since moving to Strathnaver, and certainly not to the children.

Albert had always thought that there was an aura of mystery about this Angus Smith, and it was perhaps this that had made him want to become his friend. He knew that once a fortnight he came to Golspie on business, and often joined him at the Stag Heid for one jar of the local brew. Angus would drink his ale slowly, and leave the moment he had emptied it, he never had a second one, not even if it was offered to him. That afternoon the footman made his way to the Heid, and as luck would have it, his good friend was there. Hugh got Albert a jar of the rather excellent barley ale that Daniel the landlord offered, and the two men sat down and talked.

'The Duke and Duchess are making trouble for oor Highlanders my friend,' Albert said gravely, 'and their plan is a mighty wicked one, I daresay.'

When Kitty got home, it was her eyes which betrayed her. First they tried to look away and avoid contact with other eyes, and when that was unavoidable, they stared at you and looked clean through you. Hugh noticed it immediately, you had to ask her everything twice, and she blinked when answering, got her words mixed up and blushed. Hugh mentioned this to Martha who nodded and shrugged. It was to Grand Mam that she confided.

During the school holidays, Kitty often took the cattle out to graze. She did this because she wanted to do her share of work, but she very much enjoyed the outdoor life. She had been full of silent foreboding when the family moved to the area after Fort Williams, but the moment she saw her glen, her apprehension instantly evaporated in its enchantment. She had been struck by the silence which was accentuated by the faint murmur of a stream. She loved to sit under her giant oak, feeling like Mr Cowper's Alexander Selkirk, mistress of all she surveyed. The munro at Loch Lunn seemed to have two distinct personalities, baleful and menacing when the clouds hovered above, and the exact opposite under a spring sun, almost skittish, specially when the ground started vibrating with heather. From her vantage point, she would contemplate the gentle slopes which turned gold in summer and exult in its splendour. As a child she used to think that the small nameless loch in the distance, gleaming in the sun, was a silver mine. What she liked above everything was a shock of green which unexpectedly burst out from one of the ridges, a cluster of pine trees. She often wondered, why just there? In those carefree days, she and John and other young ragamuffins from the hamlet often used to run around this oasis, up and down the undulating ridges, throwing sticks at each other, screaming like banshees, their hands spread out like birds ready for take-off.

She was almost certain on any day to catch a glimpse of the wildlife. Her heart would beat with excitement when she saw a red deer in the distance, framed by the greenness of the glen, often followed in a trice, by two or three more. It was a sight that made her wish she was a painter able to encapsulate the heart-throbbing beauty of that instant on canvas. She would hold her breath as they were such timid creatures and would disappear into the growth in one leap when disturbed. Sometimes a pine marten would dart from one end of the clearing to the next, as if pursued by a hunter after its fur. Already this year she had seen two golden eagles hover majestically in the peerless sky above. She loved to sit in the shade of the giant oak, knitting or reading a parchment scroll which Miss Black had lovingly copied in her simple but firm handwriting for her pupils, and circulated among them.

This morning she had heard a strange commotion and turning her head round, she had seen a most unfamiliar and glorious sight. She had never seen a capercaillie before, and there in front of her were two of them! They were striking looking, with red circles around their eyes, their beaks aimed at each other; it was obvious that they had been fighting, and had gradually pushed each other outside the forest into the clearing; their tails were spread out like fans and their wings trailing the ground, with the feathers round their neck puffed out. They made strange growling noises and they moved their menacing beaks up and down in unison but without making any serious attempt at having a stab at the other. Kitty looked at them in wonderment, holding her breath, wishing that they would not harm each other, and on an impulse decided that the best thing was to shoo them away as a means of protecting them against each other. She stood up and hollered at them, and they turned away from each other and clumsily flew away, making a whistling noise with their wings as they did so. She was delighted, both with the sighting and with herself for what she thought of as her good action for the day.

She watched the clouds disappear behind the mountain and leant against her tree as against a lover. She loved the Robin Hood tales, and she had been looking forward to reading the tale of the Golden Prize. She loved reading aloud, and at home felt uncomfortable doing that in everybody's hearing, with John sneering, albeit good-naturedly. She would only read aloud to Grand Mam, who had after all given her, her love of stories. She had a quick glance at the cows. They were happily chewing their cud, and were not too near the drop, which they instinctively knew how to avoid anyway. She took a deep breath and declaimed in a monotonous manner:

I have heard talk of bold Robin Hood,

Derry derry down
And of brave Little John,
Of Fryer Tuck, and Will Scarlet,
Loxley, and Maid Marion.
Hey down derry derry down

She stopped and shook her head. No, her delivery was so humdrum, she was going to do it again. She smiled, made sure nobody was within sight or earshot, and started again, this time putting emphasis on certain words.

I have heard talk of bold Robin Hood,
Derry derry down
And of brave Little John,
Of Fryer Tuck, and Will Scar-let,
Loxley, and Maid Marion.
Hey down derry derry down

She knew that she sounded ludicrous, but it did not matter, she was having fun. She did it again, and began to sing the Hey down derry derry down bit. I am losing my mind, she said to herself and giggled. She read the next bit.

But such a tale as this before
I think there was never none;
For Robin Hood disguised himself,
And to the wood is gone.

She again played with this verse, reading it in different styles. She noticed that the cows had strayed a bit too near the drop, and carefully wrapping the scroll in her shawl, and putting a stone on it for protection against the wind, she stood up and ran towards them, and tapping her crook on the ground instructed them to move away towards safer grounds, after which she went back to her cosy little seat under the oak and picked up her scroll. When she came to the bit,

Two lusty priests, clad all in black,
Come riding gallantly…

She was so engrossed by images of Sherwood Forest and the valiant men who were willing to shed their lives in the defence of the poor oppressed people, she could even hear the sound of hoofs approaching.

'Benedicete,' then said Robin Hood,
'Some pitty on me take;
Cross you my hand with a silver groat,
For Our dear Ladies sake.

She loved the word Benedicete, and she repeated it a few times, giggling as she did so. What can it mean? she wondered. To her amazement, she heard "Benedicete, fair wench!" and looking up, she saw three handsome youths in their finery, on horseback, looking at her in amusement. They were striking looking, had almost identical chestnut mounts, but she knew nothing of horses, and supposed they were Arabian. She blushed and thought of running away.

'I am sorry, your lordships,' she stammered, not feeling confident speaking English 'I, eh… I… didn't know… I mean I wasn't doing any harm…' and she found herself suddenly having to battle against her tears.

The three young gentlemen got down their mounts and in a clearly unthreatening manner took two steps in her direction. She did not dare lift her eyes to look at the young men, but felt that there was no danger.

'What is it you are reading, wench…' one of the trio asked and looking up she saw one of the handsomest youth she had ever cast eyes upon. She was too confused to answer, and was grateful when a second youth spoke.

'Don't be afraid, wench, we are completely harmless. I am Robert Helmsdale-Robertson, the Duchess of Sutherland is my godmother. This uncouth pair here call me Rob Rob. This chappie here is Shelley, Percy Bysshe Shelley. One day he will become the Poet Laureate of England, or so he tells everybody, and this runt here is George Henry Blake, who hopes to turn the Kingdom into a socialist Utopia one day. We are all staying at Dunrobin at the moment.'

And to Kitty's amazement, George Henry bowed to her solemnly saying 'Ma'am!' whereupon the other two nodded and smiled. She was confused and blushing all over, but relished this first time that anybody had called her 'Ma'am'.

'What is it you are reading... miss,' asked George Henry, and Kitty stammered her reply.

'You have a good reading voice,' said Shelley, and he extended his hand towards her in a wordless request that she let him have a look. With trembling fingers she picked the scroll and handed it over to the aspiring poet. He looked at it, obviously reading it, nodding to himself.

'Listen to this Blake, Rob Rob...'

The priests did pray with mournful chear,
Sometimes their hands did wring,
Sometimes they wept and cried aloud,
Whilst Robin did merrily sing.

'The hypocrites! Your first priority, come the revolution Blake, is to sort out those parasites.'

'Do you enjoy reading then, young... lady?' asked Rob Rob.

'What a silly question, Rob Rob! Would she be reading with such gusto if she did not?' That was the handsome one called Shelley.

Kitty wanted to ask what 'gusto' meant, but she had been dumbstruck, and felt that it would be wrong to ask questions of young lords.

'I do, sir,' she heard herself say, looking at Rob Rob for the first time. He was slim and had a noticeable tan, but his eyes were quite uncommon, very attractive, they seemed almost almond shaped.

'Miss Black…', she started but stalled. She wanted to say something about her much loved teacher, but was not quite sure what or how, so she stopped. Rob Rob was not only good looking, but everything about him exuded gentleness. Kitty did not tell Grand Mam that she had been unable (or willing) to shake off images of that young man from her mind's eye ever since she had cast eyes upon him. A worm can look at a star!

'What's your name and where do you live?' asked Rob Rob.

'Catriona Smith. We bide in Aiktree Farm.'

Rob Rob said he knew where that was.

'Will you do us the honour of reading some more of the ballad before we go, Miss Smith?' asked Blake, and Kitty did not immediately realise that the Miss Smith referred to was herself, and when she did, she blushed and knew that there was no way she was going to be able to oblige although she would have liked to. She shook her head violently and looked away. The young men who had referred to her as wench to start with, subsequently treated her like a real lady, and she was deeply touched by this. They bowed courteously and took their leave, and she could not help noticing that Rob Rob turned round several times to have yet another look at her.

'She is in love,' Mam said to Hugh. 'It's a nice feeling, it will do wonders for her self-confidence, but trust me, nothing bad is going to happen, do not spoil it for her, just let her savour the moment. Dreaming never harmed anyone. She is not likely to see the young man ever again.'

But she was wrong.

Next day Rob Rob turned up alone at Aiktree, with a bundle. Grand Mam who was outside became greatly agitated and confused on seeing the young toff. She blushed and curtsied, and to her amazement, the young man took off his fine hat and bowed to her in return.

'May I bid you a good morning, Ma'am?' said the young man in faltering Gaelic. Mam had never in her born life been called Ma'am either, and blushed some more. She had heard stories of young girls losing more than their heads to these young aristocrats, and for the first time she understood how difficult it was for the likes of them to resist these well-born swains. When all your life, you experience humiliation from all corners except from your very own, and someone from another world started treating you like you mattered somehow, how can you not lose your head? But of course Catriona had a sound head on her shoulders, and was not likely to lose it.

'I am Rob Rob,' said the young man, 'my godmother is…' he was unable to finish the sentence, but Mam nodded eagerly, making it obvious, without meaning to, that Kitty had told her the whole story. She noticed how the young man was struggling with Gaelic, and was on the point of telling him that she understood English quite well, but changed her mind at the last moment. Let the arrogant masters suffer for once.

'I have got s-s-some books and p-parchments for…' he stammered, leaving his sentence unfinished. She suddenly relented and explained in English that Kitty was out, as was the whole family apart from her. He handed the bundle over to her, bowed again, walked to his horse and skilfully manoeuvred himself into the saddle and ambled away. Mam, stood there, holding the bundle, as if paralysed, unable to move or even to think, for some time.

Rob Rob guessed that Kitty would be where he had found her the day before, and he was right. There was she, seated under her oak tree, knitting. When she heard the sound of gallop, she closed her eyes and prayed that it would be Rob Rob, and found it hard to hide her joy when her prayer was answered. Thank you God, she whispered to herself. He, wanting to impress her, spurred the chestnut on and made him stop within touching distance of her, and she was so sure of the skill of the young man that not once did she flinch. They both laughed. He patted the horse on the head, and the latter responded by neighing in his direction with obvious warmth.

'I call him Silliboy,' he said, 'but only because I love him.' She said nothing.

'Is it for me you are knitting this lovely… eh… scarf?' he asked. She blushed.

'They are mittens for the neighbours' new baby,' she said, raising her head to catch a good look at the man she had now fallen head over heels in love with. The fact that he had come looking for her was proof enough that he felt the same way about her. She nearly said that if she had the wool, she would love nothing better than to knit something for him.

'I'll ask godmother for some wool,' he said earnestly, 'then you can knit me… a scarf, can you?' She nodded, and he added, 'I'll pay you for your trouble of course.'

Kitty was a quick thinker, and instead of taking offence, she immediately thought that if she got paid for it, be it ever so little, she would be able explain to Martha and John that she was doing her bit for the family, and deviate any criticism that might come her way, to the effect that she was behaving like a romantic fool. The distant strains of a flute played by some cowherd surreptitiously strolled in on the gentle breeze, and they became aware of it at the same time.

'It'll be a pleasure, sir,' she said. He wanted to ask her not to call him sir, but Rob Rob, but he found it difficult. All his life, he had been aware of his position, there were Us and Them, and he did not know how to talk to one of Them as if he or she were one of Us. And he supposed that Kitty would experience the same dilemma. But he said it anyway.

'Kitty... can I call you Kitty?' he began, but did not wait for an answer, 'Kitty, my friend Blake has done something marvellous to me, he has shown me that all men are equal... eh... all human beings... not just men, you see, I mean all women are equal too... eh... to women... and... eh... not just women, but... Oh Kitty, if only you knew, I am in awe of you, and I am losing my power of speech...' She blushed and thought that she should not let him know how smitten she was.

'What I was trying to say, Kitty, is that you should call me Rob Rob... and think of me as a... eh... friend.'

'Oh no, Rob Rob, it wouldn't be right to call you sir,' she blurted out, meaning to say the opposite, and he burst out laughing. She did not immediately identify the cause of his hilarity, but the sentence echoed in her mind, Oh no, Rob Rob, it wouldn't be right to call you sir. And all she could think of doing was to cover her eyes, as if this negated the slip of the tongue. He bent forward and gently took her hand and pulled it away from her eyes. The contact with him made her shiver with a feeling she had never experienced before. She wished he would stroke her bare arms with his gentle hands. He too became aware of a strange sensation as they made their first ever physical contact. He wanted to keep her arm in his, and take her in his arms and hold her, but the revulsion with which he held those peers of his at Eton who boasted about how they had coerced servant girls and milkmaids to offer them sexual services made him pull away. She knew clearly why he did, and was grateful. He was indeed a sensitive soul, not someone who would take advantage of a poor crofter's daughter.

'I left some books... things to read anyway... with your Grandma. I asked Godmother for them. She is so kindhearted.' Just as she was wondering about how she would return them to Dunrobin, he said, 'The Duchess says you can keep them.'

'She is very kind... you are very kind too... thank you.' And she curtsied clumsily, and he laughed.

'You shouldn't curtsey to me, Kitty, you must not think of me as... you know... I am your friend... I mean I want to be your friend if you will let me.' She did not answer but smiled. Yes, he loves me too, she said to herself, that's the important thing even if I know that nothing can come out of such a love. Blake is right, he was thinking, we should break down those artificial barriers between people, we are all the same, our blood is of the same colour, only some people have not had their fair share of the good things of life because we the rich have taken too much for ourselves. The balance must be redressed, and I will make a start. For the first time the idea that he might marry Kitty some day, set from a wobbly fantasy into a concrete certainty. Yes, he believed in love at first sight. The girl had intelligence, beauty, and everything about her reflected gentleness and wisdom. Yes, strange to say, wisdom was the first thing that he surmised about her. It was in her eyes, and it was strange, he thought, that one so young could exhibit such clear signs of it, without doubting for a moment that someone of his tender age could have the wisdom to recognise this. This was Serendipity! He had found true love, without looking for it. A cowherd was his soul mate. He was sure that he wanted no one else to share his life. He did not know how he was going to manage that, there were many obstacles, but he felt so strong that he was sure that he would dismantle them all one by one. He must confide in Shelley and Blake.

They just stood looking at each other, silently, both yearning to be in the other's arms, but keeping sunlight between them. In the distance the cows were contentedly chewing the abundant grass of the slope.

'I am going grouse shooting tomorrow,' he said regretfully, 'with Shelley and Blake, Godmother has planned it for us and says she might join us.' He paused, and added, 'If you knew how much I care for her, she has been like a mother to me.' He looked at her to see whether she was interested, and decided that she was, so he continued. 'You know, my father is in Penang... I haven't been in years, but he is arranging for me to go on a visit next year...'

'Penang?' Kitty asked, and he explained that it was in the Far East, and that his father was the head of the British East India Company which was trying to develop that very rich part of the world for Britain.

'Blake calls it exploitation,' he laughed, 'but I don't know, I mean the natives do not have the know-how.' Kitty was lost, she had little idea of the world. At sixteen she was still struggling to learn to read and write. Miss Black taught them everything she knew, but besides the handful of books she had, it was mainly the bible, composition, and some arithmetic. She read everything she could lay hands on but there was not any great choice, so she read everything a few times over, until she knew almost everything she read by heart.

'What is exploitation?' she asked timidly.

'Exploitation?' He repeated and laughed. 'How shall I put it? It is when someone who has the power, makes other people do the donkey work for him and reaps the biggest share of the profits.' He paused for a bit and nodded to himself before continuing. 'Let me give you an example: my father goes to the colonies, he claims the native does not know how to get the best from the natural resources of his land, so he distributes seeds and seedlings of the rubber plant which he brought over from Kew Gardens and gives them instructions. Then he sits in an office, let them do all the hard work, shows them how to produce rubber, which... eh... the native doesn't know what to do with, so he takes it from him and make huge profits out of it, but the native only gets a bowl of rice for his pains.'

Kitty saw clearly what Rob Rob meant, and smiled before she spoke.

'Isn't that what is done here as well?' She asked, the young man frowned. 'Here?'

'Aye! My father, Mam, Grand Mam, my brother John and I we all work pretty hard raising our cattle, growing our oats and barley, our potatoes and turnips, making butter, knitting late into the night until the light fails, but it is the landlord who becomes rich. That's what I mean, sir. Would you call that exploitation, sir?'

It was Rob Rob's turn to blush now, taken aback by the words of the young peasant woman. He had always heard the Duchess speak of the poverty of the Highlanders, their laziness and deviousness, their drunkenness and lack of discipline, how they would be starving without the charity of the rich. Over the years this had naturally become his view too, although it was a view which was beginning to erode as Blake began expounding the theories of Hume and Locke.

'Yes, I-I-I s-s-suppose you are right…' he stammered unconvincingly. He was now assailed by emotions and doubts which set his mind in a turmoil that he had never experienced before. Surely Godmother was not talking about Kitty and her folks, and the young woman was talking generally about the landlord class, not about her dear Mother Substitute, as near a saint as can be imagined. Maybe it was not such a good idea to make friends with someone who was of such different class. Damn Blake for suggesting otherwise!

The young man who a few minutes ago was full of carefully rehearsed and lyrical sentences he was planning to say to the young lassie, now found himself tongue-tied. I must be off now, he said, walked towards his mount, and this time got on it in a less spectacular manner, nodded gravely to Kitty, then forced an apologetic smile on his lips, saying that Shelley and Blake were waiting for him, and he galloped away.

Kitty understood that it was what she had said which had produced this sudden drop in temperature, but felt that he had taken her words amiss. She did not mean to say anything condemnatory. She had always accepted the exploitation of her class as a fact of life, one complained about the weather, but knew one could do nothing to change it, so one laughed and joked about it. She had heard about the Duchess but felt no animosity towards her, although she knew that Da and John did. She hoped that she had not frightened Rob Rob away for good.

After a copious dinner, the Duke and the Duchess invited their young guests to the petit salon, and were in jolly spirits, specially as they had seen clearly — or so they thought — how they would finally turn their Sutherland property which had so far been a sponge for Stafford's not so hard earned legacy, into a profitable concern. The man had not only inherited his father's considerable wealth, but shortly after the latter's death, he found himself heir to the recently deceased Duke of Bridgewater who was equally rich, making him by far the richest man in the Union, richer, they said, than even His Majesty. In Europe, only the Romanovs in Muscovy were wealthier.

It was the first time that the Duchess was going to entertain his young guests in a fitting manner, and the Duke knew how much she valued young Helmsdale-Robertson, even wondering sometimes if she did not treasure the young man above their own.

Rob Rob had obviously written to her at great length about the young poet and his unconventional ideas. Normally she would have discouraged the friendship between the two, but her godson had mentioned that he was a descendant of the Earl of Arundel, and Elizabeth could not imagine that with such a lineage he could mean all those scandalous things the young poet claimed he would do to the ruling class. She found herself fascinated by him though, thought that his radical ideas were daring and exciting in theory, but hoped that as he matured they would make way for more sensible ones. And he was of course indubitably the handsomest young man she had ever cast eyes upon! If only I were ten years younger, she had sighed. Perhaps she really meant twenty. Strangely the Duke seemed equally fascinated by the young socialist Blake and thought he would have some fun baiting the boy.

'Tell me, Mr Blake, your Mr Hume, was he or was he not a Christian?' Blake loudly maintained that Mr Hume was definitely an atheist, whereupon the Duke shook his head and smiled.

'You're wrong there, young man, your Mr Hume definitely embraced Christianity, trust me.'

'Not Mr Hume.'

'Aye,' said the Duke who found himself borrowing Scottish words and idioms more and more often, possibly to tease his wife. 'And I'll tell you the how and the when of it if you like.' Young Blake said nothing.

Hume, he began, was having a house built in David Street, in Edinburgh, and whilst on his way to inspecting the works, he fell into a mire. As you know, since you are an admirer of the man, he was of great bulk and could not find his feet. Some fishwives happened to be passing by and he shouted for help. They came running and were on the point of rescuing him when one of them said, But that's the Mr Hume who denies the existence of our Lord, let him perish! On hearing this, the women decided to leave him to his fate and go about their business, but one of them said that they would not be doing their Christian duty if they let the man sink in the mire and drown, for all his ungodly views, whereupon the other women came up with this excellent idea. Right, Mr Hume, we will save you if you renounce your cursed beliefs and recite the Lord's Prayer and the Creed, which, the Marquess assured his young audience, he did with rare enthusiasm.

'I am sure this is apocryphal,' said Blake dismissively. The Duke did not know what that meant and shook his head dismissively.

'You're wrong, Blake,' said Shelley, 'Hume himself wrote about the incident to the Mure of Caldwell, and said that he had never met more acute theologians than those fishwives.' The Duke seemed very impressed and nodded in admiration.

They were served French liqueur and strawberries. Blake had never seen them before and asked what they were. The Duke welcomed the question, as it was not often that he was able to air his erudition.

'The Strawberry, as you can see is the prettiest of all fruits!'

'Yes,' sneered Shelley, 'but your God spent so much time making it pretty that he forgot to give it any taste or flavour.'

'Ach! That's because God did not have Lachie as his chief gardener,' roared the Duke, 'I trust Mr Shelley that after you have tasted the fruits he grows in my glasshouse, you will change your mind.' Shelley bowed slightly, half admitting the possibility.

'It came to us from the Americas. Madame Whatshername, a famous companion of Robspear used to bathe in crushed strawberries to keep her skin soft. Mind you it did not help keep her head on her shoulders when her time came, ha! ha! ha!' He paused and a twinkle in his eyes signalled the next bon mot.

'Taking baths of any sort did not do any of them any good, eh what! Look at what happened to Marat.' He expected an explosion of hilarity, but only mild amusement resulted.

'Didn't Fontenelle who lived to be a hundred swear that he owed his longevity to eating huge quantities of strawberry all his life, dear Heart?'

'You're absolutely right, dear Heart, he did,' the Duchess said this aggressively to hide the fact that she had never heard of Fontenelle.

Shelley admitted that Lachie had done wonders, that he conceded that those particular fruits were indeed more fragrant than he remembered.

'Mr Shelley,' said the Duchess, 'aren't you going to entertain us by reading one of your poems, my godson is full of praise for their excellence.'

Shelley did not want to, and shook his head, saying that having written a piece he tended to forget it as he had poor memory, and he did not carry any copies with him when he travelled. Blake interrupted him and said that he happened to have saved a copy of a poem Shelley had shown him and then committed to the waste paper basket. He had liked it so much that he enjoyed having a look at it now and then. Producing it like by magic, he gave it to the young poet. He looked at it and shook his head. No, he said, shaking his head, I am not reading this piece of trash. It is clumsy and inchoate, the rhythm is all shaky, I am ashamed of it. However after a lot of entreaty mainly from the Duchess, he relented, and read:

I met a traveller from a distant land
Who said: Two colossal legs of stone
Stand in the desert. Near them on the sand
Buried, a ruined village lies, whose frown
And wrinkl'd face and look of cold command
Show that well the artist those passions read
Which still survive, stamp'd on these lifeless thighs
The hand that mock'd them and the heart that fed
And on the pedestal those lines appear
I am Rameses the Great, King of Kings
Look on my works ye mighty and know fear
Nothing more remains but sand and decay
Of that gigantic wreck stark grim and bare
The lone and level sand stretch far away.

'What's wrong with that?' asked the Duke, 'I very much doubt that I could have done any better myself!'

'It's got some great rhymes, some excellent rhythm —' protested Rob Rob.

'For me,' the adamant young poet said, 'unless I am one hundred percent satisfied with a piece, it is worth nothing. I swear to you that this will never see the light of the day.'

'It is a great piece as it stands,' countered Rob Rob, 'it tells us like nothing else that I have read, about the impermanence of material things, that one day even Dunrobin Castle will fall into ruins.' He paused and to everybody's surprise, he had tears in his eyes as he continued.

'Shelley, you have helped me to understand that only love matters!' Everybody looked at him like he had lost his reason.

'So my little boy is in love,' said the Duchess, walking towards him and taking his hands in hers and fondling them. Rob Rob blushed, rose and walked out.

'Love is a strange potion,' said the Duke making a funny face, at which his dear Heart gave him a disapproving look. Shelley took out a little notebook and scribbled a few lines in a notebook.

When Kitty arrived home, she found the bundle on the table which John had made from wood he had gleaned here and there. It was such a pretty polished piece that it looked out of place in their shapeless hovel. She rushed to open the parcel. There were Caxton publications of Horace Walpole's *Castle Of Otranto*, Mallory's *Morte d'Arthur*, *The Three Princes Of Serendip*, but what Kitty was most impressed by a massive tome, handwritten in Chinese ink, called *Stories From One Thousand And One Nights*, Translated from French by William Gray with the gracious permission of Antoine Galland, commissioned by and dedicated to His Highness Sir Francis Egerton, Duke of Bridgewater. She knew that she was going to love this book most. She sat down on the floor and was about to start reading when Hugh entered. Everything about him reflected his gentle nature. When he walked, he did so carefully as if he wanted to avoid hurting the insects on the ground. He moved gracefully, and whatever stress he might be under, he kept his mood under control. He had a relaxed face, rarely scowled and never raised his voice.

Hugh stared at the books and scrolls sadly, and Mam explained their provenance.

'So you take gifts from my enemies,' said Hugh curtly, 'from people who wanted me and our kind dead.'

'Rob Rob is not our enemy, Da,' his daughter said softly. But he said nothing and left to go sit outside, his head in his hands. As Martha was coming from the fields, she immediately saw her husband's sorry condition and she took his pipe and tobacco to him, and he smiled at her and lit it with his flintlock. She sat by his side, as close as she could to him, but said nothing. Kitty watched them from inside the house, and was relieved when after a while she saw him begin to talk. Martha had the power to soothe all aches and pains by just listening to you. She wondered if she had loved Da as passionately as she loved Rob Rob. Da's enemy! Rob Rob could never be anybody's enemy. He had left in a huff earlier on, but she knew that he would come back. How she wished it would be tomorrow, although he had said he was going hunting with the Duchess. Forty-eight hours, over two thousand minutes! How would she manage that? She shuddered at the thought that Da could have ordered her to stop seeing the young man, and did not know how she would have responded to that.

Next day, she carefully wrapped the precious *One Thousand And One Nights* in an old shawl and took it with her when she took the cows to pasture. When they had settled down nicely in their routine, she took the book out and began reading. She began reading the story of *Aladdin and The Forty Thieves*, and had reached the point where the boy rubbed the lamp, and like magic, it was Rob Rob who appeared in front of her, holding the reins of the horse. She had not even heard the sound of the horse's hoofs, had not noticed his approach or his dismounting. She was dazzled, half by the enchantment in the story, and half by the magic of real life. How can Rob Rob appear to me when he is out hunting? Just by reading about magic? He was saying something, but she only caught the gist: the Duchess was indisposed and had to postpone the hunt. Kitty had to scratch her head in order to make sure that the presence was real. He extended his arms to her, and she stood up like a Jack-in-the-box and flung herself at him. He wrapped her in his arms and held her tight, inhaling the odours of her smoky clothes mixed with her honest bodily sweat with relish, gently stroking her back and waist. Kitty who had never been kissed before closed her eyes and raised her face to him, bent forward and he kissed her, at first tentatively, then finding her response encouraging, he put more passion in it.

'I love you Catriona Smith, and I swear that I shall always love you.' She had never heard sweeter words in her life, and closed her eyes, saying nothing, relishing the moment. She knew that the last thing she would recall before dying would be this event, these words, and even thought that if she died there and then, she would die happy.

'I love you too, Rob Rob,' she whispered, 'I'll never love anybody else.' They pulled apart at the same time as both felt uncontrollable desires rising in them and knew that it would be dangerous and wrong to pursue that path, although in the grip of passion each would have yielded to the other's wish.

Again she would confide in Grand Mam.

'Lassie,' her grandmother said finally, 'love is a wonderful thing, but nothing good comes out of a poor crofter's girl falling in love with a son of the Castle. All they want is their wicked ways with you and when they have got it, they leave you. They do it as a sport in order to go and boast about it to their friends.'

'No,' shouted Kitty angrily, 'Rob Rob isn't like that, I've told you, you're just being…' she stopped herself saying nasty, and instead said, 'overcautious…'

'Overcautious, am I?' said the old lady, taking it just as badly, not quite sure what she meant, but she stopped short of showing anger. 'Just think about what I have told you and don't do anything that you will regret for the rest of your life.' Whatever I do with Rob Rob, Kitty thought, I will never regret it.

That same night, the Duchess wrote a letter to Helmsdale-Robertson in Penang. When the two of them were teenagers, they had imagined that they were in love, but she had always been ambitious, and aspired to marry a very rich man of her own class, a duke at least, someone with the means of restoring her patrimony. He was from a more modest background had not dared risk a refusal, so their affair had been lukewarm, but both had kept fond memories of their first kiss on a boating trip on Loch Brora, the balls and picnics they had shared. At eighteen he had been commissioned and had ended up Captain Francis Light's second in command when he had landed in Penang. It was of course Light who had negotiated with the Sultan of Keddah and secured Penang for the British East India Company, and thus for the British Crown. He had been very impressed by young Helmsdale-Robertson and had arranged for his protégé to become Head of the Commercial activities of the company. He had fallen in love with a Chinese Malay woman, a seamstress, and had wanted to marry her, but there had been too many obstacles, the main one being Captain Light's intimation that should he do that, he would have to forget a brilliant career, as a native wife would be a millstone round his neck and would put paid to his aspirations of advancement. That did not stop the woman bearing him a son.

Rob Rob did not remember the first three years of his life, but Godmother told him that his mother was a Malay princess who had died shortly after giving birth to him, and explained that he had been looked after by some native ayahs. When he turned four, he was sent home where his grandmother had looked after him and when she too died, he became the ward of the Duchess, although he did not live at Dunrobin, but with a cousin of Helmsdale-Robertson in Golspie. At an early age he was sent to boarding school in the south, but spent all his holidays at Dunrobin. The Duchess had children of her own, but she always had a lot of love for the young boy. The servants used to whisper that she seemed to love the young Etonian more than her own.

9th of June 1812

My dear Robert,

I have not had the pleasure of reading your letters in over six months, and hope that before long I shall receive a packet from Penang. First of all, let me assure you that Rob Rob is very well indeed; you will not recognise him, he has grown so much in the two years since you last saw him when you were over. His school reports have, as always been excellent, as you will have seen from the copy I caused to be made and sent to you. This being the long school holiday, he is here in Dunrobin, and has brought along two excellent friends from well connected families, I can assure you.

Dear George and myself, as well as children, all four of them, George, Francis, Charlotte Sophia and Elizabeth Mary, are also in perfect health.

I have every reason to suppose that Rob Rob will turn into a nice young man, but I believe that he needs a father's guiding hand, specially when he is at such an impressionable age, if he is to avoid falling into one of the many traps awaiting to receive the innocents of this world in this day and age.

I have been concerned about an undesirable attachment he may have formed. You would be shocked to hear that the object of this unwelcome attachment is the daughter of a miserable crofter, an uneducated cowgirl. Since he allowed that girl to beguile her, he walks on air, spouts socialist nonsense, and spurns riches as being always ill gotten or undeserved, as if our ancestors accumulated their wealth by sitting in their armchairs, drinking whisky and stealing from the poor. I hope that this fancy will pass, as it usually does with young men of his age and temperament, but there is nothing like a father's stern warning couched in conciliatory and loving language to make sure that it does. To this effect, I am getting in touch with my agent in London, to book him a passage to Penang after Christmas. I know that coming to see you has been one of his dearest wishes. He will naturally miss six months of school, but with his natural propensity for learning, I feel certain that with the help of a tutor whom I shall pick myself, his chances of a place at Oxford will not be compromised in any way. I will confirm the arrangements as soon as I have the details.

Last spring, I went boating on Lake Brora with the Duke, and I remembered the very same trip you and I took the summer before you were commissioned. Naturally I said nothing of this to George. It will be our secret.

I shall write a more detailed letter in autumn when I shall have more time. As you can imagine, at the moment, with three eager young men to look after, to say nothing of some developments to our system of tenancy which you would find tedious in the extreme, I do not have too much time to indulge in letter writing.

You will, as ever be in my prayers, dearest Robert, and I wish you happiness in your work in the colonies. I should be interested to know more about the experimental projects you mentioned in your last but one letter, I seem to remember it had to do with rubber or cocoa (or both).

Yours sincerely

Bessie

(Elizabeth Gordon)

Kitty was immersed in her specially commissioned Arabian Nights book when she heard the faint galloping sound of hoofs. She smiled at herself. I am absolutely besotted by that boy, she reflected, I hear him everywhere. But she was not too surprised a few seconds later to see Rob Rob approaching. He jumped off Silliboy and she immediately knew that he was very upset. She threw herself in his arms and they held each other tight for a few seconds, until she became aware of him trying hard to stifle his sobs. She pulled away in some alarm and immediately his tears began streaking down his face. She grabbed him and they both fell to the ground. She took his head in her arms and rocked him like a baby, kissing his tears, saying nothing.

'They're sending me away,' he said finally, 'they want to keep me away from you...' She looked at him questioningly. 'Godmother! She's sending me away, I don't know what to do.'

'Sending you away? Where? To another school?' He shook his head violently.

'To Penang, to my father...'

'But they can't do that? What will happen to your schooling? Oxford?'

'I am not sure, nothing is sure yet.'

'Maybe you're wrong, Rob Rob, maybe...' her voice trailed off, and after a while she added, 'but you will come back, won't you?'

'It means I won't see you for a whole year, dearest heart,' he wailed. She immediately burst out laughing.

'A year is nothing, I will wait for you, silly boy,' at which the horse, recognising his name gave a neigh of acknowledgement. She regretted using the word silly, but the reaction of the chestnut brought a smile to both their faces.

'You will wait for me then?'

'Of course I will.' This time she said the word with emphasis. 'I will wait for you till a' the sea gang dry!'

'Father might want to keep me there, but I promise that I will not let him. I will come again, my love, tho' twere ten thusand mile.'

She smiled her gratitude at the man from Sassenach parts knowing the poems of their beloved Scottish bard, which were now so popular that even Highlanders recited them in English in taverns.

Kitty had always been aware of her sensual and passionate nature, and had always known that she would find it hard to keep her desires under control. Now that she had found the love of her life, she saw no reason why she should not do what had been foremost in her mind ever since she fell in love. The cows seemed to be looking at her, urging her on. Marigold even let out an encouraging moo. Yes, she would give herself freely to the man she loved, the only man she would ever love. It was a wilful decision, taken with complete lucidity. One did not become pregnant after just one act, she knew dozens of women who had been unsuccessfully trying for a bairn for ages.

She took his head and pressed it to her face, and kissed him on the lips, opening his mouth with her tongue, as if she wanted to get inside his body. Her body was pulsating and he was in a similar state of excitement. She felt his hardness against her thigh and smiled. He felt slightly embarrassed, and she teased him by placing her hand over this stiff presence, stroking it gently. It was obvious to him that she wanted to do exactly what he had been praying for. He, unlike the unsophisticated Kitty who thought that conception only took place after repeated intercourse, was well aware of the risks, but in the certain knowledge that he was going to come back for her whatever the obstacles, he let himself go. In any case he was in such a state that he would probably not have been able to stop himself had he wanted to. It was the same for her. She had discovered how to pleasure herself at an early age, but knew that there was much more to it, and now that the moment had arrived for her to experience the ultimate pleasure, she knew that no power on earth would have stopped her. Neither of them had had the full experience before, but when the moment arrived, they let their instinct guide them. To Paradise and Back! She thought. No power on earth can create a more delightful feeling, he felt. They lay in each other's arms under the August sun, as contented as they will ever be in this life.

Note: *The poems quoted in this chapter are Shelley's Ozymandias (presumably an early draft) and Robin Hood's Golden Prize, one of the many traditional ballads collected by Francis James Child.*

CHAPTER 16

◆◆◆

The *Startled Fawn*

RAJU WAS NOT sure where he stood with Sukhdeo, and as Jayant was going to Calcutta by boat, he told Shanti that the only way of earning some money would be to go to the big city with his young friend and try to find work there. Shri Mahendranath had told him that with the new developments the East India Company was spearheading, work was easy to find. And you could sleep in my yard if you like, the man from Gujarat had offered. When it rains you can use a little shed I keep wood in, he had said, you are like a son to me, he had added.

Raju was doing quite well in Calcutta, fetching and carrying, but his mind was made up. He was going to get on that boat to.. he kept forgetting the name of that place… wherever… as long as it was far from the place where he had suffered such stinging humiliation. One day his Gujarati friend informed him that the Startled Fawn, which had been undergoing repairs in the dry dock was soon going to be ready to set sail, and he went to Roshankali to get the family.

Jayant had also been preparing himself, and soon the time came for the family to leave. The children were greatly excited by what to them was a big adventure. Jayant had carried out some repairs to his boat, in the hope that when they had got to the city, he might be able to sell it, and get to Mauritius with some cash in his pocket. They all convinced themselves that they would not miss the old life. They had few friends and Roshankhali had always been a struggle. It was so easy to minimise the good times they had spent there. Now they all remembered the unhappy occasions, the tragic deaths, in the case of Jayant, of both his parents in the cyclone. Raju spoke of Baba's cruel end at the fangs of Dakshin Rai, of the hakeem's long painful death. Shanti remembered with bitterness how her parents had gone from riches to rags through no fault of their own, and finally had to go back to miserable Gaya, a place where her Pitaji had said, people only went to die. No one was sorry to be leaving this god-forsaken place.

They carried their possessions on their heads to the little pier on the Matla which Jayant's father had built, and where they used to moor the craft. It was a small cockpit of a boat which could be propelled by means of two oars fastened on rowlocks on either side. It was hardly big enough for the three adults and two children it was going to ferry over such a long distance, with their meagre belongings. Jayant was an expert and could move the boat at speed with one hand, with his eyes closed and standing on his head, Raju said. He was not in the same class, but was certain that in a day or two, he would be just as good, as they were going to take turns. Jayant had said that manoeuvering along the channels could be tricky, with currents changing their minds just when you had acquired a good rhythm. But there were straightforward stretches which Raju could well handle. In the event, even Shanti did some rowing, as did the children, although their contribution was more a licence to squabble.

They left Roshankhali with the aim of linking up with the Hoogli and headed for Patharparma, a tricky start indeed, but Jayant kept the craft going steadily and at a good pace, and they reached there in mid-afternoon. The children to whom Raju had boasted of his friend's skill kept pestering the boatman to stand on his head and row with one arm. They stopped at Patharparma, found a nice peepul to sit under and Shanti heated up the meals she had been preparing for a whole week before, and they had a feast. Sundari and Pradeep loved the place, its calm and its lush vegetation and would have liked to stay there much longer, but Jayant suggested that it might be possible to reach Sagar before sunset. The currents proved tricky and against expectation, the kids, instead of panicking found the pitching and tossing of the boat greatly invigorating. They managed to reach Sagar just as the sun was setting.

They slept under a keora tree after Jayant and Raju lit a fire to keep away tigers, for Jayant said that he had often seen tigers on the islands nearby, but said that as these beasts were great swimmers they could put in an appearance anytime. The little ones were very excited and said they wished they could always live like this, it was so much more fun. If only they could see a couple of tigers! They refused to go to sleep, and had to be coaxed. Raju woke up with the dawn chorus, aching all over, but the aroma of rotis which the tireless Shanti, having prepared the dough before leaving, was cooking over on an open fire, holding the rounded flour discs with her fingers, gave him new vigour.

'Rani,' he told her grandiloquently, 'when we have grandchildren, I will take them on my knees and tell them about our trip down the river and the smell of those heavenly rotis you were making,' adding after a short pause and closing his eyes, 'the aroma will live forever in my memory.'

The children could not wake up and had to be shaken, but the mood of the day before had not faded in the least, and their merriment was contagious. It was all laughter and hope. Raju's hands and shoulder muscles were aching from the previous day's rowing, but in his experience, working on tired and aching limbs often made them better. Shanti must have been tired too, but as she did not complain, Raju thought that it would be unmanly of him to start moaning. Jayant said that they had every chance of reaching the Sangam where the Hoogli took the Damodar as its wife, and together proceed towards the Bay of Bengal. They had the choice of stopping, either at Geonkhali or at Nurpur, and they could easily reach either before sunset. They planned a stop for a rest and food at Kulpi.

Everybody was excited when what appeared to be a crocodile was spotted by the girl on the river bank near Belkupur, but they could never be sure if it was indeed one. It's an old dead tree, said Jayant. What a spoilsport, thought the girl. However this did not stop Pradeep seeing crocodiles every fifteen minutes, whenever there was some unusual object that he did not recognise, some distance away. They reached Kulpi in good time, and had another long rest, and reached Geonkhali at the Sangam just as the sun was beginning to set. They marvelled at the serenity of the encounter, anybody would have supposed that the two branches would be lashing at each other in fury, like angry spouses fighting, but they behaved like a contented couple sleeping in each other's arms after a night of passion. They slept soundly at Geonkhali, rocked by the gentle chant of the rivers flowing.

The rest of the trip was mercifully uneventful, and they reached Baj Baj in the afternoon, and Calcutta the next day. The crowd milling about all over the place confused Shanti who did not even guess that there were so many people in Bengal. The place was littered with sprawling children of all ages, in rags, playing or running about aimlessly, but engaged in some ill-defined games, many laughing as mucus dripped from their noses, some crying unconvincingly as they felt abandoned by older siblings. The family sat under a banyan tree by the river with their belongings at their feet whilst Raju went to see his Gujarati friend, and Jayant set out to enquire among the boatmen plying their trade in the Hoogli river if they knew of anybody interested in buying a sound little craft.

Shanti and the kids were to wait for the men next to a Ghat with a number of banyan trees next to it, where more little children were jumping about in the water and running after each other, pushing and jostling lustily. On either side of them, as far as the eye could see, there were sheds and go-downs, harbour offices, lining up along the bank, most of them with cor-rugated iron roofs glaring in the sun, containing produce that the East India Company had stored before shipping them to Liverpool or London, tea and spices, cotton, wood, jute, raw cotton, animal skins and a large number of other produce. There were pontoons at regular intervals on the river, link-ing the two banks, with impatient crowds, bales finely balanced on their heads crossing in either direction paying no attention to each other. A large number of ships could be seen beyond the mouth of the river anchored in the open sea. Access to and from them was only possible by launches manned by skilful and powerful betel chewing Cokhan boatmen with massive oars.

The noise and bustle were nothing any of them had experienced before. Although people did not seem to be talking all that loudly, as the sever-al thousands voices of all sorts mixed, a considerable drone resulted which Shanti found overpowering. The children were fascinated by magicians do-ing incredible tricks, some swallowing fire, others throwing things up in the air which never fell back to earth and simply disappeared. Yet more laugh-ing children were running about, playing gooli or racing or standing on their heads or doing cartwheels. There were all sorts of folks there, snake charmers playing their flute and getting the cobras to dance to their tune, one-eyed beggars leading blind fellow beggars, there were hawkers hawking everything from miracle drugs to half cigarettes, singers singing ghazals and birhas, preachers preaching, there were people with no legs propelling themselves with their arms, one-legged acrobats, pickpockets, fortune tellers, and there was even a three-legged donkey walking in the most comical fashion. Mostly the people were in rags, but all the colours of the rainbow could be seen on the crowd going about on their business, whatever that may have been. There were people eating, drinking, laughing, crying, there were people quarrelling, people sleeping, and if one looked closely enough, one could see people who had hardly bothered to take shelter behind a tree, emptying bladder and bowel, unmindful of the crowd.

Shanti just sat there, fighting the mounting irritation arising from the heat, the humming and the apprehension of the unknown, and tried hard to shut herself from the noise around, moving the two little leeches away from her when one part of her body became too hot and began to itch. The crowd around her became a haze, and she was barely aware of the odours around. Every single smell imaginable was present, the most persistent being sweat. Every now and then a sudden gust of breeze wafted in a stench of urine and excrement but there was also an earthy smell like when it has rained and the earth was drying, although in fact it was quite dry. There were groups of people cooking or frying all over the place, and this provided a smell of smoke and frying which was not unpleasant, but suddenly some people started burning dried chillies in an attempt to placate bad spirits. This produced a stringent unpleasant smell which went straight to one's throat, causing the kids to start coughing. But she understood that most people around were probably also embarking on some momentous journey, and therefore were leaving nothing to chance. There was so much malevolence in this world. Angrily she pushed away Pradeep who was pulling her sari.

Raju had left some money with her so she could get some tea and puris for herself and the kids. She was terribly scared, of the people rushing in all directions, of the kids wandering away and getting lost in the crowd, of Raju getting robbed or beaten, or whatever. She tied the hands of the kids with the ends of her sari whenever she had to move. Fortunately there were vendors coming over every five minutes, offering to sell chai, nimbu pani, falooda, pakoras and puris and such things. The children wanted to do a wee wee every ten minutes, so she had to let them go the short distance towards a banyan tree with its hanging roots providing some sort of screen. They did not really want to ease themselves, they had discovered that the short walk was a sound strategy against being confined to a small area centred round their mother. When she herself needed to go, she thought that the best thing would be to tie the children to their bundles, but there was a family squatting nearby, probably also waiting for someone or something, and the auntie offered to look after the children and their things. Gratefully she accepted and disappeared behind a thick root, but she was immediately seized by panic. Were these people as honest as they appeared to be? Maybe that was how they made a living, they sat next to people who had arrived from another place with their things, offered to look after them and their children, and then the moment the adult was out of sight, they stole the children or the possessions, or both. But she bent forward and peeped, and saw the woman talking to the girl. She was relieved when she went back and found everything as they were when she had left. She began talking to the family. Indeed, it was as she had guessed, they were also Biharis and were also thinking of going to some other country, although the woman had no idea where. Ask their father, she said. Mareeshush? Shanti asked. No, she thought it sounded like Damrara. She was getting impatient when the men did not come back, and the heat was becoming unbearable. A sadhu, approached her and asked if he could pray for her and her family, and she agreed, and gave the man one pise which he gratefully accepted. I will tell you your future, the holy man said. 'You have had a tough time in the past, but now everything is going to change for the better, you have a great future ahead of you. You and your family are moving to a new place, tell me if I am right.' Shanti nodded. You will prosper there, he said, and you and your husband will live a very happy and fulfilled life. You will have three more babies and all will live, and become very successful in life. Shanti was not sure whether to believe him or not, but liked what she heard, specially as she was quite terrified of what was in store for her and her family. She parted with another pise. She forgot her annoyance at the men's continued absence for a while, she knew that Raju was not one of those irresponsible men who forget their family once away from them. Maybe he liked a drink or two, but he never went overboard, and never got drunk.

It was quite late when Jayant came back with the good news that he had easily sold the boat, and had been had paid half in cash and half in cloth and blankets. He was such a kind soul, most of the cloth was for the kids. But why did you not get any for yourself? Shanti asked. No, didi, he said, the children get dressed, and I feel the pride. And he had this endearing habit of smiling, closing his eyes slightly and moving his heads from left to right a few times before he spoke. Raju too reappeared, beaming all over. Shanti grabbed him and burst into tears, as her nerves were all frayed with the excitement and terrors of the day. 'You took your time, never worrying about us,' she said. Raju who had in fact been as quick as he could, knew that there was no point trying to defend himself and just smiled apologetically.

A hawker appeared and Raju bought tea and aloo pakoras for everybody, but Jayant insisted on paying saying that he had sold the boat for much more than he hoped for. Those Bengalis who think they are so clever are so easy to fool, he cackled under his breath. They sat down and had a little feast. The children who had allowed boredom and bad temper to get the better of their recent joyous state, soon regained their good humour and they all felt considerably cheered when Raju told them that Mahendra had arranged for them to travel in two, maybe three days' time. They found a much more secluded place and the men made a sort of shelter with sheets and blankets to keep the punishing sun at bay. Raju and Jayant spent the day smoking bidis, sometimes enjoying some toddy. The Gujrati man had explained to Raju what the procedures were. First one had to go to the Auxiliary Harbour Office next to the Ghat, a hastily constructed shed with corrugated iron roofs which made it unbearably hot, tell the officer your name and particulars, which he will write in a book, put your thumb mark on some official papers, and then you get taken to a barge which takes you to the ship anchored further away down the Hoogli, where it was deep enough and where there was a port.

They made their way towards the Ghat and waited there for a crucial announcement. They found a huge crowd, for there were three ships leaving in the next three days. Just remember your ship is the Startled Fawn, Mahendra had said. No one really knew where the tail of queue was, so what people did was to push their luck, choosing a place where there was an almost imperceptible gap and literally burrowing in. Often people would moan and protest, and then if they were bigger than you, you said sorry and moved on, otherwise, you browbeat them and stayed put. Raju was unable to find a suitable place near the Office, so the family (and Jayant) settled down in a spot which was at some distance from the shed. Someone said the officers were now dealing with people travelling on the Jupiter which was going to Fiji and that it would take anything up to eighteen hours. A man asked when they were going to process the passengers of the Sea Pride, and a Bengali clerk said tomorrow noon. Clearly the Startled Fawn was going to be some time. The moment one family went in, the people behind began pushing, squashing everybody else. Tempers were frayed and angry words were exchanged, but there were always one or two wiser heads who explained that the pushing and shoving were not going to compress the time. The time, one of them explained, was going to be the same, it's the people who would become thinner by being squeezed. Well said, Chacha, someone said laughing, and temporary good humour was restored. Raju, judging by the length of the queue and the rate at which people went inside the office, guessed that as their ship was going to be the last one to leave, it would be late tomorrow night, or even day after before things started moving for them. In fact an officious man with twirling moustaches, in some sort of uniform, had said the same.

Some time in mid-morning, while everybody was drinking chai and eating roti, which Shanti had cooked under the banyan tree, they saw a man who reminded them of Sukhdeo. They all laughed, in the knowledge that they were now out of the cruel man's reach, even if it was him.

But it was him! And he seemed to be in quite a state, sweating profusely. He gave out a big sigh of relief when he identified Raju and his family. He moved faster with a big smile on his face.

'I am so relieved to see you my boy. If you only knew how many sleepless nights I have spent... I have been looking for you all over the place... Mahendra told me you would be queuing up near the Ghat.'

'Namasté, uncle,' Raju said coldly, wondering why the old pain-giver was so relieved to see him.

'I have something of great importance to say to you, I wonder if you would like to come with me... somewhere where we can talk... privately.'

'Get lost, you old bastard!' Raju wished he could say, but he did not. Instead he said, 'Oh Uncle, I am glad to see you too, but if you have come all the way just to get me to change my plans at this late hour to come back and work for you as before, I am afraid it is too late now.'

'I know, I know, but no, I am afraid it's more serious than that, just come along for a bit.'

'As you can see, there is a massive big queue, I cannot lose my place —'

'No, people will understand, your family is here, right?'

'But the ship —'

'Your ship isn't leaving until the day after tomorrow. All I need is fifteen minutes, then you can come back here and depart with my blessing.'

'But, but'

'Just come, you will not regret it, I assure you, Shanti is well able to manage fifteen minutes without you.'

He looked at Shanti, and she shrugged, meaning do as you think fit and get rid of him as quickly as you can. Jayant gave him an encouraging look which meant, I am here, I'll make sure no harm comes to the family, so he reluctantly agreed to walk a few steps with Sukhdeo.

'I want to go with Baba,' said the girl forcefully. Raju stopped in his tracks.

'Bring the little jewel along,' entreated Sukhdeo, 'what's the harm?' Shanti demurred.

'Pradeep will want to come too, you know what he's like,' she said.

'No, I don't,' said the boy, 'I want to stay with you here, Mama.'

'Come along then, Sundari,' said Raju extending a hand which the little girl immediately seized, and they were on their way.

'Don't let go of Baba's hand whatever you do, Sweetie,' were Shanti's last words, and father and daughter and the leech walked away. She watched her man for a while, sure that he would turn round once, although usually, whenever he had said his goodbye, he seemed to forget the people and things he had left behind, so much did he hate lingering. Please Bhagwan, Shanti entreated silently, make him turn round just this once, and indeed, just when he was almost disappearing amongst the milling crowd, he turned round and as their eyes met, he gave his head a little twist to one side and winked at her. She was too far to see the winking, but knew her man's gestures inside out. She craned her neck forward to make sure he caught a glimpse of her. My dear man, she thought, I just hope that Dukhdeo fellow means him no harm.

'Sundari,' said the old friendly woman sitting beside them, 'what a lovely name!'

'No, chachi, we just call her Sundari, it's not her real name, her name is —'

'She is so pretty, so she deserves that name,' said the old auntie merrily.

The time passed very slowly. Rumours were rife and contradictory. One barge was leaving, it was with passengers travelling on the Jupiter. Shanti began panicking, but someone who looked quite authoritative explained that the barge that had left was coming back and going to do two or three more trips, and that in any case there were three barges plying between the Harbour Office and the port. The man also said that the Startled Fawn was not going to be ready until the next day. Shanti was greatly relieved to hear that, but still wished Raju would be back soon. Half an hour elapsed and Raju was not back. Suddenly Jayant became very excited.

'Look, Raju Bhai is there, can you see him?' And he pointed at the figures of a man of Raju's appearance and a little girl at some distance away.

'Are you sure it's them?' asked Shanti who was not convinced, 'what colour was the dress of the little girl?' Jayant had not noticed, but was so sure of what he saw that he tried to remember what the girl was wearing, and blurted out, 'blue.'

'She was wearing a green dress,' Shanti snapped.

'Might have been green, so difficult to say, in this light blue and green look so similar,' adding almost shamefacedly, 'also I have difficulty telling green from blue...' But he decided to go find them and bring them back. However, when he started walking, he found that it was next to impossible to inch himself forward. People reacted angrily as he tried to squeeze past them, and that made progress very difficult, and in no time he was swamped by the crowd. As Shanti could no longer see him, she thought that the two men must have met by now. Damn that giver of pain! Hope nothing bad has happened to my Sundari. Why did she want to go with her dad? Fortunately for her, in the heat of the afternoon, she dozed off for she did not know how long, but when she woke up, Jayant had not come back. That Jayant is so unreliable, she thought.

CHAPTER 17

❖❖❖

A Highland Clearance

HELPLESSNESS, UTTER AND absolute helplessness was the state Hugh was in. What Albert had told him was the saddest piece of news ever to come his way. The obstacles were too many and too arduous. What could he, to all intents and purposes, an escaped convict, do against the combined forces of landlords, their powerful allies in the government and the forces of law and order? They had all the cards and the tenants had none. No man to turn his back on a problem, he, but he prided himself that he was ever the realist. There are some battles one can never win, the dice are loaded against the poor. He knew that he would never be able to wean silly Kitty away from that toff who would bring nothing but shame and misery on the family. As he knew that one day John who was now working on the Caledonian canal, was going to leave for Canada or the Carolinas and that there was nothing he could do to stop him.

First their crops had largely failed, and famine was rearing its ugly head. Mam had a point, if God existed, he was not on the side of the poor. How can anybody fight a campaign against such heavy odds on an empty stomach? He had witnessed the rape of the gentle folks of Lairg, three hundred families dispossessed of their crofts, carted away like cattle to hastily built shacks on the northern banks of Loch Naver, with no means of feeding themselves, entirely dependent on the charity of the lairds and the church. The Cheviot sheep was everywhere, you could not sneeze without a droplet landing on one!

Hugh was torn between self-preservation and his determination to do what was right. He and his fellow crofters were under threat, and he was probably the only man around who had some experience of organising a movement to resist the onslaught. Could the so-called Improvement be stopped? Very probably not, it was like an avalanche slowly moving down the mountains, gathering speed nobody was going to stop it. You would end up get swallowed by its destructive power if you stood in its path. But does one have the right to just accept a calamity because the odds are stacked against one. He had once been a fugitive from the injustice of the strong and powerful, and if he raised his head in a crowd, his potential enemies might look more closely and discover who he was, but it would be cowardly to do nothing and watch his community decimated. For days he had been obsessed by that dilemma, and in the end he knew that he had no choice. He would be part of a movement working towards the best possible solution for his fellow tenants, but he would need to act cautiously and behind the scenes.

When a few potential victims of what was balefully looming overhead were invited to partake of some illicit brew at Tam's, the conversation immediately turned to crofters and lairds, the hated Improvement and relocation. It was easy to moot the point that crossing one's arms and waiting for the worst to hit you was not an option. Everybody agreed, and when Tam raised his tankard to this, Hugh, who was not devoid of cunning, chose his moment.

'Since brother Tam is advocating that we stick together and plan a course of action, I think we should hear what he has to say.'

Tam could be quite astute, but he was guileless, and walked into Hugh's trap.

'Aye,' he said, 'we must be united, and... eh... plan a course of action.'

'But remember, brothers, violence will get us nowhere,' suggested Auld MacDonald. This had a mixed reception. Hugh decided that his best course of action was to listen and say nothing substantial himself. He noted that the determination of the folks was pretty solid, they all execrated the notion of relocation. He thought that Tam and Auld MacDonald would make reasonable negotiators, and mentioned this to Rab who was standing by his side. He was pleased when only a short while later, Rab repeated these same sentiments. One or two people loudly agreed with this, and before long it was clear that the two men would be the voice of the Movement. Hugh felt that he had a lot to contribute, but did not wish to be a kingmaker. He was a straightforward man, maybe not without guile but certainly devoid of malice, and he thought that a little scheming when it was for the common good that was perfectly acceptable. He quickly worked out his strategy: he would waylay each man in turn, and raise some issues with them and offer some advice stealthily, and immediately after the point had sunk in, he would say something like, 'I think your idea about demanding to talk to Sellar with no preconditions is an excellent one, Mac.' Or, 'I am glad you believe that you should let it be known to the Duchess that the men all agree that she is fair-minded and will never do anything that openly went against the general interest, but perhaps you should also mention that people talk about her with great fondness for her past kindness in providing help in times of famine.' And Tam would add, 'But of course, Angus, of course I will say that, and refrain from saying that she was the root cause of the famine in the first place.' Tam was clearly no fool. And the two men would have a good laugh. Hugh felt elated at being able to put his ideas across without raising his head above the parapet.

As Tam MacDiarmidd and Auld MacDonald's leadership became more established, Hugh felt that his role in the proceedings had been kept well out of the limelight, and he felt empowered to give advice more openly, but he sometimes worried about those two worthy men shouldering the blame if things went badly. He gave the pair one piece of advice which they found particularly useful.

'Put it to Mr Sellar and Mr Young like this: say you abhor violence and that you were finding it more and more difficult to stop our people threatening to set fire to the shepherds' houses, but they were angry and you feared that you might not be able to stop a tragedy unless the Duchess and other lairds were more conciliatory.'

Tam and Auld Mac did their job very competently, and the upshot was that they wormed out some concessions from the lairds who allowed provisions for cattle to be purchased at improved rates. Further the tenants were allowed to stay in their abodes for a further six months, until proper accommodation was built for them in Caithness. But no power on earth would make the Duchess budge from her position that resettlement would be on a very fragile basis. She stood firm on her insistence that no leases would be accorded. Everybody recognised that this was a wicked strategy to ensure compliance with her every wish, that any recalcitrance however minor would be followed by instant eviction without recourse.

Then the worst famine to hit the Northern Highlands in man's memory struck, and the men became disheartened. The 42nd Regiment was again deployed from Dundee, and the soldiers made their presence felt in order to intimidate the helpless folks under threat of eviction. The Duchess did not hesitate to break the word she had given to the people and ordered instant evictions, which were enthusiastically carried out by Sellar and his team. At first they allowed the evicted to dismantle their lodgings so that they could transport them wherever it was possible to rebuild, but there were instances of some dispossessed crofters coming back and rebuilding on the same site. It was thus that Sellar decided to put into practice his brilliant if sinister plan of setting fire to the crofts. He was quite enthusiastic about the use of force to evict his victims, and on two occasions people died.

Hugh was in a state of deep despair when he heard of the death of old Mrs MacPherson who was over ninety, and senile. When he had first moved to Strathnaver from Fort Williams, she had been one of the first to help, with offerings of oats and potatoes, and looking after Kitty and John whilst the grown ups were busy settling in. Sellar's men, accompanied by a handful of fierce looking men from the 43rd, had commanded them to move outside, and Sellar himself declared in his loud whine of a voice that he was giving them fifteen minutes to collect their possessions, and warned that his men had orders to set the shack on fire after that. The MacPherson sons, knowing that the factor meant business had quickly gathered their belongings and in fourteen minutes they were all out, the old lady leaning on the shoulder of her daughter-in-law. Sellar then gave a nod, and a man, making an apologetic grimace to the family took a torch to the wooden walls, and it surprised everybody how quickly the conflagration spread. The ninety-year old woman looked at it in amazement, utterly confused, then suddenly, freeing herself from her daughter-in-law's grip, she shouted, 'We forgot Mam inside… coming to help you, Mam…' and screaming, she rushed into the flaming house with surprising nimbleness in an attempt to save her long dead and buried Mam. On the same day Hugh saw Kitty run to her Grandma in tears, and it transpired that she was pregnant.

John had not been gone a month when a penny post arrived telling the family how happy he was in Fort Williams, with a team doing maintenance work on the equipment. But from the beginning he understood that the dark clouds of downsizing hovered over those desirable jobs. The company was always short of funds, although the manager had assured them that any lay offs was likely to be short lived. It was known that the government in London was very keen for the project to go on, temporary hiccoughs notwithstanding.

Still nobody was too surprised when one afternoon, John arrived home unexpectedly, explaining that following the principle of last man in first man out, his services had been dispensed with. At first he said that he would be happy to work with his Da until he got the call to return to Fort Williams.

The boy had made some savings and was excited at being able to buy gifts to his loved ones. Even Da was forced to accept a new pair of boots.

The family soon gathered that the uncertainty in which John was living was not making him happy. Grand Mam was not too surprised when one day he spoke to her of his renewed interest in the Earl of Selkirk's scheme, and the old woman did nothing to discourage him. She had heard that the Duchess opposed emigration on the grounds that she needed a good workforce in the Highlands in order to turn it into the new Lancashire, and this was enough to convince Grand Mam that emigration must therefore be a good thing. To Hugh, the Earl had no more business getting Highlanders to leave the home of their ancestors, than the Duchess the right to "Improve". Why don't they leave us alone, and let us get on with our lives like we always have?

'My belief,' said Mam, 'is that the chance offered by the Earl is not to be dismissed lightly.'

'Mam,' Hugh had said sharply, 'oor John has no intention of leaving for the Americas, don't be putting silly ideas in his head.'

John said nothing, smiled enigmatically, but Kitty knew it there and then that no power on earth was going to keep her brother on these Scottish shores. Indeed it was not a week when John came home one afternoon, smelling of ale, and told them that he was due to sail for Nova Scotia in three weeks' time. It was all arranged, he was travelling on the *Moonglow* from Cromarty, his passage paid by Selkirk's organisation, and the shameless boy could not hide his joy at his impending departure.

San Cassimally

Hugh stared at his son for a whole minute before opening his mouth. His face was red all over, and it was obvious to Kitty that he was on the verge of tears.

'Does your family mean so little to you, John, that you could even contemplate leaving... your Ma... your family to go God knows where, and... and... be so pleased about it?' John opened his mouth to protest but could find no words. Grand Mam tut tutted, and Hugh looked at her sternly, saying nothing.

'Hughie,' she said, 'would you say I loved you any less than you love oor John here?' He said nothing.

'If after the Ross-shire Insurrection, you had been able to go to the Americas instead of facing a trial for your life, I would have been the happiest woman alive, even if I were never to see you again. Knowing that you were safe and well would have been enough for me.' After a short pause she added, 'When he is there he might look up his granda and his step uncles...' she added to the amazement of John and his sister.

John and Kitty looked at each other, dumbfounded. They had often heard their Da called Hugh, but had obviously given it less attention than it deserved. They had heard about the Insurrection, but knew little about it, and neither could imagine that their father had faced a trial for his life. Martha noticed the consternation on her children's face, and turned round to face Grand Mam, who immediately understood that she had just unwittingly broken the oath of secrecy. But she was defiant as always.

'I know, I know... I shoudnae hae said that, I dinnae mean tae, but they are grown-ups now and need to know the family history... yes, your father led the Ross-shire riots and stood trial for his life in Aberdeen. He was found guilty of rioting and sentenced to transportation.' She took a deep breath and told them the whole saga.

'But... but Da —' John was not able to finish the sentence

'And his name isn't Angus Smith either, he was born Hugh Breac Mackenzie... I've always hated the name Angus anyway.'

'Children, you must know how dangerous it still is for your father if this story gets out of the walls of this house, even after all those years. If he is caught, this time it will be the gallows and make no mistake.'

254

'We are not kids,' they said together. John, on a sudden impulse jumped up from his chair and threw himself at his father and hugged him saying, 'Oh Da! Oh Da! We never knew.'

Although Hugh had tears in his eyes and could not utter a single word because of the lump in his throat, Kitty knew that that was perhaps the happiest night of his life, his son's impending departure notwithstanding. He gently pushed John away, but everybody, including the son could see that he would have dearly loved to hang on to the boy for another hour, but proud Highlanders did not hug each other. Martha grabbed John's hand and led him to his chair like a blind man. Hugh cleared his throat and said, 'John, do what you must do, as your Grand Mam said, the important thing is for you to do something of your life, never do anything that your Mam would disapprove of.'

'No, Da, of course not.' Kitty would have bet her life on this.

'I am sorry John, I wasn't thinking straight, your Grand Mam is right... I was only thinking of your Mam... you know how much you mean to her...' and almost inaudibly he added, 'to me.'

Could it be true, Kitty wondered, that she would never see her brother again in this life, the only life one had, according to Grand Mam. John on his part could not hide his impatience at the slowness of the day. He would leave Strathnaver in two weeks, and he had worked it out, fourteen days, three hundred and thirty-six hours, over twenty thousand minutes! Then six weeks at sea. He couldn't wait to experience the sensation of finding yourself surrounded on all sides by the deep blue roaring sea, listening to the waves lashing against the bulwark, of being sprayed with invisible droplets of sea water. The fun of sailing will more than compensate for the separation from his loved ones. Of course he loved them all, he only wished that he had been a better son and brother, but he knew that in the eyes of Grand Mam he could do no wrong, although he supposed that the many stories she told them about this whinging boy in that country which was more north of the North Pole was modelled on him and meant to be moral lessons against selfishness and wickedness. I am not really a wicked person, he assured himself. If it's true that one could make good money in the Americas, he certainly will not forget his family, he would send them money and whatever he could. Who knows, he may even be able to send for them.

Suddenly there were only two days left for him to start on his journey to Cromarty, and he was filled with panic. He could not swim, what would he do if the ship hit an iceberg and sank? How was he going to bear the sadness of the separation? Could he change his mind? Da would like that, and Mam too. Poor Kitty! He had always been unfair to her, and yet she was so clearly distraught at the idea of his going away. No one can ever love you as much as your family. He doubted that if one day he fell in love and married some woman, she would love him as intensely as the family did. Poor Da! I never dreamt that he could have been involved in organising a riot against the lairds. What a crying shame that I have never really known my Da! I never knew that he was a hero, but I've always seen him act heroically all his life. He is a man of few words, and I will never have the opportunity of finding out more about him. And the poor man's trouble isn't over yet! Will he ever know peace? Already there are signs of another upheaval. That pestilential woman in Dunrobin wants more money in her coffers. She obviously does not care how much suffering she inflicts on the poor. What will Da do if he gets served an eviction order? Will he go to the coast and learn to become a fisherman at his age? Has he got the strength left in him to go kelping? What will happen to Mam, to Kitty? Suddenly he shivered as he thought of Da being involved in another movement against the lairds. They would be bound to find out who he is. No, John cried aloud, I cannot let them hang him! I must not be a coward and abandon him. Da who was outside heard him and came in. John was pale and was trembling all over.

'What's the matter, John?'

'Da, I... I am not going to leave, I want to be by your side... I don't want anything bad to happen to you... please Da, tell me you will not... expose yourself to any danger...'

'Of course not, my bonnie boy, I am a cautious man... no harm will come to me, I promise you.' He shook his head, the ghost of a smile on his face, and added, 'Don't be a softie, laddie.'

'My mind is made up now, in any case, I am not leaving.'

'Think of your future, laddie, you have a big future ahead of you, don't waste it.'

But his mind was made up now, he was going to stay in Strathnaver and if the family had to go to Wick or Caithness, then his place was with them. Hugh tried to talk him out of this stupid resolution, but seemingly to no effect. Martha likewise had her say, and finally Grand Mam. His resolution to stay was unshakeable, he swore. Maybe later when things settle down, he said, he'll think again.

However in the night, Martha and Grand Mam packed up his things, the woollen socks, hats and jumpers that they had knitted, the shirts Martha had cut and sewn by hand, the dry oat biscuits Kitty had baked for him, the bottles of illicit beer Hugh had bought from Ebenezer Reid. When they woke him up and he saw that everything was ready, he was relieved, for in the night his resolution to stick with the family had weakened, and he allowed them to talk him into pursuing the course he had been so keen on embarking upon a few days before.

The whole family went with him to Golspie by cart. Everybody put on a brave face, but John himself could not stop his tears streaking down his cheeks. They arrived at Golspie to find the boat to Cromarty was already loading. When Father and son hugged and kissed each other for the last time, he said, 'Ah dear sweet John, so you are away to an unknown land. May God look after you and make you prosper.' Even in that poignant situation Grand Mam could not stop herself murmuring that one has to look after oneself for God only looked after the rich. Hugh looked at his old Mam with loving indulgence. Then he turned to the boy and said those words he later wished had remained unsaid, as he feared that they would cause unnecessary distress to the boy.

'Can it really be the last time you and I will touch each other like this, laddie?' John was unable to stifle a sob, and the man who had defied the armed Cameron brothers broke down and sobbed like a child.

'If you do meet your granda,' Hugh heard himself say, 'give him our love.'

Kitty was distraught at not hearing from Rob Rob. Could it be that she had been wrong about him? Grand Mam had warned her about those rich young men who wanted their wicked ways with peasant wenches, promised them the earth and then abandoned them to their fate. The besotted young woman would believe that lochs would freeze in midsummer before believing that her darling had been toying with her affections. She had always had a self-assurance uncommon in people like her, and concluded that the Duchess who had long arms must have connived with the Eton authorities and with the postal service in Sutherland to deviate correspondence between the two of them, to Dunrobin, not that this stopped her, every morning, from thinking that she would hear from her lover in the course of the day.

Martha decided that Kitty was not going to do any more heavy work in view of her condition. The pregnant teenager had protested that she felt fine and that the baby was not due for a good few months anyway, but Martha put her foot down. No lassie, you stay at home and knit things for the wean and read your books, we do not want you to take any chances. In any case, Hughie had got rid of two of the cows when he was unexpectedly offered a good price for them. Kitty was surprised that no one had been angry with her for what she had done. No one accused her of bringing shame on the family. She knew of girls in her position who, ordered out of the parental house had disappeared into the Edinburgh mist never to re-emerge. Strangely, Hugh even gave the impression that he was even looking forward to becoming a granda.

What happened next was something nobody was prepared for. A few weeks later, Hugh had gone to Golspie and was drowning his sorrow in a tankard of ale at the Stag Heid when George the innkeeper asked if he had heard the news. What news? Don't know how to put this, Angus. Put it in any way you like, George, I could not hear worse, the day. Ah but you can, Angus, didn't your John go to the Americas on the *Moonglow*? Hugh stood up in panic, spilling his tankard. His body went as cold as a corpse, he did not need to hear more.

'George, you are lying!' He shouted, 'You are a lying villain, how can you?'

Other folks rallied around, trying to calm him down. The *Moonglow* had indeed gone down off the coast of Newfoundland with complete loss of life. How right Mam had always been. How can a loving God inflict so much misery on the poor of this world?

When he got home, tears were rolling down his cheeks, and the three alarmed women rushed to him and Martha took him by the arm and asked him what had happened. It's my fault, was all he was able to say. What's your fault, they all asked, and he shook his head and kept crying. They sat him down, and waited. It took a long time for him to stop shaking and sobbing, by which time, the women had guessed the truth. But not wanting to tempt the devil, they maintained their composure, and waited for Hugh to spell it out for them.

'The boy,' he said, and stopped immediately, his speech shut out by new sobs.

'The boy? You mean oor John?'

'What happened to oor John?'

'Da, it can't be true, what are you saying?'

He made a sudden lurch towards Kitty, seized her forcefully, and drawing her to his bosom he hugged her, and suddenly calmed down.

'Aye, Kitty, the *Moonglow* went down in a storm, and everybody's drowned.' Kitty pushed him away, angrily, and began shrieking, 'No, it can't be true, Da, you are lying, they lied to you, oor John can't be dead he is only young!' Grand Mam started sobbing quietly, shaking her head in disbelief. Suddenly Martha, who had never in twenty years raised her voice at her man, flung herself at her husband and with her clenched little fists started hammering the poor man on the chest, saying, 'It's your fault, Hugh Breac MacKenzie, it's your fault! You had to go and attack those Cameron brothers and get us thrown out of our home… everything you do ends up in disaster…' Then, God knows where she got the strength from, she took hold of him and shook him with surprising violence and said, 'You think you are a big man, how come you could not stop him leaving?' Kitty was going to pull her away from the helpless man, but Grand Mam stopped her, and raised her hands in a clear indication that she should let Martha say her piece. She continued talking incoherently, her words mixed with her sobs made gibberish.

When Martha had calmed down, she went and sat in a corner on the floor, her head between her knees, and she wept silently for her lost little boy. Hugh grabbed Kitty again and pulled her towards him.

'Promise me it's a boy you're carrying inside you, lassie, we'll call him John, promise me.' Kitty smiled wanly and nodded sadly.

One afternoon, a few weeks after the *Moonglow* had gone down, whilst she was sitting outside the shack, knitting something nice and warm for the baby who was now due in a matter of days, Kitty saw the postie coming over. She was not yet ready to accept that Rob Rob had forgotten her and could not contain her joy, and shouted, 'Grandma, what did I tell you? He's written!' Grandma was not even within hearing distance. The postie was out of breath by the time he reached the farm, and delivered a letter to Kitty, who was too excited to offer him a cuppa. She was surprised when she saw that it was addressed to Da. She was used to opening letters for the family, and she sat down, watched the postman disappear. Carefully she opened the letter, and recognised John's scrawl.

Dearest Da, Mam, Grand Mam and Kitty,

First of all I am terribly sorry if you have had the pain of mourning my passing, but no doubt you will be pleased that I am still alive and not only well, but prospering. Let me tell you first of all that we had so many mishaps, nearly sinking with our leaky little boat, that when we arrived in Cromarty, the Moonglow had already left. So this explains how I am still around. Lord Selkirk's agent arranged for me to travel on the next ship which left three days later. Our ship, the Highland Fling did not sink. We landed safely in Quebec and travelled mostly overland to Port Hope. I was homesick and felt lonely although I met many capital fellows during the voyage. I am now in Oxenham, Ontario. The Captain, my employer strikes me as the most fair-minded man in the whole world.

Dearest Da and Ma, and Grandmam and snotty Kitty, I worry about you all the time. I know how difficult life is for you, with threat of eviction hanging over your head all the time. You cannot fight the rich lairds Da, you do not have the means, the dice is loaded against the poor; Grandmam is right. If you allow me to give you some advice Da, the best thing you can do is to come and join me here. The Captain says he can use lots more people on his farm. The conditions are fair and square, and nobody treats you like animals. And it is a beautiful country, and I am sure you will never regret it if you come over. I am dying to see you all. Think of my proposition. I do not yet have much, but I will send you some money soon. If you decide to come over, the Captain has offered to advance the money for fares etc...

Your loving John, who is very much alive.

Kitty's first reaction was to destroy the letter, as she refused to entertain the idea of the family emigrating to Canada. What would Rob Rob do if when he came looking for her and found her gone? Then she became so angry with herself she felt like smashing her head against a tree. How could she commit the mortal sin of depriving the family of the happiness of finding that their John was still alive? Oor John is alive, she started shouting to nobody in particular, dancing about, paying no attention to the baby inside her. It was Martha who first saw her in this state as she came in from the potato field. Kitty flung herself at her mother, shouting 'He is alive, Mam, he is alive!'

'Aye, but is he going to do the right thing by you? Is he coming over to marry you as he promised?' Kitty laughed merrily.

'Mam, I am talking about oor John! He did not drown, he is alive and well.'

Martha was too confused to understand.

Kitty, in spite of her condition, fairly carried Martha over to the shack, sat her down and sat at her feet, and read John's letter.

'God be praised!' said Martha crying and laughing at the same time. Grand Mam came into the shack at the same time, and frowning asked, 'Why take his name in vain?'

'Oor John is alive and well, Mam, God be praised!' Grand Mam could not believe her ears, and making her hands into raised little fists, she turned on herself in a spontaneous sort of comical jig.

'So oor John is alive and well...'

'He missed the boat which sank!' explained Kitty.

'The good Lord made him miss that boat,' said Martha defiantly. Grand Mam nodded, then smiling almost in triumph, said, 'If that was the Lord's doing, then so was the sinking of the boat he missed, with two hundred dead, all sons of grieving mothers.'

It was Hugh's turn to come in next, and he could not believe his eyes when he saw the women laughing and dancing around excitedly.

'If you knew what I just heard, you would not be dancing about,' he said with obvious disapproval. To his surprise this reproach rekindled the hilarity. He could not remember ever seeing the dour old woman so happy. He felt his anger begin to rise.

'And if you knew what we just heard, you would join us, Hugh Mackenzie, instead of looking like you've just swallowed a mouthful of dung,' said Grand Mam merrily. Martha went to him, took him by the arm, and told him the news. Hugh looked like he did not believe this, but the women were jumping about and looking so happy that he knew that it had to be true.

When the women had calmed down, he asked Kitty to read the letter to him. He listened to it attentively, and when Kitty had finished, he nodded gravely, and it was one whole minute before he spoke.

'Since oor John thinks it's a good idea, I think we had better take him at his word and go join him... it's the only solution... I'll look into it.'

Kitty was absolutely shattered, she did not wish to leave. What would Rob Rob do when he finally made it back to the Strath? Was there an alternative? Da had already taken the decision, and nobody would listen to her. She could not run away, where would she go? How would she feed herself?

'What were your bad news, Hughie,' Martha asked him softly. He shook his head sadly, but did not reply immediately.

'They are giving out eviction orders... ours are surely due to come in a day or two.'

The straw to which Kitty had been clinging to vaporised into thin air, leaving her sinking in a bog of despair. How would she communicate with Rob Rob? Let him know where she was. Mr Shelley did not seem to have passed on her desperate message. But he was her only chance.

Book II

CHAPTER 1

◆◆◆

Leaving Inhambane

MIDALA HAD STOPPED feeling the pain in his ankle and wrist, but what was worse was that his whole body felt numb. His unjustified anger at Bomo the carpenter, the fellow he was chained to at the legs and the wrists, his twin, as he thought of him not without bitterness, had gone after he had repeated to himself that the poor man had not chosen to be tied to him. He had kept telling himself that Bomo had as much right to be angry with him, for whatever discomfort was unwittingly inflicted upon one of them, he had no choice but to instinctively react to the inevitable pain generated under the circumstances in order to minimise his own. He was surprised to discover, by his body language and the expression on his face that the carpenter bore him no grudge at all. He is a better man than me, he had thought. More in order to atone for his sullenness than for enlightenment, he whispered the blindingly obvious information, 'I think we are being taken to the ship'. This earned him an immediate hit in the ribs by the mute mulatto guard. Midala felt the sharp pain, and would have been minded to jump on his attacker and beat him to a pulp had his movements not been restricted.

The ship could sometimes be seen in the distance when the vegetation and the rocky reliefs permitted. The sea ahead was visible as a pale bluish-green blanket with white embroidered patches where two or more waves collided. A gentle breeze somewhat mitigated their misery. Do you know where we're going? asked Bomo under his breath, coughing slyly to disguise this infringement of the rule of silence, Midala shrugged. The mulatto saw nothing.

Bomo was almost the same build as him. The captors knew exactly how to pair the captives in order to convey them from the point of capture to the point of delivery most efficiently. The two men had known each other, but they had never had much intercourse, Bomo being a humble carpenter who earned his living making dugout canoes and wooden implements for pounding yam, stools, tom-toms and beds. He lived in his hut at the far end of the village, near the river, with his two wives and six children. He had no idea what had happened to any of them. The modest carpenter knew all about his illustrious twin, how many wars he had won for the tribe. He knew that whenever there was any problem, the Cojo entrusted him with the task of finding a solution. Everybody talked about the beads he had invented for the purpose of carrying out quick calculations, about his two-tiered folding ladder which made tree climbing so much easier (and to his chagrin, encouraged drunkenness, as it made it easier for people to tap their own wines from the palm trees). His other great invention was the hoe with holes in it to facilitate the separation of pebbles from earth, but it was undoubtedly his method of keeping the rogue elephants at bay which had earned him his unassailable position as the brains of the tribe. A man like him, the carpenter had surmised, is bound to be the best man to be tied to. Clearly if anybody can find the means of escaping the dire fate waiting for them, that man would be Midala the warrior.

Escape was naturally the first thing that Midala had thought of the moment he was captured, and he vowed to himself that somehow he would get out of this, but he was too shocked and angry to think of anything at the moment. As a military strategist, he never did anything impulsively, but collected all the pertinent facts first, weighed all the considerations, the risks involved and how to minimise them, and the advantages to be gained by the various courses open to him.

He was not happy with himself for allowing his plight to cloud his vision and for, thus far, not paying any attention to the misery of his brothers and sisters who had fought so valiantly and had nevertheless either been killed or captured. He never ceased to marvel at the bravery of the women generally, and of his own Rolena in particular. The cowards had felled her with their spear and stabbed her to death, and he had been unable to do anything for her, as he was himself fending off the assault of three attackers at the time. He knew why they killed her. It was clear to all that they had been ordered to seize as many captives alive, for a dead captive is worth nothing except to vultures and hyenas. Rolena had overcome two of her attackers, one armed with a gun, and killed them. They had been shamed by her valour, angry at being bested by a mere woman, and finally by the force of numbers and superior weapons, they were able to overcome her. There was no point in dwelling upon the fate of that most excellent of women. The warrior knew that death in a just war was not something to be deplored. It was a singular honour to die for the tribe, but he was a mere mortal, and the sight of the person he loved most on this earth lying on the ground covered in blood, lifeless, was unbearable, and it had quite unmanned him. He had thrown himself on her inert body and wept like a woman — which had made it possible for his enemies to overcome and capture him, thus earning a rebuke from the warrior in him. A husband reacts differently to a fighter. She had been a loving wife and mother. They had laughed together, had had a good life, he could always depend on her common sense, her loyalty to him and the tribe. It had been the dearest wish of both of them to grow old together and watch their children blossom into adulthood and give them grandchildren. A passionate and virile man, he had always laughed off suggestions by the elders of the tribe that he took more wives. Rolena was all the woman he wanted. The Spirits would surely welcome her in the Land Beyond and she will wait for him when his time came, and spend eternity together. He wished that it might be soon, but knew that it was his duty to stay alive, as he felt responsible for this brothers and sisters of the tribe. Alive he might be of some use to them. He could see his fellow tribesmen and women, shackled together, some like him and Bomo, others in threes or fours, some with wooden yokes locking their necks together, many of them bleeding as these implements of the devil tore into their skins and flesh. This was much more painful than being twinned, he imagined, for you could hardly turn round without hurting your neck as well as that of your fellow victims.

The massive Ibn Qalb, stroking his pot belly was in the forefront of the file, being carried by four Zanzibari youths in a palanquin. The English captain and his officers were in the back, laughing and enjoying the fruits of their treacherous victory, drinking masata which they had found a cache of. The burnt village was way behind them now, and it gave the vanquished warrior a sharp pain as he realised that he would never, in this life, see his beloved Mambocké where he had gone through all the stages of life from carefree childhood to lover and father.

There was an armed and mean-looking guard for every five or six groups. Some had spears and guns, which they used very liberally, prodding their helpless captives in the ribs with, often drawing blood, or hitting them in the back or in the legs, whilst others had scourges made of leather strips, which they playfully but menacingly twirled every now and then as a declaration of intent, occasionally putting their threats into action. These men were clearly not squeamish about the sight of blood. Midala was determined not to accept his fate, but he was not going to try anything desperate. For the moment he would keep his head down. He needed time to think clearly. The enemy was very powerful, and were the clear villains in this affair. He believed that the Spirits would never allow evil to prosper for long, nor the innocent and the virtuous to experience the bitter taste of defeat. You bear your tribulations with fortitude, and then as surely as rain follows thunder, your misfortune will vanish like ghosts at the first ray of sunrise.

The terrain was rocky and slippery as they were going down the cliffs towards the port, stumbling and falling and being bullied and beaten for this. To what distant land were they being taken? Would they see their loved ones again? Midala wondered whether he would see his son and two little girls again in this life. He had given them instructions, but who knows whether they had been able to do as he had instructed? They were so small and helpless, and the attack had been so sudden and had taken everybody by surprise. Had the Cojo done the right thing, the disaster that had befallen upon their nation would have been averted. Of that, he was more than ever convinced. The enemy was not invincible and that if only they had been given time to prepare…

By the look of it, half the population of the tribe, including half the children had been wiped out, and the other half captured. Ibn Qalb and Flyte-Camilton had not knowingly planned to murder little children. He would have liked to capture them, for they would have fetched a good price on the slave market. They could be trained to do any number of things. He had been told that in some countries, in the richer households, they liked having slave children perfumed and dressed up in fine clothes, serving the ladies and doing tricks for their amusement. The young girls were fed and clothed properly, and in all innocence, groomed to satisfy the sexual appetites of their masters and their friends. He wished that his daughters had been killed rather than experience such ignominy.

When he turned round to catch a last glimpse of the land of his birth, the fearless man was unable to stop his tears rolling down his cheeks. Bomo eyed him obliquely, and he too began weeping silently. The mute mulatto saw them and started laughing obscenely and this put an immediate stop to what the two men identified as self-indulgence.

As they went down the cliffs, they knew that one false step could mean a downward plunge into the abyss below. Midala had watched in alarm a pair of twins who had started at the front of the file, Wambane, a blacksmith and Biloko a medicine man, but they had gradually lost their lead. It was clear that Wambane was a very sick man, and could scarcely stand upright, let alone drag his tired body along. Biloko who was bruised all over and thoroughly exhausted, had to spend half of whatever energy he still had left, dragging his poor twin who had scarcely enough strength left in him to breathe, let alone lift his leaden legs. Blood was coming out of his wrist, his ankles and now his knees, bruised by repeated falls. Their guard had been deaf to Biloko's entreaties to get his poor companion seen to, and had paid him with a vicious stab in the rib with a stick for his pains. Finally Biloko had no more strength left in his body and the two men crumbled into one heap and stayed there whilst the other captives had to produce the extra effort to avoid stepping on them. One guard rushed to the pair on the ground and started lashing out at them with a whip, calling them lazy sons of dogs. Another one arrived to lend him support, and they discovered that Wambane had died, whereupon the first guard asked his colleague what was to be done.

'The Shaikh said not to waste time,' the second guard said.

'Let me go ask him.'

'No, you son of a diseased warthog, there is only one thing to do, throw the bastard down the cliff and be done with you.' They argued for a short while and finally agreed on this course of action, whereupon the first guard began to detach the dead man from his near dying twin.

'What the fuck are you doing, you boil on the cunt of a diseased whore?' The other tried to explain, whereupon the other guy spat on the ground.

'There is no time for that, shiteater, just push the fuckers over the cliff and be done with you.' The first guard looked incredulously at his colleague and then they burst out laughing. Just as they were about to carry out the task, Midala and Bomo drew level with them. Without a word, they flung themselves on the two guards and fell on them, overpowering them in the bargain. They would have been suffocated to death, but the furore drew the attention of other guards who rushed to their rescue. The collective wisdom of the guards decided on a whipping to death of the pair, and they immediately started acting upon their decision, taking turns, but Ibn Qalb who had been alerted by the noise, asked to be taken to the scene, and for a time he watched in amusement as the two men took their punishment, his beads in one hand and a bottle in the other. Finally by raising his hand he ordered this to stop. He stepped out of his palanquin and waddled towards the guards, every step he took, an obvious ordeal because of his great bulk. He examined the two captives who had dared to assault armed guards, nodding to himself. Suddenly he unfastened his dagger, which was obviously something he valued, as it was more a piece of jewellery than a weapon, with its silver handle encrusted with rubies and sapphires, and offered it to one of the guards, who made no effort to take it.

'Here, take it,' he said in a kindly voice, 'throw it over the cliff for me.' Everybody looked at him as if he had lost his mind. Timidly the guard stretched out his hand, but not far enough to receive the princely object. Then in an angry booming voice, the boss bellowed, 'You sons of syphilitic male whores, do you have any idea what these men will fetch on the slave market? What were you trying to do, ruin me? Take my dagger and throw it over the cliff... you may as well.' The guards bent their heads down and looked at their feet. For a moment nobody said a word, and the captives held their breaths as well, and the faint music of the waves below were the only sounds they could hear. Suddenly Ibn Qalb screamed at the top of his voice.

'Anybody ill-advised enough to damage my merchandise, will be tossed over the cliff, and I will take great pleasure in doing it myself. Now get a move on, we have no time to waste. Give those three men some water.'

Biloko was detached from his dead companion and the three men drank copious amounts of water, after which the surviving captive was tied to Midala, and at a stroke, the twins became triplets.

They reached the beach without any serious incident. A three-masted brig was at anchor, and it looked more like a ghost ship, with its paint almost all gone and weeds and barnacles covering the hulk. It was the *Coimbra*, a three hundred tonner, once a Portuguese pirate ship, now converted into a more lucrative slave transporter. Midala who had been told of the savagery of the waves in the open sea, did not believe that this cockpit would survive even a moderate storm. He knew that in a matter of days if not hours, they would be on board, heading for some foreign land where they would end their days in misery. With any luck, a storm might put an end to their misery before they reached their destination. A number of small crafts laden with people and goods were plying between the shore and the ship, no doubt fitting her for an imminent departure.

The captives were led into a massive shed, where they were given food and water. They saw a number of men waiting there, most of them white men or Arabs, and they watched anxiously whilst these men engaged in endless negotiations with Ibn Qalb and Flyte-Camilton. The men then began inspecting the captives, who were required to show their arms, their legs, and their teeth. Some were ordered to jump up in the air or do some similar feats, in order to impress upon prospective buyers how agile they were. Some were picked up and thrown on the ground in order to determine how fit they were. After a lot of haggling, the newcomers pointed at those captives they wanted to buy and small groups were led in different corners of the shed. Midala and Bomo were bought by the same man, who bought twenty more, including six women, but Biloko went to another buyer. The others in the party were likewise shared out.

Midala was intrigued by the sight of three people squatting round a stove, where a fire was blazing. The men might have been Zanzibaris or Swahilis from another part. They were smoking pipes, which they passed around to each other, and had some rods they were playing with. Midala and his batch were marched towards them, and the white man spoke to the men in a foreign language. A guard then pushed him unceremoniously towards the three men, and their intention became immediately clear to him, for it was a long tradition among the various tribes to brand their cattle with the marks of their owners, in order to stop cattle thieves operating. So, he told himself wryly, I have now been transformed from a human being into an ox. He knew that there was no way out of this, the enemy was too powerful. He therefore decided to accept being branded without a protest. He took a deep breath and braced himself. The physical pain was something he knew how to bear, it was the humiliation that he found difficult. What was unbearable was the thought that the children were also going to suffer this ordeal too. But he closed his eyes and heard the hissing noise as the hot metal was applied to his chest, and smelled burning flesh before he felt the pain. Every single captive, children included, was thus branded. Some howled in agony, many screamed and protested, but most bore their pain in defiant silence.

They spent the night in the shed, shackled together and then the people at either ends were tied to posts with metallic chains. All night long, the sailors and their helpers loaded the ship, for it was the captain's aim to leave with the morning tide. Midala found it difficult to get any sleep. First, he was feverish and aching all over, the burn on his chest pulsated with pain, and he was unable to ward off the gloomy thoughts that preyed on his mind. The unceasing din did not help. When he did mercifully nod off, he was as-sailed by nightmares in which he saw his battered children lying in a great bloody pile, bleeding to death, and he, paralysed, unable to go near them to help. Then a couple of hours before daybreak, just when he had finally fallen asleep, some guards burst in, kicking the sleepers in the ribs, wickedly smacking their whips in the air, getting them to wake up. They were released from the post to which they had been tied, and pushed like cattle towards the small crafts which were waiting to take them aboard the Coimbra.

Midala decided to do as he was ordered. He was surprised to find that they had again paired him off with Bomo. After the fracas on the cliffs, any-body would have realised that they were a dangerous pair, but they thought that they had nothing to fear from them, that they had succeeded in enslav-ing their spirits. But both men knew instinctively that neither of them was going to just accept his fate without at least trying something daring and decisive.

Before being pressed on board, guards made sure that the chains and ropes round the captives were properly secured. As they clambered on board on precarious ladders, one pair of twins slipped and fell into the sea, and was immediately dragged to the bottom by the weight of their chains. Clearly they could not be saved, but the crew did not seem to have even noticed the fatal accident. Captives who tarried to have a look and commiserate, were roundly shoved and pushed, and threatened with whipping.

Once on board, they were led into specially designed holds. Midala's heart sank as he saw the space where he knew he would be confined to for the duration of the trip, which might well be over a month. The platforms were made of rough wood, and the holds were no higher than a seven-year-old boy like his Abo. They were told to spread themselves out in very small areas, and he imagined that they looked no different from the ngaah left to dry in the sun, placed side by side, with hardly any free space between them. Already the stench was overwhelming; it was a mixture of sweat and urine, festering wounds and fear generated in the melee; as a warrior, Midala recognised the smell of fear. Above and below his own area, there were similar holds, possibly five or six, one on top of another, where more men, women and children were confined; he could hear their moans, screams and cries of despair and the frustration that he experienced at his inability to do anything for them was intense.

The ship had hardly sailed out of the harbour than seasickness set in. Everywhere in the hold, people began throwing up, and the stench in the confined space which was already quite nauseating was causing more vomiting. The moaning redoubled and soon it was the most desolate place on this earth. From the hold above where women and children were confined, the sounds of wailing and people being sick rent the air, and Midala wondered how anybody could survive this cacophony of despair any longer. He imagined that the Bad Place where bad people were condemned to spend eternity for their evil deeds on earth could not be worse. Mercifully he became so confused at that point that all this misery and despair seemed unreal.

Food was brought in later, and although they had been on a starvation diet for days and their stomachs were empty, no one had any appetite. Midala was surprised when the guards started screaming at them, but he knew that as they were commodities, it was in the interest of the captain and his associates to keep them in one piece. It was from this that his first idea sprouted. Afraid of the punishment that would be inflicted upon them, most of the prisoners, including Midala, made some effort to eat, but there were a handful among them who stood their grounds. The guards took them away and later he learnt that they had been whipped, and when they still refused, red hot iron rods were brought near their mouths until they gave up. He heard that one man choked to death as food was rammed down his throat and was thrown overboard. Also on the way back to the hold, two of them who were tied together, in a concerted action, threw themselves at the guards and overcoming them momentarily they sprang towards the railing and joyfully threw themselves in the boiling seas below. Midala naturally deplored the death of his fellow victims, but remembered thinking that with three less people, there was now going to be just that much more space for the rest of them.

About a week after they had left Inhambane, Bomo, who was familiar with the language of talking drums, noticed that two adjacent planks on which they were lying were made of different wood, and were not of the same thickness, and began tapping a message with a nail held between his two smallest fingers and a stick between his thumb and index finger: 'I am Bomo the carpenter, and I greet you all.' At the far end of the hold above, Chissane who thought he was dying heard this. He too knew drum language, and his neighbours were surprised when the young man mysteriously perked. Most people had not even heard the coded taps from Bomo, and were surprised. Chissane made a superhuman effort to raise his body just a little bit, and his companions, feeling sorry for the dying man, were willing to give up some of their already limited space for him and squeezed themselves more tightly. Weakly Chissane began tapping on the floor. Bomo smiled as he understood the response: I am Chissane and I want to die. Bomo whispered this intelligence to Midala, who immediately shook us head. No, tell him not to lose hope, tell him that we must live in order to fight for everybody's freedom, tell him that we will find the way to regain our liberty. Bomo nodded, and tapped his message, adding that Midala himself had told him to convey this message. It required little effort to communicate with the captives in the

hold above, and in the great tradition of bush telegraphy, the message was relayed to the whole ship. Soon everybody, having heard of Midala's presence
among them, began to cheer up and murmur among themselves. Ask if anybody has any idea of where we are going, Midala told Bomo, and the carpenter tapped away. The answer came back almost immediately after: The big
island, Madagascar. Midala did not know that name, but he had heard of the
big island. He wondered what was there, why they were being taken there.

On the next day, the ship began to roll rather dangerously, and this grew
more intense by the minute. It was clear that a storm was brewing. The
helpless captives were propelled one way and then the other, some failing
to avoid knocking their heads against the hull, and a chorus of agonised
screams tore the air. Outside fierce winds were howling, and there was not
one man, woman or child who did not think that their last hour had come.
Even the hardened sailors who must have been used to the vagaries of the
high seas seemed to fear the worse. The winds roared furiously and the waves
tossed the ship up like a mean cat tosses the mouse. Inside, more people were
getting their skulls and bones cracked as they were flung against the sides
of the ship. Many, weighed down by the heavy chains were unable to pick
themselves up and not a few got smothered to death. This went on for hours
and when the storm had finally abated, most people looked at each other
surprised that they had survived yet another ordeal. All night long there was
wailing and mourning for the dead, and in the morning the guards came,
detached the dead from the living, took them on the deck and unceremoniously threw them overboard to the sharks.

As people were shackled and there was no one to free them whenever
they needed to answer the call of nature, they all had to bear the ignominy
of emptying their bowels and bladder on the spot. By now everybody had
lost what little clothing they had when they came on board. When you are
covered in your own excrement, it is the most difficult thing in the world to
maintain your dignity. The humiliation brought tears to the eyes of all, and
a big lump to their throats. They felt diminished as human beings and had
to fight hard in order to stop the animal nature in all human beings from
gaining the upper hand and rise like a bilious sap up their heads and poison
their brains.

Every other day, groups of captives were led up the deck, in an attempt to keep them fit and alive. It was feared that if they died or were in a bad shape when they landed, the size of the profit for the captain and his partners would shrink. The exercise usually comprised of getting the men to jump up and down randomly and dance, to the sound of tom toms provided under duress by their fellow captives. The men badly needed the exercise after having endured almost forty eight hours of inertia in an area where they could hardly move, but it was obvious to them that jumping up and down on the deck with no clothes on was a singularly degrading sight, especially as the guards and sailors would gather around them and cackle obscenely. Often they refused to submit themselves to this, and were whipped for insubordination. It was this that gave flesh to Midala's idea.

They had gathered enough information by means of their improvised telegraphy, and they agreed that if they were to take over the ship, this would have to be done during the exercise break, when a batch of over fifty captives would have the freedom to roam the deck for about an hour, albeit under armed guard. Furthermore, the exact whereabouts of captain, crew and guards were now known to them, and this enabled them to work out a plan. When everything was ready, they would risk everything on a specified day. For the plan to work, the element of surprise was vital, but as all information transmitted were only understood by the captives, with captain and crew unaware of the signals being exchanged, there was next to no chance of their plan being known by the enemy. A date had been set, and Midala and Bomo had assigned a role to all the men and women who had enthusiastically volunteered to take part in the action. The guards and crew had not failed to notice a sudden change in the attitude of the captives who did not look forlorn and consumed by despair any more.

On the morning of the action, a dead woman was thrown overboard, and many volunteers saw this as a bad omen. Midala was shocked to find that not only were there many more guards than usual, but they were all armed with guns. It was more usual for them to have a stick or a whip. Midala suspected that luck was against them, but orders had been given. He suspected that they might have been betrayed, that someone, expecting some reward had gone and spilled the beans, and Flyte-Camilton was ready for them. He looked at Bomo who pursed his lips. There was only one thing to do, tell his followers to abort. He took a step forward and was about to open his mouth, when Bomo brushed past him and in a loud and clear voice shouted at the top of his voice: Friends, we are betrayed, do nothing. Immediately three armed guards flung themselves at him, overpowered him and led him away towards the captain who had been watching the development. He ordered that Bomo be whipped to death, unless he revealed the names of all his accomplices. As Midala knew, Bomo said not one word, and was tied to a mast and mercilessly whipped. He bled, fainted, was revived, was whipped some more, until he finally passed away. The captain talked with his officers and they decided that after having made an example of one rebel, there was no risk of further disturbance, although he did not doubt that there were many others involved. In order not to compromise the size of his profit, no further action needed to be taken.

Next Bolimbo, a fishnet maker threw himself to the sharks, and Midala soon found out why. The man had learnt by the drum telegraphy what Bomo and Midala had instigated, and as his wife who was in the upper hold was seriously ill, he had thought that if he told the officers what he knew, they would reward him by giving her some white man's medicine, but the medicine had not worked and she had died. The shame of betraying his own people for nothing was too much for the heart-broken man. It was the wretched woman who had been thrown overboard in the morning. Strangely, no one had asked Bolimbo how he had found out about the planned action.

Everyday someone died and was thrown to the sharks. By now the spirits of every single captive seemed to have been broken. No one had accepted the fate awaiting them, but they did not have the strength to hope.

CHAPTER 2

◆◆◆

Mahébourg

THE *COIMBRA* WAS going to stop at Nossi Bé on the big island of Madagascar for water and provisions. Midala had been surprised at the ease with which information could be transmitted now. The crew often talked among themselves in the hearing of the captives, in the belief that no one understood them, but there was always someone who did, and as drum telegraphy had become widespread, a few taps, and everybody was kept informed.

The warrior often wondered whether what had been happening over the last weeks was real. Perhaps, he thought, I died when we were attacked, and I have gone to the Bad Place, and I am paying for my sins, but he had not been a bad person, never knowingly done anyone any harm. As a soldier it was his duty to fight wars but he never killed wantonly. He had always been there for anybody who needed help, been kind to everybody. He loved his wife and children, never stole or told lies. He had never betrayed anybody in his life. Maybe he was not good enough to go to the Good Place right away, but the Spirits are never unjust, and he felt sure that he had not done so many wrong things that he should be punished to that extent. But he was undaunted, and in spite of being kept in chains and under almost constant surveillance, he had not given up hope of a decisive action.

Having been apprised of the stopover, he thought of the possibility of a massive breakout, in the hope that they would find the island hospitable. But the problems were many. The chains had to be removed before anything could be done. After the death of Bomo, he had not found a reliable man to discuss his plans with. He was pleased when Bomo had explained the intricacies of the drum language to him, how to produce two high, two low and a middle note by tapping on different thicknesses with different materials. He had realised the importance of this, and had not only perfected his technique, but also taught a number of people in his hold, and had urged those in the other holds, where there was invariably one or two initiated in the art, to do the same. They were all amazed at the ease with which they were able to communicate with each other. It was thus that he had learnt of the fate of Matamba, a young mother with a toddler. She was a stunningly beautiful woman, and it was not long before she had attracted the attention of the crew. A second mate promised to see that her sick and ill-fed baby was fed properly in return for sexual favours. She had lost her husband when the village was sacked, and the first time she had cried out in horror at such a suggestion, but it was explained to her that if she did not consent, she would be gang-raped anyway, and the baby would suffer. She had no choice but to submit to the demands of the man. The baby died all the same and was thrown overboard. She was then passed around from man to man, including the captain, and had learnt to accept her fate. She had always shared whatever tidbits her ravishers gave her, as a sort of reward with her wretched companions.

Midala knew that sending out messages by tapping them out was fraught with danger. Their first plan was wrecked because it had been betrayed. How could he be sure that future plans would not meet with the same fate? He had, however, felt that greater solidarity had developed between the prisoners after the death of the poor sick woman and the suicide of Bolimbo. Everybody had witnessed how a poor man had been driven to betray his own people in a futile attempt to save his wife, and no one was likely to forget it. So he decided to take the risk, but asked everybody to be vigilant, and watch for possible traitors trying to pass information to the crew. The crew totally ignored the tap tapping going on, and dismissed it: those savages, all they think about is music and dancing, they would say. It was true that one thing that allayed their wretchedness was singing and making music with whatever was available.

Midala had enlisted the help of Pumpino from Hold 2. The two had never met, but had conversed by drum telegraphy. The younger man had impressed him with his quick wit and daring words, but his actions were yet to be tested. Thus he became a natural second-in-command. They communicated several times daily, and they managed to identify and enlist four young men and two young women who seemed to have all the right qualities to carry out a lightning action on the captain and his crew. But they were only going to go ahead with this desperate plan if their fellow victims agreed that it was worth risking their lives.

He sent out a message suggesting that they should attempt a massive breakout when the ship reached the port, explaining that there was every chance that a large number of them would be shot dead. He was surprised by the reaction. Messages flooded in, all with the clear indication that whatever the outcome, doing nothing was cowardly. They had had a taste of slavery, they claimed, and if death resulted in their attempts to regain their liberty, they were willing to take the risk. He was greatly heartened. He asked if anybody could provide them with implements like files and iron bars, so they could file away their chains, and then fight their captors. That was when Matamba promised she would do all she could to help. Left alone for even the shortest of intervals in the cabin of whoever was taking advantage of her, she rummaged around and in less that a week, she had been able to lay hands on four files, a number of nails, a butcher's knife, an axe and two spare axe handles. Midala arranged for these to be collected at pre-arranged caches by people in the other holds, so they could be picked when required, and everybody set to work to free themselves and prepare for the big breakout. He had repeatedly stressed upon the merit of a concerted action, and had explained that only if people did exactly as they were told, would there be any realistic chance of success. If anybody did anything unplanned, they would bear the serious responsibility of the mission's failure. At a given signal from him, they would all rush out of the holds in an orderly fashion. The strong swimmers among them would then jump into the sea and swim to freedom, and the non-swimmers would gather near the lifeboats whilst Midala and Pumpino, and half a dozen young stalwarts would disarm the captain and the first mate, hold a knife to their throats, thus paralysing the rest of the crew, after which they would launch the lifeboats. They would then land on the big island, and go in hiding from both the crew of the *Coimbra* and the natives of the island, having no idea whether they would be hostile or not.

On the morning the ship sailed into the port of Nossi Bé, Midala, having got rid of his chains, slowly crept out of his hold. He did not expect any signs of the break out just yet. He paused as the incredible beauty of the cerulean seas and the golden sands hit him. His companions held their breaths in expectation, but suddenly a loud splash was heard. Some captives from Hold 3, in their impatience had rushed out and jumped into the sea, fatally compromising the action planned. The captain and his men surged forth brandishing guns, shooting in the air to create panic whilst making for the railing, from which they started shooting at the fugitives. Midala did not want a bloodbath on deck, and was once more frustrated in his attempt to lead his people to freedom. Clearly the Spirits did not wish it! Six of the fugitives were hit, and drowned, but three of them were unaccounted for. Did they make it to the shore? Were they able to enlist the support of the islanders? Midala would never know, but felt sure that they were much happier for having dared, even if their indiscipline was criminal.

Life on board returned to normal, and surprisingly the captain and crew, who were drunk most of the time, mystified by the severed chains, decided that it would be too complicated to do anything about it, seeing that in a couple of weeks, the troublesome captives would stop being their responsibility. All he did was to order his crew to stop "mollycoddling our guests."

After Nossi Bé, the *Coimbra* met with favourable winds, and reached the port of Mahébourg on the south-east coast of the Île de France in under a fortnight, and without any incident, if one discounts the death from cholera of a handful of captives in Hold 2. They were unceremoniously despatched to the deeps, as usual, together with one old woman who had not quite died, Flyte-Camilton having decided that it would save time on the morrow, when she surely would have.

On the final day of their journey, the captives were allowed to wash, and the sick were attended to. Those captives with visible scars and wounds were treated with a variety of products, including a mixture of mud and coal tar, applied to crevasses in their bodies in an attempt to disguise the damage done to the product, so as not to incur the wrath of their lawful owners, who had paid handsomely for it. Most of them were naked, even the women, but by now they had ceased to care about minor considerations like modesty or pride. All the scrubbing and mending could not disguise the fact that they were a sorry sight and had gone through hell. When they came down the ladders, without their chains for the first time in months, Midala thought that even if they kept him in chains for the rest of his life, he would never give up hope of liberty. However it was now known to everybody that they had been sold to plantation owners who needed them in order to cultivate their land, so there would be no logic in keeping them in chains. His course of action was clear to him, he would keep his head down and plan his escape as soon as the occasion arose. The Spirits knew that he had been a true son of the tribe, and had tried his best to bring succour to his folk, but in their wisdom they had withheld from him the means to do it right. He had tried and failed, so now he was not going to try for them anymore. Six people had died because of him, and now he was not going to do anything to risk the lives of others. He would find the means for his own salvation, and he was going to act cautiously and slowly. The sea was calm and clear, and everywhere around there was luscious green vegetation. Ahead loomed a large hill which looked like a lion at rest. In spite of his disenchantment at his condition, he had a good feeling about this place which reminded him of his native Inhambane.

He was herded in the company of the men and women who had been branded together. They were under the watchful guard of a handful of armed guards, all black men like themselves, armed with guns. It pained him that people who in all likelihood had suffered the same tribulations from the slave-traders would show so much hostility to them. No sooner were they in a large shed on land than an irate white man — he was more red than white — burst in upon them and started haranguing them in an unknown language, becoming redder by the minute, as he spat out his spiteful words. He was a stocky man with a head that was almost square, his grey eyes that were too close to each other, with thick set features, wide shoulders and disconcertingly short dumpy legs. Nobody understood a word he said. After a while he beckoned a slender and tall grey-bearded black man, and when he approached the master, Midala noticed that he walked with a limp. His beard was sparse and uneven, his eyes bloodshot. The red man spoke to him in kindly tones, and then turned round looking for Flyte-Camilton. The lame man then began to address them in Chopi language. He said that his name was Antoine Gentil. You too will be given a new name, he said in a mild and gentle voice, and you will do well to forget the name you were given at birth, because if you are heard using it, the punishment would be a substantial decrease in food rations. Midala kept his emotion under control.

The limping man said that he was glad they had survived the boat trip, he knew how tough it must have been. He explained that the irate man was their owner who had placed an order with Captain Flyte-Camilton, through an agent in Zanzibar, for a certain number of able-bodied slaves. First, one third of the slaves he had paid for were missing, and he was angry because you, the survivors all seem on the point of death. He smiled apologetically and explained that he was only translating the words of Missié de Fleury. Do not worry, he told them, your wounds will heal and you will regain your health much quicker than you think. If you do as you are told and do not rock the boat, you will be fed, given medicine and kept under a roof. What more does a slave want to survive? This white man is a tough one, so you had better start on the right footing with him, because he takes nonsense from nobody. Everybody knows the reputation of Missié Victor. Take my advice, do not under any circumstances cross him, for you will regret it. When an army has no weapons, the best course is to sue for peace. It really would be a complete waste of time to attempt to escape. Many have tried and no one has succeeded. This is a small island, and the Anti-Maroon Units are known for their vigilance and their zeal. They know all the hiding places and last time someone tried to run away, he was caught on the same day before the sun had set. The poor fellow was dragged back to the plantations, tied to a mango tree and the white man himself whipped him and finished him off. It was the law of the land. The runaway deserves no less, Gentil said, and it is in your best interest to remember this at all times. Think of Missié Victor as your father, your mother and your god. He has all the power, and if he decides to beat you to death, it is his right, there is no one to prevent him.

Antoine paused for a short while, looked left and then right to make sure that no one was eavesdropping, and proceeded in a whisper. No, he confided, it is not the law of the land actually. There is something called the Code Noir which makes it illegal for the slave owners to dish out justice themselves, but the plantation owners did as they pleased because they all drank and partied with the governor and the top administrators. There is nobody to stop them. In fact, according to the Code Noir, escaped slaves should be sent to the Bagne there, and he pointed in the direction of a building which they could not see properly. The conditions in the Bagne are much worse than any plantation owner can dish out, trust him. You work from dawn to sunset, carrying and breaking stones for construction work, you got fed the same thing day in day out, manioc and pumpkin, dal and spinach, and you are kept in chains all day long and often all night long too. You sleep like animals, twenty to a room, because there are too few guards. The hand-picked guards are sadists and are very eager to use whips, sticks and their own fists as well. But if like me you abide by the law, as it is practised, do your work with a smile on your face, you will have a decent life, you will get food which you can cook yourselves and decent clothing. If not, I pity you. Welcome to Île de France, Vive le roi!

Missié de Fleury reappeared, and as the captain had reimbursed him some of his losses, his redness had given way to pink. He made another speech, but this time did not ask Antoine to translate, not minding that no one understood. The tone of his speech was one of heightened anger, and this was all he meant to convey to the men.

The slaves were tied together securely, with a brown man with a straw hat, brandishing a whip in charge. He was followed by some black men in khaki, armed with iron rods and machetes, and they were ordered to march in silence. It was mid-morning when they started, and, with whips much in evidence, were made to walk at a brisk rate. They walked through the bush where the trees looked very different from those of Inhambane, except for the few ebony trees and aloe plants which grew here and there. Midala found that link comforting for some strange reason. They crossed some rivulets, and often the path led towards the beaches, and he thought that they looked much prettier than back home. It was much after dark when they reached their destination, when they were taken to a large room with corrugated iron walls and a straw roof. He was grateful for the yam, boiled pumpkin and pili pili sauce that they were given, specially as the sauce was how they made it in Inhambane. Some candles were lit and placed on the floor, for there was no furniture in the shed. There were some rolled gunny bags in one corner, and they were told to pick two per person, and use them as a bed to lie upon and a blanket. The men were to occupy one end of the hall, and the women the opposite. And we do not want any funny business, the guards warned them, you are here to work and not to indulge in fornication. Midala was surprised that the men spoke to them in their own tongue, but to each other they spoke a language which seemed similar to the one the red man had used. Later they would discover that the red man spoke French and the guards spoke kreol which seemed similar. They were warned that the door of the hall would be locked and that sentries would be on patrol outside with dogs which were only fed in the morning, in case anybody got some funny notions.

At dawn next morning, he was greatly comforted by the chirping of birds, and through the chinks in the walls, he could see birds he had never seen before and did not know the names of. He would learn later that they were red cardinals which were unique to the island, green parakeets, which Midala would later learn were called catteau vert, flying from tree to tree, golden yellow canaries and many others. There were tamarind trees that he had not seen before, flame trees with their distinct flaming red hues, bois noir, mangoes, avocados, papayas, and several others that he could not identify, either because he did not know them or could not have a proper view of them. In the uncleared bush, growing wild, he would discover the most succulent and the tastiest little round fruit that he had ever tasted, and he would learn that it was called goyave (guava). The guards came and unlocked the doors, and they were let out, for the first time, unfettered, but the presence of a large number of well-armed guards was more than enough to deter any thought of escape. As he emerged from the shed, he was greeted by a sight which cheered him up considerably. They were under a mountain which immediately reminded him of the breasts of a woman even if they were pointing upwards, and there were three of them. He would find out later that it was called Montagne des Trois Mamelles. In the morning hue, the mammaries appeared blue with white light reflected on a face which seemed as if they had been fashioned by human hands. Lucky devil, thought the warrior wryly. The mountain was nothing as big as those back home. All the features that he will see, will strike him as being miniatures, but he thought this was what made them beautiful. As a child, he had thought that the dwarf rooster an aunt gave him was the most beautiful bird that the Spirits had created. In spite of his small size, he was fearless and even the massive cockerels kept out of his path, and the hens simply adored him. He could hear the soft tingling of a rivulet flowing, and indeed it was a small river — everything was on a reduced scale on this small island — and its water was crystalline. He did not think that having been forcibly taken to another country he would find anything good in it, but in spite of himself, he found that he was liking his surroundings. Not that this made the slightest difference to his refusal to accept enslavement.

He had promised himself that whatever the consequences, he was going to run away at some point. Flogged to death? What is death? No man is immortal, although the soul was, and no power on earth can imprison the soul. But he was not going to run away just yet. He would keep his head down. All his previous attempts had failed, no doubt because they were carried out in desperation. His plans must have been defective and could never be reasonably expected to succeed, but the next one will be his final one. Since they had to work, they would not be in chains, or yoked in any way, and the land provided more scope than the sea. He would either make it or die! He would keep is eyes and ears open, find as much as he could about the lie of the land, ask discreet questions, and put his fate in the hands of the Spirits.

Missié Victor's appearance, with Antoine following, put an end to his musings. The red man went to speak with the guards, and the limping man approached him. He was the white man's slave, and had to do his master's bidding, but Midala did not have any bad feelings towards him. He began to ask a few questions to which the warrior replied curtly. The old man then looked away and in a stammer informed him that Missié Victor was going to be give them their names.

'What do you mean? We already have names,' he said, and Antoine laughed defensively.

'No,' he said, 'not savage names, new names, civilised, Christian names.' Then, making sure no one was listening, he whispered, 'Antoine is not my real name, I am from the royal family and my true name is Colibango.' And he smiled proudly at this, showing his near toothless gums.

'My name is Midala, and I don't want a new name.' Antoine tut tutted sadly. 'No, you must, just take the name, say nothing… or better say merci missié.'

'Missi Missé? Why?'

'It means thank you in the language of the country.' Midala shrugged, 'my advice is don't draw attention to yourself… then you will be all right. You will have two meals a day, nothing fancy, but the hyena eats the dead, and in times of need even the lion will eat grass, remember.' Midala said nothing, and Antoine went to speak to some of the others. Suddenly he turned round and said, 'Not missi missé… it's merci missié.' Midala nodded almost imperceptibly. Antoine looked at him thoughtfully, not moving, and finally said, 'And please my brother, keep your head down.' Brother, Midala mused.

Later Victor de Fleury summoned them in his presence. One of his men had a ledger, and a small coffee-coloured kid carrying a small ink pot. The master, now pink, seemed less irate than earlier on, and made a speech which Antoine translated. It was what he had told them earlier on. There were a handful of brown men who were neither white nor black, and two or three black guards in his proximity, no doubt slaves who had behaved and were given some position of trust, and they were talking to each other in Chopi. The captives were required to line themselves up, and to move forward at a sign from one of the minions. The first one to be given a name was a frail grey haired old man. Midala wondered how he had survived the horrors of the voyage.

'Look at you,' de Fleury said laughing, 'you look like you're already dead.' The guards and minions laughed exaggeratedly.

'You name shall be Mourant, Jean Mourant.'

The guards burst out laughing, explaining that Mourant means dying. The scribe wrote the names in his ledger as the names were dished out.

The naming ceremony went on at a pace. The various names Midala heard were, Marie Vache, Michel Bouteille, Henri Marteau, Denise Vilain, Marcel Mardi, Jules Crétin, Jeanne Grocul (Fat Arse). When he learnt the language of the island, he would gather that these were risible names, meaning Cow, Bottle, Hammer… When it was his turn, he took two steps towards the white man, remembering Antoine's injunction not to make waves.

'Look at the sour face of that fellow,' de Fleury said to the guards who laughed out aloud, 'doesn't he make you think that he has eaten some hen shit?'

The minions shook with hilarity, nodding their agreement with what the wise white man had just said.

'Your name shall be Louis Cacapou.'

'Merci Missié,' he said. And Antoine breathed again. He will find out later that Cacapou is a shortened form of Hen Shit.

Thus he started working for Missié Victor. It turned out that he had sugar plantations all over the island, and was in the process of building a factory for crushing cane and turning it into raw sugar. He had recently bought fifty arpents of rugged land near Sept Cascades in the region called Tamarin, and he wanted it cleared and the new arrivals, of whom a little less than half were women, were all marched there.

On the first day, they were required to build a shed. This work was supervised by a pale and callow youth in shiny leather boots reaching up to his knees and wearing a pith helmet. He shouted a lot but was not otherwise violent, his main preoccupation seemed to be keeping his boots clean. The armed guards of whom some were black, others white or mixed, were not as fierce looking as those on the *Coimbra*. They surprised themselves at the speed with which they were working. Midala marvelled at the capacity of human beings to pick up the pieces and get on with their lives. When the sun was right in the middle of the sky, they were allowed to stop and were given the means of cooking their own meal. The company had provided manioc, spinach and pulses. The women set to work whilst the men were allowed to smoke pipes which the guards produced for them. The women teased the men for being lazy bones, and this was the first time since the night of the attack that Midala had heard the sound of laughter. It took two days for the work on the shed to be completed. People allocated themselves areas of the floor without any major arguments. On the next day, they were be led to the fields, when serious and more back-breaking work was expected of them.

The callow youth was replaced by an unsmiling white man who was rather older and he shared out the work. Instead looking after the shine of his boots, he constantly followed a small party and never stopped berating them for one thing or another. He hit a man in the face with his whip because he thought he had looked at him with disrespect. He looked at Midala pointedly, but the latter kept his head down and continued digging.

Forgetting his resolution not to involve others in his plans, he thought that this time, they had pickaxes, machetes and spades, numerical superiority, and that it would be easy to overpower the supervisors, or colons, as he soon learned they were called, but where would they hide afterwards? How would they feed themselves? He might discuss this with his fellow slaves at night, but there was a danger that he might yet again be bounced into a half-baked scheme. He thought that the best course was getting to know his companions better.

The clearing work proceeded at a good rate, although the colon continually expressed his dissatisfaction. Every day he found a pretext to whip someone. He kept picking on the three men and a woman who were erecting a wall with the rocks that had been removed from the soil, saying that it was too high or too low, or maybe both, and when the leader did not immediately acquiesce, he grabbed him by the scruff of the neck and dragged him towards a bois noir. The guards ran to his assistance, and were asked to tie the fellow to the tree. He then began screaming at him, and ordered a guard to give the man twenty of the best. This, the man did this without too much relish, but when he had finished with him, left the victim more dead than alive. The colon then came to him and offered him a swill from a bottle of rum, which the man first refused, but he immediately changed his mind, in case he was given another twenty for insubordination.

The whipping and flogging was a daily routine now, but Midala had so far been spared. At night they would sing sad dirges about their lost homeland and dear dead ones, finding new words to describe their pains. The women, who were in better shape than the men, because the rape that they had endured on board, as opposed to beatings, had left them more mentally than physically damaged, began to tend the poor male slaves, and in no time couples began to be formed. Midala wanted nothing to do with women, he was still in mourning. Matamba, the most desirable woman on the *Coimbra* who had had to submit to crew and captain, had lost her erstwhile comeliness, specially since her baby died, but she had started regaining her looks. She was a good woman and had suffered a lot. One night she came to him and asked if she could lie by his side. He did not want her, but he said nothing and she took this as acquiescence. He was quite embarrassed when she began to make it manifest that she wanted him. Gently he indicated that he was not ready. She understood, nodded and went away, but she did not look for another man. She had obviously made up her mind that it was Midala she wanted. He fought hard to stop images of that most desirable woman invading his thoughts unbidden. She had high cheekbones and slightly sunken eyes, and an egg-shaped head which he found very attractive, but he thought that her full lips were her best features, vibrant and sensual. She was a strong woman but her breasts seemed small in comparison, and surprisingly long slender legs shot down from her ample behind. He easily imagined his two hands sliding up and down her frame in a sort of closing and opening flourish centred on her waist. He was a man with normal desires and knew that sooner or later he would not be able to resist her charms, specially as it was obvious that she had chosen him.

Missié de Fleury himself came for a visit the following week, and said he was shocked at the snail's pace of this useless lot. He made a speech in that sense, which was translated by Antoine, and threatened severe measures. His eyes fell on Midala as he was talking, and he got Antoine to call him. Midala walked towards the big Missié eyes on the ground, and for no reason Victor de Fleury slapped him with the back of his hand.

'That's for your insolence, Cacapou,' the red man said, 'just remember who you are and who I am!' Midala did not understand a word, and although he was boiling with rage, he kept his head down. The irate man screamed some more, and gave them some orders to the guards, whereupon three of them came towards the warrior, seized him and frogmarched him to a coconut palm and tied him there. He offered no resistance. They then took turns and gave him ten strokes of the whip each. The warrior thought that it was politic to pretend more pain than he felt, and winced dramatically each time the leather coiled itself round his bare bleeding back. He readily understood that whipping was not a punishment for slackness or for doing something wrong. It had two purposes, to show who was boss, but more importantly, to break the spirit of the slave in order to gain complete dominion over him. My spirit will never be broken, he promised the Spirits.

But his body was in a a sorry state, and that night when Matamba came to nurse him, he felt grateful and let her, and she knew that she had won. She rubbed his sores with coconut oil, and then began to caress him all over, and was delighted when he responded. He did not tell her that although she was the woman in his bed, in his mind he was lying with Rolena, who will forever be the woman in his heart, the woman who will welcome him when his time came, to travel to the Land Beyond.

The fields near Sept Cascades had been cleared and were ready for cultivation but the cane cuttings had not yet arrived from the north. So, when a ship arrived in the half-finished harbour of Port Louis on the west coast, with cattle that de Fleury's agents had bought for him in Madagascar, Midala and a party of other slaves with half a dozen armed guards were despatched to go fetch them and take them to Montagne Trois Mamelles, where his herds were kept. The men walked from daybreak until much after sunset, when they reached the new harbour town. They slept on the beach. Escape would have been possible, but Midala was still not ready for that leap in the dark. There is plenty of time for that, he told himself. Next morning, the cattle were disembarked, washed, watered and fed. There were forty of them, most of them severely ill-fed, with protruding ribs. Five had died during the crossing, for they had undergone a five day trip in their hold with no food and very little water.

It was early afternoon before they were ready to start moving. The team was quite expert at dealing with the bovines, and Midala was quite happy to follow the instructions of Georges Couillon, who had obviously been an accomplished cattleman back home. They went along at a brisk rate, and an hour or so later, cattle and men found themselves on the bank of the Grande Rivière Nord Ouest, a slightly more respectable river than the stream beneath the mountain. The cattle drank lustily, and the men cooked and ate their meals quickly. They continued along the bank of the waterway, and as the terrain was rugged and rocky, they had to proceed gingerly. Sunset saw them on the riverside and they bivouacked for the night. Couillon again proved himself a dab hand at what he was doing. The cattle were clearly disturbed after the rough crossing, and might have been nervous and unruly, but he went to each animal individually, patted them, talked gently to them, and instructed the men to do the same, and what might have ended up as an almighty stampede, turned into a peaceful night.

Midala was heartened by the almost complete absence of people on the road. It was easy to see why. There were hardly fifteen thousand people living in the island, almost all of them living in the settlements that had started springing up. Probably no more than two thousand were white men, and the rest were their offspring with black women or slaves, or so, Midala surmised from what he had heard. It seemed possible to hide in these ravines, with a proper river providing drinking water, as well as irrigation for cultivation of corn and yam. If there were just him and Matamba, it would be almost impossible for them to be detected, and if there were more, they would have to organise a watch. They could live a decent life like this for a long time.

Antoine told him that de Fleury was delighted with the team, as not a single mishap had occurred, not one cow or bull had escaped or died during the trek to Trois Mamelles, but naturally he said nothing to the men, except threatened to flog them for taking so long and wasting valuable time. Midala and his companions were kept busy doing a number of chores. A concern like de Fleury Estates with its multifarious interests depended on work rotation, and Victor de Fleury prided himself on his organisational skills. Sept Cascades was waiting for the right time for the planting of the cuttings, so some people were despatched to Flacq on the east coast where he grew tobacco, and others to Trois Mamelles to look after the cattle. Midala having been part of that successful team was picked for that, but Matamba went to Flacq. Midala did not realise how much he would miss his new woman, but he had no choice in the matter. He did not feel the time was ripe for a dash to freedom, and would bide his time.

The work on the cattle ranch was never-ending, but it kept him from thinking too much of his wretched condition. He missed Matamba, and did not welcome the advances of other women. He wondered whether he was falling in love with the woman. He hoped not, as he would not want anybody to take Rolena's place in his heart. Every night he would think of his dead wife and recall the many good moments the two of them had spent together, but often as sleep began to take over, Matamba and Rolena became confused in his mind.

When it was time to start the sowing, he was sent back to Sept Cascades, as was Matamba. She had pined for the return of her new lover, and their reunion that night was passionate and fulfilling for both of them. Why can we not be always together? she asked. Why do we have to be slaves? The man replied.

As he was a cautious man, he had not talked about the ravines and the river to her, or to anybody. Surprisingly the one person he felt the urge to open up to on this subject was Antoine although he knew that the older man had the trust of de Fleury, but he also knew that he would never betray any-body. Antoine sometimes stopped for the night at Sept Cascades, sleeping in the shed with the others, and one moonlit night the two of them were sitting under a flame tree outside, smoking their pipes when he said a sentence that he had rehearsed many times before.

'Colibango, have you tried to run away from here?' Antoine froze, looked at him obliquely and frowned.

'Don't talk like that. Some questions are never asked. And please don't let them hear you call me Colibango, Midala… eh Cacapou.'

'Have you?' he insisted. The older man shook his head and stayed silent for a bit.

'Like everybody I have thought of it, but there are so few places to hide, I told you that on the day you arrived. This is a small island.' After a pause, he added, 'What can you do with a bad leg anyway?'

'I know one or two,' Midala said, 'I mean places to hide.'

'I also told you about the Anti-Maroon Units, they are —'

'The place I am thinking of, it will be easy to play hide and seek, you see, when we went to the harbour —'

'No don't tell me any more, for I might blurt it all out if I am flogged. I am an old coward.'

'I don't think you're a coward… or old… but…' He thought it best to leave it at that.

'There are places… like the gorges in Black River, Le Morne Brabant,' Antoine said unexpectedly. He was obviously surprised to hear himself ut-ter these words, 'Eh, and… there's water there, and grottoes, I am told…

and you could grow corn and there's plenty of cocoyam growing wild... and there are fruits... but the Units will be sure to look there. And you must have seen the Grand River... there are ravines there... also a good place to hide, but again, they will look there... I could name a few other places... but I don't want to encourage you... if they catch you...' Antoine's voice was near cracking with tears threatening to cascade out, 'My brother Combasso... my uncle's son actually, he ran away. They caught up with him on that mountain in Port-Louis... the Citadel... he was half starved and sick, they dragged him up to Trois Mamelles, here... you've seen the tamarind tree? They tied him there for two nights, and on the third morning, Missié Victor summoned everybody to come and watch. He made a speech. 'I am not a bad man,' he said. Antoine stopped here, unable to continue for a big lump his throat. But he took a deep breath.

'Yes. I am not a bad man, Missié de Fleury said, I am a God-fearing Christian, I go to church every Sunday... I feed you, I clothe you, I give you a roof on your head... out of the goodness of my heart, but I expect obedience. One hundred percent, you understand. You savages cannot understand this, as you have lived in the jungle, eating each other, respecting no laws, human or God's, so you need to be taught a lesson that you cannot forget. The law of this country is that a runaway has to pay with his life. I am going to carry out this execution. Antoine... he called me.'

Here Antoine was unable to restrain himself, and his tears rolled down profusely. Midala put his arms around him and hugged him.

'I get the picture, you don't have to talk about this.'

'No, I want to,' said the older man almost aggressively. 'Antoine, here, take this, he said. And he gave me the whip. You've seen his whips, they are made of dried cow hide. You start... as he is your cousin... show them that you agree that your cousin deserves what he is getting. I told you that I am a coward... I knew that if I refused, I would end up like Combasso... so I nodded and took it. Combasso... he was younger than me, it was my duty to look after him, and there I was, helping to kill him. What was worse Midala, was that I could not show my sadness and anger to the boss, or I might have lost his trust... and I needed him to trust me... to think that I am on his side at all times... that's the worse part of slavery, your survival becomes more important than your soul… And I knew what I was expected to say, and I said it… Pierre… yes, that was Combasso's new civilised name… was ungrateful master, you gave him everything and he… spat in your face…'

'Tell him he deserves to die,' prompted de Fleury.

'I opened my mouth, but no power on earth was going to make me.' Missié Victor took two steps in my direction, and I began to fear for my life and instinctively put my hands in front of my face, but he looked at me incredulously.

'What was I thinking? He's your flesh and blood…' He shook his head sadly and took the whip from me.

'He made someone else do the job, but I had to watch…' the limping man whispered. And Antoine's tears were now beyond control, and he was unable to continue. He cried like a child, like a woman who has just seen her child killed, but most of all he cried like a man who had suddenly remembered how to cry.

'I understand,' said Midala, 'he's such a hateful man, how you must hate him.'

'Me hate him? No, Missié Victor is my father and my mother, my god.'

'What are you saying, Colibango? How can you not hate him? Do you have blood in your veins?'

'I have blood in my veins. But that man… listen, when we landed in Mahébourg… I was more dead than alive, I had diarrhoea, but worse, during the storm I had broken my leg… you know, the ship rolls and you are chained and lose control, you are thrown all over the place —'

'I know, so many people were crushed to death.'

'Anyway, my leg was broken… we had just landed, and there was this co-lon shoving and pushing me. I had fallen down and he was kicking me when Missié Victor saw us… he came towards us and slapped the colon in the face, hard like… Can't you see the man has a broken leg? He took me under his wings, ordered some men to look after me, treat my leg, threatening to flog them if anything happened to me.'

'Really!'

'Yes. Go figure.' He smiled wanly.

'And he came to see me everyday, bringing me a bottle of rum and ham and eggs... he then decided that as I was not completely fit, I would not be able to do any hard labour, and decided that I could do a good job as a sort of go-between between him and the workforce. So how can I hate him? He saved my lie, I owe him everything.'

Was this the reason why the white man seemed to treat Colibango with something like respect? It was more than respect, Midala had seen clear evidence of affection. Midala knew that when someone did a good action, the gratitude this generated was two-sided: first, the recipient felt grateful for obvious reasons, but the benefactor feels gratitude for being allowed to do something which made him feel good about himself. Being kind to Colibango was De Fleury's certificate of humanity that he awarded to himself. Since he had one, it did not matter how he treated the others!

CHAPTER 3

◆ ◆ ◆

Grand River North West

THE CANE PLANTS now growing lustily in Sept Cascades provided an impressive sight to visitors. The luxuriance was not unexpected, for the land had been fallow since it rose from under the ocean nine million years ago as a result of a volcanic cataclysm. The cane stalks in the ground were firm and dark scarlet, and the leaves fluttering in the breeze, like a green sea, the colour of jade. Flourishing above the leaves, the marble-white bloom with a soupçon of the palest pink shone proudly in the tropical sun, swaying gently in the breeze.

There is always a period of inactivity prior to the harvesting or coupe, and people who had gone to tend cattle or grow tobacco in de Fleury's other outposts began coming back, in readiness for the back-breaking task of cutting the cane with a machete. All of a sudden there were people hacking at the stems, denuding the sticks of their green stalks and loading them on oxcarts, and Midala knew that this hive of activity would provide a good smokescreen when preparing his breakaway. He had not got to know any of his fellow slaves well enough to risk confiding in them, so it was just going to be him and Matamba. After his attempts at organising escapes on the Coimbra, which had ended in catastrophe, he was not sure if he wanted to be responsible for any further tragedies. Besides deep down he must have known that two people on their own had a better chance of escaping recapture. He had carefully noted landmarks when he had accompanied Couillon to Port-Louis, noted the position of the sun at various times of the day. He had been a hunter in Inhambane since childhood, and as such had developed the skills necessary for guiding himself by land features and stars. To his amazement, on the eve of the day he had chosen for the breakaway, Antoine asked him to join him for a smoke behind the shed. I have got something I want to give you, he said, it belonged to Combasso. He gave him a flint and steel striker. You never know when you might need this, he said curtly, and not waiting for a thank you, he hobbled away on his limping legs.

On a Sunday morning, after mass, attendance to which was compulsory, he and Matamba quietly slipped away, collected the few things which they had been hiding in the bush over the last weeks, among which there were a battered old cooking pot, a kitchen knife, some dried salt-fish, some manioc, and took off. They walked briskly towards the mountain. It would take some time before they were missed and a lot longer before anybody would inform De Fleury and the Unit. In any case it would not be difficult to play Hide and Seek with them in the thickets that flourished all over the place. Soon the Trois Mammelles was behind them, and they took that as a sort of victory. They kept walking until sunset, when the rains started. They had reached Tamarin and decided that they would stop there. They were in no hurry. They found shelter under a massive strangler fig, huddling together for warmth, for the in May, the temperature drops quite a bit at night. Next morning, some monkeys on the strangler began hollering, and throwing sticks and pebbles at them, and they got up. Matamba manifested her amusement at the antics of the apes by screaming with laughter; Midala smiled happily — even at his happiest he rarely laughed — Rolena used to tease him about this.

He collected some twigs of which there was an inexhaustible supply, and proudly lit a fire by using Antoine's gift, and made tea. They drank it with sugar, from a small bamboo cup they had brought along with them. At home in Inhambane, they used wild honey as a sweetener, but this was a sugar island.

They walked briskly for a couple of hours. In the distance they could see the sea and the new but still incomplete Port-Louis harbour which Midala had seen when he went to collect de Fleury's cattle. They were not surprised, and considerably relieved when they had not encountered a single human being since they left their camp. They heard nothing but their own footsteps, birds twittering, monkeys howling, lizards tut tutting, and in the night, frogs croaking and cicadas chirping, leaves rustling in the breeze. Matamba said that if she closed her eyes, she could also hear the sound of the stars. He had not felt so lighthearted since the times when he was courting Rolena. It was mid-afternoon on the next day when they heard the flow of the river. They could contain their excitement no longer, and rushed towards where that most welcome of sound was coming from. Suddenly they saw the ravine with the river flowing below. It seemed narrower than he remembered, certainly not wider than the length of a mopane tree, ten tall adults standing on each other'e shoulders. They scrambled down the steep bank, unconcerned by scratches to their limbs and face, and exhausted by the effort, but ecstatic at finally becoming free, they threw themselves on the ground, the sun in their face and relished the moment. They found a nice pool and swam and gambolled in it like teenagers, after which they made love. Until now, they had always made love furtively, embarrassed by the presence of forty other couples, often doing the same thing. Even if no one could not see what the others were doing in the dark, the ubiquitous 'hoos' and 'haas' were off-putting. This was the first time they indulged in their passion without any inhibitions, as free individuals.

They went exploring the area, to discover what, if any, were the sources of danger and plan a strategy on the how to avoid detection.

It did not take them long to discover a grotto which seemed ideal for them. The Spirits were looking after them. Just outside there was a tree of Mother's Best Friend, the Drumstick tree — the best possible food in existence. We need never go hungry now, Midala said, the Spirits mean us to prosper. They had found their new home. Next they set out to discover where they could grow the seeds that they had brought along, and although the terrain was pretty rocky, they found patches where the soil seemed dark and fertile. They had tomato seeds, kalalu, beans, chillies, chou chou, pumpkin. They put aside half the seeds, in case they failed to sprout for some unknown reason, or were destroyed by pests, insects or birds.

He was satisfied that as they were well hidden by the luxuriant vegetation deep in the ravine, there was little risk of detection, unless it was suspected that they were there and a party was despatched to seize them. But they knew that with the coupe in full throttle, De Fleury would not be able to spare men to join the Anti-Maroon Unit, but they knew that Missié Victor often acted impulsively, and thought it best to be on their guard at all times.

There were plenty of snails. They collected them, scooped them out of their shells and roasted them over a wood fire and found them better than those back home. Then they made their most serendipitous discovery: cocoyam, the husband of all yams, growing on the river bank, just like at home. In Sept Cascades, people called their heart-shaped green fans "brède songe", dream leaves. They were delicious when cooked with a piece of fish, for on its own it gave one the itches and caused rashes. Matamba was not over-fond of the brède songe though. To her, the best thing about it was how drops of water coagulated on its waxy surface to form a small ball of liquid silver. You're just like a child, her lover teased her. When we were children, she told Midala, whenever they did not listen to their parents, they would moan. Whatever you tell the children, they would say, is like water on malanga. Midala smiled, nodded and added that in their village they used to say whatever you said to us children went in one ear and straight out of the next with the speed of a cheetah.

For the best effect, one needed salt and oil to cook malanga leaves, and they had neither. If only they had thought of bringing some salt... Still it filled space in an empty stomach. Unfortunately their supply of dried fish was limited, as they had only been able to deviate a small quantity, but they knew that living by the riverside, it would not be long before they discovered the means of catching fish. They peered into the water where it was relatively still, and indeed saw some fish there, but catching them was another matter. They found a few dried-up breadfruits still on the branch, and ate them boiled, but unfortunately, again unsalted. For some time they ate what was available, one day brède songe and cocoyam and next day drumstick leaves soup and roasted snails, and did not starve. There were wood pigeons but like the fish, they needed to be caught first. They hoped that it was a matter of time before they found the means of doing so.

Sisal grew in profusion in the area, and before long they were making yarns. Matamba did a very delicate job, and ended up with twines of incredible fineness and strength.

By now, the seedlings had begun to prosper, and the runaways felt optimism rise in them. They made some blankets with the sisal fibres, and if they were coarse at first, you soon got used to the scratching. They made fishnets and although the fish were elusive at first, they were more easily able to catch very small shrimps which they cooked with the brède songe to excellent effect, but the lack of salt made it difficult to enjoy fully. Matamba often expressed regret at this. Everyday they would look at the sea, and dream of a properly salted meal. It did not seem all that far away, but they were not going to take their chances. Still there was very little traffic in the area, except around Port-Louis, which they could see in the distance when they went up the ravine, so...

They discovered some coconut palms growing beyond a ridge they had not ventured beyond until now, and this brought a new dimension to their diet. Grounded coconut provided the oiliness that enhanced sauces. Patiently Midala detached the hard shells from their fibres, and working on a shell for hours, with his prized knife, he managed to make bowls and containers which proved very useful. They were able to make coarser ropes with the coconut fibres. They tried various spots in the river for fish, and finally found what must have been a rich breeding ground and gathering fish became a simple exercise. Back in Inhambane everybody dried their catch of ngaa in the sun for use off-season, and they did the same thing in their new abode.

One thing leading to another, they made things to wear, and got used to them after a while. As he did not have any proper tools, Midala used his trusty knife to fashion out bits of wood in all sorts of shapes, and ended up by putting them together to make stools and tables. Matamba made footwear for both of them, and they thought that they were living quite comfortably. Unless there were unforeseen changes, they thought, they could live comfortably and in freedom for years to come.

They found lots of fruit trees, and expected that when the warm weather arrived, they would have plenty of mangoes, guavas, jackfruits and some other fruits they did not have in Inhambane.

Everyday they ventured a little bit further, and were satisfied that there was not a single dwelling within shouting distance of their domain. They knew that even taking all possible precautions, even if they could stay out of sight, there was no way of stopping smoke attracting attention. This was what made them do their cooking at night, but as they felt more secure, they began gradually dropping their guards. They discovered the early stages of a track at some distance from the grotto, which they imagined the cariole of the masters sometimes used, but so far they had not seen or heard any traffic.

One day, he gave the woman he now loved more and more the fright of her life by suggesting that he would go fetch her some sea water so they could really enjoy some saltiness. Are you mad? she said, do you want to be caught? You're right, it's too dangerous, he said negligently, but already he had a plan.

There was a measure of recklessness in the old warrior which he could not always control. He had decided that he would attempt a midnight sortie. He had the faculty of waking up at the time of his choosing, and one full moon, three hours before dawn he quietly slipped out of bed with two empty coconut shells aiming for the shore which he easily reached before dawn. There was a very small settlement of less than ten huts, probably housing some freed families. There was also an official looking building, probably the army hospital he had heard about. There was not a soul in sight, but he could see smoke in the distance. Or it might have been morning mist. What looked like another larger settlement unexpectedly emerged from the dark, and he navigated very carefully round it. When he arrived at the beach, as he expected, there was not a soul in sight. First light enabled him to peer in awe at the beauty as he watched the glistening waves. He closed his eyes in order to dwell upon their music as they gently crept in and finally crashed on the sands. Suddenly he could not resist going in. Swimming in the river was nothing in comparison. He swallowed a big gulp of sea water, and although it was more bitter than salty, he relished it. He then filled his shells with sea water, and was on his way back. The first ray of the sun was beginning to peep in timidly when he heard a noise, and saw three carioles coming towards him. He was in a field with no place to hide, but a strangler fig tree, and he waited behind it for the carriages to go away. However, to his amazement, they stopped, and some men in pith helmets and shiny knee-length boots carrying whips came out with a handful of semi-clad blacks, carrying bundles and cases. There was no way to move and avoid detection, so there

was only one thing to do, the Spirits be blessed. He carefully put his two coconut shells full of sea water beneath the tree, eased himself as he knew that
it might be some time before he would be able to do it properly, and using a
hanging root, he hoisted himself up, sat on a branch, protected from view by
the thick foliage, and he did the only thing possible, watch the men at work.
The men were obviously carrying out some preliminary work in that very
field. No doubt the early start was to avoid the punishing sun. They started
working in an enclosed area of the field, measuring and digging out huge
rocks. They worked without stopping, for hours, until the sun started going
down, and he was in agony, hungry, hot and thirsty, waiting for the men to
finish, and when they finally stopped, they did not seem to be in a hurry to
leave. He had worried about Matamba all day long and expected a right telling off when he got back to her. She was a good woman, and the wise Rolena
would not mind about them being together when she watched them from the
Good Place.

The man who appeared to be the leader finally ordered his men to stack
the rocks in a neat pile in a corner, and this took over an hour. He stayed
on the tree until sunset, and when the work force had finally finished their
work, they got in the carriages and drove away. He waited for them to be out
of sight, came down but in his hurry, he forgot the sea water. He had walked
for about half an hour when he suddenly remembered, and went back to get
his coconut shells. There was no danger now. Matamba's eyes were red with
weeping; she clung to her man, beating him on the chest with her fists and
hugging him at the same time. She was trembling all over, and it took a while
before she regained her composure.

'I'll cook you some pigeon,' said Matamba between sobs, crying and
laughing at the same time, 'and tonight we will have our first salted dish
since we ran away.'

She explained how she had imagined the worse and how, distraught and
frustrated, she had angrily thrown a stick at some poor pigeons and, incredibly, it had hit one.

The two runaways lived like this for some time. Although they both
loved malanga cooked with shrimps or fish, and drumstick leaves in all its
forms, specially cooked with coconut- a recipe Matamba had invented- they

were beginning to hanker after other things. Fortunately their seedlings started bearing, and there was never any shortage of variety. It was clear that one could throw a million sticks at some pigeons and not hit any. The Supreme Spirit had intervened because He had wanted to comfort Matamba. Now, the warrior set about devising the means of capturing pigeons. He got her to weave a basket with sisal fibres and placed some left over food under it, and when the pigeons came to eat, he pulled a piece of string he had attached to it, causing the basket to trap the unsuspecting bird under it. They found some thick bamboo one day, and he cut a few of the thickest ones, and after a lot of hard work was able to make containers of much larger size than coconut shells. Matamba frowned when he brought them to her as she was sitting on a rock with her feet in the water.

'Why what's the matter with my bamboo bottles?'

'You're not thinking of going back to the sea to collect sea water, are you?'

'I know the route now,' he said, ' and above all, I know how to avoid the danger.'

They argued for a bit, but he assured her that there was no danger at all, and promised that he would be ever so careful. Again some hours before dawn, he set out, promising that he would be back early in the morning. This time he was true to his word. The people who had been working in that field had come back, and were building what looked like a big stone building, and some of them seemed to be sleeping on the site now.

'That must have been dangerous, they could have seen you?' He grinned and shook his head. She stared at him in admiration, for this was one of the rare occasions that she had seen him smile. No, it's not dangerous, once you know what to expect. This was a principle he had learnt as a soldier. Intelligence was much more valuable than weapons

Their confidence in their new environment grew from day to day, and they began venturing further and further away, never dropping their guard. Sometimes they saw carioles in the distance, negotiating the rough terrain; rarely they saw people on foot. One afternoon, they espied a man and a woman, clearly white bosses, walking in a leisurely manner, arm in arm, and they tailed them cautiously. They ended up in an alley planted on both sides by ornamental palm trees, at the end of which they saw a newly built mansion. It had a large open verandah and was freshly painted white. As there was plenty of luxuriant vegetation, they found it easy to remain unseen. There were some black slaves working in the garden, two men and three women. They watched them in silence for a time, taking comfort in the knowledge that there were people nearby they could ask for help in an emergency.

On the next day they decided to go back to the mansion, and as luck would have it, they saw a cariole coming towards them. They hid behind a tamarind tree and saw the white couple they had seen the day before. They guessed that the slaves would be on their own, and decided to seize the moment. They made their way inside the grounds and hanged around for a while amid the shrubbery, waiting for something to happen; they did not have to wait long. A round little woman emerged from the house and made for the garden where there were lots of vegetables, and they watched her collecting beans in a basket. Matamba suddenly took a few steps in her direction. The round little woman was humming happily, committing the pods to her basket in a comical manner, tossing them with a flourish, unaware of the alien presence. Matamba coughed gently, and the round little woman was so taken aback that she dropped her basket and began running away, as if she had seen a ghost.

'Stop,' said Matamba in Chopi, 'I am not a ghost, I am... Matamba.' The woman stopped, turned round to face her and looked at her in disbelief, opening her large eyes wide. How could she not be a ghost? She seemed to be telling herself.

'I am a runaway slave, a maroon.'

'Ayo,' she said, and shouted in Shagaan in the direction of the house, 'come over here, there's a maroon... she speaks Chopi...' Matamba got the gist of what the woman was saying, and was terrified; who was she calling? Were there other white masters inside? Midala, who had stayed hidden emerged from the bush, increasing the confusion of the small round woman. A small army of black slaves came out of the house, brandishing broomsticks, machetes and iron rods.

'We are not dangerous,' Midala said, 'we mean you no harm, we're runaways.'

A grey-haired man with only one eye nodded wisely.

'We suspected there were runaways in the ravine, when we saw the smoke; we even talked about it.'

'But then no more smoke…' said a thin woman with a child on her haunch.

'But of course we said nothing to the masters, we don't wish you any harm,' said a woman with a child on her back.

The pair knew that the battle was won, that there was nothing to fear. Without further ceremony, they all sat down on the dry grass like long lost friends. They were Shangaans and not Chopis, they explained, but the wars between their two nations were back there; here we are all cousins, they said. They explained that the masters had gone to Port-Louis for the day; he was the son of the richest man on the island, some sort of chief. They were called Monsieur Alexandre Taillefer de Sauvigny and the lady was Madame Georgette. They had a little boy called Bertrand, but he lived with his grand parents in a place called Moka. The lady is the daughter of the governor of the island. The name of this house is Mon Château, they added.

'I am sure you must be living under difficult conditions,' said the grey-haired man whose name he told them was Jacques Grenouille.

'Midala had to risk his life to get me some sea water,' Matamba said, and told the story to a rapt audience.

'Oh yes,' someone said, 'we have heard that they are building a factory to make sacks with the sisals near La Pointe aux Sables.'

'You must be short of pots and pans, kitchen things,' the woman with the child on her back said, 'we can give you all you need; we have everything here, and nobody knows how many; the lady never sets foot in the kitchen anyway.'

They were delighted when someone proposed to get some food from the kitchen, and came back with bits of goat meat and manioc; they ate and drank heartily, and someone asked why they had preferred to leave the comfort of their master's house to brave it in the woods, and were shocked when they were told about the conditions in Sept Cascades, the back-breaking work, the whip and the insults.

'Here,' Grenouille said, 'the master and the mistress are very nice and the idea would never occur to them to whip anybody.' Besides, they explained,

Monsieur Alexandre has said that as they belonged to his father, he could not free them, but that one day, he would do just that. They were not all delighted at that prospect.

'This is a strange country,' the round little woman chipped in, 'we did not ask to come here, they captured us and took us here against our will; if the master returns us to our home that's fine, but if they just tell us one day, look, you slaves are all free to do as you wish, what will we do.' Jacques shook his head and tut tutted.

'I have explained I do not know how many times, that when a slave is set free, he can find employment and earn good money and live where he likes, and as he likes, but not everybody is convinced.'

Midala and Matamba had clear views about this, but were sure that when the time came, everybody would seize their liberty with both hands and never let go.

The people of Mon Château gave them a large quantity of foodstuff, clothing and kitchen implements. Midala almost regretted that he need never go back to the sea to fetch salty water.

'We'd like to come visit you in your... abode...' someone said, 'but we don't think we are allowed to leave the perimeter of Mon Château.' This made Jacques Grenouille cackle with laughter.

'Proves my point,' he said, 'as free men and women, you would be free to go anywhere, there will be no boundaries -'

'He is right,' Midala said. And they went back to their home, not for one moment minding the weight of their gifts.

Life after their visit to Mon Château became much easier, but Midala could not help feeling uneasy about the new development. No one was going to betray them intentionally, but something bad was bound to happen.

At the end of the cane-cutting season, de Fleury summoned his guards and ordered them to find the runaway couple or else... As he had guessed, the Anti-Maroon unit had been completely useless. Antoine was again included in the party. Later, when he was helping the master remove his boots, he felt emboldened to emit an opinion.

'Master, there are so many places for a runaway to hide, where shall we start? We'll never catch them, it would be like looking for a cricket that has lost its song in a cane field... I mean the chirping might have led us to him...'

'The first place would be the Citadel; remember that fellow who was hiding there, before we dealt with him?' How can the man be so insensitive as to mention him, thought Antoine.

'Yes, master, but there are so many places,' insisted the slave.

'Where would you look?' asked de Fleury; Antoine winced. What if he mentioned a place and Midala just happened to be there? It would be like he was betraying him.

'Master, I have hardly been anywhere, I am an ignorant slave, I have no idea.' De Fleury laughed.

'Suppose… you decided to run away… where would you go?' He had thought of the Black River Gorges once.

'Well, he began,' but stopped immediately. No, he was not going to say. He took a deep breath.

'Master,' he said smiling, 'why would I want to run away; I am very contented here, serving you…' De Fleury nodded happily; why didn't the others realise that he was a fair man, and that all he wanted was for them to do as he said and they would never suffer any ill treatment.

'The Black River Gorges would seem like a good place to search, and the ravines… the two Grande Rivières, there are some grottoes on the coast. The island is small… it shouldn't be too difficult. If I was not so busy, I'd come myself, it should be good fun, better than deer hunting, eh.'

A few days later, four guards, three fresh recruits from France, a Créole, and Antoine, set out on their mission to put an end to Midala and Matamba's dash for freedom, under the leadership of Mr Catard, a senior colon. They scoured a good few places where runaways might find a refuge, but found nothing. Finally the party arrived in the vicinity of Mon Château near the hiding place of the couple. They were received by the young master and his wife, and they in turn ordered all their retainers to appear in front of the search party. The Shangaans were shaken and when they denied with unnecessary vehemence that they had seen the slightest unusual thing, never any smoke, may their tongue drop out of their mouths if they were lying, Antoine immediately knew that the couple were in the ravines below.

Catard suggested that they searched the ravines, whereupon the crafty Antoine casually mentioned that according to him that would be a waste of time, for if the runaways were anywhere near here, the Shagaans would have seen something, some movement, or smoke. Catard was on the point of agreeing, but changed his mind.

'We are running out of places to look,' he said, 'if we go back empty-handed, the boss is going to have the skin off our arses,' adding 'and if he heard that we did not go down the ravines here, he will think we failed in our duty... I think we had better go and see for ourselves.' So it was decided to go down the ravines.

Perhaps because he had guessed right, Antoine kept seeing signs of human presence, debris of sisals, mango stones, feathers, and such things. At one point, one of the guards stumbled on some tomato plants and gave the alarm.

'Right, our slaves are in the area,' the leader said, 'let us leave no stone unturned now... come on boys, open both your eyes wide, and your ears too.'

Antoine burst out laughing, 'here on this island, tomatoes grow wild,' he said, 'didn't you know that?' Fortunately this was accepted by the colon who had grown up in a town. Still, they looked and saw nothing. He was running out of ideas, and if the white men discovered that he had been trying to put them off scent, de Fleury might vent his anger upon him. Suddenly they came across the charred remains of a wood fire, and Antoine was sweating all over. Fortunately it was Catard himself who came to the rescue.

'I know what this is,' he said, 'people come fishing here on the riverside, and they light fires to heat their food.' Everybody agreed, except the crafty Antoine who demurred.

The fugitives had received the shock of their lives when they had seen the armed party scrambling down the ravines; their game was up, they had thought. There was only one thing to do, and that was to go inside their grotto and wait for the worse. They were not planning to fight against men armed with guns. They held their breaths, holding each other for comfort and waited. On his own, Midala would have flung himself on a guard in the hope of disarming him and then use his weapon to fight the others, but that would be madness under the circumstances. The party passed just outside the grotto, but the camouflage must have been good, for no one stopped, and finally they gave up and left. They spent another week chasing shadows, and to their surprise the normally irate man said that it was indeed a tall order, just like looking for a cricket which had lost its song in a sugar field. But mark his word, he warned, that rascally pair was bound to commit a mistake, and when they do, he will be waiting, adding his usual cryptic phrase, 'they are losing nothing by waiting!'

The pair decided to go to Mon Château on the next day to share the tale of their narrow escape with their new friends. They waited in the lush vegetation to make sure they would not run into the masters, and true enough the cariole with the young couple drove past, and they rushed to the house. They were received like long lost friends; their Shangaan hosts could not do enough for them. Midala did not say much, but Matamba regaled her audience with the story of their narrow escape. The masters were on their way to Moka, and would not come back for a few days, so they had the house all to themselves, but they were bringing back the brat Bertrand with them. Everybody ate and drank like kings, and although the pair were invited to spend the night at Mon Château, they preferred to "go back home," as they put it.

The Taillefer de Sauvigny returned in a week with the boy Bertrand. It turned out that he was fanatical about fishing, and the moment he arrived home, he began pestering his parents to take him fishing in the river. Monsieur Alexandre was not too keen, but Madame Georgette begged him to humour the boy. So father and son set out one morning and went down the ravines to the river bank. Midala and Matamba caught a glimpse of them scrambling down, and watched their progress with apprehension, when suddenly, a branch to which the boy was hanging snapped, and he began rolling down the slope of the ravine, and landed in the water, as Midala knew he would. Alexandre began shouting "Au secours, au secours!" but as he scrambled down in panic, he slipped and caught his leg in a protruding root and was instantly immobilised, possibly with a broken leg. Midala watched his face contort in agony before it changed to an expression of horror, his son could not swim. Midala rushed out without thinking and hurled himself in the torrents, swam to the boy, grabbed him and dragged him to the bank; fortunately the boy was more scared than damaged. Monsieur Alexandre watched in amazement as this saviour appeared from nowhere to save both him and his son.

The fugitives were apprehensive; their cover had been blown. Although it was clear that Monsieur Alexandre was not going to do anything to harm them, the boy Bertrand was only seven.

The inevitable happened, and Midala and Matamba were rounded, put in chains and unceremoniously carted to Sept Cascades. He knew that de Fleury was watching him closely, so he decided to lie low for a while, but the white man, frustrated in his desire to whip the man to death because he had not weighed up the new governor yet; the bastard lost nothing by waiting; in the meantime he decided to separate the pair. No one, not even Antoine had any idea of where she might have been despatched to.

Midala had never given up the idea of escaping, but the military strategist in him was biding his time, accumulating more useful facts, determined that his next attempt would be a successful one. It took him all of a year to find the right moment. This time, Midala said to himself, no one will catch me alive. This time, swore the white man, I will move heaven and earth to catch the bastard, I will go looking for him myself, and when I do, he will have lose nothing for waiting!

Obviously Rolena had pride of place in his heart, but she was gone. The passion which had developed between him and Matamba had rekindled from embers that he had thought to be cold ashes, and a whole year's separation had not cooled his passion for her. She was somewhere on the island, and he was going to do his utmost to find her. By now, he had a clearer idea of the lie of the land, and Antoine had told him a number of vital things. His friend had guessed that Matamba might be in Crève Coeur, where the master had a pineapple plantation. He also told him that as there was now an increasing number of freed ex-slaves scattered all over the island, living in small settlements, he might find refuge for a night or two, as to many of them it was a point of honour to come to the rescue of a runaway brother or sister; yes, even women ran away too. Antoine had told him of a champion escape artist called Azoline, who had escaped dozens of times. Antoine informed him about the code; it was surprising, he explained, that the Bourgeois class had not yet cracked it. If you are a runaway, and if you meet a black man whom you suspected of being a former slave, you rubbed your right eye with your index finger, as you passed him. If he does not respond, it means that he is not in the know, and had best be avoided. On the other hand, if he is willing to help, he will then rub his left eye to indicate this. When and if he does, you can follow him discreetly and he will give you food and shelter for the night, and will help you in many other ways.

With the bustle in the thriving establishment that Sept Cascades had become, it was not too difficult for a runaway to sneak out unnoticed, but it was well-known that most maroons were rounded up within one week. The slaves who made up most of the Anti-Maroon détachements having been promised freedom if they caught so many runaways, showed great keenness to rope in their fellow victims.

All the same, one Sunday morning, Midala quietly slipped away, heading for Crève Coeur. He walked carefully, avoiding public places where there were people about, although sometimes this was unavoidable, but to his re-lief, no one challenged him; Antoine had given him some decent clothing which made him look like a free man.

After four days, he found himself in the north of Port-Louis, whose im-portance was growing by the day ever since Governor Maupin had moved the capital there. A free man had advised him to go to Madame Agathe, an extraor-dinary woman who lived in Roche Bois; she was the mistress of de Metzger, a powerful Alsatian colonel of the Quatrième Régiment des Hussars, and had a string of powerful lovers besides. The lady, knew all about the suffering and humiliation of being a slave, having herself been only recently freed, at the instigation of one of her lovers. My body belonged to whoever could do her a favour, but my heart belonged to my enslaved people, she was reputed to have said. Although she was herself from Madagascar, she considered all slaves her people. It was a wonder that she had never been caught, for she was very open about what she did, feeding runaways, housing them, sometimes sleeping with them; everybody seemed to know about her habits, except the Colonel, who was besotted with her body; people said that she had given him her "dilo dire oui" to drink, and when you drank a woman's dilo dire oui, you became her slave. If she tells you that black is white, you believed her, if she said that night was day, you'd swear the moon was the sun.

Midala had no trouble finding Agathe's house, a handsome wooden edifice built at the back of a long alley in a spacious ground with luxuriant vegetation. It had originally been earmarked for lieutenant de Metzger's, but he had reallocated it to the woman whose body could arouse passions in him that he had thought had long since expired. The fugitive was surprised to find that everything he had heard about Agathe was true. To his surprise, the big-hearted woman was also sheltering Azoline, of whom Antoine had spoken.

'Go on, Azoline tell our guest how many times you have run away?' The champion escapee smiled shyly and tried to work out the answer, and finally using her fingers, indicated to the man who had only run away twice that she had run away nineteen times in four years and a bit.

'I have offered to send her back to Madagascar, but she doesn't want to go,' said Madame Agathe sadly, 'she has her own reasons.' Midala was surprised.

'Do you mean you can arrange for —'

'Sometimes,' she said proudly, 'if I can find a ship.' Midala stared at her with admiration.

'I can probably ship you to Inhambane,' she said negligently. The warrior opened his eyes wide. He would dearly love to go back to his tribe, or whatever was left of it, find his boy Abo and his little girls.

'Just say the word, and I'll start working on it.'

No, tempting though it was, he was searching for Matamba; perhaps after he had found her, he might reconsider.

'When you decide, I may not be around,' she said sadly.

Next day, he was on his way to Crève Coeur. It was one of the most beautiful sights he had seen on the island, with rolling valleys criss-crossing each other, filled with a green and luxurious vegetation. There were a number of officious people supervising black men and women planting seedlings and removing weeds, and he had to hide until he found a good moment to address a wizened old man who could hardly stand on his two feet. When he addressed the man, he jumped with fright, and was on the point of running away, when Midala caught hold of his hand and stopped him. He asked him about Matamba, and it was clear that the man did not understand a word of what he was saying. It turned out that he was from Madagascar, recently arrived and had not yet picked kreol. But he offered to find someone who could help. He waited alone whilst the Madagascar man went to find a trusted kreol speaker.

When one was found, he greeted Midala with cautious friendliness, and said that as far as he knew, a woman fitting the description, and her baby had been taken away to another place, but she was called Madeleine.

His first thought was that it could not have been her; Matamba was not carrying his baby, or was she? He would go back to Agathe to ask for her help; she had many friends, and if anybody could find a cricket with or without its song in a cane-field, Agathe would be her name.

Reluctantly he turned his back on this beautiful place, and directed his steps towards Port-Louis. In Terre Rouge, which was a hive of activity because of the mining of iron ore going on there, Midala thought that he would easily pass unnoticed. But he was wrong. He was picked up and taken to Trou Fanfaron, where he was thrown in jail, pending a decision about what was to be done with him. De Fleury demanded that the culprit be handed over to him; he would cut off his ears and brand him on the shoulder with a fleur de lys, as was his right. He was convinced that that was the only way to deal with the recalcitrant. However, governor Maupin decided that the man was an ideal candidate for the Bagne, specially designed for receiving grands marrons, habitual runaways, and as yet, Victor de Fleury had not found any hold over his new excellency.

He was therefore delivered to the Bagne on the quayside in Port-Louis. It was His Excellency's stated ambition to make this the most escape-proof establishment on any French territory, and to this effect, he had hand-picked Colonel Grapouille to be his representative on earth, naming him Surintendant du Bagne.

CHAPTER 4

◆◆◆

Leaving Calcutta

WHEN JAYANT REAPPEARED alone some time later, Shanti was filled with an inexplicable hatred for the young man, as if it was all his fault that he had not found Raju. She turned her head away as he began explaining that he had been unable to locate her husband and the girl because the crowd was much denser than he had imagined. She was not listening, and did not hear him bemoan the fact that it had been hardly possible to inch yourself forward one step without treading on someone's toes and earning a rebuke. But I am sure that it was them, he said, shaking his stupid head from left to right. Shanti went pale on hearing this, and her whole body became cold. Were it not for the lump in her throat acting like a barrage, her tears would have burst through with a force that would have made them gush out in a flood of despair. She began to panic. The little boy noticed her mother's state, and began to cry, kicking Jayant angrily when he offered to pick him up. She was only able to keep an appearance of calmness because she knew that she had to be strong for Pradeep, but after taking in a few deep breaths she regained some composure. The friendly auntie engaged her in conversation and that seemed to keep her mind off her main concern. She realised that when one is in turmoil and puts a bold face on things, stopping one's tears by a superhuman effort of will power, the body still finds a way of reacting, and in her case, she noticed that her whole body was shaking like a leaf in the breeze beginning to build up before a storm. She tried to divert attention from her trembling hands by holding one in the other. The apprehension grew worse by the minute, but Jayant thought that she had succeeded in getting a grip on herself. Things became much worse when an official appeared unexpectedly and announced that passengers travelling to Mauritius on the Startled Fawn should proceed to the Harbour Office immediately. But I can't go without my man and my little girl, she screamed at the friendly woman by her side.

'But daughter, if your brother says he saw him in front, then if you don't go, and your man and little girl get on board —'

'But what are you saying, Chachi?' Shanti snapped angrily, 'my husband will never leave without me.'

'Look,' said Jayant calmly, 'if he is ahead of us, he will surely get on the boat knowing that we can join him, what will happen if he gets on the boat and you... we don't?' Shanti's dormant hostility towards Jayant nearly broke its leash, but she managed not to lash out. It was as if he had purposely failed to find Raju, but she knew that he was right. The friendly woman nodded at Jayant's words, to show that she thought that he had a point.

'But suppose you saw wrong, that the man you saw with a girl in a blue dress was someone else?'

'Then you and I will go to Mareeshush without Raju, and all my sinful dreams will come true,' Jayant thought, for he had always been half in love with his best friend's wife. Instead he said, 'Arrey, how can Bhagwan permit the two of you to become separated?' The level-headed woman surprisingly found that thought very comforting. Indeed, how can Bhagwan play a trick like that on poor innocent souls like themselves, who had never harmed anybody? Jayant was not so stupid after all. But the latter was thinking that the same Bhagwan did allow the waves to gobble up his Ma and his Pitaji. It pained him to realise how love for one person could make you immune to the suffering of the rest of the world.

When after an eternity their turn came, they calmly inched forward, entered the makeshift shack that served as the Harbour Office, and Jayant tried to explain the situation to an impatient and unresponsive Mr Chatterjee the clerk. His Angrezi boss, Mr Delahunty enquired what the palaver was all about, and the Bengali clerk explained that the family had become separated, which made him burst out laughing.

'Tell the Bint to go to Lost Property then, Chatterbox,' he screamed joyfully. Chatterjee laughed immeasurably at his boss's joke. He did not think the appellation Chatterbox was in any way derogatory, and preferred to think of it as a mark of affection.

'What's the cove's name?' asked Delahunty, and Jayant replied, Rajendra Parsad Varma, and the Angrezi scanned a list, mumbling some names until he landed on a Rajendra, nodded and said that he fellow had been processed already. Shanti sighed with relief, but immediately wondered about the girl. She rather rudely pulled Chatterjee's sleeve and asked about the girl, 'Was my little girl with him?' to which the self-important clerk, offended by a peasant woman treating him with such lack of respect, replied testily, 'Yes, of course, now get a move on, we don't have all day.'

They were shoved towards a small door into an open veranda, joining other folks waiting to board the barge. You are so stupid Shanti, obviously Raju would not have left the girl behind, she scolded herself. The moment they had climbed on the barge which was about to leave, Delahunty, looking at the list of names, scratched his head.

'I say, Chatterbox,' he asked suddenly, 'did that cove say his missing friend was Sharma?'

'Yes, yes, sahib sir, Varma… I think… no, no… Sharma, yes, yes… quite very definitely Sharma.'

'Good,' said the Englishman, 'there is a Sharma here… we would not wish families to be separated, would we, Chatterbox?' adding, 'my good action for the day, eh.' He had stood up and taken a couple of steps towards the privy, when the clerk spoke.

'This Varma chap, sir, he had a little girl with him, didn't he?' Chatterjee asked. Delahunty made a grimace and pursed his lips, clearly not remembering, but with a shrug, he said, 'Yes, I think so…' My good action for the day, thought the Bengali clerk.

When they clambered on board the barge, Shanti became very agitated at not finding Raju there, but at a short distance down river, there was another similarly cram-packed craft slowly moving towards the *Startled Fawn*, and the friendly woman who happened to be by her side nodded wisely, 'He must surely be in that one, you'll meet on the big ship, you must have faith, Bhagwan knows what He is doing.' Yes, chachi, he must be, said Shanti.

Having survived the walk up the rickety steps and made it on board, Shanti, undaunted by the mass of people rushing in all directions, looking for relatives or misplaced possessions, began a frantic search for Raju, leaving Pradeep in the care of Jayant, and when the brig began its slow descent down the Hoogli, she became frantic, as she knew that now there was no going back. Jayant kept following her, carrying Pradeep on his haunch, telling her that Raju and Sundari were surely somewhere on board, and that once everybody had settled into the routine, they would suddenly appear. The deep resentment which had built up against the devoted family friend since their arrival in Calcutta was fast reaching its boiling point. Didn't he swear that he had seen her husband and little girl in the crowd ahead of them? May Bhagwan stop her pushing him overboard if he continues annoying her! That idiot smiling like a half-wit, swinging his head from one side to the other, who cannot tell green from blue.

She kept pestering everybody with questions. Had they seen Raju? The little girl? At first people were sympathetic to her plight, but as everybody had their own problems, it did not take long for them to become irritated by her. She began pulling her hair out, screaming that she wanted to be taken back to the harbour. The other travellers began to get seriously uneasy and complained to some officers about this mad woman who was spreading panic and despondency on board in such a stressful time. Pradeep, seeing his mother in a state he had never known her to be in, began to cry and throw a fit. Finally an Angrezi officer, accompanied by a Bengali kitchen hand appeared and Shanti explained. The Angrezi was not impressed, but assured her, that her husband was surely on board, where else could he be? Under British rule people did not simply disappear, eh what! The Bengali man dutifully translated. He then solemnly warned her that unless she calmed down, he would lock her in a dark room below. If you do not calm down, the Bengali hand translated, the Angrezi man will throw you and your little boy overboard.

They were packed very closely in the holds. The men separated from the women. There were quantities of things scattered all over the available space, and on top of that, people were unable and unwilling to stay in one place, which made circulation next to impossible. Thus the devoted Jayant took about an hour to go backwards and forwards from the men's quarters to the women and children's, looking in vain for Raju. The cramped conditions were such that once seated, people could hardly move. The moment they had been allocated their spot, an area no bigger than a small cot, tired from the waiting and the hot sun, they were overwhelmed by the smell of sweat and apprehension filling the atmosphere. Then people began to suffer from sea-sickness and the vomiting never stopped. Often the bad odours were so nauseating that they caused more vomiting, which established an unending cycle of gut-churning abomination which was to last until the very end. Nobody got used to this putrid vomitous atmosphere. Another huge problem was the lack of toilet facilities. The passengers were given buckets, and although there was a torn curtain in a corner, they had little or no privacy. The pitching and tossing of the ship caused spillage, and no matter how much sea water was used to get rid of the filth, the odours persisted adding to the hellish mix already prevalent. Many years later, the people who survived the crossing would remember it vividly.

Soon the whole ship had become aware of the disappearance of Shanti's husband and child. Most people were quick to express sympathy and say something comforting, but these produced little effect on her. The words that did produce an effect, were, unfortunately, far from consoling. An old woman from Orissa came to her, and shaking her head said that there was no doubt that thuggees must had seized her husband and child.

'Arrey, didi, what are you saying? What are thuggees?' And the thoughtless woman told her of those sinister individuals who were always on the lookout for innocent victims to kidnap. She explained that she knew all that because there were some men from her village who had been snatched by thuggees. Shanti was too stunned to respond, but although she was hating the woman for telling her all this, she was very keen to learn more. They go about in small teams, the woman from Orissa said, and one of them, an expert danta thrower aims a small thick stick with force at the ankle of a prospective victim, who when hit, falls on the ground, incapacitated, whereupon the bandits seize him, take him to their den, torture him, and finally offer him as a sacrifice to the Goddess Kali.

'Arrey, what are you taking about? People don't harm little children, my husband is with my daughter —'

'We know the Goddess has special love for little children,' the woman from Orissa said sadly, 'which is why she specially values the sacrifice of little children.'

She decided not to believe the scaremonger, but she would never again have any peace of mind.

Every night she would lie on her mat tossing, unable to sleep, and when she did, she was tormented by nightmares. They were always the same. Raju would be in a pit, blood dripping from all over his body, but he was smiling happily, and she would bend down and give him an arm to pull him up, but however much she tried, she could never reach him.

For the duration of the voyage Shanti was like a living corpse. The other passengers having problems of their own, half of them suffering from acute seasickness, ignored her completely and only the devotion of Jayant kept her and Pradeep alive, forcing food inside her, fanning her, or applying compresses of cold water on her fevered brow when the heat became unbearable, all this doing nothing to mitigate the deep resentment she felt towards him. In the first week there were a dozen deaths through dysentery and diarrhoea, and the situation did not improve as the voyage progressed. Everyday someone died of some unidentified sickness, and got unceremoniously thrown overboard.

They had been at sea for just over a week, when the storm hit, and as the ship began to roll perilously, people started screaming in the certain knowledge that the end was nigh. Some women were shouting that it was their men's fault, that they had said that they did not want to go, but the men always think they know best. The men in their quarters were blaming their women. They would not have left their homeland but the womenfolk were never contented with what they could bring home. People got tossed all over the place. Not my fault, sister, it's the storm. No, you could make a little effort, you are going to smother my little boy. You are squeezing me to death. Many got hurt, tempers became frayed, and fighting broke out among the men. Six people died of broken skulls as the force of the storm hurled them across the hold to the hull of the ship, and were buried at sea. Many more became seriously sick of a variety of ailments, some of whom inevitably passing away.

How she and Pradeep survived, Shanti, haunted by nightmares every night, unable to do anything, had no idea. Jayant it was who collected their ration of rice, dal, onion, oil, salt fish and chillies. He it was who queued up behind the impatient file of people waiting for the precarious fire to cook their meals every day. Every night she would pray that either Bhagwan returns her Raju to them, or take their lives, and as He did neither, she took it as a sign that He would give her daughter and her man back to her. Perhaps once they landed in Mareeshus, there they would be, beaming and smiling happily. Yes, definitely... perhaps... maybe...

After the interminable voyage, one morning, Mauritius was sighted. But as there were cases of cholera on board, the ship was directed to Flat Island, and after three days when the sick were first removed, and the ship disinfected, it was allowed to sail into Port-Louis harbour. It was with apprehension that Shanti walked down the steps into the barge that was going to take them on land. She carried Pradeep and, Jayant the few possessions that they had. She had no inclination to look at the new world they were coming to. Without Raju, what did it matter. But Pradeep was wide-eyed with admiration. Look, Mama, the sky is so blue, the sea so calm. Look at the mountain uncle, he shouted excitedly as he pointed to Signal Mountain, doesn't it look like a big cow resting. The Cokhan boatman smiled at him with his betel-stained teeth and patted him on the head. That man is so nice, Mama, not like the others. He meant the crew of the Startled Fawn who were always scowling and shouting.

As they were going up the steps at the Aapravasi Ghat, Shanti suddenly saw visions of the steps she took round the fire when she married Raju, with the heart-breaking difference that this time there was no Raju. Deep down she must have known that coming to this distant land was another landmark in her checkered life. Tears dripped down her cheeks, and Pradeep asked her what the matter was. Is Baba waiting for us, the boy asked. That was one thing Shanti had kept telling him, and it provoked more tears when the boy did not see his Baba. She had told Jayant that the first thing he had to do was to report Raju's disappearance. Perhaps those clever Angrezi people who write everything in their big books already knew where he was. Jayant would have liked nothing better than to carry out her orders, but he was a shy and unassuming young man. With strangers he usually stammered, and he was dreading the encounter with an official. He spoke to a peon and this young black man shook his head. He did not understand, but he went to fetch a Bhojpuri-speaking peon, but there were five hundred people to be dealt with, and the clerks were very busy. Shanti saw red. If there are clerks, she heard herself say, not quite knowing what a clerk was, then you had better get one for me now, as I have one big big problem, my husband has disappeared.

'Yes, captanine,' he said and disappeared. Shanti did not smile, but that was the first time anybody had called her captanine since she had left home to marry Raju, and she would remember that all her life. After a long wait, a white man and his interpreter came along and without waiting for Shanti's explanation, told her dozens of people had died and had been thrown over-board, and there was nothing he could do about it. She began to shout and scream, and before long Monsieur Hugon, the Protector of Immigrants himself, heard about her, invited her into his office, and listened to her atten-tively. When she had finished, he spoke calmly, and said that it was clear that her husband had missed the boat. She should not worry, because he would definitely be on the next boat which would arrive in three weeks. Shanti was much heartened by this, and calmed down.

Hugon gave orders that her registration be expedited, took down her par-ticulars, and promised that the moment Raju arrived, he would send some-one to Mont Calme where he knew she was going, to inform her. She, Jayant and Pradeep then passed their medical examination. Nothing very wrong with any of you, the medical officer said, that a little rest and two meals a day cannot put right. They received their tickets and passes and went to a smaller hall where the sugar cane planters or their staff had come to receive their new contingent of workers. Jayant would have happily accepted full responsibility for Shanti and Pradeep, at least until Raju turned up.

'So you think Raju will turn up?' Shanti asked him.

'Arrey, bhabi, the Angrezi man said so.'

When Shanti heard that she was expected to replace her husband in the fields, she said that was fine, she had a good pair of hands, and would not need Jayant's charity. Yes, Jayant had said, but you were born a lady, and grew up with naukars. Yes, one day we have servants, Shanti said, the next we become servants ourselves. In a matter of days, they were taken by oxcart to Mont Calme to join the work force of Monsieur Victor de Fleury, one of the most important sugar-cane magnates of the island. He had built a large number of very basic units to house his work force, and to Jayant's delight and Shanti's dismay, the foreman said that as there was a shortage of housing, and as Jayant was single, he would have to board with Shanti. He promptly reassured her that he would be happy to sleep outside under the jackfruit tree, or under the open verandah, if it rained. In fact, he would have been happy to sleep out in the rain for her. She had become aware of his unhealthy obsession with with her, and reacted by becoming increasingly offhanded with him. He seemed not to notice.

CHAPTER 5

◆ ◆ ◆

The Bagne

This chapter is dedicated to Laxmi Bhatt who worried about the
fate of Midala, the African warrior.

THE BAGNE WAS a desolate area on the quayside just outside the precincts of the harbour. Its construction was still incomplete, and it only offered basic facilities, and the security only worked because of Grapouille's ruthless regime. The area was spacious, and there were plans to build a Military Hospital adjacent to it. A high wall was being built to surround the prison in order to make it escape-proof, and all the present inmates, were employed in its completion. Governor Grapouille prided himself that on his watch, not one slave had managed to run away, and promised to improve on this record.

The moment Midala entered that grim place, he started looking around to find chinks in the security system. He discovered that the place was guarded by armed men, following each inmate like a shadow, and was told that they were instructed to shoot to kill anyone attempting escape. The regime of punishment for so-called recalcitrants was outrageous. They would be made to stand in the burning sun, holding a massive rock just over their heads, without water and deprived of food and sleep. Inmates worked in groups of four or five chained together at the feet, breaking rocks destined for the completion of the walls. Even at night they stayed chained. His heart sank. A planned escape seemed almost out of question. Any breakout could only be envisaged on the spur of the moment, if an unexpected opportunity arose. But a good soldier plans for all possible contingencies.

Grapouille was a drunk who swore at the men whenever he had the opportunity and enjoyed kicking them for no reason at all. He had carefully picked men speaking different languages in each group, in order to make it difficult for them to conspire. Most people, like Midala, still had difficulty coping with kreol. In his group, he was the only Chopi, the others were Malagasy, Anjouani, Swahili-speaking Zanzibari and a deaf mute. Another group consisted of a man from the Guinea coast who spoke Mandingo, a Malagasy speaker, a Shangaan man and an Anjouan man from the Comoros. But no power on earth can stop people from communicating. At first, inspired by the deaf mute, the men used sign language and made themselves understood reasonably well, and it did not take long for them to develop a common language which everybody understood, each one having supplied some kreol vocabulary known to him. Besides the guards manifested their disapproval by hitting them with the butt of their rifles if they saw the men attempting to communicate

Although the work was back-breaking, the men worked cheerfully, heartened by the sight of the calm blue sea, and soothed by the music of the waves crashing on the beach, for they knew that it was best to put up with hardships, or one ends up completely overwhelmed by them. Pastitatane, the Malagasy man was very proud of the fact that he could speak and write French, and it was Midala who suggested that he should teach them. He was delighted to do so, and often, when the guards were not actively watching them, the man from the big island arranged the small stone debris into the shapes of the letters of the alphabet. At the approach of a guard, they would cleverly mix up the pebbles as no one had to tell them that the authorities would deem reading and writing subversive acts.

Daily Midala looked at the sea, wondering if it provided a way of escaping, but with the heavy chains that he had to drag at all times, excellent swimmer though he was, he knew that it was a vain hope. They were tied together in fours even when they slept, the two middle persons with both hands tied to their neighbours on either side, and the two people at the ends had each free hand chained to a massive log by means of a heavy lock. The first step in any night escape necessarily had to be finding the means of freeing themselves from their chains. Four men weighed down by heavy appendages would not go far if they attempted to run away in broad daylight. At night they were almost completely immobilised having to empty bladder and bowel on the spot, like on the slave ships.

Everybody shook their heads in sorrow when escape was mentioned, agreeing that it was an impossible dream, but Midala, the man who had performed a number of miracles in the past, said not to despair, an idea might come to them when it was least expected.

He had wondered how the big rocks they had to work with reached the bagne, and was pleased to discover that oxcarts regularly arrived at the place with big rocks culled from the base of the Signal Mountain which they could see from their place of incarceration. One morning when six carts appeared on the precincts, the prisoners were required to unload them and take them to an area where they would be broken up by means of heavy iron mallets, hammers and chisels. It was the only time that the chains were completely removed from them and they were separated from their team mates. He thought that this might provide the means of escape that he had been looking for. However with the guards following the bagnards like shadows, their pistols poised to shoot, that did not seem viable. Still he had only been one week into the new regime. Things might develop, it was too early to give up. As a strategist who had planned, fought and won wars back in Inhambane, he was used to studying the weak points of the enemy, and this was certainly one of them. It might or might not prove decisive, and he would revisit it later.

Paradoxically, a chink of light emerged from the complete darkness in which they slept at night in their cubby holes. Because they were chained and tied, the guards, feeling safe, acting against orders, often went to sleep. The fatigue caused by the heat, compounded by the large quantities of rum which they consumed when their superiors were not looking, found them exhausted at the end of their long day. They could be heard snoring the moment they had moved to the end of the room. They usually took position near the door, where they could breathe fresh air, and benefit from moonlight when the moon was out as the atmosphere inside was almost unbearable.

An assault on the guards would not be easy to organise, but Midala had mulled over the possibility of an insurrection, which might mean certain death for at least some, if not all of their numbers. If he could find a way of minimising the casualties, he would talk it over frankly with his fellow bagnards.

Weeks went by, and although he rarely thought of anything else, he made no progress. It was like the complete darkness of the nights in his quarters, but with no compensating rays of light sneaking in at dawn through the cracks in the walls. The inmates were good company in spite of their wretched conditions. At first, the deaf mute seemed to have the most optimistic outlook in Midala's group, although he had difficulty communicating with the rest, he had frank innocent eyes and he smiled a lot, and everybody liked him and felt protective towards him.

To everyone's surprise, one day, as the oxcarts laden with rocks had entered the gates and everybody was unchained so they could unload them and take them away, the deaf mute began making desperate efforts to speak, with only pathetic incomprehensible guttural sounds coming out of his throat. He began gesticulating, turning his head left and right in what appeared comical to everybody, making frantic signs, which nobody understood. The others laughed, the guards the loudest, but Midala was perplexed, it was so unlike the fellow to behave in this strange manner. He was obviously trying to say something. If only Midala knew what it was.

They were soon to discover the reason, for suddenly the poor fellow, who was on his way towards a cart, turned round and started running in the opposite direction, towards a breach in the wall.

'Stop, or I shoot,' a guard shouted. It is doubtful whether he would have stopped even if he had heard the order, but he obviously did not, and Midala saw his jailer raise his gun, cock it, and without thinking, he flung himself at him, both crashing to the ground. But another guard did the job, fired his gun, and the deaf mute fell down, blood gushing out of a large hole in his back. Within minutes he was dead. It took three guards to neutralise the inflamed Midala, by kicking and beating him to a pulp.

Unconscious, and covered in blood, he was dragged by guards, chained and dumped in a small isolated stone cell, known as a cachot, as the other inmates watched in horror. The square base was so narrow that there was barely enough room to sit on the floor. To sleep, he had to lie across it diagonally, bending his knees. Even then, every time he moved in his sleep, he knocked his head or some part of his body against the stone wall. There was a very small vent at the top, and the massive wooden door was secured at all times. Midala was left in it for the rest of the day, with no food or water, and no one attending to his wounds. An armed guard stood outside. The heat was unbearable, and having bled profusely, he was more or less unconscious the first day, his throat parched. He had soiled his trousers with urine and excrement, and these mixed with the smell of blood and sweat, made for a stench the like of which he had not experienced even in the hold of the slave ship. During the crossing, there was at least a breeze which brought in some welcome fresh air, diluting the nauseating stench a little bit, but in the confines of the narrow cell, no such relief was available. On the ship, he had held the firm belief that the stench was due to the excrement and odours of others, for man has this ludicrous belief that his own aren't that bad. He had even sometimes relished the smell of some of his bodily excretions. However, now that he was the sole producer of these execrable emanations, this illusion was finally laid to rest. There was not a single thing to cheer one up, the darkness was almost total. He could see nothing, hear nothing. Smell was the only sense still functioning, but all it had to convey was this execrable stench. A baby in its mother's womb is at least able to hear the rhythm of its mother's heartbeat. Suddenly he became aware of the faint sound of the waves crashing against the beach, as if they were miles away and found it very soothing. All the time he had been working in the proximity of the sea, he had hardly ever paid any attention to the waves, but now, it was his only contact with outside reality, and he found some peace listening to its rhythm. Without it, he might as well be dead, he thought. Conscious of the life-giving properties of sound, he began to hear the gentle whistle of the wind among the vegetation. He had tears in his eyes when he was woken up in the morning by a dawn chorus of birds that he could not see.

In the afternoon, he was dragged to the office of the Surintendant Grapouille whose cruelty was considered an asset by his superiors. Playing with his whip, which he carried with him at all times, as if it was an extra appendage, he listened in silence to Caporal Goélard's account of the constant insubordination of the bagnard from the beginning. These were all lies, as Midala had decided not to do anything to attract attention. Mequereau, the guard who was prevented from shooting the deaf mute told another lie. Midala having caught him off guard, he said, had snatched the gun from him and would have shot him dead, were it not for Goélard who wrestled with him and succeeded in disarming him. Other guards corroborated their stories. When they had finished, the Surintendant beckoned Goélard. The latter smiled and strutted towards his superior, expecting a pat on the back, but to his shock, the moment he was near enough to the Colonel, the latter hit him across the face with his horse whip. He made futile attempts to parry the strikes with his arms, but his incensed superior continued lashing out, seemingly forgetting Midala.

'Do not talk to me of insubordination, you arse-scratching halfwit. You have powers, you dog, and any insubordination is entirely due to your uselessness. It only means that you have not been doing your job properly, full stop. Show some initiative, man!' The colonel then took three steps towards Midala, who, downcast and exhausted by the beating, was looking at his feet. Putting his whip under the slave's chin, he lifted his head up.

'Look at the state you are in,' he said, 'you people are worse than animals, dirty smelly swines all of you. What have you got to say, eh?'

'Oui missié,' he said almost inaudibly. Grapouille made a long rambling speech. He had been sent by the his majesty, halfway across the world, from the most civilised country in the world to spread light where there was darkness, but it was like filling a basket with sea water. He had said as much to Sa Majesté when he was invited to Versailles, he boasted, safe in the knowledge that no one was going to contradict him in this untruth. But does anybody ever listen to him? Even the guards thought that he was losing the plot. After going on like this for a quarter of an hour, he got back on track. Midala was to be deprived of clothing and bedding, since he thought that their purpose was for shitting and pissing into, and kept in solitary confinement in the cachot (dungeon) for fifteen days, hands and feet chained, with no more than bread and water, and with twenty-four hour surveillance outside his door.

'Should he attempt anything on your watch,' he warned the guards solemnly, 'I will peel the skin of your arse and stuff it into your useless mouth myself.' After a pause, whilst the guards were taking on board what he had just said, he screamed at the top of his voice, 'And don't anybody dare come to me and talk of insubordination!'

The guards seized Midala with singular viciousness, and were on the point of leaving, when the Colonel stopped Mequereau with his whip on his chest.

'And you, Mequereau, what kind of nose-picking, pig-dirty, shit-eating piece of vomit are you, allowing an unarmed black savage to disarm you? What happened to your balls?' He directed his whip to that area, poking it repeatedly. Mequereau was too shocked to react, and as he expected, this was followed by a cascade of blows on his face inflicted by the back of the Colonel's hands, and one final vicious kick in his backside just as the man thought that his ordeal was over.

The two men did not have to collude to come to the decision to make the slave's life hell. This was exactly the chink in their armour that Midala was praying for. The men, properly armed had twelve hour shifts, standing guard outside the cachot, and had no business going inside except to pass on to him his meagre rations twice a day. The stench alone, would have been a good enough reason for them not to venture inside, but they had a gnawing necessity which transcended all other considerations, to vent their hatred on the man who had been the cause of their humiliation, and to repay for their shame in the same currency. And what more satisfying form was there than sexual degradation! As a result, when they were bored witless, walking round and round the cachot, they thought a little fun would not come amiss. The first time, it was Goélard who set the benchmark. Having paced up and down for hours on his first shift, any idea entering his thick head quickly rushing out for fear of solitary confinement. He decided to go in and have a look for himself and indulge in a bout of taunting. Midala was a pitiful sight indeed. His body was covered in scabs, and unable open his bruised eyes he did not bat an eyelid at the guard's entry. Goélard pretended that he was going to faint and put a hand to cover his nose, decrying the filth of savages who knew nothing about cleanliness. He bent down, poked the the poor man's penis with his gun, and lifting it scornfully, he remarked on its extraordinarily small size. He expected a man like him to have an organ to match his pride, he cackled. If your mouth was not so dirty with its sores, I would make your dreams come true, Cacapou, and make you suck my dick. You would like that, wouldn't you, cock-sucking mother fucking blob of vomit? He kept swearing at the prostrate man, and spat a big gob of phlegm on his face before leaving. When he left, Midala smiled for the first time in a long time.

Goélard and Mequereau must have exchanged notes, for next day, the latter came in, and re-enacted the same little scene that his colleague had put on the day before, except that this time, when suggesting that Midala sucked his cock, he unbuttoned his trousers and displayed his erect organ. Yes, thought the humiliated man, I can hear the blacksmith forging my key.

The next day was a repetition of the previous day, but Goélard went one step further.

'You know, Cacapou, tell me what's to stop me dragging you out and shooting you like a tangue, and then tell the Surintendant that I had to shoot you for trying to escape? You heard what he said? Show initiative, man!' He did not know what to say, and kept his mouth shut. Whilst Mequereau had just cackled obscenely, Goélard kicked him a few times.

For three days, he did not have the strength to move. Although it was usually quite torrid inside the cell in the daytime, nights could sometimes be fresh enough for one to need a thin blanket, specially in view of his nakedness, and he was unable to get a good night's sleep. On the fourth day however, he was able to stand up and do some exercise, which consisted mainly of jumping up and down. That was quite a strenuous thing to do, in view of the heavy chains, but he wanted to stretch himself to his limit. His aim was to get enough strength to hoist himself up so he could reach the vent, and study the terrain. The insult and sexual innuendos became a daily routine, and so far neither had tried to translate their words into action, but to judge by the more and more obscene gestures the two depraved men were making, as well as their excited state, Midala feared the worse. He was quite apprehensive about that possibility, and did not know whether death might not be the best thing that could happen to him. He had no strength left. For the whole of the morning he was prey to this defeatist mood, but when he heard the guard outside approaching the door, he suddenly perked up. I am a fighter, he told himself, have always been, and the Great Spirit willing, I will never give up the good fight. He imagined that when the guard did decide to make good his threat, he would refuse and that his sexual frenzy might well make the man carry out his intention of shooting him. All this was out of his hands, he decided, so he was not going to worry about it.

The cell was quite high and the vent near the ceiling way beyond his reach. The wall made of stones cemented together, was fairly smooth, and did not provide any foothold. He had heard snoring and guessed that the guard normally had a nap on hot afternoons, in the shade of a bois noir tree, a little way outside the cell, so he planned to use his chains to make a cavity in the wall, below the vent. Having picked up the pattern of the waves, he found that short sharp strokes at the point where two stones were cemented together, coinciding with their crashing disguised the noise. He was pleased to find that the cement was easy to breach, and this provided the means of damaging the stone. By dint of constant tapping, the stone started frittering away and in one afternoon, he managed to make one hole big enough to accommodate a big toe. The next day, he made this bigger, and then started working on a second breach. Afterwards the operation became more arduous. He had to contend with the cumbersome chains as well as maintaining his balance on the precarious footholds that he had made. He must have slipped hundreds of times but he expected that. After one week, he ended up with four footholds and finally succeeded in hoisting himself up with his head reaching up to the level of the vent. He was filled with joy as he saw the sea, to which he had imparted almost human characteristics, since it was the only "one" who talked to him, in soft melodious whispers and had helped defeat the vigilance of the guard outside. In a week, he had forgotten the sea was so blue. He also acknowledged a debt to the filaos on the beach for providing an accompaniment to the music of the waves, as the wind blew through their needles. As a child he had wondered whether it was trees that made wind, or if it was the wind that made the leaves flutter. The position of the cell was such that the vent afforded him a limited view of the area leading from the bagne to town. He made a mental note of the breaches in the unfinished wall. A short distance away, just past the boundary of the bagne, on some as yet unused land, earmarked for a military hospital, he saw a strangler tree. At some distance he saw a few people going about their businesses, and guessed that with the activities of the ever busy harbour and the many small businesses associated with it, there would be many more around, and hoped that any escapee would inevitably meet people, some of them officials who would undoubtedly challenge him. But the difficulties were not insurmountable if he took into account all possible pitfalls. In any case there was always an element of risk, which he, as a soldier, knew he had to take.

He was not able to elaborate a complete plan, as he was not in command of all the elements involved, and accepted that he would have to trust the Great Spirit and improvise when the time came, as he knew it had to. He did not have to wait long. On the very next day, Mequereau came in, and although it was dark and cloudy, he could see the glistening face of the guard. The vent provided a little light, and he could see the man's erect cock protruding out of his trousers.

'Today's the day you have been waiting for, Cacapou,' he cackled wickedly, 'I am going to make your dreams come true, get on your knees.' Midala did as he was told, as he did not want to be beaten black and blue, having decided that he had to be physically whole and fit in order to do what he had in mind. He knelt down.

'Here, take it in your mouth, make me see paradise.' He thrust his organ forward with a quick movement of his pelvis, and Midala opened his mouth. The man gave a sigh of pleasure, but this immediately turned into a shriek of pain, as Midala suddenly bit on it with all is might. He had not expected the amount of blood which filled his mouth instantly. The man squealed like a pig, fumbled for his pistol, found it, let it slip through his trembling fingers, and the bagnard held on increasing the pressure of the bite. He was surprised to find that he had severed the cock, and spat it out with revulsion. The man, whimpering like a beaten dog, crashed on the floor trying to stem the flow of blood from where his manhood used to hang, almost lifeless, his body subject to spasmodic little jerks, like a dying chicken whose head has just been cut off. He was going to leave him like this, but knew that he would bleed to death, slowly and painfully. As a soldier he had often had to finish off an enemy out of pity, so he strangled him. It was war, and you had the right to kill your enemy on the battlefield, and if you could make it by inflicting minimal pain, it pleased the Great Spirit. He found all the keys he needed in the coat pocket of the dead guard and used them to free himself from the chains.

He then undressed the dead man, spat out the taste of blood, took his blood-soaked clothes under his arm and made a dash for the beach through a gap in the unfinished wall. He did not stop until he was out of the boundary of the bagne, at the level of the strangler fig tree that he had spotted earlier. Fortunately there was nobody around, and he was able to wash the blood off the clothes in the sea. He had already made up his mind that the strangler fig was going to be his gate to freedom. It was surprising how often that blessed tree had featured in his life. He was now certain that had he been allowed to carry out the operation to stop the attackers in Inhambane, the course of history would have been very different.

He imagined that when Goélard came to relieve his colleague, in less than an hour, he would raise the alarm and all hell would break loose. Grapouille, who prided himself on the fact that his bagne was escape-proof, was certainly going to erupt. Midala was going to hide up the tree, at a stone's throw from his office, wait for the dust to settle, and when it did, he would choose an appropriate moment to come down and make his way to Madame Agathe.

He grabbed a hanging root, coiled himself round it and hoisted himself up with an agility that surprised him. When he reached the top, he found a flat spot in the crook of a branch and sat there in comfort. It did not take an hour for the alarm to be raised, but safely ensconced among the thick foliage, he was able to watch, undetected, the clueless guards running aimlessly in all directions, often colliding with each other. At one point even Grapouille himself appeared, shouting hysterically, causing even more mayhem. When the washed clothes of Mequereau had dried, he put them on and waited for sunset. The crowd milling about in the area grew thinner at the approach of the dark, and he slid down. Since he had not seen any guards in the last hour or so he had assumed that they were looking elsewhere, and had a shock when no sooner had he come down than he came face to face with one. He was surprised at his quick-wittedness, but as he was wearing a uniform, he was well-equipped to play the part of a pursuant, and wordlessly pointed in the direction of the unfinished hospital.

'You go that way then,' said the guard pointing to the right, 'and I will go the other way, we'll nail the bastard yet.'

He ran towards the non-existent runaway, but the moment the guard was out of sight, he slowed down. He found that even if Mequereau's uniform was on the small side, people in town paid no attention to him, and he reached

Madame Agathe's house in Roche Bois without difficulty. Strangely, she had already heard of the to do at the bagne, and was surprised and delighted to see the legend who had become the first man to escape from it. She treated him to a feast, which was also attended by Azoline who had been picked up since last time, but had done yet another runner. History books would proudly recount later that in seven years, she escaped from her masters a total number of twenty four times.

'What are your plans now?' Madame Agathe asked him.

'Why, find Matamba, of course.'

Agathe shook her head sadly, and said that it was madness, for after what he had done to Mequereau, catching him would be a top priority, and once he was caught, there was only one possible outcome, and he knew what it was. He said nothing, but was deep in thought.

No, Midala would never contemplate running away. He had failed everybody so far, had not been able to defend his tribe against Ibn Qalb and Flyte-Camilton. He had done nothing for his fellow victims on the slave ship, except perhaps send some men to an early grave. There was a war between the plantation owners and his fellow victims, and he had to stay to fight. He had always known that in spite of her frivolous exterior, Agathe was a woman of wisdom and acute sensibilities, and was not surprised when she spoke.

'My friend, you are a soldier, yes?' He nodded sadly.

'What does a soldier do when he knows that the odds are stacked against him?'

'A soldier's duty is to die for the cause he has espoused.'

'Tell me one thing, how can your certain death help anybody?'

The military strategist said nothing for a while.

'What else can I do? I can't just abandon Matamba.'

'From what you've told me, Matamba is someone who is well able to look after herself... for all you know, she might be at peace now, and you would certainly expose her to danger, have you thought of that, warrior man?'

There are many things you can do, stupid man: you can go back home and see your children and their children, help protect them. And I'll tell you what your escape will do, added the formidable woman, it will bring some joy to those miserable slaves toiling from dawn to dusk with no hope of release...

you will become an icon, Midala. I will personally tell everybody about how you escaped, show them that the white man is not invincible. Agathe knew that she was on a winning streak, and as someone not averse to repeating herself, she went on for a bit.

'You may be a great warrior,' she said finally, 'but your strategy is limited to the battlefield, my friend. You forget that there are other arenas. Morale is very often more important to combatants than weapons, don't you agree?'

Midala was known for his determination, but in the end his benefactress managed to talk him out of his madness, as she called it.

'And you are in luck,' she told him, 'I am at the very moment able to organise a passage back to your part of the world, believe me, that's the only thing left for you to do.'

She warned the man that if he let that opportunity go, he might live to regret it, and strongly advised him not to let that chance slip away.

One of Agathe's lovers was Pillai, an Indian chef from Pondichéry on board the French warship *Le Quimper*. It seemed that even the King in Versailles had sampled his magic menus, and had dubbed him Pillai Roi du Pillau! Or so Pillai told everybody. He never failed to pay her a visit whenever he touched Port Louis, which was twice a year, and his ship had cast anchor in Port Louis harbour two days ago. Wasn't that fortuitous? Agathe asked the warrior, does that not mean the Spirits mean you to escape?

'Pillai is devoted to me.' she explained with pride, 'he will never refuse me anything.'

Next day, on cue, Pillai called.

'Just as we were going to bed,' she recounted to Midala later, unable to repress her triumphant laughter, 'I said, Pillai, wouldn't it be wonderful to smuggle a notorious repris de justice on one of the King's own warships? She explained to the fugitive how she had always loved to make people in authority look like fools.

'Pillai I want you to promise me one thing.'

The cook's reply was a standard one. 'My dearest woman, Pillai doesn't need to know what it is, it is accorded.'

'Are you sure you aren't going to change your mind?'

'I know I am going to regret this, but it's a promise, Pillai never changes his mind.'

'I want you to meet a friend of mine after you have taken me to paradise and back… like no one else can'.

She got Azoline to call Midala who was in another room to join them. She made the introductions, and gave him a detailed account of who he was. Pillai started to feel uneasy, but said nothing.

'I want you to take this man on board your ship and drop him near Inhambane,' she said in the most matter-of-fact manner, as if someone was asking his coachman to drop a parcel at a friend's house. The magician of the kitchen was shaken.

'Pemba,' he said, 'that's the nearest…' Then he stayed silent and pursed his lips thoughtfully, obviously troubled, and finally he shook his head wistfully.

'Do you realise what you are asking Pillai to do, ma chérie? Carry an outlaw who has killed one of his majesty's soldiers on a ship of the King of France.'

'Won't that be an absolute triumph?' asked Agathe, undaunted.

'A triumph as you say, yes, but Pillai will be risking his life, contemplating such folly.'

'So, Pillai, isn't prepared to risk his neck to please his Agathe?' The Chef demurred.

'If you can't do it, that's all right,' she said, 'I know someone else who would not hesitate.'

'Did anyone hear Pillai say that he was not going to do it?' He addressed an invisible audience dramatically, raising his hand up in the air. 'I just said that I am risking my neck, but for you, dearest, but that's a small price to pay.'

It was thus that Midala found himself on board *Le Quimper* smuggled with the provisions for the voyage.

Pillai explained to Midala that he would be safe in the store room, to which he was the only one who had access, as it was known as a prime target for larcenous and greedy seamen.

When the warship left the port, Midala was not sure if it was real, or if he had died and was on the way to meet the Great Spirit. Either way it was good, for if he had died, he would surely meet Rolena and his dead children, if they too had died. If they had not died, then the Great Spirit be blessed, for He was looking after them. If he had not in fact died, he was the luckiest man alive, as having survived incredible hardships, he was now going home to meet his beloved little ones again. He was afraid of nothing, not of the arduous trek overland to Inhambane, not of storms or disease, perhaps a few nightmares, they were inevitable even to the bravest soldier, but they were nothing compared to the living nightmares that he had endured.

CHAPTER 6

$\bullet \, \bullet \, \bullet$

Penang

Rob Rob was helpless. Godmother and Father had left him with no choice. If he knew how to make a living, he would have contemplated a break with the family, but Eton had not taught him that. Once he reached Liverpool and saw the majestic Heart of Oak, one of the earliest clippers built, a lot of the resentment arising from this enforced voyage was replaced by excitement which he could not keep the lid on. As someone who had dreamt of a career in the Royal Navy, he knew that the novelty of sailing in that magnificent ship would help assuage the pangs of separation from his beloved Highland lassie, although he saw this as akin to betrayal. Would a career in the navy make it impossible for him to marry Kitty? Yet he knew that Navy officers had wives, so presumably it was not a big problem. But he stopped himself *The trip hasn't yet started, I might become disenchanted with the sea after ten long weeks.*

Unsurprisingly he enjoyed every minute of the voyage, the simple routine, the rituals involved in the hoisting of the sails, the bells, the flying fish, the dolphins, specially as Captain Morrison had befriended him and invited him to have a go at the helm. He was immediately enamoured of the sound of waves lashing against the ship, sea water spraying his face as he leant against the railing, licking his lips to enjoy the taste of salt, and the pitch and toss of the valiant little ship. He did not suffer from sea-sickness and was very proud of himself, and found it funny when an officer said that at one time, the captain himself was not immune to this. He learnt everything he could about sailing, how to deal with gaff sail, staysail, square sail, how to rig sails, read the sextant, locate the position of the ship — everything one would expect a young man of his age to be interested in. By the time he arrived in Singapore, he felt quite certain that he would be able to take charge of clipper like this one.

It was a short journey by a launch manoeuvred by six hefty betel-spitting Cokhan oarsmen, from Singapore to Georgetown, and his father was delighted to see him. They had not seen each other for three years, the last time Sir Robert had returned to England. Rob Rob hardly remembered Penang, as he had left it at the age of three. He had no memory of his mother, although he sometimes thought he remembered a face hovering over his, an ayah, he was told, as she put him to bed. That woman was the nearest thing he had had to a mother, although he knew that she had died shortly after his birth. It was all very confusing.

The house was an extravagant wooden mansion standing on stone pillars, painted all white apart from the windows which were blue. There was a large open verandah which one got to by climbing Carrera marble steps. The large sitting room next to the verandah could easily accommodate sixty people, and he imagined that it was not uncommon for the British community to gather here for banquets and feasts. The furniture, the wall hangings, the paintings of dignitaries, vases and carpets were displayed with an ostentation which seemed to be aiming to match what he saw at Dunrobin's, but not quite succeeding. The cutlery, the china and table cloths were all monogrammed. He wondered whether Father knew all the servants, there were so many of them.

Sir Robert Helmsdale-Robertson had immediately set to work, embarking upon experiments, with his helpers, on some new seedlings from Kew which had arrived on the same ship as Rob Rob, in order to verify what earlier experiments had indicated: that there was every reason to believe that rubber would thrive here. The Industrial Revolution was predicted to change the face of industrial Britain and rubber was going to play an important part in this. The Company prided itself on being in the forefront of all modern ventures, with no new avenues left unexplored. It was the Company's policy to look at a large number of projects, carry out experiments and surveys on the most promising ones, and then invest whatever it took in those most likely to bear fruit. If ten ventures proved sterile, leaving the eleventh one viable, then it was considered a success, for the profits made when a single venture was successful were always mouth-watering. That, the leaders of the Company said, was what the British Empire was all about.

However, busy as he was, the old man still had time for his son. It was clear that his boy was very dear to him. He had been alarmed by what Bessie had written, but thought that she might have been over-protective of the boy whom he knew she thought of as almost son. He had also always suspected that she might have been more in love with him than he had dared imagine all those years ago. He told Rob Rob that he was not one who paid too much attention to the values prevalent in the Mother Country with all its snobbery and pomposity, and the boy was heartened to hear that, although the all too visible pomp and luxury around, belied this, he thought. He imagined that Father would not necessarily object to his romance and blurted it all out to him, about his great love for the crofter's daughter. The old man smiled at first, but after a moment his countenance changed. You are very young, Robert, and I have plans for you which do not include your getting married for another six to eight years. Rob Rob was stunned. He knew he wanted to be true to Kitty, but had not the faintest idea how to go about getting married. He was angry with his father, thought that he had wilfully misled him, emitting so-called liberal views in order to trick him into showing his hand, but the harsh reality was that he was wholly dependent on him.

It did not take long for Ah-Ling, one of the servants who had been beaming at him in the most friendly manner ever since he had arrived, to slowly creep upon him one afternoon, when he was sitting in the veranda, admiring the hibiscuses and jacarandas and engage him in conversation. As he had just written a letter to Kitty, he put it in a large envelope together with all the letters he had written to her which he had not yet posted, and entrusted them to the smiling man to post, telling him to say nothing about this to Helmsdale-Robertson. Later, Ah-Ling approached him again.

'The young tuan needs tea?' he asked gently. The boy shook his head without raising it.

'You must go meet your grandmother,' Ah-Ling whispered softly. Rob Rob looked at him vacantly, unsure as to whether he had heard right.

'Grandmother?' He had been told that there were no relatives from his mother's side. He had heard conflicting stories about his mother. She was the daughter of a Chinese dignitary or even minor royalty, but in either case, it had been emphasised to him that she had been an orphan. Apart from the enduring image of that woman leaning over him whom he had so long taken to be his mother, he had never given much thought to her. The story told to him, was that he had been in the care of an ayah, and then at the age of three was taken to Scotland to be raised by an aunt and his grandmother.

'Your grandmother, she live in Seberang Penai... Butterworth... across the straights... she want see young tuan.'

Rob Rob was still unable to grasp the importance of Ah-Ling's words.

'My nephew Pai will take you there... tomorrow... he come tonight... do not tell Sir Obert... Big Tuan.'

Finally the purport of Ah-Ling's words dawned upon him. He nodded absently, unsure if he should take advantage of what sounded more like an order than an offer. Why had they all lied to him?

He lay on his bed that night sweating, still unsure about what he was going to do, but deep down he knew that he had no choice. Nobody who has not known his mother would refuse to seize the chance of learning more about her. He slept badly, dreaming confused and repetitious dreams of that Oriental woman bending over him. He woke up early, got up and went outside to take advantage of the fleeting freshness of the morning, and to avoid meeting Sir Robert. He was in the massive garden and gave a sigh of relief when he saw him leave in his horse-drawn calèche. While he was eating a frugal breakfast, Ah-Ling came in smiling broadly.

'He here, tuan,' he whispered in a complicit manner, and a frail young man, hardly older than himself put in an appearance.

'Pai...' said Ah-Ling, 'he good boy, he take tuan Ob Ob Serebang Penai... Company launch... you write note for tuan Obertson, but no mention Ah-Ling.'

Rob Rob nodded, and he wrote a curt three-lined note explaining that he was taking the launch across the straits to spend a day or two at Butterworth which he had wanted to visit. He then left with Pai.

At the port, the young Penangite spoke to the boatman in Malay and they climbed aboard. It was quite hot and humid already, but Eton, with its daily cold showers, had taught him one thing: that he could put up with physical hardship. They crossed the straits, heading slightly north-east and landed at Serebang Penai in under an hour. A rickshaw took them to Butterworth where they stopped. Pai got him some Mamak roti and dal from a street vendor, which, to his surprise, he found quite appetising. A second man was hired, as the journey by rickshaw to Bukit Mertajam where the grandmother lived was too long for one man. Rob Rob shrugged. Obviously Father would not approve of his being away, but he was past caring. He had clearly lied to his son, betrayed him even, and so he owed him nothing.

The road out of Butterworth was uneven and rocky, and he could feel his bones rattle as he was regularly thrown up and down but soon they were riding across one of the most pleasant landscapes that Rob Rob had ever seen. It was as unlike the Highlands as it was possible to be but just as stunning. The lushness was of a darker green and there were trees and shrubs everywhere, flowers of all shapes, sizes and colours, and the combination of humidity and heat was both exhilarating and stifling. The hills of Mertajam loomed large, and unlike those in his native land, you hardly saw any rocky surfaces as it was all dense vegetation. He marvelled at the endurance of the rickshaw-men who took lengthy shifts pulling, and never complaining. Pai was happy to help, specially as the terrain was becoming steeper as they approached the hills. There were scattered little hamlets, and he watched small ragged Malay women tilling their vegetable patches. It was mid-afternoon when Pai smiled and explained that they were about to "leach Glandmother virage." They soon did, and he followed Pai into a little shack which reminded him of the one where Kitty lived, in Strathnaver. He shouted something in Malay and an old toothless woman appeared.

'Tuan glandmother...' Pai said happily. The old woman beamed at the boy and clearly expected him to fall into her arms or something, but Rob Rob looked at her stiffly.

'Ob Ob,' said Pai needlessly

'Dingbao,' she said almost inaudibly. Rob Rob was puzzled. 'Tuan Ob Ob,' she whispered nodding to herself, 'you big.' Rob Rob finally smiled and took a couple of steps in her direction. He first extended a hand, expecting her to shake it, but she took both his hands in hers, squeezing them fondly, and suddenly, to his alarm, began covering them with kisses. He was more puzzled than touched by this effusion. He was asked to sit down on a rickety stool, and the old lady stared at him smiling and nodding, muttering something in Malay under her breath. Then she said something to Pai and the young man went out, and came back followed shortly after by a younger frail and sad-looking woman who looked about fifty, but was in fact not yet forty. Rob Rob had the strange conviction that she was the ayah who had looked after him as a child? She stared at him, saying nothing, but he could see clearly that her eyes had welled up with as yet unshed tears. She stood there, like a statue, her hands slightly raised and her lips trembling. The young man could not take his eyes off her, and was likewise rendered motionless. Pai and the woman who was supposed to be his grandmother stared at each other, her mouth slightly open, in expectation of something monumental. The woman suddenly took one step in the direction of the visitor, and to his surprise, he did not back off this time, but did exactly the opposite, taking a step in her direction. She muttered some words which could have been in some sort of English, but Rob Rob could not make any sense of them. She raised her hands slightly to touch him, and he let her. It was when their hands touched that he knew for sure.

'Obert...' she whispered softly.

'Mother,' said Rob Rob equally softly. She drew him to her bosom and buried her head in his broad chest, stroking his hair gently. The old Grandmother spoke excitedly to Pai, and he ran out of the house.

'My son Obert,' the woman said, 'Praise God... I never think I see you in this life...'

'So you are alive,' said Rob Rob rather stupidly. She smiled, as she had obviously not understood.

'Mother, they told me you —' He stopped short, realising how cruel it would be to tell her the truth.

'Why you call me mother?' she asked suddenly.

Rob Rob looked at her questioningly, completely confused. He seemed to have gained a mother only to lose her immediately after.

'Call me Maa...' she said, managing to stop herself bursting into tears.

'Ma,' said the son, squeezing her more tightly. At this point the old grandmother took over, and made a non-stop speech in Malay which left the boy completely dumbfounded. It was clear that her mother's grasp of English, though not perfect would come in handy. She took over.

'Your grandma speak no English, just yes tuan, thank you memsahib...'

'And you?'

'I work as maid in English house... I learn... now I forget, but practise when I have opportunity, for when I meet son... you... for fifteen years, everyday I dream this, the day when I meet you.' She shook her head, not entirely believing that she was actually in the presence of her long lost son, muttering, 'Obert, Obert'

At this point Pai entered with kaya and tea on a plate, and served the visitor. When Maa was unable to explain what she meant, Pai translated.

When Helmsdale-Robertson took over the Company, Moy-Lin had just arrived in Georgetown looking for work, as her father had died suddenly leaving the family destitute. She was young when Robert saw her. She asked him for a job, saying that she could cook, clean, iron, sew, whatever was needed, and he immediately called the Steward and told him to give her a job.

She was happy in the job, she had never been afraid of hard work. She was surprised at how quickly she picked up English. The master loved to talk to her, she made him laugh by the way she spoke, not in a bad way. Then, blushing and turning her face away, she related how suddenly one day he invited her to his bed. Rob Rob felt his anger towards his father rising. Tell Obert it pains me to speak to my son about such a delicate matter, but he is an intelligent boy and should know the truth, she urged Pai. Tell him I no want lose my job, that whole family depend on me. So I agree. Besides, she explained with a coy smile, she had been smitten by this tall handsome man. Fact is, even after all the things that he had done to her, she still... loved him. Not that any man would look twice at her now.

The master was very tender to her at first, saying how he would have married her if it was at all possible, but he did not want to lose a job he liked doing, and was therefore not prepared to take risks. When she found out that she was pregnant, the master arranged for her to go Bagan Ayer Itam, where his friend the English Resident, Mr Morejohn-Quimple would arrange for her to be taken to an old Chinese abortionist, but she would not hear of it, and talked Ah-Ling, who was taking her across west into helping her. With the help of some strangers, she ended up back home in Bukit Mertajam. She did not know what she was doing, all she knew was that she would not allow anybody to kill her baby. If life became impossible, she would go deep into the forest there, climb the hill and when she reached lake Mengkuang, she would throw herself in it and drown with her baby inside her. Fortunately for her, the villagers looked after her. Grandmother sold the few possessions she had, begged and borrowed and Rob Rob was born. They called him Dingbao, which meant the one who escaped death in the local dialect.

At first Mr Robertson did not react, but when the boy was six weeks old, he arrived in the village one day. He had seemed very touched to hold his son in his arms, and readily forgave Ah-Ling for having been instrumental in saving the boy's life. He said that he wanted to take his son back with him to Georgetown, but Grandmother said that was out of question. He had wanted the boy dead, she challenged. She would look after her grandson herself. He left after giving them a rather large sum of money. He sent Ah-Ling from Georgetown regularly, with money and things for the baby but he never came to see him. They thought that was the end of the story, and were reconciled to this, thinking that the Englishman was being very fair and had accepted his responsibility.

Two years later, however, out of the blue some soldiers arrived, accompanied by Ah-Ling and an English nurse, and explained that they had come to take Dingbao with them to Georgetown. Grandmother ordered him out of her house, but a soldier produced a letter which no one in the village could read, saying that it was signed by the Governor. Ah-Ling explained that the white man had too much power and that it was useless to resist. If the villagers caused any trouble, they would all pay for it. Besides, Mr Robertson had decided that he would pay a handsome pension to Moy-Lin.

She had thought that giving her money was an insult, but it was Grandmother who pointed out that the money would come in handy, as Moy-Lin's irresponsible behaviour in the city had brought all this calamity upon them. They were warned against coming to Georgetown to see the boy.

They learnt later that Dingbao had left for England, and thought that none of them would see him again in this life. But here he was, large as life, sitting in their modest house. Rob Rob had to make great efforts during the narration of his childhood history to keep his eyes dry. Had Father really wanted him killed at birth? Was he a heartless brute, a failed murderer? How shabbily he had treated his mother. He now gave free vent to his pent up emotions, and hugging his mother, he said, rather incoherently, 'I am so sorry, Maa, I am so sorry, will you ever forgive me?' Pai had to translate, whereupon Moy-Lin cackled merrily.

'Me, no forgive you? No have to, I wrong you, you no wrong me...' she said.

Rob Rob stayed in Bukit Mertajam for a whole week, not wishing to confront his father over his cowardly betrayal of his mother. He was surprised by how relaxed and serene he was in these strange surroundings. Blood must be thicker than water.

When he reached the paternal home, his father was livid with rage, but the moment he saw the ravaged face of his son, his anger immediately metamorphosed into concern. He showed great sympathy for his boy, but the latter would have none of it. He was not used to shouting at the older generation, and thus resisted his urge to fling his contempt for what he had done, in his father's face, but it was clear to Sir Robert that his son was now privy to his guilty secret. He had hoped that, the money he scrupulously sent to Bukit Mertajam regularly, would have ensure that the shabby way he knew he had treated the mother of his boy would stay a secret. As for the servants and employees of the Company who would doubtless have shared gossip with each other, he had the certainty that they were loyal to him to a man, as their livelihood depended on his goodwill. He was surprised that they had talked. Still he would have a quiet word with Ah-Ling who had more than once proved his complete loyalty to him after the original betrayal. But who had arranged for the boy to visit his mother? But come to think about it, it was not a bad thing for the boy to have found out the truth. He could only hope that he would not hold it against him for planning to get rid of him before he was born. He had always felt guilty about depriving the boy of his mother's love. He had often laid on his bed, sweltering in the humid months, unable to find sleep wracked by guilt. First he had not had the guts to marry the woman he had indeed always loved, and then when he had been given a second chance of finding love, at the birth of his son, he had again allowed ambition and with prejudice to turn the happiness that might have been his into an Indian rope trick which he had witnessed in Bombay once, allowing it to disappear into thin air. In what way was all this wealth he was accumulating almost by the hour, the ostentation he surrounded himself with, contributing to his happiness? Bessie's crofters surely led a more meaningful existence.

When the boy had calmed down, he would have a heart to heart talk with him, and he felt sure that he would talk him into letting bygones be bygones. Now, he had an Eton education, he had grown up among distinguished people and he had a bright future waiting. He would make sure his mother would be able to live comfortably for the rest of her life. What would have become of the lad if he had grown up in this godforsaken place surrounded by, if not quite savages, but people who to all intents and purposes, behaved like children, had no sense of responsibility or punctuality, who always smiled and agreed with everything you said and then failed to deliver the goods? No, it would be impolitic to tell him that at this stage.

CHAPTER 7

❖❖❖

Mont Calme

MONT CALME WAS where de Fleury had built his extravagant home. A massive wooden edifice, big enough to house an army barracks, painted shiny white, with windows and green blinds which he thought blended beautifully with the luxuriant green vegetation surrounding it. Granite steps, polished like they were semi-precious stones, leading to an open veranda resting on stone pillars, where he loved to receive his guests, had cost him a fortune, but Victor de Fleury was a man who did not let financial considerations limit the excesses of his dubious good taste. On the grounds were gardens of flowers and shrubs, and fountains and ponds where submerged rainbows could be seen swimming lazily. His pride and joy was the maze made entirely of bougainvilleas of all colours. A man of strong dislikes, he enjoyed leading guests who he deemed to have offended him there, and allow them to get lost for a whole afternoon. His ambition was to have marble statues of Greek goddesses placed randomly among the shrubs, and planned a voyage to his homeland as soon as he could find the time in order to commission them. But who to rely on in this godforsaken place? Where to find someone he could trust to run his many concerns with something which even remotely resembled common sense?

Victor de Fleury had been an ordinary matelot from Lorient, a ship's carpenter, on the pride of the Royal French Navy, the Jean-Baptiste Colbert. When the ship cast anchor in Mahébourg Harbour, he had liked what he saw and on an impulse decided to jump ship. He changed his name to de Fleury, reinvented his past as nobility and promised himself that he would make his fortune on this island, after which he would return to France and live like a prince on the Brittany Coast.

In no time at all everybody was talking about the man of mystery. The governor who had received confidential intelligence about the man and had heard of his flair for business, invited him to a gala reception at Villebagues, and looking for the opportunity, had managed to draw him to a corner of his grand salon.

'De Fleury,' he said to him point blank, 'you are a prime rascal, and we know that your name is Férailler. You are just a vulgar little matelot, but we can help each other.'

'Causes toujours, excellence, causes toujours,' said the man from Lorient. Keep talking.

'I don't believe in taking four different routes to get to my destination… it's clear that you and I we warm ourselves from the same wood, so why don't we join forces?'

'Causes toujours, tu m'intéresses.'

'Fifty percent,' his excellency said blandly.

'I am not greedy,' lied Victor. It was not that he was not greedy, but he understood that if he had the governor as an ally, the sky was the limit.

It was thus that the most profitable — if also the most disreputable — partnership in the history of the island was born. The governor granted to the man from Lorient land rights which he then sold at excessive profit, sharing the spoils with his accomplice, then got given more land, did the same, until the pair of scoundrels had more money than they knew what to do with even after the edification of his opulent mansion. When Son Excellence left to become governor of Martinique, after two years, they were the two richest men on the island. Feelers put out to the replacement, Rémy de la Taye, showed that this one had his own agenda, and it did not include the ex-matelot. But the fully-fledged de Fleury could easily manage without patronage now.

He worked hard and played hard, he hardly slept — he did not need to. He gambled heavily; if he lost a fortune one night, he would win it back the next day. A strong ruthless man, he punched a maroon slave who had sneaked in his house looking for food one night, and killed him outright, thus consolidating his already well-defined legendary status. All this helped create for him the reputation of a man one trifled with at one's peril.

Now de Fleury had among the most profitable businesses on the island, with fingers in many pies. Sugar cane was the main one, but other interests included tobacco, tea, cattle and vegetables and fruits. The man owned more land than he knew what to do with, and had the largest number of slaves, from Mozambique and Madagascar.

Obviously there were no other houses in sight anywhere around Mont Calme, as the area, like most of the rest of the island, had been virgin territory when he acquired it. The house was surrounded by hundreds of acres of bush, some of which had been cleared to make way for small housing units for the workforce, which he had taken great care to have hidden from view, as to him, they were necessary evils. These were simply built structures, with a wooden skeleton, corrugated iron walls and roofs. The floors were earthen and plastered with cow dung. Shanti was attributed one of these.

She had grown up in her father's mansion in Roshankhali, but had moved to less salubrious conditions when she married Raju, and had not minded this simple unattractive cage. She told herself that living in the most beautiful house is like a bird in a gilt cage if there was no love in it. The day her Raju will be sent back to her, this would be transformed into their castle, and until then she would put up with it. There was a small open veranda, and it gave good shelter from rain, so Jayant was quite happy sleeping there.

Jayant, who often spent hours tossing on his mat in the night, lusting after his dead friend's widow, had to walk an hour every morning to go work on the plantations in Sept Cascades, whilst Shanti was given work in Mont Calme itself, where the astute entrepreneur had created massive vegetable patches. This suited the woman very well, as it gave her the possibility of looking after the young Pradeep at the same time. Not that it was a soft option, for the white man planned to maximise his profits, which meant that his employees were expected to deliver or else…

Although the British who had now displaced the French and seized the reins of power did not officially allow immigration from the former colonial power, many French settlers arrived, as they had cousins and uncles who had arrived over fifty years ago, and the latter claimed that the services of the new influx were essential for progress. The British, for their part, sent a large number of officials, clerks, officers of the law, and these people had to be fed. De Fleury thought that twenty tons of potatoes a year could easily be obtained with minimal work, and quickly set out to achieve this goal in Mont Calme itself. At the same time, he grew beans, cabbage, tomatoes, lettuce, groundnuts, and soon half of Mont Calme was under profitable cultivation.

Shanti, with Pradeep fastened to her back by her shawl, or sometimes tied to a tree, like a large number of women in similar situation, would dig and weed all day long, and she did not mind. She loved growing all vegetables, but tomatoes had a special appeal to her. She enjoyed plucking the "chorr," or "thieves" the little green tendrils growing at the junction between the main stem and the branches of tomato, which debilitate the plant, making it produce inferior product. She relieved her pent-up anger at her situation by crushing snails and slugs. Every stage of the development of her plants had its special attraction for her. When the seeds have been put into the earth, she longed to see them push the earth above and sprout. They reminded her of her newborn babies. Every day she would watch a plant and note by how much it had grown, and almost give a shriek of delight when two small green leaves suddenly became four. Then she would wait anxiously for the appearance of the first yellow flower, revel in this like she did when the babies took their first step, and then watch it develop and turn into a small green ball, at first no bigger than a pea but it would then grow bigger by the day, like her belly when she was pregnant, and then slowly begin to turn pink. At home in Roshankhali she never ceased to marvel at the fact that the plants that had caught her attention and which she spent most time looking at, caressing or speaking to, produced the best fruits. It was the same with all the other vegetables. It soon became apparent that the patches she had the responsibility for were spectacularly more prolific than the others. Everybody said she had green fingers.

Around each hut, there was some space which the boss had said the workers could cultivate on their own account. This was what Monsieur Hugon, the Protector of Immigrants had decreed, but his real reason for following the directive was quite selfish, for he had surmised that if they grew their own, then they would control their natural propensity for thieving. But to Victor de Fleury, indentured labour was just a new word for an old respectable practice to him. It was a law of nature that some men were born to rule and others to serve them, be their slaves — call them by whatever name, Malbars or Lascars. This had existed from time immemorial, and no one respected traditions more than he did. Never would he give up his right to give a good flogging to reprobates, law or no law. La loi, c'est moi! He used to proclaim.

He loved to repeat his rule: Anyone caught picking a single weed, or giving their plants no more than one drop of water when they were supposed to be working on my field, I will personally come and uproot all their plants and burn them, and deprive them of their privilege, because that's all it is. Hugon can shit on his own head! You people get a roof over your head, cooking oil, dal, rice and flour, free lengths of cotton sheeting, and in your country, most people would kill to change place with you... What else do you need? Silk blouses, razor blades? Oranges?

Even after a back-breaking day on the white man's fields, Shanti was never too tired to spend time with her vegetables. No wonder her tomatoes were the reddest and plumpest.

Antoine, who, after his emancipation was given a small hut (with extra facilities) in Mont Calme by de Fleury, was very impressed by Shanti's capacity for work. Daily he would drag his crippled frame towards her patch and admire the progress. At first Shanti was afraid of this black man who spoke to her in a funny language she only half understood, but it took her very little time to discover that the black man was not only harmless, but gentleness personified. It was the former slave who taught her the words in kreol for the things she was growing, enjoying a new-found vocation as a language teacher.

When Shanti began harvesting her prize tomatoes and beans, she soon had more than she needed for her own use, and very happily gave some to people like Antoine. At first the beneficiaries of her largesse repaid her with little odds and ends, and that was that. It was Antoine who suggested to her that there was more land that she could use if she wanted to. She said the bourgeois might object to that, and he said that he would ask him, suggesting that he could join forces with her. The former slave knew that Missié Victor usually said yes to whatever he asked, and he never ceased to marvel at this.

'And why does this woman want to grow more vegetables?' he asked.

'I think that she does it more for me, than for herself, bourgeois, I would not know how to start a little farm myself, and I know she is a kind soul, she will help me… it's something to do, the day is long for people like me who have nothing to do.'

'Don't feel bad about it, you have worked hard all your life, why don't you just take it easy? Or better still, why don't you read the good book… you still have the copy I gave you?' Years ago, the other black men could hardly believe it when one day, Antoine told them that Missié de Fleury had offered to teach him to read. The poor man had found it difficult, but had still managed to read after a fashion, although he often got some letters mixed up. He called them dead black ants.

Antoine explained that with his failing eyesight, reading had become laborious, and de Fleury nodded, and that was settled.

The truth was that Antoine was frail and slow, and Shanti did all the work, but she did not mind. She never tired when working on what she thought of as her own patch. And soon, the crops were so plentiful that Antoine had an idea.

'Murtaza Pirbox,' he said suddenly to Shanti one afternoon, and explained that Pirbox was one of the few Indians who had come to the island as a free man, to trade with the indentured workers. He had an oxcart in which he went from place to place, selling produce to the rich ladies of the area.

'But Missié de Fleury? He won't like it, will he?' said Shanti

'I'll ask,' he volunteered. And when he did, de Fleury flared up.

'What sort of businessman would I be, Antoine, if I was afraid of competition? Competition is the lifeblood of commerce. Only cowards want to be cocooned in monopolies.' Antoine did not have the faintest idea of what he was talking about.

'Does the bourgeois mean it's all right?'

'Are you stupid or what, man? Of course you can go ahead.' It was not that he hated monopolies, but Shanti's output was but a drop in the ocean compared to his. And he could never say no to Antoine.

Early on the next day, Antoine decided to walk to Souillac where Pirbox lived. With his bad leg, it would take him four hours or more, he explained to Shanti, and as he would need to rest, he would ask Murtaza to let him sleep in the cowshed and return on the next day. Shanti was very touched, gave him enough food for the journey and promised him some a curry and rice when he came back — he simply loved her cooking. Murtaza Pirbox had known Antoine for a long time, and he readily agreed to come have a look at those prodigious vegetables that his visitor spoke about. Yes, he said, if they are anything as good as you say, I will easily find clients for them, I will come to Mont Calme soon.

Two weeks after this conversation, a letter arrived for Shanti Varma. Antoine brought it himself, and said that it was from the Immigration Office. Shanti asked him to read it for her, he demurred but tried all the same, and gave up saying that with his failing eyesight, it looked like the dead ants were becoming alive again, and were running all over the page. Shanti knew that it was about her Raju. Had he been located? Was he on the way to join her here? She could think of nothing else, and had to make an effort not to blame poor Antoine, having to tell herself all the time that if the man's eyesight was poor, it was not his fault.

Although back home, they lived in relative harmony with the Muslims nearby, there was never any great warmth between them. You did whatever you had to do, exchanged pleasantries, but stopped short of developing friendships across the religious barrier. Even Raju who liked everybody, and defended Muslims when his friends blamed them for floods and epidemics, stopped short of having a Muslim friend apart from the hakeem, who was a sort of adopted uncle. She had been wondering who to ask to read the letter when Murtaza arrived. She was immediately struck by how handsome the man was. He was probably over forty, and had a grey stubble which contrasted advantageously with his shiny dark skin and jet black hair. He was not tall, even rather stocky, but his dress sense was faultless. He smelled of attar and had a small ivory stud tying the top of his shirt, like Pitaji. That was not the only thing about him that reminded her the latter. Poor Pitaji who lost everything and had to go back to Gaya! She was a bit wary of the Musselman at first, but if he proved to be a good outlet for their produce, she saw no reason why they could not establish a good business rapport. She had shown him round her patch, with the proud Antoine in tow, and he expressed admiration for the quality of her produce, for which, he said, he would easily find clients. They went back to her hut, and she gave him her only chair to sit on, whilst Antoine happily sat on the steps in the veranda, and she went to make tea for them. When she appeared with the refreshment, Pirbox was writing something in a notebook, and she seized the opportunity.

'Bhai, I wonder if you can do me a favour, I received a letter this morning and...'

'I can read,' said Antoine defensively, 'but my eyesight is failing more and more...'

'Ben, of course I'll read the letter for you.'

'It's from the Immigration Office,' he said when Shanti handed it over to him, and after perusing it, added, 'it's not from Missié Hugon himself, I can't see his signature... it says... signed by the Chief Clerk in absence of the Protector of Immigrants.'

'Yes, yes, but what does it say, Bhai?' asked Shanti. Pirbox had to work hard, but finally he explained that The Immigration Authorities had written to their counterpart in Calcutta, asking them to find out the whereabouts of Rajendra Kumar Varma, who had been due to leave Calcutta on the Startled Fawn on the 14th of January... and will let you know as soon as they get an answer.' She had to try very hard to stop her tears gushing out.

A bond soon developed between the two, and she knew instinctively that when she was in any trouble, the Musselman would willingly help. It was the beginning of a fruitful collaboration. Shanti found that Pirbox was very fair, and gave her a good price, and found herself confiding more and more in him about her life and her Raju.

Out of the blue one day Pirbox said to her that he knew a young Hindu man whose parents had all died on the ship and was all alone, and he had thought that he would make a good match for her.

'Murtaza Bhai, what are you saying? I have a husband already,' she said laughing nervously to hide her alarm. 'What do you mean saying things like that to me? Didn't the government say they were doing everything to find my Raju?'

'I am a foolish man,' he said, 'my wife always says that I meddle too much in other people's affairs.' And they left it at that. But the vegetable merchant had only put the matter in abeyance, waiting for a more propitious occasion.

He knew that there were a large number of possible scenarios for Raju's disappearance, and that none of them pointed to a happy reunion of the spouses.

That December, a cyclone of surprising virulence hit the island, and half the sugar cane plantations were destroyed. Shanti lost most of her produce as well, but nobody starved. To her amazement, however, whatever was salvaged, fetched two or three times the usual price, and in the end, she made almost the same as if no damage had been done to her crops. She discovered a law of business which was to serve her later: when there is a shortage of anything, the price rises inversely, so that the seller is never the one to lose.

Jayant had been working very hard too. He would leave before dawn everyday, and get back after dark and never complained. In that respect he was so much like Raju. He loved playing with Pradeep whenever he had the time, and the boy liked him very much. One Divali, when the boss allowed them a free day, Shanti, who was never in a festive mood, but thinking of her son, had prepared mithais and pakoras, and the two males had had a good time. An exhausted Pradeep had been taken to bed early, and for once, Jayant found an opportunity to have Shanti all to himself. They were both sitting on the steps of the veranda, watching the full moon, when Jayant spoke.

'Bhabi, how can I say this to you? I want to get married.' She was taken aback, praying that he was not going to declare his ill-concealed love for her.

'So, you want me to look for a bride for you?'

Jayant said nothing for a while. No, he did not want her to look for a bride for him, he wanted her to be his bride. But how was he going to tell her?

'I mean, you know, Raju Bhai and I... were like brothers...'

He is going to say something he will regret, she thought.

'Yes,' she snapped quick as a flash, 'which makes us brother and sister.'

Jayant did very well to hide his disappointment. He knew that Raju was gone for good. He also knew that no one could take his place in her heart, but he felt sure that no one else could be more devoted to her than him. When Raju had not turned up at the Harbour Office on that fateful day, his friend's fate had filled his heart with a hope which was as guilty as it was brutal. He loved Raju, he mourned for him, but he lusted after his wife too. He had always been in love with her. When Raju told him, oh, so many years ago now, that he was going to marry Shanti, his first reaction was jealousy, because he thought that once married, Raju would neglect him. Then the moment he saw her in her bridal outfit, the jealousy made an about-turn. For years he had shouldered this unwelcome burden in silence, sometimes happy when Raju told him one or two secrets of their married life, as if he wanted to share this happiness with him, although when they parted, and he was on his way home on his own, he would be invaded by sinful thoughts. Wracked by guilt, he had cried all night once when he had wished that Raju would drown in a cyclone so he could then marry her, and he had beaten his chest, slapped himself hard, asking for Bhagwan's forgiveness. He did not welcome the sinful dreams he had been having recently, but he could not control them. Ever since they reached this new country, he was tormented by his friend's absence, wishing he could trade off his life for his friend's, so he could come back and make Shanti happy, but at the same time, how much he prayed that she would of her own free will come to him, when their common love for Raju would be like a shrine in his memory, and together they would pray there. Every time he would accomplish his husbandly duty, he would close his eyes and try to pretend that he was Raju. He would never make love to her in his own name, he had no right. He did not fail to notice that she treated him with coldness, but understood that she was warning him off, because she could not have failed to read his feelings for her.

'So,' said Jayant, in an about turn which surprised himself, 'hasn't a sister got a duty to find a wife for her brother?' They said nothing for a while, then he added, 'That's all I meant to say, as Bhagwan is my witness,' but Shanti read him like an open book.

In all those months they had been in this new country, this was the first time he had seen her smile, but it was a smile of relief because he had not overstepped the boundary she had intended.

'I will do my duty,' she promised.

As Jayant lay on his gunny sacks of a bed watching the full moon disappear behind some clouds, he felt his throat ache with longing for the forbidden woman, and was happy that no one saw some tear drops trickle down his cheeks.

On her bed, Shanti for the first time began to imagine what it would be like, married to Jayant. He was not a bad looking boy — arrey he was a whole year older than her, why call her a boy? He was kind and hard-working, and if she did marry again… No, she was married to Raju and that was that. But often she felt like she wanted to be in a man's arms. Sadness and grief had not tempered her passionate nature. That night she dreamt of being in bed with Murtaza, and to her horror, she remembered that she had already had this dream and had forgotten it. But sinful dreams were like thieves who find the door of a house has been broken. They did not wait for an invitation to rush in.

She blushed next time Murtaza came, but accepted that he was not responsible for her dreams, and they carried on doing their business together. But might he be having similar dreams about her too? She wondered.

She waited everyday for a letter from the Immigration Office, and none came. A year later, she asked Murtaza if he could write to them and ask, and he said that he had a poor handwriting, but would ask one of his clients to do it. A week later, when he came, he said that the letter had been written and that he had posted it himself. No answer ever came.

One night, Antoine approached Shanti's hut, limping very badly. Shanti received him under the veranda, and seeing the state he was in, rushed to get him her one chair, which the lame man declined.

'Madame Shanti, I am not used to sitting on chairs, I much prefer the steps.'

'I will make you some tea, I have got plenty of milk today.'

'Can I just have some milk? Please.'

Shanti went in, poured him a lota of milk which the ex-slave drank greedily.

'I hope you do not mind my coming to visit you like this, but although you are from a different country, I have always thought of you as my daughter. You have always been so kind to me. I want to ask you to do me a favour… you see I am ill, and do not have long to live. I want you to do me a favour.'

'Antoine what are you saying? Missié de Fleury will take you to the hospital himself, don't talk like this.'

'Yes,' said Antoine, 'he will, tomorrow. He has always been kind to me… I never understood why.' He paused for a while and started laughing mirthlessly.

'It's funny, when I arrived, he saved my life, but has always treated me as if it was I who had saved his… he is so harsh to everybody, but so kind to me…'

'Yes, I have noticed… he respects you…'

'Many people hate him, but he… eh… has many admirable qualities.' Shanti looked at the old man dubiously.

'No, I mean, do you know, he is nearly one hundred —'

'No, really?'

'That's what he tells me … but that man can stay on his feet in the sun for a whole day —'

'Shouting at people and hitting them with his whip. I've seen him!' No, Shanti wasn't going to listen to praise being heaped on man she had detested with all her heart from the beginning. 'What is it you said you wanted me to do?' Realising that she sounded harsh, she immediately added, 'But whatever you're going to ask, it's granted in advance.'

'Thank you, Madame Shanti… I want you to do me a favour, here take this…' And he handed over to Shanti, a bundle wrapped in some dirty cloth. She was perplexed, but took it from him.

'Keep it for me, as I shall be out of the house tomorrow… I will pick it up when I come back from hospital, can you do that?'

'Why of course.' She guessed that it was his savings.

'I will smoke my pipe now,' he said. Shanti got him a flint and lock. While puffing thoughtfully, he told her how he had been captured in a war by another tribe to be their slave, and how he had eventually ended up over here. He had been separated from his wife and children. He had a woman here once, but she died many years ago, and he had not wanted to find himself another woman. He told her about the friends he had made, about Anatole who could sing like a bird, about Midala, a proud and courageous man who had risked death in order to live free.

'They say he managed to smuggle himself on board a French warship and went back to Africa,' he said laughing merrily.

Shanti hanged on to every word, and was sad when the old man decided to go. Painfully he rose, and putting a hand on his haunch, he dragged his weary frame away down the steps. As he got on the level ground, he turned round.

'And Oh, Madame Shanti, if anything should happen to me, this bundle is for you. You are my only true remaining friend.' Shanti protested, but the moment the visitor had gone, she could not resist the temptation to look inside the bundle, and marvelled at the sum she saw on there.

Antoine never made it to hospital, for he passed away in the night. Shanti found it easy to weep for him, for when one has one's own sorrows, tears for other people flow seamlessly behind. She took the decision not to mention the windfall to anybody, for that might surely have urged some people to remember that they too had been friends with the ex-slave, and cause disputes. Carefully she committed the legacy to a box where she kept her own hard-earned savings, and already in her head were the germs of untold schemes.

With her punishing schedule, she had never found the time to look into the matter of a bride for Jayant. So, when Jayant told her one evening that a friend had mentioned Jyoti, the daughter of another worker, as a possible bride for him, she claimed that she was delighted, but was also disappointed that he had not waited for her to initiate the union. She admitted to herself that she had not entirely dismissed the idea that she might have accepted him for herself one day. Shortly afterwards, everything was arranged, and Jayant and Jyoti were married. De Fleury grudgingly gave the newly-weds one of the new huts he had been building, and Jayant moved out.

The years went by and no more than a handful of people who had arrived on the Startled Fawn, having finished their indenture returned to Calcutta, but most signed an extension with de Fleury. Murtaza had never stopped suggesting that he found a new husband for her, and to his surprise, shortly before the end of her indenture, she broached the subject herself. He had just paid her a tidy sum in respect of produce bought, and they were sitting opposite each other under the veranda — she had two chairs now, and a table.

'Bhai Murtaza, you are always telling me to accept reality, that my Raju is lost to me forever. I think I have come to accept this now.'

'My Allah and your Bhagwan... the same being if you ask me... knows what he does, and has a reason for everything.'

'Yes, we have to accept his will.' Suddenly Pirbox's face lit up, as he understood what Shanti was expecting him to say.

'Ben,' he said, 'then you must take my fatherly advice… you are like my own sister… even a daughter to me… as you know…' He was hardly five years older than her.

'No,' said Shanti, blushing, 'you are not going to start again with this business of…' she could not make herself say the words.

'But a woman cannot live alone all her life, you need a good man by your side.'

Yes, Shanti was thinking, with the plans I have made, I need the help of a good man. She said nothing.

'I know a very eligible young man… he is called Kishore Brizmohan… he is so gentle, so respectful… I am sure you will like him.'

'Kishore Brizmohan?' she repeated mechanically.

CHAPTER 8

— ◆ ◆ ◆ —

Transportation

A SMALL SQUARE berth, just enough for a small man to squat was all the space each man had to himself, and they were confined there except for short periods on deck every other day. After a seemingly endless ordeal, when the Metcalfe reached Hobart, a skeletal George Loveless, battered and bruised, in a state of shock, with scabs and sores all over was taken about thirty miles up the Derwent River and arrived at the government domain farm, where he had been placed. He was to spend a long time there, under atrocious conditions, and he had little hope of ever seeing his wife and family again. He missed them terribly, and often wondered if those powerful people back home had heard of the injunction that "They who God has united in holy matrimony, none must split asunder!"

The five others, including the three Jameses had a similar fate, except that they found themselves on the brig Surrey going to Botany Bay. Their journey was no less gruelling than that of Loveless. There they were placed in various places, to serve their term. Young James Hammett was sent to Hunter's Hill, where he met his new master, Mr George Coldwell. The latter had spent some years with the East India Company in Calcutta, and was allowed to buy at preferential rate, the very big property here for which he had ambitious plans.

Whilst being taken to his new abode, James was greatly impressed by the landscape. Hunter's Hill is the peninsula between rivers Lane Cove and Parramatta, which the Aborigines call it Mooroocooboola, which means the meeting of the waters. It is lush fertile territory, able to support crops of all sorts. The mangroves extended over large stretches of the shores of the rivers, and are homes to a variety of flora and fauna. James saw wallabies and spoonbills for the first time.

363

When the party of six convicts arrived in Taj Mahal in Hunter's Hill and the constables were beginning to unshackle them, Mr Coldwell came out of the unfinished wooden mansion to greet them. He conversed with the constables and directly made for James, who very courteously bowed to him, smiling pleasantly and giving him every indication that he was going to do what was expected of him, and that the last thing he wanted was to rock the boat. He was not afraid of hard work, he would serve his sentence and the Good Lord would see to it that one day he be returned to his friends and family in Dorset.

'So you are a troublemaker, I hear,' Coldwell bawled out, 'an arsonist who burn wheat fields, a wrecker of threshing machines, a swearer of secret oaths… I have read your papers, and I want you to know that I have little time for miscreants like you who aim to destroy the established order and who do not know their place. I am a fair man but I cannot abide indiscipline. I shall be keeping a close eye on villains like you.' James was stunned. He wanted to protest that he was nothing of the sort, but the master was in no mood to listen.

'In all fairness I must warn you, the slightest trouble from you, and you will be whipped to within an inch…' James who had kept his head down all the time, nodded meekly, whereupon Coldwell put his whip under his chin and unceremoniously pushed it up in order to raise his head, so he could look at him face to face.

'And answer me when I ask a question!' he screamed, making the other convicts jump by the force of his delivery. James was not quite sure whether there was a question, so he said, 'Yes sir.'

He met his fellow workers, all transportees, all swearing their innocence, but all said good things about the master.

'Fair to middling' said toothless Bob nodding gravely, James did not understand.

'The conditions of work 'ere… fair to middling.'

Coldwell had a lovely wife, Amelia with whom, he was obviously very much in love. She was much younger than him, and they were childless. Amelia struck James as being a nice woman and noticed that she had a young convict woman, Annie Browne who was from the West Country as her maid. When called a Gyppo, she spat on the ground and said that yes, she was a Romany, but she was the granddaughter of the king of Gypsies, she was. After which she would cackle merrily. James was very much taken by the West Country girl who was seventeen or eighteen. She cast far from hostile looks at the young convict, and thereafter he sought out every opportunity of approaching her, but having decided that he would not draw attention to himself, he decided to bide his time. He expected that the bad start with the boss notwithstanding, his life in Hunter's Hill did not need to be too much of an ordeal since everybody said that Coldwell was not a bad master.

The men lived in big dormitories which housed up to ten men, and had to work from six in the morning to noon, have a twenty minute break for a quick meal, and then work until sunset. Much of the work was of an agricultural nature, consisting of clearing the bush and forest for future schemes, digging wells for household needs and setting up an irrigation system which would harness the waters of the Parramatta to irrigate the plantations that Coldwell was planning, There was also the completion of the house, which the boss wanted to be the most magnificent mansion that money could buy. James was in a small team digging wells, after Johnson Johnson, an Aborigine water diviner had pinpointed where to dig. It was back-breaking work, but he was strong and healthy even after the four gruelling months at sea.

He was sweating profusely after a full hour's digging, and taking a short breather when the master appeared from nowhere.

'Ha!' he said, 'no wonder you thought your employer was demanding too much of you. You are a shirker, Hammett, aren't you?'

'No sir, just out of breath.' Anybody could see the man was near exhaustion, but Coldwell looked at him poisonously and in a lightning move hit him on the face with the back of his hand, the blow sending him reeling as he tottered to the ground. James instinctively grabbed his spade, but immediately dropped it. Had he not stopped to think, it would have meant, at the very least, a one-way ticket to Norfolk Island. Perhaps even hanging.

Gradually he became used to the rhythm of life at Hunter's Hill, although not to relentless and undeserved reprimanding. Coldwell had clearly singled him out and went out of his way to display his fangs to him, giving him the most unpleasant chores, swearing at him, sometimes hitting him with his fist or a horsewhip which he loved to flourish as he walked, decapitating dandelions and daisies. The convict had hoped that after a while he might believe the evidence of his own eyes and discover that he was neither a shirker nor a trouble-maker, but the boss seemed to have a blind spot when it came to him, and obviously saw what he had already chosen to see.

Still it was not always doom and gloom. One night as he was smoking his pipe underneath a strange tree which had fascinated him from the very beginning, he heard a rustle in the bushes and could not believe his eyes when Annie Browne appeared in the eerie moonlight. She beamed a smile at him as she came towards him, indicating that she meant to sit down by his side. She was wearing an attractive dress with large flower prints which she had clearly inherited from Mistress Coldwell. She huddled very closely to him, and he could feel her softness against his haunch and it was a very welcome, if troubling, sensation.

'Since you are too proud to talk to me, I thought I may as well come talk to you,' she said in her bewitching West Country accent. Her speech sounded like a song and her laughter its musical accompaniment. He stared at her obliquely, as if she had just cast a spell upon him — which she had. He tried to say something but only a falsetto sound came out of his throat, which doubled her merriment. He made a second attempt to speak but she stopped him by placing her hand to his lips, and he sat there saying nothing, savouring the moment. Then as his ardour began to rise, he slyly edged his haunch toward hers, in an attempt to get a better feel of her.

'Oh you can if you want to, I don't mind,' she said, 'you can even put your arms around me.' James eagerly complied.

'Aren't you going to kiss me then, James?' His mouth dried up completely.

'Yes, miss,' he said finally, but still doing nothing. Being called miss made Annie burst out laughing once more. Miss, she repeated, pretending to look behind her, where is she? But kiss her, he did finally. He put both his arms around her waist, and she extended her mouth to him, and they kissed, he inexpertly, but she obviously knew the ropes and directed her tongue inside his mouth fetching his. Since he left Tolpuddle in chains, this was the most fantastic thing that had happened to him. No, this was without doubt the most fantastic thing that had happened to him.

'Can I smoke your pipe?' she asked, but without waiting for an answer, she grabbed it and started puffing quite expertly. She did all the talking, telling him the story of her transportation.

'I am no thief, never stole nothing for myself, I swear on the head of my poor little brother and sweet little sister... the good lord and Saint Sarah look after them now as their Annie is gone... they was always 'ungry, the mites. It were a sin to let 'em starve... I have stolen everything, bread, fruit, clothing, you name it. I always managed not to get caught, I am a crafty cow I am... But catch me, they did, in the end. A lousy 'en. That tailor said he'd take me to them if I got the 'en, you follow?' James was completely lost. 'They read the charge in court. Annie Browne, you are here to be judged on the very serious crime of stealing an 'en, valued at ten shillings and one penny, how do you plead?' The way she spoke reminded him of the ringing of bells.

'Hold on,' cried James indignantly, 'I don't understand; a chicken valued at ten shillings and a penny? Crazy... You can buy a whole farmyard of chicken for ten shillings.'

'And one penny!' said Annie laughing raucously, pushing the convict playfully on the shoulder.

'But sweetheart,' she added, 'did you not know it's a crazy world?' But whilst he was pondering on this profound statement, she interrupted him.

'Now if you steal goods worth less than ten shillings, you do not qualify for transportation, see... So I reckon they must 'ave written down, one shillings and then somebody must 'ave looked at it hard and shook 'is 'ead. That won't do, one shilling doesn't warrant no transportation.' Her eyes lit up with the hilarity that was announcing its impending gushing out. She now took a gruff male voice and an outlandish accent.

' "Ere boy, take this 'ere pencil and add a zero after the one." ' And she cackled merrily, 'That's 'ow come I'm 'ere.' James was indignant.

'Do you mean those unworthy men —' Annie's laughter gained more impetus at this. She laughed and almost choking, she spluttered 'Those unworthy men, 'e says... you mean those bastards!'

'Well, yes,' agreed James, who disapproved of bad language. When Annie calmed down, he asked, 'But Annie, how can that despicable act make you laugh? You should scream and shout and spit in their faces.' She stared at him, open-mouthed as if he had said something that defied logic, and grabbing him and squeezing him with all her might, she said, 'On the contrary, I am grateful to them you sweet boy, for how else were we to meet?' After a little pause, she looked at him in the eyes and whispered, 'That you and I should meet here, was planned since before you and I wuz born, ye know?'

After a prolonged kiss, Annie became more subdued, and finished her tale.

Seven years in Botany Bay, the judge said, and here she was in her fifth year, two more to go, but Johnson Johnson's wife had told her that she would never leave the colony alive, she said with a shrug. The proximity of warm soft flesh made him stop listening to her, and concentrate on the growing physical contact and the effect it was having on him.

'There will be plenty of time for that later, I promise you James,' she said merrily, 'now I want to talk.' James thought that he should say something too, but could think of nothing for a while. Suddenly his eyes fell on the moringa tree.

'Funny tree that, isn't it,' he asked to cover his embarrassment.

'Oh that tree... You are right, the master brought the seeds from India, it's called a drumstick tree... got a funny name in Indian... he says it's the most amazing tree in the whole world of... plants and trees... Its leaves are nice to eat when cooked, I like it, and these here,' she said pointing to the long strange looking green sticks hanging down, are the drumsticks, and when you 'ave no drums to beat, you eat 'em... yummy... He says the flowers are nice too, but I draw the line at eating flowers, I do.' And she told him a long list of magic qualities that tree was supposed to have, and promised that she would bring some for him to taste some day.

They must have been together for almost two hours, to judge by the position of the moon in the sky, but it seemed like minutes to James.

'I must go back now, sweetheart, or I might be missed... the missus must have a cup of cocoa at around this time...' She paused, looked at him with a wicked smile, adding, 'I know what you would like, but what sort of girl do you think I am? Opening my legs to you the first time we meet? Respectable I am!' She started walking away, but turned round, winked at him saying, 'Not really, not no more… not after what they did to me on the boat…' James easily imagined what that was.

Meeting Annie that night, James mused, made the whole Tolpuddle experience, the arrest, trial and transportation, seem worth while. He repeated that like a mantra a few times, but before closing his eyes that night, he winked at the ceiling, shook his head, and said, 'Not really.'

Next day, George Coldwell came towards him as he was working on the irrigation system, and his mistake this time was not to look up but continue with his work, and the boss took this as an affront.

'You scum, have you no manners? Am I the boss or are you? Am I to be ignored, you dog?'

'I didn't mean to be bad-mannered, sir, I was working.'

'Ha! You scoundrel, when my back is turned, you laze about, scratching your behind and picking your nose, and now you pretend you are working your guts out.'

'I am sir,' James replied in as a calm a tone as he could muster, 'I am not a skiver'. He knew that he did not mean to be lacking in courtesy, but one is not born servile, one has to learn it, and he had not yet done so. Coldwell pounced on him, grabbed him by the scruff, pulled him up, dragged him towards a gum tree and pushed him against it, hitting his head against the trunk. James felt the blood rush to his head, and could not stop himself glaring at the boss in anger. The latter probably regretted his violent and gratuitous reaction, but he could not abide anyone looking at him like this.

'You scoundrel, I am fast losing patience with you, and mark my word if this continues, I'll arrange for a one-way ticket to the Island for you. Would you like that, you felon?' This shook James, for he did not doubt that Coldwell could indeed arrange that, and he had heard a lot about that hell on earth called Norfolk Island. Its regime as a penal colony was the harshest that one could imagine, everybody said, although how anybody knew was a mystery, since once sent there, no one came back. It was claimed that it was specially designed for the "worst description of convicts" and for the so-called "twice-convicted," which meant convicts accused of having committed further crimes since arriving in New South Wales. The guards were the most hard-ened jailers in the colony. The men were kept in irons at all times, even when they slept. Death is much preferable to a sentence on that island, everybody said. There was a story of a man of the cloth who went to the island to bring comfort to men who were due to be executed, and also at the same time to bring the glad tidings to those who had earned a last minute reprieve. When he told one man that the King had commuted his sentence, the latter burst into tears of despair, pushed his guard and sprinted towards the cliff from which he flung himself at the torrents below.

'No sir, I will not like that, and will be grateful to you if you could forgive me for the error of my ways.'

'Ha!' said Coldwell rubbing his hands happily, 'so you agree that you were wilfully rude to me?' He had no choice but to nod his assent to an obvi-ous untruth. His tormentor walked away, leaving him shaken. He felt it in his bones that Norfolk Island was only a matter of time.

That night he went under the drumstick tree earlier than usual to keep his tryst with Annie, but she did not turn up, and he went back to the dormi-tory with a lump in his throat, telling himself that he should not allow him-self to be dragged into a one-sided passionate affair. Clearly the gipsy woman was a depraved creature who enjoyed trifling with unfortunate convicts for a little bit of sport. Or maybe she was playing hard to get. But she had made her mark, and he knew that he would find it difficult to get the saucy wench out of his system. But try, he would. He knew that he would not be able to stop himself going again to wait for her under the drumstick tree. Again and again.

Sure enough Annie turned up the next night, and explained that Miss Amelia had a headache the day before and wanted her to massage her neck and her head, and would not hear of her going to her room until she fell asleep. When she came out to meet him, he was gone. I'll never ever doubt you again, he told a bemused Annie. That night, they lay together and had carnal knowledge of each other, and when she squealed with gratification, the inexperienced James was quite bemused. I love you so much, my James, she said earnestly, you are the only man I want, and I will never love anybody else for as long as I live, and that's a promise and a Gipsy woman's oath.'

Suddenly she asked if he had enjoyed it better in the past. James truthfully answered no, for he had never lain with a woman. She talked incessantly and then stopped.

'I tell you everything, but you are quiet, you never say nothing about yourself,' she said.

'When would I have had the opportunity, Annie Browne,' he asked, laughing. She stared at him open-eyed.

'Do I talk too much then?'

'No, you talk a lot, it is true, but it can never be too much, Annie Browne. Your voice is sweet music, not just to my ears, but I verily believe that it goes all the way and enters my soul.' A true poet, you are my James, she said. She insisted that he told her about himself, and though he found it hard, he tried. He told her about Coldwell's dislike of him, and that shocked her.

'What are you saying? Master George is the kindest man on earth.' James was surprised to hear that, but Annie gave him innumerable examples of his kindness. Mr Coldwell, she continued, is a learned man, always looking at his big books. He always had a kind word for her. No, she could not understand why he disliked James so much. She told how how devoted he was to his wife, about his interest in some Egyptian carvings found in Hunter Valley, how he was always talking about them to his friends, about his time in India, his plans for the the farm.

True enough, nobody had anything bad to say about his tormentor. He could not understand it, but it became clear to him that the people with the power had written him down as a dangerous lunatic, a rebellious subversive who needed to be on a short lease. Is there a way to influence Coldwell's thinking about him? From what Annie had said, the lady was a sweet and good-natured person. She suggested that she could use her influence to get Amelia to speak to her husband in his favour. But he decided against that. If Coldwell finds out about the two of them, he might take it upon himself to thwart their burgeoning love.

On Sunday the young lovers went for a walk on the bank of Lane Cove. They walked across the mangrove trees there, letting small crabs nibble their bare feet. At first they had the place all to themselves, but some native folks appeared, collecting crabs and weeds, plants, roots and small fruits. The children, their hair red with ochre, their eyes and nose dripping, laughed and shouted a lot, running all over the place, obviously enjoying themselves. At first they were wary of the white couple, but gradually they began to venture nearer them, and finally, noticing that their proximity did not perturb the pair, they began to run around them, touching their legs, screaming with laughter as they did so. They then recognised Johnson Johnson among them, and they went to meet him. He was very pleased to see them and offered them some dried fruits and roasted roots which they happily ate and enjoyed. Johnson Johnson sat down beside them and started speaking about his people, the Koori, their customs, what they ate, how they hunted, demonstrated how to use a boomerang, gave his personal one to James, which made the latter feel uneasy, as he had nothing to give.

Johnson Johnson proudly explained that his people were the original Australians. The ancestors, who were expert sailors, had used their canoes and then walked considerable distances over what is now the sea, and which was then land, after they kept seeing smoke, presumably from forest fires, from where they had settled (which James would later learn was Borneo, South Asia). It was about fifty thousand years ago, when an ice-age was ending, with ice collecting at the poles, which had caused a drop in the sea level of hundreds of metres, enabling people to walk on the bottom of what later became sea. Johnson Johnson told him about the Songlines. James would learn that people used regularly to walk the ninety miles from Australia to Van Diemen's Land, for example.

Johnson Johnson tried to explain about the Koori concept of property, how they could not grasp the notion that anything could belong exclusively to one person. The edible roots under the ground, the fruits on trees, the wood for burning, the bark for making canoes, belonged to whoever needed them. How could they be the property of one person? He told them of the sadness of his people when the Englishman came and took possession of the land of their ancestors and drove them out. They did not even dream of asking for our permission to share it, he wailed. They listened carefully and sympathised with their plight. After a long silence, he looked at the pair, shook his head, and said wistfully, 'And they even stole my name...' James demanded an explanation.

'My name is not Johnson Johnson. The white man stole my name and gave me an inferior one in its place,' he paused, and looking away, said, 'my true name is Birumbirra…' James resolved not to call him Johnson Johnson again, but Birumbirra, but with everybody else calling him by his 'inferior' name, he somehow found this a difficult resolution to keep. From that day, Johnson Johnson and he became good friends.

When they got back to the compound, Bruce Powell, who was one of the group of convicts who had come over on the Surrey saw them and eyed them strangely. When James mentioned this to Annie, she said that Bruce had been sweet on her from the very beginning, but that she had not welcomed his attention.

'I think he thinks he is in love with me,' she cackled, 'so young James, if you misbehave, I'll know where to knock, eh.'

The weeks went by, each resembling the previous one. Christmas came and was gone without much fuss. Annie gave James leftovers from the turkey Coldwell had sent for from Cape Town (six months earlier) nurturing and fattening it. She almost always brought him things from the master's kitchen. The mistress knew that she was seeing someone on the sly but did not ask questions. Annie craftily mentioned the name of Bruce now and then, hoping that she would think that he was her mysterious sweetheart, as a means of deviating suspicion from James, in the light of the master's dislike of him. So nobody bothered James on that account.

One morning, James and Johnson Johnson were engaged in digging the canal that was to irrigate the plantations, when out of the blue the master came from behind and kicked him in his backside, shouting some gibberish at him. Clearly to the boss, he had done something wrong, but he never knew what. James turned round, and instinctively greeted his assailant with clenched fist, ready to pounce on him, before recognising who he was. The sight of this made Coldwell see red.

'So now you are threatening to assault me, eh? You lay a finger on me you whoreson dog, and I will get you hanged! Come on.'

James immediately unclenched his fist, and shaking his head, said, 'No, sir, no… I thought… I mean…' Johnson Johnson gaped at the boss incredulously. Clearly he could not understand what possessed the big white man.

'I would not dream of raising a hand to you, sir… it's just…' and he trailed off, unable to find the words.

'Now, listen to me, and listen to me with both ears, I promise you that before three months, I will see that you get your just desserts.' James knew he meant Norfolk Island! Or did he really mean to have him hanged? 'We are too lenient to criminals like you here…' and he went on incoherently for a bit before turning his back and moving away.

Norfolk Island! The man was obsessed by the idea of dispatching him there, and clearly he had the power to do so. That was when he made up his mind to abscond. He had heard stories of convicts who had done just that. Many had been recaptured, and with dire consequences. Some owners defied the law of the land and caused the renegade convict to be flogged to death. Many were sent to the notorious Norfolk Island, some were shot dead, some eaten by crocodiles, many got lost in the forest and starved to death, but a small fraction did manage to gain their liberty after all. James promised himself that he would be among those. He would plan it all in great detail, and he and Annie would find a place where they could live an idyllic life in peace, away from cruel masters. Members of the Friendly Society of Agricultural Workers, were encouraged by George Loveless to read, not only the bible, but works of literary merit. The Society was given a copy of Mr Daniel Defoe's book, The Life and Most Surprizing Adventures of Robinson Crusoe of York, Mariner. It was a book James had read again and again. They said Australia was an immense country which had not been explored properly, and many people still believed that China was at one end of it. They would find a nice quiet place, away from the wicked masters, exploit the land, live on fish and game, roots and vegetables. It would not be a lonely life because they would have each other. Provided Annie was willing.

Johnson Johnson was clearly shocked by Coldwell's treatment of his friend, and when James mentioned his certainty of being sent to the notorious island, he shook his head and tut tutted. He was sent there once to douse, and saw at first hand the treatment of the inmates there. No my friend, he urged, you must leave this place. James nodded, and admitted that he had been thinking the same thing. Yes, run away, there are many places, he said, you could also make friends with the Kouri people. We are very friendly if approached properly. He explained about their notion of territory. A person living in a place considers it to belong to his people, and nobody can cross into that land without their permission, but once it is granted, the visitor is treated like an honoured guest, even like a member of the tribe, allowed to fish, hunt and gather, offered help when needed. Anybody arriving in a Kouri site without permission is deemed to have broken the law and can be severely punished.

'You mean if I run away to a faraway place which might be someone's territory, I might be killed?' Johnson Johnson pursed his lips and made a non-committal gesture, before adding, 'But Kouri people do not kill for fun.' He explained that the custom before going on a trip, is to get message sticks given by someone known and respected by the tribe. The traveller with the appropriate message stick is granted entry and offered all help possible.

On hearing this James became very depressed, his dream of freedom evaporating like the morning mist when the sun started rising.

'I am a respected elder,' said the Aborigine smiling, 'and I can give you a message stick...' James had never been subject to such a sudden change of mood. He had witnessed on many occasions a flash of lightning in a clear blue sky, followed by a downpour, but never the opposite, the sky suddenly becoming blue after a thunderstorm.

'Can you really? Then I can go thousands of miles from here and —'

'No,' his friend said smiling sadly, 'I may be a respected elder, but not by everybody...'

'You mean he'll find me...'

'Maybe not... have you heard of Illiwarra?' James had not.

'I was born there... I am respected there... nice place. Lake Illiwarra,' he explained, 'is a salt water lake, and teems with fish and crabs and edible algae. Wild geese,' he added, 'loved the area, and I will tell you how to find goose eggs, they are very good to eat.'

'Will I be safe from Coldwell there?'

'He is busy here... he will not trouble you there... it takes days to get there... on foot, maybe fifteen...' Johnson Johnson seemed deep in thought, then suddenly added, 'Quicker if you use canoe...'

Johnson Johnson told him about the richness of the region, and it did not take him long to make up his mind. This was where they would go. At first

Annie was taken aback, but understanding James' fear, she never hesitated about throwing her lot with him. I'll go with you even to China, she said merrily. Johnson Johnson's help in the plan was crucial. He offered to arrange for his friends in Lane Cove to make a bark canoe for the runaways. Bangalay, the best canoe tree providing excellent bark abounded in the area, he said. They will also provide the couple with the best goinna to paddle the craft, and he would instruct them in that art ("one paddle in each hand, and one stroke at a time"). He would make a list of possible dangers and tell them and how to avoid them. Even a child, he said, should have little trouble keeping the craft afloat and moving in the right direction, adding with a smile, a Kouri child, I mean. In the meantime he would prepare the message stick. The pair planned their escape carefully. Whilst out courting, they had found a crack in the rocks, and decided that it would make an admirable cache for the things they planned to take with them. Annie deftly deviated the things they might need to make their lives comfortable in a faraway place: kitchen things mainly, blankets, needles and things like that. She also thought of taking some seeds from the drumstick tree. James on his part, managed to steal a few tools, rope, nails, hooks for fishing and similar things, and when they met in the night, they would go to the woods and hide these precious lifesavers, with a view to taking them on the canoe which was in an advanced state of construction. They were happy that they had thought of everything that they were likely to need in the wilds. Johnson Johnson explained to them how to catch and cook turtles, how to spear fish and trap wild fowls, although they never had the time and opportunity to put the knowledge into practice.

Annie was sorry to be leaving Miss Amelia, for she was fond of her, and knew that she would be missed too, but the moment she had agreed to go with James, there was no looking back. She had always been full of optimism even when she did not know where the next mouthful was coming from. If there were risks, she was willing to take them. If anything went against her expectations, she took a deep breath and looked at alternatives. I never cry over spilled milk, she often said, what's the point?

Over a month passed before they were ready. Johnson Johnson had said that their craft was ready in Lane Cove, that they could pick it at any time, but had warned about stormy winds. Annie, ever optimistic, said there was no point waiting any more, that they should go immediately, but the more cautious James said it was best to be guided by the wise Kouri man. So they waited for Johnson Johnson to pronounce everything, specially the weather conditions, propitious.

A week later, when the family was going to mass in the chapel which Coldwell had had built in the grounds of Taj Mahal farm itself — the servants and convicts were expected to attend a later service — the pair sneaked out. Nobody saw this as anything unusual, except Bruce Powell who followed them for a bit, and then asked them where they were going. James did not know what to say, but Annie winked at him suggestively, and playfully pushed him away.

Bruce suspected that something was afoot, but had no idea what it could be. He would have liked to go to Coldwell and have a word in his ear, but knew that if the others found out, he would be called a snitch. All day he watched for their return and when they did not, his doubts were confirmed.

The runaways reached the place Johnson Johnson had indicated, the large red rock next to a massive gum tree where the river bends, and waited there. A child seemed to be waiting for them, but the moment he saw them he bolted. A few minutes later, three men appeared, and James showed him a message stick his friend had given him. It was not really a stick, but a piece of bark on which there were some etchings of symbols. The men studied it, passing it round, nodding to each other and exchanging a few words which the pair understood not a word of. The oldest man signalled them to follow them, and after no more than a few steps, one of them began to uncover some leaves and sticks, revealing the canoe. It looked flimsy but James knew that his friend would not order a canoe that was not seaworthy. They thanked the men, who comically repeated the "Thank you," many times and helped put the stuff on board. When that was done they rubbed hands with their benefactors and climbed on board and began paddling away.

It was just as easy as Johnson Johnson had said.

CHAPTER 9

───── ◆ ◆ ◆ ─────

Atlantic

THEY HAD ALL told her that for an unmarried mother, life in the Highlands was going to be unbearable, and urged her to go to Canada with John Robert. It was a new country, and people who went there were would not have the leisure to be judgmental. If she was after a normal life, it was her only chance. The one impediment was Rob Rob. She was sure that he would come back for her, and did not want to leave him heart-broken when he found that the family had gone God knows where. However it soon became clear to her that Hugh, Martha and Grand Mam were not planning to go anywhere. They were born Highlanders and wanted to die within sights of their glens and lochs. Selfishly Catriona thought, when Rob Rob came looking for her, Da would be able to tell him where she was, and he would surely come find her. Til a' the seas gang dry! She was as sure of that as she was, of John Robert being the spitting image of Rob Rob and the prettiest baby in the whole world. Yes, she would go join her brother in Canada. With her, having once taken the decision, she did not once feel or express any regret. It was like with Rob Rob, she had decided that she would give herself to him, and she did and she never regretted the outcome.

Hugh, Martha, and Grand Mam who had urged her to go, found the thought that they would never see her again almost unbearable, but they put on a brave face, and kept saying that they would manage. They had everything they needed for a comfortable old age, they swore. In material terms that was true. It was the fact that they felt this had to be said so often, which made Kitty uneasy. She would love them forever, they had been caring and loving parents. Distance would make no difference to that love. She knew that apart from the shame of having been a wayward daughter, who, in the eyes of the world, had brought shame on the family, she had been dutiful and loving too, so there was no regret there. In any case she did not think it shameful to give yourself to the person you love. If she could put the clock back, even in the knowledge that she would never see Rob Rob again, she would not hesitate doing the same thing all over again, for at least now she would have a piece of him for keeps.

John Robert had brought a lot of happiness to the lives of the family. Grand Mam who had been gradually sliding into apathy, and had said that her time was nigh, suddenly grew a new skin, her eyes regaining their old sparkle, but even she insisted that for the sake of the little mite, there was no better option than to go away. You will both be happier there, the family said. What is happiness? Kitty asked herself? Put on one pan of the scales the happiness of having your loved ones around, minus the unhappiness of poverty and the certainty that there was no future for them, and on the other pan the knowledge that the loved ones had every chance of a good life minus the unhappiness of knowing that they would never see each other again. Which way would the scales swing? Difficult to say. Probably about an equal balance. But The Manufacturers' Committee was offering funds and Kitty and baby John were going.

The whole family set out from Helmsdale to Cromarty by boat. The parting in Cromarty was tearful, and Kitty who had promised herself that she would maintain a cheerful front was unable to stop the flow of tears, but the moment she was on board the Milton, her eyes immediately dried up, but only for a short while. When she was led to the multi-storied hold where she was going to spend about six weeks, seeing its desolate nature and the space allowed for each passenger, her eyes became once more heavy with tears, but she managed to hold them inside. Looking at the number of women and children she was going to share this space with, she made a quick calculation and arrived at the conclusion that there was room for only half the people to lie down at any given time, whilst the rest would have to sit up huddled together like spoons in a box. The height of the compartment was such that you had to move with bent legs, your head down, if you did not want to knock it against the ceiling. She hoped the women would make allowance for the babies and children and squeeze themselves a little bit more, and grudgingly they did.

Once all the passengers had embarked and the tide was favourable, the Milton weighed anchor and slowly started gliding away in a northerly direction, with a chorus of sea gulls squawking to bid them God speed, as they rose and fell with the rocking billows. Not to be outdone, a trio of stormy petrels skimming the surface of the water happily showed them the way. The winds were favourable, and in a matter of hours they were once more at the level of Helmsdale. John O'Groats came next, and then the ship changed into a westerly course, heading for the Atlantic, when a strong wind made the ship rock, triggering a general onslaught of vomiting.

Kitty and John were sharing a space no bigger than the floor of their hut in Strathnaver with twenty other women and children. A foul smell of vomit filled the atmosphere, but she herself was not seasick. It was explained to them that in order to sleep, they had to agree between themselves and take turns. There would be bells to indicate the changeover. The crying of the little ones was almost continuous, except for short periods in the middle of the night. It was like a relay race, the moment one lot stopped, like they had passed the baton to a fresh lot, another started. John Robert was quite a handful, but Kitty drew much comfort from holding him tight and cuddling him. The toilet facilities amounted to no more than a couple of buckets behind a torn curtain in a corner of the hold, and the constant rolling of the ship caused many a spill, which did nothing to improve the already foul stench. She was able to lie down for a couple of hours, after which her neighbour woke her up, apologising profusely, pointing out that it was her turn, but she took John in her arms and sat up, and mercifully he continued to sleep.

In the morning they were allowed two hours on deck, in batches, to stretch their legs and take in some fresh air, and Kitty watched in wonder the blue waves rolling and crashing against the bulwark of the Milton. The food, consisting of dried biscuits and pickled herrings, was adequate but many passengers could not keep it in, resulting in more unpleasant stench. That was going to be the pattern for another five weeks, she thought gloomily.

She had not counted on a deterioration of the weather. Fierce winds made the ship roll dangerously, and people screamed as they prayed for their lives. Dante's Inferno, Kitty imagined. As if that was not bad enough, the winds swelled into a real storm. People got thrown all over the place, and one woman died of a cracked skull. At the end of the storm, another four passengers had met a similar fate in other holds. She, who had always been full of compassion, was disappointed and shocked when she found that as people died and were buried at sea, instead of mourning for them, most, if not all her fellow passengers, herself included, saw this as a gain in space for themselves. Recognising her selfishness, her self-worth suffered a serious jolt. That's not who I am, she kept telling herself. I'm only thinking of the baby, she explained to herself.

After five weeks, when Kitty and everybody else had reached the end of their tether and some people started talking of throwing themselves overboard for a merciful end to their suffering, the Milton found itself approaching the shores of Newfoundland. This is the place where John had not met his untimely death, she reflected wryly. The brown rugged, ragged and desolate coast was one of the most welcome sights she had ever seen, and the land breeze was most welcome too. What cheered the weary travellers more than anything, was the number of birds gathering round the ship, doing acrobatics in the air, swooping down with abandon, merrily chirping or squawking. Then, re-energised, they would soar up again, only to repeat this enchanting choreography. There were ducks and geese, seagulls and cormorants, swallows and albatrosses, and they instilled in the breast of the people coming into this new unknown world some badly needed optimism.

It did not take them long to reach the Gulf of St Lawrence. Kitty gaped at the ninety mile mouth of that waterway in wonder. It looked more like the open sea than the mouth of a river. After a short while, the outlines of the coast on the southern side of the river begin to appear more distinctly.

Kitty watches in rapt admiration the clouds rolling along in colourful billows as they catch the sunbeam, giving it a rosy hue. They seem to be playing hide and seek: now you see them, now they have disappeared. It is as if they are alive and have a mind of their own. Soon Green Island emerges in a distant mist, and as the Milton approaches it, the shores with houses and farms become visible, most with tin roofs brazenly reflecting the sunlight.

As the ship approaches Gros Isle, a rocky island with attractive groves of beeches, birch, ash and fir, two ships with yellow flags are sighted, signalling an outbreak of cholera. This means some form of quarantine was being enforced. She is weary of the interminable voyage, and is impatient to be on terra firma, but for John Robert's sake, she welcomes the tedious formalities. The boy has had a bad crossing, and is lucky to make it so far, and she does not want him to be exposed to a fatal illness so near the destination. Three whole days are spent in quarantine, where passengers are checked and vetted.

John Robert had been all right when they were finally given the all clear and they set forth towards Quebec, but mother and child were admiring the Montmorenci falls when the child started fidgeting and then began screaming. It was obvious that he was in great pain, and no manner of cajoling and cuddling would make him stop. She was greatly alarmed when she found that he had become so hot that it was like holding a loaf just taken out of the oven. Next he began throwing up and had the runs. She began panicking and an officer took mother and child to the ship doctor's, although as an unwritten rule only first class passengers benefited from his immediate services, often leaving passengers from the other classes to die before they could be seen. He said that it was not unusual for a little child to have high temperatures, believed that the fever would go down of its own after making him swallow a tablet, and urged her not to worry. However, the temperature showed no signs of abating, and the vomiting got worse, as did the runs. She screamed that she needed the doctor, but confined in the hold with scarcely any room to move, nobody heard her and nothing could be done. John Robert passed away in the night. As did three adults and two more children. The captain panicked and ordered that the dead be buried at sea without delay, as cholera was known to spread like wild fire. People were quick to point out that the quarantine which was supposed to be a preventative measure, was in fact what had exposed them to the catastrophe. Prior to the forced landing at Gros Isle, there was not a single case of cholera on board. But what was the point of finger-pointing now?

Kitty was disconsolate and thought that she was going to lose her mind. She too got a high temperature and became delirious, screaming that she wanted to go back home, when she would have her baby back. People kept away from her, fearing that she would contaminate them. She did not know how she survived.

When her high temperature subsided, she had neither the inclination nor the strength to go on deck to catch a glimpse of Quebec, a majestic city built on a magnificent rock. Her neighbour, impressed by the sights, kept describing the sights in lyrical terms, with an insensitivity bordering on callousness. What did it matter to her that there was a magnificent fortress overlooking the river on Cape Diamond? Why did she not just shut up and let her die?

That night she slept fitfully, waking up in a panic every now and again, clasping emptiness instead of her little baby.

She had no inclination to watch the varied landscape on either banks when the river narrowed and when the scenery became more varied and picturesque as the Milton went further up river. The number of orchards lining the shores, bending down with rich harvests of apples and plums was astounding. Were there enough mouths in the world to gobble them all up?

The travel-weary multitudes who had braved winds and tempests to come look for a more comfortable life in unknown territory were greatly heartened by the signs indicating that poverty had left these shores forever. The soil seemed more fertile, making for a lush green vegetation. This was what had obviously attracted settlers and as a result instead of the rudimentary log-houses further down the river, there were now tastily built houses with windows and steps, mostly painted white or pale-green.

Kitty had lost all concept of time when they reached Port Hope, where John had said that he would be waiting for them. She had no idea how long it was since her baby had passed away. Very few passengers got off, and Kitty was relieved to have reached her destination. John was waiting, and brother and sister held each other, crying for a number of unsaid reasons: their much loved parents who they will never see again, her lost little boy, the glens and lochs of the land that they had left behind and which neither will never see again, her lost love, their childhood. John did not immediately register the absence of the little boy, not having known him, but she tearfully told him the story of his needless death through bad planning. John had come in a horse-drawn carriage which his employer had lent him to pick up his sister. It was a two-hour ride to Oxenham, on the shores of the Rice Lake.

CHAPTER 10

♦ ♦ ♦

Oxenham On. (1)

JOHN, HAVING MIRACULOUSLY escaped death when he missed the *Moonglow* at Cromarty, was advised that there was the possibility of catching another ship at Greenock which was sailing to Toronto in a week. He made his way to Fort William, and waited two days for a boat going to Greenock. He arrived within hours of the departure of the Highland Fling, a brig which had been used to transport slaves to Virginia, and was able to arrange a passage on board. He was shocked by the abominable conditions on board. They were not much better than on slave ships in which men had been forcibly taken across the Atlantic Ocean to become the possession of ruthless tobacco and cotton planters. It was only his good heath and his optimistic and cheerful outlook which made the rough crossing bearable. Many people on the Highland Fling were unable to finish the gruelling journey, and ended up at the bottom of the Ocean for a variety of reasons, including cholera and accidents.

On board, in spite of his own precarious situation, he was always ready to help those passengers who were suffering even more than himself. The sleeping arrangements were such that he would have been able to catch half a night's sleep each night by taking turns, but John was sometimes reluctant to wake up the men who were expected to make room for him. People did not fail to notice this, and he was much appreciated for his selflessness.

He eventually arrived in Toronto, and got casual work at the port, earning very little, and often sleeping rough or in crowded hostels. It was there that he met a man who told him about Captain Paul Cobjohn who had just bought land in Oxenham near the Rice Lake. He was told that the Captain had served in India, had been sent back to England after he had contracted malaria and was allowed to buy land in Canada at the preferential rate accorded to ex-officers. He had bought some potential prime farm land, effectively pine forests, for next to nothing, and was engaged in a massive project of forest clearance and building. John was told that the Captain had been looking for responsible people to supervise and work with the Ojibwa Indians who were engaged in a variety of work, but that the moment new immigrants landed they were snapped up by the established settlers. It had not been John's experience that any snapping was happening anywhere, and he thought that he would try his luck there. He liked the idea of Oxenham, secluded and situated near a smallish lake with rivers and lush rolling plains.

The people at the port where he was employed tried to keep him there, and urged him to come back to Toronto if his trip was unsuccessful. He embarked on a boat to Port Hope, and there, he was able to get on a coach going towards Peterborough. He got off at a point where he was told that there would be a steamboat on the Otanabee river heading for Oxenham. This was a regular service, but sometimes, owing to the shallowness of the river in some areas, in some seasons, the river became difficult if not unnavigable. The company therefore usually arranged that at some chosen point, the passengers would transfer onto scows which could cope with the shallowness, for the rest of the trip.

The steamboat, however, ran aground at a short distance from where the transfer was supposed to take place. Everybody was panicking, unsure of what the arrangements were going to be. The captain explained that everybody, men women and children had to leave the steamer with their belongings, and wade across to the shore, then walk two or three miles across the shore to where the flat boats would be waiting. The able-bodied men and women would have little difficulty doing this, but there were the extra problems of the children and the possessions. John was the first one who said that as he had no possessions, he would be happy to take care of a couple of children. He got hold of a little girl called Emily, put her on his shoulder, grabbed a boy by the hand, and started wading towards the shore, where he deposited them into the care of a couple who had arrived on the shore at the same time. He went back for more children but his good example had been followed by others and they were all taken care of. He went to assist some elderly folks negotiating the uneven terrain to the shore. He then helped with trunks and bundles, and this part of the transfer went very well, mainly because of his goodwill and organisational skills. The party finally reached the safety of the flatboats.

He slept under the stars that night, and next morning, he made for the Cobjohn estate. To his surprise, he discovered that little Emily was none else than the five year old daughter of Captain Cobjohn. The latter having witnessed the young Highlander in action only the day before, and having been unable to thank him personally because of the bustle, received him with great friendliness. When he heard what he was after, he immediately offered him a position on the estate, in the certain knowledge that he was acquiring the services of a dependable young man. There was a log-house in which the family had managed to squeeze itself, but besides there was an unfinished log cabin, which the Captain offered to him.

From the beginning, he was treated very much like one of the family, specially as Emily had grown so very fond of him. The Captain was a bit on the taciturn side, but he was obviously well-disposed towards him. Mrs Eleanore Cobjohn said that John reminded her of her younger brother she had left behind in Stirlingshire, where he was studying law with a respectable firm of solicitors. The other member of the household was Felicity, the Captain's sixteen year old sister who had accompanied her brother to Canada. Both their parents being both dead, the older brother had become her guardian. From the very first time that she became aware of John, when the steamer ran aground, she had wished that she were a couple of years older, and the young Highlander not a common working man.

The Captain had a very clear idea of what he wanted to do at Bonnyrig, the name Eleanore had chosen for the property. He was going to clear an area of the forest, and simultaneously dig wells, build a drainage system for taking water from the lake to his plantations, and proceed with the extension of his house. The Ojibwas and Cayugas having realised that they could do nothing to reverse the tide of white men with guns, were keen to work for a big white man, as they had discovered that there were things which they had only been recently introduced to, which were nice to possess, and that you needed white man's money to buy them. They had a special fondness for mirrors. Their animal skins, which had served them so well since time immemorial, now seemed to them less attractive since they had come across coloured cotton and woollen materials. Inevitably, after tasting white man's liquor, they quickly developed a weakness for intoxication too.

Although John had no special training, it was assumed that if put in charge of a team of natives, he would know exactly how to deal with them and make sure that the work was done satisfactorily. He was a white man after all. Fortunately for the Cobjohns, John proved equal to the task, thus reinforcing the Captain's suspicions about the natural superiority of the white man.

Early on, Eleanore Cobjohn expressed a strong desire to be part of the development of Bonnyrig. Not only was she not averse to putting on a man's dungaree, a worker's cap and knee-high boots, she thoroughly relished the life in the open and the challenges of activities physical, axe or spade in hand. It took no more than a day — the first day — for everybody, including Emily, although she probably hindered more than she helped, to join forces to clear an area of about a quarter of an acre, specially chosen because of the maximum sunshine it benefited from, so the family could become self-sufficient in produce. To this effect, the captain and his wife had carefully chosen seeds of various vegetables and legumes, haricot beans, cabbage, peas, tomatoes, potatoes, carrots and lettuce, which they put in the ground with an almost religious fervour. As Scotsmen, they had a particular fondness for root vegetables, which meant that turnips, parsnips and swedes were not neglected. Already on the next day, Emily began asking why the tomatoes were not ready. It was an endearing sight to watch the little girl anxiously watering this big field with a small can, in the certainty that without her contribution, nothing would sprout.

Eleanore and John were often responsible for the execution of the captain's plan. Although the Cayugas and the Ojibwas had no serious problems with each other, Paul thought that at first, that it would be more politic to get teams from the same tribe working together on one specific project. The Cayugas seemed to like building, so they were out under the charge of the lady.

At first, she supervised the repair and extension work on the house, and as she had a very clear idea of what she wanted, this went on smoothly. Big Dan was a tall well-built man with a healthy tan, and he spoke one word at a time, but had a knack for making himself perfectly understood. His men had no fear of heights and with their cat-like agility, could walk up a vertical post as if they had spikes under their moccasins. For the six months that the building activity went on, not one serious accident took place. They seemed to understand what made a perfect wooden house, which was surprising since they had been used to living in wigwams. They worked efficiently with saws, and seemed to enjoy using them. The progress on the house was clearly visible at the end of each day. Eleanore was very proud of the work being done under her supervision. She often joined in the wood sawing or the hammering that had to be done, and Paul nearly had a fit once when he saw her precariously poised on a ladder, hammer in hand, a nail in her mouth, attaching a window on the second floor with obvious gusto. No amount of reasoning would persuade her to return to more sedentary activities.

John had the responsibility of the water works. First he had to dig the wells. This he did with the help of an Ojibwa man, Wahaitiya — he had been given a Christian name, Daniel, but as he made it a point not to respond to it, even the proud captain could do nothing, so Wahaitiya it was. He was a tall thin man with an emaciated face which made him look older than he was. He had humorous eyes, and was indeed something of a wag. He sauntered comically, rather than walked, his feet hardly touching the ground, the upper part of his body stooping forward slightly. He sometimes used a Y shaped stick, but he said that he could just as well detect the presence of the water by holding his hand over the spot. He had located a few places where water was plentiful, and after consultation with the captain, John chose three strategically placed spots. Wahaitiya's dousing work was done, but a man of many parts, his advice was sought on a number of issues. He knew about wood and seasoning, which was again surprising, as the Ojibwas had no tradition for using wood except in making bows and arrows and rudimentary furniture. He knew about herbs and their medicinal properties. He knew where to get the best lake rice and how to use it to feed his fellow Ojibwas.

John had seen a picture of a lever being used to pull water out of shallow deposits when he was a child, and as the wells were hardly waist-deep near the shore of the lake, he designed and built systems based on his childhood memory of that picture, making drawing water child's play.

Meanwhile, the Captain was engaged in the forest clearing, and he had a team of ten Ojibwas working at one end of the area he planned to clear first, and a team of Cayugas working at the other end. He had not planned this, but he found that it was a stroke of luck, for a healthy competitive spirit grew out of this, fanning the progress of the work afoot, but surprisingly, no hostility.

Meanwhile, Felicity took care of Emily, and developed her latent skill at cooking and keeping house. The older girl did not have to be asked twice whenever Emily wanted to go see John at work. Often the two of them would seek him out and when they saw him digging or measuring, they would stop and watch him. John understood that Felicity was attracted to him, but thought that she was too young, and supposed that the aristocratic Cobjohns would not like one of theirs linked romantically to someone who grew up in a hovel in Strathnaver, and could just about write his name. But he imagined that in a year or two she might bloom into a very desirable young woman, and that he might then find her irresistible, which would make his position at Bonnyrig untenable. I am no romantic fool, he told himself, I am not going to allow a situation to develop, where I become attracted to a young woman only to find her swept off her feet by some toff in a plumed hat.

Clearing the forest was possibly the most arduous of the chores at hand. In the area being worked upon, there were hundreds of silver pines, spruce and hemlocks. These had not only to be felled, but the roots had to be extirpated as well. They were then defoliated, their branches lopped off before being conveyed to a specially designated area, from which they would then be taken to the lakeside where they would be loaded on scows bound for Peterborough, where only recently a sawmill had started operating. It took a couple of days for a load to be sawn into planks, half of which which were then taken back to Bonnyrig by the same route, to be used on the many construction projects now in course, the rest paid for handsomely by the sawmill.

Captain Cobjohn had a clear idea of what he wanted to cultivate, although he was less clear about who were going to buy his produce. The area was known to be ideal for the cultivation of fruit-trees, apples, pears, plums, berries, and so large chunks of land were set aside for these. Potatoes, carrots, turnips always come in handy, for personal consumption as well as feed for cattle and pigs. He knew that corn grew well, specially Indian corn, and soon he had about ten acres of it. The availability of corn made the raising of chicken an obvious choice. In the first years, husband and wife had agreed that they would try their hands at everything feasible, and then let experience dictate what future course of action to take. They readily consulted with John after it became clear that he was a sensible young fellow who had an instinctive reading of the situation. A year on, Cobjohn had been able to recruit three Irishmen from County Cork.

Captain Cobjohn disposed of a reasonable amount of cash, and he was going to invest some of it in Hereford cattle. He knew that some specimens had crossed the Atlantic as early as 1817, and that some breeders in Albany south of the waterway in America had been breeding them and might be willing to sell him a few to start his own cattle ranch. At first it would be a small affair, but he had every reason to believe that in time he would be the owner of a few thousand heads. Shortly after John arrived at Bonnyrig Cobjohn had written to William H. Sotham and Erastus Corning of Albany expressing an interest in their cattle.

When John was in Port Hope to greet Kitty, he had in fact only recently returned from New York where he had gone to talk to those two breeders. He had returned home to Oxenham, given an account of his New York trip to the captain, and on the next day, he had set out for Port Hope.

When his sister arrived at the farm, she was very heartened by what she saw. John had his own log cabin which he had built from the existing one. He had added a couple of rooms and enlarged to make it more welcoming in the hope that Kitty might come join him. One room was destined for her, and he had already made plans for an extension for young John Robert. He invited Kitty to stay with him for as long as she liked, until either of them got married, or fed up with each other. Who'll have me, said Kitty, a woman who has gone astray?

She began writing a letter home telling them about the death of little John Robert, and then found that she could not go on. John had gone out early to work on the trenches, and as she was alone, she thought that it was best to have a really good cry, clearing for good all the miseries that she had endured, all the hardships her much loved parents had gone through, her lost lover, the cruel and preventable death of her baby. Work all my sadness out of my system, she thought, and make a fresh start in this new country. From what John had said, the future seemed promising, but when did things ever turn out as planned in this life?

Eleanore had welcomed the newcomer with open arms, and said that in the beginning, at least, she could work at Bonnyrig, as there was any number of openings for her there. The vegetable concern had been a big success from the beginning, and already they had found markets for their produce in Peterborough, Port Hope and Cobourg. The farm had soon become an important supplier of potatoes to the region, and in fact demand was so great that they were unable to keep up with it. Cobjohn had to clear more land and aimed at doubling the production within a year. Soon the cattle would be arriving from Albany. It seemed to be natural barley country, and the distillery in Brighton had indicated that they could easily handle three or four times their output. Kitty could pick and choose what she wanted to do. John said that the captain had asked if they had friends or relatives back home who might wish to come over.

Kitty was not averse to working in any capacity, but with her great love of books, she had always aspired to become a teacher. There was, however, no school in Oxenham, although Cobourg and Port Hope had one each and Peterborough was blessed with two. Unfortunately there were no vacancies in any of them.

She therefore accepted Cobjohn's offer. Would she like to help Eleanore with the paperwork and the accountancy? She agreed immediately, but fired by the lady's enthusiasm for working with her hands, she felt strongly tempted to have a go at that sort of thing too, and the enterprising couple were very happy with that. She was ready for work next morning. Her hostess gave her charge of accounts and correspondence, and she began dealing with the wholesalers in Peterborough and Amherst who took their crops, the Brighton Distillery Company which bought their barley. There were letters from the sawmill, urging Cobjohn to sell them more wood, from Albany about some minor problems relating to the shipment of the cattle. What she did not learn in the office, she would learn from John, who took great pride in the success of the company which he had helped build. Felicity joined them later and helped her with accounts. Kitty thought that she seemed very accomplished, and found her friendly and warm, but she did not feel entirely at ease with her. When twice in five minutes she mentioned John to her, she deduced, rightly, that she was enamoured of her brother, and she knew there and then, that class difference notwithstanding, no power on earth was going to stop them marrying. She found that Eleanore was an ideal co-worker. She combined sound business sense with a sympathetic attitude under all circumstances.

In the afternoon, the two women donned dungarees and went to work, stacking the timber. She was surprised to see Wahaitiya at work. The wiry old man looked so frail and yet had such strength. She liked his cheerful bearing and enjoyed talking to him. The work of the two women consisted in stripping the massive fir trunks from their cumbersome branches. These twigs would serve later for the burning stages of the clearing.

The first evening, brother and sister had eaten with the captain's family. They had a Cayuga cook, Jane, who Eleanore had trained in her ways, and she had roasted a loin of beef the like of which Kitty had never tasted before. Back in their cabin, Kitty teased her brother about Felicity.

'Miss Felicity was doing the accounts today,' she said tentatively. John raised his head and looked at her in the candlelight.

'She is too young,' he said.

'Sixteen is not that young,' she countered.

'Seventeen actually,' he replied with lightning speed. Yes, she said to herself, no power on earth is going to stop them. From what she had seen of the family, she surmised, with a dose of optimism that they would probably be forced to overlook John's lowly background. Physical work must be a great leveller, she thought. Back home, a rich man would hardly speak to a working man except to give him orders. No one could imagine people from the upper classes wielding a spade or an axe.

'And there is no need to call her Miss Felicity... nor Miss Eleanore,' he said, 'Mr Cobjohn has also said to call him Paul, but I think he likes being called Captain.'

'You like her, don't you?' John ignored the question.

'I call him Captain when he is with other people, our clients or suppliers... otherwise, when there are just us, I call him Paul, he likes that.'

'I am afraid of him, I couldn't possibly call him Paul.'

'Kitty,' her brother said, looking at her intently, 'you are afraid of no one!' And he laughed a laugh which was an echo of a distant past, the sort of manifestation of joy only children remember how to produce; and each instinctively understood its magic, for in the blinking of an eye, they were in each other's arms, holding each other, tears of joy streaking down their cheeks, not even themselves, knowing why.

Although Kitty would have preferred to cook for the two of them, the Cobjohns said that would be a waste of time which could be put to better use. The two families continued to eat together. Seated at table for a roast goose that Jane had prepared that night, Felicity who was seated opposite John as usual, stole furtive looks at him, which only Kitty caught. The young girl was clearly dreading the end of a tradition that she wished continued forever, as the evening meal was the one occasion when she could see John to her heart's content. She was convinced that he reciprocated her feelings for him, but he had never said anything and usually avoided being alone with her. Why? She was eighteen... well in her eighteenth year... and many of her friends in Scotland were betrothed at seventeen, some of them married! She suspected that her brother might not like their association because of his lowly birth. She had hinted to Eleanore, whom she thought of as a no-nonsense sort of woman, about her feelings for the young Highlander, in the hope that she might give her approval and offer to talk to her husband, but she had been noncommittal. Still noncommittal was better than disapproving. Why would they object to John? He was an honest boy... eh... young man. He was as handsome as a Hussar, and he did not even need a uniform or plumes to achieve his bearing and deportment to make all the young ladies in the area swoon, except that there were very few around. If Bonnyrig was such a success, he deserved at least half the credit. There must be a reason why Paul wanted to keep the two families together, she reasoned out. It must be that he had understood where her inclinations lay, and was, in his own way, playing Cupid... yes, he is quite a romantic, my dear brother... But why did John have to hide his true feeling for her? Was he afraid that they might upset Paul? Would it upset him? She understood why he might not welcome such an attachment. She had never been too keen to encourage the lower classes to step out of line when she was a teenager in Stirlingshire. Papa who was very enlightened had said that the lower classes had to be dealt with fairness and judiciousness, whatever that meant, that excessive familiarity with them could cause confusion, and upset the natural balance between peoples of different breeding, which she had understood meant that it was best not to be too friendly with them. But that was a rule which had seemed normal for back there. This was a new country, people do things differently here. A man of high birth can often be seen sweating by the side of a rough coarse individual, doing some superhuman task together. Do the same rules need to apply? In any case, a boy of John's exceptional ability was surely going to end up a rich and powerful landowner himself some day, so why make a fuss? She must muster enough courage to corner him some day and challenge him to say that he did not love her.

Kitty was initially overawed by the surroundings, the never-ending expanse of forests. Everything made the Highland of her birth seem like a miniature of sorts. She would enjoy the new life, the friendliness, the good wholesome food. She was stunned when she heard that they were eating a goose, imagining that they only did that in fairy tales. She had never sat a table with a cloth on it, she could count on the fingers of one hand the number of times she had eaten meat without gristle and bones. The meat she had eaten was usually boiled to the point of disintegration. Conversation at table was new to her. Back home one ate in silence. I may speak differently to these well-bred ladies, but I have learnt my grammar and I know my vocabulary, and John is right, I am afraid of no one. Miss Eleanore... OK Eleanore... is a decent lady... woman. Paul is a bit stuffy, but well-meaning... he must be, to judge by how he treats Oor John! And the young princess seems besotted by him... and why shouldn't she be? Emily idolises him. In two years he will be able to buy his own land and in ten, he'd be a bigger farmer than the captain, he's so tireless. Ah there's John Smith, remember me? Aye... the owner of Bonnyrig... sure I remember you, Paul, how's things? Actually, Smith, things have not been too bright for me lately, old chap. I am sorry to hear that Cobjohn, but damned glad to see you, old chap, what can I do for you?

I hate to ask, old chap, but I have a cash flow problem, I wonder —. But my dear fellow, I will be delighted to help, I just received a handsome payment for a consignment of wheat, how much did you need? Five hundred pounds, can you afford such a big sum? But my dear fellow, it will be a pleasure, I won't hear of anything less than a thousand. Kitty… Oh, my sister Kitty is the keeper of my funds. Kitty go get the captain here one thousand pounds. This reverie was brought to a sudden end by Jane. More soup Miss? Thank you, no thank you.

Kitty got used to the routine of life at Bonnyrig. She wore fine but simple frocks in the mornings and did accounts and wrote letters with Eleanore, and sometimes Felicity. The three women worked harmoniously together. In the afternoon, they underwent their transformation and became carpenters, loggers or trench diggers. Kitty felt so healthy that sometimes it was as if she could feel the blood coursing in her veins, irrigating her whole body… if that was what blood did.

Kitty had spotted Kit, the young Irish hand since the first day, and thought that he was a rather pleasant young fellow, if a bit callow and clumsy. He loved to banter although he was not much good at it. She had noticed him leering at her, no doubt egged on by his two other compatriots, Mike and Sean, and when he approached her one afternoon, and said, 'Ach, Kitty, I, eh… I mean you… eh…' she had laughed and answered, 'You lust after me, isn't that right, Kit Mahoney?' She had no idea that she had said this. Kit had begun to protest, and had turned his back to beat a hasty retreat.

'I don't bite,' she had said laughingly. Kit had turned back incredulously.

'You mean… eh…'

'I mean, if you were going to invite me for a walk in the forest, I am not afraid of bears.'

She had been celibate for too long. During that miserable crossing, she had found that one way of coping with her pain and misery was to close her eyes and imagine that her fingers were Rob Rob's and thus soothe herself to sleep. The other women could not know what she was doing, or maybe they too, poor souls were trying to revive dead memories. Since arriving in Oxenham, she had felt deprived. She was a full-blooded woman with normal needs and she knew that she needed a man, and she was not one to beat about the bush. This fellow Kit was desirable enough, and if he wanted a bit of comfort, why she was going to give it to him. It was thus that she and Kit started their fling. It did not take the poor lad long before he said he wanted to marry her. No, she was not after a husband, she had a man somewhere, he had been temporarily misplaced, but he will come for her some day. Till a' the seas gang dry... Kit had not seemed heart-broken, when she started disappearing into the woods with Mike. She then thought that it would be mean to Sean if he was left out. She did not ask for romance, and for a time the three Irish lads took turns to satisfy her needs. Brother John found out, was not very happy about it, but thought that he had no right to put his nose in her business.

John decided that a line was to be drawn when Kitty started disappearing into the wilds with Mark, Dan Wahaitiya's son, and he thought he should remind her of some house rules. Kitty was surprised and disappointed, for she had assumed that he would have taken a different view, since she had seen him treat the Ojibwas and Cayugas with courtesy and friendliness.

He had been silent all evening, and Kitty knew what this was all about.

'John, if you have something to say to me, you had better say it now, before I go to bed.' John knew his sister's forthright ways and took a deep breath to collect his thoughts. He nodded and indicated a chair. She sat down.

'I don't know how to put this...'

'How about, Kitty, I don't like you having an Ojibwa lover...'

'Oh Kitty, how can you? I am not a... what do you call it, an Indian-hater... it has nothing to do with... different races...'

'He is a Christian... and tell me since when have you become such a defender of the Christian faith anyway?'

'No, it's not that...' But John was unable to make sense, he muttered incoherent words, and his sister knew that he was not clear in his mind what he disliked about the association. John had known about the Irish lads, and so clearly it was not her virtue that he was worried about. Suddenly the truth hit her.

'John, tell me honestly, do you think that if I associate with Wahaitiya's son, it will compromise your... I mean you and Felicity? Is that it?'

'Felicity has nothing to do with this,' he said in what was the nearest he had ever shouted at her since the time when they were bickering children. Kitty did not believe him.

'You're right, lassie,' he said in a whisper, but mumbled something indistinct about their low birth. Kitty nodded.

'John, if that's an impediment to your happiness, I will stop seeing Mark. I'll even give you my word.'

'You would do that for me?'

'Look, between me and Mark, it is different from what happened before... I believe he is the man who can make me stop pining for eh... the impossible, but yes, for my little brother, I will, it's a promise.'

For some time, the captain had been contemplating building a chapel on his land, as he felt that Christianity had to be developed in parallel with the resources of the land, specially as an uncle had died in Stirlingshire leaving him with a few thousand pounds. To this effect he had invited the Reverend Tom MacNeill vicar of St John's in Peterborough, his wife Hannah and their twins Gordon and Leah over for a couple of days. It was the first time the family would have visitors staying with them, as they now had the facility, the new extension having just been completed.

Kitty and Hannah who had also been through the ignominies of the clearance immediately warmed up to each other. She combined her work as mother and pastor's wife with running a small school, and had half joking suggested that if Kitty was prepared to take starvation wages, the church might find a way of employing her. Tom had pointed out that the Bishop in Toronto had advertised for a teacher, both in Scotland and in Toronto, so she had better be quick if she wanted to take up the offer. Gordon and Leah seemed to adore her, and they played all sorts of running and skipping games together. Father MacNeill seemed a straightforward and honest person. Having been been under the influence of Grand Mam, she knew that she had better not show her cards and decided that the best thing when it came to religion was to go along with it for the time being, and reconsider her position when she would have the leisure and the freedom to think things over.

When the MacNeills left, the twins made her promise that she would come for a visit soon. She had approached the man of the cloth, and asked him if she might become a teacher at St John's, in the light of having been an unmarried mother. He would never contemplate encouraging her to leave what was obviously a sound position here at Bonnyrig, he had said. She thought that it was his way of saying no. But on the morning of their departure, he approached her and asked if she was serious about coming to Peterborough. She had no doubt that it was dear Hannah who had changed his mind for him. She replied that she was, but would need to talk to John and to Eleanore. Well, make up your mind, and if when I get back I find that the Bishop in Toronto has not sent me someone, I'll get back to you.

Ever since the visitors went back to Peterborough, she had started giving serious consideration to going there and taking that teaching post. That would at least solve a few problems. In any case she had never expected to spend the rest of her life working with her hands, tilling the soil and heaving heavy loads, she was born to teach.

Next morning, she walked straight towards Mark's wigwam, where she had so often laid with him in the past. He beamed with pleasure.

'I often wish you can come in the morning, when I am very manly.' He tried to grab her, but she resisted. He noticed her sullen demeanour.

'Mark, I am sorry, but you and I… we must stop.'

'Why?' he asked, half hoping that she was playing some game with him. You never know with white folks.

'We just have to, I am going to move to Peterborough.' And she had turned her back on him, in an attempt to rush out, but he grabbed her arm, and she suddenly had an irresistible urge to have him one last time, so she yielded, and she experienced an orgasm which was the nearest she had ever had to an out of body experience. Mark thought that the cloud had passed, and let her go. She went on her way, promising herself that that was the last time.

'I won't let you,' said Mark almost tearfully, 'never!'

She was full of confusion. One moment she was absolutely convinced that there was no better solution than to go to Peterborough, but the next she admitted to herself that she was addicted to him like she had heard only recently about people becoming addicted to opium.

In the office, Eleanore noticed that she seemed distant and edgy and asked what the matter was.

'Tell me, Eleanore dear, I think we all know that Felicity and John are attracted to each other —'

'Yes, I think we can safely say that.'

'Do you have any objection to John?' Eleanore laughed.

'No, of course not,' she replied without thinking. Clearly she had given the matter some thought, in order to have such a ready answer, 'Why do you ask?'.

'The captain? What does he think?'

'I am not sure, Kitty, you know what men are like, they do not like to take advice from women, he has never said anything clearly, but I think, from certain signs, the way he looks at John, the way he talks to Felicity, that he knows about them and does not disapprove. But I am only guessing.'

Kitty had not finished, she had not yet started, when Felicity walked in at that moment, a good hour earlier than she was expected, explaining that she had lost her patience with the composition she had been writing for Paul, who acted as her tutor.

In the afternoon, Kitty found Eleanore taking a short rest, and broached the subject again.

'Eleanore, can I trust you?' Of course she could.

'Is the captain… likely to be… to object to John, if his sister was misbehaving?'

'Since you ask, I think Paul, like everybody else, knows that you are not an angel. Pamelas only exist in the imagination of the likes of Mr Richardson's. We know you lost your baby in the crossing… you are a normal woman… we're not living in the Middle Ages, this is the nineteenth century, gel.'

'Everybody knows?' Kitty was taken aback. Although she had been very open about her association with the Irish boys, instinctively she had known that with Mark, it was a different situation, and had taken extra care when meeting him, something that Mark, who had witnessed lynchings of Blacks and Indians readily agreed to.

'And he doesn't mind?'

'In spite of appearances, he is no prude… and we do live on a farm where he sees what the goats and chickens get up to.'

'Doesn't he mind that Mark is not a white man?'

'What? Who the hell is Mark? Surely you don't mean that Ojibwa fellow?' Kitty said nothing. Suddenly Eleanore burst out laughing.

'The Ojibwa fellow! Well I never! You are a crafty one... and I must say I think he is the handsomest man in the whole of Ontario! Such muscles, such bearing... such a nose... aquiline, I think they call it... and what a tan!'

'Are you saying that's not a problem?' There was no immediate answer.

'No. I am saying that I do not find anything wrong in it myself, but I have no idea what my dear spouse thinks.'

'You think that if he finds out about my liaison with a... eh... native he will not sanction a union between —'

'I really don't know... I... eh... think that may well be his position,' was the glum reply, 'men are so... unreasonable.'

'That's what I thought... I have already told Mark that we shouldn't see each other again...'

'You mean you put John's interest above your own?'

'It's not as you're implying. I am no saint or heroine from some book, it's just that I have no right to compromise my little brother's chance of happiness.'

'Oh, Kitty, you're such a dear wonderful person.' Kitty suddenly had an idea.

'What would you say if I told you that I am thinking of moving to Peterborough if Father MacNeill will have me.'

'Oh, as a teacher? Excellent idea,' adding sadly, 'but we will miss you.'

'You mean you really did not know about me and Mark?' Kitty asked after a moment of silence.

'No, I swear I didn't know a thing.'

'What was that thing about which you knew nothing?' asked Felicity, whom neither woman had seen or heard coming in.

'Since it's something I knew nothing about, it would be a waste of time talking about it, wouldn't you say?' replied the older woman. Felicity pulled her tongue out at her playfully. I could learn a thing or two from that woman, thought Kitty, even if I could teach her to spell.

As the two older women were unable to talk privately, they listened to the young girl complaining about the sort of things her brother expected her to learn.

'Il m'eût plu plus s'il eût plu plus! Stupid Subjunctive verbs… When might I need to use that,' said the young girl almost tearfully, 'anyway I hate rain.'

But Kitty was not listening. If for weeks nobody had discovered what was going on in Mark's wigwam, why wouldn't it be possible to carry on as before? She loved this young brave, who knows where Rob Rob is? He was so young and helpless, how could he have resisted the schemes and plots hatched by his godmother the Duchess and his powerful father, without her help. Be realistic, woman, she told herself, the Rob Rob chapter is closed. For weeks and months her tale had evolved like in those penny serials, with something new happening in every new instalment. Now the author had written THE END at the bottom, and not TO BE CONTINUED. Nobody can change the plot. The seas have gang dry! All one can do is to wait for the start of the next new serial. And it had better be a good one, with a nice happy ending.

CHAPTER 11

◆◆◆

Oxenham On (2)

KITTY HAD ALWAYS had self-knowledge, and knew that her passionate nature would have made it impossible for her to lead a life of chastity, and so, conceding to herself that she would never be able to keep her promise to John, she reversed her decision to stop meeting Mark, but increased her vigilance — at least for the time being.

Mark was a fund of knowledge of Ojibwa traditions and religions. He knew where the secret scrolls were buried. He was an expert carver and made sculptures in mica, bones and wood. He admitted to Kitty that he had converted to Christianity in name only, to please the elders who thought that there was no harm in it, as long as one did not forget Midewiwin, their own religion. He found the story of Christ being three in one confusing, and could not believe the story of the one fish that fed a whole tribe. As a skilful fishermen, he would have found it easier to believe that one man needed many fish, and not the other way round. He told her about how his ancestors had made maps on birch scrolls, of rivers and mountains, and spoke about geometrical concepts, but only as a sort of game they played.

John finally revealed his feelings for her to Felicity when she challenged him, and she was overjoyed. For over a year, the teenage girl had been dreaming of being in the arms of the man she had loved from the very beginning, of offering him her lips to be embraced. She had never doubted that he felt the same way about her, and now she knew for sure. She had guessed why he had been reticent in declaring his love, as she was well aware of the difference of birth, but she thought that he was such an exceptionally accomplished man in every way that it did not matter. Well, yes, she agreed that the lower classes were not the same, but how could she help falling in love with such a man? Love is blind, a princess can fall in love with a swineherd, or a prince

402

with a beggar girl. She will love her John with all her might, smooth out his coarseness and educate him in the manners of high society, not that they were likely to have balls and banquets in the backwoods. As a girl she used to dream about life in the high society, wearing nice gowns and pearls, and dancing with a fluttering fan, although she drew the line at masks — why would any pretty girl want to have a bird face? When father died, the family had to live in reduced circumstances, and she had thought that it was most unfair. What would she have done without Paul? He was so straightforward, such a brick. Surely he would not object to John as a brother-in-law, how could he? He had allowed, even encouraged her to work with tools on the estate, he was not someone who liked finery and silks for himself. Surely as a loving brother, he would want her happiness and there was no way she could ever be happy in this life without John. Eleanore had started encouraging her lately and had promised that if Paul was not amenable to her inclination then she would talk to him. She hoped that it would never come to that.

The Captain seemed to expect this, and when Eleanore broached the subject, he saw no objection, although admittedly he felt a little bit uneasy. Theirs was an aristocratic family with Scottish kings as ancestors, and as such, he would have preferred a man of noble birth, but on a personal level, he knew that John had nobility of character, and questioned himself as to which one was better, the latter or an accident of birth. But were there such a thing as an accident of birth? The good Lord did not do things by accident, which suggested that the Otonabee incident had happened by the design of the Creator. Overruling the inbuilt prejudices of centuries, he had come to the conclusion that in a land of harsh realities which was also a land of unimaginable potential, one had to rewrite the rules. No, John would be much better than any duke as a partner for sweet dear Felicity. Her happiness transcended all other concerns. He liked the young Highlander, had done so from the beginning, when he had shown such selflessness and such extraordinary gifts of natural leadership, not only during the crisis on the Otonabee, but in countless other situations. Without him, Bonnyrig would be neither bonny nor well-rigged! Who said he had no sense of fun, eh! He must remember to repeat this bon mot to his wife. She had been such a brick. He could have cried with joy when he first saw her in dungarees, asking for a spade so she could start working on the fields. He admitted to himself that he found his wife in dungarees a sexually explosive figure. How he wished that he had the courage to ask her to wear them in the bedroom on occasions. She, the daughter of a duke, who grew up in a house where she was served on silver plates by maids, who used to be dressed by attendants… He was the luckiest of men, and he had shown that he could adapt to the backwoods, although no doubt meeting John had made it easier. Yes, Felicity could not find a better man. They were young and obviously in love. Yes, he would give them his blessing without hesitation.

John had been so full of joy when he broke the news to Kitty, and was stunned by her silence.

'What's the matter, sister?' She raised her face to him, and he saw her tear-filled eyes.

'I am sure now that I am pregnant,' she said gloomily.

'How could you?' he asked angrily. She said nothing.

'Whose is it?' he asked with a sneer.

'John, I told you that Mark Wahaitiya was special, you are just being nasty. You were always a nasty little prick!' He said nothing, and she ran out, looking for Mark, shouting, 'Don't worry, I won't shame you, I am going away.'

The last thing Kitty wanted was to compromise John's position, so there was only one thing to do: go away from Bonnyrig, from Oxenham, possibly from Ontario. She hoped that no one had responded to the advert that Tom MacNeill had spoken about. She would take her chances and go to Peterborough on the off chance, and if the teaching post was no longer available, she would seek employment elsewhere. She knew that if one looked properly, it should not be too difficult to find a teaching post somewhere, as schools were being created all the time.

She informed Mark about her decision, and he was shocked. No, he said, he will never let her go away, and if she did, he would have nothing to live for. You can join me, she said. They argued for hours, and finally it was decided that she would try Peterborough, but she would come see him regularly.

John was equally devastated, he did not want to lose his sister. He knew that she was avoiding him, and sought her out. He found her sitting under a large hemlock and went and sat by her side. For a long while they said nothing, then they found themselves holding each other like lovers, but still saying nothing.

'I wish I could tell you that it does not matter what they think, that you come first, but I can't. If you think that it is best for you to go away, don't go too far, I can't afford to lose you again.'

'Aye,' she said, but with twinkling eyes, added, 'doesn't mean you're not a nasty little prick, though.'

A church school is never going to want a teacher with a child born out of wedlock, John said sadly. Surprisingly, Kitty who was somebody who thought all things out and from all possible angles had not considered that. She had been so impressed by the MacNeills that she had assumed that they would see no impediment to her condition. Now suddenly like a big cloud passing above can change a sunny picnic into a cold and gloomy ordeal, it dawned upon her that indeed her aspirations might come to a dead end. She now became convinced that there was no hope of a solution. The cloud had since become a downpour. Cobjohn, with his deep religious convictions would order them both out of his property. Why had she not thought things over first? She was too impulsive, too red-blooded.

'No, dear Kitty,' John said to comfort her, 'it will never come to that, go to Peterborough if you must, maybe it is for the best, but if that does not work, come back, we will talk to Paul,' adding with another twinkle, 'he'll be lost without me, you know'

When Kitty arrived at St John's she was received like a long lost relative. The twins squealed with joy when they saw 'Aunt Kitty'. Hannah reacted like it was Christmas, and even Father Tom beamed with pleasure. Hannah made some tea and produced some scones that she had baked only the day before. Kitty explained that she had something to discuss with Father Tom, and his wife took the protesting children away. She asked if he still needed a teacher, and he was delighted to say yes, the job was hers. The one young woman the Bishop interviewed, was deficient in arithmetic. He repeated that there was very little money in it, but said that she would live in a small room in the school itself, and would have her Sunday lunch with the family.

'I don't want more,' she said.

'But there is one thing, Father Tom...'

'Tom, please.'

'Tom, I happen to be pregnant,' she said, and at the same time his wife came back. The couple seemed shocked and stared at each other in silence.

'Hmm...' finally said Tom.

'That's a problem, isn't it?'

'Could be.'

'Does the father want to marry you?' Hannah asked, and she nodded.

'In that case there should be no problem,' Tom said with a tentative smile.

'There is another problem, Tom,' Kitty said, 'the father of the child is an Ojibwa.'

Another stunned silence. The three people looked at each other in turn, none of them knowing how to deal with this situation. Finally it was Kitty who broke the silence.

'I think I have wasted enough of your time, I am sorry to have put you on the spot, it was thoughtless of me.'

'Don't be silly, lassie,' said the vicar's wife, 'why should that be a problem?' Tom looked away and disguised his discomfiture in a diplomatic cough.

'The Bishop might not sanction it,' he said still looking away, whereupon his wife rushed out and the two looked at her in surprise saying nothing. Hannah reappeared with something in her hand. She came towards her husband and thrust the object in his hand. It was a bible.

'Thomas MacNeill,' she said, 'show me in here, where it says that a Scottish Christian cannot marry an Ojibwa Christian.' Kitty knew that the battle was won.

'Dearest, I am not saying I object, all I am saying is that the Bishop in Toronto is a strict —'. She wafted her hand dismissively made a face and pulled her head back slightly, and Tom said no more.

'Welcome to St John's,' said Hannah. Some woman, thought Kitty.

Eleanore hoped that since the possible source of scandal, Kitty, had gone away, Paul would not now change his mind about Felicity and John when informed of the condition of the sister of his brother-in-law-to-be. The captain knew nothing about the turn that events had taken until the night of

Kitty's departure, when they were seated in their sitting room where they often sat after a meal, reading from some book sent from Scotland, drinking a small glass of port before going to bed, and his wife went behind his chair and fondled his hair. He sensed that something was afoot, and that she was preparing him for it. So he did what he usually did under the circumstances, he hummed something tunelessly.

'Yes,' Eleanore said, massaging his neck, 'Kitty's gone.'

'And when will she be back?'

'I don't know about that, probably never.' Paul jumped on hearing this, whereupon she told him about Mark and the child she was expecting.

'And why did she go away?'

'Don't be silly, she thought we wouldn't approve of John and Felicity marrying under the circumstances.'

'Do we? Disapprove?'

'No, of course not, but she thought you might...'

'Felicity would be marrying John, not his sister,' he said, perplexed. 'I'll have you know that one of the reasons I decided to leave Perthshire was that back home people impose too many restrictions on themselves. We came to a new country, and we should adopt new, more intelligent values. I am surprised that you did not know that about me.' She looked at him, her admiration clear for the whole world to see. He shook his head slightly.

'Which does not mean that I approve of congress outside wedlock.'

'Paul,' she said happily, 'you are a strange man, and I love you for it.' He hmmed hmmed again. She felt a sudden surge of love mounting in her, for her man, like sap up a maple tree at the start of spring.

'And what if the Reverend MacNeill refuses to help her?' The optimistic Eleanore had not envisaged that possibility.

'Send her word tomorrow, that she can come back here anytime. Did we leave the conventions and false morality of dear Britain in order to fall into the same morass here?' Yes, yes, she thought happily, you made your point. A man and wife become wed at church by a priest, and indeed so were the two of them, but it was tonight, after seeing behind the dark side of the moon so to say, that she felt that Paul and her had become truly one. Had she guessed about what he thought of her in dungarees, she would have rushed and changed, but sadly he will never tell her.

'No, beloved, of course we did not.' After a pause, he hmmed hmmed again.

'Yes dear?'

'I hope they marry, the Ojibwa chappie and Kitty, I mean.'

'I expect they will want to.' After a short pause, he added.

'Now that our hands are not tied by any of the old country's prejudices, we will be at liberty to create a new order.'

O my lovely sweet pompous magnificent man!

Tom MacNeill himself celebrated the union of the Ojibwa man and Kitty, the first time such a marriage had taken place in the Maritime, as far as anybody knew.

John and Felicity tied the knot two years later after. A week after that felicitous event, a letter arrived from home, informing them of the passing away of Grand Mam.

Seven months later Kitty gave birth to her daughter Eleanore, named for the woman who was to become her best friend and ally in this world.

CHAPTER 12

◆◆◆

Young Raju's Ebony Fish

YOUNG RAJU HAD always had antennae. He surmised, made deductions, never asked questions. It was not thought proper for a child to do so. A child must always be ready to listen and obey. There was one exception. Pradeep loved to reminisce about the things that had happened to the family, and Raju wishing to know all the details was encouraged to question him then. At an early age he had already sensed his grandfather Jayant's passion for Dadima Shanti. No one had told him. The adults used to joke and say that people should be careful when the boy was around. If you mislaid a glance, they said, the boy would pick it up and learn secrets from it. He knew the meaning of two quick blinks of the eye, a hardly imperceptible turn of the head as an eye-contact avoidance measure, the slightest hesitation at the start of a sentence. He had guessed that it was a one-sided affair, and that it had never entirely evaporated over the years, like when a pan of water has boiled dry, there is always a faint white trace left at the bottom. He never openly talked about these things, but he made oblique comments which everybody understood, thought daring. However, their indulgence for the much-loved seven-year old made them pretend that they had not picked upon the offending allusions. He knew that Grandpa Jayant was devoted to Grandma Jyoti, and that he made her as happy as it was possible to be, but the fact that he fussed a little too much over when Shanti was around was not lost on him.

A word picked up here and there had informed the boy that from the very beginning, his grandpa had been dubious about granny Shanti's second marriage to the inept Kishore, the inept suitor that the Musselman Murtaza had introduced her to. Murtaza was an intriguing presence in the family. Musselman folks were looked upon with suspicion, but not him. He was perplexed and questioned Pradeep who told him what a comfort and help the man had been to the family in their needy days. But it went both ways, his father told him. In the beginning, he was a big support to Grandma Shanti, but at times he needed her help too. And with pride, Pradeep told the boy the story of how once, when he was in a real fix, Murtaza had come to Shanti who was then rolling in money and asked for a loan. Pradeep, so full of admiration for his mother marvelled at her gratitude. However her immediate response to the man who had done her a hundred favours had been negative. She had claimed that she did not have any money at the moment, but perhaps in a month… Pradeep remembered how Murtaza had said nothing and had left a broken man, for she was his last resort, and he was facing ruin. But you said Dadima was a grateful person, the boy had said. Yes, yes, listen to the rest, Pradeep had said.

In the middle of the night, Shanti came to wake her son up, and with tears in her eyes had explained that she could not sleep, so much was her conscience troubling her. How could I act in such an ungrateful manner to one who has always been a sincere and dependable friend? I am turning into a bad person, she had said as tears rolled down her cheeks. How can you say that, Ma Jaan, Pradeep had protested. I am becoming a miser, valuing money above my own friends. Anyway, she had given him a large sum of money, more than Murtaza had asked for, and asked him to set out in the middle of the night to go to Murtaza's.

'Explain to him that the moment he had left, whatshisname came in and settled his debts in full,' she had said. Such elegance, your Grandma.

Anyway Granny and Kishore had married and Jayant had wished that the new husband would help her find the happiness she deserved, but he had known from the start that he was not the man for her. He had even been sorry when the poor fellow, unable to settle on the island, and clearly accepting that the marriage had failed, finally returned to Calcutta. He was greatly relieved that Shanti had taken his departure in her stride.

Grandad Jayant never wasted time pining for the woman he had loved since time began. Once, he started telling about a dream he had had of their Sundarban days, featuring his friend the old Raju and Dadima going down the Matla River, and he had blushed and blinked and could not continue. Raju guessed that devoted as he was to Jyoti, this passion, unlike the extinct Trou aux Cerfs was a dormant one.

Raju, without seemingly listening to the endless stories of hardship and hard work, knew how proud the two grandparents were of their prosperity. Jayant never failed to mention who his inspiration was.

'If Bhabi Shanti who is only a woman, could accomplish so much, I told myself, I should aim to achieve half of what she has done,' he said merrily, tapping the space on his upturned fist between his index and middle finger of his left hand with the pointing finger of the right, producing a faint rhythmic sound resonating with the quick movements of his head left to right, but he instantly added, 'I say only a woman, but what a woman!'

He too had also managed to buy a small plot of land to begin with, and this had enabled him to make good money which he had used to buy a small sugar cane field, but as money poured into his coffers, he kept buying more. He was comfortable, but was not in the same league as her, and refused any comparison. Whilst the far richer woman counted every cent she spent, Jayant never hesitated to spend lavishly on his loved ones. He showered upon Jyoti and his daughter Prabha all manner of fineries, silk saris and gold bangles, earrings and necklaces, spectacular things that he loved them to wear, but he himself would never hear of changing his simple dhotis, coarse cotton kurtas and cheap leather sandals for more expensive ones.

Shanti never gave up working in the fields, mainly because she had always loved the open air, but above all, she loved being in charge. Besides she had discovered that when one kept a close eye on the workers, it did wonders for productivity. On his part, Jayant was content to let others do the work for which he paid them reasonable wages, and he left them in peace, and was not unhappy with the result.

His house in Floréal was quite extravagant compared to Shanti's in Rivière Sèche. She had kept the original structure and simply built extensions, and it looked a bit ramshackle. It could have benefited from a lick of paint but Shanti said that she hated extravagance. Raju thought that its chaotic exterior was what gave the place its unexpected charm. Whilst she was never really happy, never ceasing to mourn her lost husband, Jayant considered himself specially blessed. Bhagwan has thought it fit to shower worldly riches upon my unworthy self, he often said. His generosity was proverbial, although Shanti said that he was too credulous and would surely live to regret his trust in people he hardly knew.

He was surprised that being disappointed in love had not turned him into an embittered grump.

Young Raju flourished in this atmosphere where love reigned supreme. He knew that he was loved and cosseted by all, needed no encouragement to exercise his great capacity to tell stories. The old adage that children were to be seen and not heard, did not apply to him. He invented stories, mixed them with age-old tales and adages, created new words, loved to make rhymes — not all of them silly — and everybody had a good laugh. He revelled in this adulation. What the adults loved more than anything, was when the boy narrated the story of the wedding of his parents, making them all scream with delight when he claimed with a serious face that he was there, even if he had not been born yet. Those who listened to him half believed that he was indeed.

Grandpa Jayant, having sold some cows for much more than he had expected on the previous day, woke up one morning, convinced that Bhagwan was planning to further his bliss. He had always loved young Pradeep as a son, but his ambition to make him into a real son not having worked, he had always entertained what he thought was an idle dream of making him his son-in-law. Idle, not only because the boy was seven years older than his Prabha, but also because he knew that Shanti had every right to wish for someone from a better family. Shanti would interrupt at this point, blush and vehemently deny this. I was the one who had instructed the Pandit to approach Jayant to sound him on the possible union between my Pradeep and his Prabha, she said, forcing a little laugh.

Jayant thought he might burst with happiness. This union was going to be a symbol of the near mystic link between their two families. He felt that it was like bringing his old friend Raju back to life in some ways. The latter had been unreserved in his love for him. In their Sunderban days, he had been a much admired youngster and could have had any number of friends, but he had chosen the younger, lowly orphan boy. There had never been any cloud over their relationship. Although Raju was older, against custom, he never once had a harsh word for his younger friend, never belittled him, never ordered him about. Only after having Raju dancing merrily in his head did he think of the young people who were going to be joined together in holy matrimony.

'Arrey, Panditji,' Grandpa was supposed to have said, 'the marriage between our two children, is the apotheosis of my life. I can never experience anything as glorious, it is as if my soul has gone out of my body and is dancing over my head and then re-entering it again. I can hear bells, angelic children laughing, singing Oms. Our two families coming together is like Lord Rama and Sita being reunited after the vanquishing of the evil Ravanna. Of course I am delighted to give my lovely Prabha to the son of my better-than-brother Raju. Tell Shanti Bhabi, tell the whole world! We'll have the best, the most grandiose wedding that this island will ever see. In fifty years people will still talk about it. I was there, at the wedding of Jayant's daughter Prabha and Raju's son Pradeep, they will say. It was like a marriage between a Maharajah and a Princess.'

The boy narrator knew all about the todo between Shanti who had been against expensive jewellery, and Jayant with his no expense spared attitude.

'The necklace that Ma wore on the wedding day,' he said, without revealing the fact that it was Jayant who had finally footed the jeweller's massive bill, 'was so heavy that she had to make an effort to keep her neck upright as she walked seven times round the fire with my Pitaji.'

'And Nanabaji spent many a sleepless night wracking his brains about how and where to find a white horse for the groom,' the boy narrator said. Jayant laughed and said that he had known from the start that the white man Monsieur de la Varicelle to whom he usually sold his entire cane harvest would oblige him in that, albeit in the hope of getting some small discount later. Dadima Shanti was against a big wedding, but Grandpa Jayant said that it was the bride's father's call, and that happiness could not be counted in terms of money…

Two whole weeks before the big day, two baskets of the choicest mehndi arrived in Floréal, were promptly crushed by the servants on the spice stone crusher, and all the women and girls had their hands hennaed, a process which meant them holding the mushy paste in the palm of their hands for one whole night. Even the boys were indulged, but only to the extent that they were only allowed to have the tip of their small fingers painted.

Jayant had recently acquired a vast one-acre uncultivated field next door to his dwelling, for which he had big plans, but immediately after the union was contemplated, he halted the plans. He was going to use this maidan for the wedding festivities.

He arranged for the field to be shorn of all its wild growths, and made his plans. He wanted a huge marquee to seat his three hundred guests. He ordered a cartload of seating mats, hand-woven from a craftsman in Vacoas. Next to the main tent he erected a smaller tent to house the musicians and natakwallahs in drag, then some distance away, because of the smoke, two similar tents, one, exclusively for the preparation of the many dishes which he had planned for, and next to it, the eating area.

'And what a menu Nanabaji had elaborated!' And the unborn narrator made a mouthwatering list. The Musselman family friend Murtaza had married his only daughter to a bhandari who had only recently arrived from the home country, whose ancestors had been cooks for the Maharajah of Bihar, and Grandpa Jayant had secured his services. Some family friends had frowned. 'Why use the services of a Musselman?' They had asked, 'These people eat cow.' But Jayant had assured them that the Pandit, to whom Murtaza had once made a substantial loan had given his approval.

Jayant inspired by a dream, designed a decoration made of six bamboo poles criss-crossing each other near the top and tied at that point, flaunting coloured pennants in the breeze. Dozens of these were planted at regular intervals all over the maidan. Everybody agreed that it was a most felicitous idea.

The betel-chewing Gheevalla had only one eye, but in his trade, it was not sight but smell which was of the essence. The man did not judge the quantity of the salt needed for a mix by looking at it, rather he smelled a handful, and decided there and then if he needed more or less. Smell and taste. It is said that his taste buds were of such refinement, that if he but sniffed a sauce, he could tell you if the onions had been cut lengthwise or sideways. Gheevalla demanded a number of helpers, and they worked for two days and two nights to prepare the ingredients. The flour had to be mixed for the puris, and the kneading was done by three amateur wrestlers sitting round a large wooden vat which was large enough for a tall man to lie in the middle without having to bend his knees. Besan or chickpea flour for the pakoras was processed in a large degh, a cauldron. The bandhari took great care not to divulge the secrets that had kept Maharajah's palates entranced for centuries, and would prepare all the ingredients in a corner of the tent. If one of his assistants but inadvertently walked in, he would benefit from the full force of his ire.

Grandpa must have bought a whole barrel of ghee, fifty chicken, two goats, five baskets of the freshest rougets, reputed to be the best that the ocean nurtured, six hundred eggs, two sacks of flour, a sack of dal. Vegetables, peas, bindhis, tomatoes, baighan, gobi, dudhis were delivered to the Floréal house in carts. As were baskets of pineapple and lychees, fruits which they had hardly ever eaten back home. A number of three-women teams crouched on the mats were merrily cleaning and cutting the greens, humming and telling jokes. One group were shelling the peas, another peeling the potatoes, yet another scraping the bindhis. 'Bindhi must never be washed,' Gheevalla had decreed, 'they must only be scraped with a clean knife.'

We children were discouraged from coming into the working areas, Raju went on with a serious face, but nothing could stop us. What we liked most was the spectacle offered by the pineapple peeler. She was all alone on her mat, and grabbing a pineapple by the crown with her left hand, deftly turning it upside down, and wielding the sharpest knife in the house in her right hand, like an expert swordsman his sword, she would cause the fruit to swivel round, bring the knife near it, and let it do the work for her, as if by magic. The denuded fruit was left with very small hairy and brown craters all over the surface, where the seeds resided, and it made our mouths water with anticipation as the juice dripped away, leaving the atmosphere filled with its appetising aroma. We gaped in wonderment as the old lady, holding the peeled fruit by the crown, upside down, made incisions round the offending cavities by means of quick movements centred round her wrists. Only after having lopped off the bulk of the crown, leaving just enough of it for handling, was the fruit deemed ready for the degustation of Nanabaji's esteemed guests.

One man had the onerous task of keeping the many fires going. Special rocks had been chosen, chiselled with great care so as to hold the massive copper deghs, and stacks of dried filaos wood were in readiness for the fire. A holy man seated under a solitary tree kept chanting all day to ensure that rain did not spoil the party. Bhagwan must have heard him, for the sun shone all day long that day.

The whole place was turned into a hive of activity since much before dawn. Even the children were up before the cock started crowing. As both Shanti and Jayant had friends from their indenture days who were now dispersed over the island, they had already arrived a few days earlier and Jayant had moved heaven and earth to provide them with all the comforts that money could buy. Grandma Shanti would have preferred that the money which had been extravagantly wasted in a show of vanity had been given to the young couple to buy them some more land.

'But as we all know, she never interferes.' said the child narrator winking.

Although Jayant possessed banana groves, he was not happy with the state of their leaves. My guests need dark green waxy leaves to eat from. The best, he had said, and Murtaza had scoured the island from north to south to find the right banana leaves, fit to serve a Maharajah on, and they were to arrive just in time to preserve their freshness.

Early in the morning oxcarts began to pull in the through the gates of the Floréal mansion. Pails of water and bales of fodder had been waiting for the hungry bullocks. Grandpa had thought of everything.

'That boy,' said Grandma Jyoti, 'must surely have been there, how does he know all those details? He must be the reincarnation of someone who was there. I wonder who he was.' She had said this a few times already and nobody paid any attention.

As the ladies started coming down their calèches, the jingle of their jewellery provided additional music to what the paid musicians and singers were rehearsing in their tent. The natural colours of the green fields and the many flowers growing upon them tried hard to match the colours of the ladies' saris and the fluttering pennants. The arriving guests hugged and cried tears of joy. Some had not met since they had landed from the *Startled Fawn*.

It was impossible to stop the spread of smoke, but gradually it became filled with the aroma of Gheevalla's spices, and so nobody minded. Verily that man was a Magician of the culinary arts. The crowd collectively began to feel their insides rumble with anticipation. How were they going to last through the unending ceremony, with the Pandit going on forever, with all the aromas hovering in the air?

'Arrey choop, beta,' admonished Grandma Shanti, 'a wedding is not just about eating, the Pandit needs to beg Bhagwan for so many blessings.'

Anyway people had cakes and things to eat before, and lots of rose-flavoured faloodas and lassis, nimbu pani with massive quantities of white sugar, hand-pressed mango juice in which crisp burnished gold onions fried in ghee floated… but this was only for the more important guests.'

And he spoke of pyramids of golden laddoos, pink peras, green barfis, all covered in gold leaves. They were so pretty to look at in all their resplendent colours that the guests felt guilty at having to eat this beautiful sight away.

The ceremony lasted a long time indeed, the boy said. Grandma Shanti's eyes became filled with tears whilst the newly-weds were walking round the fire seven times, the bridegroom leading the bride, as she relived her own nuptials, seeing herself in the bride's place and Grandpa Raju in front of her. The old lady acquiesced.

Grandpa Jayant also had tears in his eyes, but the young narrator knew, although he did not say that the tears of joy were because as he was fantasising about being the groom to Shanti's bride.

Everybody was greatly relieved when the Pandit finally fell asleep at the drone of his own voice, or maybe he too was troubled by the aroma of almonds and raisins, saffron and cardamon, mixed with cinnamon and jeera, dhanya and methi, and decided to cut short the ceremony, the boy said brushing aside half-hearted rebukes for his supposed lack of respect for the saintly man.

Half the guests were taken to the Music and Dance marquee where men in drag were dancing to the tune of a harmonium player and a singer of bhojpuri songs, venting their acid but good-natured wit on guests picked at random. Jayant had even dared engage the services of a couple of Negro musician and singer team who were instant successes with their ségas.

In the food tent, the Wizard of the Spices and his team had already dished out generous portions of his meticulously prepared fare on the banana leaves, spread evenly on the palm frond mats.

'The guests ate so quickly they bit their fingers,' young Raju said, 'some accidentally put food in their nose and in their eyes and others bit their tongues.' His audience was in stitches on hearing this. The elderly nodded.

As Jayant had been over-generous in his estimate of the quantity of food that was needed, Granny Shanti was not surprised when more than half of the food prepared was untouched even after people claimed that they had gorged themselves to their utmost limit. They had to distribute the leftovers to the grateful population of Floréal village, attracted by the fragrance of the offerings.

His audience would often question him about the white horse, at which, young Raju would frown and to cackles of delight would say, 'Why ask me, how would I know, I wasn't even born.'

It was true that he was having difficulty being born! Pradeep and Prabha did indeed make a lovely couple. They were both easygoing and it did not take long for them to fall in love with each other. Baba Pradeep would have liked Shanti Granny to leave the running of the business to him, but although she was not as tireless as she had been, she insisted on planning everything herself. Only when I die, which will be soon, she told the boy's impatient Baba, will you be able to take the reins from my hand.

'Arrey Ma Jaan,' Pradeep said without malice, 'I fear that even after you die, your ghost will refuse to let go of those reins.'

'Sharp wit just like your father, darling boy, just like your father.' Few things gave her more pleasure than to be able to discover traits in her son which she could claim had been inherited from the anointed Raju.

But after three miscarriages which people attributed to a number of causes, insufficient offerings to the Gods, other people's malevolence, sorcery, he managed to force his way into the world. He was named Rajendra after his missing grandfather. He was a healthy little thing, drinking his mother's milk with gusto.

He grew up into a handsome little boy who loved nothing better than singing songs he made himself. He was always humming, moving his head all the time as one does when listening to music, except that in his case the music was inside his head. At an early age, he impressed everybody — terrified some — by making unexpected remarks. He was not yet four when they were on the bank of the Mesnil river one day. He was watching some fish swim in water so clear that one could see its bottom, and he said to Prabha, 'Ma, I can see the bottom of this water like I can see how much I love you.' Nobody understood what this meant, but they liked it. Baba, he said to Pradeep once, when the latter was deep in thought, your forehead, he looks like the waves on the water. He had thousands of questions: do trees hurt when people break off branches or cut them down? Does the milk you drink turn red in your body and become blood? And of course he loved making up stories and silly verses.

When a labourer made him a small flute out of a piece of bamboo, and taught him how to play it, he began saying that he was a boy, he was called Raju, had two eyes, two arms, two feet, a mouth and one flute. He made his own tunes and sang childish songs he made himself to go with alternate bouts of flute-playing. He loved cattle, and could spend hours playing with them, talking to them.

When he was three, Grandpa Jayant got him a teacher so he could learn to read and write Hindi so he could read stories from the Ramayana, but in no time at all he able to read faster than Masterji!

At nine he begged Dadi Shanti to let him take the cattle out grazing, on his own, and it soon became a routine. He would take the small herd out every morning, at crack of dawn — he slept very little — and lead them to pastures on the bank of Rivière du Mesnil belonging to the family. He would talk to each cow and bull personally, telling them not to go out of his sight, to eat and drink as much as they needed to. He would then sit down under the shade of a big tamarind tree, facing the river so he could see the water flowing, take his flute out and play on it, oblivious of time and place.

Never did anybody have to say a harsh word to him. Everybody said that he was common sense wrapped in kindness. He loved the world and the whole world loved him back. He could not remember ever being really sad, and was surprised one day when playing a melancholy tune he had made up on his flute, tears began to trickle down his cheeks. Until that day, he never knew that tears were salty, he would say. He rather liked that melancholic feeling. It is the sort of sadness that does not make you unhappy, he thought.

He had just gone seventeen when he was out with the cows one morning, playing his flute, singing a song. Suddenly his attention became drawn to something which had moved on the water. He held his flute suspended in the air, level with his face, almost like a statue and saw what he thought was a large ebony fish swimming. He stood up and went nearer and like in the stories he had heard, the fish turned into a princess. A shiny black ebony princess.

She came out of the water without seeing him, little pearls dripping from her glistening body, as drops of water caught the sunlight. In the light of the mid-afternoon sun, the picture was an enchantment, and he kept it stored in his mind's eye. He looked at her, entranced, his hand holding the flute, frozen in front of his lips. The princess was still unaware of his presence, and jumped in the air twice on her long slim legs so as to shake off the water clinging to her body, her small but fully formed breasts shaking in unison. He opened his eyes wide at the sight of the shiny jet black hair which luxuriated between her legs, and it gave him a sexual frisson, the like of which he had never experienced before. Without thinking he put the flute to his mouth and began playing a new tune, as a spontaneous tribute to the beauty of the apparition, the best tune that he had ever composed, he thought. The Ebony Fish slowly lifted her head towards him, unafraid, and watched him play, she too, entranced. Was it love at first sight? He wanted to stop playing so he could approach her and talk to her, but found it impossible. It was as if somebody else had taken possession of his body, and was playing his flute. All he did was listen to the tune he was producing effortlessly, in rapture. He did not even notice when the girl started running away. He wondered whether he should run after her, but thought that it would be scare her.

When he reached home, he was still under the influence of that vision of loveliness, and did not hear when he was spoken to. He had to see this girl again, make sure that she was no spirit or ghost. It did not take long, for next day, the girl, now dressed in a colourful cotton dress with large blue flowers re-appeared, this time on firm ground. She stopped at some distance from the tamarind tree, as if waiting for him to make the first move, and he did.

'I saw you yesterday,' he said in faltering kreol. He was used to speaking bhojuri.

'You speak funny,' she said and giggled. For a while, they just stared at each other in silence.

'You want me to play,' he asked in hardly recognisable kreol, which made the girl giggle again. He recognised that it was not a mocking laugh, it was just a manifestation of her embarrassment.

He was delighted that she was a proper person and not a spirit. She told him that she was called Hyacinthe, and that she lived with her mother and little brother in Valentina, pointing in its direction with her chin.

'Are you planning to go for a swim today?' he asked, and she cackled with laughter.

'Arrey, what's funny?'

'Maman, she said to be careful with boys.'

Anyway he soon found out that her great grandmother was a freed slave. Her father was a white man, which was surprising, as her skin was completely black, although her frizzy hair was dark brown. Raju would find out later that the father had been a colon, and had seduced her mother Hortense, when the latter was sixteen. She was the child of Agathe, the daughter that Midala never knew of, as he was separated from the mother, Matamba, by de Fleury. Hortense had submitted to the colon because she knew that she had no choice. She was afraid of getting a beating if she had resisted his advances, and that she would have been kicked out of the établissement where she had a roof over her head. Hyacinthe's father did not for a moment think that he had done anything wrong. These lewd black women, he told his drinking companions, were balls of fire, asking for it, and he was not made of wood! And if it was a sin to put pressure upon them, you could always go to confession. The priest was a good friend. Still, when the baby arrived, he agreed to provide for her, made Hortense a kept woman, and later had another child with her, the almost white boy Armand.

'What I cannot understand is that Maman loves that horrible man,' she told Raju.

On another occasion she told him that if Missié Papa, as she called him, tried anything funny with her, which she knew he would some day, she would stick a knife in him. The innocent Raju found that hard to believe, but she explained that she had heard Missié Papa and Maman argue one night, and he had said that only a fool would not wish to enjoy the first cauliflower harvested on his patch. But Maman who was always finding excuses for him, said he was joking.

Raju was seeing Hyacinthe almost every day now. They were head over heels in love with each other, but neither dared touch each other. At night Raju found it difficult to go to sleep, as he could not shake off images of the black princess emerging from the water. He was in a constant state of sexual arousal, and thought that unless they did something about it, he would die.

It was almost three months later that things happened. He was waiting for her under the tamarind tree and when she came towards him, he reached out for her, and she melted into his open arms. He pressed her to his feverish body caressing her back, her waist, and her round soft behind, and they rolled on the ground in frenzied excitement. The complicit cows looked at them placidly. He lifted up her skirt and touched her intimacy and discovered that she was… melting. They undressed and admired each other's bodies, stroking each other, kissing, and the rest happened like the most natural thing in the world.

Raju knew that he wanted no other woman on this earth, but he also knew that it was not going to be easy. For such a union to take place, he would need not only Pradeep and Prabha's approval, but Dadi Shanti's and Grandpa Jayant's as well. But he imagined that as they loved him and would want the best for him, all he needed was to convince them of the strength of the Ebony Fish's love for him. Perhaps it might be best to say nothing until he was certain of their approval.

They continued seeing each other secretly, with only the cows and the crows as witnesses. Their love for each other increased everyday. At night he would lie awake in the dark and invoke images of her. Her egg-shaped head. An egg in which her love for me was hatched. Her breasts. Two soldiers bearing the keys with which to open the gates of passion only for me. Between her legs, her chhodd, a magic furnace, which though hot one, was capable of putting out my fire. Her mouth, with which she speaks those unspoken words of love when we kiss.

Suddenly one day Dadi Shanti said to Raju that she wanted to have a word with him. He knew, by the tone in her voice and by her effort not to let their eyes meet, that she knew everything.

'Arrey Dadi, the cows have been telling you stories about me,' he said attempting to bring a touch of light relief in what he suspected was going to be an ordeal.

'Sit down!' she ordered, and when he had done so, she looked at him in the eyes and said, 'Are you trying to bring shame on the family?'

'Arrey dadima, why are you saying this? What shame?'

'You know what I am talking about —'

'Yes, I know, but what I don't know is why is it a shame?'

'Do you wish me to order the wood for my funeral pyre?'

'Dadima, you should be happy for me...'

'Chhoop,' she ordered. Silence, not a word from you.

'Your father is too distraught to talk to you himself, so he asked me to tell you his decision.'

'His decision?'

'You must stop seeing this black prostitute. Oh these black devils! They are cannibals, they eat people, you know.'

'Arrey Dadi,' said Raju hiding his anger at hearing the woman he loved called that, 'Hyacinthe is a sweet innocent girl... please don't use bad names for her.'

'So she is not a prostitute eh? Then you tell me who is a prostitute? Your mother, her mother, my lost Sundari, me?' Raju who had never been exposed to family conflict, could understand neither the words nor the anger, and was too shocked to say anything. Shanti took this as acquiescence.

'You know her mother is a bad woman, unmarried with two kids. She has a lover, a married man. She is a kept woman… a boy like you… they will turn you into a… a… pimp.' Raju was too angry to hear any more, and he stood up, stared at her and turned his back on her, about to walk away. She gasped with disbelief.

'See, she has already turned you against your own family… how dare you turn your back on me when I am talking to you?' He stopped and attempted to keep calm… and said, 'Sorry.' He had no idea what to say, how to react.

'Sit down, beta,' Shanti said, in an attempt at pacifying the boy. She was shocked by the show of rebellion from someone who had been so docile all his life.

'Beta, it's for your own good, we all want what's best for you, you know that.' Raju pursed his lips and nodded absently.

'Have you seen a cat and a dog form a couple? For a good Hindu boy from a good family and a black slave woman it is the same. It is against the laws of nature.' Raju shook his head in disbelief, what sort of argument was this? Why was it against nature? She is a woman and I am a man, and we love each other, isn't that all it needs to be about. He said nothing.

'Your father was thinking of whipping you until you saw reason. Now I can tell him to be reasonable, since you have seen the error of your ways,' she said happily. 'Don't worry, he will not touch you,' she said, adding with the ghost of a smile, 'or he will have me to deal with.'

He said nothing and left. He could not remember even a mild rebuke from his beloved Dadima, or from any adult. He had never experienced even once, any conflict with anybody. This massive eruption shook the very foundation of his sanity. He went into his bedroom shaking like he had a fever. He sat on his bed, taking his head in both hands, and unsuccessfully willed himself to calm down. Tears of frustration began streaming down his cheeks. All the bad words of the grandmother began to reverberate in his head. Prostitute. Kept Woman. Black Devils. Cannibals. Why hate so much? Oh Hyacinthe, I want you here, I want to take you in my arms and swear to you that nothing they can say will make me love you less. The silent crying turned into sobs, and he found he had no control over them.

Shanti heard them and was alarmed. She too began crying, for she hated to see the boy unhappy, but it was something she had to do, there was no choice. Raju was still a boy and needed her protection. She sent for Jayant and Prabha, and also the Pandit.

Raju must have sobbed himself to sleep, for next thing he knew, his mother Prabha gently tiptoed in his room, sat on the bed beside him, took his head in her lap and rocked him like a baby. My poor boy is so unhappy, she said. Raju cheered up. Mother is the only one who understands me, Bhagwan be praised. I thought that I had no ally, there's one, somebody who has loved me without reserve all my life.

'Ma Jaan, Dadima said such bad things about Hyacinthe.'

'I know, beta, I know.'

'You will talk to them, wont you, Ma?' She smiled.

'Come, they want to talk to you,' she said. So they must have seen reason. Prabha helped him get up, and mother and son walked into the front room where Shanti received guests and clients. He was both surprised and pleased to see Baba and Jayant dada, but not the Pandit. Not Dadima either.

Jayant looked at the boy lovingly, and tapping the space next to him with his hand on the sofa invited him to come sit there. He was grateful to him, went to sit next to him, and he, moved a bit closer to his grandson, putting his arm round his shoulder, as a show of love. Pradeep nodded at him benevolently. Pandit Naipaul had a saucer finely balanced on the three fingers of his left hand, with the cup of hot chai in his right hand, his little finger raised slightly. He poured some tea from the cup into the saucer, deftly raised it to his lips and sipped its content noisily, making an appreciative sound as the spicy and sweet liquid got sucked in his mouth.

'You make the best chai I have tasted since I came to this island, Ben, just the right amount of ilaiti, not one pinch of catcam more…' Dadima's lips twitched into the travesty of a smile.

'My boy,' he said, moving the saucer away, I understand that these ungodly black savages have been doing their jadoo on you.' Raju winced at this intelligence. What magic did he mean?

'You seem surprised, beta, but, these people are worse than Untouchables!' Then he stopped suddenly and seemed deep in thought. Nobody said anything for a bit. The Pandit then shook his head, and continued.

'No, I am telling a lie, they can't be worse than Chhamars, nobody is worse than those filthy dogs.' He had to stop himself spitting on the floor. 'But you get my meaning?' Not everybody agreed with his assessment, but no one argued with him. He continued.

'They are filthy and ungodly, and whenever they want anything, instead of working for it, or buying it, they try to get it by jadoo!' Raju frowned, unable to say anything. The Pandit pursed his lips, and recanted, 'No, they are definitely worse than Chammars, no doubt about that.' Everybody seemed to be weighing the degree of badness of those two accursed groups when the holy man spoke again.

'Yes, yes, we know you are an innocent child, and know nothing of these practices. Unfortunately our own Gods are often powerless against their demons, for as you know, they worship the devil.'

'Arrey, stop it, what are you saying? You are talking a lot of rot. You should be ashamed of saying things like that. Where's your proof?'

'He's never raised his voice to adults before,' said Prabha in an attempt to salvage the reputation of her beloved son. 'Beta, why are you talking like this all of a sudden?'

'It must be their devil speaking through him,' said the Pandit flushed with vindication. Pradeep was in shock. He stood up, turned to his son, and slapped him twice on the face.

'You make me so ashamed, is this how I taught you to speak to your elders.'

'You promised you wouldn't raise a hand to him, Pradeep.' That was Shanti.

It took a few minutes before calm was restored.

'You must promise that you will never see that black witch ever again,' Pradeep said solemnly. Raju stared ahead of him saying nothing.

'Did you hear what your Baba said, Raju?' asked Shanti severely.

'Speak when you are spoken to,' urged Prabha.

'If you refuse, then you cannot be my son, you cannot live under the same roof as me,' said Pradeep with tears in his eyes. The Pandit shook his head and tut tutted, indicating that Pradeep should not have said that.

'Panditji, I mean this,' the father said defiantly.

'No, let me handle this,' tut tutted the Pandit, convinced of his own superior wisdom and savoir-faire. He took a deep breath, and everybody waited to see the difference between his wisdom and the sad father's clumsy approach.

'For your own good, because we all love you, we cannot let you stay under the same roof as your parents and your Dadima, unless you agree to end all contact with that impure black prostitute.' He smiled with self-satisfaction.

'Promise, beta,' urged Prabha. Raju said nothing.

'We will find you the prettiest, whitest Hindu girl on the island, a real peri.'

'I think we can take that as a yes. Right?' said the Pandit exhibiting the smile of a man who has delivered the goods, convinced of being the worthy recipient of the admiration of the rest of the world. Raju still said nothing but kept staring vacantly in front of him. Everybody seemed to be speaking at the same time, it was like a swarm of flies buzzing. He shook his head violently, and immediately silence was re-established.

Raju's whole world had collapsed over him. Yesterday he was the most cherished person in the family, in the whole village, loved and admired by all, and today he was being chased out of his father's house. He stood up, rushed into his room, took his flute and rushed out. Jayant and Pradeep rushed after him, but the Pandit stopped him.

'That will undo all my good work,' he said, 'he will come back chastened, where can he go?'

But Raju was not chastened and did not come back. He walked like a madman not knowing where he was going, until exhausted he leaned against a banyan tree and with the full moon in his face and went to sleep.

Next day, he went to Hyacinthe's little house with the corrugated iron roof in Valentina, and the poor girl was alarmed at seeing what looked like the ghost of her beloved Raju. He had a fever, and Hortense looked after him, putting cold compresses on his brow, gently humming songs from the old country that Grandma Matamba had taught her, whilst Hyacinthe massaged his head lovingly. Missié Papa arrived unexpectedly in the afternoon, and Hortense explained to him who the boy was. The latter had rested and was able to speak, although he had difficulty with the kreol. To his surprise, the white man said that the best thing would be for Raju to come with him to the other side of the island, in Souillac, where his boss had his estate, and needed workers. My daughter can come with you if she wants. She did. I will follow my lover to the other side of Hell if he asks me, she said. The young couple never married, but they had a happy life.

A whole year passed and Pradeep found him after searching everywhere. He said that he had forgiven him and begged him to come back home. Everybody wants you back in Rivière Sêche, he said. Raju was pleased to hear that, for he loved his family and would have never wished to be parted from them.

'Yes, Baba, of course, I do not want to break with my own flesh and blood.'

'Any time, my boy, any time.'

'As soon as my little baby is born,' he said, 'I will take him and my wife so the family can meet them. You will love the baby, Baba.' Pradeep's face changed colour exactly as black tea does when milk is added.

'No, we cannot allow her in the house. What are you saying? She will soil it, I told you, they are worse than Chhamars.'

The baby boy born to the proud couple was named François. The grandparents never saw him. When he grew up, he married a Hindu orphan girl and had a son, Prakash, who was to become Gina's lover and thus Katrina Crialese's other grandfather.

Book III

CHAPTER 1

$\bullet\bullet\bullet$

Illiwarra

THEY FELL IN love with the place, as instantaneously as Annie had fallen for James. Here in this place they were going to live happily ever after, like in the rare fairy stories they had heard as children. There was the red gum tree Johnson Johnson had described, with a large hollow which he had said could serve them as a home until they were able to build their own gunya. If you light a small fire, they had been told, the Kouri cousins would appear seemingly from nowhere; they will naturally be suspicious, just show them your message stick.

They gathered some twigs and lit a fire with the flintstone and lock James had always had, and true enough the smoke brought the men out, reminding him of how bees were smoked out by honey pickers in Dorset. There was a large group of them, most armed with spears and sticks, and they looked none too friendly. James, following Johnson Johnson's instructions put his hands up in the air, and when he did that, the men stopped, and the scowls on their faces gave way to a look of puzzlement. He then gave the elder who clearly stood out by his bearing, the message stick. He looked at it and nodded, and said a few words to his companions, and their puzzled looks changed into wide grins and laughing sounds of welcome. One young man who was a few years younger than the pair was urged to come forward, and he offered his hand to James to shake.

'Me, Birrummbirra nephew,' he said, 'speak very good English.' And then he explained to his fellow tribesmen what he had said, and they all laughed.

'I am Billungree,' he said laughing, as if that was a great joke, 'I work in Port Jackson… but much time ago'

'Now you tell him who we are,' Annie urged her man, and James started talking about Johnson Johnson, calling him Whimbarra, explaining how they had had worked together and become friends, with Billungree translating.

To a question of James, the chief said that there were no white men close by, but he had been told that the white government had given big chunks of the Kouri people's land to some white men in Yalla, pointing in its direction, across the mountains. The couple did not like hearing this, but for the moment they were not going to let this intelligence mar their enjoyment.

The men asked Billungree to put their questions to the visitors and when he translated, James answered in his usual laconic style, but invariably Annie elaborated, which made the Kouri folks laugh, as they found it highly amusing that a woman would talk when there were men around. The Chief frowned and said that he did not think it was proper for a woman to open her mouth when there were men who were not mute around to do the talking. Billungree dutifully translated that too, but nothing would stop the irrepressible Annie. Her good humour and her laugh must have been infectious, for before long even the Chief's reticence melted away in the warmth of her exuberance.

Billungree then explained that if they were ill, they can have the service of their kadji; he was a miracle worker, he said, and can even revive a man with a droopy cock, adding that in a little while, he too would be a kadji!

'Can he do the opposite?' Annie asked, 'my man needs the opposite.' The Chief laughed so much his fellow tribesmen thought he would not stop. It was at this point that they must have realised that a woman opening her mouth sometimes made for a welcome change.

They were given the permission to stay for as long as they wanted, and promised assistance of any sort.

'We are your friends, and you can count on us, come visit us in our gunyas,' Billungree translated the chief's final words as he prepared to leave for his own dwellings.

The young man explained that their gunyas were behind the rocks towards Dappeto, pointing to its direction. The chief instructed Billungree to stay with the visitors to give them advice and help.

Together they moved their possessions to their house in the mun-um-ba tree, and James offered his new friend some ale which Annie had brought, but he declined. He explained that as someone training to be a kadji he had to forego all intoxicating substances for the time being.

'What's a kadji when he is at home?' Annie asked. Billungree looked at her disapprovingly, but he explained anyway. Very early in his life, he was found to have the magic qualities needed to become a clever man, steeped in the knowledge of dreaming, who would be able to learn how to develop the skills needed to heal the sick, judge miscreants and do a variety of onerous tasks. And he showed them his maban, a small round dark glass ball, from which he got his power.

'I found it after it fell from the sky one night,' he explained. James, who was a deeply religious man knew how easy it was to mock people with different belief systems, for he was a Dissenter and as such, subject to ridicule by other Christians who prayed in luxurious churches; he was therefore prepared to listen to Billungree.

The aspiring kadji told them about Dreaming, how the universe was created by Baiame, how He made the mountains, the stars, the seas and everything. He told them about songlines, the words which he was learning in order to be able to inform future generations of Dreaming and Dreamtime. He promised that he would come again soon, and show them what plants to eat, what animals could be killed and which ones it was sinful to kill. James was perplexed, and his new friend said he would give him an example: Never in any circumstances harm a dolphin.

'Really?'

'They are spirits of our dead warriors who protect us, and no one is more powerful than the dolphin.' And he explained that dolphins would regularly help the Kouri when they went fishing by directing the fish towards their nets, and gave examples of how they sometimes risked their lives by defending them against dangerous sharks?

When he left, Annie burst out laughing, and James said that it was best not to contradict the young man, even if we think that it's all superstitious nonsense, adding that may be it was not.

'But it is, sweetheart' squealed Annie with delight.

They made mattresses with dried leaves and grass and slept soundly after the accumulated fatigue of the past few days. In the morning they were woken up by a fearsome sound.

'Billungree's spirits have come to snatch us,' Annie cackled heartily. The raucous sound continued for a while and then they heard something like a rustling sound and it stopped. Later Billungree told them that it was the kookaburra, and explained that he was created for the specific task of waking up sleeping Kouri… and their guests in the morning.

Johnson Johnson had told them that they would be able to find all the food they needed. The lake was teeming with blue swimmer crab and crayfish, molluscs and a large variety of fish, and they had no difficulty catching them and cooking them in a pot. When some of their new neighbours called, they saw them at it, and were intrigued by what they were doing, for they, with the exception of Billungree who had worked in Port Jackson, had never even seen cooking pots; they ate many things raw, or cooked them in hot coals and ashes.

The young kadji-to-be showed them the wonderful cocoyam plants growing near the waterside in large colonies. He put a stick in the earth and pulled out the plant with the heart-shaped leaf and its corm. He explained that they cooked the yam in hot ashes and that it was delicious. The leaves they dried in the sun before eating it. Baiame, he explained, had thought of everything when he created man, and gave him the means of feeding himself.

'God is omnipotent,' said James, making the sign of the cross which intrigued his new friend.

One of the first things Annie did was to find a place which was neither too sunny nor too sheltered, where to plant her drumstick seeds.

'When that tree starts growing, we will never starve,' she said.

'I don't think we risk starving now…'

Billungree taught them the names and uses of other plants, taking them to places where they grew. He vaunted the taste and value of cattails, those long cactus type plants that they found within a stone throw form their gum-tree house. There were also some acacia trees there, and the knowledgeable shaman-to-be said that the young leaves and pods were delicious and nutritious. He showed them where tasty grubs occurred in mun-um-ba trees, baobabs whose young leaves were also precious, arrowroots, quandong, warrigal, bush coconut, which was half animal and half fruit, he said, chestnuts, wild almonds and a long list of other edible things growing within an hour's walk from their new abode. He had brought for them some blankets made from fibres of the kurrajong, and promised to show them where to find them, so they could make their own ropes and fishing nets, and clothing to cover their private parts, which offended Baiame if left bare.

That night, as the lovers lay in each other's arms after a hearty fish soup, they felt at peace with the world.

'What more do we want now?' Annie said, 'We will never starve, we are sheltered from winds and rain, we have friendly neighbours, what can go wrong?'

'The good lord is looking after us, sweetheart,' James said, but he did not share a gloomy thought which, uninvited, had sneaked into his subconscious: what about those white men that the Chief had mentioned, who had been granted land in Yalla, within a stone throw of here? Our father who protects us at all times, he prayed, I do not ask for riches and possessions, but may my Annie and I live in peace here with our simple and dear friends; please also protect my friends from Tolpuddle wherever they may be, and may we have justice some day.

But the white men in Yalla were not the immediate threat. Bruce took the escape of the woman he loved, as badly as Coldwell had taken that of the man he hated. He was not going to rest until the fugitive was caught and dealt with. In his eyes, a murderer kills someone, is dealt with and that's the end, but a subversive is out to destroy society itself; the vermin needs to be eradicated pitilessly. In Norfolk island he would be completely neutered, and daily he will pray for death and rue his perfidy.

Bruce was there when he heard this rant shortly after the disappearance. If only I can find out where the son of a bitch has gone, he mused. If I tell the master, he might reward me and make me a foreman... with James out of the way, maybe Annie will have me if I become foreman.

He was going to plan his coup meticulously; there was no hurry, or he might miss out on his slim chance of happiness. He would befriend Johnson Johnson, and as the man liked his drink, he would worm the information out of his nose.

Johnson Johnson was a simple man with malice towards none, not even the white man who had stolen his country and his name. He always spoke the truth and had no artifice in him. Bruce could tell Coldwell that the black man had been a party to the escape; the truth could then be extracted from the native under interrogation. But the Abo man had never done him any harm, and he would prefer not to see him flogged. No, he would begin by befriending the unsuspecting native...

He carried out his plan with military precision, beginning by greeting the black man with a great show of friendliness one afternoon. Johnson Johnson was surprised, but he responded to the man who had never hidden his contempt for him, with circumspection. I have got a bottle of ale, Bruce said, would you like to share it with me? Sure, he said, you are kind. And they walked towards a half-built shed smelling of eucalyptus, sat down and shared the ale. The black man expected to be asked a favour, for he was beginning to get used to the ways of the white man, but Bruce wanted nothing. There were many examples in Dreaming of people who had erred, committed a forbidden act, and after seeing the light, had returned to a path that pleased Baiame. So that was a good thing.

Bruce acted in a friendly manner in the next few days, and then on Sunday asked the Kouri man to share another bottle with him. Then they went for a walk and he told him the story of his transportation, how he had been wrongly accused of stealing some jewellery from his employers, but although he knew who the real thief was, he had not revealed his name, and taken the blame to save that other man who had a wife and kids. It was as a result of this that he was sent to Botany Bay. Johnson Johnson was not used to lies, and saw no reason to doubt the story, and his sympathy for the man grew with the spontaneity of puff ball mushrooms after thunder. Still Bruce asked nothing.

A few days later he asked the Kouri man about his life, his childhood and what took him to Hunter's Hill, and the unsuspecting man was happy enough to tell him about his clan back in Lake Illiwarra, and described with tears in his eyes what a lovely place it was, how it had everything a man needed. All you need is to bend down and pick your food, there was fish galore, nuts, berries, everything a man needed to live. Why he came north, he did not know, except that their people had a wanderlust which could not be tamed.

That night, Bruce surmised that the runaways might well be in the Lake Illiwarra region. But it was too early to take any action. He only suspected that the black man was involved in the escape, and even if that was the whole truth, he could not be sure that there was only one possible destination. Should he act prematurely and be proven wrong, Coldwell might visit his disappointment on him, and he did not relish that prospect.

By accident he happened to overhear a conversation between the master and a man everybody knew as Merchant Brown. Brown had come to see the drainage system Coldwell was installing in Taj Mahal, as he himself had been granted three thousand acres in Yalla, and he wanted to learn from his fellow Englishman.

'Yalla,' Coldwell asked, 'where the blazes is that?'

'Opposite Lake Illiwarra,' the Merchant replied, 'it's a god-forsaken place with nothing but savages and not a civilised face around, but by golly am I going to change it into a Galilee, a land of milk and honey, where cash will flow smoothly into the pockets of the deserving.'

Bruce's eyes lit up on hearing this. Maybe the master might contemplate a visit to his friend in the near future. Until now, horse-racing had been his undoing, but this was one race he was clearly winning; he could see the finishing post, and there was nothing between him and it. But he was a cautious rider, and was not going to jump the gun. He would catch Johnson Johnson unawares.

Some time later he was sharing another bottle with the black man — he considered the expenditure as an investment which would bring large dividends shortly — and as planned, he blurted out with calculated negligence.

'So, Johnson Johnson, do you reckon James and Annie are doing well in Lake Illiwarra?' And the black man replied without batting an eyelid.

'Why, I hope so, Master Bruce, there is no better place on earth for them.' Suddenly he remembered that they had never talked about James and Annie, but he did not immediately deduce that the man had set a trap for him and that he had walked into it.

'But Master Bruce, I never told you, how did you know they were there?'

'But you did, Johnny boy, you did, how else would I know that?'

Johnson Johnson knew there and then that Bruce was a villain, and that he had endangered the life of the only white man he considered his friend. He wished that there was a way of warning his friends of the danger, but he knew that there was none. The thought of killing the traitor in order to save his friend crossed his mind, but he knew that he could never do it. He stood up and walked away, and Bruce, realising that the simple man had discovered his deceit, shrugged. What the hell, the man can go shit on his own head. I have discovered the truth. I have won the race at 200 to 1! Coldwell, here I come to collect my winnings.

He was not quite sure how Coldwell would react when he told him about Illiwarra; he was a rum character, he might not like informants. He decided that he would play a subtle game.

He waited for a moment when Johnson Johnson was out of earshot, and asked Paul, who was working next to him if it was true what he had heard. What had he heard, Paul asked. Oh, nothing, only whatshisname was saying that James and Annie Browne had run away to Illiwarra. No, Paul had not heard. Next, Paul asked Peter the same question, and Peter asked Bill, and finally, Bruce knew he had won when Fred approached him and asked if he had heard the news. He was over the moon.

It was Amelia who heard from the cook, and she hesitated before telling George, but she wanted Annie back, so in the end she asked her husband if a runaway who was caught could expect justice, and he said that all his life he had fought for the respect of the law, and she took this to mean that when caught, James would be dealt with leniently. So she told him about Illiwarra.

'Isn't that where that fellow, Merchant Brown —'

'Yes, I think so.'

'In that case I think I owe the Merchant a visit, I promised...' Coldwell never suspected that Bruce was the source of the rumour.

Shortly after, Coldwell, with a party of six constables, armed to the teeth set out one fine morning towards Wollongong and Illiwarra.

The young couple had enjoyed four excellent months of freedom, and were now satisfied that this pleasant state was going to last forever. The drumstick tree was about as tall as a teenager by now. There were some rare moments, when his tribal friends informed him that some white people were prospecting the land, but they kept out of the way. It was quite easy to do that if you had friends watching over you, and nobody was actually looking for you. But when your cover has been blown, it is an altogether different situation.

Coldwell and his party descended upon Merchant, and his men confirmed that on one single occasion, one man said that he had seen what looked like a white woman by the lakeside gathering some roots, but since nobody else had seen her, he had supposed that his craving for a woman was making him hallucinate. They had a hearty meal, and early next day, Coldwell and his party, accompanied by Merchant Brown and two of his employers, with the constables in tow, set out towards the gunyas of James' tribal friends, and had little difficulty spotting the tree house where the pair were sleeping soundly. The constables burst in like an explosion, and before the lovers could even understand the enormity of the situation they had their hands behind their backs, James secured by a pair of handcuffs, and Annie by strong ropes as her wrists were too thin.

The pair was in a complete state of shock, as it was completely unexpected. They were bundled into the horse-drawn carriage and were driven away whilst the whole tribe watched in sorrow and dismay.

In Taj Mahal, Annie was treated very differently to James. Amelia would not hear of her being locked up, convinced that she had been tricked by that wicked convict. James stayed locked in a stable for two days, hands and feet tied, but Coldwell, a man who operated by the book, made sure that he was fed and was given water. After two days, he was taken to Port Jackson, and appeared before the judge, who took less than fifteen minutes to sentence him to Norfolk Island for life.

CHAPTER 2

Reverse Transportation

AFTER THE MEN from Tolpuddle had been been found guilty, workers all over the country began to fearlessly proclaim that it was a blatant miscarriage of justice, that there was a law for the poor and another one for the rich. If the law banning appurtenance to a trade union had been repealed, they asked, how was it possible for the judges, whom every Englishman knew to be the fairest in the whole world, to instruct the jury to find these men guilty? And if they were guilty, why could they not have had a short jail sentence? Newspapers published features supporting the men, now dubbed Martyrs, condemning the unfair sentence, but they had been dispatched to Plymouth in great haste in order to forestall a possible change of heart. It was not uncommon for a transportee to be left to rot in some hulk for six months or more before being taken to the convict ship, but the Tolpuddle six were on the high seas in a matter of weeks. The wicked men who had the power thought that once the men were out of the country, the protests would die down, but die down, the protests did not.

Many people maintained that the status quo was the enemy of progress and had to be resisted; the most vociferous among them, and ultimately the most effective, was George Wakley, a doctor of medicine, member of parliament and a reformer, who knew what many people chose to ignore, that there was a lot of injustice in the land, and that the system always benefited the Haves. He had created The Practitioner, a journal in which he had attacked the profession for its known malpractices, its preoccupation with making money as opposed to curing the sick. When he was elected as member for the Finsbury constituency, he chose to make his maiden speech on what he called a miscarriage of justice, to the indignation of his fellow parliamentarians. This drew even more attention to the case of the

Tolpuddle Six. He reprimanded the house for pretending that they did not know that the law which made trade unions illegal had been repealed, and for their wilfull misrepresentation of the Mutiny Act and dishonest invoking of so-called swearing of secret oaths. People believed, with reason, that it had been decided in advance to find the men guilty, he declared — like in Ancient China — where it was customary to execute the accused first, and try them later. Why else, he demanded, would the Prosecution revive a law which had been dormant since 1797? He reminded the house that the Jury consisted of farmers and mill owners, men who had close relationships with the landed gentry and who had much to lose by a process which would lead to the worker earning a fairer wage. The foremen of the Jury, he reminded the House, was the Hon. W.F.S. Ponsonby, one of the richest landowners in Dorset. That in our land, a man is tried by his peers, he said in a voice shaking with emotion, is a big lie. The men were not tried by their peers, it was a case of the poor being tried by the rich!

Although this was his maiden speech, he knew how to handle drama; he played his trump card last.

'The House was no doubt aware of The Orange Order,' he said, adding slyly, 'seeing that most of the honourable members sitting here today belong to it. Can I remind you, gentlemen, that you too swore a secret oath when you were received in that respectable Order? Yes, gentlemen, you did; I challenge you to contradict me. Why is it that you gentlemen, can take a secret oath and not be sent to Botany Bay, whilst some honest workers, in whose numbers we find preachers of the Methodist Church, doing the same thing get condemned to a sentence which many believe is equivalent to the Ultimate Penalty? Dare I suggest to you, honourable members, that in our country, reputed the world over for its just laws, that Dissenters are seen to be excluded from the benefits of its tolerance of democratic values and freedom of speech and worship? One law for the rich and one law for the poor; one law for the followers of the established church and one law for the followers of other Christian denominations?'

The embers of dissent were fanned by the increasingly vociferous controversy, and it did not take long for the king to grant a free pardon to the men who had suffered so much pain and humiliation. George Loveless, who had earned the respect of everybody in Van Diemen's Land, including the Governor's, was informed of the success of the campaign for his release by the latter himself. James was in prison in Port Jackson waiting to be taken to Norfolk Island, when the news arrived at Taj Mahal. The moment Coldwell was appraised of the king's pardon, he took prompt measures to stop his imminent embarkation; if the King had pardoned a man, it means he was as innocent as a new-born babe, and no one believed in the power of the law as fervently as he did.

James was seriously ill in prison, and the governor had feared that he might die before reaching that notorious island. He was delirious when the news came, and had no idea what they were telling him. The doctors took great care of him, and declared that he was just about fit enough to travel. He was taken back to Port Jackson where he hardly recognised George and the others. In his delirium, he kept calling the name of Annie, but he had no idea that he was being taken away from her. They were all promptly conveyed on a ship returning them home. When, with the tender care of his fellow Martyrs he finally regained both his health and his clarity of mind, and realised that he was being taken back to England, he was shattered, although until he had met Annie, his dearest wish had been a review of the trial leading to his return home. There was clearly nothing he could do, but he was determined that once he reached England, he would do everything in his power to go back of his own volition to her, at whatever cost.

Annie had been distraught at being separated from James, and soon after began to feel weak and feverish. Amelia was greatly alarmed, and called the doctor, who found that she was with child. She kept calling the name of James, and was shocked to hear that he was going to spend the rest of his life on that hell on earth that was Norfolk Island. She promised herself that she would go join him there; she would go on her knees and beg Mr George to help her in this; in spite of James' experience, she thought of him as a fair and upright man, and was sure that he would help.

In the meantime, Bruce heard of Annie's condition. This cheered him up no end, for he was sure that no one else would now want a woman with a child by another man. His blind passion for the woman was such he would have no hesitation in taking her, and she of course would have no choice. He

442

would love and cherish her child. He was reconciled to the idea that at first she would not reciprocate the great passion that he nurtured for her, but how could she not end up seeing the depth of his feeling for her?

Shortly after, a much debilitated Annie gave birth to a baby girl prematurely, and she as well as the baby were in a precarious condition. The doctors worked day and night to save them, but in the end Annie was too weak and died in the arms of Amelia. The baby survived and seemed well. When he heard the news, Bruce went mad with grief and remorse. Her death was entirely of his making, he told Johnson Johnson, the only man he considered his friend. Surprisingly he blamed the black man; why had he been so gullible? Why had revealed the secret to him? If he had been less stupid, she would still be alive, happy with another man, but all he ever asked for was her happiness. Johnson Johnson was much touched by the man's genuine grief. But he had heard that his real friend James was bound for England, and he rejoiced for him.

Annie had always marvelled at Amelia's kindness, and on her death bed, she was much comforted by her solicitude. It brought a smile to her face as she wryly told herself that sometimes a mistress and a servant can change places. She died in the certainty that the mistress would do her best for the baby. The lady grieved for the servant like for her own sister, and George was deeply touched by this. He always admired his wife for her compassion, which was why he had fallen in love with her in the first place. She had readily agreed to forego the fine saloon life of London to follow him to the outback. He had been heartened that the woman he had suspected of marrying him for his money, did truly love him. Now she found solace in the new baby. In no time at all, she was considering the baby like her own, fussing over her, hiring a native nursemaid whose own baby had died so she could breastfeed the little motherless mite. Nobody was surprised when she decided to call the child Annie. No mother could be as besotted by the little creature as she was, and George was delighted for her. It was George who one day asked her if she would like them to adopt Annie. Annie Coldwell grew up in the Coldwell household, surrounded by doting parents and not knowing that she was adopted, until her fifteenth birthday.

A Romance on the High Seas

(Extracts from the very intimate journal of Fanny Bell-Mowbray)

<u>PLEASE PLEASE DESTROY in the event of my death.</u>

<u>Nineteenth of May 1846</u>. I have never kept a journal in my life, but now that I am going to be on this sailing clipper — *The Indigo Sky* — for upwards of ten weeks, at the mercy of the trade winds I have resolved to record the events of my so-far dull, bordering on uninteresting life. I am writing this because sometimes, when one is at the crossroads, one has to take stock, and writing this is perhaps the best way of achieving this. The ship sailed out of Liverpool yesterday bound for Port Jackson, New South Wales. I would have preferred going on one of those new-fangled steamships, but at the moment they go mostly across the Atlantic. But I am not complaining; this is a gallant little English ship. The cabin is obviously cramped, but my companions are two sweet and good-natured elderly widows. I have not enquired of them to what purpose their visit to the Antipodes was, and I daresay they have not volunteered the information. Although they are dressed in fine clothes, they have a common speech. I am not a snob, I swear, but I found this striking, and took the decision to note everything interesting. I am going on a visit to my dear brother George Coldwell in Hunter's Valley, where he is a big landowner and one of the most influential men in New South Wales.

I have to laugh! Here am I talking of elderly widows, as if I were not one myself — albeit not elderly. I am not yet thirty, but forsooth a widow nonetheless. I was married at nineteen to Captain Quentin Bell-Mowbray, eight years my senior, shortly before he was due to sail for India, to join his regiment there (The 22nd Queen's Regiment). We spent no more than a week together. The Captain and I met when his father organised a ball in his honour in his Stroud home, with the view (which we now know) of helping his son find a desirable bride before he went back to join Sir Charles Napier in Poona. Mrs Elizabeth Bell-Mowbray had made sure she invited all the eligible maidens around, and I was flattered that Quentin picked me, God only knows why! I was a plain and ordinary girl with few accomplishments. I daresay my plain features have not improved with time. One does not have to look too closely to see a grey hair or three amid my otherwise jet black hair, for every time one appears and I pull it out, like the Hydra of Lerna two new ones take its place. Over the last years, I have oft asked myself if I was ever in love with Quentin, and I can verily say that I know not the answer to that. Although Quentin is the only man I have known in the biblical sense, I have no abiding recollection of the four occasions when we indulged. Maybe I am just grateful that he chose me over the likes of Pamela Wellerby-Courtney and Cicely De Vere, both manifestly much better endowed than me in every sphere. I do not recall feeling like a Hindu widow throwing herself onto the funeral pyre as her dead husband is being immolated when I heard the sad news of his passing. Sir Robert, my father-in-law explained to me (with the help of a map) how it happened.

The three amirs of the provinces of Sind, with whom we had signed treaties, started plotting with other tribes, with the intention of reneging on the undertaking they had given us (explained Sir Robert), and Sir Charles Napier, ever the man of action, decided that there was only one thing to do, to confiscate their lands: neutralise them and annex the territory.

Quentin had written to his father (a letter which we received after his demise) about how Napier had sent him and a force of only three hundred and fifty men on camels to capture the fortress at Imamghar, which they took, unopposed, after which they blew it up in order to prevent the enemy from using it if they retreated. A week later, buoyed up by his initial success, Napier decided to consolidate before descending upon Hyderabad. That was the last time we heard from Dear Quentin.

However, Sir Robert's friend from the War Office sent him a detailed letter later. The amirs, it seemed, had formed a coalition and gathered together a force of five and twenty thousand men, and they were entrenched in the bed of the Falaili river. Napier, disposing of two thousand and eight hundred men, despatched two hundred of them to help Captain Outram start a forest fire to stop the enemy using a crucial flank.

The enemy had more guns and men and were strongly posted on a curve of the river, with massive reserves in the skikargah, or woody enclosure. Sir Charles thought that the situation was desperate, but noticing a small opening in the wall in his right flank, he ordered Captain Tew to take a company into the breach, and defend the position even with his life. The good captain did as he was told, and when he died, my Quentin took command of that brave band of soldiers, and fought against overwhelming odds. He died too, but the gap was successfully held to the very last. The natives fought with valour, but we routed them all the same. The two men were both awarded a posthumous V.C. later.

And lo and behold, I, who hardly shed any tears at his death, am now crying hot tears as I write these lines. My poor brave heroic husband!

Sir Robert used to love telling visitors what a big part his dear son had played in Napier's capture of Sind for us. For once in my life, I was able to see the benefit of all those years I struggled with my latin, for when Sir Robert gruffly told the PECCAVI joke, I immediately understood it. After he had captured Sind, it seems that Sir Charles had sent a one word message to the Foreign Office: PECCAVI. I have sinned (a rather clever little pun, I thought).

Twenty-second of May 1846. It was a rough night, the sea was very choppy and my stomach churned as the ship pitched and tossed. Surprisingly the elderly dears remained serene and unperturbed.

It seems like a lifetime when the tragic events I wrote about took place, and I have been a widow since. When Sir Robert died, with George away in New South Wales, I was left with Marchmont Manor and the estate, which consisted mainly of housing and tenant farms which bring me a pretty penny without doing any work for it, which I sometimes think is grossly immoral.

The governance of the everyday matters of the estate is in the hands of the steadfast John Merryweather, as upstanding and honourable a man as breathed our English air, and for whom I have the greatest esteem. George who acquaints me in every letter of how happy marriage has made him keeps intimating that I should find myself a new husband before I get past the age, and although I am not opposed to the notion, I have not as yet met anybody to whom I have been inclined to give an encouraging nod.

Dear George humorously intimates that the deck of a clipper might well be the best place for a romance to burgeon and then blossom in the fertile atmosphere of Captain's balls and what not. So far I have not seen or spoken to any interesting prospective suitor. I despair at the thought that there might be none on board.

<u>Third of June 1846</u>. We have been becalmed. Some passengers say that this is tiresome in the extreme, but I find that lazing on a deck chair in the sun — and there is plenty of it — whilst the clipper is rocking ever so gently, watching a baleful sea, flying fishes and a few fearless albatrosses and what not displaying their acrobatic prowesses is calm-making and soporific. No, I mean relaxing. I can feel all the muscles in my body loosen, and I enjoy a sensation of well-being which I cannot properly describe, except by saying that it gives me the impression of listening to my blood coursing down my veins — if that's not too pompous a way of putting things. The Captain informed us that we are in the region of the Bay of Biscay, but although Spain is nearby, we can see no land at all, although the occasional flock of sea birds is testament to the proximity of land.

My elderly widows, two sisters-in-law, have confided to me that they were on their way to join their sons, who were cousins, who had been transported to Botany Bay in the thirties, and who, at the end of their term, had worked their fingers to the bones, and were now partners in a large sheep-rearing establishment. The boys had sent them the money for their expenses, and had insisted that they shall travel first class. They swear that their boys, as they call them, were blameless and had been wrongly condemned, on the perjurious testimony of a debauched nobleman who had found it expedient to lay the blame for his crime at their door. Even if there isn't always man's justice in this world, I surmised, there is always God's, for He, in his wisdom, had thought fit to reward those two innocent men for the iniquities done to them. I wanted to take those two dears into my arms and embrace them, but I did not dare.

I have been reflecting on my own fate lately. When you are in a confined space with nothing to do, you do tend to think about events in your life. George and I were the only children of our parents. We were always very close although he is seven years older than me. Whilst he went to Eton, I was educated at home by a Dr Washwell, a retired parish priest. He was a wonderful old man, and I have to laugh as I recall how he used to employ the same technique in teaching as no doubt he used in the pulpit, speaking in a loud hectoring voice, wagging his fingers, although I never found him threatening, as I knew that he was a gentle old dear. Sometimes in the middle of a latin lesson, he would forget where he was and start talking about Marco Polo or Chevalier Bayard, in heroic terms, as if they were some admirable saints from the bible. He encouraged me to read, but he had clear ideas about what to read and what to avoid. Captain Marryat was in, but Dickens he frowned upon — which was probably what turned me later into an ardent reader of the latter out of curiosity. I read as many of the books that he dis-approved of, indubitably because I had (still have?) a perverse nature. I must say in all sincerity that I have never in my life, come across anything in any book, which has given me any wicked thought or impulsion, and I cannot en-visage how reading can be anything but beneficial to one's soul. I often wish that I was born a man, for women are limited by the restrictions imposed by our sex. I would have liked to have been able, like George or Quentin, to fight for my country. And die even, for it's an honour to lay down one's life for one's king.

(Here follows a series of musings unconnected to the development of her history)

<u>Seventh of June 1846</u>. I am finally getting used to life at sea. I can imagine living like this for the rest of my life. We acquired fresh supplies in Aveiro, where we halted for twenty-four hours. There is a nice feel to Portugal; it is

a rugged and beautiful place, and the denizens are handsome and pleasant, albeit dark. Not that I am imputing their dark colour to negro blood, Heaven forfend! It's the work of the sun, and I daresay that their swarthy appearance make them look very handsome albeit in a threatening sort of way.

We are now being served lobsters and prawns regularly, and I relish both of these delicate crustaceans, even if the eating of them is quite laborious.

It is now abundantly clear that if I shall meet an interesting man, it is not going to be on this trip, for there is none. One or two officers have spoken to me, but although they were gallant and polite, I gave them no encouragement as I cannot see the superiority of being married to a man who was away at sea for eleven months of the year to being a spinster. I sometimes think that the condition of spinsterhood isn't as bad as that odious word 'spinster' intimates. Still, I have lived in hope, but now, dear Journal, hope it seems, there is none! Between you and me, I am not all that sold on the idea of finding any husband.

Thirteenth of June 1846. We are now in the Gulf of Guinea. We are sailing close enough to see the land, the coast mainly, but not the details. The heat is unbearable, and all one wants to do is to imbibe water, but it has a taste which I find hard to describe, which discourages one from so doing. I suppose stale is the nearest word I can think of. I have written in some details about our childhood, George and mine. Since there is not much to write about, as nothing unexpected happens on this voyage. We only had one storm which I have described in details earlier, and it was nothing as terrifying as I had hoped. I own to liking those cataclysmic manifestations of nature, storms, thunder and lightning, the sort of downpour that goes on or hours. I suspect these violent natural manifestations find an echo in my soul silently rebelling against my sedentary life.

I might as well confide to you, dear Journal, some of my most intimate thoughts about the family.

George's wife Amelia is one of the sweetest girls I know. Woman, I mean. We were delighted when George told us he aimed to marry her. I got to know her properly when George went to India on his own, with the East India Company, and she stayed with us for a while because the quarters for wives were not ready. However after a two-year stint there, having impressed his superiors with his dedication to hard work and, I daresay his intelligence, he was given an unexpected promotion, and a big house in Howrah where he was able to take my dear sister with him. Since that time the family and I have seen very little of them. We did not like the idea of their going to Australia, but Papa was convinced that the future was in the colonies, and did everything he could to encourage him to take the plunge. George was unable to resist the siren call of the Antipodes. We were all impatient to hear of an addition to the family, but it soon became obvious that she was unable to bear children. I own to a perverse nature. God knows how much I love George, but I could not suppress the question: How do we know for sure that the fault is Amelia's and not my dear brother's?

George wrote regularly, but he did not seem to have the time to go into details, so we just had to content ourselves with news that he was well and had cleared so many more hundreds of acres of land on which he was growing potatoes, wheat or breeding sheep and cattle.

The first time he mentioned little Annie, he did not go into details, and simply said that they were going to legally adopt a little girl whose mother had died. We all thought that the woman who had died might have been another English woman, wife of some other colonist, and we were delighted, both for my brother and his wife, and for the innocent little orphan child. Imagine our shock when we heard from people who had come over for holidays over here, that sadly Annie was a little girl born out of wedlock to a convict pair, he a ruffian who had been involved in plotting a revolution, and she a Gipsy thief. Of course I did not approve, but I supplicated the Lord to give me some understanding. And the good lord never leaves any prayer unanswered. One morning, as I was preparing to get out of bed, a thought struck me: a child does not bear the sins of its parents, and is innocent of their trespasses and I must endeavour to remember that at all times. But to my shame, I no longer considered Annie as my proper niece. My nightly prayers to the Lord to protect my brother and my sister-in-law and my little niece, did not sound sincere, for no one can fool the lord.

As the distance to our destination gets smaller by the day, my excitement at seeing dear George is increasing in the opposite direction. Doctor

Washwell had vainly struggled to impart to me the notion of inverse variation, and it's only today that understanding suddenly dawned upon me. I am dying to see my dear sister too, but the thought of Annie fills me with a kind of foreboding. I have gone on my knees begging the Lord to make me love her truly and without reservation. Please Lord, understand that I truly want to love this innocent child. All I ask of you is that you give me the means of doing that!

(A lot of the subsequent entries are about Fanny's impatience with herself over her uncertainty of how she was going to react to Annie, and prayers to the Lord to show her the way. There are large gaps which she explains by the absence of anything new.)

<u>Fifteenth of August 1846</u>. It seems that I have lived in New South Wales for ever! It was absolutely heavenly to see my dear brother who, if he looks older, is also much more handsome and dashing than I remembered. I had always wished that he would grow a moustache, and I am delighted that it becomes him so well. I wish he would dress himself a bit less casually, he who used to be so well-groomed. But I understand that in his new life, when he is expected to do all manner of things including manual work, a few of the niceties of life have got to give. I was discomfited and dismayed at first to see dear Amelia with a man's hat and wearing men's trousers, glowing under the midday sun as she supervises Aborigines and convicts digging the fields. I have left the best bit last. The good Lord as usual answered my prayers: I immediately took to dear sweet little Annie. She is a sweet loving and caring young thing, pretty as a picture, lissome, dark flashing eyes and although she has lived all her life in the backwoods, deprived of good society, she is naturally gifted, has poise and bearing, and talks very sensibly for a seventeen year old. But there is one thing that I simply cannot abide, she has the voice of a twelve year old, and it sounds odd. It's probably because she has always been treated like a baby. She likes to cajole everybody, not that I am saying that she has an ingratiating nature. She is just the sweetest child one can imagine. She calls me 'dearest auntie Fanny' in the most endearing manner, opens her eyes wide, bats her eyelids, pouts ever so slightly, and anyone

would feel like a brute for refusing her anything. But I know she is a good person, and I am already getting used to her. Glory be!

<u>Twentieth of August 1846</u>. This morning, when I woke up, I was full of energy, and thought that I would spend the day working with my hands on the fields, not as a supervisor, but as someone using spades and pickaxes. Nobody thought that I was eccentric or outlandish, so I spent the morning digging a trench which George hopes to use to channel water from Lane Cove river to our fields. I am already using 'our'. George has intimated that I might consider selling the cumbersome estates in Stroud and join forces with him here, but I am reluctant to contemplate this. I am sometimes aware that I nurture uncharitable thoughts about people, and nightly I ask the Lord to cleanse me of this stain. How could I have allowed the thought that dear selfless George was more interested in what my money could do to further his ambitions for Taj Mahal than for my welfare? I own that back home I am used to being Number One. Here I can never be anything but second to dear George. I would not mind that all that much, but to be honest, dear diary, I am quite keen to get myself a new husband, although I know that I have intimated elsewhere that I am indifferent to the notion; we of the feeble sex must not reveal our true nature to the world. Dear George is still so close to me that he guesses where my doubts reside, and has told me of some wonderful unattached men working wonders on the land in places like Woolongong, Kembla or Gerigong, which I had never heard of. But as he is the most honest man I know, he has not failed to mention that he sees these worthies less than once a year, so where are my chances? This is also something my dear sister has said, no doubt in the name of judiciousness, but I am ashamed of my lack of charity in thinking that deep down she would prefer me out of the way, although dear Amelia has never given me any cause to suppose that. May the Lord make me more charitable in my thoughts!

<u>Nineteenth of September 1846</u>. Understandably, I do not feel the necessity to keep my journal on a daily basis, as life here is very much the same day in and day out — not that I am complaining. It is a good life and I am perfectly

happy here. Everybody is so nice. As I said earlier, I very much enjoy helping George in the education of dear Annie, who has great aptitudes, although there are great gaps in her learning. For instance, she thought that outside England, everybody spoke French. The poor dear did not have the benefit of dear old Doctor Washwell. At first I was disconcerted by her readiness to talk about things which, according to me are best left unsaid to any but one's most intimate friends. She does not hesitate talking about what the beasts in the stable or in the backyard get up to, or about calving or lambing. I blush as I write this, but I caught her one day in the bush, taking down her knickers and easing herself. I prefer to laugh as I am getting used to her lack of awareness. I do not much care when she notices my blushes and laughs at me. I suppose I am getting to be a staid old spinster.

Tenth of December 1846. It seems eerie, but the weather is so hot that I find myself glowing all the time when I am working in the fields. Annie has no compunction in using the word sweating, which, coming to think of it, is not such a bad word, and it describes the process of losing bodily waters very aptly. I may be an old (oldish?) spinster, but I do try to not think like one. I often question myself and am not loath to changing my opinion about things. Father used to say that it was the mark of intelligence to review one's position in life, although the old dear himself never changed his position on anything, as far as I can recall. I feel so awful when I say less than flattering things about people I have loved, it seems like a betrayal of some sort.

I notice that I am rambling. I meant to say that the hot weather does not seem appropriate with the advent of Christmas. Merryweather has sent many things from home, and we are planning on a memorable celebration. George has managed to get his friend from Great Lakes, Elias Malpas to come spend a week with us. The man owns half of Great Lakes, he says, and he has hopes that the two of us might get on with each other. I cannot hide from you, dear Journal, that my heart is already aflutter with excitement. Shall Elias take to me?

Twenty-third of December 1846. I have never been so angry with George! How could he think that a boor like Elias Malpas... oh, I can't go on.

<u>Twenty-seventh of December 1846</u>. Yes, he is coarse and drinks too much, I do not much care for his leering at me, but I have arrived at the conclusion that he is an honest hard-working and hard-drinking man. He made us all laugh at the Christmas dinner, he has such a fund of stories about the Aborigines. Those that I have met over here have struck me as decent and hard-working, so I find all those stories Elias told about how stupid they were, how lazy and how dishonest, a bit hard to believe, but he has a way of making them sound very funny if not very convincing. But why do I feel guilty every time I meet Johnson Johnson or Goolagong? I used to like them a lot, but now I am on my guard. George laughed with Elias, but pointed out that as the Aborigines are not used to individuals owning property, they find it hard to believe that things they need and which are available, cannot be taken for their own use. Land, according to them, belongs to the tribe, that is to whoever needs it. I am confused. Elias has been looking at me in a manner which makes me blush. I have hardly spoken to him when we are just the two of us, but as I was helping remove the plates from the table after dinner, he found the opportunity of grabbing me by the arm, when both Amelia and Annie were in the kitchen and George was in the verandah waiting for his friend to join him for cigar and port, and said to me, 'Can I see you tomorrow when the others are having a rest after lunch? I want to tell you something important.' My immediate reaction was one of shock and horror that he should presume that I was available for the picking. Then I thought, but I was, so I relented. I do not know what to say if he does propose to me. I am filled with awe but also expectation. Maybe the good Lord wishes me to be instrumental in smoothing out some of his roughness…

<u>Twenty-eighth of December 1846</u>. It was uncanny how easy it was, George said he was not going to have a siesta, as there was some problem he had to attend to, and the gels complained of the heat and said that they were going to rest for a while. So am I, I lied. Elias winked at me. As I am not over-fond of being winked at, I blushed and changed countenance, but luckily no one noticed. He walked to his room, knocking a chair or two over as he did so, and banged his door loudly as he went in. I took a deep breath, and walked towards his door, and knocked. He came to open the door and taking me by

the hand walked me towards his bed, and made me sit down on an armchair whilst he himself chose to sit on the bed. His hand touching mine gave me what I can only call a frisson, but I stayed cool. He took off his shoes and socks, and started scratching between his toes. What an uncouth character, I thought, but decided that I shall not pay too much attention to this. At the same time, the thought that he was quite handsome crossed my mind for the first time. He reminded me of those handsome Portuguese men.

I bet you know why I wanted to talk to you, he said, looking at me in the eyes. His eyes were peerless, and not at all unattractive. No, I lied, I have no idea whatsoever. He laughed and made an attempt to catch my hand but I thought that propriety demanded that I resisted his effort. He did not seem put out in the least. I will record the conversation as faithfully as I remember it.

'I am not complaining, girlie, but it's a lonely life here.'

'Yes, Mr Malpas, I can believe that.'

'Why don't you call me Elias, eh, Fanny.'

'Sure, Elias, I will do that.'

'I will not beat about the Aussie bush, we don't have too much time left. You know I am hitting the trail tomorrow.'

'Yes, I was sorry to hear that you cannot stay longer.'

'You mean that, don't you?'

'Of course I do, Mr Malpas.'

'Then I'll have my say without any further ado.'

'Sure, I like that in a man.'

'Ever since Georgie boy asked me over, saying his sister from home was over, I have been thinking of you... I mean you and me... how does that hit you?'

'I don't know what to say, eh... Elias.'

'Say yes. Please say yes.'

'Well, yes, but... eh... yes to what.'

'I didn't know I was so shy, girlie.'

'Just say it...'

'Well it's like this... I haven't been with a woman for a whole year, would you believe that. What I am saying is... how about it?'

'It?'

'Why don't you hop in 'ere Fanny… there's enough room for both of us in this goddam sack for Christ's sake!'

I thought that I'd die before I let him see my tears, and I left the room without banging the door.

Twenty-eighth of December 1846. I resolved to say nothing to dear George. It was definitely not his fault. How was he to know what sort of man Mr Malpas was? But I cried buckets that night. I did not even like the man, and I let him humiliate me. I felt soiled and betrayed and cursed myself for betraying the memory of my poor dead heroic Quentin. I carefully avoided his gaze but could not help noticing that he had a perpetual sneer on his wicked face thereafter. When he left shortly after, I put on a brave face, and saw him off, shaking his slimy hand in the bargain, as I did not wish dear George to feel he had been instrumental in causing me grief.

Third of January 1847. After the ordeal that I went through, I wanted away from this place, but to my amazement, before I intimated my wish to George, he asked me into the small office where he did his accounts and planning away from his women. He told me that his dearest wish was that I would stay in Hunter's Valley with him, but he knew that I aimed to go back to Stroud. He asked if he could ask me for a big favour. He and Amelia had often worried about Annie's education. The poor girl had been short-changed, living in the outback, and they would be failing in their duty as parents if they did not try to remedy this sad state of affairs. He had often marvelled at how well Annie and I got on with each other, and wondered whether I would acquiesce to taking Annie with me when I went back, let her stay for a year in a civilised town, be her mentor and guardian, and perhaps do the right thing to see that she meets some eligible young man, preferably someone without too much to keep him in England, and who would welcome the challenge of Australia, where if he set about it properly, he would have every chance of hitting gold. One has got to give dear George credit for his clarity of expression and for going straight to the point. I was overjoyed, for everyday my affection for Annie had grown and grown. She and I got on very well, and I suppose I like the idea of being a surrogate mother, since any likelihood of my ever being a real one seemed to have evaporated in the glare of my silver strands.

<u>Twenty-first of February 1847</u>. Now that we are on board the steamship SS. Wilberforce, with the prospect of six weeks at sea, I have decided to come back to my faithful journal. Apologies, dearest friend, for neglecting you, and for nevertheless seeing the welcome on your frank and open page. This is one of the newest steamer built and one of the first to do the Liverpool - Port Jackson route. It is much more luxurious than the clipper and the cabins are much roomier. There is a comfortable saloon where one may spend time reading and writing peacefully, and indeed that's where I am now. We left this morning, on a southerly course, and the country seen from the ship is absolutely amazing. Annie is so excited, and I envy her the optimism of youth. The dear child thinks that nothing bad can ever happen to her, and I am pleased for her. Harsh reality will dawn upon her soon enough, so let her enjoy life until such times as she loses her rose-tinted spectacles. She is quite exhausted by the excitement of the preparation, and is having a prolonged nap. I own that I find her good-natured excitement quite exhausting too, at times.

<u>Twenty-second of February 1847</u>. Yesterday I had to end my entry abruptly, because of a most wonderful apparition. As I was busy writing my diary, alone in the saloon, I became aware of a presence, and on raising my head, there he was. The finest young man I have ever cast my eyes upon. He smiled as our eyes met, and with a bow took a few steps in my direction. He begged to be excused for his impertinence in daring to address a young lady on her own, but assured me that being discourteous to me was the last thing he intended. Did he have my permission to continue this intercourse, or should he just bow out? I felt weak at the knees and trembling all over, I invited him pray to tarry. He introduced himself, Captain Percy Robertson, late of the 23rd Regiment. My heart missed a beat when I heard that he was from the same regiment as my dear Quentin. He noticed how I had turned ashen on hearing this, and asked what the cause might be. Tears started rolling down my cheeks, but I took a deep breath and composed myself and told him

about Quentin. The legendary Bell-Mowbray! he cried. I had the honour of knowing the dear man. What a hero! He had of course only been a green non-commissioned officer himself, he owned, but he was a participant, albeit a minor one, and a witness. When historians will write about the capture of Sind, he said, they will wax lyrical about Napier and Outram, but I will tell you that we who were there will never forget Tew and Bell-Mowbray! You are making me cry, Captain Robertson, I managed to blurt out in spite of the lump in my throat. I invited him to sit down by my side, and the two of us just sat there not saying much at first. Then he questioned me, and I explained that I was going back to Stroud taking my young niece with me. He told me that his father, was the famous Sir Rob Rob Robertson of whom I must surely have heard (I had not, but nodded) Percy had been visiting him in Penang, where he runs one of the most important companies in the colony. His father wanted him to resign his commission from the army, as he had plans for him, which he would prefer not to bore me with. To cut a long story short, we seem to have become fast friends, and he made me promise that I will allow him to come talk to me tomorrow. He had a few businesses to attend to with the purser and begged my leave. I breathed a sigh of relief as he left, not because I wished him to go, but because the tension had become unbearable, with this most excellent man sitting by my side. I had originally thought that he must have been quite young, but at some point he did mention that he was just a few months short of thirty. I am twenty nine! Oh stop it Fanny, one does not lie to one's journal! I was thirty one last month. I wonder if he would not expect a much younger sweetheart. If I have struck gold, as Annie says, might he not overlook my being a few months older?

<u>Twenty-third of February 1847</u>. I confided in Annie that I had met a wonderful man, that night, and she declared that she was impatient to meet my beau (her description). He is nothing of the sort, I exclaimed, I have only talked to him for half an hour, I know nothing about him, but you are right, he seems like a very nice young man. Why did I have to add what was not even true? And for all I know, he must be years younger than me. Why are we of the weaker sex so defensive about our feelings and seek to deny them? So this morning, when we were strolling on the deck, as we were both spared the

inconvenience of sea-sickness, as if on cue, Captain Percy appeared. Annie let go of my hand and fairly jumped towards him, greeting him in her usual ebullient manner. 'Oh, Captain Robinson, my aunt told me so much about you. I couldn't sleep a wink last night, for wanting to meet you.' The Captain was slightly taken aback, looked at me, but seeing no disapproval on my face, he relaxed, and let himself be taken by the hands. Arm in arm they made towards me, and we found ourselves deck chairs on which we reclined, watching the coastline of Southern Australia disappear in the afternoon mist. I was delighted that Annie was so fond of my Captain, as I had already begun to think of him. I am sure that when I met Quentin the first time, I experienced no emotions as strong as those I was already feeling for the man. I was delighted that he and Annie were getting on so well. She would therefore give a good account of him to George when she wrote to him. Annie questioned Percy about his Indian campaign, and he was only too pleased to recount his many adventures, and I was struck by his playing down his bravery and heroism, although I am sure that he was just as heroic as my Quentin. We thoroughly enjoyed the day.

Twenty-fifth of February 1847. I cannot, must not blame Annie! She had obviously experienced what the French call the *coup de foudre*. Dear Aunt Fanny, she asked me that night as we were preparing to go to bed — I had forgotten to mention that we had a two berth cabin all to ourselves — you cannot not have fallen in love with Percy, you must tell me if you have. I laughed. Of course not, gel, I told her, love is not something you walk into blindly; for all we know the man may have a wife and three children already; he never said. Annie's face changed colour visibly. Don't be horrid, she said, he can't have. We said nothing for a while, each engaged in putting on our night dress. As long as you have not fallen in love with him, she said negligently. Of course not, I said, I am a wise old bird with a sound plumed head on my shoulders, I said, recognising the falsehood of my tone and knowing that the innocent Annie did not — or perhaps chose not to. She fairly jumped on my neck, hugged me and kissed me, after which she uttered the saddest words that I have ever heard in my life. Because then, she said dreamily, I am resolved that I shall become Mrs Percy Robertson! Don't be silly, I heard myself say — the most futile exercise ever in locking a stable door after the horse had bolted — you are too young to fall in love anyway; you are just imagining that you have fallen in love with a man we do not know from Adam. Remember looks are often deceptive, I said, repressing my tears. But Annie was not listening.

Yesterday I had a violent headache all day long and did not venture outside the cabin. When Annie came back after supper, she was brimming with joy and excitement, and explained to me that Percy had eyes only for her, responding with cold courtesy to the obvious seductive attempts of the Misses Watson, Proudfoot (she called them the Proudfeet), Amberson, Delaney and others. She was sure that he had fallen heads over heels in love with her too. I prayed to the good Lord to give me the fortitude and forbearance to deal with this calamity. Yes, dear diary, I cannot hide it from you. Had I played my cards right, Percy Robertson and I would... no, I cannot say it... it's too painful. I had to tell myself that the Lord must not have willed such a union. Thank you God, for all your munificence, may it extend to making me understand how you arrive at your decisions for us.

Twenty-eighth of February 1847. Sweet dear lovely Annie. Until today, I always thought that she was an over-indulged woman child, and I will even own to still despising her a little bit while at the same time having genuine love for her. Maybe I should also admit to slight jealousy towards her, perhaps even a little anger for being blind to my true sentiments. Yes, without her, I might easily have landed myself an admirable man; we had had the most propitious start imaginable. But clearly the good Lord did not wish it to happen. She went full tilt, as she said, and ensnared the desirable Captain into a weave of her charm, insouciance and beauty. She is undoubtedly as pretty a young lady as can grace the most distinguished salons of Knightsbridge.

Auntie Fanny, she asked me suddenly this morning — I had slept very badly last night, because I was gnawed by my conscience, and without meaning to, I had been sulking at her, although I tried to conceal this, but I pricked my ears at this point. Yes? dearest. I have an idea that I might have done something to incur your displeasure, she said. Why do you ask? I was thinking that I might have done you irreparable harm. Me? I asked. Don't be silly, how could you do me any harm? I said, still not sure whether she was referring to my initial infatuation with the dashing captain — yes I admit it, it was infatuation. She elaborated. She believed that she may have selfishly and unwittingly stood in my way to happiness, that Captain Robertson was smitten with me and that she had stolen him from me. I burst out laughing and assured her that nothing was further from the truth. My outburst sounded so false to my own ears, but Annie is a child, innocent of the way of the world. Are you sure? said the dear child, because I swear that I can give him up, if that will make you happy. No, I said forcing a controlled laugh which I tried to make as genuine as I could, why would I want your Captain Percy, when my own John back in Stroud is all I want. I was just as surprised as dear Annie on hearing these words. John? she asked, why Aunt Fanny, you are one dark horse, we never knew. Do you mean your trusted manager Mr Merryweather? I knew it, I knew it! Who else, Annie? But I made her swear silence on the subject, and she was as happy as a lark on being made my confidante and at the same time greatly relieved that she was blameless as far as Percy was concerned.

Now I do not know how I am going to spend the next 5 weeks, pretending that all I am waiting for is to be reunited with "my" John, whose face as I write this, I cannot even recall, although he is indeed a most admirable man.

<u>Tenth of April 1847</u>. It was a tour de force, living a lie for five weeks, pretending that I was basking in the reflected happiness of my niece and her new love and at the same time counting the minutes to my reunion with "my" John. I have too much pride to risk a rebuff, for I fear that even if Annie were to drown her infatuation in its infancy, Percy would not necessarily come back to me. I was definitely too old for him. So I played the game, Cupid's game, listening to Annie's confidences, advising, helping whenever I could. I must admit that Percy was no fool; every time our paths crossed, he acted like a man who thinks he has been guilty of a betrayal. He tries to look away or if he could not engineer that, he would blush uncomfortably. But why had I mentioned John Merryweather? Could it be that deep down I had always nurtured some secret affection for the man? I know that there are few men I respect more. His wife died five years ago, but I had never envisaged the possibility of us two being together, after all we come from different strata, John's father was a mere tradesman, though known for his honesty and

straightforward ways. Still 'my' Merryweather is worth ten Elias Malpas. He is as honest a man as breathed God's air, has a pleasant face and bearing, charm and wit. I daresay that his lowly station put aside, he would indeed make an excellent prospect. There, I have said it.

Now we are due to arrive in Liverpool in a couple of days. Percy has sounded me about a possible engagement between the two of them, and has even said that he realised that Annie was too young, but has given me his word as a gentleman that he would wait for her for a year or two. I said that I would write to my brother giving him my favourable opinion of him. He dutifully kissed my hand in thanks. Annie was heart-broken. Dearest Auntie, she entreated me, tell me how I am going to endure being separated from the man I love for so long. I laughed and said that we always manage. I love you so very much, dearest Auntie Fanny, you are such a brick, and I wish you every happiness with John Merryweather. I fear that Annie is going to drop a big brick which might make it awkward between me and my manager. A good manager is as rare as gold dust, I daresay.

Thirteenth of April 1847. Percy has told Annie that he was going to the Foreign Office in London, where he was to be appointed aide-de-camp to a colonial governor, although he had no idea where, and we took our leave. Merryweather had booked seats on the Lancashire & Yorkshire Railway from Liverpool for us, and his telegram had indicated with his usual precision, where to change. Finally we are to catch the Birmingham & Gloucester Railway, when he will be waiting for us in the fiacre for the final ride home to Stroud. I have had to swear Annie to discretion concerning the imaginary romance between me and dear John.

Nineteenth of May 1847. Whatever possessed me to blurt out that big lie about me and John? Annie would be discreet if she knew how, but she has an impish temperament and the wonder is that John did not immediately gather by her looks and complicit smiles that something was afoot. Then the poor fellow started exhibiting signs of confusion in our daily intercourse. The relationship between the two of us is now more than a bit strained, and John feels threatened, no doubt thinking that he as done something amiss. I cannot find a way out of this self-inflicted contretemps.

<u>Tenth of July 1847</u>. The professional relationship between John and me is becoming more and more strained, and I could see that the poor man is not happy. Still I did not expect it when yesterday, he approached me with his usual forthrightness.

'Ma'am,' he said, 'I will be obliged to you if you can find the time to hear something I want to say.' My stock response under similar circumstances is, sure, Mr Merryweather, there is no time like the present time. We sat ourselves, me at my desk, and he on a plush chair reserved for visitors. Yes, I said, I am all ears.

'Well, it's like this, ma'am,' John was not one to dilly dally, 'I have felt for some weeks now, ever since you came back from Australia in fact, that I am no longer giving satisfaction in my work.' He paused, expecting me to say something, but I was too dumbfounded to speak, so he carried on.

'If you want me to go, you must say so, and I will go without fuss, but in all fairness, ma'am, I must ask you to give me specific examples of the ways in which I have erred or been remiss.'

'No,' I said, 'you have not been remiss in anything, I swear,' but I was unable to say more, because I was debating with myself about what to say. The man had served me efficiently and faithfully, and I could not tell him that he had imagined the strain in our relationship. Did I owe him an explanation? A white lie had led to this uncomfortable situation, and I said to myself that I was not going to cover its ill effects with another one.

'Am I then to take it that I have imagined the...' the poor man was stuck for words.

'Cooling off in our intercourse?' I said. He smiled. I recognised that smile from a dozen similar situations in the past. It meant, you always know the right words, ma'am.

'There has never been any cooling off, John,' I said, possibly the first time ever that I have preferred that appellation to the more formal Mr Merryweather. I hoped that he would accept this and that would be the end of the matter, but he was not the sort of man who would accept an anodyne reassurance.

'But ma'am, I cannot see that there has never been a cooling off, I am sorry, but you always liked frankness.' I resisted the temptation of saying that I had no more to add.

'All right, John, it was a little silliness on my part if you must know.'

'Ma'am?' he said and stared at me, dumbfounded. My admitting to silliness seemed to him like the pope in Rome owning publicly to fallibility. He stood up, and was on the point of bowing and leaving, when I heard myself speak.

'You see, my niece Annie... when we were travelling home from Australia on the *Wilberforce*... Annie started teasing me about what she thought was my infatuation with Captain Percy, with whom she is now officially engaged. When I knew they were smitten with each other, and not wanting to stand in their way, I mentioned that my heart was otherwise engaged, and belonged to another... eh... and I... eh... took your name.'

'You said that?'

'Yes, John, I did; I do not know why.' He blushed and started stammering incoherently, then took a deep breath, looked at me in the eyes, and I felt hot in the face.

'Obviously you did not mean it, and that explains why you have been uneasy in my company ever since... I see.' I nodded sadly.

'Well,' said John, 'I would not want to be a source of embarrassment to you, and let me assure you that I do not for one moment think that I have been ill-used. I will go as soon as you have found a new manager. In fact I will help you find one.'

'John,' I implored, 'no, don't go, dear friend, we are grown-ups and now that we have cleared the air, I am sure that we will be able to resume our former intercourse as if nothing happened.' He said nothing for a while.

'You mean... you were infatuated with the Captain, and when you saw that Miss Annie...' he could not finish what he wanted to say, and shook his head wistfully. Then he raised his head and looked at me in the eyes, shook his head gently. 'I have always known that you were a lady of exceptional selflessness.'

I could not say anything, and felt that if he said any more, I might not be able to hold my tears inside my eyes.

'I have always admired you...' he said, 'much more than admire really, even when my dear Olivia was alive... only I never dared...'

Tenth of March 1855. I have not found time to make entries for a variety of reasons, but mainly because of all the change that has happened in my life. John and I have been bounced into a romance, because once I had told that lie to Annie, there was no way of preventing its inception.

In the intervening months, things had developed very fast, and to cut a long story short (it is not my story, so I can choose to cut it short), the sound of wedding bells is in the air. The wedding ceremony is to be held in Wells Cathedral, and the celebrations in Marchmont Manor. The illustrious Rob Rob, a youthful friend of the late lamented Shelley, Annie tells me, is coming over with Percy's mother, as are dear George and Amelia. They are all going to lodge with us at the Manor. Percy has been appointed aide-de-camp to the governor of Nova Scotia, and once married, the couple are to start their married life in the colony.

Nineteenth of November 1848. I received a letter from Nova Scotia this morning from Captain Robertson, informing me of their joy in becoming the proud parents of Rosalind, a healthy and angelic little baby girl. Dear Journal, I own to a joy not much less than theirs. Our own little boy, Edward Merryweather was born six months earlier of course. John and I daily thank the good Lord that He is watching over her.

Post Script. Rosalind Robertson and Edward Merryweather were married in July 1867. Their daughter Ann married George Robertson, a great grandson of Catriona Robertson (aka Wahaitiya) one of Don's ancestors.

CHAPTER 4

— ◆◆◆ —

Demerara

WHEN DONALD ROBERTSON finished university in Cambridge with a first class honours in Natural Sciences, he booked his passage on the Scotia, the latest Cunard liner, an iron-clad paddle steamer which was leaving Liverpool bound for New York on its maiden voyage, due to reach Toronto in good time for Granny Kitty and Grandpa Wahaitiya's diamond wedding, which was to be celebrated in the hall of the Highland College for Girls in Peterborough which Granny had created, to provide for the education of mainly Ojibwa and Cayuga children, although it was open to all.

The voyage was smooth and uneventful, with only the presence of an iceberg some distance away, causing a danger warning, breaking its monotony. Donald was not used to sitting in a deck chair for hours, but he had little else to do for the sixteen days the trip was scheduled to take. He sat on the deck, reading the many scientific journals that he had bought before leaving Great Britain. He never tired of reading and re-reading his books and papers. With his interest in birds, having studied zoology for four years, he found Thomas Bewick's *A History of British Birds* with its wood engravings and its accurate observations, completely engrossing. He hoped that he would make an enlarged copy of Mr Bewick's green finch one day, but on this ship, although he had time aplenty, his stock of material was packed in his many suitcases in the hold. He wryly told himself that in other times, he would have all the materials handy, but never the time. He wondered why he had bought *The Illustrated Book of Canaries and Other Cage-Birds*. The very idea of caged animals revolted him. *The Gardens and Menagerie of the Zoological Society Delineated* was a serendipitous find at Maggs, and he treasured this book above all else.

466

He never really liked tobacco, but a pipe gave him something to do, as he immediately started blushing and blinking at the approach of someone he did not know well. Fiddling with a pipe and a match gave him the means of minimising his embarrassment, and besides, this added a modicum of gravitas to his youthful appearance, his carefully nurtured moustache not helping much. He had contemplated growing a beard too, but as he was rather proud of his square jaw, he decided that he was not going to hide it.

Having always been bookish and withdrawn by nature, he had never developed the art of talking to the female sex. Why, he thought wryly, he hardly knew how to talk to men. He probably did not have conversational skills, for even when he talked about things of universal interest, like the behaviour of birds under different climactic conditions, (who can find that fascinating subject other than stimulating?) he found that after less than half an hour people began losing interest, and the same people, he noticed later, seemed singularly engrossed in something else when he appeared.

There were some handsome specimens of the female sex on board, and he easily imagined himself enjoying their company, but he had no idea what to do after you bowed to the young lady, smiled and exchanged information about the weather. He had promised himself that he was going to try ever so hard on this trip. He had the feeling that luck was on his side with so many desirable young maidens confined to the limited space of the decks and dining rooms. Propitious conditions indeed!

As he was reclining on a deck chair reading his Bewick, a young lady holding a fetching parasol, Miss Hilve Mortensen, to whom the captain had already presented him, and her aunt, appeared on the deck, walking towards him. He put his book down and looked for his pipe. He put it in his mouth and found a box of safety matches, in readiness. She was an American whose father had come over from Denmark and had bought a foundry in Boston. She had bouncy, bright, volatile blond hair and smiling blue eyes to match, a fine slim figure contrasting perversely with the aunt's short squat physique, and a self-assured bearing. Yes, he would not mind getting to know her. Romances were known to sprout on an Atlantic crossing, and Donald was ready. He stood up and bowed to them as they drew level with him.

'Oh good morning, Mr Robertson,' said the aunt, in a thick Danish accent, and the niece smiled angelically and bowed slightly. He wondered whether he should make an attempt to kiss their hands, but started blinking instead.

'Yes,' he said enthusiastically, 'it is a good morning indeed.' A little erudition might help create a good impression, he thought, so he added, 'The wind seems to be blowing in a north-easterly direction, and the clouds over there, which you might think are of the altostratus variety, are in fact cirrus clouds. It would interest you to know that they only appear nearer because the air is clear... what I mean is that rain is unlikely, with excellent prospects of a nice clear day.' But he did not wish to sound like a know-all. 'Of course I may be wrong,' he said convinced that he was not, 'I am sure the captain will issue a weather forecast in due course, and I for one, shall be studying it with great interest.'

'How very interesting,' said the aunt in admiration.

'Are you interested in clouds, Miss... Andersen?'

'Mortensen,' the girl corrected hiding her mortification.

'The captain was telling us that you won a first class honours degree at Trinity,' the aunt said, more as a rebuke to the young lady, than to impart the information to him, since he was already aware of it.

'Oh yes, I did, thank you. You see, I specialised in fish and birds...'

'Oh do tell us about birds, Mr Robertson,' entreated the older Miss Mortensen, 'I have always wanted to know how birds migrate. I am sure you clever scientists know everything there is to know about that.' Don failed to notice the look of despair that suddenly appeared on Hilve Mortensen's face.

'Well, this is not as much of a mystery as people might think,' he began. He was going to enjoy himself. He started by taking a deep breath and clearing his throat.

'All the senses come into it,' he began with gusto. The fair Hilve frowned. 'Vision, hearing and smell of course... but only a week ago,' he added without a pause for breath, 'I read an article in Nature, and I found it very enlightening, to the effect that earth magnetism plays a big part. You see, the earth can be considered as a big magnet with two poles...'

'I know,' said Hilve in an attempt to pacify her aunt, who she knew expected her to greet the young men she thought of as good prospects with some respect not to say friendliness. 'One at the north pole and the other at the south pole.' Donald looked disappointed. He pursed his lips and obviously regretted having to contradict her.

'Actually,' he said, 'the so-called north pole is not at the north pole per se, nor is the magnetic south pole at the south pole. That's a very interesting subject too, and if you are interested I shall be delighted to elaborate.' They said nothing, so he took that as a cue to continue.

'When we say that the needle of a compass points towards the north pole, it isn't exactly right, it only seeks the north pole.' He was now in full flow, but suddenly he was invaded by less scientific thoughts. The Captain's Ball! That would be an ideal occasion to gain further intimacy with the highly desirable young lady. He had to impress her, so he explained polarity in great details, and then remembered that it had all started with bird migration. The ladies began to fidget. No doubt like him, they were eager to get to lunch. Bird migration will have to wait for another time.

'I hope you will be going to the Captain's Ball tonight,' he said, 'may I be so bold as to...' his courage failed him. He put the pipe in his mouth and started lighting it. Hilve frowned.

'Mr Robertson, I think you should put some tobacco in the pipe before lighting it.'

'Yes, quite... quite right...'

'The absent-minded professor, eh!' the maiden aunt cackled merrily.

'You were saying?' she was determined to keep the conversation going.

'Aye, yes, yes... I hope to see you there... at the ball.' Hilve smiled and curtsied and led her aunt away.

Hilve avoided the young scientist after having verified her suspicion that there was no lousier dancer in the whole world. Donald was a bit disheartened by his singular lack of success with the girl, but that was not the first time that his earnest efforts at finding a soul mate had failed.

Still, he was not one to let desperation take hold of him. In any case, he had always been in two minds about attachments, as he feared that his pursuit of knowledge would probably come at a price. He badly wanted to find a woman to love passionately and whole-heartedly, but would she understand that sometimes, when his attention was completely taken by some investigation, he would have no time for her at all? He knew for instance that once he had embarked on a study, he could think of nothing else, he forgot to eat lunch, he was up all night, and when people talked to him he did not hear them. All those women who he had unsuccessfully tried to court in the past, might even have done him a favour by not responding to his attention. Hilve Mortensen was a case in point. She was a society beauty, and if he married her, she would expect him to attend and organise balls and soirées, and he did not expect soirées and balls to feature much in a life devoted to learning. On the other hand, a scientist is nothing if he has a closed mind. He must be open to new sensations, perhaps it would not be too difficult to juggle a social life with the seeking of knowledge. Still he wondered if the fair Hilve was at all winnable. He would discover that she was not.

Nothing much happened on board that was out of the ordinary. There were no encounters with icebergs, the sea stayed uncharacteristically calm, and the Scotia reached New York a day early. He travelled by coach to Rochester and from there took a ferry to Toronto. He stayed two days in that city and then father and mother joined him on the trip to Peterborough in their fiacre. The family had an impressive town house in Peterborough, but also possessed huge chunks of land and property spreading all the way to the Rice Lake, where great uncles John Smith and Albert Robertson (né Wahaitiya) had joined forces some fifty years ago and created their flourishing sawmill business. He was pleased to find that so much had changed, the roads were now macadamised, making the trip smooth and pleasant. The family estate had grown quite considerably. Thousands of acres of forest stretching from the Rice Lake towards Peterborough had been cleared since he was last there, and golden wheat was everywhere. Donald, who had spent almost three weeks at sea, where the unimpeded view of the ocean stretched to infinity, as if nothing else existed on this earth, had a similar sensation when passing through the cultivated fields. It was as if the globe had been transformed into a golden ocean of wheat to the exclusion of everything else, causing waves as the gentle wind dispensed with its caresses. The family owned over ten thousand acres of prime land on the banks of the Otanabee River and they had been transformed into orchards by Uncle John Smith Junior. Smith and Robertson were still the most important timber merchants in the Maritime and had a very modern plant which employed over a hundred workers, mainly Ojibwas and Cayugas. There were any number of new edifices of varying size, colours and styles lining up the road from the town to the Lake, housing the large influx of people from the Maritime who had flocked in there to find work.

Of all his family, he loved Granny Kitty more than anybody else. Mother was undemonstrative — not that he ever doubted her love for him. Father was too absorbed in the business of making money to have time for him. He regretted that he only knew one way of showing how much he loved and admired his boy, which was to lavish huge sums of money on him, often buying him things for which he had no use.

Granny claimed that the return of her favourite person in the whole world made her feel ten years younger. She was now the most respected woman in Peterborough, and Grandpa Wahaitiya glowed with pleasure every time some newspaper ran a story of one of her many achievements. He had kept a scrap book to show Donald. Father was devoted to his old man, and often regretted that following advice from his accountant, he had changed his name by deed poll to Robertson, at the suggestion of Granny Catriona. When one is in business, a Scottish name would sound more trustworthy than the Ojibwa name that he acquired at birth. Granny Catriona, like everybody else in this world, he simply worshipped. For once father seemed not to regret leaving Toronto and money-making. He much preferred working in an office and had left the practical side of the family business in the hands of his younger brother Albert and the Smith uncles who relished that sort of thing. He was so proud of his son, and expected to spend some quality time with him, not that he would be able to follow what the gifted young scientist would have to say. He wished he could hear his son disown Mr Darwin's heretical claims, but because he feared that he might not, he chose not to raise that issue with him. Granny openly broached the subject of marriage.

'You know dearest, there was a time when I was not sure if marriage was all that desirable an institution. It is even easier for a man to avoid it, as man can have liaisons without the world judging him harshly. But when I decided that my lovely Ojibwa man here, was the only man I would ever want, my soul mate, and once I talked him into throwing his lot with me, I changed my mind for good. A good woman can make all the difference to your life, trust me.'

'Granny,' Donald said laughing, 'you are preaching to the converted, I want nothing else, but where do I find such a woman… my soul mate, as you say?'

Granny walked towards him, took his head and buried it in her breast, and said, 'They don't know those hussies, what a prize catch you would be.' He always marvelled at her plummy Highland accent which she had never made the slightest effort of getting rid of.

'Just find me one, then,' he said with a laugh.

Granny did not need to be asked twice. Yes, there was Eve MacKay who was teaching at the school, recently arrived from Greenock, Scotland, and who was boarding with the headmistress, Mrs Phillips. She will arrange for the two of them to meet, specially as she knew that Mr Phillips was going to be away in Toronto on business. She sent word to the headmistress who was a good friend, and got her to arrange for the two young people to meet. Donald was delighted. He was already half in love with the charming Scotswoman whom he had not even seen yet.

Mrs Phillips invited Donald and Eve to tea on Wednesday of the following week. Donald had spent a sleepless night putting some order in the subjects he might broach in an attempt to make a good impression. He obviously knew about fish and birds, but besides, he also knew a large number of useful scientific facts about volcanoes, hurricanes, astronomy, natural selection. So when he met Eve, he was positively brimming with facts and rearing to let them loose on receptive ears.

Eve was very pretty and had high cheekbones, lips which were thin but seemed to go on forever until they seemed to reach her ears, and a small snub nose. She was just the way he liked women, slim, not very tall, auburn hair coiled in thick tresses, and crystalline black and intelligent eyes. Most noticeably, she had a bearing that was elegant without being arrogant. With her slightly pointed jaw her profile had a fetching triangular aspect which made her possibly the most attractive woman he had ever come across. When Donald went to school, teachers had no right to be so pretty. He imagined that he could indeed easily fall in love with a woman like her. She talked softly but quickly, in a determined manner, and chose her words with great deliberation.

As he would have expected in a dedicated teacher, she thought that education was by far the most important thing in the life of a child, even more important than food or medicine.

'Medicine has made fantastic progress in the last ten years. When I was in England, I —'

'Without education,' Eve interrupted, 'no one would be able to learn medicine, and...' He was not listening to her, but admiring the intensity and clarity with which she was putting across her views.

'Of course most teachers do not choose the profession in order to enrich themselves,' she said, 'it is a vocation, or it is nothing!' Don could hear the impact of the exclamation mark.

She went on without stopping, broached the subjects of morality and ethics, decried the obstacles standing in the path of women seeking to educate themselves. Did Donald meet any women students when he was studying at Trinity? No, of course you did not, because women are not allowed to go to university! He had the strange feeling that she seemed to be holding him personally responsible for this sad state of affairs. No, of course she did not hate all men, where would she be if her own dear father the Reverend Gordon MacKay had not undertaken to educate her personally?

He allowed his mind to wander momentarily, and when he urged himself to pay attention, she seemed to be holding forth about the necessity to educate adults, and was advocating the creation of night schools, not only for those adults who felt that they had missed out, but for anybody who was still illiterate or semi-literate. In her view, illiteracy was as great a calamity as consumption. Donald now stopped listening to her, and was just nodding, waiting for a moment when he might slip a word in edgewise. He found that whilst he might be in agreement with Eve, he did not necessarily want to know all the pros and cons of the matter. Good thing though education was — and he had no quarrel with her position — it was only interesting up to a point which Eve had overtaken a full two hours earlier. Seamlessly she seemed to have broken into new grounds, explaining why she thought that it might be better for children to start by learning simple words rather the letters of the alphabet. Eve seemed delighted with the way the evening had gone. She expressed her delight at meeting someone who obviously shared her passion for education and was so interested in what she had to say, and hoped that they might meet again.

Next morning at breakfast, Granny was all smiles.

'Come on now, laddie, tell granny how the evening went. What did you think of Eve MacKay? Did the two of you hit it off?' Donald pursed his lips glumly.

'Well granny, I liked her a lot at first, I thought she was very pretty, intelligent and charming, but my God, what a bore! She talked about nothing but education all evening, I was never so bored in my life. Why won't people understand that what they might consider interesting, may leave their interlocutors cold?' Granny Kitty promised herself that she would try again at the earliest opportunity.

The big party for the grandparents' wedding anniversary was a big family occasion, and everybody seemed to have a great time. Even great uncle John Smith and great aunt Felicity, who were on their best behaviour, seemed thrilled. They had always intrigued him. As a child, he could not help noticing how they could not bear to be apart, and surmised that few married couples could be so much in love, but they did not seem happy, there was always some tension between them which he could not understand. Later he discovered that John drank too much, and Felicity was given to bouts of depression. Granny Kitty who was not given to passing judgement on other people, once confided to him that although the great aunt was the one who had instigated the big romance, although she did not doubt for a minute that she loved her brother John as much as anybody could love a husband, she could never forget that she had married beneath her station, and instead of cashing the great love that they had for each other and building a happy life with it, she could not resist pointing out, even in company, how uncouth he was, always trying to change him so he would become a polished gentleman. Early in the marriage, Kitty had advised her brother to put his foot down and tell her to stop this nonsense, but dear John would never raise his voice to anybody. He so hated giving offence, that he much preferred to say nothing and bottle it all in. This, she explained was what had driven her brother to the bottle.

Father was due to leave for Toronto in the afternoon, and in the morning Donald and he had been locked in conversation in Granny's study. The old man had made it clear that he had no intention of dictating to his son what he had to do.

'I am proud, Donnie,' he was saying. He was the only man who called him by that strange appellation. 'I am proud that whatever my failings, not having followed the advice of Mam, and denied myself learning…' Donald nodded, it was true. He had been a dutiful father, he knew how much he had loved him, even if he had not been the type to give him a piggy back or go for a swim with him. He was not always there for the momentous events in his life, because he had other priorities. What was better for the family that I love, he would ask himself, to negotiate that contract worth ten thousand dollars or to take the boy out kite-flying? Money was very important for one's happiness, how can one say one loves one's family if one left them unprotected from the vagaries of life? Thus he had never flinched from spending money on his wife, his only remaining son, his father and mother. He had spent tens of thousand of dollars building them that house in Peterborough. Would they have preferred him to neglect his business and visit them more often? No, a house was more concrete. Didn't Donnie agree? He had never given this much thought, but he nodded.

'Tell me, Donnie, have you made any plans for the future?' He immediately added, 'Mind you I am not pressing you, I know how hard you have studied, I had my informants, you know,' he added with a smile, 'You need a rest. Stay with your granny here for as long as you like, put some order in your thoughts, and I know you will arrive at the right decision. When you do, just let me know.' Donald always felt a bit uneasy with the old man, but he knew that there was much unsaid love on both sides. He coughed uneasily and smiled apologetically.

'Actually Father, I rested more than I needed to on the crossing, I don't need a rest. Enforced idleness tires me out.' A chip off the old block, the old man thought happily. He too found holidays tiring, which was why he rarely took one.

'I propose to set to work straight away.'

'Are you planning to secure an appointment at some university? With your Cambridge degree you should have no difficulty at all, I daresay. I know one or two good people who will put in a good word —'

'Father, I am not planning to join any university at the moment, I want to... Oh, I don't know how to put it.' Old Mr Robertson frowned, he liked straight talking.

'I want some hands-on, eh, I think that's it's called now, hands-on experience first. The last four years I have almost always been between four walls learning from between two covers, occasionally dissecting birds and rabbits... what I want to do now is to go out in the wild and learn first hand from nature.'

'I am not sure I understand what you're saying, Donnie.' The young man cleared his throat.

'If you are agreeable to my proposition, I would like to go live in places where I might come in contact with fauna and to some extent, flora. Birds, fish, rare animals and plants, make a comprehensive study of them, photograph them, make sketches of them, that sort of thing.' The old man stared at his son, not sure about what he had heard.

Suddenly his face lit up.

'This is the ideal country to study bears and...lichens... ' He did not finish the sentence as he had caught Donald shaking his head.

'Why Donnie, you know best... Draw up a plan of action and we can discuss the financial aspect.'

Donald had already thought everything through. He would like to go live in Demerara for a while. The land there had, density-wise, a richness of fauna that had no equal in the known world. He would set up a base there, then make trips down the Demerara and the Essequibo rivers, study the land, the birds and the fishes, and then possibly use his findings towards a doctoral thesis. He thought a year there would do for a start. The old man said that he would arrange for the equivalent of one thousand pounds sterling, in Spanish dollars, to be put aside for him straight away. Would that be sufficient? One thousand pounds? I could buy half of Georgetown with that.

Madeleine Rose Robertson was disappointed about her son's hurry to leave after having been away for so many years. One week in Peterborough and then three in Toronto. He had to know how she adored him and how dearly she would love to look after him. She knew that people would find her ridiculous if she told them that the thing she missed most in life was helping her son putting his shirt on and combing his hair when he was a child. She knew that Donald would not like it now, but how she wished that he would let her, hold his head against her breast and rock him to sleep — and comb his hair — just once. He had grown up far too quickly for her. She vividly remembered the day the doctor confirmed that she was with child; she remembered his little half-formed feet kicking her, like it was only yesterday, and look at him now, he was almost twice her size. When her first born Graham died of meningitis, she thought that she would never recover, and had resented becoming pregnant gain so soon after. She was unsure about loving this newcomer whom she thought of as an interloper coming to take the place of her little angel, but the moment she heard his first cry for help, all the bottled up love for the dead child rose to the surface again and took over her whole life, like a drop of oil poured over the sea is known to spread over it for square miles. And now he was going away again. She had read about Demerara. There were primitive tribes there, cannibals, an article said, and dangerous animals, jaguars and venomous snakes. She would worry about him all the time and would never sleep again at night. Why couldn't he break a leg and be house-bound, so she could look after him? Not forever of course, but for a year only? That would be heavenly… No, she was being selfish and undignified. She could only hope now that nobody would uncover that wicked thought of hers.

'Donald dearest, have you not thought of starting a family?' Maybe it was not too late to make him change his mind. She knew about mother-in-law Kitty's unsuccessful attempt but no one had told her the details.

'To start a family, Mama dear,' the son replied, 'one needs a wife, and I don't seem to have one.' She knew that he was not being facetious, he was sometimes very opaque.

'Oh a boy of your… gifts… will have no difficulty finding a good woman… there are hundreds of eligible young women —'

'I will come back in a year's time Mama, and I daresay some of these wonderful young ladies will still be around, don't you think?'

'We missed you so much, your father and I, we counted the days.' Donald knew that he should say that he missed them too, but he had not, so taken up was he by his studies, so he kept quiet. Madeleine's face lit up, she had yet to play her trump card.

'Your gran so wants to have you around, she is getting on, you know.' This did produce an effect on him. She always knew that the boy felt more at ease with the old dear than with herself, but jealous she was not. At least she hoped not.

'Oh yes, granny Kitty... but I will spend a whole week in Peterborough before I leave.'

'She will like that,' she conceded, 'yes, do go visit her.'

'And I will spend at least three weeks in Toronto with you before I leave.'

'So your mind is made up?' He pursed his lips and nodded.

'I will write, Mama,' he said, 'to you and father,' he added, remembering that he seemed to write only to Granny when he was in Cambridge.

'Yes, dear, write often, we so enjoyed your letters.' She did not tell him that she had read all his letters so often that she knew them all almost by heart. She probably could give a better account of what he had done those four years in the old country, than Donald himself could.

From Toronto he went to Montreal down the St Lawrence, and from there father, who transacted business with the Booker brothers, had arranged for him to travel on a Booker Transport ship to Georgetown.

He landed in what was to be his home for some time, one afternoon just as the sun was setting, and he had never seen a more glorious sunset. So when Mr Emsworth, a director of Booker Brothers who had come to meet him at his disembarkation and told him that he had secured a small villa on the bank of the Demerara overlooking the ocean, he was delighted. Mr Emsworth said that someone was looking after his luggage, which consisted largely of books, his photographic equipment and his microscopes, and would take everything to his residence, but that dinner was waiting for him at his own house near St George's Church. Only when he discovered that Mr Emsworth and he did not share the same concept of the adjective small, did he express a slight reservation. How was he going to look after such a huge place? Mr Emsworth laughed; he would have to have people for that. People? Yes, servants. The concept of a single man having servants was completely inimical to Donald, although in Cambridge he had come across some insufferable toffs who specialised in speaking through their noses who had a valet in tow, who carried their books, dressed them, cleaned their shoes or their mess after they vomited after drunken bouts. He had thought that this was just a quaint aristocratic English practice. That would never do, he would not know how to deal with them. There was already a night watchman living on the premises, and he was part of the lease deal with the owner, an East Indian landowner, Emsworth explained.

Donald forgot everything when he was introduced to Emsworth's daughter Charlotte. He thought that this time it was the true thing, a clear case of love at first sight. The haughty Hilve was but a pale shadow in comparison. Charlotte was like a dream come true. She was a bit on the tall side, reaching him to the ear when she wore high heels. She was a platinum blonde and had the loveliest nose he had ever seen on a woman. She had laughing, bewitching hazel eyes, and had obviously taken advantage of the sun, for she had a healthy and fetching tan.

Emsworth's cook had prepared what was called a curry. Donald had never tasted that before, and was a bit disconcerted by its appearance. The observant Emsworth did not fail to notice his guest's reticence, and assured him that once he tasted Shankar's offering, he would become a fan for life. The daughter laughed a merry tinkling laugh which he found almost erotic. Although he had often fantasised about the opposite sex, he had never consciously entertained lascivious thoughts about them, but Charlotte aroused feelings in him that he wished he could keep under wraps — literally.

'I assure you, Don,' she said with a sweet little laugh, 'my father is absolutely right.' The mousy Mrs Emsworth to whom Donald had paid scant attention alarmed him by emitting a little squeak of a laugh, a distorted echo of her daughter's, adding, 'If you do not like it, which I promise you you won't, I mean you won't not like it… am I making sense Arnold?' Arnold smiled indulgently at her, and assured her that she was.

'If you don't like it, I will get Shankar to make you a steak… the beef here is exceptionally good.'

'No ma'am, I am sure I will like it. In my line of work, you see, I must expose myself to all sorts of new experience.'

'Yes, Donald,' Charlotte said enthusiastically, 'tell us about the things you do and aim at doing here.' But Donald who loved few things more than talking about science, was so overwhelmed by the young lady's stunning presence that he became tongue-tied. He did not know that it was this momentary paralysis of his speech faculties which had helped him in his love quest.

In Toronto, Madeleine Rose Robertson was surprised when a big envelope was handed over to her, bearing stamps from British Guyana. First, there were three stamps with the queen's head and one to make up for the full rate, was a magenta coloured 1 cent stamp with a signature. She did not expect the letter to be addressed to her as Donald usually wrote to his father with a few lines for her. To her amazement the envelope bore her name on it, in the boy's bold handwriting. By the feel of it, she thought it was a lengthy one too. Perhaps he had enclosed a newspaper cutting; did they have newspapers there? She sat down on her rocking chair in the veranda overlooking her garden to savour it. There were at least four hand-written sheets, all in Donald's bold careful script. She wiped off a tear as she remembered how she had taught him to write. She still thought that the letter might be addressed to his father, but she saw it right there: Dearest Mater!

Her hands were trembling and she made a mental effort not to cry, in the knowledge that her tears would make it difficult for her to read darling Donald's words.

Taj Mahal Villa,
Georgetown,
12, January. 1863

Dearest Mater,

I hope you and father are both well, as indeed I am. You will be surprised at receiving this, seeing that I have usually only written short letters to you. Only now do I understand that I ought to have written to you more often in the past. And I will tell you why by and by. I remember father, in one of the rare moments of intimacy he and I have shared, telling me once that the first time he saw you, his immediate thought was, and I quote: "This is the woman I want to become the mother of my children!"

She stopped reading, took her glasses off and began wiping them, because the tears of joy gushing out of her as she took cognisance of these sentiments, had quite overwhelmed her. It was not often that she had received proof of love from the two persons she loved and cherished most on this earth. Yes, she had always supposed that Edward was fond of her, he was used to having her around, but she never knew about this. She read it again:

"This is the woman I want to become the mother of my children!".

Why had he never told her that? But she loved him more than she loved God, and she had never told him that either; where would she have found the words? And Donald, whom she had suspected of not really caring for her, taking the trouble to write this long letter to her... dry up your tears gel, and read on.

The first time I saw Charlotte Emsworth, like father, I said to myself, 'Here is the woman I want to be the mother of my children!' Who is Charlotte Emsworth, you are wondering. I have decided to reveal all to you, darling mater. Mr Emsworth is the right hand man of Mr Connell at Booker Brothers, the largest English company in British Guyana, a company which he tells me was founded in the thirties. He kindly welcomed me to Georgetown when I arrived, as no doubt father has told you. He took me to his fabulous home on the night I landed and I ate curry for the first time. Curry is an Indian dish eaten with rice, and it is full of aromatic spices which are simply heavenly, although there is certain piquancy to it that I did not like at first, but found that it grew on one by the minute. I had not been three days here than I found myself addicted to the taste, and I daresay I could easily eat nothing else for the rest of my life.

I thought he loved my roast goose, she thought with a smile.

I promised myself to write a long detailed letter to you for once, and I am beginning to question myself if I am not boring you.

'No, beloved child, you are not boring me! How can you say that!' She heard herself almost shouting that out joyfully.

Anyway, the moment I perceived dear Charlotte, I thought no one can be as sweet and pleasant. She seemed bursting with intelligence and she has such bearing and presence. When I got talking to her, she confirmed my conjecture that she was an accomplished young lady. She had stayed in Somerset, England, with her cousins who were being taught at home by their father, the Reverend John Emsworth, her uncle, and she told me that she loved few things in life above learning. She asked me intelligent questions about what I had studied at Cambridge and listened very attentively to my answers. Oh, on the first day we met, I could hardly open my mouth, so thunderstruck was I by her beauty. She was kind enough to say that talking to me had made her regret that there were no colleges for young women, that if it had been possible, she would have loved to study at a university too, but unfortunately there were none that girls could go to. I spend a lot of time with her, and Mr and Mrs Emsworth seem not to disapprove of our friendship. I will no doubt be in a position to narrate to you how this true to life lovestory, not unlike one of Mr Reynold's fictional pieces that I know, dearest mater, you are addicted to, like I now am to curries, develop. I pray that there will be a happy ending. Can I beg you to wish me the best of luck in my pursuit?

I know you must be keen to know more about the place, the people, the sort of things I do. British Guyana which is the old Demerara plus some other territories as well, and which I will subsequently call B.G. is about ten times bigger than Wales, and it is very varied in its physical features. Granny told us both, if you remember, that it is the only English speaking country in the whole of South America. I was told that Guyana means The Land Of Many Rivers in some Indian language. The Dutch and the French were here before us, but it is now part of our glorious empire. Georgetown is a quaint old city, built and designed by the Hollanders; we even have canals like in Amsterdam here. They built a series of sluice gates which are called kokers, where the canals meet the estuary. They form a barrier between the Atlantic Ocean and the canals, and at high tide they are opened to allow any excess water accumulated to be drained away. So, you see, we are safe. Oh, I forgot to tell you the most important thing, El Dorado is supposed to have been somewhere in this land.

My villa, which Mr Emsworth found for me was built by a rich East Indian gentleman who came here only twenty years ago as an indentured labourer, but who is now a wealthy land owner. It is built on stilts, and do not be alarmed when I tell you why. This town happens to have been built below sea level, and as a result, flooding is a real hazard. But the stilts are there to counter the effects of possible flooding.

Mr Emsworth said to me that there are few colonies which have more natural resources than B.G. Apart from the potential for all manners of cultivation, and I can mention sugar, balata (a kind of latex which is used to make rubber, for which there is going to be an incredible demand in the near future, he says), there are large deposits of bauxite from which aluminium is made. Keep this to yourself, but my informant also tells me that some geologists have indicated that there are reasons to believe that diamond is also to be found in some parts of the colony.

There are many new buildings going up in the town, sorry, city, as it has now acquired this status. I will not bore you with a long list of landmarks in the city, but the St George's Church is one of the most impressive buildings you can hope to see anywhere in the world, it is made entirely of wood and is as far as I know, the tallest wooden edifice in the world. Incredibly there are railways operating quite efficiently here. The Demerara Railway Company operates passenger and freight services from Georgetown across sixty miles of track, down the Atlantic coast to Rossignol on the Berbic river.

The red and white striped lighthouse is an appealing sight, and I am trying to devise the means of taking a photograph of it to send you. As I will, indubitably, of all the striking buildings and monuments and landmarks.

I had the pleasure of accompanying Charlotte to a place on the river where there is the most spectacular and magical of flowers, a sort of lily which Mr Robert Schaumberg, a botanist whose works, which I read at Cambridge inspired me to come over here, named Victoria Regia, after our beloved sovereign. It has a diameter of the tallest man one can meet, and is of course circular. It looks like an enormous green plate floating on water, and at its centre is the most magnificent flower in the world, with a bright crimson centre surrounded by a pearly white ring and a rim of blushing pink. I shall paint a picture for you, for a photograph will not do justice to the colours.

As I said, I have a large house, and I rarely find use for more than one quarter of it. I have a whole room for my books! I shall convert it into a library later. I have secured the services of a cook, a young woman called Devi, who sleeps in a room in one wing of the house. She is very quiet and cooks delicious curries too, although possibly not as good as the Emsworth's cook Shankar. There is a night watchman who doubles up as gardener; he came with the house, and is paid by Mr Ramnauth (the owner).

Let me assure you as I finish this long epistle, mater dearest, that I have never felt better in my life, my health is good, and I have met Dr Laker, a friend of the Emsworths who has kindly offered to advise me on medical matters, specially as I intend to travel in some unhealthy regions in the near future.

As soon as I feel settled, I propose to go on a long trip down the Demerara, as a sort of exploratory exercise which will dictate my future plans.

Give father all my love; of course without his generosity, it would not be possible for me to lead the extravagant and exciting adventure which I am already leading.

With all my love, dearest mater

Donald. R.

When she finished reading the letter, she was in tears. It was a private, intimate letter from her son to her, and she was not going to read it to anybody else, she would only relate bits here and there to Edward. It was the happiest day of her life. It was funny how it could take a letter to do that. It was as if for the last twenty two years a mist had enveloped his filial love like her garden in a spring morning mist; you knew the spectacular irises were there, but before seeing them, you had to wait for the mist to lift; in the same manner, she could always feel that his love was there all the time, and had wished for a clearer vision of it; now that mist had cleared, no power on earth was going to make it descend on that love ever again. Although she was not sure about God, and even less sure about the power of prayers, she was going to pray hard for his success in both his love life and his professional life. *Bless that sweet Charlotte, I already think of her as my own!*

Donald hated the idea of leaving Charlotte in Georgetown whilst he went on a trip up the Demerara river. He hired a boat and a boatman, a squat Amerindian fellow who was all muscles called Yarreku, and made his first trip. Yarreku was a strange character; most of the time he had a frown on his forehead and appeared to be deep in thought, but on occasions, he was transformed into a fun loving, skittish fellow who could guffaw louder than Don's fellow Cambridge undergraduates when they went on the King Street run.

The boat was of the type called candoa made and used by Carib Indians from light wood and bark of trees, and Yarreku, who spoke in words rather than full sentences said, Unsinkable, when he showed him the boat. As the currents at the mouth of the estuary were usually very strong, the boat was moored up the river a good mile away, so the pair of them walked, each carrying enough food for a short two-day trip, and some equipment, Donald in a rucksack on his back, and Yarreku in a thick wooden box which miraculously stayed finely balanced on his head, in spite of the uneven terrain and his propensity for scampering about at a pace.

The water was dark ochre and its flow was quite ferocious, which would have made Donald feel apprehensive, but he was too impatient to start his life of adventure to let fear come into the equation. Yarreku was endowed with incredible strength.

'Sir Donal,' he said, 'you sit, Yarreku look after boat.' He had tried on many occasions to inform the Carib man that he was not yet a knight of the realm (although he fully expected that at some point in the future he would be graced with that title, for his contribution to science), but the man seemed not to understand. He was ever to remain Sir Donal. The current was so strong that the boat began by going downstream, but Yarreku only smiled and after what did not seem to the young Canadian to be a powerful stroke, he managed not only to stop this, but to make the craft creep upstream. It was like magic, the budding scientist would write in his diary. After a while, the current seemed to become weaker, and the boatman invited him to try his hand. At Cambridge, he was not prepared to neglect his studies, so he had to content himself being a mere Sunday sculler. As they went up river, the vegetation became denser and more luxuriant. He made the boatman stop now and then, hopped on the bank, set up his camera and took photographs of plants that looked unfamiliar. Flora was an area that was of limited interest to him, but he had read Schaumberg's papers and knew his Linnaeus, and he meant to show his pictures to some expert botanist friends. Yarreku was perplexed by the camera, and when Don explained to him what it did, he was not sure whether he had made any sense to the man. They stopped on the island of Borselm, which used to be the capital of Demerara in the days of the Dutch, but it was now almost deserted with most of the built-up structures in ruins. As they were sitting near the water, eating, Yarreku said, 'Look, Sir Donal,' pointing to the water, where there was a hardly perceptible ripple. A caiman, he thought, for that was something he wanted to see. No, his guide told him… anaconda. Then he saw it, a yellow anaconda, swimming towards them. As the water was clear, he could see the dark bluish patterns on its body. Yarreku was not watching the snake, but looking intently at the young scientist. Don guessed that the snake was about twenty feet long. Suddenly the serpent changed course, and they watched it disappear. The Amerindian smiled, spat in the water and dismissively said, 'Him small!'. What did he mean? He explained by pointing to his eyes, which meant that he once saw one specimen, then by tracing an invisible line between two palm trees which must have been a hundred feet apart, suggested what he thought the length of the reptile was. Later he would discover that Yarreku was not given to exaggeration. They spent the night on the island. He would not have been able to photograph the anaconda, so he sat down on the grass and made a sketch of what he had seen. If he saw nothing else of interest during the trip, this sight alone would have made it worth while.

On the island there were a large number of birds, many of which he had not even seen pictures of. Where possible, he took photographs. But the great find of the trip happened on the island as they were preparing to leave in the morning. Yarreku suddenly grabbed Don's hand in an obvious signal for him to stop. Then gingerly he inched forward, controlling the white man's movement at the same time, his free hand on his lips to demand silence. Don followed him closely, and the Amerindian bent down noiselessly and pointed to a hole in the ground. At first he thought it was a rock, but then he saw it, a grey ground-dove, resting in its nest in the ground. He was about the length of his outstretched palm, from the tip of his middle finger to the rim of his wrist. It was ash-grey, and its wings had dark violet but shiny markings. Don began to assemble his tripod, and to his surprise his companion who until a day ago, had no idea what a camera was, instinctively seemed to know how to help. He was able to see the object of his fascination through the lens. He took a deep and silent breath and pressed the shutter. Only then did the bird become aware of alien presence and took to flight.

'Lucky the dove did not fly away.'

'No luck, Sir Donal, Me make bird still.' Was he suggesting that he had some strange gifts?

'Yarreku, you saying you have gifts?' The man nodded.

'Then why did you not get that anaconda to wait?'

'Make him come forward, no can make him stop in water.' Maybe he was a joker.

The trip lasted no more than two days. Back in Taj Mahal, he had a wash, and had just finished putting on his suit when Devi knocked on the door. She seemed truly pleased to see him, and Don could see her hesitate before asking if he was staying at the villa for his supper. No, he said, he was going to see some friends. He noticed the look of delight transforming into one of disappointment. She bowed slightly and left. He went to the Emsworths, as he had promised Charlotte. They sat under the open verandah, and he gave her a detailed account of his first trip. She was very keen to hear everything, and asked many questions. She laughed when he spoke of the prowess of Yarreku.

'Yarreku? Was that his name?'

'Aye, why?'

'Yarreku means the monkey in Carib language.' Don thought that it was funny that a man would not mind being called Monkey.

He was greatly heartened to find that she was indeed his soul mate. Perhaps some day, when he felt more confident, he might invite her to join him on a trip. Not only would that be a wonderful experience which they would recount to their grandchildren some day, but she might well be of help, as she seemed to have a great thirst for learning. He caught her staring at him, and asked what the matter was. She hesitated before answering.

'Father is out, and Mum is busy in the study,' Don nodded, enquiring with his eyes if that meant anything. She nodded first.

'If you want to kiss me, I am sure it's all right.' Don had been dreaming of doing just that for days, but now he seemed shocked that she should volunteer. Yes, of course, he said, walking towards her. She stayed seated, and he bent down clumsily, put his hands behind his back and approached his lips to hers. She stood up.

'Not like that,' she said, grabbing his arms and putting them firmly round her waist. He needed no more instruction. He smiled, tightened his grip, pulled her towards him, making a sly effort to involve her pulsating breasts in the process, and that moment when the two pairs of lips met, is something which he promised he would never ever forget. She responded with equal passion, rubbing her breasts against his, and they stayed like that, holding each other and kissing, at first lips against lips, gently stroking them, and when nature dictated, they began searching each other's tongues. A fellow undergraduate had explained to him that that was the ultimate aim of kissing, that it was called a French kiss. He had also explained that a kiss was a prelude to sexual intercourse. And indeed, he felt deeply aroused, but he knew that he should not contemplate that sort of thing before they were wed. On second thoughts, not before they were officially engaged — or at least when he knew that they were going to be engaged. There was one more step, and he took it: when we get to know each other better. But even then it was going to be very difficult.

'I know what you boys are like,' she said, rubbing against his hardness, 'but my answer is no.' Don looked at her guiltily, as if he had propositioned her. 'Not tonight anyway,' she said. He was pleasantly surprised by this, but the look on his face had, as yet, only registered the surprise and not the magnitude of the promise.

'Don't look so disappointed, I will arrange it very soon... when they go to play Bridge with Doctor Laker. The servants will keep their mouths shut.'

On his way back home in the Emsworth's ghari, he could not stop whistling. He got out and almost danced his way up the steps of his new home.

Devi immediately appeared and asked if he wanted a nightcap, and he declined. He was so happy and lightheaded, he thought he had to be extra nice. The hardness was still there, and he felt a little wetness in his underwear.

'Don't run away, Devi, you aren't in a hurry?'

'No, master.' He indicated with his head that she should come into the veranda and asked her to sit down, pointing to a chair, but she let him sit down first, and then squatted opposite him, on the floor. He pointed to the chair again, but she shook her head violently.

'Tell me Devi, are you alright?' She looked behind her in astonishment, as if she would find the answer to that unusual question there. She nodded violently.

'I mean, are you happy here? Enough money? Not too much work?' She shook her head in that special manner Don had noticed East Indians did when they meant to say no. Then remembering that he had asked two questions, she started nodding, a yes to the first question. Don thought that a shy young woman saying yes and no simultaneously was a comical sight, and laughed, and she smiled tentatively, unsure about what had caused the hilarity.

'Tell me,' he said, 'what made you come to work for me?' She frowned. Why did people work for other people if not to get money so they could live, she was thinking. Why is he asking. Perhaps they were all the same, he must be after something. She raised her eyes furtively in an attempt at assessing the man. He was well-built and handsome, had a kind face, but that was not enough to make him a nice man. He was obviously well-fed, and his frank open face told her that he had never been bullied by anybody, that the whole world loved him. He had never known what it is like to feel cold or go to bed hungry. But I suppose, she told herself, that all his advantages did not stop him suffering the same as us when he has toothache. She had not realised that she had smiled as that perverse thought crossed her mind, and only became aware of it as she noticed him smiling in return, clearly not because he could read her mind, but because, she supposed, hoped, that he was probably a good-natured man after all. But that badmash, that rogue, Jeewan, had already taken her virginity, she had nothing to lose.

'My father, sir, he not working, I must earn so we eat.'

'Oh, I see,' he said. No, she thought, you don't see, how can anybody?

'My father sir, he lose mind. People at the Mandir they look after him, but I must to pay for food.'

The Pandit had said that he could stay under the banyan tree in the compound for free. He had even provided him with a piece of sailcloth for shelter in case of rain, but Baba needed to eat too. The people would give him food, but she did not want them to think of him as a beggar, so she had to find some money. Her hope was that one day she might be able to make enough money to rent a small hut where they might live together. Especially as now, after what happened with Jeewan, nobody would want to marry her, she thought. She did not plan to tell the white man all this.

'He has lost his mind? Do you mean he is...' he was unable to say the word.

'Yes sir, he mad, not know where he is, thinking he back in Calcutta...'

'I am so sorry to hear that, what happened?' No, she was not going to tell him, she shook her head, and he saw how tears had filled her eyes, and he decided to drop the matter. She stood up, and asked if that was all, and he nodded.

'Can I bring pipe, sir?' What an excellent idea, he thought and nodded.

When she brought his pipe to him, he smiled at her and said thank you, thank you, Devi, and as she was going back inside the house, he stopped her.

'Oh, Devi, I meant to tell you, you cook beautifully, your prawn curry last week was an absolute masterpiece.'

'Master what?' He explained and she seemed so happy. What an excellent day, what an excellent everything!

Devi was both relieved and disappointed. Relieved to find that the man she had admired almost from the beginning had not behaved like a cad, and also a bit disappointed, because she would have liked what she feared he was going to demand of her.

A week later, Jonathan, the young freed slave who worked for the Emsworths came with a note: Tonight is Bridge Night. There was no signature, but a tantalising print of lips as made by a very special crimson lipstick that Charlotte favoured.

He got a cariole to take him across the city to her place, his heart thumping with anticipation. He was certain that he was going to make a mess of it, but found comfort by telling himself that everybody did, the first time. He was surprised when the first thing she did was to give him a French letter, probably made of sheep intestine. He had seen one before in Cambridge when his friend Lord Blankhead produced one at a party and regaled the guests with his tales of sexual conquests. Charlotte told him that it was her cousin Clara who sent them to her, smuggled in one of the books that she regularly sent her by the post. She took him by the hand and led him into her bedroom.

He found that she was a good teacher, as obviously the mysteries of sex were not a mystery to her. She must have learned more than what her uncle had taught her in Somerset, he surmised wryly. He was too excited to give that much thought, and with her help, managed to give a good account of himself, although he was a bit shocked by her unguarded manifestations of ecstasy as she reached her climax. She lit a cigarette with a newfangled silver lamp, and they smoked it alternately. He did not really like cigarettes, he was not even sure if he liked the pipe, although he smoked one. She inhaled deeply, and pulling his mouth towards him, opened it with her tongue and blew the smoke in his mouth. It nearly choked him, and she laughed when he explained that he was not used to inhaling. It had been a memorable experience, even if it had shattered a few illusions about her. His friends at university had told him stories of their sexual encounters with so-called well-born girls, but he had not believed them entirely. Now he knew that there was so much about the real world that he had not the faintest idea about. He was pleased to find that he had not been put off by her colourful past, but he was certainly not going to confide in mother this time.

For a whole week, he never even went out of the house, so busy was he writing his notes about the river trip, making diagrams and sketches. On Saturday he went to dinner at the Emsworths'. But before they sat at table, Charlotte said she and Donald were going out for a stroll. Arnold did not even hear, but Mrs Emsworth said, We will eat in an hour and a half.

'Then that gives us enough time,' she whispered to Don with a smile.

'Time for what?' he asked.

'You'll see,' she said and he followed her meekly.

The house of the Emsworths was on very spacious grounds, and in five minutes, with the luxuriant growths around, they seemed to be on a desert island. A macaw flew overhead. Don followed Charlotte to a cosy clearing where there was a man-made grass mattress with a cotton sheet on it.

'I thought that this would make a nice little love nest,' she said, 'I made it for us myself.' Don knew that he ought to show some disapproval, but he was too overwhelmed by the prospect of what was in wait. She fell on the bed of straw and dragged him down. The world stood still.

When he went back to the villa, Devi was still up and waiting under the veranda, in case he wanted anything.

'Devi, you should not wait for me, you need your sleep, you've been up since before the cock crowed.'

'No, all right.'

'I don't really want anything, you go to bed. I am sorry I deprived you of your sleep.'

'No sleepful,' she said, beginning to get up.

'Sleepy,' he corrected automatically, adding, 'if you want, you can keep me company, and tell me about your father.' She shook her head in a determined manner.

'Of course, not if you don't want to, sorry for being…', he could not find the words, and added, 'how about if I tell you about Miss Charlotte?' She nodded enthusiastically. 'I am in love with her, Devi.' She smiled happily and bent her head.

'I am going to marry her.' She raised her head and smiled again. She obviously wanted him to be happy.

'Wouldn't you want to be married, Devi?' She did not answer, but shook her head violently.

'Why not? You're a sensible young woman, beautiful, you'll make someone a good wife.' She stood up.

'Now, I sleepful. Good night Master.'

A few days later, Donald who had been working all day was drinking a small whisky and smoking his pipe when Devi appeared, to ask if he wanted anything.

'I would really like to know why you were upset when I asked you if you wanted to marry some day.'

'An impure woman can't marry sir.'

'What do you mean, Devi? You are not impure.' He had heard about untouchability, and thought that it was a great shame.

'No man can marry me, because I am…'

'You are what? Is it a caste thing?'

'No sir. I impure.' Why is he pretending he does not understand, she thought.

'A man wants bride pure on first night, sir.' Finally he understood. What a silly notion these people have! Does that mean that I should not marry my Charlotte? She certainly is not pure. But somehow he could not believe that Devi would have had the same history as the white girl, who clearly had been all for it.

'Did you have a lover then?'

'No, sir,' she said, tears dripping down her cheeks, 'he took me by force.' Don stood up angrily, very upset, and started pacing up and down the veranda in an extremely agitated fashion.

'Who did? Who's the cad?' His anger was such that if he met the man who did this to her, he, who was not given to physical violence, felt that he could have throttled the villain.

'I can't say, sir, please don't ask me. Can I go bed now, sir?' He was too moved to say anything, he just nodded, and she left quietly.

CHAPTER 5

✦✦✦

Georgetown

WHEN HER FATHER had become mad, the company had told him that the best they could do for him was to keep him on as night watchman on the plantations, pending repatriation to India, and that exceptionally he would receive his ration of rice, dhal and oil and occasionally some lengths of cotton, but that he was not entitled to any money. She was barely five when they had arrived on the Hesperus, and it had been nothing but misery piled upon misery ever since. Because the rations were meagre, and needed to be supplemented by buying a few things from the company shop, they often had but one meal a day, and many a night they went to bed on an empty stomach, holding each other tightly for comfort, he rubbing her belly, in a futile attempt to keep hunger at bay. Still, they had survived with the help of some well-meaning people, often very poor themselves, but who still found a coin or a banana for the starving pair. Sadly their condition did not leave them immune to the malevolence of certain folks who lifted their noses at them and manifested clear hostility.

At first Baba knew who she was, and the one thing which seemed to bring some cheer to him was when she appeared in front of him, when his eyes would light up, and he would mutter some indistinct words of which only meri rani, my queen, stood out clearly. He would hold her tight, and then invariably his tears would spill out. Officially he was the night watchman. At first he seemed to know what he was meant to be guarding, but gradually he completely lost touch with reality, often chasing invisible burglars, but they only kept him on because Devi slept by his side, and they imagined that one of them had the wits and the other the brawn to handle potential burglars. Fortunately there was never any major burglary, which suggested that the unusual combination was working after a fashion. At least in the early years.

When Devi turned eleven, (having been forgotten by the authorities, they had still not been repatriated to India,) a major burglary occurred and the company said that it had no alternative but to sack them. The Indian indentured labourers who had come to the country at the same time were very kind to father and daughter, but they had very little resources themselves and although they would not let them starve, the little that they could afford to give them was often insufficient. At first the only thing Devi could do was to go out begging.

An Indian landowner saw her in the streets with a begging bowl one day, took pity on her, and asked her if she wanted to come work for his family. That was a Godsend, because most people were themselves poor and she readily agreed. Baba's erstwhile friends decided that he should be put in the hands of the Pandit at the Mandir. The Mandir was only a small one, but the government had, in a fit of generosity included a sizeable parcel of land in their official grant, as a sop to the growing population of East Indians, who were becoming increasingly important. And vociferous.

The Pandit had got some of the faithfuls to build a wooden fence around it, and allowed a few destitute people, suffering from old age or sickness, to squat under a unique banyan tree with roots extending over fifty yards, and had even provided sailcloth to make a kind of shelter with, in case of rain. Although he was known for his generous nature, he was in no position to feed those needy folks, so he demanded that the people he allowed on his patch fend for themselves, meaning that they should do the only thing open to them: beg. His one rule was that he would not provide any food for anybody, whatever the circumstances. There are only twenty four hours a day, and the work of the Lord comes before the needs of man. But he allowed them to grow vegetables wherever they found space on the compound, but for one thing, the land was sandy and not very suitable for cultivation, and for another, there was a lot of bad blood between the inmates. Still it was helpful.

Panditji was very strict in enforcing his rules. Only for feasts like Divali or Holi would he solicit subscriptions from the better off among his flock, in order to bring some cheer to those unfortunate souls. But he did encourage his faithfuls to think of the poor and help them directly, and they did.

Shri Renghanadan Pillay, a landowner, was one of the early migrants who had come from Madras. He and his wife had worked on the sugar cane plantations, and had seized the chance of making some money by raising chicken on the little compound where they and ten other families had their huts. They had been very careful, and at the end of their indenture, they had started a small poultry business which had flourished. He must have been an astute businessman, for he had ended up buying some land started growing sugar cane, and a mere twenty years after he had arrived in the colony, half-starving, with not even the clothes on his back belonging to him, he was one of the richest Indians in Demerara. His wife had died and he had married a much younger woman. He had been touched by the sight of this ill-fed little girl begging.

Devi thought that the new Shrimati Pillay was like a princess. When God took Mama away, she was only seven, but she remembered her vividly. Baba, although he had lost his mind, was not wrong in saying that she was like a queen, now this Captanine Radha was also like a queen. Shri Renghanadan clearly worshipped her and she could do exactly what she liked with him. He never said no to her slightest whims. Devi found her kind enough, but she did not think that she had ever met a lazier woman in her life. She sat on a deck chair in the sun all day long, and it was always Devi do this, Devi do that, bring me some laddoo, Devi isn't it time you made some chai for me? Put plenty of sugar. I am so tired, I have no energy.

She would have preferred sleeping under the banyan tree with Baba, but the Shrimati said she should sleep in the specially built servants' quarters, where she was given a small corner all to herself in a room where provisions were kept. She loved onion in her food, she reflected wryly, but not in her nostrils.

There were also a gardener and his wife who doubled up as cook. They asked her to call them Chacha and Chachi, uncle and aunt. They were all both kind to her, and Chachi Padma taught her to cook.

She lived a whole year like this, visiting Baba every other day, sometimes bringing him some food that she had slyly put aside for him with the connivance of Chachi Padma. Unfortunately Shri Renghanadan had a strange belief about wages.

'I am the most generous person in the world,' he told Devi, 'ask my Anuradha, she only has to look at something and the next day I have bought it for her.' Devi knew that to be true. 'Then why am I only giving you fifty cents a day for your work? Tell me?' Devi shook her head.

'Is it because I am a wicked man?' Devi shook her head violently. He was not a wicked man.

'You said it! In fact I am a kind man,' he said. Devi nodded without any great conviction.

'You see?' he questioned an invisible presence on his left. 'I will explain, listen carefully. I came in this country with nothing, and I worked on the plantations. I got next to nothing, the rice, the dal, the oil, the onions, and every year some white sheeting, and a very small amount of money, half a pound a month, or later three dollars.' Devi listened very carefully, she always did, but she did not see where this was going.

'Now, I ask you one question, did this do me any harm?' Devi knew that she was expected to say no, and answered in that sense. You see, Renghanadan again said to that invisible presence on his left. 'You are a very sensible girl, and you will go far, mark my word.' And turning to the left, he added, 'I mean this. Now, why am I telling you all this,' he asked. Devi was not sure what to say, but fortunately he was not expecting an answer. 'There is no greater harm you can do to people than to spoil them… it makes them,' turning to the left moving his hand round a few times, he asked, 'what's the word?' The invisible spirit must have whispered it to him, but Devi did not hear what he said.

'Complacent and lazy.' Devi still did not catch his drift, but the rich man must have seen the perplexed look on her face.

'If I paid you more, and Bhagwan knows I can double your wages and not feel the pinch, I will not be doing you a favour.' I must be stupid, thought Devi, I don't understand how you can be doing someone a favour by not giving them a proper wage, but she did not have to wait long for illumination. 'Only when you struggle and sweat, can you reach your…' Renghanadan pursued, turning to the left, but not waiting to be told this time, for he turned back immediately, 'Full potential!' It dawned upon Devi that she was not getting that increment that he had promised some time before.

'Then I will have to steal some more, if I am to stop Baba starving,' she thought and smiled. At that very moment, Shrimati Anuradha called aloud, 'Where are you Devi, come massage my feet, I am so tired.'

'Coming, captanine,' said Devi, wondering why somebody who did nothing all day was always more tired than those who woke up with the birds and went to sleep after ghosts started roaming abroad. Could this be what the boss was saying?

For a year it went on in much the same way. Shrimati Anuradha was becoming more irascible. She often had headaches and Devi was expected to give her head massages, shoulder massages, foot massages whenever she had a free moment.

As if all the work done in the main house was not enough, the Chacha gardener who was a soft spoken and kindly man would often come towards her, all smiles, his head moving left and right, like the pendulum of the big clock, but swinging the wrong way.

'Beti,' he would say, 'you are such a sweetie, your Auntie Padma's back is paining so much, please come and rub her. Everybody says you have the fingertips of Parvatti herself.' Devi had no idea who or what Parvatti was. One day she asked the old gardener, and he looked puzzled, 'I don't really know, I thought…' and could not find the words to express that profound thought. I am developing big muscles, Devi thought wryly, what, with all the massages, the running all day long and the kneading for the parathas which the boss and his young wife liked so much.

Parathas! It was the paratha which undid her in the end. She did not enjoy stealing, but she cried when she thought that whilst she was well fed, albeit with leftovers, she could not provide for poor Baba. The poor man was always hungry. In the compound of the Mandir, there were bananas growing, but the Pandit had the habit of counting them, and had threatened that if only half a fruit was missing, he was sure to catch the culprit and would have the painful duty of evicting them. Devi wondered whether there was a single individual living under the banyan tree stupid enough to risk incurring the wrath of the Pandit by stealing only half a banana. When there was a good crop, the Pandit said, he would himself bring some to his ever hungry guests, but let no one take advantage of his kindness! In any case, Baba did not like bananas.

Devi would quite regularly put a few things away to take with her when she went to see him: a piece of fried fish, some rice wrapped in banana leaf, a coconut, some cooked dal, whatever she could lay her hands on. Chachi Padma would smile knowingly. She had even given her an aluminium catora with a lid for the dal which was tricky to carry. But Devi noticed that when the old Chachi saw her putting things away, her back aches became more severe. Anuradha had often expressed surprise when she saw the contents of the dekhchi, saying that she was sure that there was much more of that chicken curry last time she checked. She would look at Padma and Devi sharply. Accusingly.

'I am not saying anything,' she said, 'I have no proof, but the day I catch anybody stealing from me they are out on their ears.'

'Shrimati,' Padma lied, 'I would never dream of stealing from you, I am a very pious person and I am knowing what a great sin it is to steal… I'd never steal food even if my children were starving.'

'And what have you got to say, Devi?'

'I am a very pious person too, Captanine,' she said, not sure what pious meant, 'I would never steal even…' and trailed off.

'Don't say that I have not warned you. If you need anything, just ask, I am a good pious person, I will not refuse.' Another pious person, mused Devi wryly.

'I will look this word up in a dictionary,' Devi would have said if this was a hundred years later, and she had a dictionary. The two servants looked at each other uneasily, and the lady of the house stormed away. They could hear her angrily telling her husband about thieving and ungrateful servants.

'It is you,' Padma said to Devi, 'we are only taking a few things, but you, young missy, you are thinking this house is belonging to you, and serving yourself shamelessly. Now because of you I am in trouble.' Devi did not cry easily, but this was the first time Chachi Padma, who had always so good to her had said those unkind things.

'It's my Baba, he has nothing to eat, what am I to do?' Chachi Padma was sorry she had spoken.

'I know, beti, I know… we the poor have been put on this earth to suffer… I am sorry, but be careful.'

A week later, Devi was helping Padma making parathas. She liked rolling out the kneaded dough into nice round flat cakes which Padma would then roast on the thick cast iron griddle called tawa. Anuradha, attracted by the aroma of paratha beginning to cook in a generous dollop of ghee, rushed in the kitchen and laughingly said she could not wait any longer, she had to have a taste right away. Padma was overjoyed, she loved being appreciated. With a nice flourish she tossed the flat bread over with the wooden spatula so as to let it cook on both sides, and Anuradha moved up and down in the kitchen like an excited child. When the mistress chef was satisfied that her product, now bejewelled by a constellation of dark burnished gold patches on both sides was fit for a rani, she put it on a plate and presented it to the lady of the house with a little bow.

When they were serving dinner later, Padma carried the chicken korma and Devi the parathas. They had placed everything on the table and were preparing to go out when Anuradha called them back. Devi understood right away what the problem was, but hoped that the mistress was not going to make a big deal out of it.

'What's this?' she asked pointing to the plate of parathas with her chin. The two servants said nothing.

'When I came to the kitchen, I counted how many rolled cakes there were, and I can see that there are four missing. Padma?'

'I don't know what you are saying, captanine, I —' Devi did not let her finish.

'Captanine,' she said in a clear untrembling voice, I took them, it was I.' She was a quick thinker, and thought that there was no point in them both being sacked. 'I put them away, to take to my father.'

'Arrey what's a paratha… rani…' said Shri Renghanadan, whereupon the wife turned on him.

'What's a paratha, you ask? Today it is one paratha, tomorrow, it will be the whole house… This is defiance! Only last week I told this girl you picked from the gutter that I would kick her out if I caught her again. This is not the first time, you know, I said, if you want anything, just ask. Did she ask? No, these types of people, *prefer* to steal.' Devi was singularly unconcerned. Worse things had happened to her and Baba. The young wife was in full flow, 'Take your things and leave this house immediately, do you hear?'

Since she was being kicked away she might as well take those two wretched parathas that she had hidden away for Baba, she thought. She was surprised with her own calm. The events had not taken her by surprise and she would take things in her stride. Chachi Padma gave her six dollars, half her savings and they had a good cry for a short while. She was the nearest thing she had for a mother, and she would miss her as much as she would miss her meagre wages but she was not one to waste time over the inevitable.

Wearily she made her way to the Mandir. She regretted the fact that Baba would not even understand what had happened. She thought he looked surprised when he saw her. She had bought a few sweetmeats from an old lady she knew who made mithai to the rich families; she used to be sent there by the Anuradha who had a sweet tooth. Baba gave the sweets a vacant stare but when Devi put a piece of laddoo in his mouth, he smiled and began to chew, and opened his mouth like a child to receive more.

'I have been given the sack, Baba,' she told him. He kept munching as if he had not heard.

'I have also got two parathas for you… well one is actually for me… here, have it, it's nice with the laddoo.' When she gave him the paratha, he grabbed it and tore a big chunk of it and began chewing lustily. She had tears in her eyes as she watched him eat; he seemed so happy, he who was so rarely happy. 'I have no idea what I am going to do now,' she told him. The idea that they could both go and walk down a cliff occurred to her, but it scared her so much that she chased it away with all her might.

'Don't worry, Baba, we wont throw ourselves over the cliff, we'll manage,' she told him, for a split second half believing that he could read her thoughts.

Normally, around this time one of the two women, Anuradha or Chachi would require her to do a massage for them. She smiled to herself, thinking, at least I am being spared that. But a thought occurred to her and she immediately acted upon it.

'Baba, I need to give you a massage now.' The poor man understood and smiled, and moved a bit to allow her to go behind him. She put her hands under his torn shirt. I must repair that shirt, now that I shall have plenty of time, she thought. She grabbed a lump of flesh in each hand, the poor man is becoming a sack of bones, she thought, and began to knead it. I could be kneading atta flour, she thought and grinned. Baba closed his eyes, saying nothing, but she remembered vividly how when Ma served him a lota of mango juice that she had squeezed for him, mixing it with some crisp onions fried in ghee, he would sip this, making the greatest possible noise, closing his eyes, saying to her, 'Beti, your Ma knows how to make me pass through the gate of Amarawati. ('What is Amarawati, baba?' 'A place where nice little girls like you go after they die. Our paradise.' 'I don't want to go to Amarawati, Baba, I want to stay with you.')

Early next morning, as it was Friday, she went to the little Mosque which the Musselmans of Georgetown had built. She knew that they would be going there in droves for their prayers, and that on that day, many of them had some coins for beggars. Indeed she was quite pleased with what they gave her. On a good day it was not impossible to collect fifty cents, a day's wage. On other days, she went on the main road and walked up and down, sometimes sitting in a place where she thought she could catch a few rich people. Some gave her a cent or two, many shooed her away angrily. The takings were very meagre, but come Friday she got a little bit more.

A nice bearded man in a flowing robe had given her five cents once; he had smiled and patted her gently on the head. The same man recognised her a week later, and asked if she would like to work as a maid at his house. She was overjoyed.

'But one thing, you are Musselman, yes?' he asked. She shook her head sadly. The man pursed his lips for a while, and turned his back to go away, but at the last moment, he looked at her again and smiled. 'Nevermind, come with me.' He took her home and called his wife.

'Maimoun, I have brought a maid for you.' The lady called Maimoun came in smiling, wiping her hands on her horni. She was a bit plump and very motherly.

'What's your name, little girl?' she asked kindly.

'Devi, captanine.'

'At the moment she is a cow worshipper, but she will become a Muslim,' the man told his wife. 'Won't you?' Then he earnestly explained to Mrs Maimoun that in the eyes of Allah, showing the light to an idolater, and putting them on the righteous path earned the benefactor as many sawabs or credits as if he had built a whole masjid by himself.

Devi was not sure what that meant, but smiled and nodded. 'We will call her Aisha, like the daughter of our prophet Muhammad, on whom be peace!'

'You can sleep under the table in the kitchen,' the man said, adding, 'the captanine will give you a mat and a blanket.' She found that the lady Maimoun was very kind; she did not expect her to eat leftovers, but said that she could eat the same as them. She helped her in the kitchen, at first, only cutting vegetables and kneading flour for rotis, but soon she trusted her enough to let her have complete responsibility, specially once it was established that she was a good cook, the training that Padma had given her proving invaluable.

They were also giving her a little bit more money than did Renganadhan. As the only servant she was a bit lonely, but the captanine was very kind and liked to chat.

Unfortunately this happy state was not to last. One day, Maimoun had gone to visit a sick friend, and she was alone with the Master. He had gone on a trip out of town, and had been away for two days. She made him some tea and he said that after his tiring trip he needed her to bathe his feet. She boiled some water, carried it to the back verandah, poured some in the basin and went to get some cold water in case the hot water was too hot. He patted her gently on the head.

Aisha, he said, you are a good girl; we really must get a Miaji to teach you about your new religion. And he made a big speech explaining how much better Islam was than the religion of Hindus who worshipped stones and whose gods were monkeys and elephants. In our religion, he explained, we are all the same, we do not have Chhamars and Brahmins, all Musselmans are equal. Devi smiled, doubting very much whether the likes of her would benefit from more equality under any system, whatever equality meant.

Now wash my feet gently. She proceeded to massage his feet, adding more hot water as the water in the basin cooled down. He bent down suddenly, and gently pulled her hands up, so she could massage his calves. She had never done this but it did not bother her.

'You've got a nice gentle touch,' he said, stroking his florid greying beard. She smiled. 'Are you happy here with us?' She nodded. He patted her on the head. He bent down and pulled her hands above his knees.

'My thighs are also very tired, I walked too much these two days.' This gave her a slight feeling of unease, but she did as he expected, kneading his thighs with both her hands.

'Higher,' he whispered. It was a hesitant inflexion in the whisper which alarmed her. Chachi Padma had told her that men sometimes had funny ideas, but she had taken this to mean younger men, not those who had nice white beards. She suddenly noticed that he had a hard on, and he noticed that she had noticed. She did not understand the implication of this expansion, but instinctively felt that it was not a welcome development.

'You don't have to tell Begum Maimoun about this, I will give you one dollar,' he said, directing her hands towards his erect member. Her body grew cold. Suddenly she drew back, knocking the basin of water. He made an attempt to grab her, but she was too quick for him. She was out of the house, and ran all the way to the Mandir. By the time she got there, she had stopped trembling. She had not shed a single tear.

For the first time in her life, she felt that she could not confide in Baba. He expressed no surprise and smiled at her muttering some indistinct words. It was the Pandit who, on seeing her asked if she was not working, and she said that she had been sacked.

'Don't tell me, you misbehaved?'

'No, Panditji.'

'Don't lie, I think you must have.' The saintly man was deep in thought for a bit, then nodding to himself he said, 'But if you promise me that you will be a good obedient little girl, I might get you a good post, would you like that?'

'Yes please, Panditji.' But he did not refer to that again in the next weeks. She had no alternative but to go back to begging, and father and daughter survived like this for a whole year.

'You remember what I told you,' the Pandit said to her one day, 'I said that I will find you work? Was last week, no?' She did not tell the holy man that it was more than a year ago, and nodded silently.

The Pandit had found her work with another rich landowner, but the lady beat her for nothing. When the Pandit asked her if she was happy in her new job, she told him about the beating and this really made him very upset.

'What is this world coming to? I took pity on you and got you a good position, and instead of getting thanks what do I get? Reproach! You thought fit to up and go because of a little beating? What did you expect, that the lady of the house would sing to you and rub your back? Never again will I waste my time!' And he turned his back on her and walked away in disgust.

She found work with an English doctor who was attached to a big sugar plantation. He had a wife and two children, and Devi was very happy with them, and was able to learn a little English. They were kind people, and it was the happiest she had been since she landed on these shores. They paid well and she was able to provide for Baba, buying him new clothes and plenty of mithais. Sadly his teeth were rotting away, but he had so little joy in his life. The doctor left the area after three years and she was once more without a job. Fortunately Maimoun Begum had taught her to be careful with money, and she had carefully kept her savings in a tin which she buried in the night, near Baba's banyan.

It was Chachi Padma who found her a good job at Shri Ramnath's. She said that he was perhaps the richest Indian in the country, and had a few houses which he rented out, mainly to expatriates and that he paid well. So Devi went to the house, knocked on the door of the huge house, and was told that Shri Ramnath was not going to be home until the afternoon. She sat under a mango tree all day long, waiting for the master to come home. When he arrived, he went to take a bath and do his puja and it was dark before he came out to meet her. Yes, he would be happy to give her a position, he said, and she was engaged; the wages seemed fair.

The work was pretty hard, but she was never afraid of hard work. The lady of the house was a cheerful old soul who was always chewing betel and spitting it out all over the place, but she was harmless. Ramnath had an eighteen-year old son, Jagdeo, who had gone to a school for white boys where they allowed a few rich Indians in to make up the numbers. Ramnath proudly told everybody that his son was going to London to become a doctor.

Devi thought that Jagdeo was a handsome young man, but he was very haughty. He never said things like, 'Please get me some milk,' but 'Eh you girl, go get me some milk, and be quick, I haven't got time to waste.' At least nobody hit her, and she was never afraid of hard work.

She noticed right from the beginning that although he spoke to her harshly, he liked to leer at her, and she lived in fear of the day when she would find herself alone with him. And that day came all too soon. The parents were away, but Satish the cook, as well as Rashid the mali were about. She was helping the cook, when the young master came into the kitchen.

'What are you cooking today, Satish? he asked. 'Chicken, master Jadgeo.'

'Today,' he said, 'I don't feel like chicken, I want fish.'

'O.K. I go go cook fish, we buy this morning, I was going to fry them for tomorrow.' Jagdeo shook his head. He looked at Devi, and said that what he really wanted was goat meat.

'In that case, master Jagdeo, I go go buy some.'

'Then go go, you numbskull, what are you waiting for?' Satish bowed and hurried out. Devi was beginning to tremble with apprehension. Next, Rashid the mali was soundly rounded upon because, Jagdeo said, the roses were a bloody disgrace. Go sort your mess out, he was ordered. Devi knew that he was sending him away as far as possible from the house for a specific reason. The mali had no option. She knew that there was trouble ahead, and would have run away, but she did not wish to lose another good job. Maybe the young master just wanted to tease her.

He looked at her with a wicked smile which said, now you are in my power. He looked intently at her.

'You are, a pukka jadoogar, enh!'

'No sir.' If I knew any magic, she thought, I would use it to protect myself from you.

'I know what you are after.'

'I am not after anything, master' she said looking at his feet.

'What are you looking at me like this? Remember who is the boss who the servant.'

'Yes sir, I always remember.'

'Come here,' he ordered. No power on earth is going to make me take one step in his direction, she swore to herself. He rushed towards her, grabbed her with one hand and pulled her to him. With his free hand he grabbed a knife, smiled at it, and twisted it playfully with his fingers.

'You shout, and I swear I will put that knife in your heart.'

'Please let go of me, Mr Jagdeo.'

'No, I will give you what you have been after ever since you came to work here, you witch.'

'I have not been after anything, Sir.' She surprised herself at how calm she was. Next thing he hit her across the face, not once, but a few times, almost playfully, and she felt all her energy drained out of her; she could hardly stand on her feet. Then he became all tender and apologetic. He did not want to hit her, he was just teasing her, it didn't really hurt, did it? he was not a brute, but she had made him crazy for her, and now she was pretending that she did not want it. He knew what girls were like, they played hard to get. She should be flattered, not offended, after all she was a servant girl and he the son of the richest man in Georgetown. She was limp and trembling all over now, vainly trying to kick, but her muscles would not obey her. She was unable to do anything and he lifted her sagging body and carried her to the bedroom. He took off her clothes and she had no strength to resist him. Were it not for Baba, she would have preferred death. He expressed admiration for her body, and she cursed the body which could attract such obscene passion. Who would have thought such a little treasure would be hidden under those filthy rags? He took off his trousers and threw himself on her and raped her, said he wanted to marry her, then raped her again and again.

Anuradha was shocked to see the young woman dripping blood from her thighs appearing at her gate. She was very impressed by the fact that although she was unable to keep her tears inside her eyes, the victim herself was dry-eyed. She would tell her husband later that it was her fault; had she not sacked the girl for stealing two miserly parathas, this would not have happened. The doctor was be sent for, and Shri Renghanadan kept urging him to prescribe any drugs that would help her, that he would pay for them whatever the cost. He had plenty of money, he explained, and believed that human life, even of the lowest type of people was sacred. Chachi Padma repaid some of those head massages by watching over Devi, putting cold compresses on her fevered brow. At first the doctor had expressed shock and advised police action, but when he heard that it was Ramnath's son, he changed tack, and said that since what had been done could not be undone, it would be best not to make a big deal of it. After a week, Devi seemed fully recovered, and Anuradha promptly offered her the old job, but she said no, she needed to look after her Baba.

A year later when she met Mr Ramnath senior, who was completely unaware of what had happened between his son and the girl. He told her that she was a naughty little girl for leaving a good job without telling anybody. It was my Baba, she lied, he was suddenly taken ill. But I always liked you, he said, adding that he was looking for a cook for an Englishman to whom he was renting the house on the riverside, that he had recently finished building. He asked if she would like to work there. It was up to her, he said, but advised her to hurry. I would rather die than work for that man again, she thought.

'Is he better now,' asked Shri Ramnath as he started walking away.

'Who?' she asked.

'Your Baba.'

'My Baba has never been ill,' she said without thinking, but suddenly remembering her white lie, she quickly added, 'since…' It took her no more than one minute to change her mind. The old man was not responsible for his son's crime; he was in fact a sweet old dear. Yes, she would work for the Englishman.

CHAPTER 6

◆◆◆

Essequibo

DONALD WAS TOLD that because of the rapids, the Essequibo was unnavigable, but he decided that if a circle had to be squared, he was the man to do it. He was healthy, bold and determined, had muscles, and above all he valued what he thought of as his common sense. Money was not a problem; he would get some bullocks and a cart, take along as many strong arms as might be needed, so they could help pull the craft on land when necessary. Of course the men accompanying him would have to hack and hew through the dense forest to permit displacement by rolling the craft on logs over rocky terrain. Difficult? Certainly, but what an exhilarating challenge!

Yarrekhu had also said that if that proved too difficult, it would be easy enough to locate Amerindian tribes who had their settlements along the way, and borrow, hire or buy boats from them in order to continue. If no can, we steal, he had said, you have guns, and Donald was not sure if he was joking. Yarreku had by now become his right hand man in matters organisational. He had proposed that his wife Korobona should join them and be their cook, and suggested the inclusion in the team of a wrestler by the name of Hameed who had the strength of a bull, and would be handy for carrying loads. Considering the size of the boat, the load the scientist was taking along with him, Yarreku estimated that he would need six more strong pairs of hands, and Donald said to go ahead and hire them. These people were all delighted to be able to earn some extra money, specially as Yarreku had told them the 'Englishman' paid well.

Charlotte was on the veranda looking intently at some recently arrived Illustrated London News when Donald walked in. She had not been expecting him, but was clearly delighted. She threw herself into his arms and began showering him with her hot passionate kisses. Donald was quite used by now to what he once thought of as her exuberant passion. They're in, she whispered, and our nest's too damp anyway. He smiled and shook his head to indicate that he had not come for that. He wanted to tell her immediately that he was thinking of asking her to join him on his trip, but she said that she absolutely had to show him some sketches of kangaroos and wallabies which the Illustrated claimed were the first sketches of those natives of Australia ever published in England. She really had a passion for scientific knowledge. Yes, he was sure that she would make an excellent companion, not only on the trip, but for the rest of their lives. At that point, he had never even once thought of the dangers that he would be exposing her to. He took hold of her hands, looked into her eyes, and said, 'Charlotte darling, I want to ask you something.' Her eyes lit up, she had been hoping that he would do just that very soon. She squeezed his hands in anticipation.

'Charlotte darling, I have been thinking of asking you for some time now, you know how I feel about you, would you like —'

'Yes, yes, of course,' she said happily, 'of course I would.' He marvelled again at her quick grasp of the situation. Suddenly her face darkened a bit.

'You've got to ask Père first of course,' she added.

'I wouldn't dream of not doing that,' he said, very slightly hurt that she could imagine that he would not. Then neither spoke for some time, and concentrated on the magazine. Mr Emsworth then appeared, and Charlotte's face lit up.

'Père,' she said, she loved using the French appellation, 'Don has something to ask you.'

'Yes, Donald?'

'You know I am going on a study trip up the Essequibo, and as Charlotte is fascinated by nature, she might like to accompany me.' The young woman frowned, but then looked amused, and the old man began to cough uneasily.

'These sorts of things are best handled by my dear wife,' he said finally. He called the garden boy who was pruning a mango tree and ordered him to call the memsahib. She came in a hurry. Donald repeated her question.

'Well, yes,' she said after giving the matter a full minute's consideration, 'but I could not imagine allowing that, seeing that you are not even engaged.' It was Don's turn to begin coughing uneasily and bluster.

'Oh, I… eh, I… you know, would not dream of taking a young lady along with me… unless… unless she was… were, eh… sort of affianced. I mean to me.'

'Are you asking me to marry you then?'

'I sort of thought… that would be… how shall I out it?… a sort of integrated process… engagement and… eh… the trip.' That was not really a lie; he had in fact decided to propose to her, but was not sure how to do it; he was grateful that it had happened sort of accidentally.

The old man stood up and patted the young man on the shoulder, whilst Mrs Emsworth immediately started drawing a list of who to invite to the wedding in her head.

'Oh, I… eh… sort of thought that it would be presumptuous on my part to buy a ring before knowing that you approve,' he lied.

'Well we do old chap, we do,' said Emsworth gruffly.

Charlotte loved him for his unworldliness, and thought that in return for all those things she knew he would teach her, she too would have a lot of fun teaching him the ways of the world once they were married. On the next day he ordered a diamond ring from Vaghjees, the Indian jeweller in Carmichael street, and went ahead full tilt with the preparations for the expedition. She wanted to be properly equipped for the trip, and shocked the West African tailor who had set up shop soon after he was freed by asking for man's trousers to be made for her. But he delivered six beautifully crafted pairs of men's trousers for her in two days. They were perfect, seeing that he had calculated the measures from sight, not wishing to touch a white mistress.

In a matter of days, everything was ready. Eight healthy bullocks had spent three nights in the precincts of the Taj Mahal. Food for the expedition had been bought, equipment assembled, and on the appointed morning, Yarrekhu turned up with the people he had hired, but there was no Korobona. Donald had not immediately noticed the absence, but Hameed the wrestler was very agitated, and seemed to be having an argument with the Amerindian. When Donald enquired what the spat was about, Hameed explained that he was going nowhere if there was no one to cook his meals. Yarrekhu explained that he and Korobona had had a fight, and that she had run to mother's.

That was how Devi got drafted in. She was very happy to be going, but said that she could not go without arranging for her Baba to be looked after. Donald was very understanding, and postponed the departure by one day. She went to the Mandir, gave money to the Pandit, and he promised that he would do everything needed to keep Baba comfortable. When she told Baba about her having to go away, he did not seem to understand, and just smiled. The least she could do was to spend a few hours with him, cleaning him with a wet cloth, changing his clothes, cutting his toenails, grooming him, feeding him, massaging his neck and head.

The first stage was the journey to the mouth of the Essequibo. It took them a whole day, on foot and in the bullock cart to get to the point where they were going to board the craft. When they arrived at that place, they were pleased that everything seemed in order. The craft looked frail, but Donald trusted Yarrekhu who had been responsible for ordering it from some reliable Amerindians he had transacted with in the past. There were three more healthy bullocks which were traded off for the three tired ones, and foodstuffs and other commodities like paraffin and candles and Lucifers.

Charlotte, Donald, Yarrekhu and the freed Wilson took their position on the boat, whilst Devi and the others accompanied the land party. The men installed Devi in the cart with all the equipment and provisions whilst they walked. There was enough room on the cart for perhaps two more people squeezing, and the plan was that every now and then two members of the party would take seats beside Devi for a rest. There was obviously no road, but Yarrekhu had said that his cousin Okoronote could always find a way of driving a cart, with two bullocks pulling through any forest, however thick. The two cousins were going to communicate with each other by some signals they had learnt as children.

'When I back, Korobona, she home,' Yarrekhu said with a laugh. That was probably the longest sentence he had ever used with Donald. They were on their way. Until that moment, the greatest adventure that Charlotte had experienced, was going on a picnic with her cousins back in Somerset. Now, the excitement that was generated by this expedition was like the flow of the Essequibo compared to the trench which took water from the pond to water their gardens. She decided that this was a sort of picnic on an epic scale, and her dearest wish was to be a help to the man she loved, not a hindrance. Don had briefed her on the objectives of the expedition, and she hoped that she would be up to the job of taking down notes as he dictated them to her.

Devi was quite excited too. She remembered how Baba used to take her and her brother, and Ma sometimes on trips. She never tired of those boat journeys. They had seen gharials, monkeys, gazelles, tigers, and she had always felt safe with Baba there. No harm could happen. In spite of what had happened with Jagdeo, she was not afraid of those men; they were all so strong and brawny, but without exception they struck her as being good sorts. She also had the conviction that with Mr Donald around, she would be as safe as she had been with her Baba. Okoronote seemed very sure of himself, and he directed the men to cut a path open for the ghari with their machetes. She was pleased to see Mr Donald looking so happy; he was a good man and deserved to have a good wife. It was so obvious to her that Miss Charlotte was exactly the sort of person who would make him an excellent consort; she seemed so kind, she was so beautiful, so tall, so white… She was so pleased when he told her that they had become engaged. She was not quite sure why they were going on this trip though, but knew that Mr Donald liked to study nature. Still it puzzled her that he thought it was worth spending a small fortune, just for fun.

Progress was slow, owing to the thickness of the growth. Okoronote and that other Carib were constantly exchanging signals, making sounds like owls or monkeys by whistling through their teeth. The ghari shook a lot, and when sunset was approaching, they stopped. Devi was surprised to find that the boat was already there, anchored and moored. The white couple were seated on the ground eating sandwiches and drinking tea which they had made over a spirit lamp. The men picked twigs, and she lit a fire with a stick of Lucifer, and began cooking. Yarrekhu gave her meat and vegetables that had already been cut and boiled by his wife, before she ran off to mother.

They say that Yarrekhu is a magician, that he can make birds stay still so he can catch them. She had heard a story about how once, in a jungle with some other people, a jaguar appeared suddenly. Everybody wanted to scramble away, but Yarrekhu stopped them by raising his hand and gently shaking his head. The jaguar had seen them, and everybody thought that he was going to pounce. Mothers grabbed their young ones in a vain attempt to protect them. They looked at the Monkey man, and he only smiled. Then calmly he moved a few steps forward towards the beast, which seeing him approaching, stood still. Finally, when the two were almost within touching distance of each other, Chachi Padma had said, the jaguar offered him his head to scratch, which made the killer cat purr like a kitten. He then whispered some words to him, and the beast turned and walked away slowly. She did not know if this was true, people in this country liked to tell stories like this one, but she had heard it many times. True or not, she felt safe knowing that he was around. He would not let Mr Donald do anything reckless, because you never know with him, he is the nicest man she had ever met, knew so many things because he had learned so many books, but books do not tell you everything; she supposed that he was vulnerable. He caught sight of her and smiled and waved at her. Miss Charlotte did the same. Many people had told her that the white people were very proud and haughty; indeed when she saw them on the streets in the city, they looked pretty forbidding, but those she knew struck her as the contrary of proud and haughty.

The men ate and smacked their lips to show appreciation, and as the sun was going down, everybody scrambled to pitch their tents. There were two or three lamps, but Miss Charlotte said not to waste paraffin. Yarrekhu and the men then took the bullocks to the river to drink. They did not need to be specially fed, as there was plenty of vegetation that they chewed upon on the way. Devi joined the men taking the bullocks to the riverside, and Charlotte, seeing this decided to do the same. She thought that the white lady was not only kind hearted, but also the most beautiful woman she had ever cast eyes upon. She slept like a baby that night.

Next day the land party made a quick start, and Mr Donald said that as the boat was faster, they did not need to hurry. He and Charlotte went for a walk, with Wilson carrying the photographic equipment, Yarrekhu having stayed to attend to the boat. The terrain was rocky, and they went to explore the bush. In a clearing, Donald who had the eyes of a cat saw something, raised his hands, and there, Charlotte had her first zoological epiphany: on a branch of a tree that she did not know, sat a green tree frog; she had never seen a frog of that size, he was as big as a fully grown chicken. Wilson sprang towards the creature, grabbed it by the legs, and in the twinkling of an eye he had done something to it, and the animal was dead. Donald was taken aback; at the very least he would have liked to study the creature, perhaps take a photograph of it.

'Good food,' Wilson said smacking his lips. Charlotte was horrified to begin with, but then agreed with the young scientist that it was no different from eating fish or chicken if one liked that sort of thing, and added that he would ask Wilson to let him have a taste. Charlotte pursed her lips, then her face lit up, and she said that Don was right, she will try it too. After all, the plan was to find as much food as possible en route. Wilson put the dead frog in his bag, and they made their way back to the boat.

The progress of the craft on the brown choppy waters of the Essequibo was moderate but steady. Don was becoming quite proficient at manoeuvering it under the guidance of the Monkey Man. So far Charlotte had enjoyed every minute. Although she had been fascinated by what Don had to say about his quest, she sometimes had doubts about her suitability for such a life. She knew her weaknesses; as the only girl, she had been spoiled by her doting parents who reluctantly had to let her brother Samuel go to study at Marlborough in England. She liked being served tea in bed in the morning, she had no taste for housework and got easily bored. On the other hand, she had always been fond of reading, of learning new things. Uncle Percy with whom she had stayed for a few years used to say that a day is wasted if one had not learned a new fact before sunset, and she was a staunch believer of that creed. She was as excited as Don whenever they came across anything new. Whenever they stopped, Yarrekhu and Wilson would throw a line in the water, and the latter caught a pacu, which might have weighed five pounds; another one or two, and dinner for the whole party was secured. Yarrekhu and Wilson also caught a few perai. Piranhas, exclaimed Donald, and he explained to Charlotte that they were carnivorous, usually swam in small shoals, and they could, and indeed, had been known to devour the feet of unwary people walking across their paths. The pacu was related to them, but they were mainly herbivorous although on occasions they were known to gobble up smaller fishes. Don had a number of notebooks among his things for making notes and sketches of any interesting specimens that they encountered. She asked if she could help, and he was delighted. Yes, he said with a laugh, that's why I brought you along. At first he gave her instructions on what were the important features, and she would write down some notes, which Don found impressive. She soon got the hang of this work, and in no time at all she was taking down notes off her own bat. You know, he said in admiration, you are a natural scholar. She was greatly heartened by this. Because of her proficiency, he was able to concentrate on doing sketches whilst their images were fresh in his mind.

The moment they landed, Yarrekhu saw a turtle, and ran after it, caught it and put it on its back.

'Food for when no food,' he said curtly. He then carried it to where the bullocks were, and put him in a pannier. A live turtle is easy to transport, did not go bad, and can be cooked any time. Devi cooked the pacu with a curry sauce and there was no doubt that this was the first time such aromas were entering the nostrils of the forest. Don and Charlotte went out arm in arm into the bush, which made Yarrekhu uneasy, but the young scientist had taken his shotgun with him. Charlotte felt so alive, breathing the slightly musty forest air and walking through the vegetation soaked in the dripping of accumulated dew, unbothered by branches and thorns. Suddenly on the ground beneath some vines, she saw a shiny dark purple object and bent down to pick it up. It was like some objet d'art made of porcelain that one buys at an expensive jeweller's. The young scientist was baffled, but only for half a minute, after which his frown dissolved into recollection.

'It can only be one thing, and that's a tinamou egg,' he said, and explained about that very shy bird with a genius for keeping out of sight. They scrambled back to the party, and Yarrekhu breathed a sigh of relief to see them back so soon. Donald said something to Yarrekhu who ordered one of the men to go get Mr Donald's photographic equipment, and this time the two men accompanied the young couple to where the egg was. Yarrekhu studied the terrain, looked at the trees, and nodded.

'Him here,' he pronounced dramatically. Then he started making a sound best described as 'khreeorooroo' repeatedly, and indicated that he wanted silence by putting his index finger on his mouth. Soon there was a distinct rustle in the brush, and everybody held their breaths. Yarrekhu saw him first, and pointed in its direction. When everybody had finally seen him, Yarrekhu walked towards the bird which was no bigger than a partridge, with a dark brown top coat and a tea coloured lower body. He made some soothing sounds and drew nearer and nearer to the tinamou, which seemed hypnotised by him. Charlotte would not have been surprised if he had bent down and picked the little fellow in his hands. When he was satisfied that everything was in control, he beckoned Donald who took the equipment from Wilson, and the two of them came forward. The bird stayed still whilst he fitted his camera on the tripod. He looked into the eyepiece and pressed the shutter; the bird seemed completely unperturbed, and he was able to take another photograph before, on a sudden impulse it took off. He did not fly so much as run away at lightning speed with its feet scarcely touching the ground, and finally disappeared into the bush.

'Him gone,' said Yarrekhu needlessly. Charlotte tried to get Yarrekhu to explain what he had done, and asked why he could not do that to all the other birds that Mr Don wanted photographed, and he said, 'Some family, some no.'

Later when she saw him charm a tapir, he said, 'Tapir family.' She wondered if jaguar was family.

The trip continued, not one day resembling another, but the density of chuggers was one constant. Fortunately Dr Laker had provided Donald with an ample supply of quinine. They encountered a number of birds and other creatures. There were some narrow escapes with scorpions and giant tarantulas. The men would collect palm grub whenever they saw palms; they found eggs, edible roots and greens, wild garlic, more turtles. After her initial reservation, Charlotte readily sampled everything, and did not find anything revulsive any more.

On one of the many islands where they stopped, there was a waterfall, and Charlotte decided to go take a shower there. The rest of the party was a safe distance away, and Yarrekhu had said that there was no danger on the island. She was making her way towards the waterfall when on a sudden impulse she asked Devi if she wanted to join her. Although surprised, as she never felt safe going into the pools, she said yes. The two women from two completely different worlds walked side by side, one in men's trousers, the other in a makeshift skirt, until they got to their destination. Charlotte took all her clothes off, but Devi was shy of doing the same thing. 'Go on, the men are not watching,' the white girl urged, and Devi smiled, shrugged and followed suit. Unbeknownst to them, Don was seated on a high rock with his prized Porro-Prism binoculars, studying the lie of the land with no idea where anybody was. Suddenly the two young women came into his view, and he was stunned by the sight. Side by side were a statuesque white body and a frail golden-brown body, both of the female sex allowing water to wrap round them, the flow of the water producing an eerie shine and the contrast of their hair very striking. One had platinum-blonde hair which seemed twice its real size as water flowed over it, and the other one was shiny charcoal. He could not honestly say which one was the more glorious. At that moment his dearest wish was that he had been a painter; no one but a Millais or a William Blake, would have been able to do justice to such a sublime vision. He watched them in rapture, unable to move his eyes away, like an art connoisseur, not like a man seeking a cheap thrill, but that did not stop him feeling a violent surge below, but it was beyond sexual. He knew Charlotte's beautiful body inside out, but this was the first time he was seeing Devi as a woman; so far she had only been Devi the cook, the devoted servant. What a stunning body she had too! He never guessed what perfect proportions were hidden under those drab garments that she usually wore. It was an image that he felt sure he would never ever forget. What made this even more certain was something Charlotte said that night.

'Darling, I went for a shower under the waterfalls with Devi today.'

'I know, I saw you.'

'You know what happened to Peeping Tom,' she teased.

'I wasn't peeping, it was purely accidental… I was only —' He wondered why he was feeling guilty all the same.

'I know, silly, I was only teasing.' They held each other tight; it was then that she heard herself say the most surprising thing that she had ever said; it was as if somebody else had spoken those words through her. 'Nobody can convince me that when God made us, he meant that some of us would be masters and others servants.' She had not even thought those thoughts before, they just sprouted with the spontaneity of mushrooms in summer after a peal of thunder. The power of the notion left Don staggered.

'I know you're going to say, it's not God's work, but Man's,' she added. He was not going to say that, and just signified his assent to the sentiment by saying "hmm" and nodding vigorously. He was thinking of Devi's body by the side of Charlotte's. Indeed, how can anybody from another planet, assuming that there were people on other planets — and there is plenty of hard evidence for believing that there were — coming on earth and seeing those two women under the waterfall understand that the function of one of them was to serve and be subservient to the other? What was there to tell them apart? Now, he agreed with Charlotte wholeheartedly, and nodded emphatically.

As the river became impassable at one point, the original plan was put in action The men carried the boat expertly harnessed to bullocks by Yarrekhu, and they continued their trip on land. It was then that they encountered the jaguar. As usual it was Yarrekhu who spotted the proud beast.

'Yaguaraté,' he whispered. Donald saw him in his Porro and passed them over to Charlotte who gasped as she saw the spotted beast standing proudly on a rock. She looked questioningly at the animal charmer who glumly said, 'Yaguareté only family Yaguareté.'

Donald tried to assemble his equipment, but before he had finished, Yaguareté had turned back and was gone. They saw another one shortly after, quite unexpectedly, as it suddenly came into view at a turning. He saw them and glared. Yarrekhu said 'Shout all body!' And everybody started hollering like a demented witches' convention, and scared the killer cat away.

There was no doubt about the success of the enterprise. Before setting out, Donald had said to Charlotte that he would consider the expedition a success if they encountered no more than two of the following: a jaguar, an arapaima, an anaconda or a tinamou. So far they had seen three, and they had a whole week before they planned to turn back. They had seen capybaras and manatees, giant otters, sloths and caimans. They had even eaten caiman which they found rather bland, even curried. Yarrekhu cooked turtle Carib style by killing it and cooking it in its carapace as a cooking pot, with jungle herbs; Charlotte loved it.

Magnetite

As far as birds were concerned, Donald doubted that anyone before him could have collected such a wealth of information. He had photographed hundreds of them, often with Yarrekhu working his magic on them. Many were as yet unclassified or unknown, even in scientific literature. His friend and colleague Henry Walter Bates would surely be delighted when he read his report and saw his photographs and sketches. Charlotte ended up with aching fingers, having to write down their specifications. The list was endless, and included the Spotted Puffbird, the Red-throated Caracara, Warbling Antbirds, Golden-headed Manakins, Golden-collared and Yellow-throated Woodpeckers, Black-bellied Cuckoos, Caica, Green-tailed Jacamars, Brown-crowned Motmots, Orange-breasted Falcons, Grey-headed Mites, Pink-throated Becards, Bright-rumped Attila, the Crimson Topaz. Altogether there was a list of just over one hundred and twenty birds, including many photographed and probably seen by a scientist for the first time. Each one was drawn and photographed, with approximate measurements and descriptions of their salient characteristics. Donald felt that he had only seen the tip of this great iceberg of knowledge, and was already planning many more such trips in the interest of science.

After just one more day, they were due to start on the return trip, when he would swap water for land. At one point on that last day, Yarrekhu stopped the boat; Donald knew that he would only do such a thing for a reason.

'Arapaima,' he whispered. Wilson's face lit up, and he got his gear ready; it was almost always ready anyway. Yarrekhu bent down and looked into the water, which surprised Donald, as it was pretty murky.

'Him big,' he said. Wordlessly he indicated a direction to Wilson who cast his line. Almost immediately they felt a lurch on the boat, and Wilson burst out laughing. It took him almost an hour before he was able to haul it in, with the help of everybody onboard. Charlotte screamed like an excited child when she saw the size of the fish. Donald watching her thought what a lucky man he was to have caught her. Yarrekhu stroked the huge monster, whispering some Carib words, and he stopped wriggling. The scientist managed to assemble his photographic equipment and took photographs of the huge fish from all angles. With the help of his fiancée, he measured its length and its maximum girth. It was about six feet, the height of a very tall man. He estimated its weight to be about the same as that tall man, probably one hundred and eighty pounds. As far as he knew, that was the heaviest fresh water fish in existence.

Wilson took two steps towards the monster fish, brandishing his sword, but Yarrekhu stepped in to block him. The two men exchanged some angry words, and finally Yarrekhu seemed to have won the argument, and deftly liberating the fish from the hook by a twist of the wrist, he threw it back into the waters.

'Him family,' he said, 'no eat family.'

The return journey took much less time, as many of the paths that Okoronote had cut were available, and the boats were obviously much easier to manoeuvre downstream. Devi had never felt so alive as during those weeks on the Essequibo, although she worried about Baba, but she told herself repeatedly that the poor man hardly recognised her anyway, and would not have missed her. She had been very relaxed; everybody was nice to her, no one treated her like a servant. She was so happy that Mr Donald and Charlotte ('Don't call me Miss Charlotte, we are friends, just call me Charlotte.') were going to be married shortly. She loved both of them like family, and would do anything for them.

Donald had thought that he would need a few months to work on his report and put together a massive paper that his friend Bates would no doubt be happy to arrange for publication. He would have liked to get married as soon as possible, but knew that Mrs Emsworth as well as his own mother would be disappointed if the wedding could not be celebrated in great pomp. Afterwards he would be off again; there was so much more to do. It was a huge country, and he had only skimmed the surface; there was so much more to be seen; there were reputedly over five hundred species of birds, and he had hardly seen a quarter of them; he had yet to see a harpy eagle for instance. He needed to see the Potaro river, which a fellow tribesman of Yarrekhu had claimed culminated into the Kaieteur, the mightiest waterfall anybody had even come across. There was Mount Roraima, the Kanuku Mountains, the Rupununi and Rewa rivers. And he was determined to do all this with his soon-to-be wife; they shared everything, they understood each other without words, and he also had to admit that her body no less than her intellect, excited him to the point of madness. They would get married as soon as it could be arranged. Mum and dad would certainly not want to miss it, and Charlotte's cousin Clara from Somerset would move heaven and earth to come over, seeing that she had been hoping to come for a visit for quite some time.

It would take a minimum of three months.

They reached home without any major incidents, and the Emsworths were overjoyed at seeing their beloved daughter come back safe and sound, tanned like a native and exuding good health. Her whole body seemed enveloped in an aura of happiness and her eyes had a new spark. It was so obvious that the weeks they had spent together had done nothing to dampen her love for this admirable young man who rose in their esteem every time they saw him. First they were going to have the best Christmas ever, and then they will begin to plan the wedding.

'Are there any letters for me?' Charlotte asked, and Mum gave her four of five letters, all from England. She recognised Clara's handwriting, and retired to her room to read it.

The young fiancés met on the next day, when she came to Taj Mahal Villa, and Don immediately noticed that something was amiss. He asked what the matter was, and looking away she said there was nothing. They were seated under the veranda, and Devi brought them some tea and Indian pakoras that she had made. She was surprised that Charlotte just looked at them and said thank you. Usually her eyes would beam with joy when she saw Devi's offerings. It was this which convinced Don that there was indeed something amiss. Donald looked at her, perplexed, and gradually alarm started rising in him.

'No, sweetheart,' he said suddenly, 'you need to tell me what I have done wrong.'

A tear spontaneously dripped from her left eye and she did not seem to notice. She blushed, opened her handbag and produced Clara's letter, and giving him the first page, saying, 'Read it, dearest.'

The Vicarage
Frobisher Street
Taunton
Somerset

12 October 1863

My dearest Lotte,

Let me first congratulate you on your engagement; I knew this was on the cards the moment I read your letter almost six months ago. From your description of this paragon, I already considered him my brother. I shall now begin preparing my voyage. Father is very happy to let me go, just give me ample notice so we can arrange a booking. My hands are trembling with excitement as I am thinking of crossing the Atlantic in a steamer.

You asked me whether I shall follow you into matrimony, and although Jonas Dormeuil-Thunderby is an admirable young man and we do love each other so much, I am afraid that I shall not marry him, at least not yet. I remember your meeting darling Papa's friend Reverend John Davies and his daughter Emily when they came for a visit from Gateshead some years ago, when we were both dizzy little girls. I got to know Emily over the years, and as I no doubt told you in my letters, she is one of the brightest persons I have ever met, and I could listen to her for hours. She has always been very angry that women are not able to benefit from the same facilities as men where education is concerned, and she has devoted all her life so far towards putting that pitiful situation right. It was difficult, but now, dearest coz, her efforts are coming to fruition. Cambridge has agreed to try, on an experimental basis, to allow women to study there (at Cambridge). At her instigation, a college called Girton College is going to be created, which will be dedicated to us, creatures of the supposedly weaker sex. We are only the weaker sex because men have wished us to be so! If you were not on the point of entering matrimony, I would go down on bended knees to beg you to join me there, for it is my dearest wish to have a full education. You've heard me air my views on the matter long enough. Papa is very happy for me, but that does not mean that I will miss the wedding of my best friend and dearest cousin I am so excited, and cannot wait.

'So,' said Donald, 'why should that make you miserable, dearest?'

'Can't you see? Oh Don dearest, don't for a moment doubt that I love you with all my heart, and that marrying you was my dearest wish —'

'Was? Why did you say was?'

She said nothing. There was an embarrassing silence for a while, and both had the same idea, and bent forward to grab one of Devi's pakoras, clearly for no other reason than that they were both too stunned to say anything.

'Well, Don sweetheart,' she said after munching in silence for a while, 'getting a serious education was something I had always hoped might have been possible when I was in Taunton, but got used to the idea that this was unrealistic, and I had lost my enthusiasm for learning, until I met you, when I discovered that my great craving for knowledge was not at all extinguished, but was only dormant. I now know that I could not be fulfilled unless I too, like Clara did my utmost to go to Girton. I am not breaking my engagement to you, dearest, only asking you to postpone our union.' She paused, looked at him obliquely and added, 'Only for three years... eh... maybe four.'

'I could not live without you for a week, let alone four or five years,' Don said almost tearfully, 'I won't let you go. I will teach you all I know … we will learn together _'

'But you must let me go if you love me... this is something I must do, dearest.'

'But surely you don't have to go now, the college isn't going to start for another year or so...'

'If I don't go now, I will find it more difficult... I believe the best course is to join Clara and start preparing myself... I feel so inadequate.'

Clearly her decision had already been taken. Donald knew her passionate nature and felt that once she was out of his sight, she would be lost to him. She would immerse herself in her studies, and he had no doubt that she would do as well as anybody. Why shouldn't she? He perfectly understood that his happiness was going to be swept away in the tide of her gnawing need to satisfy her academic ambition.

'I had so much hoped that you and I —' She put her hand to his lips to stop him saying any more. They both knew, deep down, that this was the end for them, although both pretended otherwise.

Charlotte left Georgetown a month later on board the paddle steamer *Albany*, bound for Liverpool.

CHAPTER 7

◆ ◆ ◆

Devi

DEVI WAS ALMOST as sad as Mr Don about the break-up of the two people she loved above everybody else in this world, apart from poor Baba. She would have liked to ask him the reason, but thought that it would be unseemly for a servant to question her master. He may be a nice man, but she was not going to take any liberty. She noticed how sad he was, and thought that there was little she could do for him, except feed him properly, see that he had clean clothes to change into — he was so absent-minded that unless Devi put a nice set of clean and well-ironed shirts and things on his bed, he was capable of wearing the same garments for weeks.

Meticulous cook that she was, she took extra care in making the things that she knew he loved, like pakoras, samosas, halwas made from chickpea flower, butter, sugar, cardamon raisins and almonds, but nothing could re-verse his ebbing appetite. After dinner, which he hardly touched, she would bring him tea and his pipe, and he would stare at them. She would sit at one corner of the veranda — he had sternly warned her once of never sitting on the floor — on a stool which some Arawak man had carved out of one piece of log and which Mr Don had bought, no doubt for twice its true price, and watch him in silence. She thought that he was glad of her company, even if no words were exchanged. Sometimes they would look at the sunset on the Demerara, and then she would say she was going to bed, was there anything he wanted her to do? He would shake his head and whisper a no thank you, Devi. This had gone on for two weeks, then one night, just as she was leav-ing, he spoke.

'I might have forgotten to say, Devi, but thank you for all the good work you did on the trip.' Of course he had not forgotten, and had in fact thanked her on numerous occasions, during the trip itself and after they had reached Georgetown.

He had not been able to find much solace in his work, and in an attempt to do so, he would sit at his desk with quantities of notes that he had made with Charlotte's help, but no sooner had he read one line, than the images of the circumstances in which the events described had occurred invaded his inward eye, putting paid to his effort. Everything reminded him of Charlotte. He was not sleeping, he was hardly eating, and worst of all he was not making any progress with his work. He knew this could not go on, but he could find no means of getting back on track. Yet never once did he blame her. He was convinced that she had arrived at her decision with utmost honesty. She had every legitimate right to aspire to learning. It was not as if she was leaving him for some other man, although he imagined that this would happen one day. He had almost completely dismissed the possibility of Charlotte coming back to him in five or six years. Learning was the most wonderful thing on earth. There were so many things Man had to learn; there were so many mysteries that needed to be pierced. He was convinced that as people learned more, they increased their chance of happiness. Learning would help Man find ways of beating diseases, of understanding each other, thus making wars obsolete and turn the world into a better place. Near future, he hoped.

That night, after sunset, these thoughts were at the forefront of his mind, and on an impulse, he called Devi.

'Devi, can you read?' She was delighted that he had spoken to her, for his silence had made her very unhappy, these last days.

'No, Mr Don, I never had the chance.'

'Not even Hindi?'

'We spoke Bhojpuri, but no, I cannot write either...'

'I can teach you...'

'Bhojpuri?' she asked hiding a mischievous smile. How relieved she was when this little joke made him chuckle. It was not a loud merry laugh, but almost an involuntary manifestation of mild hilarity.

'I would if I could, but I know no Bhojpuri, Devi. As you see, my education isn't complete either. I am afraid I can only teach you English. Canadian

English at that.' She was jubilating inwardly, hardly able to believe her good fortune, but she hid it well.

'I mean would you like to learn to read and write English?' Of course she would like that. She had often regretted her illiteracy. Instinctively she knew that having something to do, however trivial, would help the man combat his depression.

'I would love to, Mr Don.'

'Nothing to stop us starting right away,' he said. The suddenness of it all had completely confused the girl who began stuttering some incoherent nonsense, but she nodded enthusiastically when he said, 'There is no time like the present, Devi.'

Less than five minutes later, they were seated side by side at the table, with pencils and notebooks. He was very impressed with how quickly she learned. An hour after they had started, she knew how to write her name, his name, how to read the names of the various birds they had seen on the trip.

'At the rate you are learning,' he said laughing, 'you will no longer require my services in a week.'

In a week, he was teaching her to count, although he discovered that she was well able to carry out complicated calculations in her head. Still, he taught her to write out the numbers, found that she easily understood the place value of digits, and took in the multiplication table in her stride. Sometimes Don wondered whether she had not disguised the truth a bit when she said that she was completely illiterate. She had a liking for flowery handwriting, and he loved watching her, forehead wrinkled with concentration, her slightly protruding tongue held by her upper lip, bent on the table, gripping the pen too tightly, writing nicely formed letters beautifully linked together. He taught her verbs and conjugation, the meaning of adverbs, adjectives and in no time at all he had taught her nursery rhymes. How she chuckled over the comical imagery in those little songs. She was so happy that every time Don said that she had done well, she would laugh like a little child and shake her fists up and down merrily.

Don had not planned this, but after only four weeks, he found that she could be of help to him in his work. He had started using some of Charlotte's notes to make Devi read, and one thing leading to another, he found himself once more immersed in his work almost by stealth. A huge box of photographs of the expedition arrived form New York where Charlotte had sent them for processing before she left, and this gave him added impetus. He was never to look back.

By now he had found a more powerful lamp, and a bigger table, and together they read the notes and looked at the photos.

She knew that life would never be the same again for either of them when he said that they should eat together. It was whilst they were at table after dinner, he teaching and she learning that he became aware of a rising sexual attraction for Devi. He had completely erased from his memory the image of her naked body under the waterfall, but it was coming back into his consciousness by stealth. He had once thought that after Charlotte, his sexual life was over, and had become reconciled to the notion that henceforth he would lead a life of chastity. He had managed it in the past and did not imagine that it would be a great hardship. One could always sublimate libido into something creative; he had read that many a landmark discovery were made by celibate men. So his immediate reaction was to try and play down this reawakening and shoo away images of her naked brown body glistening in the waterfall. He wondered whether Devi had any feelings for him, other than gratitude perhaps. The last thing he would do was to cause her grief. When their hands touched one night, he noticed that she made no effort to pull it away; he thought he even detected a faint smile on her lips; he left his hand on top of hers, and gently increased the pressure on it, and she finally pulled it away, but reluctantly. He moved forward and grabbed her hand with determination this time, saying, 'Oh Devi, please let me.' And she willingly gave him her hand and smiled.

She had noticed that ever since he had started teaching her, he looked at her differently. Over the years, Chachi Padma, who had been in service for a good many years, had told her about male employers and what they expected from their female servants, and she had thought that as Charlotte was gone, Mr Don might have wanted to have what Chachi Padma had called his wicked ways with her. She knew that she had a passionate nature, and after what Jagdeo had done to her, spoiling her chances of a getting a good husband, having a man now and then was not an idea that was inimical to her. Besides, living on the premises made matters much less complicated, but most of all, she had always felt a strong attraction for the man from the very beginning. Now that Charlotte was out of the way, she felt free to admit that to herself. If he wanted her, he could have her!

On the very night that they made love, Don said that they should marry. At first she thought that men always said things like that, although from what she knew of Don, he was not like other men.

'But you are a white man,' she said rather foolishly.

'My grandfather was an Indian, an Ojibwa.' Devi had no idea what that was, and he jumped out of bed and went to get an encyclopaedia and read to her a none-too-short description of the Ojibwa tribe.

Next day, when Devi saw him at his desk, she thought that he had been working on his report, but he called her and showed her a letter he was writing to his mother, and gave what he had already written to her to read. She did not believe how lucky she was. A penniless servant girl who had been raped, who had begged for a living, and who only a short time ago was completely illiterate, was now so clearly the object of a profound love of one of the worthiest men existing on Bhagwan's earth.

The marriage between Donald and Devi was celebrated at the famous St George's Cathedral in Georgetown, by the Archbishop of British Guiana, William Piercy Austin. Devi got her father moved to her new house, and divided her attention equally between her new husband and the ailing and senile man. He did not always know who she was, or what he was doing in this strange place, but he was kept in the most comfortable state possible.

Just under a year after the marriage, Devi gave birth to a boy, who was called George Rajendra.

Twenty years later, George married Ann Merryweather, granddaughter of Percy Robertson, whom she met when this family came to Toronto on a visit. The latter had been promised a colonial governorship by The Earl of Derby, but here is an extract from a letter found in the archives of Lord Palmerston some years after his death:

"... before any appointment to the governorship of Ceylon is finalised, I would like your Lordship to take cognizance of two important factors, viz: (a) That the aforesaid Percy R. Robertson has a Malayan grandmother, to

whom his grandfather was not married, and (b) That his wife was also born out of wedlock, to convicts, a Gipsy mother, and a father who were transported, she for theft and he for sedition of the British Empire. I suggest to your Lordship that these considerations outweigh by far, any merit on the part of the candidate, accruing from his excellent military record, even taking his Victoria Cross into account."

Percy and Annie settled in Halifax, Nova Scotia where he bought a thousand acres of prime land in the Annapolis Valley.

CHAPTER 8

$\bullet\,\bullet\,\bullet$

The Life and Times of Gina

ON THAT CLEAR sunny afternoon somewhere in the Highlands, Katrina Crialese had no clear idea about the route she was going to take. Contrary to her nature, when travelling, she never made plans set in amber. She went where her fancy took her. She could start in a certain direction and then find herself changing it on a vague hunch. As long as she made it to Ullapool at some time, she did not mind where she went. Anywhere you went on this enchanted place was a treat. She had no idea that the Scottish Highlands were so magical. She still had a few weeks of freedom ahead of her before settling down in new surroundings and she had no anxiety about this. In her experience there had never been a problem with fellow academics, people speaking the same language, and no doubt fired by the same thirsts. She often heard negative things about a colleague, about people delegating work to juniors, or even doubts expressed about the complete authenticity of their papers, but she paid scant attention to gossip. If there was jealousy and back-stabbing, she was never the target of any, as far as she knew, and never in a million years would she say anything behind someone's back that she would not say in front of them.

Having been born in Britain, she was always considered by the Italians as a glamorous Saxon and she thought that they treated her with more respect than she deserved. Having grown up in Italy and acquired a much-admired tan (although she knew of an Italian emeritus professor who whilst doing a Ph.D in Bristol in the seventies was told, Sorry, we do not rent our rooms to coloured people) and speaking perfect English, albeit with a slight Italian accent, she had acquired an exotic aura in anglophone circles, which she found pleasant to bask in. She had very little recollection of Dunstable where she had lived until she was four. Gliders? She planned to go have a look at it some time, now that she was going to be in the British Isles for a couple of years at least. She might look up granddad Rudi if he was still alive.

If Gina never tired of telling Katrina almost everything about herself, including bits that someone with her history might have been excused for keeping to herself, the young scientist, when not yet a teenager never had enough of her tales. Gina's mother was born out of wedlock, she revealed without batting an eyelid. What's wedlock? The little girl had asked. Look at it this this way cara mia, she had started, there are two types of bastards in this world and she had elaborated in details, to Maria's alarm. After a while Maria, Katrina's mother gave up trying to stop the older woman giving her daughter uncensored accounts of her life, in the knowledge that it would make not the blindest bit of difference.

The family farm in a village upon whose name no two families agreed, on the edge of Montepulciano, which was even then one of the most backward places on earth, produced far too little for a comfortable life. Wine, she told the wide-eyed toddler, was so cheap most people used it to brush their teeth with — those who bothered at any rate. They even gave it to the cows! Oh the fun Gina and her little friends had watching their drunken antics!

Gina's very first memory was of her mother crying on the way home one morning after Sunday mass. She did not understand the reason then, but Padre Pietro had based his sermon on the theme of girls without morals who did not think of the consequences of their sinful folly, and everybody had turned round to look at her Mamma. This was a favourite subject of the holy man. When she was unlucky enough not to fall asleep in church, she would hear him tell the congregation how girls followed their mother's example as surely as water flows down the ditch that's already there. Gina suspected that whenever he was too drunk to prepare a fresh sermon on Saturday night, he rehashed that old theme.

She had never felt at ease in that place full of morons, and as the farm was not doing at all well, she decided to leave home, doing a variety of jobs as laundress, maid, kitchen hand, flower seller among others, sending a large fraction of her meagre earnings home.

'You name it, ragazza, and your grandma has done it,' she told Katrina who never failed to detect some pride in the assertion.

During the war years, she found work quite readily and ended up working as a kitchen maid for the British troops after they arrived in Monte Cassino.

They had set up camp in the Trocchio Hills, and hired a small number of locals to do various odd jobs, as there were not enough auxiliaries. When they were available, they were usually privates from the colonies like Ceylon, Fiji, British Guyana, Mauritius, Trinidad. They wore uniforms but they did not carry guns and were not trained for military action.

'Most girls dreamt of attracting the notice of some blue-eyed Yorkshireman, a Gary Cooper or a Jean Gabin, and would have nothing to do with the darkies,' she said. Not her! There were so many people she knew that she could look down upon for their lack of charity and other real failings, so why pick on skin colour? In any case she always thought that there were some shades of brown which were was much more attractive than pasty white. Many of her fellow workers thought her a proper hussy for befriending the colonials, even if she spoke no English and they no Italian.

Then Prakash entered her life. He was small and thin and looked like a hungry teenager, and she thought that he was the most beautiful young man she had ever set eyes upon with his shiny brown skin. 'You are such a sharp little missy, you must have noticed that I always put the same quantity of milk in my coffee, no? Today I will tell you the reason: because that was exactly how my Prakash looked, the only man I've ever loved.' He had peerless dark brown eyes, long eyelashes and the most perfect nose. And he began to chat her up. 'His voice was like music I tell you, and his laughter — why, cara mia, after all those years I can just close my eyes and hear it ring like little bells.' He spoke little English and less Italian, but that did not stop him trying his luck with the girls, oh yes, all the girls. He was irrepressible. Somehow he managed to make himself understood by using words from his own language, adding an "o". The first thing he said to her was "to bello," then correcting it to "to bella mo to aimo". He came from Mauritius where they speak a patois of French. It did not take a genius to make out what he meant, nor what he was after, Gina explained. She never made any bones about her past history, not stopping at giving her granddaughter graphic details, including how they did it the first time, clearly relishing the telling.

Whenever they had some free time, they met, sat under a tree or went for walks on the hills overlooking the villages, smoking, talking gibberish before they developed their own brand of esperanto. But more than anything they laughed. It was the laughter which cemented their relationship. 'You know, cara you can build the best possible relationship with a man based on laughter.' And of course the inevitable happened.

"'Why would I not give myself to him?' She said flinging her arms up, 'Why would I deprive him of what I had generously given to others before him? I was unmarriageable anyway! So why deprive myself of something I wanted with all my heart? I might be lots of things but hypocrite I am not, Katia mia!' Yes, it was a moonlit night, and they had arranged to meet behind the kitchen. To be honest, she could not remember the sex, only the smell of decaying potato peelings. Truth is, she confided, one does not remember the sex, only the after-sex glow… like food, you remember it was good, but not the taste. You will understand later, she assured her pre-pubescent granddaughter.

He claimed to have fallen in love with her and wanted to marry her. He showed her a photograph of his family home and promised that she would live like a princess on that paradise island. She thought she was too clever to fall for Prakash's talk, but he was a fine talker, and she realised soon enough that she was smitten with him. She loved listening to the stories of his childhood in Mauritius, of his ancestry, the stories his parents had themselves been told by their ancestors, which had survived many generations. He had an excellent memory and so was able to recount the histories of his ancestry. Gina had an excellent memory too, and she would later tell Katrina everything she remembered.

She was becoming starry-eyed about the notion of going to a foreign country with a brown man who had promised him that she would be treated like a queen by his family in their stupendous mansion. One day, when you see that film, Son Of The Sheikh, with Rudolph Valentino, you will understand what I am talking about, she told her grandchild. However the moment she had become responsive to the idea of marriage, he started having second thoughts. He was not dishonest, she told Katrina vehemently, but it had dawned upon him that there would be too many obstacles in front of them. To begin with they were in the middle of a war; where would they find the money for the passage to the island? Once they arrived on the island, where would they live? He admitted to her that the mansion he had shown her was the Plaza Cinema in Rose-Hill — not that she had completely believed the tall tale initially. In the sort of house he lived in, the roofs leaked, the floors were cemented with cow dung, they had no electricity, did not even have proper toilets, just a hole in the ground. In our little village outside Montepulciano, we slept next to the cowshed she had countered. Then he declared that his people would not take kindly to his marrying a foreigner, a Christian. He was not only expected to marry a good Hindu girl, but one from the same caste.

He told her how his ancestors had arrived in Mauritius in the early nineteenth century with just the rags on their backs, having mislaid the head of the household on the way. This had not stopped his great great how ever many great grandmother from working her fingers to the bones, and ending up making a fortune, owning hundreds of arpents of sugar-cane fields, houses and stocks and shares. Only his father, the grandson of the matriarch had done the inexcusable, running away with the daughter of an ex-slave, a black African, and had been disowned. So, he had to admit that the stories he had told her about his family were a bit exaggerated — to the extent that hm... hm... they were in fact all lies. He had not inherited anything, and his family had remained poor. But he had sort of inherited the most valuable heirloom, a gold earring. Actually Prakash admitted that nobody gave it to his grandfather. When he the family banished him, as he knew where his grandmother kept it, he simply pocketed it as his due. Yes, just one of a pair. 'You've caught me looking at it, but I never wear it.'

By now, she was completely besotted by her brown man from the Indian Ocean, and believed that when you are in love, all those obstacles that Prakash mentioned were minor irritations that could be brushed away. Gradually the young private caught some of Gina's optimism and made up his mind that they were going to marry at the first available opportunity and tackle the obstacles as and when they arose. The fact that they had found each other convinced them that they were born lucky and for such as them, no difficulties were insurmountable.

But the war was still raging on, with all its uncertainties. The Germans had rallied after initial setbacks. Then out of the blue, they decided to retreat, leaving the Allies free to attack the Gustav line. Then General Lucas ordered his regiments to move. 'I am not stupid, I listened and followed the development of the war, you know.'

She saw her lover for less than fifteen minutes before he was due to leave with his company. He was in such a state, trembling all over, trying so hard not to show her his tears. She knew there and then that it was the last time they would see each other. He had no idea where they were going. She knew that he would have tried to contact her, but was unable to. Neither were great writers. As he was leaving, he pressed his most valuable possession, the earring into her hands. 'So you will never forget me,' he cried. Even if they took her brain out she cannot forget that lovely man! Prakash will always be her first love, and her most treasured possession was a badly faded photograph of the two of them taken by an English private with his Brownie camera. She proudly showed it to Katrina, and she dutifully went through the motion of admiring the pair, but in fact one could hardly recognise anything. Of course she never told him that she was carrying his child — Katrina's mother Maria.

'What about the earrings, Grandma,' little Katrina had asked, 'why don't you wear it?' She had cackled merrily, 'Do I have only one ear? How can I wear one earring?' And she promised that Katrina would have it on her eighteenth birthday.

Katrina had always felt very close to that mysterious soldier, and as the photograph revealed next to nothing, she felt free to imagine him as Gina had described. It was this man who was her grandfather, and she was sure that he was no wife-beater like Rudi was. Might he still be alive on his island? Was he still in Dunstable?

Gina went back to the village to deliver Maria, and was surprised when Papa and Mamma did not throw her out. The baby was darker than the other little girls in the village, but although some people whispered wicked things behind their backs, she grew up into a normal hard-working peasant girl who could hardly read and write. Maria, her sweet, prudish lovely self-effacing mother. The fact that Katrina seemed to love Gina more, did not mean that she was indifferent to her mother. She had a different personality, she was more serious, vulnerable, not much given to laughter, but she respected her and admired her more than she knew.

'Your other grandfather Rudi,' she told Katrina, 'said that he had been an Ukrainian resistance fighter against the Germans, but he never showed me no papers to prove that. One thing I can tell you though, Katia cara, he did not act like no war hero.'

He had spent the last days of the war in Istanbul, doing what, he never told Gina. He went back to Kiev when it was all over, but could not fit in. He thought they owed him a job for fighting the Germans, but there were no jobs. When he heard that there was work in England, he decided to take the plunge.

The new government had promised to build new homes to replace those that had been destroyed by the Luftwaffe, and there was a huge demand for people to work in the brick and cement factories. He came to Bedford to work for the Marston Valley Brick Company where most of the work force were Italians who had been encouraged to come over in the mezzogiorno, with their passage paid, hostel accommodation guaranteed, usually on the Midland Road which would soon be known as the Via Roma.

The Italians tended to mix only with people from their own villages, and avoided other Italians, but funnily they had no such reservation when it came to Poles and Ukrainians. Why they took Rudi to their bosoms, Gina would never understand; it was certainly not for his charm.

Rudi easily made friends with some boys from Chianciano and was soon able to string together a few words in Italian, but he never spoke about the war. He helped build the Santa Francesca Cabrini church and developed a taste for pasta. After a year or so, Giuseppe, Aldo and Roberto, who were cousins, his three best friends decided that as they were earning good money and were in a secure job, it was time to find brides for themselves and that was where Gina came in. Rudi would have liked a bride too, but he hardly knew any girl. The lads then revealed that they were going to send for brides from their village. Their folks at home would make sure they chose good women with strong haunches and big tits. And if you want to, Rudi, we can ask them to choose someone for you too, they offered.

Ravaged by the war and by Mussolini's excesses — Gina never understood how that flat-headed bastard had come to power — the country was on its knees. What had Italians done, she asked the little girl, that we deserved leaders such as il Duce or Il Divo? Anyway, most men were unemployed, unable to support wives and children, and those who had jobs had their pick of the girls. As a result, there were plenty of young Italian women who were less marriageable, for a variety of reasons, who would be willing to go to the end of the world to find almost any husband.

A few months later, four fresh but slightly shop-soiled peasant women arrived at Victoria Station in London, among whom Gina, with what reputation that she had acquired in the village — totally justified, she assured Katrina.

'If I was a man, I certainly wouldn't want a woman with a bambina,' Gina said.

Anyway, three of the women were from Chianciano, and as the families had not been able to get sound local women, they had agreed to extend their horizons and go to that village without a proper name outside Montepulciano and found her. Maria was left behind with Gina's mother for the time being, but Rudi knew of her existence and he had said it did not matter. There was an understanding that Gina would go fetch Maria at some point.

At first they were happy enough. She found him austere and humourless but soon enough began having doubts about the wisdom of the union. He seemed to be living in the past, and often had nightmares. Sometimes he would wake up in a sweat in the middle of the night, and when she pressed him, he would talk about Babi Yar and admit his part in the massacre, but spared her the details. He never laughed and rarely smiled, and complained about everything. But she was used to hardships, and was willing to put up with him. She loved to laugh and tell stories, and nothing he could do would change that. If he likes to sit and sulk, she had thought, he was welcome to it, but do it on your own, man! He rarely spoke about his Odessa days and she only heard about it from the girls who themselves heard about it from their husbands, to whom he would tell everything when they went drinking. Still, he was quite a handsome man with bluish-grey eyes and blond hair, and people who did not know him all told her how lucky she was to land herself such a catch. Yes, she had thought, if he had been a fish, he would have had the distinction if being the first blue-eyed fish.

Only a few months after their marriage, however, he began complaining that with a wife who did nothing he was hardly able to save any money. Contrary to his expectations, Gina greeted this news with relief. She was many things, but work-shy was not one of them. So you want me to go work? Why you no say so? I'll find myself work if that's what you want, you blue-eyed fish. Meltis was always looking for women workers, and she got herself a job with them. The pay was not much, but the combined salary was enough for a comfortable living, and they were able to save ten shillings every week. But the very best thing, she said, was that they could eat all the sweets they wanted. The broken bits that could not be sold.

'Did I tell you that as a child, I never had any sweets, cara? So you see, I had a lot of catching up to do.'

She became the most popular woman with the neighbourhood's children as well. One day, out of the blue he brought up the question of little Maria.

'What sort of woman are you?' he asked, spitting on the floor, 'having a little bastard like this. How many men have you fucked? What possessed me to marry a whore like you, a woman who was not a virgin? Who had fucked every soldier on the front'.

'You no spit on floor!' she screamed at him. She did not know it then, but he was already humping his best friend's wife.

The war hero sprang up, threw himself at Gina and slapped her with the back of his hand. She reeled back with the force of the hit and banged her head against the wall. Whatever hope she had entertained of falling in love with the man one day evaporated on that night, like water poured in a hot pan. It took one slap. A man slaps you, cara, slap back, you are fit and strong. Anyway, she was trapped and there was no way out. She did not know how to get out of the country, but here at least she had a job. She would put up with him for the time being, she thought, and bide her time. One day she might end up sticking a knife in him, but not just yet. As a small child, Katrina was quite surprised to hear her grandma say things like how much she hated it when he demanded sex. Yes, Gina said with a shrug, she had to submit herself, and allow herself to be humiliated. It was a man's world. How she prayed nightly that she did not become pregnant again.

To her surprise, one day, after he had been drinking all night with the cousins Giuseppe, Aldo and Roberto, he called her, and said that if she wanted to go collect Maria, that was all right, adding, 'But don't expect me to pay for your tickets.'

So she went with Sofia and Assunta who had also left their babies behind, and she came back with Maria. She had fully expected Rudi to ignore her little bastard, as she herself constantly and lovingly referred to her, but to her surprise, he took a shine to the little girl, and the two of them have always got on quite well. This made the relationship slightly more bearable to her, and a year later, Uncle Vittorio was born.

Katrina was very fond of the mentally handicapped uncle. He was sweet, always smiling. People think of them as unfortunate, but Zio was the happiest man she knew, loving his food, the sunshine, music and laughter. Nothing in the world gave him as much pleasure as to fart loudly in company, and laughing himself silly afterwards. Once he realised that the boy was not normal, Rudi lost interest in him, but he was never nasty or mean to him.

When Mamma was twenty-two she married Papa, second born son of Giuseppe Crialese, son of Rudi's friend, although he was a couple of years younger than her. They had grown up together, with Maria treating him as a younger brother, but at an early age they both knew they were made for each other, and the relationship changed. Neither had done well at school. Papa got a job as a waiter at the Arrivederci near Bedford Station, but had hopes of becoming a chef; Rossano the proud owner encouraged him to go into the kitchen and learn. Maria trained to become a hairdresser. Katrina was born two years later. She remembered that they filled the house with toys that, to Mamma's chagrin, she had little interest in. She was always bookish; when she was four, Papa was made redundant. People could no longer afford going to the restaurant. For a while the family survived on Maria's meagre earnings, seeing that even the recession could not stop hair growing on peoples' head. Then Papa got a job at Vauxhall's in Dunstable, and the family moved to a rented flat near the

Downs. Giuseppe was never happy cutting plastic foam to make car seats, when he dreamt of carving meat, fish or poultry, and when because of the recession, they cut the working week to three days, money became even scarcer. Katrina remembered the change in the atmosphere at home. In Bedford, it had been laughter and joy, but in this strange place it was long faces and sulks all round.

Gina had wanted out of her miserable life with Rudi almost since the first day, and as luck would have it, her only remaining brother who lived in the family farm in Italy died, and she was his sole remaining heir. When she said to Rudi that she was going home, he shrugged and said nothing. He was neither upset nor pleased. When the time came for the departure, it was done without acrimony and without tears. The two of them parted, and neither demanded that the other wrote or kept in touch. She told herself that she would send him a Christmas card every year but never did. They did get his news from Auntie Assunta who wrote two or three times a year. They later heard that he had moved to Dunstable too.

Katrina had been looking forward to start going to Icknield Primary when all of a sudden Papa came in smiling one day and said that they were all going back to Italy. She remembered the exact words, 'We are going back home to Italy.' Giuseppe had had never been there, nor had Katrina.

'Zio Enrico has found me a job as waiter in Siena, we are all going back home to Italy.' Mamma dropped a cup of tea that she was holding and threw herself at him, grabbing him by the neck and kissing him full on the lips, something she never did in front of her daughter. In the beginning they would stay at the farm with Gina, and Papa would cycle to Siena to work. Maria hoped to make the farm produce a few marketable products like cheese, butter, eggs and tomatoes.

Katrina had always thought that home was Bedford or Dunstable, but she had no difficulty accepting Gina'a little village. Maria and Giuseppe knew just enough Italian to converse with each other, as Gina had insisted on speaking Italian to anybody who had the faintest Italian connection. Even Rudi ended up with a good grasp of the language. If he had not seemed upset about Gina leaving, he was clearly sad to lose Giuseppe and Maria of whom he was very fond as well as the handicapped Vittorio. The latter did not seem to care.

The four year old girl remembered the journey on the Orient Express, the night train to Dover, the ferry across the channel at dawn, and the excitement, the noise, the shoving and the pushing, everybody making a fuss over Zio Vittorio, and him enjoying every bit of it, even if he did wet his pants. The moment the train arrived in Domodossola, she understood what they had meant when they said, "We are going home!"

She loved the village, the open air, the fields, the woods. She loved the pigs, the ducks and the goats. She loved the smell of manure in the morning, the cows mooing in the distance and then there were the bells tinkling merrily. She loved the simple kind-hearted peasants. Papa had promised Gina that once he began to earn serious money, he would buy a cow or two, as an investment, and true enough, in less than a year they indeed had two cows and a bull on Gina's patch.

She had loved her little school and was surprised when Signorina Lumini told Mamma that she had a seriously clever little girl who would go far. In her whole career, she said, she had never come cross anybody who was so bright and so hard-working. She should go to university, Signorina Lumini had said, and everybody wondered what a university was.

Papa ended up by achieving his life-long ambition of becoming a chef. His next ambition was to own his own restaurant one day, a big place in Siena or Florence.

After primary school, they sent Katrina to Scuole Medie in Siena where she did brilliantly, and finished her secondary education at the Liceo Scientifico. Then Bologna university, followed by a scholarship to Harvard.

CHAPTER 9

❖❖❖

Babi Yar

EVERYBODY HAD BEEN expecting it, the Ribbentrop-Molotov pact notwithstanding. His sister Olga had come for a visit from Odessa with her Captain and their three kids. Anton loved playing with them and Father had sternly warned him not to get them overexcited just before being put to bed. Suddenly the radio which was cracking away in the background started broadcasting martial music, and a solemn voice announced that the Nazi invaders had crossed the border and taken Lvov. There was little doubt that in a matter of days they would be in Kyiv.

Rudi was surprised that Father, who hated the Russians for what they had done to the Ukrainians, causing the holodomor, which cost three million lives, did not rejoice on hearing the news. He was very suspicious of the Germans and knew about their racial laws. Not only was his grandfather a Tatar, but Mama had a Jewish grandmother, and feared that past slights with neighbours and the need for ration coupons might bring these things out in the wash. Anton who ignored family history was over the moon. The Germans will help us liberate ourselves from the yoke of that murderer Stalin, he said. Anton was studying Law at Taras Shevchenko and his fellow students had convinced him that there was a big chance that this fellow Adolf Hitler, ridiculous though his moustache was, would help them get rid of the commies. Father had his doubts. Rudi who had never been interested in studies, but was a good enough car mechanic, tended to follow his big brother in everything. If Anton said Hitler was a good thing, then he went along with that. Mama said nothing — whatever Father said must be right. But then Anton, her favourite son said the opposite, so he must be right too. The Captain was obviously in a high state of bewilderment, and had been pacing up and down the floor for some time. He had decided that under the circumstances, he had no alternative but to rush back home to join his regiment.

'Olga, take your brother with you when you go back to Odessa, it will be safer for him,' mother had entreated. Rudi was not sure.

'Whatever for? Why do you want me to go to Odessa?'

'First, it will be safer for you, then you can more easily cross over into Turkey, and then go to America… this country is fucked up,' said his father. He trusted neither side.

Rudi shook his head, he was going nowhere, he would stick with Anton and go wherever the latter decided. Finally the Captain, Olga and the kids left, and Father acted like a punch drunk boxer, staring in front of him, saying not a word, not even when spoken to. Then suddenly, for no reason that Rudi understood, Anton made a U-turn. His friends must have told him to be wary of the Nazis. They were patriots who hated the communists and the Nazis about equally. So he and Rudi put a few things in their bags, and left. We will link up with the Ukrains'ka Povtans'ka Armiya, he finally decided. That's our best bet, he assured the younger brother. He had been told to go to Park Askoldova Mohyla where he would meet some like-minded young men who would then proceed together to an address where they would become members of the Armiya. But when they arrived in the park, they were met by some fierce-looking individuals, some of whom knew Anton, and it turned out that they were committed to the Nazi invaders. To Rudi's surprise they talked Anton into changing his mind once again and the brothers ended up joining them. Rudi felt that he had no choice. They were taken to a secret camp where they met a huge army of volunteers, a sort of welcoming party for the Einsatzgruppen, little knowing what their real agenda was.

Anton was recognised as excellent material, and when the Germans arrived, he was recommended to them as officer class. He was subjected to the intense propaganda necessary to revive the dormant anti-semitism that Ukrainians had been disciplined into controlling by the Bolsheviks who even sent people to prison for saying the derogatory "Zhid" rather than "Evrei". Anton conveniently wiped off any lingering memory of their Jewish ancestor. He was promptly made an officer of the Waffen SS of the Einsatzgruppen and in time, had 1000 men under his command. He relished his new uniform and Luger, and gloried in the company of his new friends, drinking vodka and schnapps every night with them. Rudi had to satisfy himself with being a foot soldier, but he was happy to bask in the glory of the illustrious brother.

The Germans were firmly ensconced in the city before the end of July, and as pockets of resistance began to mushroom up almost everywhere, especially among party members, harsh measures had to be resorted to. Thus hostages were taken and summarily shot pour l'exemple, which Rudi found difficult to accept. He was not entirely an enemy of the communists, and he began to wonder why the Germans who had supposedly come to liberate his nation were now shooting them dead for something done by someone else.

One day, when he was repainting the walls of the mansion on Naberezhne Shose which the Germans had taken over, he heard Anton laughing in the next room, and peeping inside, he saw him drinking with his crony Herr Major Werner Weisskopf; the latter caught sight of him, and called him in.

'You are the brother of that famous man here, ja?' he asked, pointing at Anton. Rudi did not know enough German to understand all that was said, but enough to nod assent to this.

'I say, Anton, why don't you ask your brother to go get us a couple of nice Ukrainian chicks with big tits for tonight?' Rudi understood every single word this time, and that proved a turning point in his attitude to the invaders. Ukrainian women were not de facto whores! He was pleased that the German had so clearly overstepped the mark. He had expected that his fearless brother would tell the man in no uncertain terms where to get off, but Anton only burst out laughing and ordered his brother to get back to work. In German.

Anton's success seemed to have gone to his head, and the younger brother could not understand his devotion to those arrogant foreigners. However, the fact that they were both in the Einsatzgruppen meant a few privileges for the family, extra coupons, protection from possible harassment, and in those increasingly difficult times, one wore a nose peg and learnt to smile mechanically.

Rudi did odd jobs for his new masters, fetching and carrying, a bit of car maintenance, and was glad that he was not officer material. If he had been asked to do anything overtly militaristic, he would have run away. He could not fail noticing that people who had more or less welcomed the invasion, had soon had a change of heart. Father who had kept quiet at first was now calling the Germans the enemy, and begging Anton to dissociate himself from his murderous friends. Rudi was shocked when he heard the brother talk about the necessity of breaking eggs if one wanted to eat an omelette. But the younger brother had little choice doing what he was doing, although running away to Odessa was something he often thought about. However, Odessa was faraway, and the only possibility of getting there would be across the dense forests, as the roads would be teeming with Anton's friends. If only I could steal a boat and sail it down the Dniepr... he began dreaming. If only...

Then came the bombshell. The family with its Jewish skeleton in the cupboard had neither loved nor despised the Jews of the city. True Jews and gentiles did not really mix much socially, but he had had some good Jewish friends at school. There had been some acts of sabotage in the city, which everybody understood to be the work of the communist partisans, which must have included Jews. As far as he could see, they were like everybody, most were hard-working and honest and all loved telling funny stories. So, he was bemused, to say the least when one late autumn evening, he read one of the many posters the Germans put out in public places, to the effect that all Jews of the city of Kyiv and its environs had to come, on Monday the 29th of September 1941 by 8.00 a.m., to the corner of Melnykov and Dokterivsky streets near the Jewish cemetery, with documents, money, valuables, warm clothes, linen etc... for relocation. Whoever of the Jews, the notice went on, does not obey this order, and is found in another place, for whatever reason, shall be summarily shot. Any citizen who enters an apartment that has been vacated, and takes ownership of items will likewise be shot.

Suddenly he remembered that he had been asked by his team leader to be early for work on that Monday, and he wondered whether he would be working for the relocation movement mentioned on the poster. Once he was in the depot to which he had been assigned, some trucks came and they were ordered to climb aboard, and were taken to the corner of Melnykov and Dokterivsky streets, where already some apprehensive Jews were beginning to collect, loaded with suitcases, bags or bundles. They exchanged glances with each other but scarcely said a word. He had somehow gathered that something even more sinister than deportation was afoot.

There were enough people, men, women and children, to fill the Lobanovsky Dynamo Stadium twice over, gathered in the area, and they were ordered to line up and proceed along Melnykov Street in the direction of Kurenivka. They were accompanied by a large number of armed Einsatzkommando. Every now and then, a soldier shot someone for no apparent reason, and the sight of the corpses on the road must have struck terror in the breast of everybody — which was obviously the aim of the Nazis. They walked in silence, full of foreboding, and Rudi was ordered to follow in the truck. They overshot Kurenivka and in the distance ahead, they could catch a glimpse of the ravines of Babi Yar. Babi Yar! Where he and Anton and other friends used to play cowboys and Injuns. They had spent days there during the school holidays, he knew every ridge, every dip, every rock. It had been a place of fun. What were they going to turn it into?

By now everybody had realised that the invaders had a whole new meaning for the word relocation. Rudi realised that he was powerless to do anything. He was no hero. He suspected that he might even be a coward. He kept marching, hoping that it was not going to be as bad as he feared. First the Jews had to deposit their belongings in a large cordoned area, after which they had to take off their shoes and all their clothes including underwear, after which they were taken to the ledge. He saw someone he had seen at Naberezhne Shose and knew as Standardtenführer Paul Blobel who seemed to be in charge of the operations, give the nod to a team of subalterns, and they in turn gave the order to their team of trigger-happy shooters with machine guns to start the execution. As the victims fell on the ground lifeless or dying, other members of the Einsatzcommando pushed them down the ravine with their feet. They did this with an incomprehensible viciousness, as if it were the dead who were the guilty men. The sound of gunfire would not cease for a single second until it was dark on that dark day in September. Rudi would always be shocked when he remembered how, in view of its enormity, the massacre generated such little wailing and screaming. They were stunned into silence, he thought.

He watched this scene in a state of shock. Someone pushed a bottle of vodka towards his mouth and he took a swill. At first he thought he was going to be sick, but a second gulp put him right. Some people in his group seemed just as shocked as he was, but there were others who seemed to be enjoying the spectacle, like something they would like to tell their grandchildren some day. Yes kids, your granddad was there at Babi Yar, on that great day when we shot thirty thousand "Zhids" and kicked them into the ravine. The order came that Rudi and his team, provided with pistols, were to go down among the dead and dying and finish off those who had not yet died. In later years, every time Rudi remembered that day, the people he had finished off, although he knew that he was putting them out of their misery, he would feel sick in the stomach, and six decades later, he still had nightmares.

He had no choice. Had he refused to obey orders, he would have joined the thirty thousand. Maybe he would have been better off. As he descended down the ravine he was assailed by images of him scrambling down there in his carefree childhood days, and he felt guilty of committing a crime against childhood. With trembling footsteps he approached his first victim and shot him as he raised his head with a look of entreaty in his eyes. He convinced himself that the dying man was begging him to put him out of his misery. He shot about twenty more telling himself that he was carrying out an act of kindness, avoiding them a prolonged agony or stopping them being buried alive. He will swear to his dying days that he experienced no thrill of any sort. He had wished that a man had many lives, so he could have allowed one of his to be used in an act of defiance against those Nazi murderers, but you have only one life, and he did not have the wherewithals to be a hero of the Soviet Union.

At first Rudi had not been able to believe the evidence of his own eyes when he caught sight of Anton There he was, his big hero of a brother, laughing his head off, armed with a Luger, shooting Jews in the head and kicking them down the ravine with the same gusto as he used to kick a ball into the goalmouth of the opposing team. He was enjoying himself and relishing every moment.

That night, Rudi slept not a wink. He had a temperature of 41, and was delirious. He kept seeing the images of the day. His German officer had warned them against taking a day off on the next day. You haven't seen nothing yet, he added with a laugh, there is more vermin to exterminate. Father was so worried that he sent for Anton, but the moment the older brother came into the room, Rudi became more disturbed, shouting, I don't want to die, tell him not to shoot me, Father. Anton laughed, and said, silly boy, I ain't shooting nobody, I am Anton, your loving brother. Rudi was sure he saw a gun in his hand and that he was going to put a bullet in his head. He was terrified, and buried his head in Mama's breast. Mama, help me, tell this man to go away. Father explained that the boy had been worried about going to work. Tell him not to worry his silly little head, he told Father, what's the point of having a powerful brother if he will let small things like that worry him? he asked. Later when Dima came to visit, he was almost lucid. When the two were left alone, Dima said that he had made plans for them.

'We are going down the Dniepr to Odessa.'

'There will be Germans all over the place,' Rudi said, but hope was already penetrating his soul, like the morning sun forcing its way in across a chink in the curtain in the morning.

'Fuck the Nazi pigs,' said Dima, 'if you don't take risks...' He left the sentence hanging in the air.

'We can row at night,' Rudi said suddenly, and Dima laughed.

'Who's talking about rowing? My boat has a motor, and we'll have plenty of fuel as well.' Rudi was now quite excited by the prospect.

'Do you mean the boathouse at Naberezhne Shose?'

'Where else?'

There would be a third man, Dima explained, Grigor, a communist with a price on his head.

Rudi said nothing to Father and Mama, and next morning, he met Dima and Grigor outside the burnt café in Dnieprovskaya just before sunrise. Together they walked to the Club and Grigor opened the boathouse with a skeleton key. There was nobody around, making it child's play to drag a small boat out to the water. Then they went back and took some fuel cans and some tools, and in less than half an hour, just as the sun was beginning to rise, they started the motor and were on their way.

They were amazed at how simple it all seemed so far. In no time at all the green domes of the Vydubychi Monastery became visible on the left, and they forged ahead at full speed. They took evasive action, and avoided detection for a good hundred kilometres, not encountering a single German. The locals sometimes gaped at them in surprise, but that did not worry them. It was not until they were approaching Hrebeni that they saw what appeared to be a lone German soldier patrolling the river bank. Grigor said not to worry, and he directed the craft towards the shore where the man in uniform was. The soldier shouldered his gun and took aim, but did not pull the trigger. There was nobody else in sight.

'Tovaritch, kamerad,' Grigor shouted merrily, 'wollen sie mit uns, ein vodka trinken? Is it too early for you? Or would you prefer schnapps?'

'Juden raus!' shouted Dima, and the German laughed.

'Heil Hitler,' said Rudi, feeling he had to join in.

The soldier moved his gun away to have a good look at the three men.

'Heil Hitler,' said the German happily.

'Good perches, in the Dniepr, ha, ha, ha!' Grigor said. The German nodded, and by now the boat was within metres away from the bank.

'Come on board,' Grigor said, 'if you are not seasick.' For the first time the German smiled, and he indicated his willingness to do that. Grigor signalled to Rudi to help the man on board, and he offered the man his hand, but he frowned and refused, he was quite able to do that without help, thank you. Grigor stood up and offered his hand to shake. The German extended his hand with a laugh, whereupon Grigor pulled him forward violently with one hand, and to Rudi's amazement, he had plunged a long knife carefully hidden in the other into the man's heart. The invader died silently and instantly. Dima and Rudi stared at the dead man in disbelief, and then laughed. Grigor was beaming with the satisfaction of a job well-done.

'We'll take him with us for a while yet, sixty kilometres or so, and then we'll dump him into the river. There are some islands near Kaniv… the body won't be found for months… we won't get there until around sunset.' They began by taking his Luger, his binoculars, his boots and Grigor signalled to take his clothes as well.

The mysterious Russian then explained about the partizans, the Cata-combs in Odessa where they usually hid.

'The fatherland is in danger,' said Grigor, 'and we are needed'. Rudi was impressed by these words, and felt that he had no choice but to go along with him.

Using the binoculars, they saw a small group of men in uniform. They were either Germans or Ukrainian volunteers. Traitors, spat Grigor. It can't be too far from Rzysciv, he said, adding that he knew that they had a battal-ion there. Not for the first time, Rudi marvelled at the precision of Grigor's intelligence. They decided to switch off the engine and take shelter in a small inlet. The dead German was now completely naked, and there was little they could do to explain his presence on the boat if the German patrol saw them. Rudi, who had the binoculars, was greatly alarmed when the men seemed to be looking in their direction. Suddenly someone pointed in their direction, and Rudi stammered out this information.

'If we go down, we take a few of the bastards with us,' said Grigor mer-rily. He struck Rudi as a man who not only was not afraid to die, but who would be disappointed if he survived the war. Even if by a stroke of luck they managed to kill them all, Rudi thought, the gunfire would surely alert other Germans likely to be in the area, and it would all be over in a matter of minutes.

The Germans then took a few steps in their direction, and Grigor's face lit up. He fine-tuned the position of the gun, and gave Dima the Luger. Rudi now began to seriously feel fear. He did not want to die. Oh God, he said to himself, I have not even fucked a woman, surely my time can't have not come yet. If he could swim, he might have thrown himself in the water to escape the inevitable fate of having a bullet in stomach. Then he too started laughing hysterically as he saw the Germans laughing. Their presence had not been detected, the soldiers must have been sharing funny stories. Grigor looked disappointed, and Dima exchanged a look with his friend suggesting that he shared his fears. Rudi was greatly comforted knowing that Dima was also afraid; lately he had been acting as if he was made of a different clay, pretending that he was more like Grigor. Perhaps he had just been put-ting it on to hide his fear; maybe he should try this as well. They sat in the gently swaying craft in silence, watching the soldiers through the binoculars in turn.

The men in the green uniforms seemed in high spirits, laughing aloud and singing, until finally they settled down drinking and eating. The three fugitives were hungry too, but had come prepared. They ate some black bread and cold meats and washed it all with some vodka. Rudi was much calmer now, although for a long time after the looming danger had passed, his heart was still beating furiously.

After a long while, the soldiers decided to move on and walked away, and they soon disappeared from view. Wordlessly the trio landed on terra firma and gathered some stones, and tied them to the dead man's body and arms, and cautiously, they manoeuvred the craft forward gaining speed. The engine droned on monotonously, making them feel sleepy, but it did not take long before they were in Kaniv. As Grigor had said there were many uninhabited islands and he pointed to one, saying that it was one of the smallest and nobody lived there. The moment they felt the coast was clear, they dumped the body overboard, and Rudi could not help signing himself and making a silent prayer for his soul; even the hardened communist Grigor looked wistful. The body hit the water, making a gulping sound and at first seemed to hesitate between floating and sinking, but after a short while it got pulled down by the stones it started zigzagging its way downwards.

The way ahead now seemed pretty clear, and they filled the tank with more fuel and got the engine started and gained speed very quickly. The red sunset on the Dniepr was something Rudi and his fellow Kievlans had always cherished, but this particular sunset became burnt in his memory for ever. They ploughed on in the moonlight which spread broken bits of gold on the waters. It must have been in the early hours of the morning when they saw the lights of what they surmised was a major town. Cherkassy, Grigor muttered. He then said that a few kilometres down, they would stop for a two hour sleep as it would be madness to sail in the dark. They landed again and huddled closely to keep warm on this cool autumn morning and went to sleep. Grigor woke them up exactly two hours later, at first light. Having swallowed some cold coffee which Dima had brought in a bottle, they were once more on their way.

They were now in the waters between Kremenchuk and Komsomolskaya, when out of nowhere a German patrol boat appeared. There was no doubt that they had been spotted this time. The boat had a speed at least double theirs when on full throttle. There were four men on board, and through a loudspeaker, a clear message rang.

'Achtung! Achtung! Stop immediately or we shoot.' Dima and Rudi did not see Grigor take aim, but suddenly the patrol boat exploded. The speed with which the man had carried out his action was almost unearthly. Luck must have been on their side, for it took but one shot, and it must have hit the petrol tank of the enemy ship. Instantaneously bodies were seen shooting up as the flames rose and falling down again; it was obvious that the enemy were turning to ashes.

'Now they are going to send the Luftwaffe after us,' said Rudi, in the prey of both elation and fear.

'No they won't,' said Grigor, 'they prefer to use their planes to bomb cities and towns, it's more cost effective.'

'But they might send their patrol boats,' ventured Dima.

'That's a certainty,' said Grigor. Rudi began to become irritated by the communist who spoke like an oracle.

'So what do we do?'

'Nothing!' said Grigor with a laugh. That was the first time that Rudi had seen him laugh. The younger men looked at him.

'Well, not quite nothing,' Grigor conceded. 'Those idiots will send a patrol after us, but we will stay put right here, and they will be chasing a ghost boat.' He explained that they would lie low between the islands at Cykalivka, where they would have a good vantage point. The patrol boat would leave from Kremenchuk, and they would be able to watch its movement as it went down river. After less than a day, they would come back empty-handed, tail between their legs, when the trio would be free to continue their odyssey.

They found a good hiding place between the islands as Grigor had said, and did not have to wait long before a heavily armed patrol boat raced down the river and disappeared from view.

'They will be back in less than forty eight hours,' said Grigor. Feeling safe the three men played cards, cooked and ate their meals, tried unsuccessfully to fish and waited. Thirty six hours later, they heard the sound of an outboard motor, and shortly after saw the boat heading back towards Kremenchuk. Dima and Rudi watched them in the binoculars, and Grigor shook his head when he was offered a peek.

The moment the German patrol boat had disappeared in its own wake, Grigor indicated that there was not a moment to lose, and they set off for what they hoped would be the last leg of their journey. They forged ahead all day and for part of the night, stopping for some rest on a river bank near Novomikailovka. In the morning, Grigor said that they should expect a significant German presence when they were near the big towns like Dniprodzerzhinsk and Zaporizzja, and Rudi feared the worst. So far they had been lucky, their good fortune was not going to hold. All afternoon he waited apprehensively for the sword to drop. They went past Dniprodzerzhinsk, and saw no Germans, and Grigor felt cheated. His discomfiture was more pronounced when after Dnipropetrovsk there was still no impediment to their progress. He shook his head; I was sure they would be everywhere, he said gloomily. Then suddenly his face lit up; there is Zaporizzja yet! I guarantee that they will be there, the Germans or their treacherous Romanian allies. When they reached Zaporizzja there was no sign of enemy presence either, and Grigor resigned himself and they forged ahead. I suppose it will be all clear now until we get near Odessa, he said, the picture of dejection.

They had taken just five days to get to Odessa, and when they landed, Rudi declared his intention of visiting his sister Olga, and Grigor said he had three days. Our Soviet forces are going to evacuate the city to regroup, he explained; the Germans and the Romanians are about to occupy the city. Could Rudi and Dima meet him under the Richelieu statue on the Primorsky Stairs at sunset in three day's time? Rudi had no intention of doing this. Unlike Grigor he had every intention of surviving the war. But he nodded. Dima tagged along.

When they got to Olga's, she tearfully told them that Igor had been sent to Leningrad and that she had not heard from him. Go to Istanbul, she urged, or the Germans will draft you into their slave labour units. She had some money for him, for his boat fare.

'I can't afford to lose both brother and husband,' his sister wailed.

Rudi was very tempted to take the money and escape, but could not arrive at an immediate decision, one moment putting personal safety first, then the next telling himself off. I am no hero, he conceded, but that does not mean I have to be a coward. Then he began telling himself that he had a duty to atone for what he had done in that accursed ravine, and finally that was what made up his mind to cast his lot with Grigor.

On the day he was due to meet Grigor, the Germans and Rumanians did indeed march and occupy the city. As the Soviet troops had retreated, there was nobody to resist them, and in the elation following their quick success, they let off their guard, making it easy for the two young men to keep their tryst with Grigor. When a country is invaded by a foreign enemy, one would expect the population to fall prey to gloom and despondency, but Rudi had not seen Grigor looking as healthy and optimistic since when he shot the German patrol boat's tank and blew it to smithereens.

'As I told you, those sons of bitches have invaded us,' he said. Then he laughed a mirthless laugh adding, 'Now our job is to make them regret the day they were born. Follow me.'

He signalled the young men with his chin and made for a side street, where a decrepit car was waiting. They clambered aboard, and Rudi recognised that they were going towards Nerubaiskoye. He had never been inside the catacombs, but Olga had told him about it. Odessa was built with sandstone which was in abundance underneath, and the builders had paid for it by leaving massive caves and a gigantic labyrinth.

These catacombs, had been for centuries a haunt for vagabonds and smugglers, cutthroats and wayfarers. It was so tortuous and haphazard, that it was littered with the skeletons of dead people who had incautiously wandered inside and then could not find their way out.

Grigor put them in the picture in less than fifty words. We, the patriots of the Soviet Union, he said, use the catacombs to hide from the enemy and plan our action from here. We know our way inside out, but any German or Rumanian bastard venturing inside would be irrevocably lost. Welcome to your new abode! It made sense to Rudi, for Odessa and the regions were singularly free of forests and hills, and there was no other place to hide.

When they were inside, they were greeted by a number of partisans, all in high spirits and rearing for action. They greeted Grigor with veneration, 'Welcome back Yakov,' they kept saying. Rudi felt proud to be a companion of this much admired man. Then from a small recess an impressive man came out and wrapping Grigor/Yakov in his arms gave him a resounding kiss on both cheeks.

'Yakov Gordienko, I knew you would do it. Welcome to the Unit.'

'Thank you Comrade Moldotsov, thank you. May I congratulate our new Hero of The Soviet Union! No one deserves thisaccolade more. Can I introduce you to my young friends Rudi and Dima… two heroic young men with whom I travelled down the Dniepr from Kyiv.'

And the Comrade Hero of the Soviet Union grabbed Rudi rather forcefully, he thought, and planted two resounding kisses on his cheeks too. It was thus that Rudi became part of the Partisan movement fighting for the liberation of the fatherland. It was the first time that a Hero of the Soviet Union had kissed him, and in all probability the last time too.

He was much impressed by the eagerness of everybody to die for the fatherland, although he never craved for such an honour for himself. I will do whatever is necessary for me to do, he told himself, but once I die, I wont be in any position to serve the fatherland, so my first priority is to stay alive. I will live for the fatherland. For the duration of the war, he lived in fear of his life, and every night he prayed to the Archangel Michael to spare him when on the next day when he had a dangerous mission to carry out. And the first lesson he was to learn was that a mission which was other than dangerous was a contradiction in terms.

After the first day, he hardly ever saw Gordienko or Molodtsov again. His immediate commander was someone he was told to call Captain Marlov. He was a ragged rough-looking and speaking man, but like Gordienko, he was fearless. It occurred to Rudi that it was not that these men were not unafraid of death, they had an absolute belief in their invincibility.

Rudi's first job seemed easy enough on the surface, but if caught it would have been torture and death: the resistance wanted to enlist the support of railwaymen and longshoremen in order to find out the times and destination of trains, the contents of cargo arriving in the Odessa ports, so commandos could go blow them up. It was anonymous young men like Rudi who were chosen to distribute leaflets. Not once did anybody betray him, and as a result of this sort of work, a number of trains were indeed blown up, a good few rowboats sunk, killing a large number of Rumanians and Germans and destroying ammunition and equipment. As a result the enemy found that their transportation and communication schedules were severely disrupted.

Yakov Gordienko had said that one important job of the resistance was to keep enemy troops pinned down in Odessa, so they could not serve elsewhere. To this effect, a number of actions which might be regarded as pranks were devised and Rudi and Dima were part of that too. They were given the task of getting volunteers to put sugar in the gasoline tanks of enemy officers, sticking wrong labels on goods due for transportation, putting a knife in enemy tyres, scratching their shiny limousines with a nail, and a host of similar pinpricks which demoralised them considerably, as they hated being ridiculed.

A short time after he had started his resistance work, Gordienko and Molodtsov were closeted in a cave and were obviously planning a big coup. A couple of hours later they asked Marlov and a few other officers to come in, and later, the officer briefed Rudi on a major operation that he was to be part of it. The Rumanian Kommandatura had taken over the old NKVD building in Engels street, and had demanded renovation works. Rudi's mission was to infiltrate a group of workers that he had already established contact with through his leafletting work, and place toluene in places he was shown on a map. Other operators were likewise entrusted with similar missions. Rudi got in touch with his contact who agreed to let him join their team, and he easily found the places Marlov had indicated and was able to place the explosives in. Later that afternoon at half past five, someone using an electrical device set the bombs off, and the building blew up, killing fifty seven enemy soldiers, including the Rumanian general Glogogianu, sixteen officers and thirty five soldiers.

Rudi felt proud of his part in this action at first, but when later thousands of Odessans, mainly Jews were rounded up and killed in retaliation, he was not sure. Once more he was riddled with guilt for causing innocent deaths. Telling himself that it was war and that he was doing his patriotic duty helped but little.

Finally he completely lost his nerve, deserted and ended in Istanbul, and there he sat out the war doing a variety of jobs.

After the war he went back home, and was surprised nobody came to arrest him. But Kyiv and the Ukraine had too many painful memories for him. Anton ended up by blowing his brains out with his prized Luger. When an opportunity arose he took it and found himself on a boat to Turkey once more. From there, he jumped on the Orient Express to Victoria Station.

On the night before Katrina was due to leave for Washington to take up her fellowship at the Smithsonian Centre, Grandma Angelina, who did not do solemn, called her and said that she had a family secret to tell her.

'Swear you will never mention this to Giuseppe,' she said in English, presumably because she thought that would baffle any potential eavesdropper.

That was her Papa, she was talking about.

'You know, your Grandpa Giuseppe… he is not your grandpa.'

Katrina was too stunned to take it all in.

'Granny Assunta told me before she died… Giuseppe, your dad… he is Rudi's child… the two of them… she made me swear… she and Rudi, they had been humping each other like rabbits… crafty buggers they were… they did it for years… no one knew. I always knew he was a bastard… do that to his best friend, pteh!'

'So Rudi is your grandpa after all,' she spat on the floor, and added, 'I am sorry.'

Book IV

CHAPTER 1

From Allapur to Ullapool

KATRINA HAD CYCLED extensively in the Highlands and had spent three days in Ullapool. The town was charming enough but not what she would have called riveting, and feeling a bit blasée she had thought of giving a miss to the usual tourist sites. She had checked in at the Eilean Doran Guest House, and had been quite content to take things easy, and catch up with her reading and watching television. One of the articles she had read only last night, was Donald Robertson's paper on the Godwit. He had something of a reputation in ornithological circles. She had obviously read most of his other writings and had been impressed by the clarity of his exposition, his lucid and intelligent conjectures. She remembered how disappointed she had been when at the Smithsonian, she was told that she had missed meeting a man whose work she admired so much, by just a week.

She was fetching her bike from the garage, aiming to go south, although as yet she had not decided where, when suddenly the Canadian cyclist appeared at the gate, pushing his bike which he had just dismounted. He took a deep breath and made for Katrina.

'Ex-ex-cuse me, is this the the the… Eilean Doran?' They both laughed as they caught sight of the massive billboard with the name EILEAN DORAN writ large, under which they were. On a sudden impulse and the vaguest hunch, Katrina, knowing that he was Canadian asked, 'Excuse me, are you by any chance Donald Robertson?' He dropped his bicycle which went crashing to the ground, and he made no attempt to pick it up. He stared at her, dumbstruck, craning his neck in her direction, opening his eyes wide. Any onlooker might have taken him for a half-wit.

'D-d-d-d-doctor C-c-c-crialese?'

As Don was still thunderstruck, Katrina decided to put him out of his misery.

'Only last night I was reading your paper on the Godwit. Tremendous!' Don took a deep breath, and reminded himself of his many strategies to speak without stammering.

'Oowhen Aye oowas at zthe Sim-mithsonian, Aye heard sso mmuch aabout you… always oowanted t-to emmeet you.' In his estimate his strategy had worked, and that alone gave a big boost to his confidence, which facilitated his delivery. Katrina found his speech pattern strange, but did not immediately recognise it as an allotropy of the stammer. After talking shop with the man whose work she had always admired, and having learnt that they were going to be colleagues at Aberdeen, she took the decision to extend her stay in Ullapool.

They had tea and scones in the dining room of the Eilean Donan, and in the afternoon, they went round Ullapool on their bicycles. That evening they ate lobster and drank Viognier.

On the next day, they cycled the twelve miles to Braemore to visit Corrieshalloch and the suspension bridge. They left their cycles in the car park and walked the narrow path to where the mile long gorge began. Neither of them, seasoned travellers though they were had seen anything so breathtaking — or so they claimed. The walls were almost vertical, and the river Droma flowing over a number of waterfalls below was a stunning sight. It was whilst walking on the suspension bridge that Donald, who had been thinking of nothing else since the start of the trip, managed to grab hold of Katrina's hand. She reacted with mild hostility to that, as she did not like the idea of the male offering succour to a damsel in distress, but almost immediately after she identified this for what it was, a tentative attempt at establishing physical contact, and she smiled. Besides it felt nice. She was a sensual woman. It was more than the warmth of his hand that appealed to her, everything about the contact was pleasant. The pressure on her hand was firm without being aggressive or possessive, and when inevitably, shortly afterwards he began to gently play with her fingers, she closed her eyes and enjoyed the moment. They found it difficult to part with each other that night.

On the next day, on Ullapool Hill, they walked among the pine trees hand in hand, for long periods saying nothing. When they saw the place where as part of a project, some school kids had planted trees mirroring the vegetation that their ancestors migrating to Nova Scotia would have first seen on landing in Pictou in the late seventeen seventies, Don became a tad thoughtful.

'One of my g-great great...' he said, making a flowing gesture with his hands to indicate he wasn't sure how many greats he should say, 'grandfathers sailed on the Hector from Loch Broom.'

'One of my ancestors was a slave from Mozambique,' said Katrina.

Two young people in the prime of life, at the pinnacle of their profession, with the world at their feet, reflected on the long voyage that took their ancestors, from places that most people had never even heard of, to that spot in Ullapool. Each was thinking of their ancestry: the destitute Indian family who had mislaid their father, the near starving Highlanders forced out of their land, the proud slave ancestor who had refused to accept bondage, the original Steve McQueen, for whom no jail was unbreakable, the gipsy woman transported for stealing a chicken to feed her younger siblings, the Ojibwa man who knew about geometry, the labourers who tried to stand for their rights, the great great great grandmother who had had to submit to rape and violence before marrying the eminent scientist who had sailed up and down the Essequibo. The hero of the battle of Sind. The simple peasant grandfather who was forced to carry out the orders of the Nazis at Babi Yar and then ended up a hero at the Odessa Catacombs. So many others who must have had similar histories but about which they knew next to nothing.

It was at this spot that the pair exchanged their first kiss. The sun was hidden by a dark cloud, and a cool breeze was trying to subvert summer. Don had a hand over Katrina's shoulder, and he squeezed it gently, which made her lean over helpfully, making the kiss the next obvious and inevitable move.

'I've I've b-b-been looking for you all my life,' said Don almost without stammering, 'and f-f-fell in love with you in the Hamish. D-d-de you remember our paths c-c-rossed there?' Katrina nodded, laughing at the memory. *Hope he doesn't come and sit at my table...*

Although no words were said to that effect, at that moment, they both knew that they would spend the rest of their lives together.

After the Highlands, they still had a few weeks before Jolyon came back from Australia, and they were free to travel south of the border. They found railway travel was not cheap. They visited Bedford and Dunstable. Katrina could not decide whether she truly remembered Dunstable Downs with its gliders, or if they were false memories based on photographs and stories heard.

When they finally arrived in Aberdeen, they found accommodation in Beach Boulevard, from which they could catch a glimpse of the Esplanade. They decided against living together, and took separate flats in a newly built apartment block, on the same floor, opposite each other. Conveniently, Ananda Garg who was going to be part of their team was able to get a flat in the same building, but on a lower floor. They all settled down and started working on their exciting new project with the enthusiasm of the dedicated scientists that they were. They worked hard and during weekends, Don and Katrina either went hill-walking or cycling. Sometimes they went camping on the Cairngorms. Ananda's wife Roopa who was a television producer in Delhi had not joined her husband, but planned to come visit him twice a year. On some occasions he joined them, but he always seemed to be either on the phone to Roopa or expecting a call from her. As a rule the three of them had one meal a week together at home, during the weekend, usually Sunday late lunch, as they called it. Late, because it started late, giving everybody time for a lie-in, and it spilled until late afternoon, making dinner unnecessary.

Don had no culinary talent whatsoever. Katrina was good at following recipes (Gina had dictated a good few to her), and Ananda used to say that if he had not become a zoologist, he would surely have followed in his father's footsteps and become a Chef. He was indeed an excellent cook, if a bit on the fastidious side. Indian cuisine, he explained, was designed to keep our virtuous Indian girls virgins until they married, by tying them to the kitchen in order to keep their minds off sex, so that the more time-consuming and complicated the method of cooking was, the more popular it was with the anxious parents. As a consequence, with all the time in the world available, he explained, elaborate recipes evolved through fine tuning, which is why, Indian cuisine is the best in the world. Don't take my word for it, he said, that"s what Einstein said. To anybody unconvinced by his oratory, he would give a discourse on Indian spices. Not only did we give all its known spices to the world, from aniseed to Zaffran, we also have the honour of not including horse radish in our cannon! Ananda loved an audience when he was cooking, so he could display his artistry, and at the same time, regale it with tales of famous bhandaris and their oeuvres.

The Indian ornithologist was an aficionado of pasta, and Katrina almost always cooked fusilli or macaroni for the boys when they met at her place. He said spaghetti reminded him of worms. Alternately they would invade Ananda's kitchen and help the Bengali expert make kormas, biryanis, koftas and what not, peeling onions or potatoes, squeezing lemons, or mincing lamb (he did not eat beef). He did everything with a certain panache, holding the handle of the frying pan above the flame and twirling it round with studied insouciance. He always claimed that the end product was not quite what he had hoped for, but he now knew how to make it better next time.

He was a lover of good whisky, and said that this was why he had been so keen to come to the land which produced the finest single malt ever distilled this side of Svarga, the Hindu paradise. Don and Katrina were not averse to a tot or three of Glenfidditch either. Interestingly the Canadian never stammered on Sundays. Ananda would regale them with stories of his Saurkundi Pass Trek and the birds he saw and photographed there. Himalayan Bulbuls and Himalayan Griffons, Bonelli eagles, Hume's warblers, pink-browed rosefinches, among hundreds of others. He had a fund of stories about India, the Kolkata of his birth and his adopted city of Delhi. He loved telling old Indian folk tales, and his guests loved listening to them. One day Don, having imbibed rather more single malt than usual, suddenly declared that he knew the best Indian tale ever, and bet that Ananda did not know it.

It was a story an ancestor used to tell the children, and was like an heirloom, being passed from generation to generation. Surprisingly he was told it by his rather austere father.

'There was a man who p-p-possessed a unique well,' he began, 'and for some reason, he d-d-decided to sell it.'

'Oh, I know,' interrupted Ananda, 'it is a Birbal story, go on.'

'I also know a story about a man who had a gold well—' Katrina said, 'my grandma Gina was told it by... eh, my Indian ancestor. Sorry, go on, Don.'

'Yes, it was a gold well... anyway... a man from Bihar b-bought it, paid his money and the v-vendor seemed happy enough.'

'A man from Bihar? That was in my story too, how extraordinary.'

'Birbal never told stories about men from Bihar!' said Ananda with finality, 'so it cannot be the story I know.'

'In my story,' Katrina went on, 'the seller came back and—'

'In m-mine too... to c-c-claim the gold...'

'In Birbal's too,' admitted the expert.

It turned out that Don's version was identical to the one Katrina knew, and this left the lovers perplexed for a while. Surprisingly the idea that it might have emanated from a common source did not seriously attach itself to either of them. Admittedly they each had Indian ancestors, and from Bihar too. Don never knew the circumstances in which his great great... however many... grandmother Devi found herself in Demerara, as his parents and grandparents did not remember or did not know. The mist of time had thickened into a pea-souper. Katrina only knew what Gina had told her, and many of the facts had got filtered away as one generation retold the tale to the next. She knew that there was an ancestor called Shanti who had mislaid her husband whilst catching the boat to Mauritius; that was what Prakash had told Gina.

One day, Katrina asked Don why he had decided to go to Ullapool. Because his great... grandmother Devi had once said that although she and her father had migrated from the Sunderbans, they had originally come from a place called Allapur in Bihar.

'That's uncanny, Gina also said that my soldier grandfather had ancestors who came from there, I thought Ullapool and Allapur seemed quite similar, so... call me stupid—'

'Could it be,' wondered Don aloud, 'n-n-n-o, how c-c-ccan it be? This is real life, not Mills and Boone.'

Ida, who exchanged emails with her brother almost daily, had often said that she would seize the first opportunity to come visit them in Aberdeen. *I am so keen to see for myself this paragon who seems to have ill-advisedly fallen for your hidden charms — hidden to me at any rate*, she had written. Don was overjoyed when she phoned at three one morning to announce that she had booked herself on a flight to Glasgow. And good soul, he had rushed out and knocked on Katrina's door, not wanting to keep that exciting news to himself.

Ida had rented a car and driven to Aberdeen.

'I don't believe this,' she exclaimed the moment Katrina and Don opened the door to her, 'you look more like his sister than I do.' She elaborated.

'I mean you do not have the same features, but I am talking about the overall picture, the bearing… know what I mean?'

'All ornithologists all look alike.'

'No, all Indians look alike.'

'One of our ancestors must have misbehaved,' Ida said.

'Definitely an Indian one,' said Ananda merrily, 'if you only knew what goes on in those gaons.'

It seemed that Don had urged Ida to come over in time for the celebration of the first anniversary of their first meeting in Ullapool, although why this had taken such an overblown importance, Katrina could not fathom out. Unbeknownst to her, Don had planned to pop the question, and had wanted to share his happiness with his sister.

The Italian woman planned an Italian meal for themselves and Ananda on that Saturday. She was useless without recipes but with her scientific habit of following clear instructions, she did not feel daunted by the task. Usually when she set her mind to it, she made quite acceptable — Don said excellent — dishes. Also she prided herself on always carrying out her tasks in the most rational manner. She told the others that she wanted no help from them at all, preferring, as always, to work by herself as she found it easier to concentrate. She gave Ida the choice of sitting in the kitchen watching her cook or watching the Old Firm match with the boys on STV. Ananda was a great fan, and welcomed the opportunity of showing off his reading of the game but Don and Ida hardly understood the rules. Still they were happy to sit in front of the telly with cans of beer for a change. Don had got a few bottles of San Miguel in the fridge. Ananda agreed that whisky and football were incompatible.

She had planned everything perfectly, and everything was ready exactly at the end of the game. They ate heartily, drank Chianti, and ate Ras Malai which Ananda had brought for dessert. After the meal they played Upword, a multi-storied scrabble game for a bit, and Ananda kept making words which the others had never heard of, swearing that they were perfectly valid Indian spellings of words they knew differently. It was good fun.

When Ananda said he was going, Don said to hang on for a bit, he had something to give Katrina, and he wanted him to see it too. Typical of him, instead of producing it, he had to say a few words about it first.

'It is s-s-something special… even unique I would say. You m-m-might say it's incomplete, but it's special just b-b-because of its… incompleteness. It is my most prized possession, I have it in my personal luggage w-w-whenever I travel… Ida knows what I am talking about. She was so jealous when Mum gave it to me instead of her.'

'Not true,' said Ida weakly.

'M-m-mum ss-specifically said I should give it to my wi-wife… she…'

He stopped suddenly at that point, possibly overcome by emotion, and started blinking at a furious rate — something he had more or less stopped doing. Katrina put her hand on his arm and gently squeezed it.

'I wished I knew its full history,' he continued, 'all I know is that it b-b-belonged to our Indian ancestor… my great great g-g-g-reat grandmother Verity—'

'Her real name was Devi,' corrected Ida, 'They forced her to change it to Verity.'

'I n-n-never-knew that,' said Don.

'You were never interested in the notes and diaries of the ancestors,' she challenged.

'Anyway… at her death it was given to my… great great grandfather… also called Donald… and… eh… to cut a long story short, m-m-mother gave it to me, and said I should give it to my wife… I want to give it to Katrina… as an anniversary present… eh…' He fumbled in his pocket for a bit, became alarmed when he could not find it.

'I c-c-can swear I p-p-p-ut it in my pocket when I left the f-f-f-f-flat…'
He stormed out in a panic.

'Trust my dear brother,' said Ida laughing. Don stormed out of the room.

Katrina and Ananda exchanged smiles, and waited for him to come back.
He did almost immediately.

'As I said, I n-n-n-knew I had it in my p-pocket, it was there all the time,'
and he produced a small plastic pill box and gave it to Katrina. She took it,
studied the box, not rushing to open it.

'C-c-come on, open it,' urged Don.

Katrina shook her head. Her eyes were filled with unshed tears and she
felt a big lump in her throat. 'No,' she said finally, 'I know what it is.'

'I can't bear the suspense,' said Ananda with pretend impatience.

'You said that it's a family heirloom, from your Indian great great great
great grandmother. Let me see, it's a small item, and you said you always
have it with you… funny, but I too have something I always travel with…
eh… also something which comes from an Indian ancestor.'

She could not continue, so great was the emotion. But she took a deep
breath, smiled apologetically and made an effort to pull herself together.

'That is such a coincidence… that the two of us should have… no, it's too
far-fetched.'

'What's so far-fetched?' Ananda wanted to know.

'Everything! First, we meet in the Trossachs, and have the same bikes…
we are both working on bird migration, we are both joining Jolyon's team…
we both did a stint at the Smithsonian… it's never-ending… uncanny.'

'W-what is it that you always t-t-t-travel with?' asked Don.

'I'll show you,' said Katrina. Her expression had changed suddenly. It was
as if she was scared of something, and her hands began to tremble. The two
men were surprised to see her bend towards the bottle of whisky, and her
whole body shaking, she poured some in a glass and topped it in one go into
her mouth. Even Ida seemed a bit lost.

'What's the matter, s-s-sweetheart?' asked Don.

'I'll show you mine first,' she said, and opening her bag with trembling
fingers, she produced one gold earring, the one with a small crown with
small chains dangling from its equator. It had somehow fell into Prakash's

hands. With her incredible memory Gina had remembered everything her Mauritian sweetheart had told her and had in turn told it to Katrina. Don stood up, and looked at it in amazement. He tried to speak, but no words would come out of his mouth.

'It's a piece of jewellery Dr Robertson, not an apparition.'

'It's magic! Teletransportation,' said the Canadian without stammering. The others looked at him, expecting him to elaborate. He was in fact trying to, but could not speak. Ananda came to the rescue.

'Open Don's present,' he urged.

It was the other one of the pair, the one which the remorseful Sukhdeo had travelled all the way to the harbour to return to Raju. Like hers, it had a small gold crown with small chains. Don watched her, like in a dream, as she held each one between the thumb and the index fingers of each hand and raised them for all to see. The gold in each piece was exactly of the same hue, and it did not need an expert to discover that they were made by the same craftsman. They were identical in every way.

'This tells us without the shadow of a doubt, that you Don, have for ancestor, the villainous uncle of Katrina's ancestor who demanded his pound of flesh when his cow died and had to be given one earring.' They had shared whatever they knew of their histories with their Indian friend.

'What do you mean?'

'Yes, Prakash told Gina the same story.'

Katrina was a bit sorry that Don was a descendant of Sukhdeo, but one is not responsible for one's ancestors. It was clear that Verity/ Devi was a descendant of Sukhdeo.

Ida had remained uncharacteristically quiet, but everybody almost simultaneously noticed that she had one of her superior smiles.

'OK,' she said, 'are you ready for this?' She stared at each in turn, and continued, 'It meant little to me when I read uncle Aloysius' account of some of the tales Ancestor Verity aka Devi aka Sundari told him.

CHAPTER 2

— ❖❖❖ —

Hesperus

(Calcutta, India, 1840s)

THE MOMENT THE family was out of earshot, Sukhdeo was all smiles and backslaps. The best thing was for them to go to a place just round the corner where they could indulge in some toddy, he said, to bury past grievances. Raju did not feel like drinking, specially with Sundari in tow, and with the man who had done him so much harm. However, he reasoned, whatever may have happened between the two of them, he was an elder, had been a friend of Baba's, and in any case after today, never again in this life would their paths cross, Bhagwan be praised. That, he told himself wryly, was something that needed to be celebrated. Besides, in the apprehensive state he was in, a little drink might calm his nerves. So he allowed the older man to grab hold of his hand and lead him to the stall away from the bustle of the riverside where a sinister looking one-eyed man in a red turban, with thick twirling moustaches was serving drinks. Raju was seized by panic and found himself covered in a film of cold sweat. Had Sukhdeo brought him here for some villainous purpose? Could he get out of this situation without causing any upset? But the toddy was ordered and he imitated Sukhdeo and swallowed it in one gulp.

'I needed that,' said Sukhdeo, smacking his lips, and he signalled the one-eyed man to bring some more.

'What I wanted to tell you, beta — I always thought of you as my own son — was that I am so sorry things have come to this between us. If only you knew how many sleepless nights I have spent, gnawed by regrets! As you know your father and I were distant cousins, but that was nothing, we were friends, better than brothers, like this.' He made crooks of his index fingers and pulled hard, showing that no force could wrench them apart. 'And I honestly used to think of you as my own son,' he said, 'honest I did.' Raju knew this was true, but hoped that the old man was not going to keep saying this. He knew that it was his refusal to endorse this sentiment was at the root of all their problems.

'I am not saying it's your fault... your Aunt Lalita interferes too much, and she is always having a go at me. So and so is a thief, such and such is a slacker, that one has shown us disrespect... you know what women are like.'

'My Shanti is not like that,' thought Raju but thought it best to say nothing, in an attempt to keep this unwelcome encounter short; instead he just nodded in a neutral manner.

'I know your Shanti isn't like that,' said the older man, seemingly reading his mind and agreeing with him, 'but trust me, all other women are.' I must remember to tell her that, the proud husband told himself.

'But my boy, who knows eh? Give her time and she too will learn...' Raju smiled and acknowledged the old man's little joke.

'Arrey, no, I am not blaming nobody, all I am saying is that I never really believed that you stole those things. Why, beta, you have never stolen in the past... I was not doubting about the goondas, you never tell lies, although you are often exaggerating, don't you?' And as the effect of the toddy was beginning to make itself felt, he gave a raucous short laugh, and presented his open palm for the younger man to slap. Raju complied it with singular lack of enthusiasm, and for a little while neither spoke. Then Sukhdeo shook his head wistfully, and continued, 'But... ach... I shouldn't have accused you. And the cow, as you said was old, she didn't have long to live...'

'If you have come to say you are sorry, OK, thank you, now I must go.' The next round of toddy arrived.

'Drink up.'

'I am glad you realised I am no thief, but I must go, I don't want to miss my ship, Shanti will be worried.'

'Arrey, there is plenty of time, they told me at the harbour. Drink and I am coming to the point.' Raju drank. To his surprise, Sukhdeo was suddenly holding the golden jhumka that Shanti had been forced to part with in his hand, its tasselled chains glinting seductively at Raju. Surprisingly the other drinkers seemed not to notice.

'Here, take this, I should never have taken it from your Shanti in the first place. Tell her how sorry I am, and promise you will both forgive me.' Raju could not quite believe he was hearing this. He drank his toddy in one gulp again. He took possession of the earring and kept staring at it like one hypnotised.

'Did you say there's plenty of time?' he asked the older man.

'Arrey, the man said the ship was not leaving until tomorrow. Late tomorrow.'

'In that case, maybe you should let me buy the next round.' Sukhdeo shook his head. No, he insisted, a young man should not stand an elder a drink, it was disrespectful.

Raju liked his drink, but he never drank irresponsibly. He liked to believe that he knew when to stop. But the excitement and the stress of the situation were too great, and he needed something to relieve the tension. He promised that this was the very last, final and ultimate one, knowing that he had already stepped over the mark. Sukhdeo wished him a good trip, and hugging him, tears dripping down his cheeks.

'Ya Bhagwan, Parsad, your father was…' He could not finish the sentence, shook his head, clearly choking with emotion.

Putting the earring carefully under his turban, Raju grabbed the girl by the hand and fairly ran towards the riverside, but the crowd seriously impeded his progress. Regardless he pressed on and brushed past a tall well-built man with a handlebar mustache, a proper pahelwan. He didn't even stop to say sorry. He heard an order being shouted, 'Catch that Chootya,' and a companion of the irate man tripped him over. He crashed to the ground, just avoiding smothering the little Devi. He hurt his forehead slightly and a trickle of blood was coming out. The ruffian bent down grabbed him by the scruff of the neck and pulled him up until his feet were hanging in the air. The girl began crying in panic, whereupon one the goondas gently pinched her cheek and said, Don't worry we don't harm little sweeties like you, but that did not stop the scared little girl.

'Do you know who I am?' the Pahelwan asked fiercely, whereupon, four or five men who were obviously associates of his began laughing. All I know is that I wouldn't like to share a toddy with you, thought Raju wryly.

'Boss, if the chootya knew who you are, he would have been more care-ful,' one of them said, to renewed laughter.

'What do you lot think,' the Pahelwan, feeling his side whiskers, asked his sidekicks darkly.

'The chootya needs to be taught a lesson, boss,' chorused four men who all looked the same to Raju.

'No please, Sarkar, be kind, Bhagwan will repay your kindness to me a thousandfold, please just let me go…' He was on the point of delivering a long-winded entreaty, but the offended man turned to his associates and laughed obscenely.

'Another madr chodd from Bihar! I knew there was something wrong with him from the moment I caught sight of him' Raju grinned foolishly, in the hope of an early reprieve.

'Ek Bihari sau Bimari!' One Bihari, one hundred diseases!

'Them's worse than those fuckin' intouchables,' spat the smallest of the four.

'What do you people hope to find in our sacred town? You're polluting this city with your presence, why don't you piss off back where you came from?' Raju thought that he had finally found his way out.

'Sarkar, actually I am on the point of leaving Calcutta… my wife and family, we are moving to—' He could not finish his sentence, as a resounding slap on the face shocked him into silence. Also, he had momentarily forgotten the name of that place they were going to.

A small crowd was watching this scene passively, neither enjoying it, nor outraged by the sight of five men victimising a small undernourished man and his little girl.

'You only speak when you're told to.' The girl was so shocked to witness this humiliation of his father that she stopped crying. Raju was heartened to note that she had formed her two hands into fists.

'It's all right, little girl, you can continue crying now,' said one of the badmash kindly, but she did not take up the offer.

'What's your name, little sweetheart?'

'My Baba calls me Sundari, but—'

'Her real name is Devi—' Raju was not allowed to finish, as another re-sounding slap followed by yet another reminder of when he was allowed to open his mouth crash-landed on his face.

'Yes, he needs to be taught a lesson,' the Pahelwan said, 'bring him along… take the child.' Wagging a finger menacingly to the man carrying Devi, he added unnecessarily, 'See no harm is done to her. We never harm children. Don't cry little one.' Then angrily turning to his men, he said, 'If she starts crying give her a sound slap to shut her up.'

And Raju was forcibly dragged away, the girl in the arms of the goonda. Bhagwan save me, he prayed inwardly, you are the only one who can now. What's going to happen to my Shanti and my little boy now? He knew about thuggees who kidnapped strangers, robbed them and killed them as a sacrifice to the Goddess Kali.

'Please sir, kill me but spare the girl, she is so young and innocent, she has never done harm to nobody…' He saw the boss nod, and one of the men punched him and he collapsed on the ground, and lost consciousness.

When he regained consciousness, he found himself being dragged by two men, one on either side, his knees bleeding through rubbing against the rough ground. He had lost his champals. They seemed to be aiming for a little maidan next to a Jain temple. He started whimpering. Please sirs, let me go, I will miss my boat. No one seemed to hear or care. As the crowd thinned out, Raju's fear for his and his little girl's lives increased in inverse proportions. Ya Bhagwan, let them kill me, but don't let them take my girl and sell her. Why did this madr chhod Dukhdeo appear in my life at a time like this, like a black cat heralding a big disaster? What business did he have, becoming repentant? That man has been like a burden the family has had to bear since the beginning of time.

Finally they were under a big banyan tree and a goonda pushed Raju roughly against it. There were half a dozen stragglers watching proceedings, and they too said nothing and watched passively.

'Teach him that lesson now, boys,' ordered the Pahelwan, and the men closed upon the poor Bihari, and began slapping him on the face, whereupon the boss cleared his throat and spat his contempt at such a poor show of force. 'I said teach him a fuckin' lesson, not caress him.' The men redoubled their effort, joining kicks and punches to slaps, their faces contorted by the most vicious expressions they could muster. The fellow who was holding the girl looked on sadly and asked if they did not think that the man had had enough.

'Yes, yes,' agreed the poor victim, 'I have been a bad bad man but I have learnt my lesson now—' The Pahelwan took a couple of steps in his direction, looked at him in the eyes, then punched him twice in the stomach in quick succession.

'So far you have learnt shit, madr chott you have learned your lesson when I say you have, not one second before, not two seconds after!' He cleared his throat menacingly, and his face reflecting the venom he had built up for the man he had never seen in his life, he spat a large gob on Raju's face. Then he turned to his minions, 'If there is anybody I hate more than a Bihari piece of shit, it's a grovelling Bihari piece of shit.' The four men almost shrieked with laughter.

'The boss is so funny,' chorused the men.

'Now go back to that revolting Gaya and stay there. If I catch sight of you in our sacred Calcutta, I will personally cut your balls off.' And they let him go. The man who was holding Devi seemed reluctant to let go of the girl, and pinched her cheek again in what he thought was a token of avuncular affection, before allowing her to slide down. Raju was hurting all over, but relieved that no bones were broken. Best of all his turban with all his possessions was still miraculously on his head. Now he was lost, slightly concussed, not knowing how to retrace his steps to the Harbour area. His clothes were blood-soaked and he was still bleeding in places. If Shanti saw him like this, she would have a fit. And the people in the Harbour Office would never let him go through in the state he was in. So he stopped at a ghat, washed his clothes to remove all traces of blood, and cleaned his wound, then he bought himself wooden clogs. Devi was dry-eyed but looked scared, and he patted her gently on the head every now and then, calling her a brave little girl. He hoped that a black eye might just pass muster. He squeezed the clothes dry and put them on whilst some giggling kids watched behind a banyan.

When he finally arrived at the spot where he had left Shanti and the boy, he was surprised to find that they were not there. He, started to panic and began shouting, Shanti, Pradeep, Jayant. The people in the line did not fail to notice that he was in a bad way, and allowed him to join it, and he joined the fingers of his two hands together, and bent forward slightly towards them in a thank-you gesture. He had no idea if this was the right place to be queuing up, but thought that the best thing would be to join it, in the hope that it would lead him to the office where he might ask about Shanti. The girl behaved very well, and after a long wait they made it to the office, where Delahunty and Chatterjee looked at his black eye and shrugged.

'Name?' Chatterjee asked.

'No, you see, Sahib—'

'What's the cove saying?' asked Delahunty.

'I am not quite too very sure, Sir, he is speaking Bhojpuri which I am not very understanding.'

'My Shanti and Pradeep… giya, na ?' Giya na?, in bhojpuri means "are they gone?"

'I think he's wanting to be going to British Guyana, Sir,' Chatterjee said.

'Aren't they all? Check his name, we don't have all day man.'

'Your name?'

'My Shanti and my boy, are they gone?' Giya na?

'Naam kya hai? Kon chi ba?'

'Rajendra Sharma, Sahib.'

'I can see a Rajendra Varma here, the idiots can't spell…' said Delahunty checking the passenger list, 'Let him through. Jaldi, jaldi!'

'My Shanti, she gone? Giya na—'

'Yes, yes, Guyana, Demerara… *Hesperus.*'

It was thus that Raju and his little girl found themselves on the *Hesperus,* bound for British Guyana, whilst Shanti and Pradeep were on their way to Mauritius. Later, the two ships, the *Startled Fawn* and the *Hesperus* exchanged greetings as they crossed each other in the Bay of Bengal.

Raju pestered almost everybody on board asking about Shanti and Pradeep.

Everybody's temper was frayed by the heat, the anxiety and the waiting, and if there was one thing nobody wanted, it was to shoulder someone else's problems. However once everybody was settled in the harsh routine on board, and had got used to the smells and discomforts of seasickness, people began to sympathise. You must go talk to the captain, they all said, but how?

Every time he accosted an officer, he was sworn at and ordered to go back to his hold downstairs.

He had only survived the gruelling voyage by convincing himself that on landing he would be reunited with his family. Although he had lived on the sea, he now suffered from seasickness, with the attendant vomiting, bellyache and loss of appetite. He had no energy to cook his meagre rations of rice, dal, onion, but his fellow passengers, taking pity on his daughter more than him, had helped. Devi, on her part had quickly become a firm favourite of the other passengers, and had borne the voyage quite well, ending up by being possibly the only passenger to have gained some weight.

When they finally landed in Georgetown, he was as thin as a drumstick, could hardly stand on his two legs, having been battered by the storms which had flung him from one side of the hull to the other, nearly cracking his skull on more than one occasion. Besides, he had been ill almost all the time, with diarrhea, headaches, and even a bad cold.

He was taken to a plantation on the Demerara. He hoped that Shanti would be around somewhere, and badgered everybody about her. People started looking the other way when they saw him nearby. Then the rumour spread that he was feeble-minded. Not everybody treated him with compassion, not even for the sake of the little girl. He knew that he was not going mad, but when everybody became convinced that he was, he began to doubt his sanity too. That was a known trigger to madness.

Still, he started working on the fields, but obsessed by his lost wife, he would drop his pickaxe and stare at the sky, in the middle of some task, talking to himself, saying things like, "I know you are somewhere, my Rani, please don't hide from me." People who were not yet convinced that he had lost his mind required no further proof. Gradually the bosses began to say that he was unfit to work on the fields, and out of kindness, the manager gave him a night watchman's job, so that at least he could feed himself and his lovely Devi who was now too grown-up to be called Sundari.

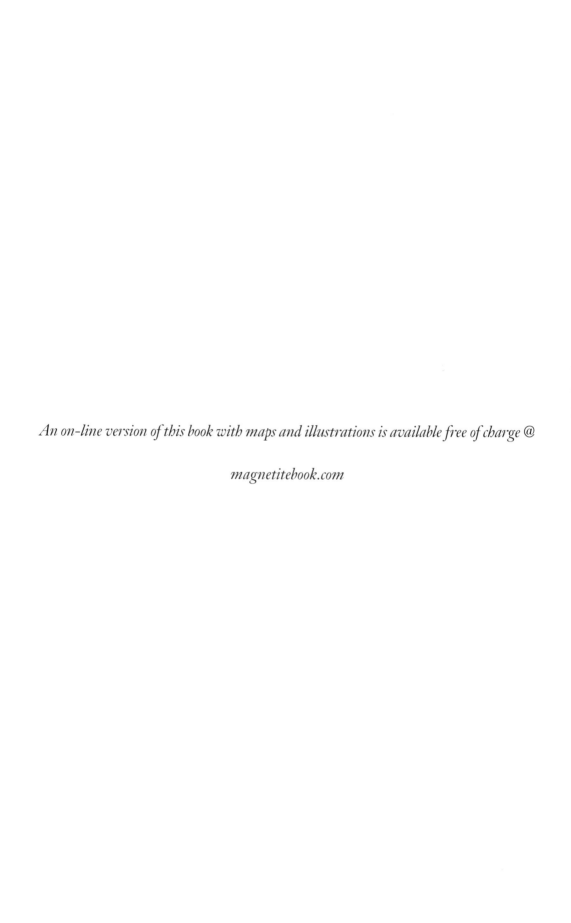

An on-line version of this book with maps and illustrations is available free of charge @

magnetitebook.com

Other books by San Cassimally

The Case Book of Irene Adler
The Memoirs of Irene Adler
The Adventures of Irene Adler
Sherlock Holmes Vs Irene Adler
    (*A duel of Wits*)
Trumped
    (*A Sherlock Holmes & Irene Adler Investigation*)
Samosas and Ale
    (*Stories with an Indian Flavour*)
Sarah Bernhardt: My Erotic Life

San Cassimally welcomes comments from readers @

sancass@blueyonder.co.uk

82346836R00322

Made in the USA
Columbia, SC
09 December 2017